Florence James was born in Gisborn
graduated from the University of S
children, *Four Winds and a Family* (1...), with Dymphna Cusack.
Her other collaboration, *Come In Spinner,* won the 1948 *Daily
Telegraph* competition, and was published in an abridged edition in
1951 to great acclaim.

Dymphna Cusack was born in Wyalong, New South Wales, in 1902.
She published twelve novels, including *Pioneers on Parade* (1939) with
Miles Franklin, *Southern Steel* (1951), *Black Lightning* (1964) and *The
Sun is Not Enough* (1967). She also published eight plays, three travel
books, and two children's books. She died in 1981.

The unexpurgated edition of *Come In Spinner* was first published in
1988. It was filmed as a two-part mini-series and broadcast on ABC
Television in 1990.

"And, sometimes, 'Come in Spinner',
laugh the gods.

Yet the felled tree ever sprouts from the lowly butt.

And, 'Come in Spinner', laugh the gods again.

'Well, who'd believe it — tails!'
my empty pocket cries.
But still there blooms my unabated spring."

IAN MUDIE

IMPRINT CLASSICS

COME IN SPINNER

DYMPHNA CUSACK
FLORENCE JAMES

Introduced
by Florence James

ANGUS
& ROBERTSON

A division of HarperCollins*Publishers*

AN ANGUS & ROBERTSON BOOK
An imprint of HarperCollinsPublishers

First published in an abridged edition by William Heinemann Ltd in 1951
Published in Australia by Angus & Robertson Publishers in
Pacific Books edition 1966
A & R Classics edition 1973
Sirius Quality paperback edition 1981
Complete edition first published in 1988
This Imprint Classics edition published in 1990
Reprinted in 1990, 1991
CollinsAngus&Robertson Publishers Pty Limited (ACN 009 913 517)
A division of HarperCollinsPublishers (Australia) Pty Limited
25–31 Ryde Road, Pymble, NSW 2073, Australia

HarperCollinsPublishers (New Zealand) Limited
31 View Road, Glenfield, Auckland 10, New Zealand

HarperCollinsPublishers Limited
77– 85 Fulham Palace Road, London W6 8JB, United Kingdom

National Library of Australia
Cataloguing-in-Publication data:

Cusack, Dymphna, 1902–1981.
    Come in spinner.
    ISBN 0 207 16948 9.
    1. James, Florence. II. Title

A823.3

Front cover illustration: Ponds advertisement from
'Australian Women's Weekly'. 21 April 1945
Back cover photograph of Rebecca Gibney, Lisa Harrow and
Kerry Armstrong by Martin Webby.
Courtesy ABC Television.

Printed in Australia by Griffin Press

5   4   3
95 94 93 92 91

INTRODUCTION

"Spinner is a winner"

This exciting news was cabled across the world from Dymphna Cusack in Sydney to me in London. *Come In Spinner* had won the *Daily Telegraph* Australian novel competition. The prize was £1000 and, much more important, the novel was promised publication in Australia, the UK and USA with a minimum printrun of 100 000 copies. That was in the days when 3000 copies was an average first print run and Australian novels were fighting an uphill battle on their home ground in a market flooded with imported fiction.

Winner of an Australia-wide competition in 1948, it was not until nearly three years later, in January 1951, that *Come In Spinner* became a winner in the bookshops. When English publisher William Heinemann launched the first edition on the English market, it was greeted with rave reviews led by the prestigious *Sunday Times*:

> To lose oneself in *Come In Spinner* is indeed a stirring and memorable experience. Here is something of the clatter and jostle of *Manhattan Transfer*, something of the rackets and undercover miseries of *Alexander Platz*, something of the suave and raffish luxury of *Grand Hotel* and— something plus.

February publication in New York was heralded by equally enthusiastic reviews. It was not until March that the English edition reached Australia, where it met with a very mixed reception.

On radio Vance Palmer gave it a splendid send off. He too had picked up the "something plus", commenting that "the social implications of this book are many and thought provoking".

In his report to the competition judges, the *Daily Telegraph*'s literary critic had said: "This is the best novel of modern Sydney yet written by anyone." On its publication, however, the newspaper took a different view. The *Daily Telegraph* had never announced the winner of its novel competition and now, astonishingly, called it a muckraking novel fit for the literary dustbin. Their critic was not alone in wanting to keep the rackets and the greed and the ugliness of wartime Sydney hidden beneath the good-time surface; Melbourne commercial radio station 3UZ cut short a serial broadcast of the novel in response to public complaints.

However, disapproving critics notwithstanding, the public cleared out the bookshops and waited impatiently for fresh supplies. From that day to this, *Come In Spinner* has been in demand. Why, then, this new and enlarged edition? I wonder how many *Come In Spinner* fans know that the book they have enjoyed so much is in fact a severely abridged version of the original story. And why, they will ask, were the cuts made in the first place? There hangs a story.

When Dymphna and I set up temporary housekeeping in the Blue Mountains outside Sydney during the last year of the war, we had not thought of collaborating on a novel. Dymphna had recently been invalided out of the Education Department and I had given up my wartime job in Sydney and was waiting to join my RAAF husband who had been posted to London.

We took with us three small girls aged between nine and seven—Dymphna's niece and my two children—and planned a few weeks' bush holiday together. However my husband's posting was changed, Dymphna's health began to improve wonderfully, the children loved the carefree life, and friends who visited us on weekends kept us in touch with the wartime Sydney we had escaped from. So we stayed on in our rented cottage, sent the children to the local school and had great fun writing about their adventures. Our collaboration was simple: we would each choose a story, write it up, then edit the other's work. In no time at all *Four Winds and a Family* was finished and had found a publisher.

This was our *Come In Spinner* gestation period, when Dymphna and I were gathering together the threads of our lives, our first real opportunity since the days of our friendship as undergraduates at Sydney University. Letters had kept us in touch through the years, and it was not surprising to find how our interests had coincided under very different conditions.

During the Depression, Dymphna had taught in country high schools and found herself greatly depressed by the hardships her pupils and their families were suffering and often barely survived. At the same time she was writing, and her plays were winning prizes in national competitions. Her novel *Jungfrau* was published by the *Bulletin* in 1936. "I'm going to write—and I'm going to write a story of real women," she had said. *Jungfrau* was the story of the friendship between three young Sydney women and was hailed as breaking new ground in Australian writing. Genteel readers were shocked. Dymphna's next book was her first experience of collaboration; she and Miles Franklin together wrote the novel *Pioneers on Parade*, airing wittily their indignation at the social pretensions of the sesquicentenary celebrations.

Meantime, I had been establishing myself as a freelance feature journalist in Fleet Street, interviewing newsworthy people from all walks of life. There was a time when I shared digs with Christina Stead before she left London to work in Paris and when she was writing *Seven Poor Men of Sydney*. During these years, I ghosted two adventure books for a well-known African explorer and had the privilege of writing popular articles on pre-school education for Dr Maria Montessori, Italy's first woman doctor and internationally renowned educationist. At this time I was doing voluntary social work among East End school children and their parents.

When I returned to Sydney in 1938, I joined Dymphna and her friends in a little group of keen Australian writers who were fired with Miles Franklin's burning conviction that "without an indigenous literature people can remain aliens on their own soil. An unsung country does not fully exist nor enjoy adequate exchange in the inner life."

During the succeeding war years, Dymphna continued

to teach in country schools, lectured for the Army Educational Service and also had the unforgettable experience of a brief spell as caretaker of a block of Kings Cross flats. And all the time she was writing.

My war had been spent in Sydney with my two young children. Accommodation was a constant problem and my work as Public Appeals Officer for Royal Prince Alfred Hospital, which involved me in social functions and erratic hours, often made life complicated. Outside the windows of my Martin Place office, where I edited the RPA Gazette and organised fundraising committees, every kind of military activity took place and the air was alive with the shouting and laughter of the crowds. This was often a poignant reminder of the Children's Court, only a mile or so away, where Dymphna was involved in school counselling and I did voluntary PR work.

Now that we had time in the Blue Mountains, why not tell the Sydney war story? Why not write about the women's world we knew, where men's labour was in short supply and women were "man-powered"? We would keep within the range of our own and our friends' experiences. We would tell the Sydney story as we knew it, pulling no punches.

How to begin? First came the planning. We worked out the chief characters and the broad lines of their stories and decided the action would take place during the course of a week. Then we began to fill in the detail and build up our common references. We charted the weather during the first week of October 1944. We cut out pictures of clothes suitable for our characters' special occasions and collected a whole gallery of photographs until the pin-ups on the large board in the hallway between our two rooms began to jostle each other for space.

It was now time to start writing. We began by each choosing a character and sketching his or her story and family background, and before we knew it our characters began to take charge of their own plots.

Dymphna was subject to recurring bouts of acute neuralgia and could not stand using a typewriter. But she could dictate to my typing when she was well enough, and when she was not I got on with my own writing. Working hours extended from the.children's departure for school until lunchtime, after which Dymphna rested and I edited and caught up with the housekeeping.

This worked splendidly until we had nearly finished the first draft, when Dymphna became uncomfortably aware that she had not even begun the novel about wartime Newcastle for which she had received a Commonwealth Literary grant. She couldn't type, and writing by hand was too laborious—what about a dictaphone? A splendid solution. With both of us able to work independently, that speeded the winding up of the *Spinner* stories. Dymphna began dictating *Southern Steel* while I got stuck into the sorting and weaving of the complicated *Spinner* plots.

It took almost two years to complete the original manuscript and its first massive revision, but we achieved this in time to enter the novel competition which closed in October 1946. Then we worked on another revision until I finally got my RAAF summons to England and left in July 1947 taking with me a copy of the second revision, little knowing the problems I was leaving behind.

A few weeks later, Dymphna was called into the *Daily Telegraph* for the first of many consultations. She was told in confidence that we would be the prize winners, but until the huge manuscript was cut by at least 50 000 words—to a length considered publishable by the newspaper—there would be no announcement.

Dymphna agreed to try, wrote to me and got to work. Cutting for continuity and balance was a big job and there were many problems. We cross-edited by airmail, being scrupulously careful to retain the truths and tone of our story, and the final revision was sent to me to deal with in London, where the *Daily Telegraph* had a publishing affiliate. The publisher wanted another 50 000 words cut! I refused but agreed to consider further editorial suggestions. How nervous of possible obscenity the publishing industry was.

We now entered the realm of comic opera. The English

publisher decided to do some editing of his own and spent weeks changing racy Australian idiom into ladylike English dialogue. I changed it all back again and, for good measure, asked Christina Stead to vet the American dialogue. She was delighted with the book and agreed with me that there should be no further revision.

The *Daily Telegraph* countered by proposing to withhold the prize money until publication. I consulted the British Society of Authors and Dymphna saw our Sydney solicitor, with the result that we were paid our £1000. When Dymphna joined me in London in 1949 (travelling on her share of the prize), the London and Sydney offices of the *Daily Telegraph* again put pressure on us to make further alterations, but we stood firm and, finally, in October 1949, three years after the competition closed, *Come In Spinner* was released to us to find our own publisher. This meant that we would forgo the *Daily Telegraph*'s promised publication of 100 000 copies. But we believed our novel had something valuable to say and so did the London publisher, William Heinemann, to whom we offered our final revision. It took them just one week to accept *Come In Spinner*, without asking for either cuts or alteration.

Eventually the first edition reached 100 000 copies, and lest anyone may think the authors made a fortune, those were the bad old days when English publishers wrote "colonial" contracts for Australian authors, under which Dymphna and I shared the handsome royalty of 6 pence a copy on Australian sales.

Since then, *Come In Spinner* has been spinning steadily. Over the years eight translations have been published in various European countries and a variety of paperback editions have succeeded each other in the bookshops.

When Dymphna died in 1981, neither she nor I had given any thought to including all the original stories in a new edition and, in fact, the question of the whereabouts of the original manuscript arose only when a mini-TV series was in prospect. It was Richard Walsh, the publisher of Angus & Robertson at that time, who contacted me about the possibility of including all the *Come In Spinner* stories in a new edition, and who tracked down the original manuscript in the National Library.

I am not going to write in detail about this new *Come In Spinner*, only to say that it is truly a new edition, complete and unabridged, that includes whole stories that had been cut out and much more about the adventures of the chief characters. What fun Dymphna and I would have had working on it together. By happy coincidence, I was able to take a cottage in the Blue Mountains for the months I spent shaping this new *Come In Spinner*, often remembering the time when we were writing together and our friendship through all the years.

We dedicated the original edition of *Come In Spinner* to a great Australian writer and a beloved friend, Miles Franklin. I would now like to add a further dedication to this new edition:

> To my two daughters, Julie and Frances, who loved Dymphna and who shared our friendship.
> To their children, my three granddaughters: Pippa and Robin who, now in their early twenties, have shared *Come In Spinner* with their friends and assure me that the problems of young women are not so different today, and to Erica who, in her early teens, will no doubt read this new *Come In Spinner* when she is ready and will give me her honest opinion.

Florence James
SYDNEY 1988

FRIDAY

I

Angus McFarland stepped out of the private hire car at the main entrance of the Hotel South Pacific and snapped a brusque reply to the commissionaire's "Good evening, sir." The chauffeur pocketed his tip, touched his cap, and the car moved smoothly down Macquarie Street.

Angus was hot and uncomfortable. The unseasonable heat of the spring afternoon beat up from the pavement, and across the street the glare from the setting sun blazed back from the fan-shaped transoms of Parliament House. He noticed with rising irritation that the sky was angry with clouded fire, and flaming mares' tales rioted in the upper air. That would mean another hot day tomorrow — probably a westerly, judging by the sky.

What a fool he had been to let his sister persuade him to go to Wahroonga on a day like this, even if Ian and his family were down from the country on one of their infrequent visits. It had been damned boring as well as uncomfortable — nothing but family business and gossip. Serve him right for going; he had nothing whatever in common with Virginia or Ian, and he ought to have known better. He should have spent the afternoon up at the Continental Gymnasium having his usual Friday Turkish bath and massage to get himself in form for his evening with Deborah. A man wanted to feel at his best with a girl as vibrant and beautiful as she was — particularly when he was seventeen years older.

Not that that really made any difference, Angus told himself hastily. His middle age was a thought on which he did not care to dwell and he smothered it immediately under a number of customary private reassurances. Why, a man was in his prime at forty-nine if he looked after himself properly. And he had always done that. He had never spared himself on the golf course, nor had he once failed to fit in his massage twice a week ever since he had decided some years ago that this was essential if he was to keep his waistline under control and at the same time continue to enjoy the quantity of whisky he was used to and the choice food which a lifetime of delicate eating demanded. Other men might go to seed in their forties, but not he.

Yet, in spite of his satisfactory statement about himself to himself, Angus turned to go up the steps of the hotel with a sense of personal injury which vented itself on his sister and the heat. It almost seemed as though Virginia had deliberately planned to upset his massage routine out of malice, and the weather had perversely arranged to be hot and windy tomorrow in order to ruin the spring race meeting for him.

His irritation sharpened to distaste as he was forced to join the stream of people who were moving up the hotel steps with the ragged purposefulness of ants. There had been a time when a man could mount the steps of his hotel with dignity. After all, when one had patronised the same hotel on and off for twenty-five years, one had reason and right to expect to enter as an honoured guest, not merely as one of a jostling mob clamouring for a drink before six o'clock closing. There was some comfort at least in the thought that all but a privileged few would be disappointed.

Angus picked his way fastidiously round the outskirts of the crowd in the vestibule. No better than an Eastern bazaar, he said to himself. Utterly repugnant, all of it. The prowling servicemen with hot inquisitive eyes: the girls dawdling by, welcoming obvious pickups with the assumed warmth of old acquaintance: the drawled compliments of Americans: the clipped greetings of a few British naval officers: the casual Australian voices; guttural Dutch and nasal French. Revolting. He would complain again to the manager. Not that that would be of much use. Sharlton was always promising to do something about it and always excusing his failure, which all boiled down to the fact that it was deliberate policy. The directors ought to be ashamed of themselves for allowing the hotel to become a place of common assignation. If it were not for Deborah he'd move to the Australia tomorrow.

He made his way with impatient authority through a crowd waiting round the lift doors. Neither lift was down. He put his finger firmly on the call button, the bell buzzed surprisingly close at hand and he was astonished to hear an American voice only a little above his head call with an impatience matching his own: "Say, buddy, instead of ringing hell out of that bell, you'd do better to spend your energy looking for an elevator technician. We're marooned."

Angus stepped back a pace. Someone behind him tittered.

"Better see if you can find the manager," a second voice advised. "This flaming old rattletrap's stuck again."

He recognised the voice as that of the insufferable relieving liftman whom everyone called Blue. Angus moved to the other lift and put his finger on the button, looking fixedly at the indicator as though he was not only deaf to the men in the lift but blind to the gathering crowd as well. There was no response from the second lift. It seemed permanently stuck at the top floor.

This was intolerable. In no country in the world but Australia would a man have to put up with service like this. Unquestionably the South Pacific was going to the dogs. If it weren't for Deborah he would stay at the club — anywhere rather than endure this sort of thing every time he came in or out. Quarter to six! He had already been waiting for five minutes. Anger mounted in him. He had come back early especially to have a rest before dressing for the evening and he had to waste his time standing round waiting for a lift.

It was true he was not meeting Deborah until eight o'clock, but the whole evening would be ruined if he had to rush and he wanted to be at his best for her. She was always so exquisite, poised — utterly different from the upstart women who invaded the South Pacific nowadays with their interminable high-pitched laughter. He felt again a sense of incongruity that Deborah's position on the staff of the hotel's beauty salon should place her at the beck and call of such women as these. All the months he'd known her he had never become reconciled to the thought. It was time he did something definite about it.

When Blue had opened the lift door at the second floor two American officers lifted a finger in friendly greeting. "Just hold her, will you, Blue?" one asked, looking along the corridor, "Homer's still round in the Wellington Room saying his goodbyes. He won't be a minute."

"Good-oh, Loot." The lift bell buzzed. Blue looked at the indicator and jerked it off. "You can wait," he said amiably to the invisible caller.

A lanky sergeant pelted down the corridor and into the lift. "Whew! I w-w-was afraid you'd be g-g-gone," he stuttered.

"Trust us, serg." Blue clapped him affectionately on the shoulder. "Wait all day for you, we would."

"That's real nice, B-B-Blue," the sergeant grinned and flicked a cigarette towards him. "Butt?"

"Thanks." Blue opened the maroon tunic of his uniform and tucked the cigarette away in the pocket of his khaki shirt, buttoned up the tunic again and started the lift. "How did the shivoo go off?"

"Swell. N-n-nicest party I've been to since my kid sister graduated. Ellery sure is a lucky guy to get a g-g-girl like Constance."

"And boy! Is she easy on the eye!" The lieutenant clicked his tongue admiringly.

"She sure is," drawled the young airman, "and sweet as they come."

The sergeant drew a deep sigh. "That's love for you," he said. "C-c-can anyone tell me why no g-g-girl ever looks at me the way Ellery's girl looks at him?"

"You want to eat more spinach, Homer," the airman advised.

"Babes in the wood," Blue said sentimentally. "I

brought 'em up in the lift together and they stood there lookin' into each other's eyes and floated out on air holding each other's hands. Fair give me a lump in me throat it did.''

The airman shook his head mournfully. "When I think of the luck of the stiff getting a wife like that *and* a Purple Heart!''

They all sighed together and caught their breath short as the lift stopped between floors with a jolt. Blue swung the handle over. Nothing happened. He pressed each button on the automatic indicator in turn. The three Americans followed his movements. The lift stayed stuck. He ran his fingers through his scanty ginger hair.

"Sorry, pals. I've pushed all the buttons. I've pulled all the gadgets and it's no go. Anyone got any ideas?''

"Maybe if we all jumped together," the airman suggested.

Blue cocked an eye at him. "This is a lift, Corp, not a kite.''

"*On* the elevator I mean, Buddy. Not out of it.''

They all jumped up and down together solemnly. The lift remained where it was.

"Stuck! I had a car when I was out on dates at college used to get stuck like this," the lieutenant said. "She sure was a fine car.''

Blue tried the handle again. Half a dozen floors were ringing on the indicator. He jerked it clear.

"Where are we?''

"Between first and ground floor.''

"I'll t-t-take a peek." The sergeant knelt and put his face down, looking out through six inches of iron grille that had cleared the first floor. A buzz of voices rose from the vestibule. "So n-n-near and yet so far," he mourned.

"What can you see?'' demanded the lieutenant.

"Just enough of the Cockpit to put my blood pressure up. Gosh there're a lot of b-b-blondes in this town.''

The airman knelt down beside him. "Drugstore," he said. "Look at their partings.''

"Move over, you old son of a gun," the lieutenant

nudged him.

Blue gazed down on the pink-beige bottoms of the kneeling men. "Easy seen you boys ain't spent the war shiny-bumming."

"You n-n-need t-t-talent for that, Blue," the sergeant replied without moving his eyes from the crack. "Us b-b-boys haven't got it."

"You've said it." The lieutenant shouldered his way to a better view. "I reckon sixty years from now I'll still be crawling through jungles when those guys at HQ have grown fast to their chairs."

"That's what you call the seat of war," the airman commented dryly.

"I know," Blue agreed. "We breed the kind here at Victoria Barracks."

"It's a fine war for them. I wish I had what it takes to get me a job at the base."

"Maybe you could learn it by correspondence. . . . Gosh, look at that coppertop!"

"Listen, boys," Blue broke in. "You keep your minds on the job. If you don't want to be here all night you'd better give someone a call for a lift mechanic while you're down there."

"That's no use, Blue. What you want is an elevator technician."

"Move over," Blue gave the sergeant a nudge, "and let me see if I can get someone to give us a hand." He knelt and squeezed himself down at the end of the row.

"Hey," he bellowed to the sea of heads in the vestibule below. "We're stuck! Will somebody send for the manager?"

The buzz of voices continued unheeding.

"All I can see now," the lieutenant tried to get a better view, "is the top piece of that gold statue that stands up in the middle of the Cockpit fishpond."

The airman laughed. "Good old Bouncing Belle. I've never seen anything so curvaceous. What a girl!"

"Grandpa's idea of female pulchritood," the lieutenant

6

chuckled. "What did they stick her up there for, Blue?"

"Aw . . . she was a figurehead on a sailing ship called the *Bouncing Belle*; belonged to the old joker who built the first South Pacific pub down near the docks. She's in the contract and they can't get rid of her."

"Boy, what an armful!"

"She bulges," the airman said critically.

"Matter of taste," said Blue. "When I was a kid, if a girl didn't have bulges, she made 'em."

"A few more dames like that around and your poppa'd be a billionaire, Homer, instead of merely a millionaire." The lieutenant dug the sergeant in the ribs.

Homer got up and dusted the knees of his pinks. "I w-w-wish you wouldn't always keep bringing my P-p-poppa up," he said aggrievedly. "I can't help him being a m-m-millionaire."

"Crikey!" Blue exclaimed. "If I had a poppa a millionaire I'd put a placard across me bloomin' back to let everyone know."

"So would anyone else but Homer. He's kinda shy about it. I never know whether it's the dollars he's bashful about or the product that brings 'em in."

"I d-d-don't mind my Poppa making b-b-brazeers at all, it's a national utility, and if I ever get out of this war I'm going to do the p-p-p-publicity for the firm. It's just I don't like having P-p-p-poppa's money thrown up at me. It makes me unp-p-popular."

"You act like a crazy man, Homer." The airman clapped him on the back. "What do you think Spen here and me stick round you closer than a brother for? Love?"

"I d-d-don't mind you guys knowin'. It doesn't stop you from slappin' me down."

Blue flattened out on the floor and let out a piercing: "Ho-ho-ho! Ho-ho-ho!"

The buzz of conversation below the lift stopped for a moment and a shrill, affected voice called angrily: "What are you doing up there, pray? We've been waiting here for hours."

"Listen, lady," Blue explained, "we don't like it any better than you do. But she's broken down. Hop round to the manager's office, will you, and tell him."

"Really!" The shrill voice came to them full of pained astonishment.

"Lady, if you ever want to travel in this lift again," Blue implored, "get somebody to get a mechanic. It won't go, see?"

"Denny, darling," he heard the voice coo, "would you run round to Mr Sharlton's office and tell him to send someone immediately? Tell him the lift's been stuck for hours."

"Oh, Mummykins," they heard Denny darling complain petulantly, "there's always something wrong with the lifts in this wretched place. Next time I come into town I'm going to stay at the Australia."

Blue straightened himself as the voice faded. "Well, that'll certainly be a break for the South Pacific."

Homer cowered behind the airman. "D-d-did my ears deceive me," he whispered, "or was that that D'Arcy-Twyning d-d-dame?"

"Too right it was."

"Help! You c-c-can keep me locked up here for life, Blue, but d-d-don't let her get at me."

"OK, mate. Looks like the lift'll do the trick for you. Seems like we're going to be stuck here all night if I know anything about this rattletrap."

"Five-thirty," exclaimed the airman, looking at his wristwatch. "We ought to have been round at the Carlton five minutes ago."

"I d-d-don't like to think of those g-g-girls waiting there in the foyer for us."

"As this is our last night in Sydney town for God knows how long, I don't like to think of them not waiting," the airman said gloomily.

"Well, you've just got to resign yourself to it," the lieutenant cheered him up. "We're going to be late — but late!"

"We might as well settle down for a quiet evening at

home and make ourselves comfortable," Blue suggested. "How about a game of swy just to pass the time?"

"What's swy, Aussie?"

"Two-up."

"I seem to've heard of it."

"It's the great Australian pastime. Fairest game on God's earth. Just a matter of spinning a couple of brownies."

Blue fished in his trouser pocket and brought out a handful of change from which he selected two pennies.

"Is it on the level, Blue?"

"Too bloody right it is. You could play it in your mother's parlour. I'll show you how it goes." He held the pennies up for the Americans to see. "This is heads and this is tails, see? And you put 'em on your hand like this."

He extended the first two fingers of his right hand and placed the pennies on them, tails up. The Americans leaned over, deeply interested.

"Now watch carefully." Blue flicked the pennies into the air and let them rattle on the floor of the lift. "There you are, see!"

The three Americans gazed on the two tails with growing interest.

"I'd lose on that toss," Blue explained, bending to turn the two pennies over on the floor so that the two heads showed. "If they'd fell this way I'd of won, but if they'd fell this way..." he turned one coin over to show a tail, "that don't count."

"I g-g-get it," exclaimed Homer delightedly, "a kind of crap, eh?"

"That's it, serg. You start this if you like, pal, just to show the game's on the level." He handed the two pennies to the sergeant.

"Now how about a little bet? Better make it easy, eh?"

Blue suited his words by placing a ten-shilling note on the floor. The sergeant obliged by immediately covering his bet and placing the two pennies on his hand, looking uncertainly at Blue.

"Right. Now you're spinner, see," Blue told him. "Come in the ring, give him some room, boys."

The sergeant tossed the pennies clumsily in the air.

"Two heads," cried Blue. "Cripes, can you play! Right. I'll cover the quid." He placed the note on the floor; the coins soared again to show a head and a tail.

"No go," said the sergeant while the lieutenant and the airman looked on.

A couple of heads and tails came next and then two tails.

"Bad luck, pal," Blue said, gathering in the money. "Now I'll have a go if you like," and, withdrawing three pound notes from his pocket he placed them on the floor. "That's so you can all have a bet," he added in explanation. "You guys don't want to feel out of it."

The two others each drew out bulging wads that made Blue's eyes goggle and his fingers itch. A thrill of anxiety went up and down his spine as he heard the lift clanging next door. Cripes, he hoped they wouldn't be able to dig up a mechanic.

The bets were covered. Blue called happily, "Let the angels see 'em," and the pennies spun again. They came down to rattle and roll on the floor, and four eager pairs of eyes waited for them to settle. A head and tail.

"No go," said the sergeant.

The pennies went up again.

"Come on babies, speak to me," crooned the lieutenant.

"Two heads," said Blue with satisfaction, gathering in the six pounds booty. "Right now. Like to double up, gentlemen?"

There was a slight pause while the sergeant explained to the others that to double up meant adding two pounds each to cover the six pounds that had now become Blue's property.

A burst of laughter came from the unseen crowd waiting for the lift and a piercing whistle disturbed the game.

Blue put his nose down to the narrow grille. "Is that the mechanic?" he enquired anxiously.

"Are you the ringie?"

"That's me."

"I want to have a bet with you," the voice called.

"Sorry, mate. School's closed here, but you can set 'em on the side between yourselves down there if you like."

There was a roar of laughter from the crowd.

"Good," another voice called. "Here goes."

Blue saw a hand waving a ten-shilling note, then he saw two brown faces under RAAF forage caps peering up at him from the outskirts of the little crowd.

"All set on the side?" he called.

"All set."

"Right." He stood up again. "Come in, spinner."

Angus heard above him, with incredulity that amounted to horror, the jargon of a game he had not heard or seen played since the days of the First World War. When the rattle of the pennies first caught his attention he had deliberately taken no notice, but now no one could disregard the noise. Or the language. If this was a sample of what the South Pacific was coming to, the sooner he — and Deborah — got away from it, the better. He would sound her out about a flat tonight.... He frowned. It would take some skill to do it. In all the months he had been taking her out he had not been able to bring himself to the point of asking her. There was something about Deborah that eluded him: she was not like any other woman in his wide experience. He could never make up his mind just how much a woman of the world she was. And, since Angus was used to making up his mind on every matter that came under his notice and he was strongly attracted to Deborah, he had lately found himself venting his annoyance at his own indecision on any irritation that presented itself.

He decided to walk up the stairs, remembered the six flights to his suite and decided not to. His anger grew, fanned by his indignation for Deborah, on whose erratic hours of work in the Marie Antoinette Salon he had so often to wait, and resentment at his own deep involvement which gave him no choice but to wait. He turned a contemptuous glance on the crowds milling around the Bouncing Belle. Really, he did not know what Sharlton could have been thinking of, to have had that vulgar figurehead regilded. It had always been an eyesore, and now, with the lights gleaming on every golden curve, it was positively offensive. But no doubt it suited a crowd like this.

Vulgarians, that's what they all were, with neither knowledge nor taste; chasing showy pleasures, swallowing any liquor they could get. All they wanted was a stimulant and an aphrodisiac; though what need there was of either he could not see, with all these trollops flirting their bottoms under swinging skirts, their breasts impudent and aggressive under skintight frocks. People said the breakdown in manners and morals was due to the war, but he had been young in the last war and he would take an oath it had not been like this. Women had dignity then, and mystery. Open parading of lust there might have been in some places, shameless soliciting — that was inevitable in war — but it was kept in its place. It did not intrude into decent society as it did nowadays. The Americans were responsible for it, in Australia at any rate. They had too much money. Until they came, hotels like the South Pacific were not frequented by other ranks, and at least officers in the last war had thought enough of their uniforms to behave like gentlemen, even if they were not.

He started as a hand touched his arm. An affected voice gushed over him: "Oh, Mr McFarland, isn't it all frightfully inconvenient! Denise and I have been waiting here simply hours."

Angus turned, lifting his hat and bowing an acknowledgment of the greeting. "Mrs D'Arcy-Twyning. Miss Denise....most inconvenient."

Blue's voice came down to them. "A quid wanted," he called. "A quid in the guts to see her away."

"Right!" The voice rose jubilantly. "Come in, spinner!"

The rattle of coins sounded again.

Mrs D'Arcy-Twyning shuddered. "That awful language! What are they doing?" She craned her long, crêpey neck upwards.

"Playing two-up, I'm afraid." Angus's mouth set in a tight line.

Mrs D'Arcy-Twyning gaped incredulously. "No-o-o!"

"The whole thing's perfectly ghastly," Denise pouted. "I had an appointment at half past five at the Marie Antoinette for a manicure, and if I know those girls they simply won't wait back a minute for me, and I'm bothered if I'm going to climb the stairs after the ghastly time I've had trailing around that orchid show the whole afternoon."

"Denny darling, you're really very naughty. It was a perfectly enchanting show, Mr McFarland. Lady Govett was the president, you know. Sir Frederick's just back from India ...that big conference...what was it about? Anyway, he's just back. A horrible place, he says, beggars everywhere, you couldn't move for them. He's sure we're going to have trouble there soon, they've got quite above themselves."

"He brought Goldie back the divinest saris, she's going to have them made into evening frocks." Denise's voice was full of envy.

Mrs D'Arcy-Twyning held out a transparent plastic box to Angus. "Look at my prize cattaleya. Isn't it magnificent?"

"A fine specimen."

"It's quite a thing," Denise trilled, "and it cost her seven guineas at the auction afterwards."

Her mother tee-heed. "I told you not to say anything about that, you naughty little girl. It was for charity and you know your father and I never begrudge money for a good cause."

"Well, all I wish is this silly old lift'd come. I simply must have a manicure before the ball tomorrow and I don't know where I'll fit it in now."

Angus's irritation increased irrationally. To think that every little chit like this D'Arcy-Twyning girl could order Deborah around. "I shall see Sharlton myself," was all he could trust himself to say.

"Oh, he's not in the office. Denise has just been and Mrs Molesworth says they've sent for a mechanic, but you know what it is to get a man at this hour."

"Surely both lifts can't be out of order." Angus held his finger on the second bell.

"No, but the other driver got out to see if he could do something and one of the American boys took his lift up and must have left the door open at the roof."

"Is there no one to go up and see?"

"They said in the office they'd send one of the porters."

"That's typical," Angus muttered, all his annoyance focusing itself on the lout who had left the door ajar. A burst of laughter from the marooned party above his head made him feel that it was all part of a deliberate plan to ruin his evening. It was already five to six.

Mrs D'Arcy-Twyning went gushing on. Angus disentangled from the spate of words her thankfulness that at last all these Americans were going home and we were to have the British Navy here. They, at least, would never leave lift doors open on the roof and disrupt the social engagements of the guests for whom the South Pacific used once to be run — not, as it seemed now, for a horde of jumped-up baggages and servicemen.

He glanced at the enormous square sapphire on Denise's left hand, pledge of an American colonel, and waited for her protest. But she only opened her eyes in ecstasy and lisped: "Isn't it too marvellous? I simply adore the British."

"Ah," said Mrs D'Arcy-Twyning rapturously, "there'll always be an England. Or should I say — Britain?"

"It's a matter of taste. You'll be in the fashion if you do."

"Oh yes, we're all British now."

Angus winced. "Personally I deplore this wartime breaking down of traditional distinctions."

Mrs D'Arcy-Twyning went off at a tangent. "I'm so glad to see you've booked a table for my OBNOs Ball to-morrow evening. I was hoping you might join my party at the official table. We did so look forward to having Prince Alexander — he's on the *Impenetrable*, you know — but he'd already arranged to fly down to Melbourne. Such a charming young man, so democratic. But Commander Derek Ermington will be there — his father, you know, is Lord Weffolk.''

"Thank you. But my brother and his wife and daughter are down from the country and I'm taking this opportunity of entertaining a family party.''

"How charming! We're booked right out, you know. It's so nice to think Australians are rallying so generously to help the orphans of British naval officers.''

"Splendid,'' Angus murmured. Confound the OBNOs. He had booked thinking it would be an ordinary Saturday night dinner dance at Who's Who, now it looked as though there was going to be a disgusting social crush.

He had let himself in for a wretched evening, he thought morosely. Already he was regretting having asked the family. It was bad enough to have had to spend the day with them! Ian, his brother, soured and aged by the problems of running a property with all this damned government interference: his sister-in-law, Olive, more irritating than ever, with her eternal preoccupation with the affairs of the Country Women's Association. She and his sister Virginia were a pair; no style, no poise, nothing but good works and sentimentality. And their husbands were as bad; Ian and Lawrence actually backed them up. Lawrence, with his exaggerated ideas of giving back to the community the extra income he was making out of war contracts, and Ian, with that bee in his bonnet that absentee landlords were the curse of the country. Why, Ian had actually suggested that he should leave Sydney and lend a hand on the property! A lot of good he'd be on the land after thirty years of civilised living, and besides it was ridiculous to think he could cut loose from all his interests at a word from Ian.

Angus made an impatient movement, reached out his hand to press the bell again, and thought better of it. By God, if people had to put up with what they suffered in

France in 1917.... Women were losing their femininity nowadays and their husbands and fathers encouraged them. Look at his niece Helen. Positively weatherbeaten and no sense of style. It was a pity she couldn't take a few lessons from Deborah on how to look after her skin and hair. The way Olive let a young girl neglect herself like that was positively wicked. It was no excuse that she had to be up early and late, mustering, trucking, working like a man. She needn't do it if she didn't want to, and if she hadn't enough sense, her mother ought to put her foot down. There was something abnormal about this fervour on the part of women for the war effort. Probably sex compensation.... Well, he could tell them, as a soldier, how men preferred to find their women when they came home. Certainly not like Helen; no polish, not a spark of charm, nothing attractive about her.

Mrs D'Arcy-Twyning gabbled endlessly. He brought his mind back with an effort, but the clink of coins against the floor of the lift kept distracting him.

Blue's voice rang down the lift well. "Stand back, boys! Fair go for the spinner!" The coins rattled again. The people pressing around the lift doors were listening with upturned faces. The cable ropes of the second lift began to sway. "Whoopee," someone called, "she's coming. They must have moved the body."

The crowded lift shot down, the door opened slowly and a flustered lift driver looked out.

"Sorry, sir," he said, "but it got held up."

"We've been waiting hours," shrilled Mrs. D'Arcy-Twyning.

"I'm very sorry, madam."

At least he was apologetic, thought Angus. Not like the fellow in the other lift. He could still hear the clinking of coins and bursts of raucous laughter. It would serve them right if someone sent for the police...playing an illegal game in public!

"I shall certainly speak to my husband about it," Mrs D'Arcy-Twyning said severely. "There's a directors' meeting next week. They must be told about this."

"I don't know what the Britishers would think," Denise chanted in her singsong treble.

The last passenger stepped out and the waiting crowd surged forward. The lift driver barred the way. "Guests first, please. This way, madam. This way, sir."

Mrs D'Arcy-Twyning and Denise swept in disdainfully. Angus followed.

From the marooned lift Blue's voice encouraged the unseen players. "OK, fellers. Let the angels see 'em!"

The pennies went spinning up again from Blue's practised·fingers. Down they came and the spinner collected. The rolls of the Americans decreased steadily, and by the time Blue spun out at last, there was a big bulge in his shirt pocket.

The lieutenant and Homer took their turn and the young airman crooned to the spinning coins in his drawling southern voice: "Do it for Daddy, babies; do it for Daddy."

"Bad luck," Blue consoled him, collecting the last of his roll. "You're a hell of a fine player; I've never seen anyone pick up the game so quick in me life. It's just that these Aussie brownies don't understand the crap language."

"You've c-c-cleaned me right out, Blue." Homer turned out his empty pockets.

"I'll give yer a loan for the night," Blue offered. "I know what it is to be stone motherless broke in a strange city."

"That's OK, Aussie. My b-b-buddies'll see me through. But I'll give you one last t-t-toss." He opened his wallet and took out a lottery ticket. "I'll play you for this. It may bring you five thousand of your m-m-money. And we'll be back in Manila by the time it's d-d-d-drawn."

"Looks like they're starting the last big push in the Pacific, eh?"

"That's right," the airman agreed. "All the big shots are moving up from the base."

"Well, that oughter cheer you up; things must be getting safe!" Blue generously covered the lottery ticket with a pound note and handed Homer the pennies. "You take the last toss for luck, serg. Stand back, fellers, and give him a fair go. Now! Come in, spinner!''

Homer placed the pennies reverently on his outstretched fingers and breathed on them: "C-c-c-come on, you little b-b-brown sweethearts," he pleaded and spun the coins.

"Up where the birdies fly, you beauts," Blue's strident voice cheered him on.

The pennies rolled to his feet.

Homer solemnly picked up the lottery ticket, flattened it against the wall, and wrote across the back: 'To my old pal Blue'..."Say, what's your other name?"

"Johnson," Blue supplied. "Come out with the First Fleet."

"Blue Johnson," the sergeant continued, "from Homer P. Alcorn in settlement of a d-d-debt of honour." He turned to the other two. "C-c-come on, you guys, witness here, so it's all legal."

Blue pocketed the ticket and buttoned his tunic. The lift gave a jerk. Slowly they began to descend. When he opened the door the manager was waiting, his thin face pale with rage. Crikey Blue thought, old L.F. looks like murder. Aw, what the hell. "Well, here we are at last, Mr Sharlton!" he announced cheerily.

The manager ignored him. The crowd jostled forward. "Now then, now then," Blue waved them back. "No pushin' and shovin'. Make way for our allies."

The Americans filed slowly out, each pausing to shake his hand. "Good luck, Homer P." Blue smiled up at him warmly. "Come and see me when you get back, mate!"

"S-s-sure," said the sergeant, "it's a date."

The manager gritted his teeth and stepped back to allow the lift to fill. He followed the last passenger in and stood beside Blue, lean and forbidding.

In the Marie Antoinette Salon on the second floor of the Hotel South Pacific the process of beautifying the last client of the day went through its complicated routine.

Claire came wearily into the boudoir, now free of waiting patrons, and crossed the mushroom-coloured carpet to the large Louis Quinze mirror which reflected the whole luxurious room within its gilded frame. The pink light from the sham wall candles suffused her with a flattering glow, softening the sharp contours of her face and burnishing the formal curls of her upswept chestnut hair. I'm looking better tonight, she thought, enjoying the colour scheme of the gleaming curls above her turquoise blue overall, not nearly such a hag. She gave a short laugh and turned from the mirror. Fancy you falling for your own stuff, Claire Jeffries. Keep that for the patrons, my girl.

She collected the scattered sheets of an evening paper and put them on the settee to take home with her, picked up copies of *Vogue* and *Harper's Bazaar* thrown carelessly down on the carpet, and gathered the *Tatler* and *Country Life* from the lounges and chairs, smoothing their dogeared covers. These damn women...careless devils they were. They'd squeal loud enough if the magazines weren't there for them, but did any of them ever give a thought to all the time and trouble it took to get round the wartime ban on their import? Serve them right if they had to put up with local stuff — and it looked as though that was what it was coming to. She'd stake her life that hers was the only salon in town where the patrons still got the really good overseas periodicals — for that matter there wasn't another salon in Sydney that had succeeded in maintaining its old air of elegance through all the difficulties of war.

She shook out the folds of the heavily draped turquoise curtains, musty with stale perfume and cigarette smoke. She wished to God they'd relax some of these idiotic restrictions on dry cleaning so that she could get the place freshened up. The oyster-grey brocade on the chairs and lounges was positively grubby.

She went over to the elaborate showcase beneath the great mirror and ran her eye proudly over the rows of exotic jars: cleansing cream and muscle oil, complexion milk and skin tonic, facial packs, pore cream, astringents; lotions to remove suntan and lotions to simulate it; deodorants to remove the human smell and perfumes to replace it; powder bases for dry skins, for greasy skins, for skins in between; makeup to obliterate shadows under the eyes and makeup to shadow the lids above them, blue, mauve, green or silver; dry rouge and moist rouge; powders to warm pale skins, powders to cool the florid; concoctions for encouraging coveted curves and concoctions for taking off superfluous ones; lipsticks for strawberry blondes, platinum blondes and natural blondes, for brunettes, brownettes, two-tones and inbetweens; everything redolent of the heavy perfume that pervaded the salon, and every pink and gold label bearing as the symbol of feminine beauty the ill-fated head of Marie Antoinette.

Claire opened the glass front. Now just what would she unload on Mrs Dalgety this time? That Mystery of the Orient line had been a bit of a flop since the Jap war had taken the lid off Eastern glamour. She'd stock her up with that; the old girl was never sober long enough to get her eyes focused on the labels anyway.

As she stood up with the bottles in her hands another reflection fell across the mirror.

"Have you finished Dalgety yet, Guin?" Claire asked the girl behind her.

"Not quite. She's got a bit longer in the sweatbox." Guinea thrust her face closer to the mirror. "Holy mackerel! I look as though I've been boiled!"

Claire looked at the two reflections and her nervous fingers tightened round the jars. Hell! she said to herself. What's the use? All the cosmetics in the place won't make me look like Guinea, even when she's giving that lump of lard a sweat bath. Skin with the bloom of twenty-two on it, hair curling around her shoulders, gold as no expensive touching-up could make it.

"How long will she be?" Claire nodded towards the curtained cubicle.

"Another five minutes and then Deb can have her. I've got her on top heat, and I hope she busts. She'll holler for help in a minute or two. Jeepers! How she stinks. Gin oozing out of every pore!"

"Serve her right if she has a stroke," Claire said viciously, packing half a dozen jars in an elaborate pink and gold box. "Coming in here at five-thirty and throwing her weight round to get the whole works. Old Mother Molesworth may be hostess of this pub and the manager's girlfriend, but it's over the odds when she lets us in for this kind of thing right on closing time."

Guinea's voice rose half an octave. "Reallah, Miss Jeffrahs, you must understand there is no closing time for the Marie Antoinette Salon where our distinguished guests are concerned."

"Distinguished me fanny, Dalgety's only a jumped-up bitch."

"But a rich bitch."

Guinea flopped on to the settee and picked up the evening paper. She took a glance at the headlines and shuddered. "'END OF GRIM ARNHEM BATTLE'," she read aloud. "My God, listen to this: 'Three thousand of the original 8000 members of the British First Airborne Division who landed at Arnhem on September 17th were withdrawn to the south bank of the Lek on Monday night.' When the hell is it all going to end?"

"When they've got nobody left to fight, I suppose." Claire looked over her shoulder. "Ah! Look at this! 'GREAT BRITISH FLEET FOR PACIFIC.' That ought to cheer you up, with Sherwood on the move."

"Not me." Guinea pulled a face. "I know the British. Nice boys but they've got no money. Front stalls at the movies and a bunch of violets is their idea of a big night. I've been spoiled for that."

A wailing voice came from a cubicle. "Miss Mal-o-o-one

...I'm fainting..."

Guinea shrugged. "I must have left her on too long. She's probably grilled." She strolled unconcernedly across the thick carpet and down the corridor, switched off the power in the sweatbox and ran a wet towel over the protruding apoplectic face.

"You're all right," she said professionally, swinging the box open and revealing Mrs Dalgety slumped on a chair with the sweat trickling down her parboiled body.

"I'm sure you've left me too long," she spluttered as Guinea poured some ice water between her lips.

"Oh no, Mrs Dalgety, not a minute too long. You've lost pounds, and think how good that'll make you feel when you get into that new model of yours for the races tomorrow."

Mrs Dalgety blinked red-rimmed eyes as she looked down at her drooping breasts and slack belly. "Do you really think so?" she asked doubtfully. "I'd give anything to lose some of this weight."

"Sure thing, and the massage'll take off a few pounds more. Now in we go to the shower."

Mrs Dalgety waddled into the shower room. Soon, yelps of protest announced that Guinea had turned off the hot water and was letting the cold needles play on her with full force.

"Were you christened Guinea?" Mrs Dalgety inquired when at last the vigorous towelling was over.

"Good lord, no. My name's Margaret — Peg for short."

"Well, how did they come to call you Guinea?"

"I used to be on the Bouquet Boutique in the vestibule, and one of the Yanks did a painting of me. He called it Guinea Gold because of my hair."

"How romantic! Was he in love with you?"

"Gosh, no. He was a dried-up little bozo full of ideals."

"Tut, tut, what a pity! I hope he gave you a copy."

"Not him. He published it in *Down Under* and that's how it caught on." She sighed. "That was in the great days before the 'Fall'."

"Naughty, naughty," Mrs Dalgety twinkled lasciviously
and whispered, "How did you fall?"

Guinea shrugged her shoulder. "Very simple. One of
those shiny-bumming old brass hats from Victoria Barracks
got his knife into me. He kept pestering me to give him a
date." She shuddered. "Ugh! I got so fed up that when he
said at last I could pick my own time because he had every
night off, I told him he was damn lucky, that was more than
the boys in New Guinea got. He got rather hostile about it,
and the next thing I found myself up here."

"Serve him right," Mrs Dalgety said virtuously. "I can't
bear old men myself." She shuddered sympathetically as she
settled down on the massage table and leered pointedly up at
the masseuse who had just come in with cream and talc powder in her hands. "I think old men are revolting, don't you,
Miss Forrest?"

Deborah gave a strained smile. "You're probably
right," she said, beginning to sprinkle her with powder.

Mrs Dalgety sighed luxuriously: "I don't know what I'd
do without you girls. You keep me young."

"*And* beautiful," Guinea added, winking at Deb.

Mrs Dalgety chuckled till the loose flesh wobbled.
"That's what Alistair says, the naughty boy!"

"He should know. When's he coming?"

Mrs Dalgety moaned. "Oh my dear child, don't you
realise that's what all this fuss is about? I've just had a wire
that he's coming tonight! And I've simply got to be fit for the
dinner dance." Her face puckered as though she was going
to cry, and she looked anxiously at Deb who began to pound
her belly with firm rhythmic movements.

"Honestly, Miss Forrest, honestly now, I'm not too bad
for a woman of forty-three, am I?"

Deb caught a glimpse of Guinea grimacing in the doorway and lowered her head. "You're wonderful," she agreed
mechanically.

Mrs Dalgety examined the masseuse through half-closed
lids. So this was Angus McFarland's latest. That accounted

for the way Liz Destrange had been going on the last few months; they said she was drinking like a fish. There was no doubt Angus was a good picker — when it came to looks anyway. What a beauty Liz had been when she'd first got mixed up with him — that must have been ten years ago. It had been an unlucky day for her, poor devil; Angus obviously wasn't the marrying sort. Here was Liz now, looking like a hag and high and dry, while he was running round after something young enough to be his daughter.

She relaxed under the kneading of Deb's strong fingers. *Miss* Forrest. What was she doing with a wedding ring on then? There was no doubt about it, she had a lovely figure . . . good-looking too, though not in the pin-up class like Guinea. Reserved type, more of a lady than the other girls. Trust Angus, the old dog, to get something out of the box. He wasn't a day younger than she was — fifty next birthday. She knew; they'd both had their twenty-first birthday parties in London in the middle of the last war. She sighed regretfully. Life was most unfair; no one would throw off at him going round with a girl twenty years younger, and yet look at the way they stared at her and Alistair. Oh God! she thought, belching loudly, it's enough to make a woman take to drink in earnest.

"Life's very unfair to us women, I always say," Mrs Dalgety spoke her thoughts aloud. "You'd think the prime of life was invented for men only. Once a woman's forty they expect her to retire to the junk heap, while they start all over again on the young ones."

"Too right," Guinea agreed fervently. "Seems like it's the way the male's made."

"It all boils down to money in the end," Mrs Dalgety snorted indignantly. "A man can go through three generations just because he holds the purse strings." She gave another snort. "Monkey glands! All the fuss and money men spend to keep themselves at stud a few years longer!"

"It's a pity someone doesn't start something like that to pep up women."

Mrs Dalgety cocked a bleary eye at Guinea and

brightened. "That's an idea. I'll think about it."

"It'd be a nice change, Mrs Dalgety. Fancy you and me prowling round snatching baby boys out of their perambulators. We might even start harems!" They both went off into peals of laughter.

Deb turned Mrs Dalgety over distastefully. It was bad enough to have to put up with her disgusting breath without having to endure this sort of conversation. She began to massage her back and thighs. Only tonight and tomorrow morning, she told herself, with a sudden passionate desire to be out of the stale perfumed air of the salon. Then, forty blessed hours with no one to massage, no idiotic stories to listen to; fresh air and sun and wind. If this heat kept up, maybe a swim with Angus. He talked of a run to Palm Beach on Sunday. It would be lovely. . . . She kneaded the pads of fat across Mrs Dalgety's shoulders and her own arms tingled as she thought of plunging into the stinging October surf.

Claire looked round as Guinea drifted back to the boudoir. "How long will Deb be?"

"She's whacking into the old girl like the devil, so I shouldn't think she'll be too long. Gee, Dalgety must have had a soak this time."

"Elvira says she's been on a binge ever since she came to town and that's nearly a week ago."

"Whew — what a stomach! She must be tanned inside! I hope Alistair hasn't got a dainty nose."

"You needn't worry about Alistair. He should be used to it by now."

"How long has he been the boyfriend?"

"Must be fifteen years since he went out to their station. It used to be one of the show places of the northwest, but they're in the banks up to the neck now. Mrs Dalgety fell for him straight away, and he graduated from jackeroo to gigolo in one season."

"Nice work if you can get it."

"He's about twenty years younger than her — she's got a son older than him."

"She evidently reads the ads. 'Make yourself beautiful

for the returning hero'," Guinea quoted mincingly.

"Hero be blowed. He's a choco. Caught in the draft. They say her old man put the military on to him but she's succeeded in keeping him in Melbourne so far. The bitter pill there is that he'll never get above a private."

"How can he stick her?"

"Bank books are more than beauty, dear."

"Forty-three, Miss Jeffries. Forty-three, aren't I wearing well?"

"Forty-three! She'll never see fifty-three again."

Guinea leaned back on the boudoir stool and swung her legs in front of her. "It's funny. Even when you've got to work back and miss a date, it's funny to see the old cow hanging on to forty-three and going through the sufferings of the damned to get herself in shape for that gink. It's really funny."

Claire watched Guinea's reflection in the mirror, balancing perilously on the stool, legs outstretched, wedge-soled shoes raised in the air. The pink glow deepened her mushroom pink overall and gleamed on her bright hair. Claire looked again at her own face, tired and sagging, all the stresses of thirty-eight hard years showing in the sharpening contours and fine lines. No trick of lighting, no rosy illusion could change that. All the massage, all the cosmetics, all the care that the Marie Antoinette lavished on its wealthiest patrons could never again make her look as Guinea looked. Never. No, she said to herself, it's not funny. Not a bit funny. It's hell. What was it really worth to Mrs Dalgety to be mistress of a sheep station when her life was one long struggle to hold the man she loved? And if it comes to that, what is it really worth to be you, Claire Jeffries? Founder, life and brains of the Marie Antoinette, with your own line in cosmetics, your own line in glamour and your own life an endless struggle against the encroaching years and the insecurity of love?

She set her jaw stubbornly. It was something to have created the Marie Antoinette. It was a symbol of something important; of the beauty so necessary if a woman was to be desired, of the luxury which should be every woman's birth-right, of charm and sophistication, of gracious living, of all the things a woman needed if life was not to close over her like a tidal wave when once her youth was gone.

Guinea put her feet down with a thump. "You doing something special tonight?"

"I was. Nigel and I were going to have dinner at Rom's and then go on to the game. But I'll never make it by eight now, I'll have to give him a ring."

"You'll still have time."

"Time?" Claire laughed. "It's all right for you, my child. A wriggle of the hips and the pull of a zipper, a dash of lipstick and the whole South-West Pacific Command is at your feet. But I need rest and makeup and clothes if I'm not going to look a hag."

"Do you have to go home first?"

"I intended to, but I can't manage that now. I think I'll skip dinner and go on after. Deb's asked me to lie down in her room, but that means I'll have to wear my old suit. She's offered to lend me her lamé blouse to freshen it up but I'll still look like a hag and Nigel's so fussy."

"It's a nice suit. And with the blouse and a shoulder spray it would be OK."

"By the time we finish here, there won't be a decent flower left in the town. I rang down to the boutique and they've got nothing but red roses left. Huh! Can you imagine me in red roses?"

"Oh gosh! That reminds me. I'll have to wander down to the Cockpit myself and tell the boyfriend to park himself somewhere till I'm finished. He'll be there any minute now. Blast that Ursula, I wish to God we could get someone else on the desk. It was twenty-five to six when old Molesworth rang down about Dalgety and she could have said we'd gone, instead of pooling us for this."

"The trouble is, Old Mole has Ursula in her pocket, and since the reception desk isn't part of the Marie Antoinette staff and, if you come down to brass tacks, Molesworth prac-tically runs the pub, there's nothing I can do about it."

Guinea clicked her teeth. "I'd like to be under the reception desk when those two are having a pow-wow on the phone while we're slaving. I'll bet the wires run hot."

"If Ursula had to stay and do the job herself it'd be a different story."

"Alice Parker walked out pretty neatly, too, didn't she?"

"I'm sorry about that, Guin, but you heard the fuss she made. I just felt I couldn't cope with her again tonight and I couldn't possibly ask Val to stay back after last night."

"Aw, I'm not blaming you, but I still think it's pretty tough. Whenever we're rushed at lunchtime Alice is always the one who manages to wangle time off to go shopping for that flaming bottom drawer of hers and she's never worked a minute after five-thirty on a Friday night yet."

"I've been wondering what I can do about that. You know she and the boyfriend always go off to the last half of a five-o'clock session on Friday night and have dinner afterwards because he goes home to his mother at Gosford for the weekend."

"Jeepers, what a hell of a way to spend a night out! No wonder the girl looks as though she suffers from night starvation!"

"The price of virtue, my girl, and the path to respectable wedded bliss."

Guinea laughed. "She can have it for mine."

"But seriously," Claire said, "I did mean to take a stand about it tonight but she told me that that young sister of hers in the AWAS is coming home on leave and she and Ross had promised to meet her train at six. The kid's coming all the way from north Queensland and hasn't been home for six months, so what could I do?"

"That is rather different," Guinea agreed, somewhat mollified, "but why all the secrecy about it? If she'd told us we wouldn't have minded."

"Well, you know what an oyster she is."

"Oyster? Bloody little snob. Thinks she's too good to speak to the rest of us!" Guinea pursed her lips reflectively, swinging her feet up and down.

"Anyway, you'd better hop down and see that man of yours," Claire advised, "or some of the wolfesses will have eaten him alive before you get there."

"I'll have to change first in case I run into Old Mole on the prowl."

Guinea sauntered into the dressing-room and came out with a brightly coloured floral frock over her arm. She threw off the crumpled linen uniform and stood there in scanties and brassière kicking off her white wedgies. With a supple gesture she slid the gay frock over her head, wriggled it down and pulled up the zipper at the side.

Guinea walked quickly along the corridor towards the front lifts.

"Cor lumme!" gasped Elvira, the ancient room-maid from the sixth floor, sidling out of a passage and almost bumping into her. "You ain't going down in one of them, are yer, with the shindy wot's going on about Blue?"

"Why, what's happened?"

"Tell yer after." Elvira rolled her eyes dramatically. "Can't afford to be caught 'ere." She scuttled down the corridor towards the Marie Antoinette.

Guinea pressed the button and waited. She knew none of the liftmen would split on her, and anyway, what the hell! She craned froward as the lift came up, alert to skip round the corner if the manager or hostess should appear. L. F. and Mother Molesworth were a pair of prize snoopers.

The lift doors slid noiselessly open and Blue's hatchet face split in a wide grin at the sight of her.

"Hiya, Blue?" she said, stepping in.

"Miserable as a bandicoot."

"What's wrong?"

"L. F. says I've ruined the pub's reputation, though I'd have thought Old Nick himself couldn't do that."

"What yer been up to?"

"Aw...lift stuck and I helped some Yanks to pass the time, teaching 'em swy." Blue opened his tunic and showed her a roll of notes in his shirt pocket.

"Holy mackerel! You're certainly some teacher."

"Everything on the level too."

"Crikey! L. F. must have nearly pupped on the spot."

"Ain't got it in him. Where y' going?"

"I want to go down to the Cockpit to get a message to me boyfriend. I got to work back and I can't meet him till later."

"Aw, come up and have a yarn first."

Blue swung the handle over and the lift shot upwards. He opened the door at the top floor and looked up and down the corridor. There was no one about. The lift bell buzzed. He put his thumb on the indicator button and kept it there.

"Rush on face-lifting tonight?" he asked conversationally.

"And how! I can't stay more than a minute, Blue. I've got to get back."

"Well, I done y'r a good turn. That D'Arcy-Twyning sheila was hopping around downstairs like a cat on hot bricks for half an hour waiting for the lift."

"Pity about her! She gets her face plastered all over the papers for ski-ing up and down mountains half the winter and then can't walk up two flights of stairs."

"All them society coots is the same. Old McFarland was there too. Nearly burst a blood vessel, the paddy he got into rather than walk up to his suite. And you ought to hear him telling his brother what he went round the links in!"

"My God, he must be just about due to go round in a bathchair!"

Blue fished in his trouser pocket and pulled out a pound note. "Be a sport, Guin, and give this quid to Elvira to put on Stormcloud tomorrow, will yer?"

"What about Doss?"

"It's all above board. That's not out of me screw, nor tips this time neither. It's swy money. As soon as the bar closes, Doss'll be up to frisk me for me wages, and she'll pinch me roll too. So if you don't take it now, I'll never get a chance again. And I've got a corker new system, can't be beat."

"I've met lots of that kind walking home from Randwick," Guinea said sceptically. "You'll never get that country pub of yours at this rate, Blue. Why don't you chuck the gee-gees?"

"Fair go, Guin. A chap's got to have a bit of a punt. Yer might as well be dead as not take a chance now and then. Go on, give it a burl, kid. I'll buy yer a mink coat on the proceeds."

"You can keep your mink," Guinea laughed. "I don't want Doss scratching my eyes out. I saw her handling some drunks one day. Phew!"

"She's a wonder, ain't she? A bloke's lucky to have a wife like that. Ever seen her do me over? Gawd, if I've got so much as a deener in the cuff of me pants, she gets it. She's determined we're going to get that little pub she's got her heart set on, but I tell her it'll take a hell of a long time on the lousy screw we get, even allowing for the tips she picks up from the Yanks down in the bar."

"How much do you need?"

"We could do it on a thou. We got just on two hundred in the bank."

"Well, you won't keep that long if you play two-up in the lift."

"Easy money. The Yanks are mugs, nice blokes but mugs. This bunch is going north tomorrow. I won a lottery ticket off one of 'em. L. F. can't complain about me not being nice to the guests."

"It's time we got going," Guinea said. "I gotta put off that date."

Blue took his finger off the indicator button and the numbers went up for every floor. "Aw, break it down," he said to the invisible bell-pushers, as the doors slid shut. "A man can't be in two places at once. You better get off at the first floor, Guin. L. F.'s got his Gestapo out in the Cockpit."

At the first floor Blue poked out his head. "All sereno! So long, and don't forget about the quid."

Guinea looked cautiously up and down the corridor. She

went swiftly to the head of the main staircase, her feet sinking into the thick maroon carpet on which the golden monogram SP was sprayed like a monstrous orchid. The Friday evening crowd had welled up from the vestibule and overflowed into the upper corridor and lounges. Women and girls surged towards the powder room like high-stepping ponies on their stilt heels, their brief skirts flipping the back of tanned knees.

The sight of a pair of sheer silk stockings sent Guinea's eyes flying to the face of a pretty redhead. Any girl who had real sheers these days must have what it takes. Once, a ferry pilot had brought her two pairs of nylons. Ah, but that was in the great days of '42 when the American forces first spread over the country in a wave of superbly tailored beige-pinks, olive-drabs and light khakis; a wave that bore on its crest orchids, nylons, exquisite courtesy, Hollywood lovemaking and a standard of luxury that had never before penetrated below the privileged ranks of the socialites whose fathers and husbands really had the dough.

Guinea paused at the top of the stairs and looked down on the vestibule. She knew every detail of it by heart from the days when she had been the decoy at the Bouquet Boutique. Gilt-framed mirrors gave it a deceptive spaciousness and the restless figures were repeated like some fantastic moving mural along the mirrored walls. The air hummed with the incessant clamour of the crowd. Khaki was the major note in the colour scheme; khaki in all its tones from beige to olive, in all cuts from the lounging GIs to the perfectly tailored higher ranks. The dark blue of the RAAF was almost black under the electric lights, the grey-blue of the New Zealand airmen and a group of RAF officers showed up soberly against the bright florals of the girls.

Guinea stiffened and turned sharply as a voice spoke in her ear. "What are you doing here, Miss Malone?"

She looked into a mocking face with prominent brown eyes. "Jeepers, Mrs Cavendish! You did give me a fright. I thought for a moment you were Mrs Molesworth."

Mrs Cavendish drew her lips back in a thin smile. "If

you want to know where she is, I just saw her escorting Mrs Ainslie along to her office — you know, the one whose daughter's landed that American fellow whose father's such a big bug. That's the girl along there, isn't it?" She glanced along the corridor to where a laughing girl stood gazing up at a young American officer.

"Yes, the fair one's Constance Ainslie and that's the hero. Real young love, they tell me." Guinea gazed with pleasure at the young couple so completely absorbed in each other. "They are sweet, aren't they?"

Mrs Cavendish raised her brows critically. "Well, if you like that style.... Who is that dowdy-looking girl beside her?"

"That's Helen McFarland — you know, the Ian McFarlands. They're just down from the country."

"Oh, them! My dear, wouldn't you think with all their money they'd do something about her? Or maybe they'll be able to buy someone for her." She gave a throaty gurgle of amusement at her own wit.

Guinea frowned. "She's a nice kid. She comes into the Marie Antoinette and you couldn't wish for anyone nicer. Not a bit of nonsense about her."

"Isn't there? What a pity!" she said without interest and peered over the railing. "All these young things look the same to me. I can hardly tell one from the other, what with their peroxided curls bobbing around their shoulders and the terribly healthy look they all have nowadays."

Guinea's eye slid up and down Mrs Cavendish's slender black crêpe elegance. Skinny hag, she said to herself, she looks like one of those walking skeletons out of *Vogue*. She ought to talk. To hear her you'd think she'd never had her hair touched up in her life.

Mrs Cavendish looked coldly over the stream of young girls passing her on the stairs. "They look so terribly alike," she said plaintively, "as though they all come out of the one mould. I suppose it's all part of the feminine pattern men on leave are supposed to fall for."

Guinea laughed. "I don't think the boys prancing

around on leave are interested in the pattern. It's the girl they're after and a good time."

"So far as I can see they're all after one thing."

"And why not? Fun today and curtains tomorrow; that's what it is for most of them."

"Gather ye rosebuds..." Mrs Cavendish murmured.

"Sure," Guinea said briefly. Her eyes ranged from the Bouquet Boutique back to the bookstall, over to the cloakroom and across to the booking desk. OK, she said to herself, it's all right for you, Mrs High-and-Mighty, criticising us. You were lucky enough to have your fling before the war... you've had all the fun you're likely to get. Gather ye rosebuds! OK, I want two dozen roses, put my heart in beside them.... And why not? Better than working in a factory, better than being jammed up in a dingy house with a bunch of howling kids. Of course, there's no future to it — but what the hell? Mum had all the future in the world when she got married and look where it got her — seven kids and a husband on relief.

"Why don't you bring some of your boyfriends along to the school one night?" Mrs Cavendish gave her an ingratiating smile. "It's awfully good fun."

"Not for me, thanks. If a bloke's going to do his roll, I like him to do it on me so's we both get some fun out of it."

"Oh, but darling, you get tons of fun out at the game. Baccarat's terribly exciting, you know."

"Too right it is. An old bozo took me along one night and had a heart attack when you cleaned him out."

Mrs Cavendish looked pained. "Oh, but it all comes right if you go along often enough. What you lose one night you win back another."

Guinea laughed amiably. "Yeah. And you win all the time."

Mrs Cavendish glanced at her tiny platinum and diamond wristwatch and made a little shocked sound. "Heavens! I had no idea it was so late. I simply must rush, and I did want to go up to the salon, but I won't have time now. Do be a darling and give Claire a message for me." She opened her expensive black bag and scribbled a number on a card. "Tell her we're in a new flat and to give us a ring at this number and we'll send a car round for her and Nigel whatever time they want to come over tonight."

"OK, I'll tell her."

Mrs Cavendish patted Guinea's shoulder and drifted down the stairs.

To hell with her, Guinea said to herself. Slinking along like a pre-war eel. Too bloody refined for words but doesn't mind touting for a baccarat joint. She glanced at the clock ...five to six. The swirling stream, intent on crashing the lounges for a drink before six o'clock, crowded the over-worked lifts and jostled on the stairs. One good thing early closing did for pubs — it pepped up the drinking rate and everyone was so anxious to get a drink they never questioned the price or the quality.

There was no sign of Sherwood yet. She'd give him another three minutes, then she'd have to beat it. It wasn't fair to leave the whole job to Deb and Claire. Cripes, fancy having to go back and get that old bag of a Dalgety into a sufficiently presentable state to totter round Who's Who with her boyfriend. Guinea had never danced at Who's Who herself. It was practically the only nightclub in town she had never been in. But that was one point L. F. was really solid on. No member of the hotel staff dared set foot in Who's Who except when they were on the job. She giggled as she thought how it would rock him if Deb Forrest ever dined up there with the pub's star boarder, old McFarland. That would be a poser for 'Ladies First' Sharlton. L. F. and his bowing and scraping! "The guest is always right." But what a deuce of a headache it must be when the guest is right in the wrong way.

The Cockpit was in great form tonight. Whacko! No wonder poor L. F., with his worship of cash plus class, tore what was left of his hair over it.

He'd never been the same since the night an enterprising young air gunner had decorated the Bouncing Belle with an OS brassière. Now the Belle stood in the middle of a marble fishpond, constructed to protect her from even more ribald touches. Great old girl, the Belle.

It cheered you up — if you ever wanted cheering — to think that a pub like the South Pacific should have been landed for life with the figurehead of an old sailing ship as one of the terms of its survival. Say what you like, nothing could make the Belle respectable, not all the gilding could hide the fact that, in spite of copious draperies, she definitely bounced and, what was more, bounced in the wrong places. From the viewpoint of the Marie Antoinette, she was a wench whom you'd have strongly advised to go in for foundation garments in a big way and to hell with the expense.

Guinea had once had a poetic boyfriend in the Navy who used to amuse himself wondering what the old Belle thought there on her pedestal, long retired from her honest life when she breasted the spray as her ship went bouncing over the waves. Did the fog of cigarette smoke filling the air seem like some sea fog? Did the gabble of the crowd sound like the crying of sea birds? And did she, with her gilded sightless eyes, still gaze upon far horizons? Had she also gathered from her pedestal, with her unhearing ears, that bouncing was a word no nice girl mentioned publicly nowadays without grave danger of being misunderstood.... At which stage he usually remembered what he'd come for and forgot the Belle in a firm resolution not to waste any more of his leave. He had been a nice kid — went down on the *Canberra*.

At that moment Guinea caught sight of a tall, uniformed figure making his way through the crowd towards the telephone boxes just below where she was standing on the stairs. "Pss-tt," she hissed loudly, leaning over so that she could almost touch the gold leaves on his cap. "Pss—t—Sherwood!"

He looked round quickly, and at last, after another hiss, looked upwards. His face, round and tanned under the peaked cap, broke into a smile. She beckoned and he came up the stairs to her two at a time.

"Honey," he began, squeezing her arm, "I'm sorry."

"I know — but I have to beat it. I can't get off for about

an hour."

His eyes clouded. "I say..." he expostulated, pressing closer to her.

Guinea disentangled herself. "I've got to go now," she insisted. "If you like to wait I'll meet you in the Madrid Lounge about quarter past seven."

"Wait? I'd wait for you till the cows come home."

"Quarter past will be plenty...and don't get stinko!"

"Ah...Guinea," he protested, then lowered his voice persuasively. "Gee, you're a swell dame. Clark's gone to Brisbane. What about coming up to the flat for the night?"

Guinea frowned. "Aw, I dunno. Last time you drank too much."

"Anything you say. Coke if you like. Say you will."

She hesitated.

"You're so sweet I could take a bite out of you right now."

"Well, don't start cannibalising on the stairs."

"Gee, Guinea, I'd almost go AWOL for you. Say you'll come."

"Maybe. If you're sober when I've finished, I'll think about it."

"Tell me you love me just to keep me going while I'm waiting."

"Get along with you."

His face grew suddenly grave. "I've got to be on my way north tomorrow."

"Oh gosh, Sher!" She looked at him in dismay. "Gee, I'm sorry."

"You'll come?"

She squeezed his hand and nodded. Then she turned and ran swiftly up the stairs, pausing at the top to touch her fingers to her lips as he looked after her.

At the top of the staircase Guinea stopped suddenly beside an enormous bowl of flowers. Green tulips! Jeez! She drew in a deep breath. She hadn't seen a tulip tree since the weekend she'd spent with Kim Scott up at his grandfather's farm, four . . . no, five years ago. The year war broke out. What a kid she was then. Kim too. Proud as punch of his new Air Force uniform and rarin' to go.

She touched the cool green cups of the flowers. Kim had made a crown of them for her . . . all young love, high romance and . . . moonshine. Crikey, to think she'd been faithful to him for two years! What had happened in the haystack at the farm had been like a marriage for her. "This'll last forever," he'd said. Forever . . . that was how she'd felt about it, too, until he came back from the Middle East two years later, making a big mouth about himself as the great lover. "Love 'em and leave 'em, that's my motto," he'd boasted.

OK, if that was how he wanted it he could have it. Two could play at that game. What was sauce for the gander was sauce for the goose. She wasn't pining. My God, it made her sick the way the Aussies came back and squealed about the Yanks getting off with their girls. You'd think they were a lot of monks themselves.

She snapped off a flower, she'd press it for a warning. Better still, three of them would make a wow of a shoulder spray for Claire's suit. She removed two more swiftly, endeavouring to look as much like a member of the staff engaged in her lawful duties as she could.

Good lord! Was that Old Mole? It was, and on the warpath, too, judging by the tone of her voice uplifted to reprimand a harassed drink waitress. Caught with the booty on her! No time to get to the stairs, impossible to reach the lift. Nothing for it but the Powder Room. Bessie would be on duty now and she'd be safe with her, even if Mother Molesworth did poke her nose in.

Bessie's round plump face creased into an accomplice's smile as she opened one of the lavatory doors and pushed

Guinea in. "This is the only place in the whole pub you'd be safe from Old Mole. Shoot the bolt and I'll give you a call when the coast's clear. Val'll keep nit in the corridor."

"You're a sport, Bess." Guinea closed the door.

Bessie dragged her feet wearily over the tiled floor to her little office where Val sat smoking on the edge of the table.

"Hop out in a few minutes for me, will you, dearie?" Bessie sank into a chair sighing: "Gee, my feet's aching tonight. I got a corn under me big toe that's giving me gip."

"You poor old thing, I'll bring some of that foot powder along on the weekend." Val stubbed the butt of her cigarette and went out.

A woman appeared at the door. Bessie passed out a hand towel and dropped two pennies into a box with a clatter.

When Val came back she had just finished stitching up a ripped hem for a young girl who went off into hysterical giggles every time she tried to explain how it had happened. The girl went out grateful and still giggling. Val shrugged her shoulders. "Tiddly already," she commented casually and reported the coast clear.

Bessie got up and knocked on the lavatory door.

"Gee, that was a narrow squeak," Guinea breathed as she came out.

"Now just what have you been up to?" Bessie asked affectionately.

"I skipped down to the Cockpit to warn the boyfriend I'd be late, pinched these tulips on the way back for a shoulder spray for Claire, and just missed Old Mole by the skin of me teeth."

"She's turning on the dentures for the benefit of some of the squattocracy in the Madrid Lounge," Val informed her, "so you'll be OK for a while."

"Thanks, kid."

"Nearly finished Dalgety?" Val asked.

"Finished! There's an hour's solid hard work still to be done on the old girl."

"It's a damn shame. It was a bit of luck for me I beat

it when D.D.T. didn't turn up for her manicure on the dot or I'd have been there still myself."

"Blue told me she's back now, so you'd better get while the going's good. Old Mole'll drag you back to do her if she sees you."

"Not me. I've done all the overtime I'm doing this week."

"Indeed you have," Bessie was indignant, "you're looking far too pale. Isn't she, Guin?"

"She looks real nice to me," Guinea said. "Gee, Val, red suits you. Wish I could wear it."

"You don't think it's too short?" Val wheeled slowly to let them get the full effect of her new linen suit.

"It's perfect."

"Well, I'll have to be skipping along. Are you sure there's nothing you want me to buy, Bessie?"

"No thanks, dearie, I've got everything for the weekend except the meat and I'll get up early tomorrow morning and get along to the butcher before I come to work."

"I'll pick you up at nine then."

"Have a good time at the pictures," Bessie called after her.

"She's positively pretty when she's dressed up," Guinea remarked.

Bessie nodded vigorously. "And just as nice as she looks. I've got real fond of her. She reminds me of my own girl with those big dark eyes and her lovely skin, though I wish she'd put a bit of colour on meself."

"Rouge'd spoil her, she's got all she needs with that bright lipstick. You see a lot of each other, don't you?"

"Yes, I'm taking her home with me for the weekend. And I had a hard job persuading her to come, I can tell you. It's the anniversary of her wedding, and with him still missing up there in the Islands I don't like her being in that flat by herself."

"It's a wonder she doesn't get someone to share it with her."

"I did suggest that, but she nearly blew me head off at

the idea. Do you know, she keeps the place exactly the same as it was on his last leave? Gives me the creeps to think of it.''

"She's one of the faithful kind all right.''

"Faithful's faithful, but you can get too fond of your own company and that don't do no one any good, not even the person you're being faithful to. Though from what I can hear he seems to have been a real nice chap. Not the kind of Yank you see around here mostly. One of the serious kind. I seen some of the letters he wrote to her and they'd fair break your heart. There was poetry in them too. Real lovely, and he made it up himself.''

"So far as I can see all the wrong men get bumped off in this war.''

"If the whole lot was bumped off the world'd be a lot happier for women, from what I've seen of them.''

"Oh, they have their uses.''

"That's right. Get all you can out of them while the going's good, Guin. Only don't you be fool enough to go fallin' in love.''

"Not me. So far as love's concerned, I've had it.''

"You take my tip. A bankbook's a woman's best friend. When you get a bit older, if you were starving and went down on your bended knees to them to save your life they wouldn't give you what they'd spend on you for a night's fun, now. And stick to your money, too. I know, I been through it. Once this war's over, all the promises the government's making now'll go down the drain just like they did after the last war.''

A tightly waved, yellow head came round the door. "Bess, old girl, you've said a mouthful. That's what I'm always telling Blue.''

Bessie beamed a welcome. "Hullo, Doss.''

Guinea started in alarm. "Holy mackerel! Is the bar closed already?''

Doss nodded. Guinea grabbed up the tulips. "Claire'll cut my throat for staying so long.'' She peered round the outer door, looked up and down the corridor and disappeared.

Doss subsided into a chair, opened her purse and brought out a roll of notes. "Take a look at this, Bess."

"Gawd! Haven't been frisking the Yanks, have yer?"

Doss laughed. "Not me. But the old man has."

Bessie gasped. "Don't tell me Blue got all that roll when he was playin' two-up in the lift?"

"That's right."

"We-e-ell!"

Doss kissed the roll and laughed, then put it carefully back into her bag. "I heard them talking about the two-up business down in the bar and I was that mad with him that I tore up as soon as we closed to get his wages off of him, like I do every Friday, and blow the tripe out of him. But when he hauled this out of his pocket, well, you could have knocked me down with a feather, and I didn't have the heart to say a word. A few more windfalls like this and we'd soon have our pub in the country."

"That's all right when you're on the winning side," Bessie said cautiously, "but it's not likely to happen that way twice."

"Oh, I know that! That's why I never give Blue a chance even to have a punt if I can get in first. But it gives you a bit of a kick all the same."

"It'll perk him up too. He's lookin' a lot better lately, isn't he?"

"Yes. It's that last treatment they gave him at the Hundred-and-Thirteenth. Done him a lot of good, though the doctor says his back'll never be really right again. That's why I'm keen for him to keep on that front lift where he doesn't have any heavy carryin' to do. I'm only hopin' L. F. won't do his block over this swy business. After all, it wasn't really Blue's fault; them Yanks are on for anything."

"I'll say they are. Do you think there's any chance of L. F. keeping him on permanent?"

"I dunno. Blue's not suited for this kind of job, y'know. Too independent. He wouldn't crawl to the king to save his life. L. F. only put him on for the fortnight because he was absolutely stumped with Roly sprainin' his ankle and the rush of the long weekend. And now with this swy business, he'll be lucky if he sees the fortnight through."

Bessie nodded sympathetically. "I'm afraid you're right. But it's a pity, he gets on so well with everybody."

"Not everybody," Doss laughed. "If people have got any tickets on themselves, Blue don't get nowhere with them. He don't know his place, old Mother Molesworth told him the other day."

"Maybe he don't," Bessie said warmly. "There's too much boot-lickin' around here, as it is."

"Funny, y'know, Bess. You couldn't wish for a nicer chap than Blue at home. I never seen any other man with less nonsense about a man's work. He'll hoe in and help me with the washin' and cleanin' up the house and make no more bones about it than if he was sittin' up in front of the fire watchin' me do it, like most men." Doss groaned and eased off her shoes.

"Tired, dearie?"

"Flat out. The public bar gets more like Taronga Zoo at feeding time every day." Doss rubbed her ankles tenderly.

"Feet gone on yer?"

"Giving me hell."

"So're mine." Bessie rubbed a swollen ankle in sympathy. "They've never been the same since I got them bunged up the time I was working down on the quay in the old *Captain Phillip* during the depression. Short-handed we were all the time and run off our feet. The only thing there wasn't any shortage of, so far as I could see, was beer."

"Why don't you go to a chiropodist, Bess? I'm going in the morning and I'll make an appointment for you."

"Seems a waste of money to spend it on your feet. I'm trying to put away all I can so's when my Ken comes back he won't have to put up with what his father put up with after the last war. Chucked out on the scrap heap, he was."

"Well, at least they'll have their deferred pay this time, which is more than they had in 1918. But still and all, you've got to look after yourself, Bess, and just you remember this war won't last for ever, and once it's over, what's going to happen to the over-forty-fives like you and me? They'll turf us out the moment the Manpower releases all these young-sters from reserve jobs, and you and me'll still be a long way off the pension.''

Bessie sighed. ''Yes, it's going to be a bad time all right, but I suppose it wouldn't be fair for us to keep the jobs when all the young fellers and girls come out of the Services.''

''And believe me, we won't. But we've got to live, haven't we? And who's going to care two hoots how we live? That's what I'm always trying to drum into Blue's thick head.''

''He got knocked about in the last war too, didn't he?''

''Yes. He was only a bit of a kid when he got wounded in France, and then gettin' blown up in Greece this time and bein' out in the mountains in the cold done him no good. He's never been the same. Christ, if we could only get enough money together to put into a nice little country pub, I wouldn't call the queen me aunt.''

''I'd be frightened to take a man of mine into a pub. It's a terrible temptation.''

''Well, thank God, that isn't one of Blue's failings. He'd gamble his shirt off on any damn thing that's got a leg to run on, but he doesn't shicker. With a good cook and me in the bar I'd have no worries. Blue's got a way with people when he likes.''

Bessie sighed deeply. ''I always used to hope that was what me and me old man'd do, but it'd never of worked. I was as smart in the bar as you are, but he was the kind that'd drink all the profits. Couldn't have wished for a kinder hus-band and father, but there you are.''

''That's right,'' said Doss. ''If it's not one thing with men it's another. But Blue and me, we know each other and we could run a real nice little pub. Y'know, one of the homely kind. Not like these beer houses the breweries run. All they're interested in is how to get the fellers to swill as much liquor as they can hold between the bar and the Gents.''

''How much would it take?''

"At least a thousand. There'll be a hundred or so from his deferred pay, but with only two hundred in the bank, God only knows where the rest of it will come from. Though this'll pep it up a bit." She patted the roll of notes in her bag.

"Well, I'll have to get along now, we're going to celebrate. Blue comes off at half past six and we're having dinner in town and going to the flicks for a change."

"What yer seein'?" Bessie asked.

"We're going to try and get in to *The Man in Grey*. Blue don't like war pitchers."

"I've heard that one's real exciting. Well, have a good time," Bessie called cheerfully as Doss went out.

Val set off up Macquarie Street with the long, firm stride of her Service days. Three hours on her hands before she called for Bessie. What would she do? Go to the pictures? That was what she had told Bessie, and anyway there wasn't much else for a girl to do on her own.

She stood irresolute on the corner of Martin Place and watched the people streaming past to ferry and tram and train. All going home. . . . She should have been going home too, instead of waiting for Bessie. The trouble was Bessie was so kind, you just couldn't go on refusing her invitations. But at home, among all the familiar things you'd shared with Ven, with every corner of the little flat reminding you of him — his books on the shelves, his pipes on the mantelpiece, his dressing-gown in the wardrobe. . .there he was with you.

Someone brushed her in passing. She looked up and saw the pedestrian light signal CROSS NOW and let herself be carried along with the stream of people crossing the street. On the footpath in front of Sydney Hospital she hesitated again; downhill led to the ferry and home. . . . With an effort she turned away and walked slowly in the opposite direction, letting the crowd hurry past her.

Two years ago, this had been her wedding day. The interminable months slid away and, as though she was actually present, she was back in New Guinea living through those few enchanted weeks when she was nursing Ven. Again she was walking eagerly along the jungle path that led from the AAMWAs' hut to the hospital where he was growing stronger each day as blood transfusions and careful nursing won a battle against fever and a bullet wound under the shoulder. How happy she had been when at last he was out of danger and the overworked sister had handed him over to her care! Then one morning he had said quite suddenly,'' I wrote you a poem làst night, do you mind?'' And her joy had been so sudden and overpowering that she had upset a basin of water and had to crawl round mopping it up. How they'd laughed together when the sister had finished her scolding! And then he'd shown her the poem. The words rose to her lips and she spoke them softly to herself as she walked along the city footpath:

> *Two worlds have met*
> *Here in this alien land.*
> *Yours, sun-drenched South...*
> *Mine, fast locked by Northern seas.*
> *You waked my winter heart to life,*
> *You are my Spring.*

Three weeks later they had been married, in the afternoon, two years ago. Everybody had been sweet about their wedding. The girls had made her a wedding dress out of parachute silk — she had it still. And the boys had gone out and collected orchids, masses of them, so that there were enough to make a bouquet that showered to the ground and a tiny skullcap for her hair....

At the top of the street the hooting cars and clanging trams of the busy intersection brought her out of her dream and her eyes were caught by the Gothic spires of St Mary's Cathedral and the mellow stone walls glowing warmly in the last fire of the sun. She crossed the road and stood watching the endless stream of people that flowed up and down the broad, shallow steps to the side door. Perhaps it was only her imagination, but those coming out looked comforted. She took a step forward and hesitated, then turned and went up the steps and pushed open the padded leather door. It swung behind her and she stood a moment in the shadowy dimness of the aisle accustoming her eyes after the strong sunlight. The sanctuary windows above the high altar glowed in the gloom with jewelled fire and the great chancel was ribbed with sunset gold from the narrow windows in the clerestory. She went quietly to the back of the cathedral and down the winding stone stairs to the tiny crypt.

Whenever she came here to watch the sleeping Anzac on his tomb, every nerve quivered with certainty that Ven was alive and would come back to her. It could have been Ven lying there; the long limbs, the lean young face, broad hand nerved and vital in bronze as if in actual flesh. She gripped the railing and looked down to where he lay sprawled in the abandon of sleep — not death; his proud face turned, the eyelids closed. So Ven used to sleep. That was how she had first seen him when he was brought in on a stretcher to the hospital in Moresby, his tin hat beside him, the waterbottles still slung over his shoulder.

Her tears splashed on the cold railing. It didn't matter if she cried here, lots of women cried here; perhaps that was why they kept the little crypt so badly lighted. Perhaps the men who went through the cathedral in their long black robes, dedicated and aloof, knew that women like her, who never went to any church, came here to weep and be comforted, and knew too that sometimes there is not only comfort but strength in tears. She wiped her eyes and took out her compact, powdering over the signs of weeping.

She turned and went up to the cathedral again. The air was heavy with the smell of incense and the sanctuary lamp glowed before the high altar like a beacon. All this was too splendid for her, too vast and impersonal. She skirted the gleaming brass rails and the marble steps.

Behind the great altar she found what she was seeking and kneeled before the sorrowing Virgin. "Mother of God," she prayed. "Keep Ven safe for me. Just safe. Let him come back. Please, Mother of God, let him come back. You know what it's like. You lost your son. But you had Him for thirty-three years and I only had Ven for one year, not all the time then. Three weeks in hospital, then our honeymoon up in the hills and just one month back here. Please let me have him back."

She went to the little table, dropped a coin in the box and lit two candles, placing them in the branched candlesticks where other candles were guttering out. "This is for Ven," she whispered, "to bring Ven back. And this one's for me. Make me brave so I'll be worthy of him."

It was dusk when she went out onto the great steps at the front of the cathedral. A few high clouds still held the fiery afterglow. She crossed over to the little park and walked through the unkempt grass, scattered with Moreton Bay fig leaves that the wind had brought down. The swishing of the leaves against her shoes and the smell of the bruised grass took her back to New Guinea. They'd had to keep the vegetation cut back from the path that led from the hospital to the AAMWAs' hut and there was always the smell of bruised leaves. At the end of the muddy road was the sprawling hospital, where Ven was waiting for her...

Caught in her memories, she went down through the drab streets to Woolloomooloo, and only when the gates of the wharves barred her way did she come back to the present. That was where his ship had berthed a year ago when he came south just in time for their first anniversary. She gripped the iron railings as she stood looking through at the busy wharf. They were loading a ship now, the kind of ship that had brought him home. She had stood like this the afternoon he came in. There had been other women too, women with children, women alone, all with their faces pressed against the bars. And he'd come down the gangway at last, and over to her, and he'd kissed her without saying a word, the bars cold between them.

Heavy footsteps startled her. "Better move along, Miss." A policeman spoke behind her, and added more kindly when she turned, "not a very nice place for a lass like you at this time of night.''

She mumbled an explanation and turned to go back. She could hear his footsteps echoing, heavy and measured behind her, as she walked towards the city.

As she opened the plate-glass door of the Marie Antoinette Salon, Guinea heard a familiar cackle coming from Claire's office. She stuffed the green tulips into a vase of flowers on the reception desk and went down the corridor to the office.

"Ha, still here, Elvira?" she called cheerfully. "What's the dirt?"

Elvira was rocking to and fro on her chair, her shrunken little body twitching helplessly with laughter. At the sight of Guinea she started off again.

"What's it all about?" Guinea insisted.

Elvira got her breath at last. "I just been tellin' Claire about Blue playin' two-up in the lift. You should've seen L. F.! 'E nearly 'ad a stroke. And that D.D.T.! 'Er and 'er ma waitin' for the lift and listenin' to 'em yellin' 'Ten bob in the guts!' I nearly yelled down the lift well meself, 'Put somethink on for me, Blue!'"

Mrs Dalgety's fruity voice came from the massage cubicle: "You girls come right in here and tell me what's the joke. It's the least you can do after making me suffer like this."

Elvira's mouth shut like a trap, the lipstick still visible in a smudge above her thin lips. Her dark opaque eyes slid round towards the cubicle. "'Oly Moses," she whispered. "I fergot all about 'er," and added aloud: "It's just a story I 'eard from the bar, Mrs Dalgety. 'Ave you 'eard this one?" She dropped her voice to a confidential key.

Mrs Dalgety laughed explosively. "Now isn't that just like a man."

Deb slapped her fat buttocks and, in a disapproving voice, requested her to turn over.

Elvira came over to Claire. "Lady Forrest's gettin' uppity these days, ain't she?"

"Now then, bush telegraph, lay off the staff here," Guinea warned her, shaking her shoulders with a joviality that took the sting out of her words.

Elvira slipped her black-sleeved arm through Guinea's.

"Get along with you, luvvie," she cawed, nudging her in the ribs. "Don't try and tell me you don't like a bit of gossip?"

"Too right I do, but not in the home paddock. Now what else have you got?"

Elvira withdrew her arm and smoothed down her white apron. She set her cap at a rakish angle on her dyed black curls and rolled her eyes languishingly at them both. "It's love," she said, raising her upper lip in a sentimental leer that revealed her yellowed false teeth and brick-red gums.

"Yeah?" said Guinea, sitting down and preparing to enjoy one of Elvira's acts. "But whose?"

Elvira minced to the desk and opened a cardboard box that lay on it. She drew out a diaphanous black nightdress patterned lightly in red and white and held it up against herself, moulding the shaped bodice over her sagging breasts.

"Whew!" whistled Guinea, "where did you get a nightie like that?"

Elvira paraded round the office with an obscene swagger of bony hips and stopped in front of Guinea. "Wouldn't you like to have one like this for your first night, luvvie? Just look."

Guinea lifted up the full skirt and it slid over her hands in a transparent ripple. She shouted with joy when she examined it more closely and saw that the design was a delicate tracery of 'YES' patterned in red and 'NO' in white.

"Gee, that's a stunner all right," she said enviously. "Where did you get it from?"

Elvira folded the nightgown carefully and slipped it into its box, her eyes modestly lowered, her lips drawn primly together. "D.D.T.," she whispered.

"Oh! Denny darling!" Guinea shrugged her shoulders. "I might have guessed. She gets them easy enough. That American fiancé of hers has sent her enough undies for a lifetime — even allowing for hard wear."

"Want to buy it?" Elvira inquired.

"Who, me? Good Lord, no. Anyway, you can't sell it if you took it out of her room."

"I didn't. You don't think I'm that dumb, do yer?"

"Where'd you find it then?"

"To be perfickly accurate, at the bottom of Commander Derek Ermington's bed — when I was making it this morning."

"No!" Guinea gasped. "Cripes, she's got going there in double-quick time. His ship's only been in ten days."

"And wearing the nightie 'er fiancé sent 'er! It don't seem decent."

"That must be the one she was showing to the bunch of girls in the picture in last Sunday's *Star*."

"The hidentical. 'Pickwante', the paper said. Huh, disgusting, I call it. Not that she 'ad it on long, judging by the bed this morning. Battle of Waterloo, I'd say!"

"They say the British always win the last battle."

"I wouldn't bank on that," Elvira remarked darkly, "not till we see what other h'allies we're gonner 'ave 'ere. One of these mornings I'll probably be taking an 'ammer and sickle out of 'er bed if the war goes on much longer..."

Guinea shouted gleefully. "So long as it's not a rising sun," she said.

Elvira sniggered, "'Ot stuff, she is. None of the hopposite seck ain't safe with 'er unless 'es paralysed." She opened her owlish eyes wide, "What I'd like to know," she whispered, "when I read all them warnings in the paper about you-know-what, is how they don't ever seem to get a dose — all them snooty silvertails. It beats me."

"I've never heard that blue blood was any specific against the spirochete, so it must be just luck," Claire remarked drily.

"Garn," Guinea broke in, "these fellers are pretty careful — for the sake of their hides more than anything else. They ought to raise our war memorials to the blue light kit."

"That's a bright idea," Claire agreed. "Blue light rampant on a green field."

"Well what can you expect? There's a war on, isn't there, and only the rich like D.D.T. can afford to make love indoors."

Elvira closed her eyes piously. "Ugh!" she grimaced.

"Immoral I calls it. Interfering with natcher, that's what it is. That sort of thing is anathemia to me. 'Er and 'er Pick-Pockettes with their phizogs plastered all over the noospapers!"

"Now, now, Virus, remember your place. Respect for the director's daughter. You know what L. F. said in his pep talk this morning."

"L. F. — 'im with 'is Ladies First. Fine one 'e is to talk. Sunday nights and 'im and old Molesworth. Seen 'er crawling to D.D.T. and 'er mother when I come up. Give me a lecture on treating 'er with the respect due to 'er position, she did. I nearly said: 'Which one of her positions, may I hask?' 'Orizontal hor hotherwise?'"

"Them and their 'en-roost. D'Arcy hyphen Twyning. Why can't they be satisfied with a straightforward name? A good old English name like Beauchamp with a 'p' don't need no trimmings. Mr Beauchamp always says 'e's goin' ter take me 'ome to see 'is people — real well-connected 'e is — only come out 'ere on account of 'avin' a weak chest."

"I didn't know your old man was a Pommy," Guinea remarked.

"'E's English," said Elvira, drawing herself up. "And I'd 'ave yer know, Guinea Malone, I'll 'ave nobody callin' Mr Beauchamp a Pommy."

"No offence intended, old girl." Guinea slapped her on the back.

"And none taken." Elvira smoothed her apron smugly like a hen preening its feathers. "That there D.D.T.," she picked up the conversation again, "you oughter see 'er. Comes into the SP for a rest, she says, and lies in bed 'alf the day ringin' the bell. 'See this is pressed for me, Elvira,' she says, and 'Send me up some morning tea, Elvira,' she says, and 'Wake me at half past three and bring me a tray, Elvira,' she says."

"It's a great life," Guinea sighed enviously.

"Too blooming right! But I know what would 'appen if any of yous tried to get it. You'd 'ave the Manpower down on yer in two ups."

"And how!" Guinea snorted indignantly. "Look at what they did to my kid sister, Monnie. She's been stuck in a lousy woollen mill and they won't let her get out because it's a reserved occupation, and they won't even give them rises because they don't come under the new regulations for women in industry."

"Appalling," Claire agreed.

"Just wait till they start on yous girls," Elvira winked broadly and motioned over her shoulder towards Mrs Dalgety's cubicle with a short, roughened thumb. "They'll probably stick you in as rouseabouts in a lunatic asylum, seeing the experience you've 'ad 'ere." She picked up the nightdress and raised her eyes piously: "The goings-on in this place! I dunno what the world's coming to, I don't. Now, when I was a girl, if I'd gone on the way some of them bright young things round 'ere goes on today..."

"Get out," Guinea poked her in the ribs. "I bet you've been a high flyer in your time, Virus."

"My time!" Elvira snapped indignantly. "I'd 'ave you know my time ain't over neither, not by a long shot. Mr Beauchamp 'as 'is marital rights regular as clockwork every Monday night and no nonsense about it neither."

"You'd better wear that nightie next time."

"Me wear a thing like that? Not me. I'm respectable, I am. Married twenty-five years I been and three children, but Mr Beauchamp ain't never seen me in the nood yet and I wouldn't let 'im see me in a thing like that. Not for all the rice in China — if you know what I mean."

"We know," Claire said soothingly, putting the box away in her drawer. "And I'll see what I can get for this and let you know on Monday. There's a woman in our flats who's collecting a trousseau and I think she'll jump at it."

"Righteo!" Elvira agreed, moving towards the door. "See you termorrow, luvvie. I oughter know a good thing for Randwick be then. He's a roughie so 'e'll go out at long odds."

"Not for me, thanks," said Guinea. "The last one you gave me ran like a hairy goat."

"Could yer blame 'im?" Elvira asked reproachfully. "Raining like it was last Saturdee? 'E's no mudlark."

"I don't care if he has webbed feet. But that reminds me, Blue gave me this quid for you to put on Stormcloud."

"Stormcloud? 'E's wastin' 'is money."

"Well, it's his money and that's what he said."

"Don't you think she's any good?" Claire inquired.

"No-o-o. Ain't got Buckley's chance. Seems like there's a 'indoo on that 'orse. Never 'as 'ad any luck."

"Miss Malone," Deb's voice came sharply.

"Coming!" Guinea handed Elvira the pound note and disappeared into the cubicle.

Elvira scuttled out.

"How's it going?" Guinea asked Mrs Dalgety.

"I feel like a new woman. You were right, Guinea. I'm sure the sweat bath and the massage have taken pounds off me."

"Now if you'll let us help you to dress," Claire said sweetly as she came in, "I'll do your makeup and Guinea'll fix your hair. You don't want to be late."

"Gracious no! What time is it?"

"Nearly quarter to seven," Guinea lied, winking at a startled Deb and Claire.

Mrs Dalgety heaved herself upright and sat panting from the effort, with legs hanging over the side of the table. "Oh dear," she moaned, "and Alistair said he'd be here at half past."

"Then we shall have to hurry," Claire said briskly. "Where is your foundation garment?"

The three women struggled to lace Mrs Dalgety's sprawling body into a foundation garment, whose delicate hue and exquisite lace trimming covered a corset as unyielding as any of Queen Victoria's day.

"Ah," sighed Mrs Dalgety when the struggle was over and she could draw her breath again. "It always seems so unfair that women have got to work so hard to keep themselves looking presentable for men." She snivelled with self-pity. "Every time I put on a pound it nearly breaks my heart — but does it worry a man how he looks? Not him. He can be as thin as a skeleton or as round as a barrel, and all he does about it is go to his tailor and get his suits built up in the right places. So long as he can go out looking like a tailor's dummy in public he doesn't care what he looks like in bed. But he still expects every woman to be a Venus."

"Too right," Guinea laughed. "They can be wall-eyed and bald, flat-footed and hamstrung, but so long as they can still crawl into bed they all think they're irresistible."

Mrs Dalgety sighed again. "That's the trouble, we just can't do without them."

"Well now, come along and we'll get on with your makeup," Claire said persuasively.

But Mrs Dalgety was feeling the need to assert herself in view of the sad case of women.

"I think Guinea had better do my hair first. Perhaps I'll need a different makeup with the new rinse she gave me. One can't be too careful, can one?"

Guinea rolled an eye of sympathy at Claire and pushed a chair unceremoniously against Mrs Dalgety's thighs. She collapsed with a grunt and gave herself up to Guinea's swift fingers.

When all the little reddish bronze curls had been firmly pinned into a fashion-plate arrangement on the top of her head Claire came back and looked at her in the mirror with a detached professional gaze.

"Yes, that rinse has made a difference to your whole personality and you're going to need a complete new set of makeup — for day as well as night. Don't you think so, Deb?"

"I do indeed." Deb put down her nail file and placed Mrs Dalgety's fingertips in a bowl of warm water.

"I have a wonderful new line just in," Claire continued, "but it's frightfully expensive. You know how hard things are to get..."

"Dear me, I do hope it is not some of that stuff they've been selling on the black market? I heard it was terribly bad for the skin.''

"Oh no! This came off one of the American ships. I was very lucky to get it. Though they certainly made me pay through the nose.''

"That's different. Then you can make up a full set of everything. Goodness knows how long the war is going to last and I simply can't risk being without it.''

"I can't spare *very* much, I'm afraid.''

Mrs Dalgety clamped her jaws obstinately and narrowed her eyes at her reflection. "Be a good girl and let me have a full supply,'' she ordered.

"Well, in view of your difficulties, I'll spare you just as much as I can,'' Claire conceded. "I'll let you have everything new from the base up.'' She began to pat foundation cream into the heavy face with its sagging jowls and veined nose. The powder base, thick as greasepaint, produced a startling, expressionless mask on which she proceeded to paint a new face. The shading of eyelids, the rouging of cheekbones, the painting of eyelashes and eyebrows over the sandy wisps of hair, the expert touching with darker cream and darker powder of the loose flesh beneath the chin worked a miracle. A new and fashionable mask emerged to face the world.

"You're simply marvellous, Miss Jeffries.''

Claire gave a last touch with the powder puff. Guinea adjusted a curl. Deb smoothed her frock and stockings and fanned the freshly lacquered nails.

"I can't thank you girls enough.'' Mrs Dalgety rose with difficulty from her chair. "I'll be in again tomorrow morning to get you to fix me up for the races.''

"What are you wearing?'' Claire inquired.

"'My London tan and beige.''

"Lovely,'' Claire said warmly. "You'll need quite different makeup, though.... Manchu rouge and Cathay lipstick, I'd say.... Anyway, come down dressed and bring your hat and we'll try it out.''

Mrs Dalgety collected her purse and looked round for her discarded clothes.

"Don't worry," Claire said amiably, "I'll have them pressed and sent to your room."

"You are the sweetest thing, Miss Jeffries...and so good of you all to look after me at this late hour."

Claire, Deb and Guinea held their smiles in place and strove to look unconcerned while she fumbled in her purse. After a struggle she waved a five-pound note at them. "This is just for you girls. Put everything else down to my account."

The three women cooed their thanks and escorted her to the door with murmured assurances that it was a pleasure to have had to stay back till seven o'clock for her. Mrs Dalgety swept out in a flourish of night blue crêpe.

"Gawd!" Guinea wiped her hands over her brow.

"This is easy to take, anyway." Claire was changing the note at the desk. She handed them each thirty shillings.

"Whoopee!" said Guinea. "Seems like our luck's changed. Somebody must have taken that hindoo off us that Elvira's always talking about."

"My horoscope promised me a lucky week." Claire pocketed two pound notes and began to count the money in the till. "About time, too. There's definitely been a hoodoo on Nigel and me for months."

"The stars must be on the side of the working class then. Blue's got a roll like a bolster."

"Blue? Don't tell me he really made a packet playing two-up in the lift."

"Too right he did."

Deb stopped in the middle of counting the soiled towels. "You don't mean to say that Blue's been playing two-up in the lift?"

"That's it. I'd have given quids to have been there," Guinea burbled.

Claire snapped a rubber band round a roll of notes. "Me too. You should have heard Elvira's account of it, Deb. I nearly died laughing."

"Oh, was that what all the noise was about when I was doing Mrs Dalgety?"

"Yes, funniest thing I've heard in years."

"Well, if you ask my opinion," Deb said stiffly, "I think it's absolutely disgusting."

Guinea shrugged her shoulders. "I don't see what it's got to do with us, except it makes a good story."

"I think it reflects on the whole hotel. I don't know how we're ever going to attract tourists to Australia after the war with the standard of service they're accustomed to in other places."

"Oh, phooey!" Guinea exploded. "Let 'em stop at home for a change and spend some of their cash on making conditions a bit better for Welsh miners and dust-bowl farmers. Sherwood reckons there's more baloney talked about the American standard of living than anything else except the British Empire. His Pop was out of work for years and they didn't even have any dole in their state, and when the men tried to form a union they sent out the militia to beat them up with steam hoses and tear gas."

"Come off it, Guin," Claire gave her a friendly slap as she passed. "They ought to give you a soapbox in the Domain, my girl. And my God! look at the time."

"Ten past seven!" Deb gasped.

"Jeepers!" shouted Guinea, "I'll have to hop it or my bloke'll be grown to the seat and it'll take a crane to get him across the street to Down Under." She stepped out of her overall, kicked off her shoes, discarded scanties and brassière in one swoop and scampered under the shower, pushing her hair under a cap as she ran.

Claire went round, systematically locking cupboards and drawers. "I don't mind Elvira getting her whack out of the Marie Antoinette rake-off the same as the rest of us," she remarked, "but I'd hate to think of her getting off with any of our stuff to do a spot of black marketing on her own."

"I can't understand how you can put up with her," Deb said distastefully, pausing to throw a towel to Guinea, who came skipping out of the shower room.

"Better to share in the fun when she's plastering others with dirt than stand back and get it yourself. Don't you agree, Guin?''

Guinea tossed off the shower cap and began to towel her glistening skin, which was golden tan except where the brief brassiere and trunks of her bathing suit had protected it.

"I'll say. Get on the wrong side of Elvira and you can expect anything from the Manpower to the Vice Squad on your doorstep.''

"But she's so disgusting,'' Deb insisted. "She's got a mind like a sewer.''

Claire shrugged. "But she's very useful.''

"Anyway, I like a bit of dirt myself,'' Guinea laughed, dancing naked round the boudoir. She paused to do up a frail brassiere of black lace and draw on the matching scanties.

Claire looked at her admiringly. "They're a pretty nifty set.''

"Aren't they?'' Guinea answered complacently, bending to fasten her high-heeled ankle-strap sandals. "Alfalfa sent 'em up to me from Melbourne.''

"With the purest intentions, no doubt,'' Claire smiled, collecting her own clothes from their hanger and calling to Deb, who was tidying the massage room.

"Not on his side. Gee! Does he write slushy letters? I only ever read the beginning and the end.'' She zipped up her frock, ran a comb through her shining hair, flicked a powder puff over her face and applied her vivid lipstick generously. "Will I do?''

Claire glanced up and nodded. "Super. Now you run along. Deb'll help me lock up before we go to her room.''

Guinea picked up her bag. "'G' bye now. Be good girls, you two.'' She paused at the door. "Oh, Claire, I nearly forgot. I pinched some of Old Mole's favourite decorations when I was down below. They're in the vase here. They ought to look swell on your suit.''

She was gone before Claire could answer.

Deb waited while Claire closed the door of the Marie Antoinette Salon behind her. "Thank God we can forget about that till tomorrow."

They turned down a side corridor and walked up the back stairs to Deb's bedroom, placed between a bathroom and the goods lift on the third floor. Deb switched on the light. "Whew! This room's like an oven." She opened a window on to the light well, and the curtains moved in a slight draught that brought with it the smell of the kitchens. She closed it quickly again.

"Oh, don't worry about me," Claire said, "all I want is to get my feet up." She dropped into a chair and kicked off her shoes. "God, I'm tired, and my veins are giving me hell."

"I think you're awfully silly not to get a pair of flat shoes for the salon."

"My dear, I look a positive frump in flat heels. Nigel says they simply ruin whatever poise I might have. Besides, it's not only my feet, I'm aching all over. I could fall flat on my face and sleep for a week."

"Well, stretch out on the bed now and get all the rest you can."

Deb turned to the dressing-table and saw the letter with a small square packet beside it. She deliberately looked away from the familiar ACF envelope with her husband's writing on it. She didn't want to think about Jack tonight. She went to the wardrobe, took out a bottle of sherry and poured out two glasses, handing one to Claire. "Drink this up, you've got nearly an hour and you can stretch out flat on the bed for a while when you've had your shower."

Claire sipped her sherry and leaned back in the chair. "I hope old Ma Dalgety drops dead on the floor of Who's Who tonight. To think we sweat our lives away for hags like her." She swallowed the sherry. "God! that's a reviver." She put on Deb's bathrobe and went out.

Deb turned slowly and picked up the envelope. She

weighed it thoughtfully in her hand, putting off the moment when she must open it. . . . Was Jack coming on leave at last? The news for which she had been waiting so long she no longer wanted to hear. It was impossible to believe that she had not seen him for seventeen months — the longest time they had been separated in all the years they had known each other. She began to slit the envelope and then changed her mind and put it down, propping it up in front of a framed photograph. Better see what was in the parcel first. *Miss Forrest*. She undid the wrapping with pleasant anticipation. Only one person ever sent parcels to *Miss* Forrest.

She unwound the thick paper and uncovered a small gold box, opened it and took out an exquisite little flask of perfume. . .Chanel 5. Angus was amazing. However did he manage to get Chanel 5 in wartime? She undid the stopper and the heavy perfume rose to meet her. This was the kind of thing girls dreamed about — finding tiny packages containing rare and almost unprocurable perfumes when they came in from work. No, not from work. Somehow that didn't go with the picture at all.

Her pleasure was dashed as she picked up the letter again. The thought of opening it depressed her. She didn't want to open it. Why should she? All Jack's familiar arguments would be there to spoil her evening.

Well, he could argue about going back to the Vineyard till he was blue in the face. Her mind was made up. She would never go back! She picked up her glass and finished the sherry slowly, then sat down and slit the envelope.

The words leapt out of the page and sent the blood in a wave over her face and throat: "Down the weekend after next. . .probably Saturday. . . . Twenty-eight days' leave. We'll spend them at the Vineyard. . . . Bring Luen up with you. Wire me Brisbane if there is any change in plans. . . ."

She folded the letter angrily. Not a word of whether he might be upsetting her arrangements. Not a single word asking what she would like to do during his leave. Nothing. Just at the end: "We'll leave all our discussions till then."

Discussions! She knew Jack's idea of discussion. Giving her all the reasons why he was right, and if she didn't agree with him telling her she was being feminine and wrongheaded! This craze of his for going back to the Vineyard was sheer sentimentality. Up in the New Guinea jungle he'd idealised the place until he'd forgotten what it was really like. You could see from his letters that he'd got the idea into his head that they only had to get back there again and life would be as simple and free of problems as it had been when Luen was a baby.

That was Jack all over. Let him want to do something badly enough and he'd ride roughshod over everybody, her included. He'd had just as many arguments when he wanted to leave the Vineyard as he had now that he wanted to go back to it. They'd had their first row over that. She loved the little cottage that she'd made into a home and she was completely happy there looking after Jack and Luen and Uncle Dick. Jack had seemed happy too, the way he was always talking about planting more vines and how they ought to go in for wine-making and heaven knows what. Then suddenly he'd swept all their plans aside by announcing that he thought it was time they went back to the city. When she begged him to stay he told her that she was just being sentimental about a few vines and a pretty cottage when she ought to be thinking about the future. How could they give Luen the advantages they wanted for her on a vineyard? he'd asked her accusingly. And wasn't it time they had a little fun themselves? Not that he wanted to hear what she thought about it because he had already accepted a sales job in a motor firm in town.

Well, she could tell him there were no more opportunities for any of them on the Vineyard now than there were then. Because they'd had one good season and they'd been happy there, that was all he remembered. It was like expecting a holiday to last for ever....

"Oh God, what's the use of arguing..." She leant her head back against the chair and closed her eyes, trying to empty her mind of problems. She was tired, tired....

But instead of the peace of mind and body she ached

for, the Vineyard sprang to life against her closed lids. What a dump it had been when they first arrived, and how proud Jack was when she made it comfortable and homely so that Uncle Dick wondered how he had gone on for so many years without a woman around.

Then the spring had come, and she had watched the bursting buds on the long rows of vines, and the early blossoms came on the orange trees and their perfume lay sweet and heavy on the night air. They had banked everything on the crop and it promised to be a bumper one.

She remembered the October days when she'd sat reading and knitting on the sunny veranda. . . and the cool nights. It was late spring when the last frosts came and the vines down the valley were scorched. It was only a miracle that had saved theirs. That second night none of them could sleep for fear of another frost, and she and Jack had got up and gone out in the moonlight to see. There was a little wind and the lawn was soft and watery with dew under their hands. It was bitingly cold, but there was no frost and the crop was safe.

Luen was born at Christmas time when the grapes were swelling and the vines were full of the hum of bees. . . . Oh they'd been on top of the world that year when their whole life was full of the baby and their home, and there'd been wonderful January rains and a record vintage! It was easy to believe that every season would be a good one when you had spent only one there, and that life would be full and happy again because everything had been wonderful when you were young, and had your baby, and you saw the whole world in a glow of romance.

Deb sat up and jerked herself back to the present. She wasn't going to fall for that sort of thing again, however much Jack romanticised it. Why should she throw aside all her prospects only to have her whole life upset for a few years until he got some other bee in his bonnet?

She heard Claire's hand on the door and pushed the letter deep into her pocket, picking up the bottle of perfume swiftly. "Guess what this is?"

Claire took the flask in her hand as though it was a rare

antique and whistled enviously. Chanel 5! She closed her eyes and drew a deep breath. "Where the devil does he get hold of such things? It must have cost him twenty quid if it cost him a penny."

Deb looked astonished. "Four times my wages," one part of her mind said. "Twenty pounds for a tiny bottle of perfume for you, Deb Forrest," exulted another. And still another: "What would Jack say to this?"

"Use what you want," she said, picking up her towel and turning to the door. "We might as well go out smelling as though we really belong to the luxury class. I've hung your blouse up there."

Deb's lamé blouse was swinging on a coat hanger attached to the window curtain and Claire's eyes brightened with delight.

"It's a gem, Deb," she cried, touching its severe tailored lines gently. "It'll look super."

"You're lucky I bought the gold. I was torn between that and a silver one, and that'd have been no good with your hair."

"With a gold blouse and Guinea's tulips, nobody'll notice my old suit."

"Lie down and have a rest. I'll have my bath and you can get thoroughly relaxed. Put these pads on your eyes."

Claire sighed luxuriously as she stretched out and Deb laid astringent pads on her eyelids.

"This is heaven," she murmured. "I wish I could stay here for a week."

Claire lay trying to rest, trying to still the twitching in her knees and the nervous fluttering in her stomach. Another drink would fix that. She got off the bed and listened. The bath was running next door. Quickly she poured herself another glass of sherry and gulped it down, carefully putting the glass back where it had been before, and hurried back to the bed.

Oh God, her heart was going like a sledgehammer now. If she hadn't been to the doctor, she'd have thought she really had something wrong with it. Just nerves, he'd said, over-fatigue...not enough rest...take more care. Early nights, plenty of fresh air and sunshine. Huh...sunshine in the Marie Antoinette! That was funny. Early nights.... Early to bed, early to rise. Good advice. No doubt infinitely better than going to an endless round of parties and night-clubs. Dancing too long, drinking too much, gambling too often.... Much better. So what?

Lights played against her closed lids, changing from gold to green and blue and red, swirling circles, throbbing stripes, scatter of sparks like a firework display. She was looking a hag and she knew it. Thirty-eight wasn't old — nearly thirty-nine, to be honest. Deb was only a few years younger — thirty-two — and she looked as fresh as twenty-two. But Deb hadn't been in the racket as she had. Racket, racket, racket.... Party, party, party...drink, drink, drink ...gamble, gamble, gamble.... Keep up with the young ones, show them you're as good as they are. Show them a woman's only in her prime at thirty-eight. She'd have to take a pull, she thought, adjusting the pillow so that she could breathe more easily. The works were running down, some day they'd stop altogether. Morbid to think like that. Life begins at forty! Who wrote that? What goddamned fool wrote that?

But why should she worry? Was she ever short of a date? Did she ever miss a party? Dressed up, slim, soignée, her hair still the chestnut red that used to send men mad. No, not the same chestnut red.... Now she had to have a rinse to bring up the lights. There were fine lines at the sides of her eyes and the skin beneath them was beginning to sag. Once you got blue bags under your eyes you might as well throw in the towel.

She should worry! Nigel still thought she was stunning. He'd been telling her for years she was stunning. How long would he go on thinking that, if they didn't soon get a run of luck that would give them the thousand they needed to get married? No, she said to herself, be honest, he thinks it's necessary, but I don't. I'd marry him if he didn't have a

66

bean. Yes, I'd marry him and keep him if that was the only way I could bind him to me for ever. If I could only feel safe. Seven years of this dangling and I still feel the same about him. Worse. I've never been able to take him for granted, one touch of his hand and my heart turns over.

If only he'd marry me. Oh, darling, darling, darling Nigel, ask me tonight. Please God let him ask me tonight!

The tears started to her eyes under the astringent pads and she squeezed her eyelids together hard. This was no way to start an evening. She'd only make herself look worse. She cupped her palms over her eyes as the door opened quietly and Deb slipped in. "It's all right," she mumbled, "put on the light. I'm not asleep."

Deb switched on the light above the mirror and put her towels away. She shook her hair out of the shower cap and began to brush it. Claire watched her from between her fingers. She didn't look a day over twenty-five.

"Feeling better?"

"Much.... Though I still wish I could fall into my bed and sleep for a week. Old Dalgety was just the last straw."

"She was the limit," Deb agreed, handing her a cigarette and lighting one for herself. She had a shrewd suspicion that there was more to Claire's red eyes than overwork. Maybe it was just that she was nervy and worn out. She looked ghastly without makeup...almost plain...hard to tell what lay behind that sophisticated air of hers.

Deb settled herself in the chair, turned the wastepaper basket upside down and put her feet on it. She had worked with Claire for nearly two years and she still did not know her. Now, as she watched her dabbing the cool pads against her eyes, she felt a surge of curiosity. When she had first come to the South Pacific two years ago, Claire had represented for her the highest pinnacle of sophisticated elegance. The patrons of the Marie Antoinette might rank higher in the social scale, their clothes bear the tabs of world-famous designers, their beauty might be the product of Claire's thought and skill, but even privilege, wealth and leisure could not give them greater elegance nor more certain poise than Claire.

Watching her as she smoothed the foundation cream over her face, Deb acknowledged how much she owed to Claire for her initiation into the world of fashionable society. She would never have been able to hold her own with Angus without Claire's training and Claire's advice...probably she would never have attracted him in the first place if he had met her before Claire got to work on her, and made her diet that half stone off and buy some smart clothes. Angus took for granted the things that it usually took years of experience and training to give a girl if she wasn't born to the purple.

Claire wrapped a scarf round her hair before pressing the powder heavily into her skin. Deb was shocked to see the pallor of her face when the burnished hair was hidden, the dark smudges under her eyes, the hollowed cheeks. All the qualities that gave her face distinction when she was made up reduced it now under the hard light to a haggard mask.

"Why don't you try to have a rest this weekend?"

Claire laughed without mirth. "My dear," she said, "why don't you?"

Deb smiled self-consciously in answer.

Claire held up a thin hand and ticked off the fingers. "Tonight, dinner at Rom's and baccarat till God knows what time. Work tomorrow morning, Randwick in the afternoon. The game tomorrow night again and, if we're lucky, on Sunday night as well. According to our latest horoscopes, it's a wonderful week for both Nigel and me and we can't afford to miss out on a lucky break. And in between times, I've got to clean up the flat, do my washing, fix up some summer clothes in case this heatwave lasts, feed us both and you know what that means in shopping queues — and keep an eye like a hawk on Nigel to see that he gets some rest. He's got to be at the top of his form for some film tests on Sunday. And I'll be back in the bloody salon on Monday although it's a public holiday. Six-hour day! I'd like some of those unions to see the hours we work."

Deb sighed. "I've got a terrific time ahead of me too. I simply must get up to my sister's tomorrow or Luen will be terribly disappointed. And with tonight and Sunday booked up with Angus, it won't leave me a minute."

"It's just as well your man is comfortably middle-aged as well as wealthy," Claire went on with a faint tinge of malice in her voice, "otherwise you'd never be able to keep up with him. Elvira said he's been having a luxurious forty winks since six o'clock."

Deb felt a stir of resentment at the thought of her affairs being discussed with Elvira. Still, no use to say anything. It was one of those things you just had to take.

"I find it hard enough to keep up with Nigel as it is." Claire's mouth curved happily as she spoke of Nigel, her eyes softened.

This was love all right, Deb thought rather enviously, something perhaps you never felt for anyone but your first love. Though Nigel wasn't Claire's first, from what she could make out — far from it. "My fatality," Claire had said, "one of those things."

She finished pencilling the thin slanting line of her eyebrows and pulled the scarf down loosely to cover her face before turning to slip the golden blouse over her head. Her face under the green georgette had the mystery of some old Egyptian head — the lift of the chin, the sculptured cheekbones, the heavy-lidded eyes. Deb caught a glimpse of herself in the mirror and regretted that there was nothing exotic about her. She had always been told she was pretty, but it was only when she came to the Marie Antoinette that she had learnt how much more than mere prettiness a woman needed.

"You don't know how lucky you are," Claire's voice came blurred through the veil. "I'd take a bet on it that if you play your cards properly you might even be able to land old McFarland. . . . It's obvious he's potty about you."

"You forget I'm married."

"Being married needn't stand in the way of your sharing his bankroll. It's not marriage men like that are after." Claire's eyes grew hard, her mouth tightened. "Just think of never having to worry about money or clothes or anything any more. . . . And to have them all handed to you by a man who's been Sydney's most eligible bachelor for the last twenty-five years. I'd take it on myself if I got the chance, I can tell you."

"What about Nigel?"

"My dear, if a woman has all that old McFarland can give her to play round with, she should worry. Most men I know wouldn't mind playing second fiddle, in name at least, to a fortune like his. They'd find it very useful."

"Not Jack," Deb said firmly, "I certainly can't see him playing second or any other fiddle to anyone."

"Oh, Jack!" Claire dismissed him with a shrug. "He's just a boy full of old-fashioned bunk about love in a cottage — or a vineyard." She picked up the framed street photograph from the dressing-table. "He's terribly attractive, I'll admit, but he's not properly grown-up yet."

"Still, he is my husband. And I have a daughter, too. Don't forget that."

"Luen's the image of him, isn't she?" Claire held the photograph away to focus it better.

"Mmm...I suppose there is a resemblance."

"That's Dr Dallas MacIntyre with them, isn't it? She certainly knows how to wear her clothes. It hardly seems fair for one woman to have all she's got. Looks...brains...and a clothes sense like that." Claire look enviously at the bright smiling face. "Have you told her about Angus McFarland?"

"Good heavens, no! That's not the kind of thing I'd confide to her."

"Straitlaced?"

"No...not exactly. That is, she always seems to have queues of men friends, but...well, she just simply wouldn't understand."

Claire put the photograph back. "It's all right for her, she's not in the same boat as us. Every year spends a bit more of the only capital that ordinary women like us have got ...youth and looks and the power to hold your man, but for women like Dr MacIntyre with a profession, every year brings something more to them, whether it's knowledge, experience or simply a bank balance." Claire laughed. "I'd think twice about letting my husband out with her."

"Oh, Dallas is almost one of the family. We've known her since we were kids. She was a marvellous help to me when I was doing my massage course and she still looks after the family's ailments. She made all the arrangements for Luen's tonsils last year and I didn't have to worry about a thing, and she's looking after my young sister, Nolly. Fixed up a hospital bed for her and everything. The baby's due any time now."

"How many's that?"

"This'll be the fifth."

"God!"

"What can you do? Both Nolly and Tom want them. Personally, I feel that Jack and I have got enough on our hands to give one child everything she ought to have."

"All I can say is, if I had a daughter, nothing on God's earth would persuade me that it was better for her to be brought up as you and I have been, struggling all the time for our existence, instead of having the kind of life money can give a woman. When I think of what a thousand would do for Nigel and me..." She threw up her hands and turned away sharply.

"You mean, he still thinks its absolutely essential to have a thousand in the bank before you get married?"

"Oh, it's not only his idea," Claire said defensively, "I think so too."

Deb smiled. Claire's face darkened. "I don't see anything amusing about that."

"I'm sorry, but I was smiling at the thought of us — Jack and me — getting married on three pounds twelve shillings a week and not another penny to bless ourselves with."

"Yes. And look where it got you — out on the dole before you were married a month."

"That's right. But somehow, it didn't seem so bad then."

"Would you like to risk it again?"

"Heavens, no. I wonder our parents didn't try to stop us, hot-headed young fools that we were. But I suppose they couldn't have. We were young — and in love."

"Nigel and I are in love, but we're not young. He has expensive tastes and so have I. He went to the best schools, mixed with the best people and was brought up to expect money all round, then his old wretch of a grandfather in England married a young girl and he got none. Poor boy, he had a terrible time. He just can't adjust himself to not having the best. And that's what marriage without a sock in the bank would mean if either of us got sick."

She sat still, looking into a future that brought a shadow to her face. A life down to bare necessities. Neither of them could endure it.

"But your luck's changed, hasn't it?" Deb tried to introduce a cheerful note.

"At baccarat?"

"Yes."

Claire smiled. "Not so bad. Nigel won twenty-five smackers on Wednesday, and we've got the tip that Stormcloud's going all out tomorrow at Rankwick. But for God's sake keep that to yourself. I don't know where Blue could have got it. The owner told Nigel in absolute confidence at the game on Wednesday. Bit of luck for us, but he seems to have taken a great fancy to Nigel."

"Oh, don't worry about me, I don't know one end of a horse from the other, and I'm too mean to gamble."

"You don't know what you're missing. I'm all excited about tonight already. I'm certain we're going to be lucky. This weekend's under a marvellous vibration for both of us, and once you get a good run of luck, it seems to hold. That's all we need, a run of luck."

A run of luck.... Luck! "Oh, God," she prayed soundlessly, "give us a break. Just a run of luck. What's a thousand pounds? Mrs Dalgety can chuck it away on a new car for Alistair. Angus McFarland can write a cheque for it without noticing the difference. Just one thousand pounds...it would set me and Nigel up for life. Please God, this *is* my life. I've paid for everything.... Just a run of luck...."

She put on the black jacket of her suit. "I suppose it'll all come out in the wash, but don't forget that while love on the dole might be romantic at twenty, it'd be hell at forty."

Deb sighed: "It's all very difficult."

"Let me help you into your frock."

Claire lifted the long black dress from its hanger and slipped it over Deb's head. The heavy crêpe rippled down over her hips and fell to the floor in a sweep of concealed flares.

Deb preened herself at her reflection in the long mirror. Black georgette high to the throat shadowed the skin of her back and arms, her shoulders and bosom, down to the boned bodice of the underlining that covered her breasts in two daring curves.

Claire looked over her shoulder. "Satisfied?"

"I adore it — so long as I don't think about the bill."

"Bill be blowed! It's an investment. . . . You can take me on as dress adviser when you're in the money."

Deb laughed. "I hope I won't feel uncomfortable with most of the women in short frocks."

"With your escort? Don't be silly. If Angus asked you to wear a train and court feathers it would be all right. It's only the climbers who have to conform."

Claire perched a tiny toque of soft green feathers on her own chestnut curls.

"How does it look?" she asked.

"It's absolutely enchanting on you."

"It's terribly good with this blouse. You can borrow it sometime when you want a change."

Deb grimaced. "Thanks all the same, but you know how silly I am about green."

"Well, it's my lucky colour," Claire laughed.

"Guinea certainly had an eye for the right colour when she chose these." Deb picked up the tulips and pinned them high on the shoulder of Claire's suit. "Aren't they perfectly lovely? I've never seen anything like them before."

Claire looked at her reflection in the mirror. "Guinea's quite astonishing. She goes out with orchids splashed all over those dreadful florals she wears, and then she chooses the perfect flower for me."

Deb looked at the two figures in the long mirror. "You are tiny, aren't you?" she said. How she envied Claire's poise and the sophistication that, by some trick of carriage and personality, lifted a year-old suit and an improvised posy to the ranks of a *Vogue* fashion plate.

Claire, eyeing the tall figure beside her, felt a pang that her own glamour was so patently manufactured. Simplicity and freshness. That must have been what caught the old boy.... She sighed and turned to pick up her gloves and bag. "I'll have to rush. Thanks awfully for helping me out. And have a good time."

"I ought to thank you." Moved by an unexpected impulse, Deb bent and kissed the pale beautiful face. "Have a good time yourself. And good luck..."

"My God," Claire rolled her eyes, "do I need it!"

Monnie Malone peered out through the glass doors of the ladies' waiting room on Central station. The clock in front of the train indicator said quarter to eleven. She gnawed her fingers nervously. If she hurried, she could still catch the ten to eleven train, but then it would be after twelve by the time she had done the long walk home from West Hills station, and that meant there'd be another row.

It was all Bridie's fault, what had happened. If Bridie hadn't told Mum on her for getting home a bit late from the dance the night before and saying goodnight to Bob over the front gate, there wouldn't have been any row. Monnie rubbed her ear, which was still sore from the slap her mother had given her at the breakfast table that morning. Gee, she wished now she'd caught an earlier train, but she'd been that mad at Mum for nagging at her all through breakfast. She was getting on for seventeen and surely it was time she had a bit of fun. She might as well be dead, the way Mum went on about her going out anywhere. Why, this was only the third dance she'd ever been to, and if they hadn't been held in the church hall she'd never have got to any of them. And Bob was real nice, he never even wanted to kiss you goodnight like the girls at the factory said other boys did. If it had been only Dad there wouldn't have been all this fuss, he didn't treat you as though you were still in the infants' school. But even Dad wasn't much help, he always gave in to Mum.

When she had rushed out from breakfast in a temper and vowed she'd never go home again she hadn't bargained for being landed on Central station late on a Friday night with only a few shillings in her purse and nowhere to go. After work she had waited outside Peg's place for hours it seemed, and when at last she knocked timidly on the landlady's door, it was only to be told that Peg would not be back that night. Then she had gone to the post office in William Street to ring up Aunt Annie, but the phone just buzzed and buzzed and nobody answered it. She must have gone up to the Scotts' farm for the weekend, so it wouldn't be any good going to her place. There was nothing for it but to go home.

As she peered out from the waiting-room at the people hurrying across the station, her heart was still hot with resentment at Mum and Bridie, but she was getting more and more worried. By now the ten to eleven train had gone and there would not be another for an hour. She went back into the washroom. It might be only her imagination, but it seemed that everyone in there was staring at her, though some of the other girls had been there for ages, too. For a dreadful moment she wondered if Mum would go and put a police message out, like she'd done once when she was mad at Mick for going off with some of the boys. But Mum wouldn't do that to her — not the first night anyway.

The washroom was a cheerless place with the naked lights glaring down on porcelain basins and white tiled walls. Her own small face peered back at her from the mirror, rounded and babyish still, with brown hair curling to her shoulders, and blue eyes frightened under their thick brows. Bob said she was pretty, but what chance did you have of getting anyone to look at you twice when Mum wouldn't even let you put on a bit of lipstick? "Time enough to be going out with boys when you've got rid of your baby fat," Mum always said. How she hated her chubby chin and her smooth, plump shoulders. Gee, what did they expect you to do, stuck at that old mill all day on a machine you hated the very sight of and not able to change to a better job, because the Manpower was always on your tail on account of textiles being a reserved occupation? It was all right for Mum and Bridie, look at the wages they were getting in munitions.

The waiting-room was almost empty now, and the platform was growing more deserted every minute. Oh dear, what could she do? She'd never meant it to end like this.

"Well, if it isn't Monnie Malone!" a voice exclaimed loudly behind her.

She had a confused impression of painted faces in the mirror, and turned quickly. "Oh, Shirley, I am glad to see you. Gee, you look different."

Shirley laughed loudly. "Six months in the bright lights sure makes a difference to a girl after wasting the best years of her life in a dump like West Hills. Doesn't it, girls?"

"I'll say," they chorused.

"This is Monnie Malone, kids. We were at the same stinking mill. Meet my pals Betty and Fay. Us girls have got a flat together up at the Cross."

"Hiya, Mon," Betty said, laughing loudly as though there was some joke.

"Can it," Shirley warned. "What yer doing here at this time of night, Monnie? Did the Manpower give you a release too?"

Betty went off into peals of laughter.

"Oh no," Monnie explained earnestly. "I'm still at the mill. I often wondered how you got away, Shirl."

Shirley dug her in the ribs. "Urgent war work," she said, winking.

"How wonderful. Is it good pay?"

"Marvellous. Plenty of overtime." Betty burst out laughing again. "Anyway, what are you doing here this time of night?"

Monnie dropped her eyes. "I had a row with Mum and I came in to stop with my sister Peg, but she's away for the weekend, and I stayed round town so late and now...I'm... scared to go home."

"You poor little sap. What about taking her home with us, girls?" She looked at Fay inquiringly.

"Sure, baby," Fay said in broad Americanese. "Grace will probably offer her Betty's job!"

"You're a wunnerful pair of pals," Betty muttered.

"Are you certain I wouldn't be a trouble?" Monnie asked breathlessly.

"Not a bit. Come along, kid. We're just on our way to a party," Shirely explained.

"Isn't it terribly late?"

"In West Hills maybe, but at Kings Cross the night's just a pup. Let's go down and get a bus."

Going down the station steps, Betty tripped. Fay and

Shirley grabbed her and saved her from falling, but she flopped back on to the steps and went off into another peal of laughter.

"Shut up." Shirley's voice was savage. She pinched Betty's arm with her long reddened nails, and the two girls hoisted her to her feet. She whimpered a little as they marched her down the steps.

"The poor thing," Monnie murmured, full of sympathy. "Did she twist her ankle?"

"She's tiddly."

"Oh!" Monnie exclaimed in shocked surprise.

"Somebody poured hooch into her lemonade," Shirley lied glibly, shaking her head and frowning at Fay.

"Oh, isn't that wicked! Poor girl. If you like you can leave her at home with me and I'll see she's all right and if there is any work I could do in her place...."

Betty gave her a startled, owl-like glance. "Jesus!" she croaked.

Fay shoved her into a seat at the back of the bus. "Another sound out of you and you'll get what you're looking for."

"Oh, don't worry about that tonight, kid," Shirley said generously. "Though later on maybe they'll want someone."

Sitting opposite the three girls in the bus Monnie thought how wonderful and glamorous they were. Shirley was awfully pretty and so grown up! Even her voice was different — she spoke like the films. Her hair was much fairer than it used to be, too, and it was piled up in a high pompadour with a blue bow, and she was awfully smartly dressed. Betty and Fay were older and even smarter, though they weren't so pretty. A green ribbon was threaded through Fay's thick coppery hair and she wore a low-necked black satin frock which was the smartest dress that Monnie had ever seen except at the pictures. They all looked like something out of the films to her, with their heavily painted lips, their carefully rouged cheeks, their plucked and pencilled eyebrows and their startling mascaraed lashes. She resolved to find out from Shirley just how she had managed to get round the Manpower and find a job in the city that was obviously so much better paid than the woollen mills. Her heart soared at the thought that somewhere there might be just such a job for her.

Betty went off to sleep on Shirley's shoulder with her scarlet lower lip hanging slackly open showing the pale pink inside; the posy of frangipani on her shoulder was crushed and bruised. Whisky in her lemonade! What a wicked thing that was for anyone to do.

As the bus drew up at Kings Cross they shook Betty roughly and her head lolled on to Shirley's shoulder.

"Give her a hitch," Fay ordered, "and you take her bag, kid."

Shirley and Fay lowered her, not too gently, down the steps. Her legs crumpled under her as her feet touched the roadway.

"Oh Christ," Shirley said, "how the hell are we going to get her home?"

Two policemen standing on the corner of the footpath observed without interest the girl staggering helplessly between the other two. Betty straightened up at the sight of their uniform and fixed them with a drunken glare. "God rot the bloody cops," she mumbled and let out a yelp of pain as Fay's heel dug sharply into her ankle.

"Better get her home as soon as you can," one of the policemen said ponderously.

Shirley and Fay cringed as though they had been struck and hurried Betty along, murmuring frightened apologies. The two men looked after them, then turned and went heavily down Bayswater Road, eyes fixed rigidly ahead as though it were still midday and the jostling throng just an ordinary business crowd. Monnie trotted after the girls, clutching Betty's large red shoulder bag in both hands.

"Wanna hand, sister?" an American sailor asked, blocking their way.

"Mind your own bloody business," Shirley spat at him.

"And get outta the way," Fay said belligerently, "or you'll get my toe where your mother never kissed you."

"OK. OK, sister." He moved aside nimbly. "Only tryin' to help."

"By the living God," Fay muttered as they hauled Betty along the footpath, "if this bitch ever mixes her drinks again I'll cut her bloody throat. I've just about had enough of her muckin' things up for us."

Betty began to whimper.

"Shut up," Shirley snapped.

Monnie clung closer to them. She wondered what so many people were doing out so late at night; of all the crowd only she and the three girls seemed to be going home.

Men in all the uniforms that the war brought to the southern seas lolled in doorways and against shop windows, ogling the parading girls. Their eyes swept up from feet prancing on stilt heels, over rounded bare calves to swaying buttocks, and lingered on pointed breasts. Others smoked and balanced on the edge of the footpath with pretended nonchalance. Girls stopped to talk with them; couples went by, arms entwined, staring into each other's eyes, and there were snatches of strange conversations and the chatter of unfamiliar tongues.

Two swarthy sailors with striped vests and red pom-pommed tam o'shanters blocked her way. She could not understand the words they rattled out, staccato as machine guns, but she dodged round them and darted along the crowded footpath, bumping into strange, laughing men.

The shop windows were brilliant; some were piled with exotic fruit, others gleamed with sparkling silver and gaudy jewellery. The ham-and-beef shops were still open and filled with all sorts of foods she had never seen before. Spotlighted dummies displayed hats and frocks behind plate glass, and there were windows full of flowers. Every girl, it seemed, wore flowers, shoulder sprays, single blossoms in elaborately piled hair, even little floral hats, enchanting as a dream, and the air was full of the heavy sweet perfume of frangipani. Floating over everything was the sound of high-pitched laughter, like the chirruping of birds at sunset. How she envied the girls, all so pretty, so smart, so gay. What splendid, well-paid jobs they must have.

Taxis hooted as they crawled down the road, stopping to spill a laughing couple from one door while another piled into the emptying cab. Shirley and Fay clicked firmly along, ignoring whistling and wolf calls. Monnie pattered behind, keeping as close as she could. A police car cruised slowly past, its occupants all eyes in the darkened interior, its loud-speakers blaring out a disembodied warning. Nobody seemed to be taking any notice.

The street lights sifted through the plane trees, illuminating their young leaves to a ghostly green and casting fantastic shadows on the pavement. On the corner of a side street an Air Force boy was playing a mandolin, and girls and sailors danced on the footpath with skirts whirling and legs out-flung, their wild yells punctuating the gay strumming.

The sound of the music roused Betty and she struggled to join the dancing. Fay and Shirley dragged her past with difficulty. "Here, take our bags," Shirley ordered. Monnie obeyed. With arms locked around Betty's waist and holding her flailing hands, they dragged her down a laneway like a dark canyon between high walls, full of darker shadows. Monnie clung closer to the three girls for protection.

Halfway down they propped Betty up against the wall beside a doorway flush with the street. The light behind the fanlight showed a black-painted 78A.

"Here, open my bag and get out the latchkey. It's in the purse part," Shirley ordered.

Monnie fumbled with the catch on the smart white patent bag. When she opened it, the smell of strong perfume rose. She unsnapped the bulging centre compartment. It was stuffed with crumpled banknotes. Gee, Shirley must have a good job. She felt carefully among them with embarrassment and something like awe. The key wasn't there, it must have fallen down to the bottom. She fumbled among damp hand-kerchiefs and face powder spilled from a compact.

"For Christ's sake hurry up and find that bloody key before somebody comes," Fay muttered.

"I've got it," Monnie cried, extracting the key from a

corner where it was half-hidden in the torn lining. She slipped it into the lock with shaking hands and pushed the door open. A narrow staircase, lit by a subdued light, rose almost from the doorway. They pushed Betty towards the stairs, their footsteps muffled by the thick carpet, and, as they passed the half-open door of the lounge, she caught a glimpse of three men sitting in chairs pushed stiffly back against the wall, like a dentist's waiting-room.

The whole house was quiet, and Monnie wondered when the party was going to begin. Then suddenly, a high laugh shrilled from behind a closed door.

"The party's on," Shirley whispered nervously, "we'll have to hurry, and for Christ's sake don't make a noise."

Fay pushed Betty roughly ahead of her, and opened the door of their flat. They lowered her on to a tumbled double bed, stripped off her frock, and dropped her shoes to the floor. She lay snoring and relaxed, her flesh pale through her black lace brassière and scanties.

"Fay and I have promised to go to a party in another flat," Shirley explained to Monnie. She was restoring her makeup with swift, practised fingers. "Think you'll be OK here with Betty?"

Monnie glanced at the girl on the bed and her fear showed in her face.

"You don't have to worry about her now; she'll sleep till midday if you let her alone. You get yourself something to eat and tuck up on the settee there."

"But what about you two?"

"Don't worry about us. These parties go on all night sometimes. Anyway, if we want to go to bed we'll pitch Betty into the bath and bloody well let her sleep it off there. Just help yourself to anything you want. See you in the morning."

Monnie stared at the snoring Betty and round the untidy flat. She felt a pang of fear. Shirley usen't to swear like that, but then neither did Peg when she was at home. But all the girls swore now. She'd heard Peg and her friends talking once when she went up to the salon and she'd thought their language was terrible at first, but nobody else seemed to take any notice of it.

She tiptoed back into the bedroom and drew a dirty sheet and grey blankets over Betty, took off her own clothes and hung them neatly behind the bathroom door, putting on her slip again to sleep in. She found a blanket and a pillow and curled herself up on the settee. Gee, wasn't she lucky to have met Shirley! And weren't they all terribly kind?

Deb came out of the cloakroom and flickered a glance through her lashes to make sure that Angus was already waiting for her. Yes, there he was at the foot of the curved staircase. He really was distinguished, standing there half a head taller than most of the other men. Claire was right, he was like something out of the *Tatler*. He stepped forward and she smiled up at him.

Henri hastened forward to welcome them. "Good evening, *madame*," he said, bowing from the waist with a continental grace Deb found pleasantly flattering after a day kowtowing to Marie Antoinette patrons. She returned his smile with what she hoped was the right mixture of warmth and condescension, and followed him among the crowded tables. The red carpet, the white tablecloths, the gleaming reflections in the mirrors, the soft music, the air of luxury, the deference of the waiters — this was the setting she loved.

Henri bowed them to their table. It was against the wall, and in the enormous mirror beside it the world of the fashionable restaurant went through its routine of dining and wining and dancing.

The table gleamed white and silver in the reflection from a shaded lamp which poured down its light on a flat crystal bowl of lily-of-the-valley. Angus disliked the fashion of women wearing flowers, but he always ordered the rarest and most fragrant blooms to give a note of distinction and difference to his table.

Deborah glided into the chair Henri pulled out for her, with a faint inclination of thanks. The delicate perfume of the lily-of-the-valley drifted up to her and she bowed her head to the tiny bells. Cool, like the cool smell of ferns and wet underbrush. Not a perfume for a nightclub. They must have cost pounds, too, judging by the price of a single spray at the boutique.

"I thought you'd like them." Angus's eyes lingered on her gleaming hair, the whiteness of dropped eyelids, all her vibrant grace.

"They're lovely. I didn't know you could get such masses as early as this."

"I ordered them specially."

Two waiters appeared beside them.

"Everything is ordered." Angus seldom bothered with menus. "And take away these tumblers," he gestured contemptuously at the common wartime glasses. "Where are my own?"

The waiter murmured apologetically.

"Send Jacques to me." He turned to Deb. "Shall we have a cocktail now and dance before the floor gets too crowded?"

Deb nodded, half smiling. Jacques placed the cocktails beside them in fragile glasses. Angus raised his glass to touch hers. Their eyes met and he murmured: "I feel this is going to be a special night."

She smiled in answer and sipped her cocktail with the same casualness with which Angus sipped his. A special night? What did he mean by that? Every night that he took her out was special in a way she could hardly explain to him. Special, because she went with a rising excitement each time, and a sense of enchantment at seeing Angus's world from the inside. He would never know that it was all rather like a fairy story — Cinderella's story — to her. Even after six months she couldn't help feeling guilty when she caught a glimpse of the sheaf of banknotes he placed on the bill at the end of the evening. Not that it mattered to Angus, she knew that. It wasn't like the times she and Jack went out together, when she felt personally responsible and got indignant when the costs began to mount up. It was nice to think that even if you went on going to expensive places with Angus for years, you couldn't ruffle the surface of his income.

The orchestra started up. He raised his brows. "Shall we dance?"

When they rose, the full-length mirror beside their table showed her the perfect couple; his broad shoulders and perfect carriage were those of a young man, and the grey at his temples only served to make him look more distinguished.

He looked his best in evening clothes and the fact that hardly another man there wore the conventional black dinner suit didn't seem to worry him. They were mostly younger men in uniform, and the sprinkling of civilians in lounge suits had the guilty air of men who felt they should be in uniform too. Only a few of the women were in dinner frocks. Thank goodness Mrs Dalrymple and her daughter from the SP both wore them too. It would have been embarrassing, she felt, for all Angus's insistence, if she had been the only one there in formal dress.

The saxophonist moved to the microphone and began to croon:

> *The southern stars are bright above,*
> *Pale frangipani fills the air,*
> *Its blossoms star your perfumed hair. . . .*

As the music sobbed out its sentimental refrain, the pressure of his hand strengthened on her back.

> *The night is made for you and love. . . .*

Through the thin material of her frock, she could feel the warmth of his hand. She wished men hadn't given up the old fashion of wearing gloves, although thank heaven it wouldn't hurt this black dress.

> *Your lips are warm and soft, my sweet,*
> *As frangipani in the night. . . .*

She felt his lips against her hair. The singer's voice melted away in a dying cadence:

> *Your touch is music — all delight.*
> *I scatter stars around your feet. . . .*

Deb sighed. Jack would be back next week and all this would come to an end.

Angus really was wonderful, she thought, as they sat down at their table again. There was absolutely nothing he couldn't get, from unobtainable perfumes to the best table at Prince's. Every time she went out with him her amazement deepened at the way people could get anything if they had the secret of commanding it. She caressed the lily-of-the-valley. How utterly right it was; less ostentatious than orchids, but harder to get. And the oysters on their bed of cracked ice... Angus said it was sacrilege to eat oysters soaked in piquant sauces, and though the dinner menu said 'oyster cocktail', on their table the oysters were ungarnished except for the slices of lemon beside them.

"I always say Sydney people don't really know what oysters are like," he remarked, "they want to taste them fresh from the rocks as one gets them down at Bermagui. Those are oysters."

Deb smiled. "I don't know the Bermagui ones but I'm certain they couldn't be better than those at Bateman's Bay."

He lifted his eyebrow questioningly. "Oh, you know the far south coast?"

"Yes." Deb wondered what he would think if he really knew just how and when she had been there. A picture of Jack flickered across her mind — Jack, tanned like leather, in a pair of ragged shorts, making his way around the rocks, and getting their dinner with an old oyster knife. Not oysters for an appetiser, but oysters to fill up the emptiness of your stomach when your dole rations were running out and the southerlies made it too rough for fishing.

"We used to go camping down there quite a lot," she said airily. Only a white lie, that 'quite a lot'. It sounded as though they had gone there often instead of staying a long time because Jack was unemployed.

With a certain malicious amusement she saw again in her mind's eye the shack they had built out of stringybark on the edge of the beach. Once they had got over Jack losing his job and their first shame at being on the dole, they were as proud of the tricks they learned from the fishermen as if there was no better life in the world than beachcombing, and no greater excitement than selling a catch of fish to motorists up on the highway and actually possessing a few shillings of their own.

Oh, yes, she knew the south coast.... She'd lived there for nearly a year, and she would have stayed longer if she'd had her way. When she knew she was going to have a baby Jack wanted to go back to town, but she didn't want to leave the camp and so they had stayed on into the winter until the shack had been blown down over their heads in a gale and Jack had insisted on taking her back.

She wondered how Angus's knowledge of the south coast matched up to that. Had he ever got as much fun out of the drive to Sydney in an expensive car as she and Jack had got out of hitch-hiking two hundred miles on milk wagons and timber jinkers? For the first stretch they'd huddled on a utility truck against the back of the driver's cabin, watching the road stream away between the undulating paddocks, green under their winter grass. The piled stone walls the convicts had built ran down to the cliff's edge, and beyond them was the deep winter blue of the sea. South coast names rippled through her mind: Kioloa, Ulladulla, Tomerong, Nowra, and the train terminus at Bomaderry.

She could see Jack now standing on the station and looking at the list of fares. He wanted to go back by train to save her, but she was more interested in saving the money, and while they were still arguing a big lorry drew up beside them and the driver leaned out and said: "Like a lift, kids?"

That was luxury. They sat in the front with him right back to Sydney and had lunch by the roadside and laughed and sang all the way up the coast. Wollongong, Woonona, Corrimal, Bulli...and then the familiar road through National Park and the white sandhills of Cronulla coming up in the distance.... Yes, she knew the south coast!

An imp of mischief prompted her to say casually, "We spent part of our honeymoon there before we went to Uncle Dick's vineyard." But she stopped herself in time. Any reminder that she was married or had a child always put a damper on Angus. He would lapse into silence, almost as though he was jealous. Well, he'd just have to be jealous.

Men, as Claire said, were the devil. They wanted your company and anything else they could get, and they were damn clever at not being compromised themselves, but jealous of any suggestion that you might have other attachments. It was all take and no give. Not that she could honestly say that of Angus; he'd never made a pass at her. All the times he'd taken her out he had behaved with a flattering deference. And that, judging by the stories other girls told, was almost a miracle.

They continued to eat their oysters in silence. Deb had learned that food was a serious matter for Angus, to be treated seriously. You danced and enjoyed it; you talked or listened, and appeared to enjoy it; you ate and enjoyed it; but you did not chatter over your meal, except for an occasional expression of appreciation, nor did you get up between courses or in the middle of them and dance. The waiters at Prince's knew his tastes; they knew the minimum and the maximum service he required and, judging from the notes they pocketed at the end of the evening, they were well recompensed for remembering.

Dining with Angus always made her feel that she had been transferred to another world. She had to remind herself constantly that this was the standard which Angus regarded as his right. Inferior, of course, in these deplorably rushed war days, as he had often explained to her. Only a shadow of what service had been in the great restaurants of the world — Claridge's, the Meurice, the Adlon, Raffles, Hotel des Indes.... She loved to hear his stories of the parties in a world so far removed from her own as to sound like a fairy-tale, yet close enough for her grasping if she was to believe his veiled hints and casually dropped comments.

Of course, on the other hand, he might merely be taking for granted that she came from a world like his own. After all he knew nothing of Jack except that he drove a cream Oldsmobile — she hadn't said that he was a car salesman and it belonged to the firm — and little of her except that she flitted off mysteriously to a job in a luxury salon during the day and at night wore clothes that, thanks to Claire, were right in his world.

For her to have a job probably didn't seem odd to him when so many leisured women were in munitions or other essential jobs for the war effort. But hers was no war effort. It was solid hard need. She'd like to know just where a sergeant's allotment would go in Angus's scheme of affairs. She felt a sudden pang of guilt to think she'd drifted so far from her original intention of putting away a sock for the postwar days out of her earnings. Why, this very frock she was wearing had knocked her back twelve guineas and it would have cost twice that if it hadn't been for Claire's connections. Oh, well, no use crying over spent guineas! It was worth it.

Angus's voice brought her back with a start. He was in the middle of grouse shooting.

"How wonderful," she murmured to hide the fact that she had not been listening.

"Some day perhaps you'll taste how they cook pheasants at Gleneagles. And London — I'd like to take you dancing at the Dorchester." He smiled at her warmly, then his face darkened. "Though heaven only knows what will be left of them all when the V-bombs have finished."

"Poor things, it's too awful."

"One wonders what will be left of all the lovely old places one knew. I had aerograms from England only this week and they tell me the destruction in London is appalling. Middle Temple and the Temple church.... When I think of the destruction all through Europe, I wonder if I can ever bear to go back."

The wine waiter was standing beside them, holding a silver bucket in his hand. As he placed it on the table, the light gleamed on the tinsel-covered cork.

"A special celebration," Angus smiled across at her.

The waiter handled the bottle with as much care as she used to handle Luen when she was a tiny baby. He began to remove the wire.

"A good year, eh, Jacques?" Angus said complacently.

"A meeracle, sir, a meeracle to see such a dr-rink in such

times as zees.''

"Ah, miracles are only good management. I have three others put away, and I doubt if there are another three in the whole of Australia.''

"I'ope in ze safe dee-posit, Mr McFarland, sir. For I warn you, Jules and ze ozzers — zey would stop at nuzzing for soch a t-treasure.'' Jacques turned his eyes heavenwards as he eased the cork out and the champagne foamed from the bottle. *"Enchantant*, sir!'' he whispered in an awed voice. *"Suprème!''*

Angus smiled warmly across to Deb as the sparkling liquor bubbled in their shallow glasses.

"For a very special occasion,'' he said, raising his glass and smiling at her over the brim. "Our anniversary! Six months since fate brought me to your table.''

She took a sip. "Mr Sharlton would hardly recognise himself in that rôle.''

"Fate wears strange disguises, my dear.''

The pale, bubbling drink was dry and cool. Rather like sparkling hock, she thought. Really, there was a great deal of fuss made about things that didn't live up to expectations. Honestly, she wouldn't have known the difference if there hadn't been all the build-up.

"Like it?''

"Delicious.'' She smiled at him over her glass. Fancy you, Deb Forrest, drinking vintage champagne rarer than gold with one of the McFarlands, and having the nerve to criticise it just because you haven't got what they call a palate!

"Then I shall keep the other bottles specially for... other special occasions.''

"That will be lovely.'' The champagne fizzed up the back of her nose but she managed to conceal it under a little laugh.

The dinner was 'austerity' only in name, and by the time they had finished and got up to dance again, the champagne was singing in Deb's head. It was wonderful to be swept out of the rut of everyday living; dining among the socialites at Prince's, drinking priceless champagne that enveloped the world in a rosy glow, dancing to the music of a wonderful orchestra with a man who considered your every whim. This was how Cinderella must have felt.

The sight of a khaki tunic beside them reminded her that it was an enchantment as brief as Cinderella's — finished when the clock chimed midnight. Her midnight chime was the letter on her dressing-table. A week, maybe less, and Jack would be home again. What would he look like after this long time in the jungle? Would he have changed? One thing she knew well enough, he wouldn't have changed sufficiently to appreciate her going out with Angus. She could imagine the way his jaw would set and the furrow come between his brows. She set her own mouth mutinously. Who was he to dictate to her the kind of life she should live? Wanting to take her back to the Vineyard! She'd be a drudge, that was all. And Luen. What prospects would there be for Luen growing up on a place that had never done more than keep Uncle Dick, and he was born to it?

Jack had given his ultimatum. Well, she would give hers when he came back, and she wouldn't argue about it either. One thing was certain, she could never tolerate that life again.

Back at the table, Angus drank his steaming black coffee and laid the cup down with a gratified "Ah!" The first lot had not been hot enough and he had sent it back. This was so hot that it burned Deb's mouth. She wondered how he could swallow it. He sat looking at her, smiling the one-sided smile that gave his face a quizzical charm.

"It was a fortunate day for me when my table at the South Pacific was taken that Saturday. Otherwise I'd never have met you."

"If you could have seen poor Mr Sharlton's face when he realised that there was only one vacant seat and that with a member of the staff! He'd have asked me to leave the table if you hadn't been standing there."

"While I was wondering what I had done to deserve not

only such a companion, but a respectable introduction to her as well.''

''I'm sure that in all your time at the SP nothing quite so unconventional ever happened to you.''

''They say there's no armour against fate.''

''Apparently not even Mr Sharlton's superb organisation.''

''Apparently not. I shall just be grateful to fate and drink to our next anniversary. I think we'll make it the first of each month so that we don't have to wait too long for an excuse for a special party.''

''I'm afraid that mightn't be possible. You see, my husband's coming home on leave next week.''

Angus raised one eyebrow in the quirk that emphasised the sardonic mask he presented to the world. ''Really?'' He sounded quite uninterested, but when he offered his cigarette case to her, Deb was astonished to see that his hand was shaking.

That's torn things, Deb thought regretfully. Still, it had been a lovely interlude and she had been mad to think it might go on. But what a fool she'd been to tell him about Jack tonight and spoil everything.

Angus prided himself on his control. It was not solely that his ancestors had given him a nervous system set firm by generations of good feeding and secure environment. Old Angus McFarland, his grandfather, had once encountered Captain Gilbert and outshot and outdared the bushranger. It was a good inheritance, to which his grandson had added the traditions of Oxford, the friends he had made there, the security of his investments and the boundless sureness of his own value and his place in the world. ''Nothing can throw Angus McFarland off balance,'' they said at his club. His company on Gallipoli once paid him a similar and more virile tribute. Angus was proud of his ''nerve'', complacently aware of his reputation. There was confidence in the set of his head and the ironic detachment with which he viewed the world from his six feet two. There were a lot of men, now dragging reluctant middle-aged bodies through the involutions of VDC drill and manoeuvres, who swore that a company of the "Old and Bolds" led by Colonel McFarland DSO could have done more than a battalion of the Second AIF.

Angus had so long been aware of his own imperturbability and privately proud of the way he could light a cigarette in the teeth of a crisis without so much as the visible twitching of a muscle that he was all the more astonished at his reaction to Deb's words.

He drew on his cigarette and beckoned the waiter. What he needed was a stiff drink — champagne wasn't a real drink at all. He'd had half a bottle of whisky sent round with the champagne and God help Jacques if he'd touched a drop of it. He continued to talk pleasantly about the difference between this war and the last. Then, leave had been a different matter. He told several anecdotes of leaves he'd spent in England and described the places he had visited. He drank a double whisky in silence.

He was angry, angry with himself for this betrayal, angry with this husband who could shake his whole world to its foundations with a breezy announcement that he was coming home on leave. Above all, angry with the whole undignified situation in which he found himself. Watching Deborah's downbent head he was astonished at the strength of the emotion which flooded him. Good God, he hadn't known he could feel this way. Like a boy! Like a boy in the urgency of his desire, like a boy in the complete disregard of all the material factors that stood in the way of its satisfaction.

When their association started, he had visualised a pleasant relationship. He'd played with the idea of Deborah becoming his mistress; she was damned attractive. But that was only in the early days. Lately he'd put that thought away; she wasn't the kind of woman to be taken casually. He even toyed with the idea of marriage. He hadn't seriously considered marriage since the last war, not since Noreen Remington and he had announced their engagement just before the first troopship sailed, back in 1915. Nearly thirty years ago. He had been too honourable to marry her before he left, but Noreen had had no delusions about honour when she married young Marston who had too much sense to go overseas and plenty to cash in on war contracts. That had put him off marriage. And if once you were set against marriage, the other way was so much more exciting; it offered so much greater variety, and so much more freedom from personal responsibility. Not that a gentleman didn't see that a woman was suitably rewarded for her favours.

Damn it, he felt as he had felt that day in hospital in Cairo when he'd opened his sister's letter that had brought the news. Pain, frustration, the need to kick something — or someone — good and hard.

It was with amazement therefore that Angus heard himself say "Of course, my dear. . . ." he broke off. There was a strange note in his voice when he went on again: "Of course, your realise, my dear, that this has not been merely a casual acquaintanceship for me?"

Deb looked up surprised. "It has been delightful for me, too."

"I should perhaps have given you some clearer hint of my feelings." He began again and stopped. His voice was unsteady. Deb was silent. "Deborah," he said urgently, "I am asking you to marry me."

Deb sat quite still, looking at him. No, she said to herself, I don't believe it. It's fantastic. Not Angus McFarland. It's like Cinderella. . .I *am* Cinderella!

"I should have preferred to do this more formally, shall we say," Angus added in a tone more like his own. "I didn't want to rush you. But I feel you should know exactly what my intentions are."

"But I'm married," Deb said, and immediately thought

how ridiculous such a remark was. It broke the tension and Angus laughed.

"I'm only too aware of the fact. But there are such things as divorce."

"Yes — that's right." She stopped herself in time from saying: "I don't think Jack would like it," and finished lamely. "Please, could I have another cup of black coffee?"

Angus ordered the coffee and found himself drawing a long breath with relief from tension. He should have said this weeks ago. Then plans for the divorce could have been under way and he wouldn't have had to endure this moment of uncertainty and frustration. Absurd, when all his life he had acted on the principle of making up your mind about what you want and going straight for it. What he wanted now was to marry Deborah.

Angus took a last drink, leaned over and put a hand on hers. "Do you mind if we go?"

"Just as you please."

"I must have you to myself."

He rose and stood smiling down at her. When she got up her head was whirling and her knees felt like cotton wool. His hand under her elbow steadied her.

She sank into the cushioned seat of the private hire car. Angus murmured directions to the chauffeur and sat back beside her, his arm firm around her shoulders. The big limousine purred softly down Castlereagh Street to the Quay and the wind was pleasantly cool on her flushed face.

The lighted ferry wharves slid behind them as they swung in a wide curve across Circular Quay and up the short steep hill into Macquarie Street. The world was drowned in moonlight. Deb saw, as in a dream, the battlements of the Conservatorium rising white among a circle of dark trees, palms pirouetting like ballet girls the length of the street, a tunnel of stippled darkness beneath the avenue of Moreton Bay fig trees in the Domain; she smelled the scent of magnolia drifting from the Botanical Gardens and the fresh-cut lawns. The night was heady with perfume and moonlight.

As they cruised round Mrs Macquarie's Chair the harbour unfolded below them, silver light and broken shadow. Peace. Easy to forget there was a war on, if it weren't for the battleships swinging in the tide. Peace, too, in the car with Angus's arm around her, his other hand resting gently on hers.

"A night for love," he whispered, his lips against her ear.

This was heaven, flying through the night, dreamlike, enchanted. Her head drooped against his shoulder. She hiccoughed. Heavens, she thought, I'm drunk!

His lips against hers were full and warm. "Little lovely one," he murmured, "I think I'd better take you home."

SATURDAY

I

"God! What a morning!" Claire ran her finger down the list of appointments. "Not a spare minute, and we'll simply have to fit old Dalgety in somewhere. I can't see myself getting to Randwick till the races are half over."

Guinea turned over a page of the morning paper and grimaced. "Wouldn't it make you sick?"

"Who's made the headlines this time?" Claire inquired without raising her head.

"That poor little devil of an AWAS who died in Brisbane."

"That abortion case?"

"Yeah. The trial's started and it's plastered all over the paper. Why the hell do they have to go dragging in everyone from the bloke and the girl's roommates at the barracks to the poor old hag who did the job? What good does it do?"

"It's the law, my pet."

"Damn the law!" Guinea turned over the pages indignantly.

"Turn to the social page and see who's hit the news."

Guinea flipped over war, politics and disaster, literary reviews and sporting fixtures, stopped and clicked her tongue, "Old Ma D.D.T. and Denny darling have got their faces in again." She whistled through her teeth. "Listen to this, my girl. Who do you think this means? 'It's amazing how youth is flattered by old vintage and vice versa. There's a certain well known man about town, tall and greying but still a divine dancer who seems to have that something that charms all femmes. A little bird tells me that one of our most beautiful station homes, long closed up, may at last have a permanent hostess. Well, he seems to have all the answers to any girl's prayers, though we understand there is a slight obstacle. Maybe it's merely the old story that beauty on one side and experience on the other seem to make a perfect temporary combination.' I'd take ten to one on they're having a crack at old McFarland and Lady Forrest.''

Claire drew in her breath. "Whew. She's moving up in the world all right. Sh, here she is.''

As Deb emerged from the massage cubicle, Guinea shouted with delight, "I say, this'll put old Ladies First's blood pressure up.'' She gurgled maliciously. "Large as life in the Weekend Diary. 'The Belle Bounces Again!' Now, do you think they mean D.D.T. or the old Bouncing Belle downstairs?''

"If you'd read it we'd know,'' Deb suggested.

"'Few places of historical interest have such buxom skeletons in their cupboards as Sydney's Number One Glamour Pub, known familiarly to its habitués as the SP. Despite all attempts on the part of the directors to rival the Savoy and the Waldorf-Astoria, and all the manager's efforts to counteract the Belle's influence, she keeps popping up in unexpected ways. If you belong to the Society for Psychical Research you'll probably say that it's too much to expect the Gilded Girl to adjust herself to the upper crust of café and pub society, considering that she started life on the prow of the fast schooner that brought its owner such riches blackbirding round the South Pacific in the good old days.' What's blackbirding?'' Guinea looked up.

"Something like slave trading. The best people used to do it.

"Oh! Well then,'' Guinea went on reading. "'After that she adorned the bar of the original "South Pacific" which her owner built down near the docks when he decided to turn to more legal forms of piracy...' Jeepers! there's still plenty of pirating goes on in the Cockpit, if they'd like to know.''

"Well, get on with it,'' Claire urged.

"'The Bouncing Belle next accompanied the son (by

parental command) when he turned respectable and moved up-town to the site the SP now occupies. She was inherited, along with the name, as an inseparable part of the bargain when he eventually sold the pub to a brewery in the 20s, himself retir-ing from vulgar trade to good works and a knighthood. Blackbirding seaman, dockside tavern keeper, respectable Sir...they have all passed. But the Bouncing Belle still goes on bouncing, to the unending mortification of her directors. Not even the acquisition of such a superb site for Sydney's premier hostelry, nor the wartime dividends pouring into their coffers entirely compensate for this perpetual reminder of their low origin. We can readily sympathise with their desire to rake in the shekels by providing a home from home for our gallant allies, but I ask you, isn't it rather over the odds to establish a two-up school in the lift as one of the attractions? A strange place, those of us who number swy among our accom-plishments would say. But maybe it's easier to dodge the Long Arm of the Law that way, for — in case you don't know — even the SP lift can't make the game legal! Has anyone told the manager?'''

"Phew," Claire whistled, "I hope I don't cross L. F.'s path to-day."

"Blue should have had more sense," Deb said crossly, disappearing into the cubicle. "It makes us all look ridiculous. If we're ever going to attract tourists here after the war we'll have to give them something better. The British and Americans have been accustomed to very different standards of living."

"If there's anything that makes me puke it's all this hooey about the British and the American way of life. What's it all boil down to? Same as here, only on a bigger scale. Oodles of unemployed, and a few ginks lousy with money loping round the globe from bars to brothels, and criticising us mugs who've got to work for a living."

"Don't be ridiculous. Everyone knows travel is highly educational."

"It all depends what you want to be educated for. Per-sonally I haven't seen much sign of it in the wenches that come in here, whether it's Ritzes or ruins they babble about."

"Well you must admit they have got very different standards abroad from ours."

"That's what Nigel's always saying," Claire agreed.

"Yeah? Standards who for? Not for mugs like us. I'm fed to the teeth with these Britishers who mistake ruins for civilisation, and I don't find it any easier to take the Yanks who think it's spelt plumbing."

"They ought to give you a soapbox in the Domain, my girl." Claire picked up the paper and read the last lines over again with relish. "It's clever, you know. Personally I think it's the best joke I've heard in years. God, the *Daily Sketch* has got its knife into the place!"

Guinea chortled, "Serve them right. Fancy any lounge supervisor being nuts enough to refuse to serve one of their reporters just because he wore a sports shirt.

"Wasn't he the fellow who did those hair-raising reports on the Kokoda Trail?" Claire asked.

"Yeah. He bought into a slap-up row with the brass hats too. He reckoned practically everything he wrote was censored out of sight. Funny, the boys up in the jungle seem to get quite a different line on war to the showground commandos."

"Well, frankly, I don't see what good all that horror stuff does," Claire said.

Deb agreed with some heat. "Personally, I think it's a pity they don't censor a bit more. It's so distressing to read."

"It's a damn sight more distressing to go through it, I'd say. So far as I can see, a hell of a lot of people are enjoying a bloody good war, and I can't raise a tear over their second-hand sufferings. You should hear Mum on it, and she's taken enough knocks what with Jim lost on the *Sydney* and not a word about Mick since the fall of Singapore. She'd have all of us who are sitting pretty at home lined up for a true-to-life newsreel once a week, mud and blood and guts and all."

Claire shuddered. "Well, maybe she could take it, but to be perfectly honest I couldn't."

"I can't see the need for it," Deb agreed.

Guinea shrugged. "Maybe if you'd had your husband injured in one war and lost two boys in another and dragged your kids through a depression in between, you might feel the same. All these old bozos, sitting on their backsides deciding what we should and shouldn't know about make me puke. If they spent their time trying to stop war and depression and all the filth that goes with them instead of trying to make us believe that going to war's a game of ring-a-rosy and life on the home front nothing but kiss-in-the-ring...If we'd had a bit more truth from the beginning, we wouldn't have had twenty thousand men trapped in Malaya."

"Oh, come off it, Guin," Claire laughed. "We've heard all this before. All I'm sorry for is that I missed seeing L. F. lick the dust off the fellow's boots when he found out who he was."

"Well," Deb said, "while I've got no sympathy for L. F., I must say I think it's time they took a stand on the way some of the men around the place dress."

Guinea snapped back, "You can't expect all the troops to have their prewar Savile Row suits laid away in mothballs like Alistair. Why the hell can't a journo wear what he likes so long as it's decent?"

Deb shrugged her shoulders. "It all depends on how you look at it. Personally I wouldn't like my escort to come along looking like a tramp."

"I like a man to be well-dressed myself," Claire agreed.

"Ah, phooey! You can booze, bludge, bounce or blacketeer in this pub and get away with it — so long as you appear in public with your collar and your fly done up." Guinea emitted a giant raspberry at the SP and the world of fashionable appearances in general.

Deb picked up a bundle of towels and went out.

Guinea looked after her with a puzzled expression. "I don't know what's come over her. She used to be quite human. But I can't open my mouth lately without she jumps down my neck."

"I don't think she means it. Probably just finding things larger than lifesize at the moment. She's expecting her husband home on leave any time now."

"Whacko! No wonder she's looking down in the mouth.

From what I saw of him last time he was on leave I can't imagine him taking too kindly to the present situation."

"Oh, well, you can't blame a girl for having a bit of fun while she can get it."

"I don't blame anyone. I only think it'd be damn funny to see old McFarland with his snooty air taking a kick in the pants from Sergeant Forrest."

Claire laughed. "I'm afraid you won't have the pleasure, my dear little angel child. It'll probably just fizzle out like the rest of these wartime affairs and nobody'll be any the wiser."

They started at a cold voice behind them and looked round, the laughter dying out of their faces and their eyes suddenly guarded.

"Oh...Miss Jeffries." Ursula Cronin stood at the door, tapping her teeth with a pencil and frowning at them as though she resented the world in which they found reason for laughing at nine o'clock on Saturday morning, and resented still more being shut out of it.

"I hope I'm not intruding," she said, in what Guinea called her "prissy" voice. It accompanied the air of superiority with which, as receptionist, she regarded the rest of the Marie Antoinette staff. Claire swore that it was that air that had got her the job, but Guinea was convinced Mrs Molesworth had put her there because of her capacity for belly-crawling, which Ursula constantly referred to as her "loyalty to her employers". In addition she had a flawless skin and natural brown curls that tricked all the patrons into believing that the Marie Antoinette products and treatment would do as much for them.

"Mrs D'Arcy-Twyning is on the phone," she continued, "and wants to know what time you can fit her in for a facial and shampoo and set."

"This morning?" Claire asked incredulously.

"Naturally this morning. She specially wants it because of the OBNOs Ball tonight."

"Then why couldn't she have booked it weeks ago? Doesn't she know this is one of our busiest mornings, with women piled up three deep all wanting facials and hairdos and all the rest of it for the races and the ball and every other bloody thing?"

Ursula looked pained. "Naturally, I didn't ask. In any case, we can't refuse; after all she is the wife of a director and we'll have to fit her in somewhere."

"We'll have to!" Claire said explosively. "You mean you'll fit her in and we'll have to stay on to do the work. If you had to cut your own dates when you graciously take extra bookings, we wouldn't have so many of them. Do you know what time we left here last night?"

"If that's how you feel about it, perhaps you'd like to make your complaints to Mrs Molesworth. After all, the Marie Antoinette is run for the guests. I'm only trying to do my duty in assisting them."

Claire turned away impatiently, swore under her breath, and picked up the book again.

"What does she want?"

"A shampoo, set and facial."

"The bloody old hag. She would!"

Ursula bridled. "Good grief! If you can't be ordinarily civil..."

"Civil me foot. Tell her to come down here at nine thirty and get the damned thing over."

Ursula tapped her teeth again, and lowered her eyes. "She specially said *not* before ten thirty. She wants to have a good rest."

Claire steadied her voice. "All right, quarter to eleven... Ask Miss Parker to come to me please, Miss Cronin, and next time you want to suck up to a director's wife, just remember we're the poor bloody mugs who've got to do the work."

"And I'd ask *you* to remember please, Miss Jeffries," Ursula drew herself up, "that I'm not accustomed to having language like that addressed to me." She tossed her head and went out.

Claire threw the appointments book on the desk. "Blast that woman!" she muttered fiercely.

Alice appeared at the door. "Is there anything wrong?" she asked, looking anxiously from one to the other.

"Only that that bloody Ursula has rung in Mrs D.D.T.

for a shampoo and set and facial this morning. Can you fit her in at quarter to eleven?''

Alice's pretty curved lips took on a stubborn line. ''Oh, I can't possibly. I have Lady Leeper from half past ten and you know she simply won't have anyone else but me.''

''I thought you always insisted on having the D'Arcy-Twyning hag,'' Guinea put in.

''It's not fair to say I insist, just because I usually have her,'' Alice smoothed back her soft blonde hair from her forehead and gave the suggestion of a sniff. ''Besides, Lady Leeper...''

Claire tapped her foot impatiently. ''Oh, for heaven's sake,'' she interrupted, ''Guin, will you do the shampoo?''

''OK. I'll chop five minutes off Mrs Ranken, she's a good sport, and old Mrs D.D.T.'s only got about six hairs left, so they won't take long.''

''You'll have to do her set, Alice, so for God's sake don't moan about it. You got out of Dalgety last night.'' Claire turned away and stabbed at the book with a pencil.

Alice looked hurt. ''That wasn't for myself. I told you I had to meet Mary.''

''Oh, you've always got a cast-iron alibi.''

Alice ignored her. ''And about this morning. It's only that I can't do justice to my work if I have to rush and I don't see how Guinea can either...''

''I'm not interested in what you see. You'll have to do it, and that's all there is about it.''

Alice opened her mouth to speak, thought better of it and went out.

Ursula came in again with her superior air. ''Mrs D'Arcy-Twyning said to ask would you send one of the girls up to do a manicure for her daughter.''

''Did you tell her we're short-staffed and busy as blazes?''

''I said we'd do what we could.''

''Why can't she come down here? Is she crippled?''

''Pleasure bent,'' Guinea suggested. ''The Navy are very wearing.''

A dull flush covered Ursula's throat and face, but she ignored the comment, merely asking in a tone of patient long-suffering, "When will someone go so that I can tell her?"

Claire walked to the door and called. "Val, will you take your manicure tray and go up to D.D.T.'s suite?"

Val's voice came, lifted in surprise. "What, now?"

"Yes, now. She wants a manicure for tonight and you might as well get her done before the rush starts. We haven't got an appointment for you till nine thirty, and they'll just have to wait if you're not back."

Val came out, her dark pageboy bob swinging heavy and lustrous round her face. She raised her eyebrows questioningly. "Why can't she come down here like other people? Is she bedridden?"

Guinea gurgled. "Hit it in one, sister. And how!"

Claire lifted her hands helplessly.

"Good grief," Guinea mimicked, "don't you know your place, Miss Blaski?"

Ursula turned sharply and went back to her desk and they heard her voice on the telephone, smooth and ingratiating, regretting that she had to send Miss Blaski immediately and she hoped it would not be too inconvenient.

"Sounds like a turtle dove," Guinea commented. "Born crawler, that woman."

"I hate having to ask you, Val," Claire said.

"Cut her claws off," Guinea called, as Val went out.

Ursula's voice welcoming the first patron warned them that the Marie Antoinette was launched on another busy day.

Up in Denise D'Arcy-Twyning's suite Val Blaski sat on a low stool beside the bed and proceeded with the work of bringing already beautiful nails to a state of even greater perfection. Beside her, Denise lay stretched on the bed like a golden cat, all sinuous grace and purring comfort.

She really is awfully pretty, Val thought, looking up and catching a glimpse of pale hair streaming over the primrose bedjacket. Too thin though, she'll go scraggy like her mother.

In the bed beside her, her mother, unflatteringly exposed in a pink sheer nightdress, sipped her coffee and read out snippets from the morning paper in a querulous voice. They spent a long time criticising the pictures of the Ainslie party and commenting with malicious delight on the general unsatisfactoriness of press photographs.

"Not a thing about us." Denise's voice was petulant. "Not even a par. And after what you paid for that orchid, too!"

"Huh!" Mrs D'Arcy-Twyning interrupted her. "Just listen to this. 'Lady Govett's beautiful orchid shoulder spray was much admired when she came on after the orchid show to the farewell party which Judge and Mrs Oscar Ainslie gave for their only daughter Constance and her husband, Lieutenant Ellery Carter of Baltimore, at the Hotel South Pacific yesterday afternoon.'" Mrs D'Arcy-Twyning glared at Denise through her bifocal glasses. "So that's why she was in such a hurry to get away from the show. And you should have got an invitation."

"Oh, pooh, that Constance Ainslie! You know we've never exchanged two words since the first meeting I called to form the Pick-Pockettes when she wouldn't join, and she said right out in front of everyone that she thought the whole idea was vulgar. You'd never think we'd been at school together since she's been to the university and become her father's associate. She's only married a lieutenant, anyway."

Mrs D'Arcy-Twyning looked up from her paper again. "I see Helen McFarland was there, too. I expect she's up in town with her mother for the Country Women's conference.... That'll be the family party Mr Angus McFarland's bringing to the ball tonight. He's booked a table for six, though...I wonder who the other three are...probably his sister Virginia Halliday and her husband, and probably Mr Ian McFarland's in town too..."

"How nice it'll be for Helen at the ball with those five old frumps. Just about suit her. She's as lively as a suet dumpling."

"Oh Denny darling, I wouldn't say that just because she's shy, and after all she is a country girl. You can't expect her to be up to your standard. Besides, if she is the only young one in the party I think it would be a good idea if you introduced some of your naval officers. Yes," she went on thoughtfully, "I'd like to get Virginia Halliday on to one of my committees. Her husband's doubled his business since the war, your father says, and he gave a thousand pounds to the Far West Children's Homes last year. Besides she's got money of her own...She'd be a splendid treasurer. Yes, you must be nice to Helen tonight."

"Oh Mummykins, I couldn't. Why, the English boys would get a totally wrong idea of Australian girls. And I have got my own reputation to think of."

"Yes, Denny, I insist. It's most important. And I do think you ought to be more careful how you speak about Constance and Helen. After all, they belong to very good families."

"Oh, stop lecturing, Mummy," Denise said rudely. "That stuffy North Shore set think they're too good to live — joining the VADs and working themselves to a standstill at the Anzac Buffet. The way they look down their noses at those of us who think it's not a crime to amuse ourselves while we're doing our bit for the war is simply infuriating." Denny darling's voice was thin and envious. "Hateful prigs, the lot of them."

Really, Val thought, lifting Denise's delicate pink fingers from the bowl in which they had been soaking, really, listening to the two of them you'd think I wasn't here. The smell of fresh coffee as Mrs D'Arcy-Twyning poured herself a third cup made Val remember that she had left home in a hurry without a proper breakfast. But they were not interested in whether she was thirsty; to them, she was neither mouth to be filled nor ears to listen, only hands to serve.

"Ooo-er, you're straining my wrist," Denise whined.

"I'm sorry, but this position is so much more difficult than at a manicure table."

"There should be one in every suite," Denise pouted. "Why don't you tell Daddy, Mummy?"

"I will," Mrs D'Arcy-Twyning promised, her mouth full of buttered toast. "But first of all I'd like to know how I'm going to break it to him about your engagement. If you'd listened to what I told you, you wouldn't be in this position."

"What did you tell me?"

"I told you from the first that you shouldn't take those Americans seriously, and you with your grandfather on the D'Arcy side a Scottish laird."

"Ouch!" Denise shrieked. "You hurt me."

Val muttered an apology.

"Didn't I?" Mrs D'Arcy-Twyning insisted.

"Oh, Mummykins, how could I help it? They were sweet while they were here. They had a way of making a girl feel so important — all those flowers and gifts."

"Anyway, the point is if you'd listened to me you wouldn't be in this awkward position of having a fiancé returning from the States expecting to marry you, and you just about to become engaged to an English naval officer."

"Oh, Mummy, the English are wizard!"

"Wizard or not — you'll have to do something about it."

Denise pouted. "Aren't I doing the best I can? You never stopped nagging me when I wanted to marry an American, and now I'm giving him up and going to marry an Englishman you nag me just as much."

"Well, I must say, I'm not satisfied. It's much too indefinite. He hasn't even spoken to your father yet."

"Oh, but he will, darling. The English aren't impetuous like the Americans. We must give Derek time, that's all."

"Well, all I can say is, I hope it's all right."

"Anyway, Mummykins, you ought to be grateful. After all, his father has got a title. I bet that counts for more than an old laird. And think how much better it will look for you as President of the OBNOs to have your daughter marrying a British commander. I think you're terribly unfair."

Denise's pout turned to a quiver and her voice trembled. Val, looking up, caught her sidelong calculating glance, but Mrs D'Arcy-Twyning had not her advantage.

"There, there, Denny darling," she patted her daughter's shoulder, "don't cry. I am very happy about it. I think Commander Ermington is a wonderful match — so distinguished too — and I'll be very glad if you marry a Britisher after all. It's just I want everything settled and I don't want us to appear ridiculous. You don't want a scandal on your hands, sure-ly? The commander wouldn't like it. Think of that American arriving and suing you for breach of promise or whatever they sue you for in the States."

Denise yelped again, and glared down at Val. "Do please be more careful," she said petulantly, "that's the second time you've hurt me."

Val bit her lips. Oh God, she prayed, why must I listen to this?

"But Mummykins," Denise went on in her high-pitched whine, "Dwight wouldn't do that to me, he's too sweet for words."

"If you hadn't made all that fuss about getting publicly engaged to him, it wouldn't have mattered so much. I don't know how I'm going to break it to your father."

Denise held up a hand and let the light play through the square sapphire on her third finger. "It was a super party, wasn't it? We'll have to think up something terribly special for my engagement to Derek. I think I'll have emeralds next time. They're so fashionable just now."

"Really, Denise, you shock me at times. Haven't you any sympathy at all for your poor mother who has to go through all the agony of explaining that we're giving a party to an-nounce your engagement to a commander in the Royal Navy when they're all expecting invitations to your wedding to an American lieutenant-colonel? By the way, have you sent him that cable I told you to send?"

"Oh, I'll just explain when he arrives...anyway he mightn't get here before the wedding and then I won't have to explain." She dismissed the matter. "And d'you know what, Mummykins?...I think I'll have an all-white wedding — something terribly picturesque. Puffed sleeves and bouffant skirts." Denise murmured dreamily, "It'll be summer and the Navy'll be in white. And gold flowers...Mummy, darling, could I have twelve bridesmaids?"

"Twelve bridesmaids? Good gracious, child, who ever heard of twelve bridesmaids?"

"That's why I want to have them. Besides, you forget

there are thirteen of us Pick-Pockettes and they all expect to be asked.''

"It'll take a terrible lot of coupons."

"But darling, Mrs Molesworth can always get them for us. I say, did you ask her about some more?"

"Yes I did, and I was shocked to find that she now wants two pounds a page. Thirty shillings was bad enough before...but two pounds! It's positively black market.''

"The greedy old thing. Someone ought to tell the Prices Commissioner.''

"I told your father. Raising the price on us indeed! Unpatriotic, I call it.''

"But you do like the idea of an all-white wedding, don't you, petty-pie?''

"Yes, it sounds very nice. Nothing vulgar about it.''

Val's throat contracted. She set her teeth.

Denise grew starry-eyed. "Think of us coming down the steps at St Clement's — all white with long spray bouquets of gold flowers. Can you get gold orchids, do you know?''

"I'm sure I have no idea, and if you think your father and I...''

Denise rolled her head lazily on the pillow and looked down on Val, now putting vivid lacquer on her nails.

"Have you ever heard of gold orchids?''

"No, Miss D'Arcy-Twyning.''

"What other gold flowers are there?''

"Dandelions are in flower most of the year.''

"Dandelions!'' Denise gasped and raised herself on one arm. "Dande...'' She stared at Val's grave face, the wide mouth set firm under the brilliant lipstick that masked its real expression. She hesitated. But Val went on lacquering her nails with quick, expert strokes. "Oh,'' Denise laughed, "you must mean calendulas — marigolds most people call them.''

"Oh no,'' Val answered in a cool even voice, "I mean dandelions, 'pee-the-beds', most people call them. You must know them, the same pale gold as your hair, with big black centres.''

Denise's cold blue eyes met the manicurist's, still as brown pools in her pale face. If she was trying to be funny...But no! No one ever tried to be funny with Denise. Not in the South Pacific. No one would dare.

"What did they say your name was?"

"Blaski."

"Blaski? You're a refugee, are you?"

"My husband is in the American Army."

Denise looked at her for a moment. "Oh! How odd!" She stretched luxuriously and cuddled back into the pillows, her eyes closed. Then she smiled, opened her eyes and drew a thin white foot from out of the bedclothes. "Would you do my toes now?" she commanded. "The same colour as my fingernails, I think, don't you, Mummykins?"

Ursula came to the door of the cubicle where Guinea was putting the finishing touches to a hairset. "You're wanted on the phone, Miss Malone."

"Oh, thanks. Excuse me, Mrs Armstrong, I'm afraid this is an urgent call."

Outside, Ursula used her injured voice. "I told him it was most inconvenient, but he insisted."

Guinea slid down the passage as though on skates.

"Please don't stay long on the phone," Ursula called after her.

"Hello! That you, Guinea? You know who this is?"

"Sure..."

"Lew Alfrickson here."

"Oh! Welcome back, big boy. This is a surprise. When did you get in?"

"Hey, don't you read your mail? I wrote and told you I'd be up from Melbourne for the weekend."

Guinea chuckled. "I must have missed that bit."

"I hope you saved me tonight."

"What's on?" Guinea asked cautiously.

"I thought you might like to come to the barn dance up top tonight."

"Up top?"

"Yeah. Who's Who."

"You mean — the OBNOs Ball?"

"Nothing else."

"Not a hope of getting in there, they've been booked to the roof for a week."

"Well, I've got four tickets. A friend of mine booked them last weekend and now he has to catch a plane north this afternoon, so I thought we'd get hold of another couple. Would you like that, baby?"

A series of mad pictures slid across Guinea's mind.... L. F.'s face... D.D.T.... Mrs D'Arcy-Twyning's skinny neck... Old Mole... The forbidden glories of Who's Who. It'd probably mean the sack.

"Sure," she said enthusiastically, "sure, Alfalfa, I think it'd be swell."

"Good for you, kid. I've got some orchids here for you to wear."

"Oh thanks."

"You know how I feel about you, honey, it's always orchids to you. Well, eight-thirty tonight outside your place."

"That'll be fine." She hung up the phone and sat still a moment, blinking, then leapt to her feet and rushed into the office, where Deb and Claire were trying to sort out some double bookings which Ursula, as usual, had rung in on them at the last moment.

"Girls!" she gasped... "Girls! I've got an invite from Alfalfa to the OBNOs Ball tonight!"

"Phew!" Claire whistled.

"The OBNOs? But it's being held in Who's Who," Deb expostulated.

"So what?"

"Well, you know the rule about the staff dancing at Who's Who."

"That wouldn't make any difference to me," Guinea groaned. "What rocks me is, here's the chance of a lifetime and I'm stumped. I haven't got a long frock."

"Nothing of mine would fit you," Claire said regretfully.

Guinea squeezed her shoulders. "No. I'd bust all your seams, pet, and your longest'd only come to my knees!"

Deb was silent.

"It's a damn shame," Claire turned back to the desk. "I'd have given a quid to see Old Mole's face when her eyes fell on you."

Ursula appeared in the doorway and whispered in the awed voice of one announcing royalty. "Mrs D'Arcy-Twyning has arrived. She's earlier than she expected. I hope you can take her."

"Shove the bitch in a cubicle," Guinea said. "Tell her she'll have to wait till I've finished Mrs Armstrong."

Claire turned back to the appointments. What rotten luck for Guin to have to turn down the ball.

Fancy Guinea being asked to Who's Who, Deb thought, with a wave of irritation. Angus had never asked her there.

Val came in and slammed her manicure tray down with a clatter. Her face was white and her eyes blazing.

"How'd you get on with D.D.T.?" Deb inquired.

"I should have killed her, not manicured her."

"As bad as that?" Claire looked at her in surprise. Even an hour with D.D.T. seemed scarcely sufficient to rouse such passion. Val was usually so unruffled.

"D.D.T. and her men and her wedding and her Pick-Pockettes and her OBNOs...I,even had to do her toenails."

"Well, the OBNOs isn't turning out as exclusive as they intended." There was a note of envy in Deb's voice. "Guinea's Alfalfa rang and asked her to go with him."

The tension went out of Val's face and happy malice bubbled up. "Whoopee! I could kiss him for it myself. That'll take the starch out of them."

"Of course she can't go," Deb said. "She hasn't got a long frock."

"Hasn't she?" Val thought a minute; then her eyes danced and she laughed aloud. "Well, I'll be Fairy Godmother. I know just the thing. Nobody'll even see Denny darling when Guinea turns up. I'll give that little slut a white wedding."

Deb cast a warning glance at the nearest cubicle. "Sssh, Mrs D.D.T.'s in there."

Val drew her face into a semblance of seriousness and went to the door. "Can I speak to you for a moment, Miss Malone? It's urgent."

Guinea came out and Val drew her aside and whispered, "I can get you a dress for tonight if you'll go."

"What?"

"A friend of mine runs a hire service for bridal gowns. It'll set you back two quid but you won't have to leave a deposit. What about it?"

Mrs D'Arcy-Twyning's voice came to them in a rising wail. "Miss Malone. I'm most uncomfortable."

"Oh, go jump in the lake," Guinea muttered under her breath. Aloud, she replied: "I'm just fixing a fuse, Mrs D'Arcy-

Twyning. We could all have been electrocuted." And softly, "The current'd skid off her hide."

"Well?"

Guinea nodded. "It's a deal."

"What size are you?"

"Thirty-six bust and five foot eight in me socks!" she whispered back, her eyes sparkling.

"Good."

Guinea jitterbugged ecstatically along the narrow corridor and disappeared behind the curtain.

Mrs D'Arcy-Twyning stared into the mirror and saw the girl's golden hair lying artlessly on her shoulders, the graceful bend of her head, her peach bloom skin — vulgarly robust, of course, compared with Denise's fragile beauty. She bent her head again to the shampoo hose with unaccountable bad temper. She closed her eyes and as the warm water flowed soothingly over her head and firm fingers stimulated her scalp and the fragrance of the shampoo filled her nostrils, she forgot the youth and beauty of the girl which had so disturbed her, and let her mind sink into delicious contemplation of the evening ahead.

What a triumph it had been to get Who's Who for the ball, the most exclusive dance floor in Sydney's most exclusive hotel! No other society hostess had ever managed that. And she wouldn't have got it either, even with Daniel's seat on the South Pacific's board of directors, if he hadn't promised to do a little judicious investing for Mr Sharlton...And who, after all, could blame the manager for humouring the wife of that shrewd investor Dan D'Arcy-Twyning? Tonight would be her triumph, she'd show them all. With viceregal patronage, Who's Who in her pocket, the name of Mrs D'Arcy-Twyning featuring discreetly as president on tickets priced at two guineas, and the resources of the South Pacific to ensure her success, there wouldn't be a social climber or publicity hunter in Sydney who wouldn't cut the throat of their dearest friend to be in her shoes.

Guinea broke across her pleasant thoughts. "Will madam have her usual rinse?"

"Of course," she replied curtly, "and I'll need my parting touching up."

"Certainly, madam."

Mrs D'Arcy-Twyning's ear, trained to catch the slightest intonation of disrespect, was doubtful of the tone of the girl's reply, but as she was doubled over a wash basin she had no means of seeing her expression. Impudent hussies the girls were today. Bad enough before the Americans came, but now they were fit for nothing — though she had to admit that even the Americans hadn't succeeded in spoiling her Denise.

She slid back into her former mood of irritation and consoled herself with the thought that they would all come down to earth pretty painfully when there weren't any more US paybooks around. It was positively revolting the type of girls who were now brazenly flaunting themselves in the hotel foyer where once only the socially élite had gathered. The foyer was nothing but a common pick-up place these days. Soon she would be ashamed to have her husband associated with such a hotel, but it wouldn't be any good talking to Dan about it; he didn't care about such things so long as the dividends kept rising. Ordinary shares up to the limit allowed by wartime regulations, and thousands of pounds socked away into the sinking fund or whatever it was they used for camouflaging their profits. And singing Mr Sharlton's praises to the skies — never knew a fellow like him, couldn't bribe him if you tried...best hotel manager in Australia...lucky they got him to take over just before the Yank boom.

She caught another glimpse of Guinea in the mirror. It was a wonder the Manpower hadn't got her for a canning factory or something. A strong, healthy girl like that ought to be doing a job to help the war effort. Look at the way Denise worked with her Pick-Pockettes. Never spared herself at all.

Guinea squeezed her hair gently and wrapped her head in a warmed towel. "If madam would sit up now, Miss Parker will be in to set your hair in a few minutes." She turned away swiftly, leaving her customer alone in the cubicle.

Mrs D'Arcy-Twyning took one look in the mirror at her sharp drawn face, steamed free of makeup and framed with straggling wisps. She closed her eyes to shut out the unlovely reflection and let her mind dwell instead on the figure she would cut that evening. She thought of the pearl grey satin, so elegant and daringly cut to show off the girlishness of her figure, the perfect background for the prize cattleya orchid of regal purple that she had chosen for her shoulder spray and paid such an exorbitant sum for. Against the surrealist murals of Who's Who — which she could condone only because of their fashionable success, but deplored for their lack of true art — among all the gold braid, the uniforms and glamour, she would look every inch a lady.

She was just running over the list of names for her official table with satisfaction when Deb came in and, with a word of excuse, took a jar out of the cupboard. Mrs D'Arcy-Twyning watched her with avid curiosity. Whatever could Mr McFarland be thinking about? She'd heard he'd been taking that girl around everywhere for the last six months. A masseuse in a beauty salon! And to think of all the suitable women he could have had, with his money and family. It showed complete lack of consideration for his class when he allowed himself to be so indiscreet.

Alice came into the cubicle in a little flurry, breathless and apologetic. "Good morning, Mrs D'Arcy-Twyning. I'm so sorry I had to keep you. I didn't realise till this very moment that it was you who was waiting."

Mrs D'Arcy-Twyning accorded her gracious forgiveness. "I was just spending a few minutes checking my final arrangements for this evening."

Now this was a girl of whom one could approve, quietly-spoken and refined, with the right shade of deference. "I would like my hair to look particularly well tonight," she went on, "something striking, yet suitable, of course. How would you suggest doing it? I thought Edwardian perhaps, it shows off the jawline so well."

Alice lifted the hair, exposing fully the stringy throat and neck, and quickly brought it down again, bunching it to one side. "Perhaps Edwardian curls on top and the side swathed across the back of the head. It's very flattering, it gives both height and softness."

Mrs D'Arcy-Twyning graciously acquiesced. "Madam Lucretia always cuts my frocks for softness round the neck. She says it's a shame that swan necks went out with the Victorians."

Alice murmured agreeably while she rolled the little flat curls with her skilled fingers and pinned them down for the drier.

Mrs D'Arcy-Twyning rambled on: "I was just going over the official table for the ball. The difficult thing really is to keep the numbers down. One has such a reputation for one's success in these affairs that the girls were positively clamouring — especially when they heard I had a commander from the *Impenetrable* and two lieutenant-commanders from the *Incorruptible*! Charming boys...so different to the Americans, don't you think?"

Alice had met no Americans, but she agreed warmly. The flat curls were now pinned in a row above Mrs D'Arcy-Twyning's hollowed temples and Alice began to set the waves across the back of her head. "I am sure it will be a great success..." she murmured. "It's for the orphans of British naval officers, isn't it?"

"Yes, my dear. That's a charity very near to my heart. I remember my own happy childhood so well...ah... Scotland."

She broke off as Val drew aside the curtain. "Your daughter is on the phone, Mrs D'Arcy-Twyning. Will you take the call here?"

"Tell her I'm busy. I'll ring her when I'm finished."

Val withdrew. "The old girl's dancing the Highland fling over the family estates," she said to Claire.

"Huh! Pure romance. She was born in Manly, and never been outside the heads except on a Saturday afternoon cruise to the Hawkesbury."

"You don't say?"

"I do. Mother knew their next-door neighbours."

"Don't tell me they've never made the grand tour to the dear old homeland with all their dough? It'd shatter my last illusion."

"No. They were waiting to take 'Denny darling' to be presented at court when she left school. But of course the war hit that on the head."

"What did he make his money in? Beer?"

"Partly, but that's only the last few years. He got his start in a grocery shop at Newtown. Worked like a nigger, they say, and finally started a chain of them — you know — the Kookaburra Cash and Carry places. They're everywhere now."

"Oh, so that's his line."

"Not now. Mummykins didn't think it was smart enough, so he got rid of them and landed a packet of shares in Frith's Brewery. They reckon Horatio Veale got him on the board because he's such a good front for any dirty business. Honest as the sun and just a sucker for those social-climbing bitches of his. Listen to her in there. I wonder what tale she's putting over now?"

In her cubicle Mrs D'Arcy-Twyning sighed. "And now when I think of those poor little British children whose fathers have gone down defending our Empire — my heart bleeds for them. When this terrible war is over we must have them out here. It's little enough we can do to repay our debt to the mother country and, besides, we must keep up our British stock."

Alice smiled sweet acquiescence as Mrs D'Arcy-Twyning went on. "Yes, I'm only doing my duty. Charity balls are most exhausting, but no D'Arcy has ever been known to turn her back on duty."

As Claire passed the curtained cubicle she caught the last words, spoken as though addressed to a public meeting. "You'll be pleased to know," she said to Guinea, who was gulping a cup of tea in the office, "that no D'Arcy has ever been known to turn her back on duty."

"You're telling me," said Guinea, "especially when the Navy expects."

Mrs D'Arcy-Twyning's monologue went on relentlessly like the buzz of a saw. "Of course I can always gather a very influential committee. Not like these women who tackle social functions quite outside their scope. One must be able to call on the best people, Miss Parker, if one is really going to do anything substantial for charity. Take tonight. We've sold Who's Who right out — five hundred tickets at two guineas each and all by invitation. We could have sold twice as many, only frankly, we wanted to keep it exclusive."

"How wonderful," said Alice as she fixed the earpads and swung the dryer into position. She handed Mrs D'Arcy-Twyning a folder of *Tatlers*. "I think you'll like these."

"Oh, I shall be quite happy with any English papers. A touch of home, my dear."

In the outer office, Ursula's voice was raised in greeting. "Good morning, Mrs Molesworth." Alice stopped dead.

Mrs Molesworth's commanding voice came clearly to the cubicles. "Good morning, Miss Cronin. What number is Mrs D'Arcy-Twyning in?"

Ursula cooed directions.

Alice stepped aside to make way for a maid carrying a tea tray. She set it down and withdrew. A tall, handsome woman entered, seeming to fill the cubicle with her presence. "Ah, good morning, Mrs D'Arcy-Twyning," she purred. "Is everything going satisfactorily?"

Mrs D'Arcy-Twyning smiled up at the hotel hostess. "Yes, thank you, Mrs Molesworth. How thoughtful of you to send along a cup of tea." Good gracious, she thought, the woman puts on more weight every time I see her.

Thelma Molesworth busied herself with the tea tray. "I knew what an exhausting day you would have before you and I thought this would help to soothe your nerves." She straightened herself with an involuntary sigh. Mrs Molesworth was a big woman and to the feminine eye there was no doubt about the rigidity of the corset that kept her hips and waist under control, or the expensive brassière that gave shape and support to her heavy bust.

"You're sure there's nothing else you want?"

"Nothing, thank you."

"The waterlilies have arrived for your table. Would you like to come up and see them when you've finished? I'm standing the bowls on mirrors.''

"How original! I do appreciate your assistance. I'll come up later.''

Mrs Molesworth withdrew deferentially. She made a royal progress along the corridor, lifting aside each turquoise curtain with her plump white fingers and making honeyed inquiries of the patron within. She finally paused at Ursula's desk. "How are you, my dear? Everything going satisfactorily?''

"Well...yes,'' Ursula said with a quick glance over her shoulder, "but there are just a few things...I feel I'd like to talk over with you.''

Thelma frowned. "It's too bad. I haven't got a minute to spare today. Can they wait till next week?''

"Oh, yes. It's nothing urgent,'' Ursula reassured her. "It's just, well, you know, little things like private phone calls. I don't feel it's fair to the hotel...''

"I understand perfectly,'' she patted Ursula's hand. "It's such a comfort to me that you're here. You must come up and have coffee with me as soon as the weekend rush is over.''

A few seconds after the outer doors had swung behind Mrs Molesworth, Elvira sidled in. She threw Ursula a wheedling "''ullo, luvvie'', ignored her frown, and scuttled down the corridor.

Claire was alone in her office finishing a cup of tea.

"Hullo,'' she said briefly, "what are you doing down here this morning? Old Mole's snooping around.''

"'Oly Moses, yes. I nearly run into 'er.'' She lowered her voice to a hoarse whisper. "Did y'ear the news?''

"What news?''

"Old McFarland proposed to 'er.'' Elvira motioned to the massage cubicle with a stubby thumb.

Claire put down her cup abruptly. "I don't believe it.''

"Cross me 'eart.''

"Where did you hear that?''

"From the 'orse's mouth.''

"I still don't believe it.''

"Spit me death, I did. I was doin' 'is bathroom this mornin' and I heard 'im tellin' 'is brother. 'E didn't know I was there, o' course. And did they 'ave a regular go-in over it!''

"But did he say definitely it was her?"

"'E said Deborah Forrest and there ain't no other Deborah Forrest I know what 'e's been runnin' round with."

"My God!" Claire sat down, gazing up into Elvira's eyes, opaque and mischievous as a monkey's. She felt dizzy with the shock...hollow. Of course, it was wonderful for Deb...

Elvira leered, baring her brick-red gums. "She's got a nice welkim waitin' from the family. 'Is brother's mad as a snake."

"Ssh!" Claire frowned warningly as Ursula's voice rose in greeting. "I think that's Helen McFarland coming in now."

"Cor, so it is. Elvira peered round the door. "Not much to look at, is she?"

"Well, she mightn't be in the glamour class, but she's a nice lass."

"Yeah, I'll 'and it to 'er and 'er mother," Elvira conceded. "Not a bit of swank about the pair of them, and that considerate! A pity Uncle Angus wasn't a bit more like 'is brother...'Oly Moses!" She went back to her original topic. "Asking 'er to marry 'im! Can yer beat it?"

But Claire refused to be drawn. She got up in a businesslike fashion. "I have to go to Miss McFarland now, and you'd better hop it, my lamb, in case Old Mole takes it in her head to pay a return visit." She drew back the curtain of the cubicle and Elvira scuttled out.

"Good morning, Miss McFarland," Claire warmed to the flash of white teeth in the tanned face reflected in the mirror. Really, she thought, the girl has a lovely smile. It's a pity she's so shy. She adjusted the cape around her shoulders. "I suppose you want something special for the ball tonight?"

Helen gave an embarrassed laugh. "That is mother's idea, but I don't want you to go to a lot of trouble. Just a shampoo and a set."

"I suppose you're awfully excited about the OBNOs?"

"Well," Helen began uncertainly, "I suppose I should be. But frankly, Miss Jeffries, I'm not. I'd rather a thousand times be going to help my cousin Susan. It's her weekend at

the Anzac Buffet and I went with her last night. It was —"
she hesitated, and ended lamely, "it was great fun."

Claire caught the note of excitement in her voice and looked at her reflection. . . Her eyes were closed and she was smiling as though at some secret vision. . . Enraptured.

Oh, oh, Claire thought. I'd take a bet it wasn't only the
Canteen that was great fun. Then suddenly, seeing the brown,
work-roughened hands clasped together, the crinkly hair tucked
into an unbecoming roll, the look of excitement, she felt a pang
of pity. Life was hard enough if you knew how to make the
best of yourself.

As though she had read her thought, Helen opened her
eyes. "I know there's not much that can be done about me,"
she said shamefacedly. "But I wonder if you could — well
—" She caught a glimpse of Claire's face, frowning and
speculative as she examined her hair, and flushed a deep brick-
red. "It doesn't matter. . . Just a shampoo and set."

Claire shook out the fine hair and curled it round her
fingers. She lifted it higher showing the clean line of the jaw
and the beautifully shaped head.

"You're very lucky to have naturally curly hair, you
know."

"That's about its only advantage. It's so mousy, and it
looks awful loose on my shoulders like most of the girls are
wearing it." Helen gazed at her reflection mournfully.

"Look," Claire said on an impulse. "You don't give
yourself a chance. Your hair is really very pretty but it looks
nothing in a roll. What about letting me cut it short? You've
got a well-shaped head and you carry yourself beautifully."

Helen's face brightened. "You mean — quite short?"
Claire nodded.

"Oh, I'd adore that. I used to have it like that at school,
and it's the only time it ever suited me. But I thought now
with everyone wearing it on their shoulders, wouldn't I look
odd?"

"Pouf!" Claire picked up the scissors. "You only want
to bother about a fashion if it suits you. . . Here we go." She
cut the hair quickly while Helen watched her with fascinated

hopeful eyes.

Claire gave a last snip, ran the comb through the short, crisp hair and gave it a few professional pushes with her fingers. "There, what do you think of that?"

"Oh, it really does look nice, doesn't it?"

Helen could hardly believe that the reflection in the mirror was her own. The springy waves framed her face softly and gave her a young, eager look. "It makes me feel as if I was still at school."

"There are a lot of women who wouldn't mind looking like that," Claire smiled, "and it's absolutely right for your type. Now we'll finish it off with a brightening rinse — and, if you don't mind my saying so, I think a brighter lipstick and a shade darker powder than you're wearing will work wonders. Would you like to try them?"

"Yes, I would if you think so."

"Good. I'll come back and give you a makeup when your hair's done. Miss Malone will be in for your shampoo in a few minutes."

Claire went out briskly and left Helen smiling at herself in the mirror.

It was astonishing what a difference the new cut made. She twisted her head round trying to get a side view. Had she really got a good-shaped head or was that just the sort of thing hairdressers always said? She picked up the hand mirror and studied the back of her head critically. Yes, there was no doubt her hair looked much better this way with the short ends curling at her neck; even from the back she looked somehow younger and more exciting. She had a new feeling of confidence.

If she'd only had her hair cut like this yesterday, she thought, perhaps she wouldn't have behaved so stupidly. As the memory swept over her, a blush rose up her throat and mounted to the roots of her hair. She hadn't meant to be rude, it was only that she was suddenly shy...but she couldn't expect Alec to know that.

She put down the mirror with a feeling of hopelessness. Oh! what did it matter whether she looked her age or ten years older, whether she had an attractive haircut or a dowdy one. She'd always be shy and do the wrong thing. Uncle Angus was right, she had neither looks nor charm, and the sooner she faced up to the fact and stopped worrying about what Alec must have thought of her the better. He'd probably been glad to get her off his hands if the truth was told. . . . But although she tried to believe what she was telling herself, she knew it wasn't true. Alec had enjoyed dancing with her, she knew that, and he was just about as shy as she was. . . . Her mind slipped back to their meeting.

Susan had brought him up to her in the crowded Buffet. "Alec and I are old friends out at the Hundred-and-Thirteenth," she said, "but this is the first time he's ever danced in here, and he dances beautifully, so I'm going to pass him on to you. Now don't let him get away by himself in a corner again. Helen, this is Sergeant Alec Campbell. My cousin, Helen McFarland. You two Scots should get on well together."

For a second neither of them had spoken.

"Perhaps you'd rather not dance. . ." he began uncertainly.

"Would you rather not?"

"I'm a bit clumsy," he said hesitantly. "That dance with Mrs Ainslie was the first time I've danced for ages. Really, I'm badly out of practice."

He had serious brown eyes and a shock of dark hair that had been punished severely with hard brushing and hair cream, but it was wavy and inclined to break loose in a way which she found rather pleasant and small-boyish. She heard the diffidence in his voice and took it for shyness. That was something she could understand and she tried to put him at his ease. "I'd like to dance, but I've never danced here before either."

"Well. . .in that case, let's."

They moved on to the floor. There was not much room and Alec put his hand round her waist rather tentatively. Immediately she was bumped against him and they both laughed. Then he took her hand in his.

The fingers lying in her lap curled involuntarily as she felt again the touch of his mutilated hand. Unconsciously she had glanced at their joined hands and saw that he had only the two first fingers and thumb. He caught the movement of her head.

"You don't mind Algy, I hope."

"Algy?" She was glad of something to say.

"Yes. That's what we call him up at the hospital. He's a bit stiff, but they tell me he'll work again if I do my occupational therapy like a good boy and make innumerable tea trays and toys that I don't want." He spoke with a little defiant laugh.

"I've heard about that sort of treatment. My cousin Susan goes out to help with the weaving at the Hundred-and-Thirteenth and she says it's wonderful how they get stiff fingers working again. But of course, that's how you know Susan, I expect."

"Yes, I started on weaving."

While they were talking Helen was painfully aware of the stiffness of his hand and found her own fingers stiffening in sympathy. She loosened them and tried to talk to keep her attention occupied.

"You do dance beautifully." She caught a serious look in his dark eyes. "You even make me feel that I'm a good dancer. And I know perfectly well I'm not."

"Don't you dance much?"

"No. I live in the country."

"Do you mind if I make a suggestion?"

"No, of course not."

"You'd be much better if you let yourself loosen up a bit."

Helen let herself relax. Her hand lay more naturally in his.

"There, isn't that better? Now don't think about dancing. Just talk and your feet and I will do the rest. Whereabouts in the country do you live?"

"Forty miles the other side of Bathurst. Do you know it up there?"

"I'm afraid I don't. I've lived on the east coast all my life — at Grafton, except for six months I spent jackerooing up near the Queensland border out of Warialda."

"Were you with sheep?"

"Yes. Merinos."

"We've got Corriedales."

"Have you, by Jove!" She heard the eagerness in his voice.

"Did you like the life?"

"Like it! I've never enjoyed anything half so much as I did those six months. And I worked like a slave."

"We all do. Why did you leave? Was it to join up?"

"No. My father died and I couldn't afford to go on with the job. You see — there was Mother — so I went back to Grafton where she was living and started pushing a pen in an accountant's office by day and swotting at night. Something with a future!"

"And you liked it?"

"I hated it. It wasn't the actual work. I wasn't so bad at figures, strangely enough. But it was being closed in all the time — nine to five thirty with nothing but figures representing things that were real for other people and never dealing with anything that was real for me...if you can understand what I mean."

"Yes, I think I can. I help Dad with the bookkeeping a bit since our manager joined up, and I keep the stud records as part of my job, but I know I could never bear to be boxed up in an office doing it all day long."

"That's how it was with me. And I can tell you I jumped at the chance of joining up."

"But you'll go back to the land when you're out of the Army, won't you?"

"I wish I could, but I'm afraid those days are over for good."

"But why? We're all so terribly shorthanded, we're simply screaming for manpower."

"It's not that. I'd planned to do vet science at the uni after the war — I'd have been able to manage it with the training they've promised to give returned men, and my deferred pay..." He broke off abruptly, then added, "But Algy's put the lid on that little plan."

"But even if you can't become a veterinary surgeon you

could still do a practical job," she insisted. "Dad says there's going to be a lot of places on the market with the boys coming back unsettled and wanting the excitements of city life."

"It's just the other way round with me. Tough, isn't it? But I'm afraid deferred pay and gratuities wouldn't go far along that line...and that's all I have. After Warialda, I couldn't take up one of those soldiers' selections they doled out for the poor wretches to break their hearts over after the last war."

"No, of course you couldn't. But surely they won't cheat the men like that this time."

"Won't they? Perhaps not. But I'm not banking on it. And anyway, they go by ballot. No, I've got to help Mum, so I can't go off jackerooing for little more than my keep. I'll just have to think again." His voice had a jaunty defiance.

Sitting in her chair in the Marie Antoinette cubicle, Helen ached with sympathy for him. To want to go on the land and to have to work in an office! She knew exactly how he must feel. She wanted to tell him that his hand needn't really matter. Even if he couldn't do vet science, he could be a good enough practical vet for a general job when he'd learnt to use his fingers a bit more. She wanted to tell him she understood how he felt, as she had wanted to tell him last night.

He had broken across the conversation with a self-conscious laugh. "I seem to have been doling out my life story in pretty fat slices."

"But I'm awfully interested..."

The music stopped. "That was good," he said enthusiastically. "Shall we have another?"

He clapped his good hand on his stiff one and Helen saw that he had a dark weal running out from his cuff up the centre of his palm to where his two outside fingers and part of his hand were missing. A wave of pity swept over her.

The encore started up and she held her hand out to take his. This time she clasped his fingers with a friendly firmness and she felt his arm tighten round her waist as they swung into an old-fashioned waltz.

"You know, I did forget about my dancing while we were talking. It was better, wasn't it?"

"Much. It's only practice you need. Come, shall we let it rip?"

He swung her between the other couples once round the floor, then to the door, where they came to a stop.

"I say, let's go out and get a breath of air, shall we?"

She hesitated. "I mustn't lose sight of the others."

"They're too busy to miss you. We'll only go for a little stroll."

But she did not move. Suddenly, when they stopped dancing, Alec had become a stranger to her again and she panicked. "I'm terribly sorry, but I really must find the others. Thank you so much. Excuse me, won't you?" And without waiting for his reply, she had darted back into the room and was hidden amongst the dancers...

Guinea came into the cubicle with fresh towels over her arm. "Sorry I had to keep you waiting," she said pleasantly. It was nearly closing time and the last patron was undergoing a process of rapid dehydration in the miniature sirocco of a hair dryer. "Oh no. Certainly not," Guinea assured her with a quick glance at the clock, "if you dry this kind of set slowly, it'll be hanging around your heels by Monday." The victim submitted; it was a long time between sets these days.

She went out at last in a flurry of compliments, slightly dazed and dry as a chip. The door closed behind her and the latch went down. Ursula put on her hat, picked up her bag and gloves and remarked disapprovingly to the rest of the staff, still busy with the cleaning up, that she thought this clock-watching was frightfully bad for the Marie Antoinette's reputation.

"I hope she falls flat on her puss," Guinea flung at the closed door. "She beats the gun every time herself and she's not coming in on Monday."

"Have you ever known her to come in on a holiday?" Val asked.

"Not her. Every day's six hours for her, and Alice too

for that matter. I wish I knew how these virtuous virgins get away with things."

"What's this she's left behind? Don't tell me someone's sending her flowers from Marina's?" Val picked up a silvered box tied with green tinsel and read out from the card: "'Miss Mallon'. Who the dickens is she?"

"What d'yer know?" said Guinea. "They must be from Alfalfa. He never does get me name right. That cow of a Cronin never said a word about them coming."

Guinea untied the tinsel ribbon round the box. "Corks!" she gasped, gaping at two exquisite mauve and purple orchids on their bed of cotton wool.

"Whew!" whistled Claire. "Cattaleyas! Alfalfa's certainly in the money today."

"They really are beautiful." Deb went to open the outer door to an insistent rapping.

"A parcel for Miss Blaski," said the messenger.

"Whacko, that must be the dress. Here's a bob for the kid," Guinea fished a coin out of her pocket. "I hope the damn thing fits," she said fervently, fumbling with the string.

"Here, let me," Val took the box. "You get your uniform off." She shook out the frock in a rustle of stiff white taffeta. "Ah, that's the one I asked for. It's only been worn once."

"Gee!" Guinea looked at it doubtfully. "It looks terribly young and innocent-like."

"Hurry up and slip it on, Guin," Claire urged.

Val and Deb lowered the dress over her head. The skirt billowed out like a crinoline, the corselet bodice nipped her waist to delusive fragility and moulded her high young breasts. The little-girl neckline and enormous puffed sleeves gave her an air of touching childishness.

"Whacko-the-diddle-oh!" she whooped, twirling on her toes.

Val stood off and looked at her with complacent admiration, as though she had wrought the miracle herself. "That'll lay them in the aisles."

"Is it really all right?"

Claire viewed it from all sides. "Perfect. It makes you look like dreamdust and dew on the grass."

"It's lovely, Guinea, and it doesn't need a thing doing to it." Deb stood off and looked at her critically, "but you certainly can't wear orchids with it."

"You watch me."

Guinea picked up the orchids and held them against her shoulder.

"Not there," Claire cried aghast. "Don't you dare wear anything with that frock."

"Not even my diamond watch?"

"Most certainly *not* your diamond watch, my girl. Now look how I'm fixing these," Claire laid the orchids against Guinea's shining hair. "High up and to the left. That's the spot. What do you say, girls?"

Val hugged herself with delight. "Gorgeous. Fairy princess with a dash of the devil. That's your line. And lay off your usual language."

"Aw, gimme a chance. Expect me to be dumb? Alfalfa wouldn't know me."

"Well, just say 'yes' and 'no'."

Guinea gurgled, "It'll be mainly 'no'."

"It takes you to land orchids and Who's Who for nothing," Val laughed.

"Well, that's what he'll get. Fancy having old age creeping over you. Ugh!"

"Alfalfa's not old," Claire protested.

"Forty-five if he's a day, and nothing but a wornout old wolf at that."

Deb turned sharply away and picked up the orchids, her cheeks hot with a telltale glow.

"That's not old for a man," Claire argued. "Lots of women marry older men."

"Maybe for a meal ticket," Val said. "When they can take their pick, it's the young ones they go for."

"Too right," said Guinea. "My God, I've got a chest like Lana Turner."

Deb recovered her composure and laughed. "You be

grateful for it. D.D.T. has to wear cheaters.''

Val grinned with happy anticipation. "I'd give a quid to see D.D.T.'s face when you come in. Couldn't you make a set at her admiral just to please me?''

"Sorry, he's got whiskers. I had a naval boyfriend once like that and it was like kissing a prickly pear.''

"You're hopeless," Claire laughed.

"Anyway," said Guinea decidedly, "I always think beards make them look like pansies.''

"I think you've got it wrong, but have it your own way.'' Claire got up. " And now we've seen the mannequin parade, you'd better hop it, kids. If I don't lock up now I'll never get out to Randwick, although with this filthy westerly blowing I'd just as soon stay at home if Nigel wasn't mad to see Storm-cloud run in the Epsom. I hope you have a wonderful time, Guin." She turned to Deb. "Give me a hand in the office, will you?''

Claire changed quickly while Deb nervously rearranged the already tidy office. She felt she ought to tell Claire about Angus; it seemed only fair. But somehow she didn't know how to begin. It was all so different from yesterday when they had discussed him in her room. And she was still so bewildered she hardly believed it herself.

Claire's voice came to her from the dressing room, muffled and a little too casual, as though she had been reading Deb's thoughts. "I hope you won't feel I'm butting in, but I think you ought to know that Elvira's gossiping about you and Mr McFarland.''

Deb swung round startled. "What about?''

Claire came to the door pulling on her gloves with elaborate care. "Well — she says he's proposed to you!''

Deb's face flushed. "Someone ought to strangle that woman, she's a menace.''

"That's not the kind of gossip that can hurt your reputation, even if it isn't true.''

Deb's colour deepened. "It is true, Claire. I'm sorry Elvira got in first. I've been wanting to tell you all the morning, but I never seemed to be able to get a minute with you alone. Angus did ask me to marry him last night, but I don't know how Elvira knows anything about it unless she was under the table at Prince's."

Claire came over and kissed her with a sudden warmth. "I'm so glad for you, Deb. It's wonderful. It's the most wonderful bit of luck I've ever heard of." Her voice was unsteady.

They stood facing each other, Claire with tears suffusing her eyes, Deb self-conscious as a schoolgirl caught in some childish fault.

"I haven't said I will, you know."

Claire's eyes widened, her face was blank with astonishment. "But you will," she cried, grasping Deb's hand. "Oh darling, say you will."

It was daylight when Shirley and Fay came back from their party and they sounded so tired and cross that although Monnie wakened when they came in she gave no sign and lay quietly on the settee with her eyes closed till they were sound asleep. Then she got up and went into the kitchenette to make herself a cup of tea and get something to eat, but she could find only a few scraps of food and some sour milk.

They must have forgotten to do their shopping yesterday, she thought, but then they had so little time with their work and overtime and all the parties they went to. Well, thank goodness this was Saturday and they could have a good sleep-in and she would go out and buy some food so that she could have a meal ready for them when they woke up. She dressed without making a sound and crept out of the house.

How different the lane looked in daylight, not frightening any more, but gay in the sunshine. She wandered along Darlinghurst Road, fascinated by all the exciting things in the shops — not that she could afford to buy them. She bought only the most necessary things at a ham-and-beef shop — eggs and milk and crisp new rolls. She'd have got more, only she was horrified at the prices. Things cost twice as much here as they did at West Hills.

The thought of West Hills reminded her that they would be worrying about her at home. She'd ring up and leave a message with Bridie's friend on the switch at the factory, telling them she was staying with Shirley and that she'd be home with Peg for Dad's birthday tomorrow. She wouldn't be afraid to go home now she had a place to come back to and the promise of a good job. Even Mum wouldn't try to interfere with a chance like that!

When she came out of the telephone box she stood for a moment in the sunshine. She had never seen such a gay crowd doing their Saturday morning shopping; women in slacks and sandals and brief beach dresses; men in bright shirts and shorts, choosing their meat and vegetables and groceries with as much care as the women. And there was so much chatter and laughter

— it was more like a picnic than a weekend shopping rush. The striped awnings shading the little shops made it different too, like something you'd see in a technicolor film. And the windows glowing with colour; the greengrocers where strange fruits were piled among the familiar ones; great yellow globes of pawpaws with dewy black seeds, knobbly green custard apples, scarlet chillis, purple eggfruit and young sweet corn hanging silvery tassels above boxes of mushrooms. The homely things, like potatoes and beans and pumpkins, did not seem to belong to the same family.

She stopped at every flower shop. Someday she might dare to go in and buy a spray, just a little one to pin on her shoulder. She looked at the orchids, long sprays of them, cream and green and delicate pink with brown spots, and single slipper orchids, green and brown. They were for the glamorous women she saw going up and down the street. There were gardenias and brilliant spikes of gladioli, and cyclamens, heliotrope and purple in their red earthenware pots. Pink boronia and godetias and broom were bunched in buckets round the doorways and there was one little place that was a cave of flowers, tier upon tier right up to the ceiling.

The plane trees lining the street had their new leaves and the breezes from the harbour kept them perpetually dancing, a scatter of tender green in the spring sunshine. They made her feel like dancing too.

There was a man standing at the corner of the lane with a basket of frangipani blossoms. "'Ere y'are lady," he said as she lingered. "Only sixpence a spray."

She hesitated. Sixpence was an awful lot for a few blossoms. Then, on a sudden impulse, she handed him the money and took the spray. The maidenhair fern with it was curling a little and there was a bruise on one of the flowers, but the perfume was heady and she skipped down the lane holding them against her cheek.

It was after one o'clock when she got back, and the girls were still asleep. Betty was on a pile of cushions in the bath, where the other two had dumped her.

Monnie made herself a cup of tea and buttered a roll that

melted in her mouth. She tidied the tiny kitchenette and washed up piles of greasy dishes, the saucers filled with sodden cigarette butts and the cups with the dregs still in them and lipstick stains on the rim. It was a joy to work at the sink under the flowing hot water. Imagine running hot water! That and some soap she found, and her overflowing desire to repay the girls, started her off on the washing.

It was not hard to find their soiled clothes, they were scattered all over the flat. There were scanties under a cushion, others soaking in the bathroom basin, a pair thrown across the chair in the bedroom; brassières dropped just as they had taken them off, lying on the floor like sucked grape skins, and a whole pile of dirty clothes behind the bathroom door. How careless they were with their clothes! They were all so pretty too, georgette and lace and gay spotted cottons. Monnie wondered how they managed to buy so many clothes on their coupons. She filled the sink with suds and washed them carefully, trying not to notice their stale, unpleasant smell. It wasn't that the girls weren't clean, she was sure, just that they didn't have time to look after their things properly. She put up a string line across the bathroom where the sun was streaming in on to Betty, wrung out each fragile garment carefully and doubled it over the line.

Then she scrubbed and polished the flat and at last, tired and happy, lay down on the lounge and looked through the film magazines, the *True Romances*, the *Oracles* and *Miracles*, that lay scattered all around.

It was late afternoon when Shirley stumbled sleepily out of the bedroom, her black georgette nightdress dangling from torn shoulder straps. She rubbed her knuckles into her eyes and slumped down onto the settee. "Jesus," she said, "what time is it?"

"It's about half past four. You all seemed so tired out that I didn't like to wake you."

"Tired out! You're telling me! Oh Gawd! I've got a mouth like the bottom of a birdcage."

"Will I get you something? I went out and got some eggs and fresh bread for lunch."

Shirley groaned and turned her head away. "Eggs . . . ugh!"

"Would you like a cup of tea?"

"Oh, a cuppa sounds like heaven to me."

Monnie made steaming tea and cut paper-thin fingers of bread and butter. Shirley gulped it down. "Gorgeous. I feel different already. Got any more?"

"Plenty."

"I'll swallow an APC in between."

Monnie ministered to her tenderly. Nothing she could do could ever repay Shirley for rescuing her from that awful waiting-room at Central last night.

Shirley drank three cups of tea and stretched herself with a drawn-out yawn. "Gee, the place does look different. You must have had a cracker under your tail this morning."

"Oh, I loved doing it. I know you simply haven't got the time and it's really an awfully sweet flat." Monnie rubbed at the marks of glasses on the table. "I couldn't get these off but I've made a difference to the carpet, haven't I?"

"I'll say," Shirley agreed. "It's the first time I knew it had roses on it." She wandered into the bathroom. "Crikey! Am I seeing things?"

Monnie followed her. "I hope you didn't mind me washing them, but I know you haven't got much time."

"Take a look at this," Shirley called to Fay.

"Christ almighty!" Fay said. "Who owns all those duds?"

"We do. The kid washed them out for us."

Fay looked at Monnie rather oddly. "I hope you enjoyed it."

"Oh, yes — they're so pretty."

Betty opened bleary eyes at the voices and let out a yell. "Jumping Jesus! Have I got the DTs? I lost that blue and red bra, a week ago. Who found it?"

"The kid did."

Betty stared at it foolishly. "Whaddyerknow! Did you find the scanties to match?"

"No."

"Oh well, I must have left 'em at the party."

Shirley laughed rather boisterously and turned to Monnie. "You don't want to take any notice of the things Betty says. That's her idea of a joke."

They all drank tea and nibbled thin bread and butter and drifted round the clean flat uttering cries of astonishment. Monnie tended them like a hen feeding her chickens and there was laughter and joking and she was utterly happy. How different it was from home! No one to nag at you. Just friendliness and fun.

A tall, grey-haired woman came soundlessly into the room, a smile curving her thin lips as she greeted Monnie. "M-m-m," she said, her voice running up and down the scale, "so this is the little girl you told me about?"

"Yeah," Fay nodded. "Yeah — this is Monnie... And this is our friend, Grace, Mon. We were at a party in her flat last night," she added hurriedly.

Grace looked down at Monnie and smiled. Monnie smiled back at her shyly. She was so beautiful and dignified in her plain black frock. Not at all the kind of person you'd expect the girls to know so well.... She glanced uncertainly at Shirley, stretched lazily on the settee in her draggled black nightdress and smoking without any embarrassment. If they were friendly with someone like Grace, everything must be wonderful.

Grace slid an arm protectively round Monnie's shoulders. "I'm so glad the girls were able to help you last night, darling. Did you sleep well?"

Monnie nodded.

"And I don't wonder, after all you'd been through, you poor little pet. I'm so glad Shirley brought you home. She knows I'm always interested in little girls like you who have been unlucky enough to get into trouble at home without meaning to. You can trust me to help you."

The woman tightened her hand on Monnie's shoulder and turned to Fay. "Isn't she pretty? You didn't tell me she was so pretty. But such a little thing," she added doubtfully.

"Strong as a horse," Fay reassured her. "You should have seen the amount of work she got through in the flat this morning."

Grace looked round approvingly. "M-m-m-m. . ." Her voice went up and down like the cooing of doves. "It looks wonderful." She held Monnie closer. "Poor darling," she crooned, "were they horrid to you at home? How old are you, dear?"

"I'll be seventeen in March," Monnie mumbled, hope rising in her.

The woman put a plump, perfumed hand under the child's chin and tilted her face up to her. "Is your hair natural?"

Monnie nodded.

"Aren't you lucky," she said smoothing the hair back gently. "Shirley was telling me the bad time you've had. M-m-m-m. . ."

Tears came into Monnie's eyes and she could not speak for the lump in her throat.

"It's a shame. I cannot understand how some mothers can be so cruel to their daughters. Now, my little girl — you're rather like her when I come to look at you. She's at boarding school in the country." Grace eyed her speculatively. "Just about the same size, I would say." Her face lit up and she tucked her hand under Monnie's arm. "I'm quite fond of you already, darling. You be a good little girl and Aunt Grace will see that everything is all right. Perhaps you'd like to come to a party with the girls tonight, would you?"

Monnie breathed an ecstatic "Yes."

Grace squeezed her arm. "Splendid! And later on, I want you to meet a great friend of ours, Sport. She'll love Sport, won't she, girls?"

"Sure." Fay gave a little dry laugh. "Sure. She'll love Sport."

When Deb opened the door of her room a cool fragrance greeted her. One of Marina's familiar silvered boxes, tied with green tinsel, was on her dressing-table, filled with lily-of-the-valley. Good Lord, she thought, there must be pounds' worth! She slit the envelope and read the card: "Twelve hours. Another anniversary."

Angus certainly had tossed caution to the winds this morning, telling his brother about his proposal and now sending flowers to her room. It must be all over the SP. Oh well, she should worry, though, the way she was feeling, a bottle of iced champagne would have done more for her at the moment than any box of flowers. She was too tired to arrange them, so she put them in the washbasin just as they were. She took off her overall, kicked off her shoes, and slumped onto the bed. It was heaven to lie down.

All the morning, as she had massaged and patted, rolled and pummelled heavy, hot flesh, murmuring amiable nothings in answer to the small chatter of the salon, the secret thought of Angus had kept flickering through her mind like summer lightning.... Angus's hand firm on her back as they danced; Angus toasting her in champagne; his proposal...always it came back to that. Angus had proposed. Angus had proposed...

She settled herself more comfortably on the bed and wished she could stay there the whole afternoon.

There was no doubt she was burning the candle at both ends. Wednesday night at a show, last night at Prince's...and though it hadn't been very late when they had got back to the hotel, the memory of Angus's kiss on her lips had kept her wide awake for hours and taken all the rest from her short night.

Her head still ached. It must be the champagne. How she wished she didn't have to go to Nolly's that afternoon. How glorious it would be to have a hot bath and get into bed. Already, in fancy, she could smell the perfumed water and feel the silkiness of her nightdress and the cool sheets.

Sleep, sleep...she didn't even want to eat, just to rest, utterly and completely, and then tomorrow morning she would wake refreshed, ready for the day with Angus.

For half an hour she lay drugged with her own exhaustion and the memory of the night before, until she fell asleep. Almost immediately, it seemed, she woke again, stabbed by a sense of urgency. There was something she had to do. She must wake up, she must get up. She opened her eyes with an enormous effort of will, blinked them against the light and glanced from force of habit at the little travelling clock on her bedside table. It was two o'clock. Realisation flooded over her. She had told Nolly she'd get the two-thirty train to Pymble. If she didn't catch that she'd miss the bus connection out and there wasn't another till the evening.

Oh damn, she'd never make it. "Damn!" she swore aloud, and felt better. She couldn't possibly get dressed and down to Wynyard station in half an hour. Well, she'd just have to catch the next train and take her chance of getting a taxi at Pymble station...and that'd be at least another five shillings to add to her rapidly mounting expenses. "Damn and blast!"

It seemed mad to go rushing up to Nolly's when she'd have to leave again tomorrow morning at the crack of dawn. Oh well, there was no getting out of it. Luen would be disappointed enough when she found that she was only staying the night, but she'd be broken-hearted if she didn't turn up at all...and she really ought to give Nolly a hand. Families were the devil, always expecting you to be at their beck and call. They never seemed to realise you had a life of your own, and after all, you couldn't be expected to run your life only for your child and your sister, however fond you were of them.

Heavens, she hadn't bought a thing to take up to the children and the shops would all be closed. She pulled out the drawer of her dressing-table and sighed with relief. There was the huge box of chocolates Angus had given her on Wednesday with only a few out of the top row. She fumbled in the lower layer to refill the empty places. That'd have to do — they were damn lucky to get it at all; it must have cost at least a pound and most people couldn't get chocolates anywhere these days, for love nor money. She pushed the box into her overnight case, slammed the lid down and looked at the clock. She'd have to rush if she wasn't going to miss the next train.

As the electric train roared out of the tunnel and on to the Harbour Bridge, the salt breeze off the water fluttered through her hair and she relaxed against the back of her seat. It was a blue-and-gold day: washed blue of a hot sky, deep blue of the harbour patterned with billowing white sails and busy ferryboats; smoky grey of a battleship swinging at anchor off Kirribilli Point; foreshores olive-green where the bush ran down to the water's edge; clusters of red roofs and white houses; every colour shimmering in the sunlight with a sharpness that hurt.

She closed her eyes against the glare; the rhythmic beat of the steel wheels, the swaying motion of the carriage, lulled her to sleep again.

She woke with a jerk as the woman beside her rose to get out at Chatswood, and realised that she had slept through half the journey. Only five more stations and she would be at Pymble. Then there would be Luen...Luen. How would Luen feel if she married Angus? Of course she adored Jack, but children soon adapted themselves to changes. Look how fond she'd got of Tom and Nolly, though when she first went there they thought she'd never settle down. Nolly and Tom. How would they take the news? Badly, she imagined. Though heaven only knew what right they had to order her life, even if they had helped her out with Luen when she gave up the flat after Jack had sailed and then couldn't find a place where they could afford to live. It was hard to remember now that there had ever been a time when she had thought going to live at the South Pacific was a hardship. Of course she'd been just a suburban simpleton then, like Nolly was still. Well, one thing she was certain of now, she wouldn't let anyone make up her mind for her.

The train rumbled through a deep cutting and came out again among gardens and shrubberies. Red flowering gum trees bordered the line, delicate mauve-blue jacarandas in full bloom floated like misty clouds above close-clipped lawns, purple bougainvillea spilled over fences, and Illawarra flame trees flaunted their orange feathers in the sunshine.

Deb let her imagination invade the prosperous brick houses, the bungalows of cream and white stucco set among their lawns and flower beds. Angus's sister would have such a house, servants too, from casual comments he'd made about her difficulties with the Manpower. In a dream Deb saw herself in her new white slacksuit stretched elegantly on a swinging lounge, and Angus standing beside her with a cocktail shaker in his hand...the cool clink of ice...negligently she reached for the glass he offered...

Her daydream carried her into Pymble station. When she got out she had to deal with the unpleasant reality of persuading the driver of the only taxi to take her the three miles to Nolly's, and then had to wait, hot and impatient, in the shade of a flowering box tree while he did half a dozen runs with short-distance passengers. When at last he picked her up, it was with a bad grace and he let her open the door for herself while he lit a cigarette. Bloody nuisance these long trips, he thought, but you daren't refuse them. This kind of dame would report you as soon as look at you.

Deb felt his bad manners were a personal insult and tried to think up a cutting and dignified reproof. He took a few leisurely puffs before he started while she sat fuming in the back, wishing that Angus was with her to deal with the fellow's insolence.

The car left the suburban asphalt for the bush road to Nolly's with a bump that tossed her off the seat. There had been no rain for weeks and the powdery dust rose in choking clouds. She held on to the arm rest to try and steady herself and grew more furious with every bump.

The fibro cottages scattered among the bush looked cheap and flimsy after the substantial houses nearer the railway station, and soon the grey-green eucalyptus gave way to rows of orange trees, their shiny leaves glinting in the sunshine. The taxi pulled up beside a double gate and the driver leaned back over the front seat and pulled down the handle of the door, letting it fly open. Deb straightened herself and got out with as much dignity as she could manage and handed over the exact fare.

"Struth! Thinks she's a bloomin' duchess!" the taxi driver threw after her as he turned the car.

Deb opened the gate and caught sight of Tom between the trees. He was wearing an old khaki shirt and an ancient pair of trousers and was leaning on his spade, watching her with a broad smile. "Hullo! Chucking your money round on taxis, I see! Won the lottery?"

She bit her lip. The hide of him! Whose money was it, anyway? Before she could think of a cutting retort, a crowd of yelling barefoot children came galloping down the dusty drive.

"Oh, Mummy, Mummy!" Luen called, as she raced ahead of the others and threw her arms round Deb's neck, knocking her hat sideways and kissing her cheek with a hearty smack.

"Hullo, my pet." Deb kissed the only place she could reach, which was the parting of her daughter's sun-bleached hair. "What a little tomboy you're growing." She put up her hands to loosen the arms twined tightly round her neck.

Luen held a fist close to Deb's ear. "Listen, Mummy," she whispered ecstatically. There came the piercing crackle of a cicada. "He's a double-drummer."

Three other small children were now jumping round her, pulling at her skirt and holding up grimy fists.

"Mine's a greengrocer — look!" Durras opened his hand carefully, showing a cicada with iridescent wings folded back on a body of delicate green.

"He's a fine fellow, Durras," Deb agreed, removing a grubby paw from her skirt.

"Mine's a floury baker...and mine's a black prince!" Young Jack and Andrew held up their fists for her to peep at their treasures.

"We got hundreds and hundreds this morning," Luen went on, "and we put them in a kerosene tin with a board over it, but Nimmy got in and ate them and then he was sick all over the kitchen floor, and Auntie Nolly said it served him right for being such a greedy cat."

"Chooks don't get sick when they eat locusts. They eat lots and the empty shells off the trees too. I've seen them," Durras informed her importantly.

"Nasty old Nimmy," scolded four-year-old Andrew.

"He's not, he's my best pussy. Nasty old locusts," little Jack challenged his brother.

"That's enough, you kids," Tom broke in. "Take Auntie Deb up to see Mummy now." The children seized her hands and began pulling her up the drive. "Tell Nolly I'll be up for a cuppa in half an hour," he called after her.

Luen snuggled under Deb's arm. She was growing so fast, she would soon be up to her shoulder. Deb noticed that she had practically grown out of last year's shorts and her hair needed cutting. Of course, you couldn't expect Nolly to look after her the way she used to; here the child was only one of five. All the same, she didn't have to look like a ragamuffin.

When Luen looked up at her, with a face full of laughter, Deb caught her breath at the likeness to Jack and a wave of tenderness for them both swept over her. The same grey eyes, the sun-bleached hair, the same full underlip and stubborn chin...

The three boys ran ahead and Deb and Luen followed them up the dusty drive between the orange trees that led to the square fibro cottage with its corrugated iron roof shimmering in the heat. Nolly came to the top of the steps leading down from the wide veranda, carrying little Deb. The minute Luen saw her, she broke from under Deb's arm and ran ahead shouting, "Mummy's here, Auntie Nolly!"

Nolly settled the baby more comfortably on her hip, dragging the crossover cotton dress tight across her swollen belly. Deb took in her sister's ungainly figure, her bare legs and old flat-heeled shoes at a glance, and her greeting was touched with irritation that Nolly had not troubled to wear the maternity girdle she had gone to so much trouble and expense to get for her. Her flushed face was still girlishly pretty but she'd soon lose her looks if she wasn't careful.

Nolly kissed her warmly. "It's good to see you, Deb. I'd just about given up hoping when you didn't come on the bus."

There was nothing but welcome and relief in her voice, but Deb's touchy conscience heard a rebuke.

"We were so busy this morning, I simply couldn't get away earlier," she explained.

"You poor kid, you look worn out. Come along in and take off your hat while I get a cuppa."

Luen clung to her mother. "What have you got in your case, Mummy?"

Deb opened it. "Look! I've brought up a lovely box of chocolates for all of you."

The children's eyes goggled. "Corks, what a whopper!" Durras gasped.

"Shall I give them one?" She handed the box to Nolly and five grubby hands reached out and solemnly took a large chocolate each.

"They're delicious." Nolly bit into hers. "I haven't tasted anything like this for years. Where did you get them?"

"Oh..." Deb hesitated. "Oh, one of the SP guests..."

"Run along now, nips. Say thank you, Auntie Deb. And Lu, you and Durras take the children outside, so I can talk to Mummy a little while."

Deb caught the soft tone of Nolly's voice when she spoke to Luen, saw the answering glance and smile on the child's face as she held out her arms for the baby. "Can I take Debby too?" Debby leapt into her arms and gurgled "Lu-lu" happily, over and over again.

"Isn't the baby rather heavy for her?"

"Oh no," Luen put in quickly. "She's always my baby in the games, and mothers always carry their babies round. Come on, Durras, we'll go on with hospitals and I'll have a new baby." She led the children to the side veranda, where a hospital ward was rigged up with half a dozen kitchen chairs covered with cushions and rugs.

"It's wonderful the way Lu manages Debby, she simply adores her." Nolly straightened herself up and smoothed out her dress. "Come on in and I'll put the kettle on then you can change. There's no sense in wearing your good clothes around this place, the children will only mess them about. I don't know why you wear them up here."

"You forget I've got to look decent when I leave the hotel."

"Yes, I suppose you have." Nolly's casual tone, which Deb was growing to resent, dismissed the Hotel South Pacific, guests, management and staff alike. She took some scones from a tin and got the butter out of the cool safe. "Look at that," she said distastefully, putting a half melted mass on the table.

"I don't know why Tom doesn't get you a refrigerator."

"Don't say that to him. He's likely to blow the roof off. He's been trying and trying for the last two summers and I haven't been able to make him buy a new thing for himself, so he'd have the cash on hand in case we got a chance of a secondhand one. But even though we've had a priority for ages they say there's no hope of a new one till after the war."

"It's an absolute scandal," Deb said indignantly. "Here, pass over the scones and let me do them for you."

Nolly handed over the knife. "I'll set the tray and then we can all sit down together. You're looking quite washed out."

"We've been working very hard."

"Oh well, the air up here'll set you up over the weekend."

Deb let the reference to the weekend pass with a twinge of guilt. Time enough later to tell them she was going back tomorrow morning. No use starting a fuss now when she'd just arrived.

Nolly was pouring the boiling water into the teapot when Tom came in through the back door. He wiped his heavy boots on the mat and crossed over to the sink. "Phew! What I'd give for a shower!" He washed his hands in an inch of water. "Tank's down to the last two rungs and it's the hottest spring in ten years. One bad bushfire through French's Forest and the shire'll lose enough timber in one day to pay for the water mains ten times over. But it's always the same with those blokes. They sit round a council table quibbling over a few thousand pounds until they've shined the seats off their pants and the fires have burnt out thousands of acres of bush and a dozen orchards or so, and then they make speeches to the firefighters about their heroic efforts, and damned well sit down and do nothing for another year."

"You're all right here though, aren't you, with the pump from the creek?"

"Yes, we're all right so long as the creek holds out and there's enough wind to keep the pump going. But that's not the point. Half the other orchards and farms have to depend on their tanks, and what's going to happen to them if a fire comes along at sixty miles an hour?"

"Well, stop worrying and have a chocolate to cheer you up." Nolly offered the large gold box.

"Thanks. Gift from the black market, eh?"

Deb stiffened. "Not so far as I know."

"We're grateful, anyway. Haven't been able to get a bit of chocolate for the kids in months."

"One of the customers gave them to Deb," Nolly explained.

"Good work," he looked over at Deb with a laugh. "I don't suppose they gave you a bottle of beer for me as well?"

Deb hesitated, then lied feebly, "I did try to get one for you, but they won't sell bottles, even to the staff."

"I suppose they've got to make all the money they can out of the Yanks while the goin's good." He looked at her with a grin. "Been dyeing your hair, I see."

"I don't dye my hair," Deb answered with some sharpness, "that's just a henna rinse to bring out the lights."

"What's the difference?" he asked airily and picked up the tray. "Where'll we have it? You lead the way, boss."

"On the veranda, it's coolest there."

They went out to the wide veranda, where the glare was sifted through passionfruit vines spilling from a high trellis and starred with cream and purple flowers. The heavy scent of orange blossom was on the wind. Tom put the tray on a little wicker table, and Nolly sat down with an unconscious sigh of relief. Deb pulled up her chair, the slight irritation over, her mind on hot tea and buttered scones. She was famished.

Tom sugared his second cup of tea. "So Jack'll be down any day now."

"Yes," Deb was caught off her guard. She hadn't meant to tell them anything that would involve her in questions about Jack's leave. It was all too complicated. She went cold at the very thought of them knowing about Angus.

Nolly went on: "Tom had a letter from him early last week. He said he'd probably be able to give you the exact date in a day or two. Have you heard yet?"

With Nolly's eyes looking into her face, Deb's carefully planned evasion refused to frame itself on her lips. "Next Saturday," she heard herself saying.

"Oh Deb, how wonderful! A week today! It must be almost eighteen months since you saw him."

"Seventeen."

"Yes, of course. It was May, the Valencias were in bloom. Do you remember, Tom? He loved it here. I believe he'd put his deferred pay into an orchard out this way if he hadn't already got the Vineyard. It would have been fun to have you near us."

Fun? Fun to live in this god-forsaken spot? Fun to spend your life cooking and charing and looking after kids? Deb looked over at Nolly, who was drinking her tea unconcernedly, as if no one would think of disagreeing. Deb's glance took in her brown hair carelessly cut, with a bobby pin holding it back to one side, yet still curling prettily round her face. Her skin still had its fine texture and there was a radiance about her that made you forget she had no makeup on. But there was a new line forming from nostril to mouth and a fine tracery gathering round her eyes, although you didn't notice it when she was talking, and her face was alight. She looks older than me, Deb thought.

Tom was speaking again. "I wasn't sure when Jack was here last just how much of this back-to-the-land business he really meant. I thought it might only be that he was fed up with not having any home and you not being able to get off from your job."

"You can hardly blame me or the South Pacific for that," Deb said defensively. "After all, he got his last leave right over the Easter rush when we were terribly busy. And he was pleased as punch when I first got the job. I wanted to go into munitions, but he was too high and mighty in those days."

"I don't know anything about that, but I do know that in his last letter he's keener than ever about the Vineyard. He's got great plans for fixing it up when he gets back."

"It'll be lovely for you to go up there with him." Nolly's voice was warm with happiness. "And you'll have it to yourselves too. He said Uncle Dick was going to board with the Duggans so you could have the run of the house."

"I...I may not be able to get off for a while." Deb heard the smallness of her voice and was ashamed at her own cowardice.

"Oh Deb, that's the limit! Surely they won't try to keep you this time, too?"

"Well, I didn't know the exact date he'd be coming, so I couldn't fix it up in advance, and now it's just caught us in the middle of our busiest time."

"But couldn't you leave? There must be plenty of other jobs you could get when Jack goes back and it's not as though you'd be caught by the Manpower with Lu only ten."

"I suppose I could get another job; but where am I going to get a room to live in? Besides, it isn't likely I could get such a good one and you know we'll need every penny to start again when Jack gets out of the army."

Deb hated herself as she said it, but in the same flash of thought she knew that she couldn't say anything else. They would never understand. How could they, with their smug little plans to drag her life down to the level of theirs?

"I wonder if Jack will see it that way," Tom remarked drily. "I'm afraid I wouldn't."

"Why shouldn't he? That was our idea when I first went to work and Luen came here. It'd be silly to give up a good job like the one I've got. You'd never get the tips anywhere else. Why, last night..." She stopped in some confusion and added lamely, "though the work's terrific. Last night we had to work till after seven."

It had been on the tip of her tongue to tell them about Mrs Dalgety and her five-pound note. But it wouldn't be tactful to mention a tip of thirty shillings when she was only paying fifteen shillings a week for Luen. When she first got the job she used to send Tom and Nolly into gales of laughter with her stories about the Marie Antoinette; then somehow it didn't seem funny to her any more, and these last months she'd hardly told them anything. It was Nolly's maddening way of dismissing all the things that were important in civilised living that annoyed her, she told herself. She hadn't minded at first, but since she had been seeing so much of Angus, the way they poked fun at the hotel and its guests no longer amused her.

Tom chipped in now: "Tips! Don't tell me you're prepared to spoil Jack's leave for a few tips? What's come over you?"

"I don't know what you mean," she parried defensively.

"Oh, don't you? Well, it ought to be obvious to anybody with half an eye that if they're working in a pub that's making its money out of war profiteers, tips are only a genteel form of rake-off."

"You don't know what you're talking about," Deb said loftily. "Not all the South Pacific guests are that type. Many of the old pioneer families stay there when they're in town, and they dislike the war profiteers as much as you do."

"Jumping their claim, buying the best girls and the best liquor — they're the only reasons the pure merinos can't stand 'em."

"You don't seem to realise they belong to entirely different worlds. They're cultured people and widely travelled."

"You don't have to tell me. In the good old days the Australian plutocracy did the big world in a big way — the good old absentee landlord game. Till the bombs started dropping, that is. Then they beat it for home and cover."

"You're most unjust. A few social climbers may do that sort of thing but it certainly doesn't apply to the well-bred people."

"Wonderful how wealth becomes breeding when it's a couple of generations old. Even the Bouncing Belle is respectable now, and as for the son of the bushranger who built the first SP on the profits of blackbirding and rum running —

why, his illicit still was just back in the bush from here and he used to take the stuff down the Lane Cove River under a load of wood to his little pub in Sussex Street. And he became an alderman of the City of Sydney before he died.''

"Well, isn't that better than going on rum running?'' Deb felt she had scored there.

"It all depends on the kind of alderman he was. In any case it doesn't give them the right to look down on the new rich. Their sons'll be just as respectable and the SP'll be delighted to lick their boots in turn and forget that they made their money out of the war and black marketing.''

"You're just prejudiced. Have you ever met any of the best families?''

"Too right. Look round you, madam, meet one of Australia's best families — Mum and Dad, four at hoof and one in the bag.'' He put a calloused brown hand across the table and squeezed Nolly's hand firmly. "We're the real pioneers, aren't we, Noll? Put more into the country than we take out of it.''

Nolly laughed. "There's something in that. Maybe the SP will give us all a free meal if we ever get to town.''

"We'll have worked harder for it than a lot of your pals ever did, Deb.'' He looked at his hands. "You'll have to get the Marie Antoinette to give me a manicure first, though.''

"Oh, you and Jack get on my nerves. You talk as though there was something particularly admirable in this back-to-the-earth thing of yours, instead if it merely meaning that we all live without any modern conveniences and you and Jack look like a pair of navvies.''

"What's wrong with looking like navvies? Where'd we be without navvies, anyway? You wouldn't be able to come out here in a taxi if navvies hadn't made a road for you. It's a damn sight more honest way of earning a living than the blokes who sit on their backsides at the SP and rake in the dividends.''

"Well somebody's had to do the work for there to be dividends, haven't they?''

"That's right. But who? Not the blokes who live on them,

they're just parasites on the country."

"Well, there's one thing the South Pacific has taught me, however biased your ideas may be about it..."

"What's that? Carry your liquor like a lady?"

Deb ignored his comment. "That there are a lot more ways of doing something for your country besides burying yourself in primitive holes like this and the Vineyard."

Tom's jaw set hard. He poured himself a cup of tea and stirred it noisily before he answered. "I've never held any brief for unemployment myself," he said, "but if you ask me which type of unemployed I prefer as a human being, the bloke on the dole or the bloke on dividends, I'd plump for the dole every time."

"Now you're merely being offensive."

"Sorry. I'd have thought from your father's experience in the depression you'd feel the same. And frankly, it gets my goat to think of all the chaps who never had a fair go in peace and have given up everything they've got, to go and fight...It's always the same. War is only government policy continued by another means, and the people who are exploited in peacetime are exploited in war. Whichever way it goes, big business is on the receiving end!"

"What about the enormous taxes they pay? And the interest-free loans?"

"I don't know what friends you've picked up, my girl, who would be likely to present the government with interest-free loans. But next time they boast about it, ask them what it saves them in taxation."

"All I know is that people with big incomes are hit very hard."

"Down to the last yacht. Breaks your heart, doesn't it?"

"You have no idea of how the price of everything has gone up."

"Haven't I?" said Nolly. "Take a look at my housekeeping bills."

"Don't be so narrow, my pet," Tom said, looking at her affectionately. "Your sister doesn't mean necessities, she's referring to the luxuries no well-bred person can do without.

A couple of houses apiece and two cars, one for light work and one for heavy."

"If they own them I don't see why they shouldn't use them. And the government regulations simply force them to buy petrol in the black market, no matter what it costs. It's scandalous."

"What? The black market or the people who buy in it? The ones who buy are as bad as the ones who sell. Black market petrol at ten bob a gallon pinched from Army trucks, black market liquor sold only to the most valued patrons, clothes...don't forget the racket in clothing coupons, and the factory that supplies your precious Marie Antoinetter with hocus-pocus all done up with pretty labels to be sold at ten times its cost. Black markets couldn't run without black buyers, and that's just where your well-bred best families get off at the same stop as the common blacketeers — and that goes for your high-class pub too."

Deb poured herself another cup of tea and drank it slowly to cover her silence. What right had Tom to talk? Tom, who was content to be stuck in a garage at Hornsby doing a mechanic's job until he got the orchard going? Not a spark of real ambition. What did he know of the world that Angus came from? Tom would have everyone get their hands as horny as his if he had his way. She looked across at the ingrained dirt that no amount of washing could remove from his strong hard hands, and gave an imperceptible shudder of distaste. Jack's hands would be like that if they went back to the Vineyard, and she'd be no better than Nolly after a year of scrubbing and cooking. She wanted to tell them both they could have it all, she wasn't going back to drudgery. Tom called it doing an honest job. Being a fool was her name for the same thing. But she could never get the best of an argument with him. It wasn't that there weren't plenty of good reasons she could give, only when Tom bullied her she just couldn't think of them.

Deb had a sudden sense of panic that she had said too much — given herself away. But she need not have worried. Nolly laughed comfortably and squeezed her hand. "Tell him to mind his own business, Deb," she said, smiling warningly at Tom. "I've no doubt you and Jack will settle everything quite amiably between you once you get together again."

"No doubt you're right. Sorry, Deb." Tom smiled at her in a way she found infuriating.

Nolly changed the subject. "Did you notice the orange trees as you came up? We've got great hopes for them. If we get a good winter crop, Tom thinks he'll be able to leave the works."

"What about the Manpower?"

"I'll have no difficulty there. I'll be a primary producer."

"Do you think you can make the place pay?"

"Depends on the season, of course, but everything's looking fine, and, bar accidents, we'll have a bumper crop. As soon as I start work here in earnest, I'm going to put a couple of acres under vegetables."

"How'll you manage about water?"

"Piping's frozen at the moment, but as soon as they release some I'll get water laid up from the pump. It's all a matter of how soon I can get the place going properly. I'm not going to let another depression catch me."

"From what I can see, there needn't be another depression. If the workers would only behave a bit more reasonably..."

"Well, no one could ever have accused your father of being unreasonable — there wasn't a harder-working man going, and what good did it do him when they closed the Government Savings Bank in the last depression?"

"Poor old Dad." Nolly's face was tender. "Dallas was only saying the other day that losing everything like that helped to kill him. He was hurt so deeply in his pride."

"That's right. He never knew what hit him and there were a lot of fellows like him who took it as a personal failure instead of realising that they were victims of the system."

"I don't see that there's any resemblance at all between what happened to Dad and the way the workers are going on now. All these strikes in wartime..." Deb parroted Angus glibly.

Tom lit a cigarette before he spoke. "Now just what would you know about the workers, cooped up in that hothouse of yours?"

"Hothouse or no hothouse, I'm quite sure I see much more of the world than you do in your workshop."

"All depends on what you mean by 'the world'. The way you've been going on the last couple of months you seem to be labouring under the delusion that the SP is the world. The life of that pub of yours is as far removed from the life ordinary Australians are living today as your big business man is from the working man."

"I don't notice them killing themselves with work. If they really wanted to stand behind the boys at the front there wouldn't be all these strikes."

"Oh bunk! Take off your SP specs and have a look at things as they are for a change. And when you feel you can afford to miss the tips, take a day off and have a look in the factories. Get around the suburbs and see the women lugging heavy parcels home and struggling to keep their families going on a soldier's allotment."

"That's just why I'm not going to give up my good job at the Marie Antoinette till I know something a bit more definite about my future. Where would Luen and I be, stuck up on that Vineyard, if there's another depression?"

"Where you ought to be, in your own home. And damn lucky to have it. Jack sees a slump coming too, that's plain," Tom went on. "He says he's finished with the car racket, and a good thing too. He wasn't made for a boss's man any more than I was."

"Jack never was a boss's man," Deb countered with heat.

"What can any salesman be but a boss's man? Out to put the sales figures up, by fair means or foul."

"Well, if none of us had any ambition, it'd be a tame world," Deb threw at him.

"Tame? That's what a decent world ought to be — a place where you can live decently without having to behave like a savage; where kids can grow up healthy and free. That's my ambition, to give my kids a chance to be civilised human beings. If I can give them a decent home and a happy life, they won't want to live at someone else's expense. No," he went on without giving Deb a chance to interrupt, "old Jack's come to his senses up in New Guinea and you're a lucky woman that he has, if you only knew it."

Deb was boiling. What right had Tom to lay down the law to her and walk roughshod over all her opinions? That's exactly what Jack would be doing when he got home. Hot tears of injury pricked her lids.

A gust of wind swept the passion vine. Tom went to the corner of the veranda. "I don't like this change in the wind." He looked over the sloping orchard to the bush-covered hill beyond. "And that yellow haze doesn't look too healthy to me."

Nolly got up and stood beside him, following his gaze. "You don't think it's fire, do you, Tom?"

"I'm not too sure, but I don't like the look of it."

The three of them stood with the wind in their faces, shading their eyes and trying to see against the glare beyond the windmill, which clanked in a sudden gust. Tom sniffed the wind. "There's bush burning somewhere. I can smell it."

There was a thickening of the haze above the wooded hill that rose steeply beyond the orchard. It might simply be a trick of the sunshine, Deb thought. She could smell nothing.

"There's no need to worry yet," Tom turned to reassure Nolly. "But I think I'll get out the utility and see what's up. There's fire somewhere and I might be able to give a hand. I don't think there's any likelihood of it coming this way, but there's no harm in being ready here, so I'll fix up the hose to the pump line and with this wind you ought to get decent pressure hosing this side of the house. Deb had better do that. You look after the kids, Nolly, and see they keep near the house."

"You don't think there's any danger?" Deb was anxious for reassurance.

"Not here. The land's well cleared round the house and I've burnt a good firebreak on the other side of the creek. But you never know what tricks the wind will get up to. You'll be able to keep things under control, Deb, we can't have Nolly dragging the hose around. Just keep the windward side of the house soused with water, that's all you can do.''

Tom put his arm round Nolly's shoulders and dropped a kiss on top of her head. ''I'll be off now and don't worry, old lady. If I thought there was any real danger I wouldn't be going. And Deb'll look after things outside. We can't have you needing an urgent trip to hospital while I've got the bus out.''

''I'll be all right.'' Nolly looked up at him with a smile. ''Are you going like that?''

He glanced at his stained khaki shirt and trousers. ''No sense in dressing up if there's a job to be done. Durras!'' he called. ''Put my leather fire-beater in the back of the truck, son, and fill the satchel pump. I'll take that.'' He ran down the steps from the veranda and round the back of the house to the shed which served for a garage. At the sound of the utility starting up, the other children ran out.

''Where is Daddy going? I want to go too. Is he going to take us?'' they all clamoured.

''No, he's got to go by himself. He'll take you next time,'' Nolly soothed them.

''D-a-a-d!'' shouted Durras, following the truck out of the shed, ''can't I come and help?''

Tom stopped the truck at the steps. ''Not today, son, next time. Mummy might need you, so I'm leaving you in charge here. Will you do something for me?''

''Let me, too,'' begged Luen.

''Both of you, then. There's a pile of sacks at the back of the shed. Stick them in one of the laundry tubs and soak them right through with water. Stir them round and squeeze them up and down till they're sopping. Can you do that?''

''Of course we can,'' the two voices shouted.

''Then I want you to leave half a dozen of them soaking and take the rest back to the shed and wrap them round that drum of petrol under the bench. Do you know which one I mean?''

''The new baby's petrol,'' Luen said.

"That's right. We want to keep it cool so it'll be ready if the baby needs it in a hurry. Can you do that for me?"

"Oh yes, Dad," Durras answered, full of importance at his job.

"Do you think the baby might need it today?" Luen asked Nolly, her grey eyes wide with excitement.

"Well, you never know with babies and it's just as well to be ready."

"And when you've done that, bolt the shed doors and go straight back to Mummy and not one of you kids is to go near that shed again until I come home. And don't go down in the long grass near the creek, this is just the kind of weather to bring the snakes out. Do you understand?"

"Yes, Daddy," chorused four trebles with an "Uncle Tom" sounding below in Luen's husky voice.

"Good. It's young Jack's turn to open the gate, isn't it? Hop on, son."

The little boy jumped on to the footboard. Tom leaned out and looked at Deb with a twinkle in his eye. "Of course, if we are really stuck for some extra petrol, I'm sure Auntie Deb could touch one of her rich friends for a few black market coupons."

Without giving her a chance to reply, he let in the clutch and was off down the drive in a stir of yellow dust.

For an hour, Deb had played the hose on the roof and walls of the house, soaking the veranda and showering the dusty Christmas bushes in the garden below. The hot wind brought with it a choking smell of smoke and the scent of burning gum trees. She was streaming with sweat and Nolly's old cotton frock stuck to her back and thighs. She felt the moisture gather and run down her body, little rivulets dripped off the end of her nose, and her hair, under the old cabbage tree hat, was gummed together in draggled wisps. Her shoulders and back were aching and her arms felt as if they would drop off.

At last the sun was sinking down to the bush-covered hills. Deb turned her face to the wind and watched the yellow haze in the western sky deepen to a menacing red-gold. At one minute, the hot wind in her face was like a blast from some great oven, at the next it had dropped and there was only the still heat around her.

"No-o-olly," she called, "the wind's gone down!" She held the hose upright and the water shot up like a flagstaff and fell back again on her head and shoulders.

The children heard her voice and came running round the veranda.

"Look," Andrew called, "Auntie Deb's having a shower." He was down the steps in a flash and plunging into the spray.

"You little scamp, you'll get your clothes wet."

"I don't care, I don't care. Shower me, Auntie Deb," he begged.

Nolly came and looked over the veranda.

"The wind's gone down," Deb called up.

"That's a relief. They must have stopped the fire beyond the far ridge. Good heavens," she laughed as she caught sight of Deb's bedraggled figure. "You look a wreck."

"Well, I've cooled the place down at least, even if I've nearly drowned myself."

Andrew hopped up and down in the spray and the other three came tearing round the corner. "Hose us too," they shouted, leaping round her.

"Go on," Nolly called down, "it doesn't matter about their clothes."

Deb made an arch of spray for the children, who ran in dancing and squeaking with delight. Durras kicked off his shorts, Luen tossed her shirt and shorts into the air and little Jack came to her to have the buttons of his sunsuit undone before he danced into the spray. The children dodged in and out, shrieking and chasing each other, their naked brown bodies glistening in the red glow, their hair stuck to their heads like tight, glossy caps.

Dusk was settling down when at last Deb turned off the water. "Come on," she called to them, "we'll all go and have a good rub down." But the children scattered in front of her, darting among the orange trees, calling to her to catch them.

She gathered up the sopping clothes and looked up at Nolly. "I'm all in. You'll have to use your authority now." She came up the steps with the water dripping from her hat, her shoulders drooping and her sodden frock flapping against her legs.

Nolly took the bundle of small garments. "The children can romp for a while. You get out of that frock and give yourself a rub down. There's an old dirndl of mine at the back of the bathroom door you can put on; then stretch out on Lu's bed on the veranda, it's coolest there. I'll just see that Debby's asleep and then I'll get you some tea."

When Nolly came back with the tray, Deb was lying in a pleasant doze. She could hear the voices of the children still in the orchard. "Oughtn't they to come in?" she murmured without stirring.

"The mossies'll drive them in once they stop playing. They'll be vicious in this heat." Nolly sat down on the bed at Deb's feet.

"It's a wonder we're not being eaten alive out here."

"They don't worry us much in the house. I think it's being so high off the ground." Nolly poured out the tea and Deb propped herself on one elbow and balanced her cup on the edge of the bed. She looked out over the veranda railing to where the rounded edge of the moon was just showing above the bush. Nolly's gaze followed hers and together they watched in silence while a copper moon lifted itself above the tree tops.

"It's a bushfire moon," Deb broke the silence.

Nolly spoke the troubled thought that she had put aside all the afternoon. "I do hope Tom'll be all right."

"Of course he will. It's not an hour since the wind dropped. It'll take longer than that to get a big fire under control and, judging by the glare in the sky, it's been a pretty big blaze."

"I know it's silly to worry. Tom's not the one to leave while there's anything to be done."

"Of course he won't. You can't really expect him for hours yet."

"No, I suppose not."

Deb could hear the droop in Nolly's voice. "You're just tired, that's the only reason you're worrying. Drink up your tea and come and lie down beside me." She put her cup on the tray and moved against the wall to make room. "Do you remember the last time we watched a bushfire moon? We were really worried then...and we needn't have been."

"I'll never forget it." Nolly stretched herself out beside Deb. "I'll never forget a single minute of that holiday. If it hadn't been for you and Jack, I don't think Tom and I would have had the courage to get married."

"Oh yes, you would. You were made for each other."

"But we might have wasted so many precious years saving up if we hadn't seen how happy you two could be on nothing...and after that bushfire, I could hardly bear to let him out of my sight. The moon was copper that night, too. Remember how it rose out of the sea, and you and me sitting at the foot of the cliff with the water lapping at our feet and all our camping gear around us?"

Deb nodded.

"And we talked and talked all night, until the moon went down behind the blazing ridge."

"Why, Nolly, the moon's making you quite poetic," Deb

cut across the emotion she heard in Nolly's voice.

"I knew that night I would marry Tom. Although I could hardly speak of him for fear, somehow my mind worked perfectly clearly. If he came out of that fire alive, I knew I would marry him. I knew then that we belonged to each other and nothing in the world mattered but having the man you loved."

Deb stirred restlessly. Her physical tiredness and the moon shining on her face drew her into the memory of the Deb and Jack of the first Christmas after their marriage. But something else pulled her just as strongly to the present. That year was lovely while it lasted, she told herself, but life's not all camping and moonlight. You can't go back. That's what Jack's trying to do, that's why he wants to go back to the Vineyard to the time when Luen was born and we were utterly happy. But that was ten years ago and it's no good trying to go back.

Nolly was silent. She'd never forget a single hour of that Christmas holiday with Jack and Deb and how she and Tom had first come to the camp at sunset. For the last half mile they had caught glimpses of the sea above the low scrub, through the great trunks of the spotted gums. Then the forest cleared suddenly and they came out on the ridge above the bay. She would never forget that first moment of breathtaking beauty, when they had stood silent, the sun hot upon their backs. Below them, the ridge plunged steeply down into a green twilight of burrawang palms and dark shadow that stretched to the edge of the beach where the sun burst out again in a burning crescent of sand, and lit the surf to a fringe of dazzling white on the vast blue carpet of the sea.

Deb fought against Nolly's mood. She sat up. "Don't you think the children ought to come in?"

Nolly pressed her back on the bed with a firm hand. "Another half hour won't hurt them. They're cooler outside on a night like this anyway."

"But they haven't got any clothes on."

"Well, you don't think they'll catch cold in this heat, do you?" Nolly ran her fingers through her damp hair and lifted it off her face.

Deb made a last protest, "But they haven't had any tea..."

"They won't go hungry. Can't you hear where they are?" The children's voices had moved further away and Deb could hear them shouting to each other round by the loquat tree. Nolly laughed. "They're filling up on loquats. If I know them there won't be any room left for tea by the time they've finished. Anyway, they'll come up when they're tired, so let's have a bit of peace while they're happy."

Nolly lay stretched out on the bed completely relaxed. Deb felt her baby move in the slight touch against her side. Nolly put her hands behind her head and drew up her knees to lie more comfortably. The rising moon bathed the two faces in bright golden light and threw the shadow of Nolly's bulk over Deb's slim figure. With her eyes fixed on the moon Nolly spoke of a Tom who was just twenty, a Nolly not yet seventeen, and Deb let her own memory flow back with Nolly's to Jack and her own young love.

How long ago it seemed, that New Year's Day eleven years ago — a whole lifetime away. It was at the end of the Christmas holiday that Tom and Nolly had spent with them. What kids they'd all been, she and Jack behaving as though they owned the sea and the forest because they'd been beachcombing there for three months.

That was a time you couldn't talk about to other people, except Tom and Nolly who'd shared it and were filled only with wonder and admiration for their poverty-stricken, makeshift life. As if it were yesterday, she saw again Jack and Tom set out along the forest track early on that New Year's Day, with their rucksacks full of freshly caught fish to sell to the motorists returning to Sydney after the holiday.

The night before, the heat had been unbearable with the same oppressive feeling as tonight. Next morning they had all wakened heavy and tired, and not even a dip in the surf could cool them for more than half an hour. Then Jack and Tom had left with their fish. Nolly suggested taking a last look from the top of Durras Mountain before she went back to Sydney next day.

It was a steep pull up the side of the mountain and they took their time. When at last they broke out of the forest, the sun was high overhead and veiled in a golden mist, and the fiery breath of a wind newly sprung from the west scorched their faces and brought with it an acrid scent.

Nolly had wrinkled her nose and sniffed the wind. "Smells like a bushfire."

"It is too. Let's climb up a bit higher and see where it is."

They scrambled up the wall of boulders that brought them out above the treetops and a rising westerly whipped the hair back from their faces. They shaded their eyes with their hands and looked into the wind. The forest ridges were wrapped in a thick haze, and far off a smother of blue smoke shot with flashes of yellow flame curled like a trail from an enormous engine. Nearer, they could hear the crackling as the tree tops caught.

Nolly had turned to Deb, her eyes wide and panic in her voice: "The boys. Suppose they're in that."

They had taken one last look at the fire leaping towards them, then they'd run, slithering down the giant boulders until they reached the bush, plunging down the mountain side, slipping, steadying themselves against the tree trunks, tripping over the undergrowth, unconscious of scratches and cuts, sweat running down their faces, their shirts sticking to their backs, hearts pounding, breath coming short. When at last they reached the camp there had been no sign of the boys and the fire was still beyond the ridge that bounded the bay.

All the afternoon and all night they had sat in unendurable suspense on the rocks at the foot of the cliff. They watched the tide go out as the moon rose higher, bleaching the sand and the cliffs. They watched until the sun came up, a flaming ball in the smoky haze that the wind had blown out to sea.

Then at last they had seen the boys, two small figures rounding the far headland, and they leapt up shouting and raced along the sand to meet them. Deb could still feel Jack's prickly cheek against hers and his arms tight around her. His face was streaked and dirty and his eyes reddened, and he smelled of smoke and singeing...and he was safe!

Deb found that she was lying stiff and tense on the bed and her heart was thumping as it had thumped that morning. If Jack had been in that fire it would have been the end of everything for her. That was how she'd felt too when he left for the Middle East, as though she was torn in half... She made herself relax. How stupid it was to get worked up like this.

Nolly eased her position and straightened out her legs. Eleven years ago... Why, it seemed only the other day. What full and happy years they had been, too. She felt she had only to put out her hand to take the hand of the sixteen-year-old girl sitting in unendurable suspense all that night, the forest beyond the clifftop a wall of flame against the lurid sky, the surf, white in the moonlight, lapping the rock where they sat among their few possessions. She'd known then what she felt about Tom.

After that wonderful meeting, they'd gone back with the boys to the camp and made tea and wolfed enormous sandwiches and sat close to each other and heard each other's stories. It had been a narrow squeak. She'd often said to Deb in those days when the long casualty lists were coming back and you never opened a paper without having your heart in your mouth, that Jack would be all right. Nothing could touch him after coming through that fire.

The wind had changed when the boys were halfway back to the camp and the fire was almost on them before they knew. It was impossible to see anything in the thick forest. When they had turned into a gully they had heard it racing down the mountain, roaring and crackling, less than a mile away, and they had crashed wildly down into the narrow gully where a thin trickle of water ran between the rocky sides. It had been pure instinct, Jack said, but Tom always swore Jack had gone straight as an arrow to the only shelter that could have saved them. Whatever it was, they had made the clearing where the old well was sunk beside the deserted farmhouse.

The fire had been roaring down the gully behind them when they plunged into the scummy water and dragged the half-rotted well cover over their heads. The water had reached their shoulders, green and stinking and they sank as low as they could. They heard the roaring crescendo and the crash of beams as the flames raced across the clearing and engulfed the old house. The long, dry grass went up like a torch and the bushes around the well writhed and crackled. Under the well cover, the reflection of the flames broke the dank gloom, the moss shrivelled from the stones, the boards above them caught fire, and the air was full of the stench of charring wood. They were half suffocated by the smoke and the water grew hot and they flailed it with their arms to keep it moving.

They had been there hours, it seemed, with the steam rising from the surface of the water, and the stones on the side too hot to touch. Even after the fire had passed, the forest around them was full of the sound of crashing branches. And when at last they had crawled out, the moon was high and lurid in a smoky sky, the old house was a blackened ruin and the clearing smouldered as if the very ground was burnt. A long way off they could see the fire riding the night along the ridges.

It wasn't till dawn that they could risk walking through the burnt underbrush in their thin sandshoes and they had followed the rocky gully down to its outlet on the next beach. Singed and blistered and dirty, smelling of smoke and sweat and stagnant water, they had come back.

Nolly began to talk. "You know, Deb, I've been thinking of the fun we had that year, bushfire or no bushfire. I never told you, did I, how shocked I was that first day when the boys were fishing round the headland and we went into the surf without our bathing suits. I saw you were tanned all over and I realised that you and Jack must have spent most of your time naked."

"Oh! That all began when I lost my costume. There was no harm in it."

"I never felt there was. After the first surprise, it seemed a perfectly natural part of your Garden of Eden."

"Garden of Eden! That's all very well when you're young, but it's a different matter when you have responsibilities."

But the old enchantment was strong upon Nolly and she went on: "Remember the Christmas pudding we made in the billy?"

"Yes, and I remember too that our dole rations and our few shillings would never have run to the ingredients if everybody back at home hadn't sent down something towards it. Goodness, what a pair of beggars we must have seemed."

"You seemed wonderful to Tom and me. I remember it all so well, nobody could afford much. Tom's mother sent half a dozen eggs that I carried carefully packed with paper in our billy and Jack's mother sent currants and sultanas and I had bought a tin of condensed milk so we could make Mother's recipe."

Deb was touched in spite of herself. She remembered how thrilled she'd been as the packages came out of Nolly's rucksack. And when the oranges and apples were added from Tom's, she could hardly believe her eyes. "We can't just eat them," she had said as she picked up the oranges and smelled the pungent oil in their rinds. "We must hang them on our Christmas tree."

It was all so long ago and so childish, Deb said to herself fiercely, and aloud to Nolly, "Heavens, what a lot of sentimental nonsense it all seems now."

Nolly was silent. Deb's changed, she thought, stealing a glance at her sister's set face. She's got hard somehow. We can't even talk about things any more. It was as though each time she came out they had drifted farther apart. And now, this business of not being able to get off for Jack's leave, what really lay behind it? Nolly had a feeling that Deb was holding back something important. And saying she wouldn't go back to the Vineyard after the war . . . That wasn't like the old Deb at all.

There was a thumping of bare feet along the veranda as the children burst round the corner of the house. Luen climbed onto the bed at her mother's feet, Durras got up beside her and Andrew followed with little Jack, who was lugging a tabby cat half as big as himself.

"What are you two talking about, Mummy?" Durras demanded.

"The wonderful Christmas tree."

"The one when you and Uncle Tom and Mummy and Daddy were all at the camp?" Luen asked eagerly.

"That's it. The wonderful tree on which your Mummy and I found the nicest little girls and boys in the world."

"Tell us about it," they all begged. "Do tell us about it."

Luen hugged Deb's feet. "Oh, make her, Mummy! It's nicer than all the fairy stories."

"Of course, we know the part about the babies being on the tree is a fairy story. Mummy's told us all about where babies really come from," Durras explained seriously.

"But we like it that way just the same," Luen put in hastily.

"Do tell us," they all begged again.

"Don't you think it's time they were in bed?" Deb said rather sharply. It was ridiculous, turning the whole thing into a fairy story.

"No-o-o! No-o-o!" The shouting went through her head like a knife.

Nolly laughed. "Well, I'll tell you what we'll do. You children run in and put your pyjamas on and Lu will pour you out a glass of milk each, then you can come and sit here and we'll have the story of..."

The children finished the sentence for her. "The magic Christmas tree!" they all shouted together.

"Come on," Luen cried, jumping off the bed, "beat you to it."

Little Jack carefully gave Nolly the cat to mind and ran after the others. Laughter and squeals came from the house.

"You don't really give yourself a chance to get a rest, do you?" Deb said rather crossly.

"Oh. I don't mind this kind of thing. This is fun, but I must admit I'm looking forward to letting up a bit on the routine now you're here for the weekend. It's the cooking that get's me down. You've always got to be at it with a hungry brood like this."

Deb had no answer.

"And the shopping," Nolly went on. "It's the housewives they ought to be giving Victoria Crosses to in this war. Though

I'm one of the lucky ones, Tom's a wonderful help and we have the utility whenever we've got a bit of petrol."

"I'll see. I think I may be able to get you a few coupons."

"That'd be marvellous. We'd all be grateful. You see we've got a sort of co-operative arrangement out here; when we've got the petrol, I shop for the women who can't get any transport and they do various things for me. One of them minds the kids sometimes and another one comes over and helps me with the children's sewing and they take it turn about to come in on the truck and help."

"You seem to be on quite a good wicket."

Nolly laughed lazily. "It suits us all."

Deb stirred uneasily. She really ought to tell Nolly that she wasn't going to stay over the weekend, but the words wouldn't come. She knew how Nolly woud take it, how she'd look up astonished and open her eyes incredulously. "But why?" she would say; or "Lu *will* be disappointed." Deb found herself wishing they could have a dingdong row like they used to have when they were kids and it would all blow over and each would go her own way. But Nolly, the mother of a family, would never be drawn into a proper row. She always manages to put me in the wrong, Deb thought resentfully... Heavens, how tired I am... And anyway, whatever happens, I'm not going to let this sentimental Garden of Eden stuff get hold of me. I'm going out with Angus tomorrow even if the skies fall.

Nolly, pursuing her own thoughts, added the final touch to Deb's guilt. "Such luck. I've managed to get a woman to come and do the washing the fortnight I'll be in hospital. She'll come on the first Monday. There shouldn't be any hitch. I'm booked in on the twentieth — that's three weeks today — and I've always been pretty well on the date before."

Deb deliberately misunderstood. "That's fine. It'll make things a lot easier. Tom's so good with the kids and he's pretty handy in the kitchen. You really won't have anything on your mind."

"Tom? Of course he's good... But what's that got to do with it?" Nolly looked across at Deb with a puzzled frown.

"Well...I...what I mean is...you can leave the house with a much easier mind." Deb kept her face turned away.

"Deb..." Nolly's voice was bewildered. "Deb, what are you trying to get at?"

"What do you mean — get at?"

"Are you trying to tell me you're not coming here while I'm in hospital?"

Deb spoke with a voice of elaborate forbearance, but her hands were shaking. "My dear, I thought I made it quite clear this afternoon that I could not get off, even for Jack's leave." She was glad Nolly could not see her face.

"But I thought you meant you couldn't get the whole twenty-eight days off...and it was only the first fortnight at the Vineyard you were talking about." Nolly's voice caught, she swallowed and went on: "I was thinking it was pretty decent of you to make it the last fortnight, but I knew from what Jack said in Tom's letter that it'd be all right with him."

"I think at least I might have been consulted. Jack never wrote a word to me about it." Deb made a show of indignation.

"But of course he didn't think there was any need. Neither did I. I just took it for granted."

"I think there's been rather a lot taken for granted between Jack and you folk."

"But you always said you'd come when I had this baby. Right back when I first knew. And Tom simply can't get off from his job, there's no one to take his place."

"Well, I'm in the same boat," Deb heard her own voice hard and steady and hated herself and Nolly and the whole humiliating situation. "But my job's not important, I suppose?"

"My children are important, that's what I know," Nolly's eyes flashed.

"You wouldn't think so, the rate at which you have them," Deb flared back.

"So long as we don't ask you to help us keep them, that's our business. And anyway, you and Jack had none of this nonsense about only children until he got that car salesman's job and you both got too big for your boots. The war's brought him back to earth, and if you're not going to make a mess of things you'll have to come back too."

Deb ignored the attempt to carry the quarrel on to her own ground. "If you go on having babies at this rate, what chances will you be able to give them?"

"We give our children love and happiness, and that's more than you do for Lu."

"I do wish you wouldn't call her Lu. Her name's Luen."

"I thought it was Araluen."

"I think it's hateful of you to speak like that when you know exactly why I had to let her come here...and I pay for her, don't I?"

"Yes, you pay for what she eats — but what about fares and school books and other expenses? I don't get those out of fifteen shillings a week, and I wouldn't have Lu feel different from my own kids for anything."

"If she's such a burden on you, perhaps I'd better take her away then, or," Deb added hastily, "perhaps you'd let me have an account for her full expenses, and tell me what you really want for her board."

"Oh, get off your high horse! Though, as a matter of fact, that is one of the things Tom asked me to speak to you about this weekend."

Deb controlled herself with an effort. "I'm sorry, Nolly. You've been awfully good to Luen and I do appreciate it. It's been a hectic week and I'm a bit nervy, that's the trouble."

Nolly capitulated, she never could keep up a row. "We're both on edge, I know. I'm sorry too...but," she persisted, "that doesn't solve the problem of what's going to happen when I'm in hospital. And I'm simply not going to have Tom worried any more than he is. Honestly, Deb, I don't know what's come over you lately. You don't seem to care about any of us any more — not even Jack or Luen."

Before Deb could reply the children were back on the veranda clamouring for their story and she was immediately occupied in keeping her feet out of the way of the three boys jostling on the end of the bed while Luen squeezed in between her and the wall. Nolly helped them all to get settled.

"Ready, my little gumnuts?" Nolly asked.

There was a chorus of "Yes."

"Once upon a time a sapling grew in a spotted gum forest by the sea. He was a fine little tree with a straight, slim trunk and leafy branches that ended in a topknot of red tips. And he was just about as tall as Durras and Luen put together.

"Now, one hot summer day there was a rustle in the forest and the sound of dry leaves crackling and twigs snapping, and another sound, a strange one that none of the trees had ever heard before. It wasn't the rabbits nickering or the mother wallabies talking to their babies, though sometimes it sounded rather like them. And it sounded just a little bit like the tiny birds twittering at dawn, only it wasn't dawn. And it wasn't the galahs screeching in the tree tops, or the crows cawing, or the currawongs calling, or the bower birds clearing their throats, or the magpies warbling, though every now and then the little tree thought it was just a bit like all of them. And he was so curious that he strained his leaves to listen and his slim trunk bent over so far that his roots began to complain.

"All the time, the sounds were coming nearer and nearer, and the little tree was getting more and more curious, until at last, just when his roots were quite sure that if he bent over any farther they couldn't hold on to the dry earth another minute, he shot straight up again with a jerk, because what do you think he saw?"

"*Two strange animals walking through the forest!*" all the children shouted together.

"And what strange animals they were! They stood up straight and they had two legs like a kangaroo, but..."

"— *they didn't hop!*" chanted the children.

"— and they had fur on their heads, but..."

"— *none on their faces!*" the children chorused.

"— and a strange sort of bark wrapped round their middles that the little tree —"

"— *had never seen before!*" the children finished triumphantly.

"'Look!' said the tall one, 'this is a fine little tree,' and she pointed to the sapling. 'Look at his straight, smooth trunk and his fine topknot of leaves.'"

"And then, of course, the little tree knew what the strange sounds were. They were the noises these new animals made when they talked to each other. And he found out, too, that the tall one was called Deb and the short one was Nolly.

"'Yes,' said Nolly, 'he is a beauty. Just right for our Christmas tree.'

"The little tree didn't know anything about Christmas, but he was quite sure it must be nice when they admired him so much.

"Then Deb took some great golden oranges and tied them to the branches, and Nolly took some beautiful rosy apples that she'd polished till they shone, and she tied them among the pointed green leaves. And just as soon as they were all hanging on the tree, the sun touched the young red gum tips with his golden fingers and turned the little tree into..."

"— *a fairy tree!*" sang the children.

"And he turned the oranges and apples into..."

"— *gold and rubies!*" they finished.

"Then Deb and Nolly called very loudly down to the sea...."

"*Coo-ee! Coo-ee! Ja-ack! To-om!*" the children called between cupped hands.

"In no time Jack and Tom came up from the beach with their fishing lines and a basket of beautiful silver fish, and they admired the little tree too and they joined hands round the tree with Deb and Nolly and they all sang a Christmas song."

Nolly looked around at the excited faces. "Now, little gumnuts, are you all ready?" She started to sing and the four children joined in:

> *A little gum tree grew straight and strong,*
> *Straight and strong, straight and strong,*
> *A little gum tree grew straight and strong*
> *On Christmas Day in the morning.*
>
> *And what do you think was on that tree?*
> *On that tree, on that tree?*

And what do you think was on that tree
On Christmas Day in the morning?

Gold and rubies were on that tree,
And Christmas presents for Daddy and me
Five tiny babies too little to see,
On Christmas Day in the morning.

One golden orange for baby Lu,
An apple for Durras of ruby hue,
Andrew and Jack and wee Deb too,
On Christmas Day in the morning.

Luen broke in almost before the last word had been sung. "But Auntie Nolly, what about the new baby?"

Durras dismissed the interruption: "Mummy will just make up a new verse. Now finish the story," he commanded.

"Well, there's not much more, is there? Only that the great big rubies and the golden balls shone in the sunlight all through the day and the little tree grew prouder and happier every time one of the creatures told the others how lovely he was. But when evening came, then everything was changed.

"When the sun went down behind the forest he took his magic with him. And the young leaves of the little tree turned back from crimson jewels into red gum tips again, and the rubies became shining, rosy apples, and the golden balls were oranges once more. Then they each took an apple or an orange from the tree and ate it, and the others they put away carefully in case possums should come out for a midnight feast. And when they had eaten the fruit, they all laughed and put the pips in the ground and told them to grow into apple and orange trees for the little girls and boys who were hiding among the leaves of the Christmas tree. And they promised the little tree that if he grew straight and strong, one day, when all the children had been born, they would bring them back and once more turn him into..."

"— *a magic Christmas tree!*" the children finished the story with ringing voices.

"But, Mummy, you haven't kept your promise to the little tree, yet," Andrew said solemnly.

"Silly," Durras told him, "we can't go till Mummy's got all the children."

"Can we go next Christmas when we've got the new baby?" Jack begged.

"My Mummy might have another little baby too," Luen said hopefully. "Mightn't you, Mummy?"

"She might too," Nolly laughed. "You never can tell. Now off you go to bed, the whole lot of you. And one sunny day we'll all go down to the spotted gum forest and find our magic Christmas tree."

A motor horn played a familiar signal and Guinea put her head out of the dormer window of her attic room and whistled a reply. In the street light she could see Major Alfrickson standing on the edge of the footpath.

"Can I come on up? I've got something for you," he called.

"Sure. So long as it's not alive." It'd be safe enough with the door open and her dressed up like a sore thumb; even an old wolf like Alfalfa would hesitate before he ruined a frock like this.

Major Alfrickson crossed the footpath and came panting up the narrow flight of stairs to Guinea's room. He put down a duffle bag with a gasp, and collapsed into the only comfortable chair. "Say, Guin, why don't you live in a place with an elevator?"

"Garn. This house is a hundred years old."

"Then it's time they gave it back to the Abos." He spread himself more comfortably. "Say, you look swell. Turn round. Honey, you look just like an angel dropped down from heaven. Come over here and sit on my knee for a minute. I want to get my arms around you and I'm too darned blown to move."

"The heck I will," Guinea retorted unsympathetically. "You're getting fat."

Alfalfa patted his waistline mournfully. "You've got something there, honey. It's the good living down in Melbourne that's done it. Boy, do those guys at the base live high?"

"What have you been doing? Shiny-bumming?"

"I've been putting in a goddamned lot of overtime. We had to work practically every afternoon getting the handouts ready for the press... communiqués from HQ and all the rest of it. You know the sort of thing."

"Oh sure, I know the sort of thing. Quote: 'Americans winning the war from the South Pole to Tokyo. Our allies also ran.' Unquote."

"Hey, Guin, that's not fair. We do at least admit you Aussies can fight — sometimes. But we got to keep the corn belt back home interested in this war."

"Maybe. And I don't mind admitting you saved our skins when the Nips were on our doorstep, and Churchill gave us away, but I take a dim view when you claim you won the Battle of the Boyne and Waterloo as well."

"Come off it, Guin. Gimme a kiss, anyway."

"So long as you don't disturb a hair of my head," Guinea warned him, bending down and brushing a kiss across his cheek.

"You smell like new-mown hay," he murmured, his arms closing round her waist.

"Lay off, you'll ruin my dress." Guinea pushed him firmly in the chest and the sank back in the chair.

"Gosh," he exclaimed, "you've got a hand like Joe Louis."

"And don't you forget it."

"OK then, for the time being. I hope you don't intend to wear that fancy dress all night." He kissed her fingers sentimentally.

She flipped her hand away and tweaked his ear. "What have you got in the bag? A body?"

"Pass it over here and I'll show you."

She picked up the bag and swung it on to his knees. "Jeepers, it's heavy enough."

He opened it, rummaged inside and took out two cartons of Chesterfields. "Thought you might like these."

"Thanks. They're always welcome." She craned her neck with undisguised curiosity to see what else was in the bag. He took out shaving gear and toothbrush. She looked at them suspiciously.

"Are you spending the night at Who's Who?"

"Well, you never know." Alfalfa looked up at her and grinned.

"No, you don't, do you? What's that?"

He took out two bottles of whisky.

"Well, they'll keep you warm wherever you are."

"They nearly gave me apoplexy. I paid five pounds a bottle to that gangster taxi driver who delivers the 'milk' at our flats. That comes of not getting in in time to pick up my quota.''

''You're a mug. I could've got them a lot cheaper from Elvira, if I'd known you wanted them, but you guys always seem to have it laid on.''

''Not real Scotch, you couldn't.''

She unscrewed the cap and smelled it. ''Phuff! Real Scotch! You could run a jeep on it. Elvira'd sell you that brand of Scotch for three quid. She pays five bob an empty Scotch bottle and her husband mixes the hooch. Got anything else?''

He drew out a tiny mantel wireless. ''Thought you might like this to remind you of your old Alfalfa when I'm gone.''

''You're a sport, Alfie,'' she said, slipping her arm round his neck. She dropped a kiss on his forehead where the hair was receding, and evaded his grasp before he could draw her onto his knee.

The sound of the horn rose again. ''We'd better get going,'' she said, picking up her evening bag and deftly sliding past him to the door. ''Pack up your nightshirt and come along. I don't want to miss any of the fun.''

''Gee, Guin,'' he said plaintively, ''you're hard on a guy. Here I've spent all the leaves I could in Sydney taking you round and now you're going to let me go back to the States without so much as a real cuddle.''

''Petty-pie,'' she murmured, blowing him a kiss, ''don't you know I'm a good girl? My mother warned me never to sleep with strange men.''

''A nice future for a guy,'' he mourned, ''and me with a wife that doesn't understand me.''

''Well, I do, honey bear. So let's get crackin'.''

He dropped the shaving gear back into the duffle bag with a hollow sigh and joined her on the landing.

''Say, did you ever lose any of your boyfriends on these stairs?'' he asked, looking down the steep, narrow flight.

''Plenty. They take 'em away with the garbage.''

''I don't favour the ashcan as my destination.''

''Well, that depends on you.''

They came out into the quiet street. ''Not a military car,'' said Guinea, "my mother warned me against them, too."

"It's strictly illegal," Alfalfa laughed, "but Byron and I will be on our way before these guys at base get round to courtmartialling us. This is Byron, Guinea. Colonel Maddocks. We come from the same home town. Bit of luck, he just flew in from the north this morning after I rang you. He was going to join us, but when we went to pick up his girlfriend she's got ptomaine from some prawns she ate last night and can't lift her head off the pillow."

"Too bad. I could have got someone for him, if I'd known!"

Guinea stood beside the car, white and ethereal in the street light.

Colonel Maddocks caught his breath. "If that someone would be like you I'd have been a happy man. It's pretty dull to spend your first night back in civilisation alone."

Guinea liked his lined face, yellow from atabrine, and the slow drawl of his voice. "Why don't you come with us then? We're sure to pick up a partner for you." Gosh, she suddenly thought, maybe we won't. Who's Who isn't like the Frat or the Coconut Grove.

"If Lew doesn't mind me tagging along, I'd be happy just to look on."

"Sure," said Major Alfrickson with false heartiness, "though I'm afraid there won't be much fun in it for you, By," he added warningly. He opened the back of the car and Guinea spread her wide skirts over the seat. "You'll have to sit in front with the Colonel, Alfalfa. I can't have my dress spoiled."

"I don't blame you, it's poetic," Colonel Maddocks remarked, turning the car in the narrow street. "Do you know, I have an intuition that I'm going to enjoy this night."

Major Alfrickson did not respond.

The best orchestra in Sydney — so the publicity said — had just finished the second dance, when Guinea and her two escorts burst on the OBNOs Ball like the Aurora Australis. Mrs D'Arcy-Twyning watched them go slowly across the empty floor to a position second only to those occupied by the official table and the family party of Mr Angus McFarland. She looked at her booking plan to confirm what she had seen. "Colonel Sorenson." That was right. She had placed them there herself. But neither of the men was Colonel Sorenson — though one was certainly a colonel. And the girl with them? Who was she? No! It couldn't be that brazen chit from the Marie Antoinette. Just a resemblance, some trick of the light. But not. . . never. . . that Malone girl, who only that very morning had shampooed her hair.

She glanced at Denise, whose eyes were lifted adoringly to Commander Ermington's bearded face. Mrs D'Arcy-Twyning murmured an excuse to her partner, so happily absorbed in his glass that he did not notice her going, and moved along to Denise.

"I don't want to spoil the lovely talk you and the commander are having, darling, but if he will excuse you for just one little minute. . ."

Denise squirmed under the firm grasp of her mother's fingers, pouted prettily and rose, touching the commander's hand lightly as though to confirm a pact. "Just a teeny-weeny minute, darling."

"Tickety-boo, my sweet."

Mrs D'Arcy-Twyning drew Denise aside and bent to whisper to the commander: "Doesn't my little Denny look a dream tonight?"

"Ineffable," he agreed, with his eyes glued on Guinea.

She hissed in Denise's ear: "Look over there beside the McFarland's table. . .keep smiling." They both beamed with deceptive sweetness. "Do you see what I see?"

"Hell! It's that bitch from the Marie Antoinette."

"That's what I thought. I'll see Mrs Molesworth. I'll have her thrown out."

Denise clawed at her arm. "Don't be a fool. You can't do anything. That's Colonel Maddocks she's with. Why, it's practically diplomatic."

"Colonel Maddocks? Oh, is that who it is?"

Denise's china-doll face looked thunderous. "Oh, Mummy," she wailed, "that's just the kind of dress I wanted for my wedding." She bit back an oath as her mother pinched her sharply. "Go back to Derek. She won't get away with it, don't you fret."

Angus McFarland's party gazed across the official table at the new arrivals. "Oh, Ian, look," Olive touched her husband's arm. "That's the man we saw in the newsreel the other day with General MacArthur. Colonel Someone-or-other."

"Maddocks," Angus said. "Byron Maddocks. He was with the Americans in France in the last war. General Staff."

"Really, he doesn't look old enough, does he?" Helen's eyes watched the party wistfully. "Did you know him, Uncle Angus?"

"Yes, yes," he dismissed her shortly.

Helen sighed. "What a pretty girl with him."

"Looks young enough to be his daughter," Ian said disapprovingly.

"We're behind the times, old man," Virginia's husband, Lawrence, put in laughing.

"And a good thing too." His wife gave him a brief, intimate smile. "I'd like to know how you'd get on running round night after night at the pace these young things go."

"Doesn't go with a job like yours or mine," Ian laughed across at Lawrence good-humouredly. "Leave the youngsters to the fellows with soft jobs. General Staff, eh, Angus?"

Angus ignored the remark. Although Deborah was certainly not a youngster like this girl, Ian's remark was in extremely bad taste.

"Her face is very familiar," Olive persisted. "Do you know who she is, Angus?"

"I haven't the faintest idea."

Helen looked across the room at Guinea. I'm sure I know her, she thought, then her face lit up. "Why, Mum, no wonder her face is familiar. That's the girl they call Guinea from the Marie Antoinette."

Angus frowned. "From the Marie Antoinette? Oh, nonsense!"

"But it is. I'd know her anywhere. She shampooed my

hair only this morning."

Olive stared. "You're right, Helen. 'Malone', I think her name is. What a difference clothes make! I've always thought she was attractive, but tonight she looks a real beauty."

"Doesn't she?" Helen's eyes were shining. "Oh, Uncle Angus, do ask them over, since you know Colonel Maddocks. I've never seen anyone lovelier in my life." She smiled as Guinea looked over towards their table.

"I'll do nothing of the sort." Angus's voice was harsh and his face dark with anger.

Helen threw him a rebellious glance but was silent. It was ridiculous the way you were expected to kowtow to Uncle Angus. You'd think he was God. Anyway, he took that pretty masseuse from the salon out, didn't he, so what difference was there in asking Guinea Malone over to meet them? At least they'd meet someone bright! The least he could have done was to ask someone young for her, instead of making her waste an evening like this. She'd have gone to the Anzac Buffet with Susan again only for her mother saying it wasn't fair to Uncle Angus after he'd gone to the trouble of arranging the party for them. Party! It wasn't her idea of a party to be tied up all evening with someone who wasn't only her uncle but older than Dad. If only she could have gone to the buffet... She had a feeling of desperation at the thought that perhaps she would never meet Alec again even if she did go back. But she must try... she would ask Susan to take her again. Yes, that's what she'd do and next time she'd go, whatever arrangements Uncle Angus had made for her.

Helen rested her tanned young face on hands as hard as her father's and watched Guinea. It would be lovely to look like that, she thought with a pang, and have all those marvellous men clustering round. Perhaps after the war. ...Don't be silly, Helen, she told herself. It isn't the war that made you a social flop and you know it. You also know perfectly well that you'd rather be Dad's right-hand man at home than the belle of all the balls going. But all the same it made you feel rather out of it in Sydney. Still, with young Angus a POW in Malaya and young Ian dead, the least she could do was to stop grizzling. Angus asked her to dance. Oh dear, she thought helplessly, he always makes me nervous, I feel positively bumble-footed! She cast a despairing glance at her mother, who smiled back encouragingly.

It was astonishing what Helen's new hairstyle did for her, Olive thought. She looked young and attractive in a boyish sort of way. . . and her hair was really pretty with all those soft curls clustering close to her head. It was a pity Angus hadn't thought to ask a young partner for her.

Virginia and her husband got up to dance.

Olive watched Helen unhappily, as Angus pushed her resolutely before him. "I wonder if we're being quite fair to Helen, Ian," she murmured. "She's twenty-three now and she's missed so much. She never even had a coming-out party because of the news about young Ian. And she really is getting so shy and difficult. I simply had to make her come tonight. She wanted to go off to the Anzac Buffet again with Susan. Really, she's getting that way she thinks of nothing but work."

"Nonsense," her husband growled defensively, wishing he could get out of his damned stiff shirt. "She's worth a dozen of any woman here and she does the work of two men."

Olive sighed. Somehow, for a girl of twenty-three, doing the work of two men did not seem good enough.

Angus looked more intently at Colonel Maddocks's partner. It couldn't be the Guinea Malone that Deborah had spoken about. Deborah always said she was handsome in an obvious sort of way, but dreadfully common. This girl in white, smiling so demurely at Maddocks, might be out at her first ball. She was a beauty all right, but he couldn't see Maddocks taking up with a girl from a beauty salon. No sooner had the thought crossed his mind than he was jerked to a stop. They might say the same of him. Deborah worked in a beauty salon, after all. Yes, but that was different. Deborah didn't belong among that class of girl, hers was just a war job. . . semimedical too. After all, she was a trained masseuse, she might have been working in a hospital. No! that girl couldn't be from the Marie Antoinette. Deborah had told him it was one of the strictest rules of the hotel that no member of the staff was allowed to enter Who's Who as a guest.

Helen danced awkwardly. Angus did not seem to notice it. He danced with authority. Relax, she told herself, you got on all right last night when you relaxed and didn't worry about your feet. Deliberately, she tried to forget that she was dancing with her supercilious and rather frightening uncle and let her mind go back to Alec. Angus was occupied with his own thoughts and as they circled the room together in silence Helen was at the buffet again. Her strong fingers were curved round Alec's stiff ones and she was trying to put him at his ease. Susan had told her last night that he never talked about the war or how he got wounded, but a pal of his said he'd had his hand nearly cut in half by a shell splinter in Syria and the regimental doctor had performed a miracle, and he was lucky to have a hand at all, if he'd only realise it instead of being so damn sensitive... Then she had to go and put her foot in it like a clumsy fool. Oh, would she never have the social poise to do and say the right things the way other girls did naturally? She hadn't minded holding his hand; it didn't give her any feeling of repulsion, only a longing to make up to him for it. But running away like that... Perhaps he thought she couldn't bear to go on holding his poor hand... Oh, how could she have been so gauche? She wished she could see him again and they could dance just once more so that he'd know it wasn't his hand... She must, she simply must go to the buffet again.

Olive watched Angus and Helen dance by, both of them with their eyes fixed on something far away. She turned to her husband. "What exactly did Angus say to you about Burramaronga this morning?"

"He said that as he was going to get married he'd probably want to open up the old home."

"But didn't he say anything about young Angus? After all, it's always been understood that it would go to him after all the work he's put into the property. If it hadn't been like that, he'd have started out on a place of his own long ago."

"Angus didn't even mention his name till I put it to him straight out, and then he had the bloody hide to tell me that of course he'd keep him on as manager when he came back from the war."

"But...about afterwards. After all, Angus is not a young man, and he can't live for ever."

"My dear, the fact of it is, he's so completely infatuated with the woman that he's lost all sense of proportion."

"Helen's seen her a couple of times in the Marie Antoinette and says she's very attractive and quite young."

"Young enough to have a pack of kids," Ian said glumly. "Come on, we'd better dance, I suppose. Damn this collar."

It was not until the violins led the orchestra softly into "Pale Frangipani" and the lights dimmed in sympathy with the romance of a tropic night that Thelma Molesworth, on re-entering Who's Who realised that something had occurred compared with which the breaking of all the Ten Commandments was practically negligible. A member of the hotel staff had dared to crash Who's Who! She thought at first it was a delusion, the result of overwork and worry, but the gasps of admiration that went up from all round the room as the spotlight focused on the first couple on the floor, made her realise that it was only too horribly real. She sent a waiter for the manager.

For a moment, Guinea and Byron had the floor to themselves. The colonel, tall and saturnine, his tunic beflagged like a ferryboat on Regatta Day, had learnt more than the military arts in his West Point days, and the social campaigns between two wars had brought his dancing to perfection. Guinea, magically etherealised, moved with the effortless grace bestowed by years of practice at the Trocadero and Coconut Grove. She seemed to float in his arms, so perfectly they moved in unison.

"It's Colonel Byron Maddocks," Thelma heard someone near her whisper in awed tones.

"Not *the* Maddocks?"

"Yes, he's been up with MacArthur. Who's that with him?"

"Never saw her in my life before. Probably someone from the American Legation."

"Whew! What a beauty!"

The spotlight held Guinea and Byron in an enchanted aura while they circled the floor. The man at the switch had a sense of drama and he dimmed the wall lights still further, until there seemed only the two dancers in all the world.

The saxophone player put down his instrument and sang as they passed the platform. "Your touch is music — all delight. I scatter stars around your feet..." And it was so romantic that every woman there wished she was in Guinea's place. The rhythm grew faster, her stiff skirt went out in a great arc, her flying hair was like a golden banner in the spotlight, with Alfalfa's orchids a fairy crown; her bright young face was uplifted with eyes ashine, lips half-parted in a smile... Oh yes, it was high romance...fair women and brave men...

With perfect timing, Colonel Maddocks swung her out of the spotlight to their table. The lights went up in a burst of clapping.

"I think that rates a drink," the colonel said, pouring her a stiff whisky and himself a stiffer one.

Alfalfa filled up her glass with ginger ale. "Gosh, Guinea," he said, "I wouldn't have known you. You looked like an angel."

Guinea turned on him a wide-eyed smile of tremulous innocence. Major Alfrickson spilled his whisky in surprise. She lifted her glass with slow grace, saw out of the corner of her eye that Colonel Maddocks was being greeted by several new male arrivals, put her glass to her lips and winked: "Here's the skin off your nose, honey bear!"

It might have been Colonel Maddocks's military reputation, or the fact that he had been the hero of two of the most spectacular divorces outside Hollywood, or merely the repertoire of off-colour jokes that Major Alfrickson was reputed to possess that brought a swarm of high-ranking servicemen to their table claiming acquaintance, however brief. But when Alfalfa managed to secure Guinea at last for the sixth dance, he was vehement and frank in his commentary on the loyalty of brother officers and the fraternity of the Allied forces.

"You ought to be grateful, Alfalfa," Guinea reproved

him. "If you'd had me on your own all night, you'd have been just a wornout old wolf before the show was over."

"I'll hand it to you kid," he said generously, "you sure done 'em in the eye. They all seem to think you're a debutante let out of the convent for your first party with your dear old Uncle Lew. It's almost worth having to queue up for you to see their faces." He beamed at her with fatuous pride.

"Nerts," said Guinea, "I wouldn't trust any of that bunch as far as I could kick 'em."

Alfalfa felt a sudden pang. I'd marry the girl, damme if I wouldn't — if I wasn't already married, he thought. He breathed whisky fumes close to her ear. "Baby," he said, "I'll miss you something awful back in the States and I'm going to miss you something awful tonight."

"I owe this to you, Snugglepot."

Alfalfa's mind reverted hopefully to the shaving gear and his grip tightened.

When they returned to their table, Commander Derek Ermington, RN, was there, rivalling the colonel in braided lustre and beribboned glory. They had already cemented Anglo-American relations over a drink and were now happily saving Australia for democracy by shooting all strikers and proclaiming martial law.

The commander acknowledged his introduction with a formality Guinea felt almost called for a curtsy. Gawd, she said to herself, I wonder how D.D.T. lives up to that? But, to the commander, she only smiled a deprecatory smile and, remembering Val's advice, kept her mouth shut. The English weren't like the Yanks. They'd pick her accent in one go.

A princess from a fairy tale could not have sunk with more exquisite grace to the chair the commander held for her, nor turned upon him a glance more virginal. It brought blasé photographers in a rush across the floor. It halted Alfalfa in the act of pouring her another whisky. It brought Colonel Maddocks to her side, determined that no British straight-striper was going to come horning in where he himself had so successfully poached. They made a perfect foil for her, the three men rivalling each other in the splendour of their service plumage.

"Just hold it one moment, madam... Back a little, sir."

Alfalfa's blood pressure rose, but he backed. Guinea smiled at the colonel. A flash!

Commander Derek Ermington bent to whisper to her, she lifted a childlike, serious face to his. Another flash!

Mrs D'Arcy-Twyning piloted Denise to the ladies' room. L. F. hissed cutting reproaches in Thelma's ear. She left to loosen her corsets, she could bear no more.

The orchestra sobbed out the opening bars of a Viennese waltz and Guinea rose to dance with the commander.

Watching the girls dress up for the evening, Monnie thought, was like pressing her face to a shop window when she was a child, longing for the things she couldn't have. She had ironed their frocks for them and they pirouetted round the lounge when they put them on and said she was a prefect lady's maid. She helped Betty to roll her brassy hair into a high pompadour and tucked in a velvet bow that matched the green bows on her floral frock. She combed the stiff bob out on Shirley's shoulders, gently smoothing out the tangles and explained how she'd learnt about hairdressing from Peg. "Gee, kid, y're a wonder. When my ship comes in you can come and valet me." She rolled Fay's thick copper hair round her fingers and pinned a diamanté clip in the upswept curls, watching Fay's thin mouth curve delightedly at her reflection in the mirror.

"We'll see you have a whacko time at Grace's party for all you've done." Betty giggled as she made the promise.

"You won't be lonely till we come back, will you?" Shirley asked. "There's tons of mags to read and maybe you'd better have a bit of a sleep. You had a late night last night — for you."

"Oh no," Monnie assured her, "I won't be lonely. As a matter of fact," she added, "I thought, as soon as you were gone, I'd run over to Peg's place and tell her I'll be going out home with her tomorrow. You see, it's Dad's birthday."

"Peg?" Shirley frowned. "But you won't catch her now. She'll have gone out."

"Then I'll just leave a note for her telling her what time I'll be there in the morning so she doesn't go home without me."

"Oh!" Shirley looked at Fay questioningly.

Fay shrugged her shoulders. "It's your pigeon, Shirl."

"Listen, kid," Shirley said impulsively, "how'd you like to come along to the Coconut Grove with us tonight?"

"Tonight?" Monnie was incredulous.

"Sure. Tonight. Seems a damn shame leaving you here all on your lonesome while we're out having fun, doesn't it, girls?''

"That's right!" Betty jitterbugged into the lounge. "What's life on your lonesome?''

Fay was stubborn. "I don't like the idea of taking her with us at all. Grace said to bring her to the party after we came back.''

"Oh, hell, Fay, don't be such a sourpuss. You had plenty of fun yourself. Besides, it'll put her in the mood, whereas if she goes round — to her sister's..."

"I could wait here just as well till you come back if you think there wouldn't be a partner for me," Monnie said diffidently, not wanting them to think she was taking advantage of Shirley's generous impulse.

Betty hooted. "Don't worry about partners. There'll be no trouble finding a partner for you, kid. You'll be lucky if you don't have to beat 'em off with a fly swat.''

"I'll ask Grace," Shirley said suddenly and ran out and down the stairs.

Monnie shivered with excitement while she listened for her return. Grace came back with her, smiling and gracious, a froth of clothes over her arm.

"Of course you should go with the girls, darling. I think it's a splendid idea," she said, warmly patting Monnie's check. "I don't want you to get lonely waiting for the party to begin. And I've got just the things for you to wear — they belong to my little girl.''

Monnie protested half-heartedly. Grace squeezed her shoulder. "Oh, darling, you mustn't rob me of the pleasure of seeing just how pretty you can look. And these undies are hers too.''

She handed Monnie a pair of embroidered pink silk scanties and a matching brassière. She held up a pale-blue silk frock and Monnie slipped her arms into the tiny puffed sleeves. Grace zippered it from hem to neck and patted the little flat collar into place while Monnie looked at herself in the mirror. Why, she thought, with a touch of disappointment, it was the kind of frock Mum would have picked for her, it was so plain and done right up to the neck.

"There," Grace said, "don't you look sweet?" She dusted Monnie's face with powder. "What a lovely, fine skin you have, and such a pretty mouth. Just a little lipstick and a touch of perfume." She held the stopper of a small flask to Monnie's nose. "Isn't that lovely?"

"Oh, wonderful."

"It's something very special. Have you ever heard of Chanel 5?"

"No."

"I don't wonder. It's very rare nowadays and frightfully expensive. This flask cost twenty pounds. If you're a good girl you might be able to buy it for yourself some day." She dabbed the stopper behind Monnie's ears. "Now you smell just as sweet as you look."

"Doesn't she look a honey?" Shirley exclaimed.

"Just the cutest doll," Betty agreed, looking up from fastening a gold chain round her ankle. "But those shoes won't take her far."

"Have you got anything suitable?" Grace asked.

Shirley dragged out a pile of shoes. "There's a pair of blue sandals here that ought to fit her. They pinch my little toe. I never could wear 'em."

Monnie slipped on the high-heeled, ankle-strap sandals. They were a bit loose, but she buckled the strap tight and declared them a perfect fit. Grace pinned the frangipani in her hair and stood back to admire her.

"Whacko!" Shirley cried. "Doesn't she look super?"

"Swell," Fay agreed. "Gives her a bit of zip."

"All ready for the kill," Betty laughed.

Grace kissed Monnie affectionately. "You look perfect, darling. Now have a nice time." She turned to the others and there was a different note in her voice. "And don't forget to come back to the party on time."

"I only hope to Christ it'll be OK," Fay snapped with sudden change of mood. "I'm taking no responsibility for her."

"Of course it'll be OK," Shirley snapped back. "You just stick close to me, Mon."

Monnie danced after them down the stairs.

Monnie floated light as air in Calvin's arms. Her head was leaning against his shoulder as they danced, his lips were on her hair and he was singing under his breath. A girl was crooning into the microphone and the world seemed full of music and singing.

She was overwhelmed with wonder that she, Monnie Malone, should be dancing with a "Lootenant" who had a double row of ribbons on his tunic, called her "angel" and sang, as he drew her tightly to him:

> *Pale frangipani fills the air.*
> *Its blossoms star your perfumed hair,*
> *The night is made for you and love. . .*

Calvin bent over and she felt his lips against her eyebrow.

> *Your touch is music — all delight.*
> *I scatter stars around your feet. . .*

he crooned softly, rubbing his cheek against hers.

She had never felt like this before. They were dancing divinely and there was a tingling feeling all through her. She was awfully glad that Calvin hadn't been annoyed with her for refusing to have some whisky. She'd thought at first he was going to be, but then he'd laughed and gone off and got her some Coca-Cola. Now she felt as though she was floating on a cloud, there was a lovely warm feeling in her stomach and she could feel her cheeks glowing. Calvin snuggled her close to him, his lips nuzzling her ear. Oh, this was paradise! She wasn't even worrying any more that the girls didn't seem to know the men they were dancing with; if they were friends of Calvin's, it must be all right.

When the music stopped, it was like being wrenched out of a dream. She stood rocking unsteadily. Calvin tightened his grip around her waist. "You're so sweet," he whispered.

She dropped her eyes under his gaze. He gave a funny

little laugh. "I just can't wait to tell you how sweet you really are."

When they got back to their table, the others were already there. Shirley looked up rather crossly. "We've been waiting for you two. We're moving on to the party now."

"OK by you, Calv?" Hank inquired.

"If I can bring my Irish rose with me, anything's OK. How about it, honey-babe?" He squeezed her waist and she slid out of his grasp giggling.

"You needn't worry about that," Fay said. "She's coming along all right."

"Just one more for the road," Jules insisted heartily. "Everybody fixed?"

"Here's looking up your kilt," Betty called.

Monnie lifted her glass which someone had filled up for her again and clicked it against Calvin's. She threw back her head and tried to drink as the others did, with long smooth swallows, but she choked on the first mouthful and they laughed at her as Hank and Calvin patted her back. Jiminy! This time her drink tasted horrible; the coke must have gone flat. She didn't like to say anything when they'd been so sweet getting it for her specially, because she said she didn't drink. When she stopped coughing and Calvin had wiped her eyes tenderly, she finished the drink in little difficult sips, puffing clumsily at the cigarette he lit for her between his own lips.

She wished that they weren't going to leave the Coconut Grove, it was more wonderful than anything she had ever imagined and she wanted nothing better than to go floating round the floor for ever and ever with Calvin holding her closely and whispering lovely things to her.

But when the glasses were empty, Fay and Shirley got up purposefully and Jules pulled Betty to her feet. She did not want to leave either and began to protest till Shirley dug her sharp heel into her instep.

Monnie floated to the door with Calvin's arm tightly round her waist. She had not remembered that the broad steps were so high and, as the cool air hit her face, the footpath went up and down like a wave and she rocked on her unaccustomed high heels. Her head was whirling. "Gee, I feel giddy." she giggled.

Calvin clasped her tighter, Jules let out a bellow of laughter. A taxi drew up at Elmer's hail and they all piled in. Calvin put Monnie in beside the driver and slid in after her, lifting her on to his knee.

"Elm Lane," Fay called, "Kings Cross."

"Yeah! I know," the driver let in the clutch.

Monnie's head dropped against Calvin's shoulder; he cuddled her close, his lips sucking at her throat, his hand cupping her breast. Oh dear, she thought, plucking feebly at his arm, I shouldn't let him, I shouldn't let him.

Shirley was furious. "Damn you, Hank. How much of that Scotch did you put in the kid's coke?"

So that was why the last drink had tasted so horrid. She tried to tell him she was all right, but her tongue was thick. Their voices came to her as though they were wrapped in a fog.

Fay leaned over and put a finger under her chin. "Christ, you're a fine lot of bums, you are! You've just about passed her out on us."

"I'm all right," Monnie mumbled, terrified they'd lock her up in the flat instead of taking her to the party with them, the way they'd locked Betty up last night.

Hank's voice was apologetic. "Aw Jeez, Fay, I just freshened it."

"Bloody fresh is the word. I can just imagine what Grace will say when we take her home like this."

Monnie clung closer to Calvin.

"Don't worry, sister." Calvin squeezed her to him. "You drop us off at our apartment, I'll bring her to."

"OK," Shirley agreed unwillingly, "but don't knock her about."

Calvin directed the driver: "Drop me off at Martini Mansions first." He swivelled round in the seat. "That's a dumb trick, Hank, she's passin' out on me. I ought to give you a sock."

"Keep your shirt on, brother," Elmer smoothed, "if you don't know a pick-me-up, I do."

"Do you know where we can get hold of any of the real stuff?" Jules asked the driver.

"Yeah. Whaddayawant?"

"Scotch."

"No Scotch, but I got some gin in the boot. Five quid a bottle."

"OK. How many've you got?"

"Two."

"That'll be swell."

The taxi turned sharply up a hill, flinging Monnie against Calvin. He kissed the V of her throat and she did not mind. It pulled up in front of a tall modern building. The driver looked at his meter: "Two dollars." Calvin passed him a ten-shilling note.

"Not bad, for a two-bob trip," Betty remarked loudly.

"Shut up," Fay flung at her.

"Jesus," she screeched, "I might as well be dumb!"

"Who said you're not, honey?" Jules slapped her bottom as she got out of the car.

"Step on it," Fay urged Hank, who was at the boot with the driver. "We haven't got all night and we can't keep the party waiting."

"Got a queue lined up, eh?"

"You'll see for yourself. Anyway, we've got to get the kid off our hands one way or another. Grace'll go mad if she sees her like this."

"Aw, she'll be OK with Calv. He's got a couple of kids like her of his own back home. Show you a picture of him with the missus any time."

So Calvin was married! Monnie tried to struggle out of his arms and stand up, but her legs crumpled and he gathered her up again so gently that she forgot to be worried.

"Want a hand?" Hank inquired.

"Nope, kid's light as a feather."

Shirley peered into her face. "Looks bloody crook to me."

Monnie made a tremendous effort to speak. "Mmmmm. all right...mmmmmmmm...allrigh...."

"Just plastered," Calvin said comfortingly. He dropped

a kiss on her nose and turned to Jules: "You take a look and see if all's clear. I don't want nobody after me for chicken-stealing."

Jules beckoned them from the doorway. Monnie had a dazed impression of being carried up wide steps past glass showcases and going up in a lift, then Hank, flinging open the door and saying with a flourish: "Come on, Calv. Lift her over the doorstep." They all laughed loudly at that, and Calvin lowered her gently onto a divan bed. "How do you like our little home sweet home?" Hank was saying to the others.

"It'd do me," Betty went over to the huge windows. "What do they sting you for it?"

"Twenty quid in your money. Ain't that right, Jules?"

"It is seventy-nine dollars if you want it in real money."

"That's more than twenty quid."

"Probably. But your landlords always take ten dollars extra just to be on the right side of the exchange."

"Twenty quid a week! Are you buyin' the joint?"

"Sure," said Jules, "we're goin' to crate it and take it back to the States with us."

Through mist, Monnie saw Fay bending over her. Her face was angry and her voice sharp. "Listen, Monnie, you gotta get back to our flat."

Monnie struggled to sit up, but her head lolled against the pillow.

"She'll be OK after this," Calvin insisted, sitting down beside her and slipping an arm under her shoulders. "Here, drink this up." He held a bitter-tasting drink to her lips and she swallowed it, protesting.

"I don't like the look of her," Shirley's voice was anxious. "At the rate you silly bastards poured hooch into her the kid won't be fit for anything till tomorrow morning. I told you to lay off."

"Well, kid or no kid, we got to get going. Sport'll raise hell if we're not there by eleven." Fay's voice was angry.

"You don't have to worry," Calvin reassured them. "I promise you I'll have her along to the party before you're on your second round. See, the stuff's beginning to work already."

Monnie sat up. For a moment, she saw everything very clearly. Jules was getting ice cubes from the refrigerator and dropping them into the glasses. Hank uncorked a bottle and read the label. "'Pure Jamaica Gin'. Whadderyerknow? Cheap at the price."

"Huh!" Betty scoffed, smelling the liquor, "never been outside the three-mile limit. I know that recipe: metho and water laced with a spot of oil of juniper from the chemist."

"What the hell," Hank shouted recklessly, "it's got a kick in it, hasn't it?"

"Like a mule."

He filled the glasses. "Here's to 'ee!" Shirley cried as they tossed down the drink.

"Now for Christ sake let's get going," Fay went to the door. "And Calvin, mind you bring the kid along to No 78A Elm Lane just as soon as she comes round."

"You can rely on me," Calvin assured her again. "I will be there in an hour. I'll make it snappy."

The voices came to Monnie blurred and far off, the room spun round her, there was a whirring in her ears — and darkness.

SUNDAY

I

Guniea wakened late. The sun was streaming across her bed. She yawned ecstatically. What a gorgeous morning. She threw back the bedclothes and lay there with the sun burning through her pyjamas. This was the kind of day to spend on the beach. She thought regretfully that she'd been a dumb cluck to knock back Byron's idea of a picnic. But it was her father's birthday and in the Malone family, come hell or high water, you wouldn't dream of missing Dad's or Mum's birthday or Christmas, even if General MacArthur asked you out on the loose.

As she sat up, her eyes fell on the mantel wireless Alfalfa had given her. That'd be Dad's birthday present...he'd be thrilled. The memory of the night before came flooding back. Whacko! What a night it'd been! There was the bridal dress hanging from a coat hanger, with moulded bodice and stiffened skirt keeping its shape even while it was hanging up. It looked as though it could hop down and go skipping off into a waltz, headless and legless just as it was.

She had Val to thank for that and even though two quid was an awful lot to fork out for the hire, it'd been more than worth it to see the look on D.D.T.'s face, and old Mole standing there like a stuck pig.

Guinea's little attic room with its sloping, angled ceiling was already hot, and the air was full of the ringing of church bells. They floated high and clear from the ridge of Darlinghurst, and the big bell of St Mary's boomed from the cathedral tower. From the dormer window that looked out over the top of the girls' college and down the steep drop of

Forbes Street to Woolloomooloo, she could see a tangle of masts and giant funnels above the roofs of the wharf sheds. The harbour was dazzling in the sunshine and beyond the shelter of the wooded headland it was whipped by a fiery westerly.

She picked up her watch. Ten o'clock! She'd have to step on it. It was a beaut little watch — diamonds and platinum, must have cost a packet. And just her initials on it and the date. That was like Sherwood. Gosh, she was going to miss him, a really decent bloke he was. If he'd still been here she could have rushed up home and had dinner and torn back on the excuse of work, and they could have had a wow of an afternoon at the beach. He was the kindest guy she'd ever met. Gentle. When he made love to you, you felt like a cross between Betty Grable and the queen. He'd asked her often enough to marry him and he was that damn nice and generous you'd like to have done it just to please him. Had she been a mug to turn him down?

Somehow she just couldn't come at the thought of going off to America and leaving everybody. Besides, what the heck was the use of going ten thousand miles to live in a small town with a chap who wasn't even sure of a job to go back to? Sherwood wasn't the kind to shoot a line and he'd had a damn bad time before he joined up. And Sherwood was no bonehead either. "Listen to me, baby," he'd said the last night when they'd lain close together in that strange quiet mood, half passion, half tenderness, you felt when you slept with a man for the last time before he went back to danger, "this war's only going to be half over when we start plastering the world with Vs for Victory. I don't know so much about you here, but back in the States we've got a hell of a lot of guys who're prepared to give GI Joe the State Building and the Statue of Liberty when he's on his way out to fight the foe, but once the fighting's over and the GI Joes come streaming back, they'll sing a different tune. We don't mind fighting for the American way of life, but there are a lot of guys like me who are going to expect it to be a damn sight better way when we get back home than it was before we left."

She sighed and commonsense came to her rescue again, as it had when she'd said no. If you were going to get tied up among the basic wagers and the dole queues again, you might as well do it in your own country. Now, seeing New York with Byron Maddocks would be a different matter altogether. Glamour with a capital G and luxury, if you were to believe what the papers said. He was the answer to every gold-digger's prayer, maiden or otherwise, and if she was to believe what he'd said in the car on the way home after they'd lost Alfalfa, shaving gear and all, New York was hers for the taking. Mind you, she told herself as she began to sort out her clothes for the day, you had to take everything the Yanks said with a grain of salt. It wasn't that they were liars — at least not any more than other men, or insincere. It was just their way of being nice and friendly.

Holy mackerel! What was she doing mooning around like this? If she didn't get a move on she'd miss the eleven o'clock train and there wasn't another till after dinner. She stowed the watch carefully in a carved cigarette box in the corner of a drawer. Crikey, what a lot of junk was in that box. A couple of rising suns, a gold pin, a tiny marcasite naval crown, half a dozen heavily monogrammed frat rings — she only recognised a couple of them — an embossed silver bracelet.... Now, who the devil had that come from? At the bottom there was a pair of silver RAAF wings, with a pin clumsily soldered on — that had been her first scalp.

To hell with men! She slammed the box to. One of these days she'd dump the whole damn lot into some pop shop. Not Sher's watch, though, that meant something. But if she wore it home Mum would just about read the riot act to her. She could easily pretend she'd bought the radio and apart from a lecture on extravagance she'd get away with it. But let Dad or Mum so much as get a glint of those diamonds, and twenty-two or no twenty-two years old, it'd be paddywhack-the-drumstick for her.

She ran down the stairs, showered in the poky bathroom and rushed back. She slipped into an old frock that wouldn't attract her mother's attention, crammed the family gifts into a string bag, tucked Alfalfa's wireless under her arm, and was off.

As Guinea walked along the barren platform of West Hills station, the westerly hit her face like a blast out of a furnace and the grit oozed into her sandals. "Jeepers," she groaned, "fancy having to walk a mile in a wind like this."

Before she had gone a quarter of the way the string bag was cutting into her fingers and Alfalfa's portable wireless had become a ton weight. She cursed loudly when she found that the sweat from her arm had damped the blue paper it was wrapped in and stained the sleeve of her white suit. Lucky it was three years old. It was more than your life was worth to wear anything new to go home. Mum always acted as though a smart turnout was a sure sign you'd be up the spout next week. She had saving on the brain, Mum had. Jeepers, what was the use of saving, and anyway, what was there to save for nowadays?

Half a mile off she could see the square fibro house set among straggling trees at the top of the hill. Crikey, what a hell of a pull it was, she'd never make it with all this junk. She sat down on a log to empty the pebbles out of her sandals and try to find a better way of carrying the wireless. She moved her string bag to the other hand and rubbed her numb fingers. All she hoped was that the family would appreciate what she'd gone through to get home and bring these damn presents.

The twins, the youngest of the Malone brood, saw her coming and ran whooping down the hill, with their mongrel blue cattle dog yelping beside them. "Gee, Peg," they shouted, still fifty yards away, "what'd jer bring us?"

Guinea put the wireless down and braced herself for the impact. Grimy hands pawed at her and the dog slathered her bare legs with a tongue like wet flannel.

"Lay off, you kids," she commanded, landing a neat kick on Kevin's shin as he grabbed for the string bag, "and carry this wireless carefully or you won't get anything at all."

"What have you got for us?" they persisted.

"Nothing, unless you carry these parcels for me. And keep your noses out of things or you won't even get a peep at them."

They gave in, took the parcels, and started on the last pinch to the top of the hill in an incoherent jumble of questions and conversation, punctuated by Timothy's ecstatic woofs.

Mrs Malone was in the kitchen and the air was full of the heat and smells of cooking. Hell, Guinea thought, fancy a baked dinner on a day like this!

The sweat was running down her mother's face as she closed the oven door and straightened her back. She poked out a hard cheek for Guinea's kiss. "Nice to see yer, Peg. Expected you fer your father's birthday. I got a pair of chooks in the oven he's been fattenin' up for the event."

"Trust Dad to see he gets a proper celebration. I managed to get a bottle of whisky for him at the pub. It's nearly cut me fingers off carrying it."

"That'll be a real treat. Your father hasn't tasted a drop since I dunno when. Here you, Kev, take your fingers out of that basin or I'll tan the hide off of you. And Maura, you go round the side veranda and tell your dad Peg's come, though from the noise you've all been making, he'd have to be deaf not to hear it himself. He's having a lie down."

"Here, take your chocolate with you," Guinea said, handing them a slab each.

"Gee, you're a sport, Peg." They seized the chocolate and tore out of the door.

"How's Dad been?" Guinea asked.

"Not too good. This heat knocks him out and it don't matter what I say, he does too much."

"You're looking a bit peaky yourself, Mum. Why don't you lay off in the weekend instead of frizzling yourself to death over the stove?"

"Now look here, my girl, we've had all that out before. Whenever there's been money in this house to buy a weekend joint, a weekend joint we've had — or poultry as the case may be. Your father wouldn't consider it Sunday without his good hot meal. Neither would I, for that matter." She basted the fowls lovingly.

Maura came through the kitchen door like a willy-willy. "Here's Dad."

"Hullo, my girl."

Guinea felt the familiar stubble of the grey moustache against her cheek. She put her hands on his shoulders. "Let me have a good look at you, you old sinner." She eyed his lined face, bloodless under its tan. "You've been getting a bit of sun, I see?"

"That's right. I'm thinkin' of joining the lifesavers now they're short of men."

"That'll be a thrill for the girls," she laughed, slipping an arm around his waist. "I brought you a bottle of whisky for your birthday."

"Whisky! Well, what do you say to that, Mum! Trust our Peg. A sight for sore eyes, isn't she? Do you know, Peg, you get more like your mother every day, and when I married her she was the prettiest girl this side of the Blue Mountains."

She felt a sudden lump in her throat as she pressed a kiss on his hollow cheek. Gee, it did something to you when you saw Dad like this, and never so much as a squeak out of him. "Look at what else I brought. And here's wishing you many happy returns of the day."

He took the little cream radio in his hands, his eyes bright with excitement. "Dual wave! You don't tell me it's dual wave! Gosh, Peg, I'll get some fun out of this."

"Well now, you sit down and fiddle with your present, Father." Mrs Malone pushed a chair to him and exchanged a warning glance with Guinea.

"Fancy me listenin' to Tokyo, Mum! You know, I never listened in to Tokyo in me life."

"Tokyo, Berlin, London, San Francisco...you can get them all."

He tilted the radio back with two bony yellow hands. "It's the neatest little bit of work I've seen. I hope it didn't cost you too much, I don't want you to be wasting your wages on me."

Guinea hugged his broad shoulders. "Ha, ha, I know something worth two of that. I won it in a raffle at the pub. Sixpenny ticket and here you are! Aren't I clever?"

"You're a wonder, isn't she, Mum?" He hugged her in return. "I'll get all the more pleasure out of it, thinking it's one of the few times in life you get something for nothing."

"You're right there, Dad," Guinea agreed fervently, "and here's what I really did pay for." She produced a pair of slippers.

Her mother had taken down the big aluminium teapot and was measuring tea into it carefully.

"And that reminds me." Guinea opened the string bag and dived into it again. "You can have a beano on tea. I managed to get a pound specially for you. I had some coupons given to me."

"Now that's real thoughtful of you. If there's one thing I do miss with the rationing, it's me tea."

"And here's some cigarettes." She handed her father four packets she'd taken from Alfalfa's carton.

"American! How did you manage that?"

Her mother slammed the lid on the teapot. "I hope you haven't been going out with any of them Yanks. From what I hear they're no fit company for any decent young girl."

"Not me," Guinea said firmly. "One of the girls in the SP is married to a Yank, we get all kinds of perks through her. He's a real decent bloke. They're not all as black as they're painted."

Mrs Malone banged the teapot and milk jug onto the table. "You take my advice and stick to your own kind. If Aussies are good enough to go out with in peacetime, they ought to be good enough to go out with now."

"OK, Mum, keep your hair on. I know my way round."

"That's right," her father said approvingly, "I could trust my girls anywhere."

Mrs Malone snorted. "It's not the girls I'm worrying about, it's all these young fellers gallivanting round with too much money to spend and not enough to do. You're home all day, Dad, you don't see them like I do, waiting outside the works every afternoon and whistling to the girls when they come out. The way they go on, I'd skelp the backsides off of them if they were my sons. Not that I don't say Peg can't look after herself, she's got enough sense to come in out of the wet; it's the bits of girls who haven't been brought up properly that I'm worried about." She turned a sharp eye on Guinea. "Has Monnie been round to see you?"

"No she hasn't. Why, where is she?"

Mrs Malone hesitated. "She's staying with Shirley McGovern. Do you remember her?"

"Oh, yes, she was in the same class as Monnie, they started work together too. You remember, her father's a POW in Malaya. A mass of yellow curls, pretty little thing."

"Well, it don't seem right for two girls their age to be alone in a flat in the city."

"Aw, Monnie's nearly seventeen."

"I still don't like it."

"It's the way she went, Peg, I think, that's worrying yer mother. They had a bit of a row, you see. Not that I'm blaming yer mother, but Bridie exaggerates and Mum takes too much notice of her. You know what a soft little thing Monnie is mostly, but rub 'er up the wrong way, and before you know where you are, whoosh! fur and feathers flying everywhere."

"If a woman can't give her own daughter a clip over the ear without her flying off the handle and running away from home, I'd like to know what the world's coming to."

"I know, Mum, I know, and I'm not blaming you. It's just...well...that Monnie's a touchy little thing and nagging's not the way to get the best out of her."

"You'll be telling me how to bring me own children up next, Michael Malone."

"Now, now, Mother. Have I ever interfered in all me life? I'm just saying, yer can't treat 'em all alike. Now Peg here took a belting like a boy and none the worse for it."

"I don't know about that," Guinea interrupted, "but I certainly took it. How did you know where she went?"

"She rang up yesterday morning and left a message for Bridie, and all I have to say is that when she comes home today — birthday or no birthday — I'll give her a piece of my mind. I'm the one to decide what's the right time for her to come home from a dance, and so long as she lives under my roof she'll do as I tell her."

Mr Malone sighed and slowly stirred his cup of strong sweet tea. "Maybe you're right. I don't know. But I kind of brought Monnie and the twins up meself after you had to go out working, and me too sick to do a man's job. Mind you, I'm not saying I made as good a fist of it as you would of yourself, but I find you can lead those kids practically anywhere, but the moment you start pushing them round they sit back in the britching and you have to light a fire under 'em to get 'em moving."

"Here, you take this, Peg." Her mother handed her a slip of paper, "and go along and look her up at this address if she doesn't come today. Bridie got the address from Shirley's aunt."

Guinea looked at the paper before she put it in her pocket. "OK. I'll do it on my way home tonight."

"And how often have I got to tell you not to say 'OK'?"

"OK. If you give me the cloth I'll start setting the table."

"And father, you go and have a lie down before your dinner, and just because it's your birthday, I'll get Peg to take you out a drop of whisky and milk."

"Now that's talking, mother. Wonderful woman she is, Peg. I'm a lucky man." He raised his gaunt frame from the chair and went slowly out of the door.

"Gee, Mum, he looks crook."

Mrs Malone slammed the oven door. "You don't have to tell me. I've been trying to get him down to the doctor these last two weeks, but you know what he is as well as I do."

Guinea began to set the things out on a tray. "I'll smooge to him after," she said. She went to her purse and took out three pound notes. "Here you are, Mum, I didn't have time to post it last week."

Mrs Malone tucked the notes into the old teapot. "You're a good girl, Peg. Your thirty shillings every week makes all the difference. Did you see the sleepout we got put up?"

"Yeah, looks good. Took 'em long enough to do it, though."

"Well, you know what it is to get labour. It was only because Bridie happened to know a carpenter that we got it up at all. But it makes a lot of difference, I can tell you. With a room to herself, Bridie doesn't feel she's crowding us out so much now."

"How's she getting along?"

"Oh, all right. She's doing oxy-welding now and she's real good. We got on to different shifts and it's much better for yer father, there's always one of us home at night and he hasn't got all the worry of seeing the kids to bed."

"She must be making a pretty penny."

"She's doing well enough and she looks after her money better than some I know."

Guinea ignored the thrust. "Has she heard from Ted lately?"

"Had a letter last week. Up at Finschaefen. He's hoping to be home for Christmas."

"Whacko! isn't that wonderful! He won't recognize young Teddy when he comes back."

"Bridie's living on her allotment and putting everything she makes into War Savings certificates." Mrs Malone was not to be diverted.

"Oh, Bridie always could live on the smell of an oil rag."

"You ought to take a lesson from her yourself, my girl. These good times won't last for ever, and you saw enough of what we had to put up with in the depression to know that when the bad times come again, the girls'll be the first to get put off. Like Bridie was."

"Gee, it all seems like a bad dream now, doesn't it?"

"Not too much of a dream about it. It was bad enough

when your father was on relief work, but when his old wound came against him on that road job and we just had to live on the dole ticket, that was when the pinch came."

The brightness went out of Guinea's face, her eyes were sullen. She did not want to listen or remember.

"Three pounds twelve and six a fortnight coming into the house for the eight of us and the endowment going to pay the rent."

"I still hate the smell of fried bread." Guinea's mouth was set in a tight line.

"Then you just bear in mind what I'm saying, my girl. If we're not very lucky it'll be the same thing over again when this war's finished, for all their highfalutin' talk about the New Order. They want every pair of hands they can get to turn out war materials now, but as soon as the last gun's fired, it'll be back to the dole for the likes of us."

Guinea went into the dining-room feeling suddenly hollow. It was like hearing again Sherwood's bitter, drawling voice. "God damn the lot of them," she said under her breath, moving the vase of paper flowers from the centre of the table.

"Set a place for Monnie, and don't forget to put a rug under that cloth," her mother's voice followed her from the kitchen, "I'm not going to have my best table ruined."

Guinea smiled ruefully. That warning had gone forth ever since Mick had got his first job and saved up to buy the highly polished table with the two extra leaves for his mother's birthday.

Guinea collected a rug from the sleepout and spread it. Her mind was suddenly tender with memories of Mick and Jim installing the table in the dining-room; the effort to get it through the narrow doors without scratching the top; small fingers slapped when they smeared it; storms precipitated when an unfortunate child spilt water on its shining surface; and the family gatherings round it — the last complete one just before young Jim went back to join the *Sydney* on its last voyage.

She looked at the enlargement of Jim and Mick in the

place of honour above the mantelpiece; Jim, baby-faced under his sailor cap, Mick's slouch hat set rakishly above a laughing face, so strangely like her own. They'd given up hoping about Jim now, and Malaya had engulfed Mick along with all the rest of the Eighth Divvy. They'd heard nothing, not a word, not even the comfort of his signature on a formal card. But to Mum, he was alive and so close to her that they all accepted her high faith. His clothes were put away in mothballs, not to be touched, and Guinea felt that if the whole family went naked, Mick's clothes still would not be touched. In spite of Mum's passion for saving every penny, she still put the same ad. in the *Saturday Herald* once a month — *NX163090 2/19th, Michael Malone, last heard of at Parit Sulong.*

They had dinner late. Mrs Malone would never have admitted that she was putting it off, but Guinea knew by the way she kept going to the front door and looking down the hill towards the station that she was giving Monnie a last chance of being there for Dad's birthday dinner. They sat down at last and nobody, not even the twins, mentioned that Monnie was not in her usual place.

When everything was cleared away and Guinea and the twins had done the washing-up they all stretched out in the shade of the side veranda. Guinea, tousled and barefoot, sprawled in an old deckchair and chatted lazily with her mother and father. They had hardly settled down when they heard the clamour of the twins and Timothy announcing a visitor.

"That must be Monnie now." Mrs Malone sat up on her stretcher and peered out under the sun blind.

"I told you she'd be certain to come," Mr Malone said triumphantly, "I knew she wouldn't miss her old Dad's birthday."

The jabber of voices and Timothy's sharp yelping grew louder, and they heard footsteps on the front steps and the thudding of bare feet as the twins stampeded round to the sleepout. A stocky figure in Air Force uniform followed them.

"Holy mackerel!" Guinea exclaimed under her breath. She tried to pull her skirt over her knees and tucked her bare feet under the chair.

"Hullo, Peg."

The colour went up her throat in a sudden wave at the familiar voice. "Oh, hullo," she said with pretended casualness.

"Why, if it's not Kim Scott," her father cried. "Now this is a nice surprise, son." Kim was shaking his hand and smiling down at him, his square teeth white against his bronzed skin.

"I'm that pleased to see yer, Kim," Mrs Malone was pumping his hand enthusiastically.

He bent and kissed her. "That goes for me too, Mum."

Guinea leaned back in the deckchair. She put her hands deliberately behind her head, remembered the blue stains on the sleeve and immediately put them down again. Kim made no attempt to shake hands with her.

"How long are you down for?" Mrs Malone asked.

"Got another ten days."

"How's the war going to get on without you?" Guinea inquired dryly.

"Aha, I left directions. They'll manage." He screwed up his grey eyes and looked down at her with a broad tantalising smile.

"One of these days, me lad," she said to herself, "I'll wipe that cocky grin off your mug."

"What have they made you now, Kim?" Mrs Malone asked. "You've got a different sort of braid on your sleeve, haven't you?"

"Flight-lieutenant."

"Well, that's real nice."

"Oh, that doesn't mean anything, it's just a case of living long enough." He turned to Guinea. "And just chickenfeed to Miss Malone. Moving in high society nowadays, I see, Peg."

"Who told you that one?"

"Well, judging by this morning's paper."

"What's that?" Mr Malone lifted his head from the pillow and peered over the top of his glasses.

"Don't tell me you didn't see your daughter's photo taking up half the *Sunday Star*, Mr Malone."

"I did not. We get *Sunday Topics* here. What's it all about?"

Mrs Malone sat up. "If you've been going in for any of them beach girl competitions, Peggy my girl, I'll belt the soul case out of you. Same as I did before, when you were sixteen."

"Oh, pipe down, Mum. Who said I've been going in for any competitions? Don't you know this big drip can't read? What is it anyway?"

Kim unfolded a paper. "No need to be able to read to know who this is." He held it up for them to see.

"Jeepers!" Guinea groaned to herself. "Isn't that just my luck!"

Mrs Malone grabbed the paper. "What's all this about?" she demanded, fixing an accusing eye on Guinea and stabbing the picture with a hard forefinger.

"Oh, that old thing," Guinea dismissed it lightly. "They were stuck for partners for some of the official guests at Who's Who last night and the hotel hostess hauled a couple of us in from the salon."

"Humph," snorted her mother.

"Now, I call that a real good likeness," her father said, "and if you could get me a copy of it I'd like to frame it."

"Nice work," Kim grinned at her.

"Sure, if you can get it."

"Don't tell me you've been wasting your money on evening dresses like that?" her mother persisted.

"Good lord no, Mum. It was hired."

"Well, you look real nice in it, Peg," she conceded, "and I must say I like a simple modest dress like that after all the naked things you see around."

"That's why I picked it."

"Would you let me have the paper, Kim? There's a lot

of people I'd like to show it to.'' Mr Malone read the caption over to himself. "Oh, they've spelt your name wrong, Peg," he said in disappointed tones.

"Gosh, it's a wonder they bothered putting it in at all. They wouldn't if Mrs Molesworth had anything to do with it.''

"Do they pay you for overtime?'' asked her mother.

"Sure. Overtime and expenses.''

"Well, don't let it go to your head, my girl. It wasn't you the photographers were after, it's these cock-a-hoop admirals and generals wanting to show their fancy uniforms off. So long as you remember you're just a paid employee like the waitresses, you'll be right.''

"American,'' said her father. "Big bug, too. What are the Yanks like, Peg?''

"Real gentlemen, Dad. Real nice and kind, they are, treat you like a lady.''

"You don't say.'' Kim's voice was politely sceptical.

"I do. Gimme the Yanks every time. Though Colonel Maddocks wasn't a Yank, he was a Southerner.''

"Well now, would you tell me what's the difference?''

"I'm not sure, Dad, except that they don't like Lincoln and they're still fighting the Civil War.''

"Ah. Like your grandfather about Cromwell. And what's this fellow with all the whiskers and the embroidery on his coat?''

"Royal Navy.''

"What was he like?'' asked her mother.

"Aw, you know. All 'quaite-quaite' and 'tickety-boo'!''

"You certainly get round.'' Kim had seated himself on the side of the bed near her father, who hospitably offered him a cigarette.

"American? I am in luck.''

"Peg brought 'em out.''

"Did she? Hard to get?''

"Not if you know the ropes.''

"Is that so? You must teach me.''

"Go and put the kettle on, Peg," her mother commanded. "Kim must be dying for a cup of tea after that long walk."

Guinea got up angrily. She was furiously aware of her crumpled skirt and bare feet. The hide of him to sling off about Yanks. As she went in she heard him explaining that he'd just dropped over to know if they'd heard anything from Ted. Oh yeah! She slammed the kettle onto the stove. She'd forgotten she hated him so much.

The conversation came to her clearly as she prepared the afternoon tea.

"Haven't seen any of your folks for a month of Sundays, Kim," her father was saying.

"No. Aunt Annie was telling me they hadn't been over. You know the old man's been laid up with arthritis most of the winter and it takes Aunt all her time with the garage."

"I imagine there's not much doing in the car line."

"That's right, but they manage to keep going. Dad wants to hang on so I'll have something to come back to after the war."

Mrs Malone snorted approvingly. "He's got his head screwed on the right way, your father has. You want to take a leaf out of his book. You're all heroes now, but six months after the war's finished you'll be out on the scrapheap. Same as after the last war."

"Aw, I dunno."

"Mother's a terrible one for crossing her bridges before she comes to them. Meself, I've got hopes that we may have learnt something this time."

"Huh! Learnt! All they've learnt is how to kill more people more quickly. You mark my words, Kim Scott, and don't go splashing your money all over the country like these Americans. They'll regret it."

"If we let it happen again, Mother, it'll be our own fault. If the ordinary people, like you and me and Kim here, haven't learnt enough to stick together when the big bosses try to put in the boot, then we deserve what we get. There's a terrible lot of power in human beings if they'd only learn to use it the right way, and I have a feeling that this time they may have realised that if they can win the war by sticking together, they can win the peace the same way.''

"You've got something there," Kim agreed. "A lot of the blokes I know who never did any thinking before the war except about what was going to win the next race have had to do such a hell of a lot these last years to keep their skins whole that I don't see them settling down when it's all over and just taking what they like to hand out to them.''

"It'll be just the same as it was after the last war, you mark my words," Mrs Malone reiterated gloomily.

Guinea buttered fresh scones savagely and thought that if she had to live at home and listen to her mother making that remark at least ten times a day, she'd go off her rocker. No wonder Monnie had beat it.

The late afternoon sun poured in through the kitchen window. Jeepers, it was hot! The blasted room was like an oven. She wished to God she was on the beach with Sher. Suddenly she was overcome by a sense of desolation. What a mug she'd been not to marry him and get out of this darned country for ever. The place'd soon be overrun with blokes like Kim all coming back too big for their boots. Nothing of the smart Alec about Sher.

Through the window she could see, beyond the scattered houses, the parched paddocks from which the westerly had burnt out the last vestige of green left by the winter drought. The undulating plains stretched away to the Blue Mountains. That's where Grandfather Scott's farm was, tucked away between the Nepean River and the foothills. The mountain scarps towered above it and the broad river washed almost to the foot of the orchard. She pulled the blind down with a jerk. To hell with the Scotts. She'd had the Scotts and so far as she was concerned they could take themselves and their farm and all go jump in the river. It made her puke to hear Kim out there on the veranda buttering up Mum and Dad. He ought to sling off at the Yanks! She'd met a pretty fair sample of them from Brooklyn to Texas and she'd like to see one of them who could get away with what Kim could.

"Mother's right, up to a point," Mr Malone was saying reflectively. "Promises are not enough. They'll have to do things. Nationalise the banks, that's the first move. And then all the other things that ought to belong to the people, coal mines, land...everything that really belongs to the people."

"Oh, you and your nationalising, Father. Put your money in the bank and keep it there, that's what I say."

"There's more to it than that, Mother. If you go down to the root of things, it's money — which means trade and profits — that makes wars...and depressions too. And until the people who've got to fight the wars have the biggest say in who's going to provide the money for them, I don't see how we're going to get much farther on. Take over the banks, that's the first thing the government'll have to do."

"Maybe," Kim said, "but sometimes I think we ought to shoot all the politicians and start right back from taws. And all the racketeers who've been socking away a wad of money out of this war. It'd give me a lot of pleasure to put a bullet through them. A lot of fellows think my way too."

"Suit you better to be putting your money away, Kim, and when you come out of the Air Force you'll have all your deferred pay to put into the garage, and then you needn't worry what anybody else is up to."

"Sounds heady when you put it that way, Mrs Malone, but there've been a lot of other blokes in this war besides me, and if I come back to collect my deferred pay I'll owe it as much to them as to luck. And what am I going to feel like, building up a nice fat business through no credit to myself, when my cobbers are hoofing it from door to door selling pot scrapers and reels of cotton?"

"You can't save the world, my lad, so just you look after yourself. And anyway, this is no way to be celebrating Father's birthday."

"What do you know! What a bit of luck I dropped in. I brought some cigarettes over for you, so now they'll do for a present. Mind you, they're only Australian."

Guinea caught her father's low reply: "I'd rather have 'em, but don't let Peg know. Not after her buying them others."

"And what are you doing with your leave, Kim?" Mrs Malone asked.

"Aw — giving Dad a hand round the place, and getting in a bit of surfing. Tomorrow I'm going to have a look at the six-hour procession."

"Well, indeed now. I'd like to be going with you. Many's the time your father and me marched together in the great days of the AEU...Those were the days — great men, great fights. And now the pair of us couldn't put one step in front of another unless we were pushed along in a wheel-chair."

"We'll manage that yet too," Kim laughed. "When I'm demobbed, I'll make a twin one and the three of us'll go along together and sing the 'Red Flag'."

"Get along with you, Kimmie Scott. There's not one of you could keep in tune for more than two bars, I'll be bound, even if you knew the words, which you don't. Stick to your unions if you like but leave them Commies alone. Your Aunt Annie and I aren't going to spend our housekeeping money bailing the three of you out of gaol."

"Tough, aren't they, Pop?"

Mrs Malone's voice changed to matter-of-fact sharpness, but Guinea could detect an undertone of anxiety. "Your Aunt Annie didn't say anything about seeing Monnie lately, did she?"

"No. As a matter of fact she told me to tell her she'd like to have her over next weekend. She says she hasn't seen her for weeks. I mustn't forget to give her the message. Where is she?"

There was a long silence. At last Mr Malone spoke. "We've been expecting her home all day, but she's sharing a flat in the city with a girl she used to work with and maybe she didn't like to leave her on her own."

Guinea came out with the afternoon tea.

Monnie came out of a sodden sleep as though she were emerging from an anæsthetic. Her brain seemed stuffed with cotton wool. There was a foul taste in her mouth and she shuddered as she ran her tongue round her teeth. A steel band pressed into her head and when she forced open her heavy lids the room swayed sickeningly. It was a strange room with big windows through which she could see sky and clouds and a giant clock face. She half-opened her eyes again and tried to focus them. Half past six. Did that mean six in the morning? Or had she slept on till half past six at night?

Someone stirred in the bed beside her. Her brain cleared as though a light had been switched on, and terror ran through her. She sat up, pressing away from the horrid snoring body. The wall was cold against her naked back. She tried to draw up her legs, but they were caught in a tangle of bedclothes. She dragged at the sheet to cover herself, and stared down at Calvin's face, dark against the pillow. Calvin who? How did she get here? It came back to her slowly and she recalled each incident: dancing with him, drinking the last coke and going out into the cool air, the pavement swaying up and down, snuggling against him in the taxi, being carried into his flat. His flat...that's where she must be now. She'd been here all night. Her clothes were scattered round the floor. Calvin had taken them off. Calvin!

All the horror of the night came back to her. Calvin naked beside her, Calvin's hands fumbling at her body, his mouth hard on hers, bruising her lips. Her struggles and his brutal strength. His arms pinioning hers, his body pressing her down, her powerlessness and the pain, the searing pain...

She could smell the sickly perfume of stale frangipani. She pulled the bruised blossoms from her hair and flung them away from her with loathing. She was shivering, the morning air struck cold. If only she could creep out of bed and dress, perhaps she could get away.

She tried to slip down to the end of the bed without waking Calvin, but he turned and the covers slid onto the floor. She saw the hair black on his chest and belly and made a frantic grab for the sheet to cover him. He woke at the sudden movement. Her startled eyes looked down into his and saw recognition dawn in them. His arms came out to clasp her. "Monnie Mavourneen," he yawned sleepily, "gimme a kiss." She strained away from him. "Come on, baby." He drew her back into the bed beside him and his mouth came down on hers, wet and open, sour with smoke and stale liquor.

"Let me go, let me go!"

Sobs broke their way out of her throat. She could feel the trembling of his laughter turn to something urgent and frightening. She pressed her palms against his shoulders and dug her nails into his flesh. His dark face was above hers as it had been last night, his strong body pressing her down.

She lay spent and weeping. Calvin lit a cigarette, sliding an arm around her shoulders and drawing her close to him. She could smell the strong smoke of the cigarette and the pungent sweat in his armpits. The tears flowed unchecked under her closed lids and rolled down her cheeks. He drew her head onto his shoulder and rubbed his chin against her forehead. It was bristly and hard and her tears flowed faster.

"Ah, can it, kid. It won't kill you. Ain't I been nice to y'?"

She moaned wordlessly.

"Goddam," he said, pulling his arm away and sitting up. "What more d'ya want? Y're damn lucky when y're starting on this game to find a guy as considerate as me. You want to wake up to y'rself."

Monnie buried her face in the pillow and wept until she had no more tears.

When she looked up at last, Calvin was sitting on the edge of the bed, shaved and dressed, a cup of coffee in his hand. "Sit up and drink this, honey."

She obeyed and he held the cup to her lips, the strong black coffee burning her mouth and throat.

"Listen, baby, I'm on the job this morning, so I got to

be on my way. You skip into the bathroom and get yourself dressed. I ran a bath for you and I'll drop you off at your place."

She was dressed and ready before he had finished his breakfast.

"You're a real pretty kid." He tipped her face up to his. "If I wasn't going north again you'd be having me tagging around. There's a lot of things I'd like to teach you and we could sure have a lot of fun." He kissed her unpainted mouth lightly. "That's to remember me by, honey."

They went out of the flat and down to the street, and the air was full of the ringing of church bells. Monnie shrank from the sound as though from a physical blow. It seemed that they were ringing for her alone, and that everyone must hear them shouting aloud her sin and disgrace. She tried to pray: "Dear Mother of God..." but the words died. She shook her hair forward to hide her face. She could not look at the people hurrying to the churches nearby. She was shut out of all that forever. She had never missed church before in her life except when she'd had the measles.... But now, how could she ever go again?

Calvin put his hand under her elbow and they crossed the street and went through the little park. The air was bright and full of the feeling of spring, and the young poplars rippled in the breeze, but the light hurt her swollen eyes and her desolation shut out the morning.

A taxi pulled up beside them. Calvin asked for her address and directed the driver. As the car turned up Martin Place on its way to Kings Cross, he put his arm round her shoulders and drew her to him, without memory or desire.

Monnie stood on the doorstep of 78A and fumbled in her bag for the key of the outer door. Calvin's taxi had gone and the lane was empty. The church bells were ringing and in a moment of agony she put her hands to her ears but she could not shut out the echoes of the bells beating down between the crowded buildings. Somewhere near at hand one clanged monotonously; another, farther away, sang on a pure high note; still farther off a chime of bells floated clear and sweet, while through them all, rising and falling with the wind, the big bell of St Mary tolled.

For a moment she wondered if she had got hold of someone else's handbag. There was a bundle of crumpled notes pushed into it — more money than she'd ever had in her life — two five-pound notes, three singles, and a torn ten shillings. She stared at it unbelievingly. It was her bag all right, there was her handkerchief and her powder puff.

She turned the latchkey of the outer door and went in. At the foot of the stairs she stopped short. Suddenly, she knew everything — the notes in Shirley's bag! All the notes in her own bag! She dropped them back into the purse with loathing and shut the bag with a snap.

She flew up the stairs, along the passage, and pounded wildly on the door of the flat. No one answered and she banged again. It seemed ages before Shirley opened it; she was only half awake.

"For Christ's sake, do you have to knock the bloody door down?" she grumbled angrily and flung herself down on the settee again. Monnie shook her furiously by the shoulder.

"What the hell's the matter?"

"You've got to wake up." Monnie went on shaking her.

"Jesus! What's biting you?"

"Why did you leave me there last night?"

"What else could I do? You passed out."

"Someone must have drugged me."

"Hooey, you were stinko. Babes like you shouldn't drink."

"I didn't want to drink...only..."

"Well, find yourself a bed and shut up about it now. You've got all day to bellyache." Shirley rolled over and pulled up the bedclothes.

Monnie dragged at her again.

"But Shirley," she wailed, "something terrible happened. That lieutenant... You don't know. What'll I do?"

Shirley disappeared beneath the sheet. "Go jump in the lake for all I care."

Monnie threw herself into the armchair and sobbed aloud.

"Gawd Almighty," Shirley groaned, unwrapping herself from the bedclothes and sitting up. "How long are you going to keep up that blubbering? I gotta head like a watermelon and this is what I gotta listen to. Haven't you got any consideration?"

Monnie went on sobbing loudly, all her control gone. The noise brought Fay from the bedroom. She strode across the room and shook her by the shoulders.

"Stop that bloody row, stop it, or by the living God I'll slit your throat." She gave her two stinging slaps across the face.

"Oh, Christ," Shirley groaned. "What'll we do with her?"

"Didn't I warn you we'd have something like this on our hands? Bringing your bloody babes-in-the-wood here." Monnie still sobbed. "Shut up, you idiot, shut up, I tell you! Next thing we know someone'll send for the cops and then where'll we all be? Get her a drink, Shirley."

Shirley got off the settee heavily and poured out a stiff dose of Betty's sal volatile. "Drink this up," she ordered, jamming the glass against Monnie's teeth and holding it there until she swallowed. Her sobbing grew less.

"Now what the hell's all this stink about?" Fay demanded.

Shirley gave a helpless gesture. "What d'ya think? The loot, of course..."

"Jesus, is that all? I thought the Vice Squad musta been on her tail."

Shirley was apologetic. "Aw, she's only a kid, and after all it's the first time."

"Well, there's gotter be a first time for everything, hasn't there? And if every kid went on like this over her first man the place'd be a flaming madhouse."

Betty appeared at the door of the bedroom, yawning and querulous: "What the hell's all the row about at this time of the morning?"

"The kid," Fay was contemptuous, "raising a stink over last night."

"Oh, that!" Betty yawned again, "I thought something must be wrong. Christ, am I tired!"

"Aren't we all! But there's no chance of sleep till this mug stops bellowing."

Fay shook Monnie angrily by the shoulder. "Did he knock you about?"

Monnie shook her head.

"Did he bite you?" Betty inquired. "I reckon a girl's got reason to squeal then."

"Did he pay yer?" Fay asked.

"Yeah, that's the most important thing," Betty said, picking up Monnie's purse. She counted the notes. "Take a look at this. Pretty good for a first, eh, Shirl?"

"What did I tell you?" Shirley said triumphantly. "Didn't I say she'd be a wow?"

Fay took one of the five-pound notes and threw it on the table: "That's for your share of the flat," she explained. She stuffed the rest of the notes back and threw the purse over to Monnie, who let it slide to the floor.

"You've been damned lucky, my girl. You take my word for it. Not many of us get paid the first time, I can tell you."

Betty laughed mirthlessly: "Too bloody right. Get yer to do it for love, that's the usual lark."

"Listen, kid," Shirley put an arm round Monnie's shoulders, "you roll onto the settee and I'll give you a nice glass of hot milk with a stick in it and when you've had a good sleep, everything'll look different. I know how you feel, you're worn out. Men never bloody well know when to stop."

"That's a real good idea," Fay agreed. "Your eyes look like two burnt holes in a blanket. I'll stick on the milk and you get her into bed, Shirl."

Monnie looked up at them as they sat one on each arm of her chair. Their clinging nightdresses stank of stale powder and sweat, she could see their bodies gleaming through the transparent black material and their hot sweetish female smell rose up and sickened her. She got up.

"I'm going," she said flatly.

"Oh, no you're not," Fay made a grab at her as she turned to the door, but Monnie was too quick for her and slipped behind a chair.

"Get hold of her, for Christ's sake," Shirley panted. "She's such a bloody sucker she'll spill her guts once she gets out of here."

Fay and Shirley dragged her from behind the chair, struggling and screaming as they tried to pull her into the bedroom. Fay clapped a hand over her mouth and Monnie drove her teeth into it savagely.

"You little bitch!"

"Well, keep your dirty hands off me. I may be a sucker, but I'm not the kind of sucker you think I am. And I'm going to my Aunt Annie."

"Take it easy, kid," Shirley pleaded, slipping an arm round her.

Monnie caught her a blow across the face that sent her staggering back. "Touch me again, either of you," she yelled, "and I'll tear your eyes out." She stood panting, watching their movements warily.

"What's all this noise about?" Grace's voice came, silky and menacing, from the doorway.

Monnie swung round, and in that moment Fay caught her arm, swinging it behind her back and holding it there in a lock.

"It's all the kid's fault." Fay turned an accusing glance on Monnie. "Came tearing in here like a mad thing screaming about what the bloody loot done to her last night and woke the lot of us up." She licked the bleeding palm of her hand.

"So that's it?" Grace turned to Monnie. "Haven't you got any consideration for anyone at this hour of the morning?" she demanded. "And where are you going?"

Shirley sank back onto the settee and lit a cigarette. "She's going to beat it," she said.

"Yeah." Fay's voice was full of scorn. "Reckons she's going to tell some flaming aunt or other she's been ruined."

"Oh, she is, is she? Just fancy that!" Her hand closed round Monnie's arm like a vice. "Here, Shirley, pour me out a double dose of that stuff we give Betty."

Monnie struggled, but Fay grasped her other arm. The spoon loomed up before her, enormous, distorted, and gritted against her teeth. She shook her head violently. "I won't take it, I won't take it!" She aimed a kick at Grace's shin.

"Ouch," Grace swore under her breath. "Here, stretch her out on the bed."

Fay straddled the struggling girl. Grace held her nose. Shirley pushed the tablespoon between her teeth. Monnie felt the liquid running down her throat. She lay there, spent and helpless, the taste lingering unpleasantly in her mouth.

"Cover her up," Grace commanded. She stood gazing down on Monnie, rubbing her bruised shin. "And one more squeak out of you, my girl, and we'll have the police in on you before you know where you are."

It seemed to Deb that she had hardly gone to sleep before she was awakened by an ear-splitting crackle. She opened her eyes with an effort and turned her head. On the pillow beside her was a little fist from which the deafening row came. Luen laughed and poked her tousled head under the mosquito net. "Isn't he a beauty?" She uncurled her fingers and showed the jewelled head of a cicada. "He's a yellow mundy. I kept him in a box under the bed all night."

"Ssssh," warned Deb irritably, "you'll have everyone awake. It's much too early."

"They're all awake now. I've been up simply hours and I thought you'd never wake up."

Deb heard giggles and the drumming of cicadas on the veranda. She looked up into Luen's excited face and her own broke into an answering smile. She put out her arms and pulled the child down for a good-morning kiss. "Nice way to wake your poor wornout mother," she teased, half in earnest, running her fingers through Luen's tangled hair. The cicada started crackling again.

"Put that noisy creature away and run and get your brush. I'll give that mop of yours a really good doing for once in its life."

Luen dropped the mosquito net and skipped away, returning with the brush and a gurgling baby which she pushed in front of her under the net. Deb sat up and started to brush Luen's hair with strong swift strokes while Debby bounced and grabbed after the brush and all three went off into peals of laughter.

"There, that's enough." Deb gave way in a tug of war with little Debby, who immediately started banging with the brush at her own silky curls. She glanced at her watch. "I'll have to get up."

"Oh goody! Then we can get the picnic ready."

"What picnic?"

"Auntie Nolly promised to take us for a picnic by the creek today when you're here, and we've got simply millions of sausages to cook on the fire and she says we can have billy tea and..."

"This is the first I've heard of it."

Luen caught the tone in her mother's voice and the light went out of her face. "But you do want to come for a picnic with us, don't you, Mummy?" she pleaded in a small shaky voice.

"Of course I do, darling," Deb reassured her quickly and put an arm round her shoulders. The baby clutched happily at her hair. "It's only that I didn't know about it and you see I'm terribly disappointed because I simply have to go back to work today."

"Oh Mummy, you're not going back today." Luen looked up at her with a quivering mouth; the tears glistened in her eyes and spilled down her cheeks.

"You must be a big brave girl, darling. I wouldn't go if I didn't have to. You don't think I'd rather go back and work in that old hotel instead of having a lovely picnic with you, do you?" Deb lied, almost persuading herself as well as Luen. "Now you show me what a brave girl you can be."

Luen wiped her hand over her cheeks, leaving a grubby streak; she tried to smile up at Deb and snuggled against her shoulder. Deb pulled her close and kissed the top of her head. She felt mean — so mean that she let herself go in a burst of irritation at the baby, who had crawled onto her knee and was jigging up and down.

"Oh, take her off," she said, exasperated.

"But she only wants to play." Luen looked at her mother with puzzled eyes and took Debby onto her own knees.

"Well, she'll have to play somewhere else. I've got to get dressed."

She remembered that she still had to break the news to Nolly that she wasn't going to stay. Heavens, how was she going to tell her? "Is Auntie Nolly up?"

"No."

Good! That's what she'd do. Take a tray in just as she was leaving. She would get the children's breakfast first and then take Nolly's tray. Tom would be sure to be dead to the world after coming in so late after the fire-fighting, so she'd just creep in and tell her quickly and she needn't stay and answer questions. Just say she had to go back and work, and that would be that.

"You go quietly in to Auntie Nolly now," she told Luen, "and tell her not to get up. I'll fix breakfast and take her a tray in bed. And don't say a word about my going back. I'll tell her later. Now off you run, I'm going to get dressed."

Luen put the baby on her hip and staggered out of the room, her thin little body bent over to balance the weight. Deb frowned as she watched her. It's really appalling the way Nolly lets the child lug that heavy baby round, she thought, whipping up her sense of shame at her own meanness into indignation against Nolly. And the way they're letting her grow into a country bumpkin — it's high time I sent her to a decent boarding school where she'll have a chance to make some worthwhile friends. I will, too, just as soon as things get straightened out. Straightened out... Everything had looked clear and straightforward enough yesterday before she came; it had all seemed quite plain that when she married Angus, with his money and position she would be able to give Luen every opportunity in the world, and her responsibility as a mother really left her no choice. But here at Nolly's with the children, where everyone was happy even though they had none of the things that counted in Angus's world, she could not rid herself of the feeling that they had something precious outside his reckoning.

Why couldn't she have both? she asked herself passionately. It wasn't fair that she should have to choose. And she wouldn't have to now if it wasn't for the ridiculous way Jack was behaving. Oh God! she mustn't let herself go over all that again. She picked up her brush and attacked her hair vigorously.

She felt awful about Nolly. No matter how she tried to argue it out, she hated herself for letting Nolly down about the hospital: there had always been that sort of trust between them. If she was ever in a tight spot she could count on Nolly

— and on Tom too, even if he was getting so insufferable with his set against anyone who had a bit more money than he did. Look how they had taken Luen... She pushed the idea away from her quickly, it was too uncomfortable and confusing. What she had to think about was Luen's future and her own. She couldn't afford to be sentimental. Just because Tom and Nolly were happy under these appalling conditions, that didn't say she and Jack would be. Far from it.

She stopped quite still, her hand holding the brush raised halfway to her hair. That was it! Of course. If she did that, it would show Jack just how appalling the whole idea was. Yes. She'd take her holidays the last fortnight of his leave and they could both come to Nolly's.

It would serve a double purpose, she thought grimly. Here at Nolly's with all the children milling round and all the work to do without any conveniences at all and no help, she wouldn't be likely to get sentimental as she might do up at the Vineyard with just the three of them. Up there, with the long peaceful days, the nights together after so long apart, Heaven only knew what Jack would talk her into... But looking after Nolly's house with a brood of children and two hulking men would keep her reminded that life wasn't all sentimental reunions. Yes, that's what she'd do. She'd show him. Her uneasiness slid away. She put on an old wrap of Nolly's with a defiant air, seized a towel, called cheerfully to the children outside and plunged into the morning jobs.

Luen and Durras helped her to get the children's breakfast and looked after them while she prepared a tray for Nolly and Tom. How the devil was she going to tell them she was leaving? She had pushed the thought to the back of her mind during the whirlwind of the last hour, but now she'd have to take the tray in herself and tell them. Even with the good news that she was coming to look after the family while Nolly was away, she felt mean about the picnic. Oh hell! She'd just have to tell them plainly that this was her only chance of catching L. F. and Molesworth on their day off duty, and if she didn't take it she mightn't get another chance, and then she positively couldn't come.

She went soft-footed down the hall and listened at the door. Tom was snoring regularly. She turned the handle without a sound and opened the door wide enough to put her head in. Nolly had put the mosquito net back from the double bed and she could see them both lying in the relaxed attitudes of sleep. Nolly's brown hair was fanned out on the pillow and her face looked full of hollows in the dim light that came into the room below the half-drawn blinds. Tom was lying beside her, snoring gently in a deep sleep, his face against the white pillow dark with unshaven stubble. Thank heaven they were asleep. She withdrew her head, closing the door with a feeling of intense relief and tiptoed back to the kitchen.

"They must be dead tired," she said sympathetically to Luen. "Sleep's much better for them than breakfast, so we won't wake them and I'll just write a note to Auntie Nolly to tell her I'm going back to fix up the arrangements about coming here to look after you all when she's in hospital. Won't that be lovely?"

"Yes Mummy, oh yes."

"And will you and Durras keep the children outside so they don't make a noise in the house?"

"Won't Auntie Nolly be taking us for the picnic even?" Luen looked at Deb with big disappointed eyes.

"I'm sure she will when she wakes up, darling, but think how much more you'll all enjoy it if she isn't tired."

"Yes." Luen said doubtfully, and added, "Auntie Nolly always makes picnics such fun."

"Yes, she makes them fun for you," Deb said severely, "but what about being fun for her? It's not much fun for her if she's tired. You want to think of that, dear, and be a little considerate."

Luen looked at her bare toes, and her lower lip shot out just like Jack's.

"Good heavens, what's the matter?" Deb said irritably. "You don't think a sulky face like that would make Auntie Nolly happy, do you?" Luen didn't answer. "And it's not a very nice face for Mummy to remember when she's back at the hotel working and thinking of her little girl having a lovely picnic.''

Luen threw her arms round her mother's waist. "Mummy darling, I do wish you could stay. Please stay with us, please, please.''

"Sssh, you'll wake Auntie Nolly,'' Deb gently unclasped Luen's hands and held them in hers. "Next time I come, perhaps we'll all be here together with Daddy. And then you'll be glad I went back today, won't you darling?''

Luen nodded, and Deb bent down and kissed her forehead. "Now, I've simply got to fly. I'll write that note for Auntie, and then I must be off. I'll put it on the breakfast tray and you can make her a nice hot cup of tea and give her my letter when she wakes up. Will you do that for me? Come on, say 'Yes Mummy' and give me a smile.''

Luen raised her face and looked at her mother. There was a gallant little smile on her lips. "I do love you, Mummy darling,'' she said.

Deb dropped a kiss on her nose. "That's my little daughter. Now come and help me get ready.''

Deb was out of the house before there was a stir from Nolly's room. She took the children down to the bus stop with her and waved them goodbye as it moved off. It was less than half full when she got in, but by the time they reached the outskirts of Pymble it was crowded. Girls got in with black prayer books, looking fresh in their pretty summer frocks and shady hats. Middle-aged women, hot already from their tight corsets and best shoes, and boys and men uncomfortable in dark Sunday suits, sweltered in the heat. Family parties with picnic baskets and babies and bathing costumes clambered in after them, and young girls in gay beach dresses and youths with open-necked shirts, with their trunks and towels rolled in a tight bundle under their arms.

It was as hot as Saturday. The sun poured into the bus and by the time they arrived at the station, Deb was sweating and uncomfortable. She went across to the bookstall for a

Sunday paper, but they were all sold out. The train came in and she got a seat out of the sun, but the whole carriage was hot and stuffy. My God, she thought, what a way to start a day. I must get in a good rest or I'll never be fit for anything. She wished she had a paper to keep her mind off things.

In fairness to Angus she would have to tell him what she had decided about Jack. That was only decent. But, however hard she tried, she could not recapture the nostalgia that had moved her at Nolly's with Luen lying asleep beside her. Just as last night she hadn't been able to keep Jack out of her thoughts, so today it was the thought of Angus that dominated everything.

Soon she would be at the hotel relaxing in a scented bath. She would rest, perhaps sleep for half an hour before she got into her new white suit, and then she would go down to meet Angus, and he would tell her how attractive she looked...

She pulled herself up. Stop it, Deb. This is no way to go woolgathering when you've got to think out how you're going to tell Angus that you must keep your promise and look after Nolly's family while she's in hospital...and Jack will still be on leave so he'll be there too, and there's nothing you can do about it.

Jack. She opened her bag and took out Jack's letter. She hadn't looked at it since that first hurried reading on Friday ...Vineyard...Vineyard...the word sprang out at her five times on the single page. She felt absolutely exhausted even thinking about the fortnight at Nolly's. She'd be completely fagged out and it would be ghastly for all of them. The thought of Nolly's family with their bounding energy and Jack making a fuss over the lot of them and specially Luen — the way he spoiled Luen when he was on leave was always hard to take — and her cooking for the whole brood, and cleaning...

Oh, well, no good worrying about it now. She'd written the note to Nolly and even if she wanted to she couldn't pull out now.

And then, supposing going to Nolly's didn't work and

she lost Angus. Wasn't she being an impulsive fool if she told him today? Wouldn't it be better to wait till Jack was actually back? After all, Angus didn't expect an answer until then...

The thought of telling Jack about Angus gave her goose pimples. She steeled herself. For nearly five years now Jack had left her to make her own life and it had been a pretty thin one until she got this job and sent Luen to live at Nolly's two years ago... When all your life was wrapped up in your husband and your child and suddenly you were left to make a life for yourself and without much money at that, there wasn't much to it if you were the faithful kind and your husband was as bad at writing letters as Jack was. You couldn't go on sharing your life with him if he didn't give you anything to share, and you couldn't just live for your child, making her clothes and cooking her food in a couple of poky rooms with no freedom or the money to keep up with your old friends. She couldn't stand it anyway, and when she'd taken the job at the SP, it had been with the idea of saving money for when Jack came back. After she had been there a little while, she knew that having the job was her only chance of keeping herself from growing into one of those possessive mothers who can't bear to let their children out of their sight... She could imagine how Jack would have liked it if she'd gone on like that!

Well, he'd find she was a different person when he came back this time. And he could like it or lump it. After all, he was as much to blame as she was. When he had come back on his last leave nearly seventeen months ago he'd been critical of everything she did, of her job at the SP and of Luen being with Nolly, and he hadn't even tried to understand. She could do nothing that was right and it was only towards the end that the difficulties had been swept away in the anguish of his going back. Then he'd gone, and there had been blankness again. Sometimes when she waited weeks for a letter she wondered if he was being deliberately cruel, or whether she just had no part in his life any more.

For the first couple of years when he was away she just

lived for Luen, and even the first year at the SP, she'd only gone out occasionally with other men. It had all been very harmless. If the men showed anything more than friendliness she'd countered with snaps of Jack and Luen, and if they didn't like it that way they hadn't asked her again. But with Angus it had been different. When she met him, she was thoroughly down in the dumps and Jack hadn't written to her for a month. Not that there was anything extraordinary about that, although she wrote regularly every week. It had been lovely going out with Angus. He always treated her as if she was important to him.

She wouldn't let her mind run back to their last night at Princes, nor to the day ahead of her, but pulled it back to Jack. It wasn't her or Luen that was most important to him, they had to fit in with what he wanted. Jack wanted to go to the Vineyard, Jack wanted his wife and child there with him... It didn't matter if a depression hit them again and it was the same old story, out of a job, on the dole. Insecurity. No decent start for Luen, herself worn out with drudgery...all the things he'd sworn he'd never let happen to her. But he'd let her take the full responsibility for Luen these five years and she wasn't going to spoil Luen's chances now by dumping her out on a vineyard that couldn't provide a decent living for one, let alone for three.

By the time the train left Milsons Point and was running up the approach to the Bridge, she had made up her mind. The moon and Nolly and memory had put a spell on her last night. This morning in broad daylight she knew that Jack was being selfish and irresponsible, and that Angus was offering her everything she wanted for herself and Luen; security for them both and all the opportunities she wished she had had, and she wasn't going to let Luen miss them.

The train ran off the Bridge and into the tunnel. She got off at Wynyard station with her mind made up.

A stale, sweetish smell met Deb when she opened the door of her room. Phew! Made you think of death. She switched on the light. Damn, the water had drained out of the basin and Angus's lilies-of-the-valley were brown and wilted. She flung them into the wastepaper basket; she must remember to take them out to the housemaid's cupboard before she went out, or she wouldn't be able to sleep in the room that night.

The telephone rang. She reached for the receiver and paused a moment. If it was Angus, she didn't want to talk to him. Not yet. It rang again, she braced herself and picked up the receiver. "Is that you, Miss Forrest?" a strong, affected voice asked.

"Yes," Deb answered with relief.

"It's Mrs Molesworth here. I'm so glad you're at home. I have a message from Mr Sharlton for you. He would like you to come up and have a sherry with us before lunch. . . say at twelve thirty in my suite."

Deb thought quickly. What did he want her for? He must have heard the gossip about her and Angus. Yes, that's what it was. "That's very kind of Mr Sharlton, but I'm sorry, I have an engagement at twelve o'clock."

"Oh," Thelma's voice held a faint tone of annoyance, "would you hold on a minute?"

Deb had an inspiration. "Could you call back again later? I've left my bath running," she said. That was one for Molesworth! But the voice held her against her will.

"Just hold on one minute. Mr Sharlton suggests that you might come up for a cup of coffee before you go out. Say half past eleven. Now, don't let your bath run over." Deb heard the click of the receiver almost before the last peremptory, honied word was finished.

Old Mole was used to getting her own way all right! But she needn't think she could put it over this time. Today was Sunday and the Marie Antoinette masseuse was off duty, her time was her own. She'd ring back and say she hadn't time — that'd be one in the eye for Ladies First Sharlton and his girlfriend. Yes, that's what she'd do, ring back at 11.30 and say she couldn't make it.

Deb went over to the wardrobe and paused with her hand on the door. Trying to get in on the ground floor with the future Mrs McFarland, that's all they were doing. They wouldn't invite her to take sherry with them on Sunday in the holy of holies for anything less than that. No member of the staff had ever penetrated the sitting-room of old Mole's suite on a Sunday except the waiter, who took up meals for two and carried back titbits of gossip to the kitchen for the staff to paw over. The Marie Antoinette had Elvira's authority for that. And Elvira, for all her malice, was generally pretty near the mark. Yesterday, the whole staff must have heard the news of Angus's proposal. A succulent bit of gossip like that would run like a bushfire, from basement to roof garden.

Deb took her new sharkskin suit out of the wardrobe and laid it on the bed with the matching slacks beside it, standing a moment to enjoy their gleaming white. She turned away with a little smile of satisfaction at their absolute rightness for Palm Beach.

She ran her bath as full as she dared. What heavenly luxury to lie soaking in hot water up to your neck with the perfume of wood violets drugging you to laziness. Heaven only knew where Claire had managed to get bath salts like that for her birthday, they hadn't been in the shops for simply years. But Claire managed to get most things one way or another. Deb waggled her fingers in the pale green water and released a fresh wave of heady fragrance.

Angus wouldn't have the faintest suspicion that the whole staff of the SP was buzzing with his affairs. He felt himself so far removed from the people who served him that he never seemed to suspect that behind their discreetly veiled eyes they were simply seething with curiosity, and the minute they left him their tongues would be wagging nineteen to the dozen. That was what came of being born to the purple, she thought. She'd never make that mistake, not after two years in the Marie Antoinette. He thought he could fall in love with the masseuse in the hotel beauty salon, propose marriage to her and get away with it! It really was ironic, she thought as she reached for the plug chain with her big toe, that with all Angus's discretion, he should have been the one to let the cat out of the bag.

She rubbed herself dry and felt deliciously refreshed. She really would have to tell Angus some day how the news had got around. But would she? There were many things, she realised with a start, that she would never tell Angus, even if she did marry him. Somehow she didn't think he'd be amused to know that the floor maid had overheard him telling his brother in the retreat of his private sitting room that he was considering giving up the pleasures of bachelorhood at last. "Don't be surprised," Elvira reported him as saying, mimicking his English voice with cruel fidelity, "don't be surprised if I call on you one of these days to be my best man."

By the time she got back to her room, Deb had decided it would be amusing to go up to Thelma's suite in her new outfit and find out exactly what it was all about and, by the time she'd finished dressing, she was looking forward to putting in the next half hour playing her new part as Angus's fiancée. She had no illusions about her stocks as SP masseuse, they were the same as they'd always been, but it would be fun to borrow Angus's glory for half an hour and treat L. F. and Molesworth to a little bit of the future Mrs McFarland.

She took one last look at herself in the long mirror and checked over every detail. Claire had been right, there was nothing quite so good as dead white against her olive skin, and the tan and blue blouse that showed between the straight open edges of her box coat was the perfect colour note. Her rough white straw hat, utterly simple — but heavens, how expensive! Her pale tan stockings, white shoes with tan heels, white doeskin gloves and, final luxury, the elegant tan leather duffle bag that opened into a circle and carried her wisp of a bra-swimsuit against one side, and her sharkskin slacks in the flat pocket against the other without a bulge in its elegant shape. Thanks to Claire's introductions and discounts,

Mrs Angus McFarland with an unlimited dress allowance couldn't have been turned out better.

Blue was on the front lift. He raised an eyebrow when she asked for the sixth floor. "Visiting royalty?" he said, swivelling a mischievous eye on her.

"Looks like it, doesn't it," she replied amiably.

"They do say negligy is the correct wear for Sundays."

"So I've heard," Deb smiled. She didn't want to get on the wrong side of Blue with all the gossip flying round the place.

He picked up the Sunday paper and unfolded it at the social page. "Ain't it a corker picture of Guin?" he said proudly.

Deb took the paper from him, "It certainly is," she agreed. "Heavens, this'll rock the place!"

"You're telling me. You should have heard D.D.T. Did she carry on a treat. Rang down for all the papers about half an hour ago, and then had hysterics. Had to get her mother in. Old Molesworth has had her work cut out with her I can tell you. God, I'd have given my deferred pay to have seen them silvertails when Guin walked in up top last night."

Deb stared at the pictured faces. My God, she thought, with her hide, Guinea could get away with murder. This'd take the D'Arcy-Twyning bunch down a peg or two, and so much for Angus's family party and their exclusive Who's Who. She handed the paper back to Blue. "It's a lovely photo," she said. "She certainly must have been a success."

"I'll say," Blue agreed heartily. "Like to take it along to old Mole for her gallery?"

"I'll leave that to you." Her laugh was rather strained. Blue really was getting over the odds.

He opened the door for her. "Well, so long. Don't forget your curtsey."

Deb knew exactly where to find Thelma Molesworth's suite, although she'd never been there before. As she walked along the heavy piled carpet, she could hear again Elvira's description and her obscene cackle: "Turns sharp, the corridor does, and there's a board with STAFF on it. 'Oo's 'Oo staffroom at the end, they come down the fire stairs. But do they sleep there? No luvvie, they don't. They go off respectable to their wives and husbands to sleep. Do they work there on Sundays? No luvvie, they don't. Nice goin's on there of a Sunday. Mrs Molesworth and Mr Sharlton dinner for two, luvvie, ever so nice and cosy — just as if they was a respectable married couple theirselves. Disgustin' I calls it, and them alone there with 'is door just hopposite 'ers acrost the passage.'' Elvira always gave a wink and a leer before dishing up the tastiest titbit. ''And 'im with his 'ay fever. 'e don't go to bed in madam's flowery bower. All them flowers is just a halibi! Mrs 'igh-and-mighty Molesworth 'as to go visitin' 'im and then go back and cool off in 'er own bed so's she'll be there when Chrissie takes in the mornin' tea.''

Deb turned the corner by the STAFF notice, and walked past a door on the right. A few steps further, she stopped before the word HOSTESS in discreet gilt lettering and knocked firmly.

Thelma opened the door. She was dressed in a magnificent housecoat of cherry red and seemed to fill the doorway. She inclined her head in gracious welcome and smiled her dazzling smile that showed an upper set of beautiful dentures.

"Do come in." She held the door wide open.

Thelma Molesworth was tall and had the full-busted, sternly disciplined figure of a prima donna, to which she added a permanent inclination of her head which was always elaborately coiffured. The Marie Antoinette girls used to swear that the raven black hair that never varied in its elaborate pattern of waves and curls was a wig, until Elvira brought them the juicy titbit that her husband's partner's girlfriend was the trusted hairdresser who touched up Thelma's parting twice a week and gave her a special set at nine o'clock every Monday morning.

"We're delighted to see you. I'm so glad you managed to come." For so many years now, Thelma had flashed her smile and dropped honied words in the sacred cause of hotel service that even when she was sincere, her graciousness gave the impression of being carefully cultivated. "Now, where will you sit? Over here." She patted a pale blue satin cushion which half filled an overstuffed chair.

The whole room gave Deb an overstuffed feeling. The chair seemed to swallow her, the heavy pile of the royal blue carpet sank richly under her feet, she seemed surrounded with bulging chairs and lounges piled with enormous satin cushions. Even the polished wood of the radio was curved and gleamed with a fat glossiness.

Thelma swept over to the telephone which stood on a writing desk in the corner. "I know you're short of time, so I'll order coffee immediately and ring through to Mr Sharlton."

Deb's eyes fixed themselves on the walls. She'd heard about Thelma's gallery of photographs often enough, but she'd never really believed that they completely covered the walls of her sitting-room and overflowed on to the radio and mantelpiece. But it was true. From the tops of the chairs to the picture rail, the walls were covered with photographs of men and women of various ages and types, all wonderfully free from wrinkles and other facial blemishes, and unmistakably stamped with the applied glamour for which the social photographers charged fabulous prices.

"Do have a look at my photographs," Thelma invited, "they're quite a unique collection, you know."

Deb got up to see the photographs more closely. It was an incredible array. Quite impossible to pause and decipher the hieroglyphic signatures, though here and there a clear message in bold handwriting leapt out: "For Thelma in happy memory", "To our darling Miss Ashcroft", and a whole new group, obviously of wartime vintage: "For Mrs Molesworth, in warmest appreciation".

"It wasn't no more than six months after she'd got hitched and swep' off to the country in great style, that she come crawling back to the pub," Elvira had said. "But neither hide nor hair of Mr Molesworth did we ever see!"

Deb gave up looking at faces and let her eyes sweep

over the gallery, every photograph frame to frame against its neighbour. Court feathers jostled ballet skirts, prima donnas posed in operatic get-up, officers' uniforms from two wars and all the services flaunted their ranks and ribbons; there were visiting actors and actresses, conductors from overseas with dramatic batons, fat shanks and skinny shanks in knee breeches and white stockings, an imposing collection of women's evening fashions over the last twenty-five years and a variety of tails faultlessly sheathing distinguished and nondescript gentlemen alike.

"I know you're in a hurry this morning, but you must come up some other time and I'll tell you all about my celebrities." Thelma took Deb's arm and led her back to the chair. "Did you tell the switch to put your call through here?"

"Oh no, I was in such a hurry getting dressed, I quite forgot."

"Then I'll do it for you."

"Thanks." Managing bitch, Deb thought. But she had forgotten to ring down and anyway what's the odds? Let her hear Angus's voice asking for me if she wants to.

While Thelma made the call Deb slid a quick glance through the half-open bedroom door where a tall crystal vase full of glorious blue irises was reflected in the long mirror of the dressing table. A sweet perfume drifted out from a bowl of violets on the bedside table. Of course, she remembered Elvira again. "L. F.'s 'ay fever's the grand halibi." She looked back to the lounge. Just as Elvira said, there wasn't a single flower in the room. Even the low table in the centre that would have looked lovely with a bowl of flowers, held only an ivory figurine.

Thelma followed her glance. "That's the Picadilly Eros — the god of love, you know," she smiled archly, fingering the exquisite figure poised for flight. "Madame Donna Bella gave it to me when she stayed here on her last Australian tour. There she is." Thelma pointed to a large full-length portrait conspicuously displayed above a fragile walnut escritoire. "Such a charming woman, so simple. I always say fame never spoils the really great."

Her recital was cut short by a knock on the door and L. F. came in with a soft tread. The staff swore his walk was specially cultivated for snooping. His high shoulders with the head set low between them and carried slightly forward, his ascetic features and spare tall frame gave him an air of deceptive fragility. "'Im delicate!" Elvira scoffed. "Eats like an 'orse and can work the 'ole staff off their feet without turning a single one of the 'airs 'e's got left."

He greeted Deb with his special bow from the waist. Among the staff it had caused his given name of Lancelot Frances to be changed into Ladies First, or L. F. for short.

"Good morning, Miss Forrest. I am so glad you could come. I always regret that my work leaves me so few opportunities of seeing the members of my staff personally." He crossed to the settee beside her and sat down, carefully picking up the creases of his grey worsted trousers and showing heather mixture hand-knitted socks above his brown suede shoes.

Astonishing what a difference clothes made. Deb took in every detail of his brown sports jacket and cream silk shirt. His weekday suit, black with a faint chalk stripe, his white shirt with the onyx cuff links, his black socks, discreetly speckled with silver above the slim black oxfords, his tie shot with silver to match the patent leather gloss of his black hair streaked with grey, which he wore in a MacArthur part above the left ear and glued across his bald pate to meet a wispy fringe a hemisphere away...they were all part of his personality for her.

It was quite true that in his formal clothes he did look like General MacArthur, as far as the neck at least, with that aquiline nose and his hairdo arranged so carefully to hide the bald pate, but in his sports clothes you only thought what a silly vain fellow he was with those absurd long hairs across his pink dome.

He offered Deb a cigarette, lit it and leaned back at his ease, one long fine hand fingering the satin cushion beside him. It was a beautiful piece of quilting. Thelma's work, Deb thought. Everyone knew how proud she was of her needle-work and her domesticity. "My little home" she used to call her suite. With that gallery round the walls! It would have been pathetic if old Mole wasn't so obviously proud of it.

Thelma plunged into the silence. "It's a lovely day for a run," she said conversationally. "I do envy you."

"It is a lovely day," Deb replied with composure. Obviously Old Mole hadn't put her nose outside and felt the westerly.

L. F. looked from Thelma to Deb with obvious admiration. "Really," he said, smiling paternally, "this charming picture you two ladies make, shows me what I miss by having so little opportunity to meet my staff informally."

Compliments from L. F., Deb thought. What next?

A knock came at the door and a waiter entered with a silver coffee service, putting it on the table beside Thelma.

L. F. continued when he had gone out, "Mrs Dalgety asked me to tell you how much she appreciated the treatment you gave her on Friday evening. She says you have a particularly soothing touch."

"Thank you. It's always encouraging to hear good reports of one's work."

"And I must say," he added, "that I'm very pleased with the spirit in the Marie Antoinette Salon. Of course, I know that is Mrs Molesworth's special interest," he inclined slightly in Thelma's direction, "and I'm sure she gives you full measure of encouragement, but Mrs Dalgety asked particularly that I should myself thank the girls for staying back so cheerfully. 'To get the gum leaves out' was, I think, her phrase."

Gum leaves, Deb thought, that's not what she smelled of!

L. F.'s voice was measured and patronising. He might have been passing on a vice-regal message. Deb well understood the game: Mrs Dalgety's wealth and social position kept her safely outside the range of criticism. She felt an imp of mischief rise. "I'll tell Miss Jeffries so that she can pass on your message to the girls," she said sweetly.

"Oh, I'm sure Mrs Molesworth will see to that." L. F. was the manager again.

Thelma handed round coffee and hot teacakes dripping with butter. Deb declined. Thelma nibbled a plain biscuit and L. F. methodically emptied the silver dish, carrying on his monologue. "Mrs Molesworth is very happy about the staff at the Marie Antoinette. She has always agreed with me that in the intimate relations of a beauty salon, the guests should be attended only by women of refinement."

Deb smiled sweetly, sipped her coffee and wondered where it was all leading.

Thelma cut in, "I'm afraid that doesn't apply to all of them — not after last night's unfortunate incident. Have you seen this morning's paper, Miss Forrest?"

Ah, Deb thought, Guinea! She turned an innocent face to Thelma. "Is there something I should have seen?"

"The Malone girl from the salon not only gatecrashed Who's Who last night, but she's got her photograph splashed all over the paper this morning. Just look at this."

Deb took the paper. "She photographs beautifully, doesn't she?"

Thelma swept on. "The only one they published of the OBNOs Ball. Such an insult to the ladies of the committee." Her voice and look told Deb that the future Mrs McFarland would be wise to take her direction in matters of social behaviour.

"But why?" Deb enquired, and her voice held no more than the simple question.

Thelma shot a look at her. She fought a desire to put the Marie Antoinette masseuse in her place, but remembered in time her social duty to the future hostess of Burramaronga, and spoke with gracious forbearance. "Perhaps you didn't know of the unfortunate incident last night."

"No. I wasn't in the hotel."

"Miss Malone had the impudence to attend Mrs D'Arcy-Twyning's charity ball."

"But surely she was with a party," Deb said sweetly.

"A party! It was absolutely brazen. She came in with

two high-ranking American officers. That's why we couldn't do anything about it. And she knows perfectly well the rule about the staff not being allowed in Who's Who.''

L. F. discreetly interrupted her with a fit of coughing.

Suppose I turned up with Angus? Deb thought. ''But surely, Mrs Molesworth,'' she said, with a shade of Thelma's own accent, ''anyone who buys a ticket is entitled to go to a charity ball wherever it's held.''

''Of course,'' Thelma's voice held a new note of conciliation, ''technically, I suppose Miss Malone was probably within her rights, but to allow herself to be photographed. . . and with Miss D'Arcy-Twyning's fiancé.''

Deb gave her a surprised look. ''Oh,'' she said, ''I didn't know he'd arrived from America. Did he come unexpectedly?''

''That was broken off,'' Thelma explained. ''She is going to marry Commander Ermington. Quite shortly, I believe. He's the youngest son of Lord Weffolk, you know.''

''Really.''

''So you understand how awkward it all is.''

''No, I really don't — if she hasn't announced her engagement. And anyway, everyone knows what press photographs are worth.''

Deb smiled at both of them sweetly. L. F. nonchalantly waggled his free foot and watched the toe of his shoe. Thelma bit her lip. It was wonderful being treated as the future Mrs McFarland; it made you feel as important as if you really were.

''I'm afraid the official guests won't take that point of view,'' Thelma spoke stiffly, ''and the girls who work so hard for charity should at least have their work acknowledged.''

''Of course,'' Deb agreed, ''but I don't think that's the real trouble, do you?'' She looked again at the paper in her hand and smiled charmingly at Thelma. ''Guinea Malone is a beauty and I expect jealousy is at the bottom of it, really. She must have looked glorious in that white frock with her gold hair. . .and with two distinguished escorts of her own in a practically manless world! I can imagine there was more than a little gnashing of teeth amongst Sydney's society lovelies last night — the Pick-Pockettes wouldn't take it too well!"

While Deb was speaking Thelma's face took on a pop-eyed look and her lips were pressed thinly together, as though she was straining physically to keep her mouth shut. L. F. was watching her with a malicious smile.

The telephone rang. Thelma took up the receiver, her voice all honey. "Miss Forrest? Yes, one moment, I'll ask her to speak."

Deb went over to the phone. "Hullo. Yes, good morning." She smiled into the telephone and there was a gay ring in her voice. "Right now? Yes, I'll be down."

She replaced the receiver and turned to Thelma with a sweet smile. "You will excuse me, won't you, I've a car waiting."

Thelma opened the door for her. "Goodbye."

Deb left like a queen. The door closed behind her a shade more sharply than was necessary.

"Well...such nerve! Criticising Mrs D'Arcy-Twyning's guests to me. The upstart! Who's she to talk about the Pick-Pockettes, anyway!"

"It doesn't seem much more than half an hour ago that I heard a pretty frank criticism of the D'Arcy-Twyning family in this very room," L. F. remarked quietly, picking up the Sunday paper which was turned back at Guinea's photograph.

"That's quite different. Deborah Forrest telling me my business! The next thing she'll be running Who's Who for me."

"Tut tut, Thelma. Exaggerating as usual."

"Me exaggerating! I never exaggerate. And what Mr McFarland can see in that underbred young woman..."

"What any man sees in a pretty woman twenty years his junior, my dear."

"Serve her right if I fired her tomorrow."

"But you won't, so why mention it?" L. F. said lazily, turning the paper over to the sporting section.

"And did you see her clothes? Not a penny less than thirty guineas for that turnout, or I'm no judge."

"I reckoned thirty-five," L. F. said blandly, without looking up.

"Where does she get the money? That's what I'd like to know. Not from her husband's allotment or her wages, although I always said we pay those girls in the Marie Antoinette too much with the tips they get. And if she's letting Angus McFarland anticipate his husbandly privileges... she may find she's making a great mistake."

"Think so? Well, you'll soon know whether she's going the right way about it. In the meantime I wouldn't let my imagination run away with me if I were you. If she marries McFarland, you'll want to add her to your gallery after she's been presented at court." He turned a page of the paper with a crackle, folded it in half and plunged into the important matter of Saturday's winners at Randwick.

Thelma bit back a retort. The one occasion on which she would never dare to disturb Lance was when he was carrying out his Sabbath ritual of reading the racing news. Gold pencil in hand and notebook by his side, he went through every race with meticulous care, jotting down the starting prices of the horses he fancied and calculating the fortune he would have won or lost if he'd really made the bets. His temper for the rest of the day depended on these figures: if he won, he was plunged into gloom because he hadn't put the money on, but if he lost he was equally elated to think he hadn't been mug enough to put money in the bookies' pockets. L. F. had never attended a race meeting in his life, Saturday afternoons were far too busy, but he read the stable news and studied form and weights with such attention during the week that he could have floored half the owners in a racing quiz.

Thelma sneaked a glance at him over the top of her own paper. She wanted to read him the letter from the agent about the place he'd found on the mountains for their country club. It had been burning a hole in her escritoire ever since she got it yesterday, but there simply hadn't been a minute when Lance wasn't preoccupied, and it was no use bringing it up today unless his mood was going to be receptive.

After the interruption of Deborah Forrest, she'd be lucky if he finished his calculations before midday dinner. She fingered the letter in her pocket. Perhaps it would be better to wait till after dinner. She noticed that he was smiling to himself as he jotted down figures; it looked as though he was losing.

He looked up at her. "Good day for the bookies yesterday, with Stormcloud coming home at fifteen to one. She was a surprise packet, all right."

"I've never heard of Stormcloud."

"Not many people had before yesterday. She was a rank outsider. And there seems to be a bit of mystery about her owner; she used to belong to Doctor Smithers."

"Oh, the man who had the Coconut Grove," Thelma sniffed. "I bet there's some dirty work if the horse had anything to do with him.''

L. F. smiled at her amiably. "Well, I'm five pounds better off today than I would have been. I had my money on Velie.'' He went back to his calculations, humming to himself tunelessly.

For twenty-five years Thelma had had to listen to the prices Lance would have got if he'd been at the races the day before, and for twenty-five years she had consoled herself with the thought of how lucky she was that he was content to make bets with himself in a notebook and spend Sunday morning working out the odds from the paper instead of spending Saturday afternoons losing money on the course. Every Sunday morning she listened to his complaints about different starting prices for his winners with the same angelic patience.

She felt more cheerful, picked up the paper again and went back to the social news. She clipped out a paragraph about the former luxury yacht that had just come into the harbour, and the two bachelor playboys who had handed it and themselves over to the American Little Ships when the war broke out. They were the Morgan twins, of course, such dear boys. She must make sure to get an autographed photograph of them for her gallery.

She looked up at her latest photograph — a group of pretty girls posed round Denise D'Arcy-Twyning. Below were scrawled the bold, untidy signatures of the thirteen Pick-Pockettes. Lance had thought she was lowering her standards when she hung that one. "After all," he'd said disapprovingly, "what have they ever done? We'd never have heard of them if their fathers weren't making money out of the war. And while I don't mind letting them have the run of the hotel, I don't see why you should put them in the gallery." But you never knew who they'd marry, Thelma had argued, and she'd been right. Look at Cheryl Parmetter, married to that free French marquis, even if she had been divorced within a year. And now Denise engaged to Commander Ermington. Perhaps one day she'd be Lady Weffolk — you never could tell in wartime, even if he had three older brothers.

Lance always spoke to her about *her* gallery with an amused tolerance and pretended it was beneath his notice, but Thelma knew that the photographs were for him as much a symbol of his success as they were of hers. And they were more than that, they were the history of their twenty-five years together.

She had begun the collection in the very first hotel Lance had had, when his father bought the lease and had the licence transferred to him for a twenty-first birthday present, and had thrown in his own capable barmaid Thelma Ashcroft to help the boy run it. She was worth her weight in gold, the old man always said, and she was proud of his praise. The girls in the bar didn't get away with anything while she was at the till, and what she didn't know about running a hotel staff was nobody's business. Lance had been such a kid then, although he was only three years younger than her, and she'd mothered him. But he hadn't been in the hotel business with his father since he was fifteen for nothing, and between them they'd made a name for the Duke of York and a pile for the old man into the bargain. There he was, in the top row, pompous and magnificent in his lord mayor's robes. That was the year he'd sold the Duke at a pretty profit and bought the rundown Commercial for them to work up.

L. F. looked up with his gold pencil poised and an irritable frown between his eyebrows. "I wish these papers'd make up their minds. Three Sunday papers and three different starting prices for Flying Angel. If I'd got the *Star* price I'd have made a tenner, but she's only eight to one in *Sporting Topics*." He went back to his figures.

Thelma went back to her papers. After glancing through the headlines of the Sunday papers she settled down to her morning's work in earnest, and took the top paper from the pile with a sigh. Twenty-seven newspapers to get through before midday dinner — four papers a day, six days a week and three on Sunday! Certainly newspaper rationing had reduced her work by limiting social publicity to war workers, but it had also robbed her of many interesting titbits.

She ran her finger along each line in the social columns, so that there wasn't a name that missed her eye. Any mention, however small, connected with the South Pacific and its guests, was carefully pasted into a huge cuttings book with stiff covers, which she slid in between the back of her desk and the wall. There was no nubile young socialite in Sydney whose friends and enemies, prospects financial and matrimonial, were not charted in Thelma's cuttings book. She knew all the eligible bachelors from the best squatting and professional families; her country list was a miracle of completeness, and she even managed to keep up with he wartime rise of industrial and black market fortunes, and had a special index for the strange individuals who were constantly being thrown into the social limelight of the expensive nightclubs. Thelma filled on an average two books a year and indexed them meticulously so that she could turn to a full newspaper biography of any of her portraits at a moment's notice. Today, however, any pleasure she might have taken in snipping out the week's cuttings was overshadowed by that frightful article in the paper on Saturday and today Guinea's photograph. How could that new supervisor, Faulkiner, have made such a stupid mistake over the journalist — an ex-war correspondent at that? Certainly, it was hotel policy that the guests in the lounges must be properly dressed, but there were always exceptions and a good supervisor should know where to draw the line. But there was no pleasing these newspaper people...when Lance said he'd deal with Faulkiner, the journalist had had the hide to stick up for him and tell the manager it was his fault for having such bloody silly rules.

Thelma frowned at the recollection. Lance couldn't fire Faulkiner with the Manpower difficulties, so he had taken it out on her. It had been quite useless reminding him that only the week before she had warned Faulkiner about the new director of the Art Gallery who was reputed to have nothing but open-necked shirts in his wardrobe. Oh well, Lance was tired and nervy, he needed a rest pretty badly after the last couple of years with the Americans. Not that profits hadn't soared but you always had to be on your toes, and anyway the profits didn't come Lance's way. How glad she'd be when she and Lance were out of it all and in their own place. She simply must talk to him about the agent's letter; Wentworth Falls would be a perfect place for their country club and this property sounded ideal.

Of course, what she would really like would be to get married first and go away somewhere for a long holiday. Lance needed a holiday and so did she. They could have a long, lazy honeymoon, somewhere away from everybody. Perhaps in Honolulu or New Zealand...they'd have to wait until after the war for the trip to England that they'd been promising themselves for so long. How wonderful it would be if they could go abroad before they settled down to work up the club. If this property was as good as it promised, they could buy it and hold it, and then open it up in their own time when conditions were better. Mr Veale would finance them, he'd promised as much when she came back to the SP after her awful experience with Harry Molesworth. If they went abroad first, they could see the great hotels of Europe and maybe cross to the States and get all the latest ideas about country clubs.

Before she'd finished dreaming, Thelma had travelled round the world with Lance. And while she was lost in her dream, twenty-five years fell away and she was in her twenties and Lance was the eager, intelligent boy he'd been when they started at the Duke of York together and she had first fallen in love with him.

She came back to the present with the Saturday cutting in her hand. That Bouncing Belle article in the Town Crier's Diary — of course everyone would read a juicy morsel like that. "Two-up in the lift"..."illegal!"..."Had the manager heard about it?" A gratuitous insult! She read it over to herself again, looked up to speak to Lance and thought the better of it. As if it wasn't bad enough having had to take that awful Albert Johnson on the lift — "Call me Blue" indeed! He had the whole staff and most of the Americans calling him Blue, but he'd be Albert to her as long as he stayed. And it didn't seem as though they'd ever get rid of him with the Returned Soldiers' League behaving so unreasonably. And with Doss such a good barmaid, they couldn't afford to have a showdown. She'd have to talk to Lance about putting him somewhere where he'd have no contact with the guests. That whistle in a South Pacific lift! It went through her head like a red-hot needle every time she heard it. And his "lady" instead of "madam". What Manpower brought you to! Well, they'd get rid of Doss as soon as this stupid ban on employing women under forty-five was removed and they had their pick of young girls again. And once Doss went, Albert wouldn't stay.

That was one cutting she wouldn't put in her press book. She folded it neatly and tucked it into a pigeonhole in her desk. And here was another. Guinea Malone — "Malon" if you please, trying to give herself an aristocratic name into the bargain. The brazen little bitch! After all the care they'd taken to keep Who's Who exclusive, she had to crash into it with an American colonel and get herself photographed with the son of a lord, and Denise D'Arcy-Twyning's fiancé at that. Thelma squirmed at the memory of the appalling things Denise had shouted at her hysterically less than an hour before, and her threats to tell Daddy. If she got old Dan Twyning on the warpath, that might be goodbye to the parcel of brewery shares he was going to get for Lance. . .Thelma carefully cut out the picture and put it in the pigeonhole beside the Town Crier's Diary.

She looked at her wrist watch. It was five minutes to one. Just on lunchtime; no wonder she was getting restless.

Thelma had a stomach that registered mealtimes with the accuracy of an alarm clock. From her early twenties when she had begun to put on weight, through thirty years of increasing girth, she had fought a losing battle against her appetite.

Already her mouth was watering in anticipation of the Sunday dinner that would be served in a few minutes. "Five to one," she reminded L. F. He grunted but did not look up from his paper. Thelma went into her bedroom and closed the door behind her.

She crossed over to her dressing table and picked up a hand mirror, scanning her heavy makeup carefully in the strong light from the window, turning her head to catch the light on her parting. She peered at it anxiously. Not a sign. There was no doubt that Simone was doing a good job with the new dye; it had been so difficult during the war to keep her hair the lustrous black which had been its glory all the years that Lance had known her. Having to get it touched up every four days was a nuisance, but it was worth it. It was ten years since she'd first started dyeing her hair and she preened herself that no one had ever guessed.

Not that it seemed to matter to Lance nowadays how she looked. Once he had taken a pride in her appearance, but now he never commented on anything unless it was to say unkindly that he thought she was putting on weight. To think that twenty-five years ago he'd given her her beloved lapis lazuli earrings, "to match her fathomless blue eyes", he'd said. She smoothed the heavy silk crêpe of her cherry house-coat and turned her head so that the earrings caught the light in the mirror.

What a mess she'd made of things, marrying Harry Molesworth. She knew now she had done it as much to pro-voke Lance as anything. They should have got married right at the beginning, back in the Duke of York days when they were first in love. She had always wanted to marry him, but he had so many reasons why it would be bad for business. She was much more attractive in the bar if the men thought she was free, he told her, and it was better for the manager not to be married. They'd only been at the Duke of York a year, when some wag christened him "Ladies First" and it had stuck ever since. And there was no doubt it suited him. Even when he had been quite a youngster older women had fallen for his grave courtesy, and the young ones had always fallen in love with him in a safe kind of way.

At first she had been jealous, but she never really had anything to be jealous about over Lance. If he'd mar-ried anyone he'd have married her, she knew that. But he didn't seem to want a wife and a home and family like most men. He didn't seem to need a woman, not the way Harry Molesworth did. Even when he was young he'd never been passionate.

Although for twenty-five years she'd been his wife in everything but name, she had come reluctantly to realise that Lance's work mattered to him more than anything else in the world, and that the only family she would ever have so long as they were together would be a series of hotels. During all those years she had worked beside him, bolstering his confidence, helping to build up his reputation as one of the shrewdest managers in the hotel world. She'd been his mistress for twenty years when she told him she was going to marry Harry Molesworth and leave the SP. She had been so certain that the threat was all that was needed to make him marry her himself. Well, it hadn't.

So she'd married Harry and she'd honestly tried to make a success of her marriage and prove herself a model wife. But it hadn't worked. Harry Molesworth didn't want a model wife or a model home, he wanted a place where he could take off his collar and tie and put his feet on the mantelpiece, and ask his mates around.

At the end of six months she'd put on a stone in weight snacking in the kitchen for solace, and had begun to devour whodunnits. When she finally made up her mind to leave Harry, instead of the pleading she expected, he laughed his head off and told her she could have a divorce any time she managed to bring that stick of an L. F. up to scratch.

She had come back to Lance and the South Pacific on the verge of a nervous breakdown. He had fired the hostess as well as the head housekeeper, whom he suspected of keeping her family in linen on the side, had taken Thelma back to fill both jobs at just a quarter of his own salary, and introduced into their private relations an unfortunate habit of referring to the mess she had made of her marriage.

Thelma heard the waiter knock on the outer door and went back to the lounge. Lance came to the lunch table silent and preoccupied, his mind still on starting prices. With firm righteousness Thelma refused crisp sauté potates and told herself that if Gladys Moncrieff had taken off a stone on grilled chops and pineapple, she could do the same on steak and watercress. Really, it was maddening.

The delicious luncheon spread a comfortable feeling through her and her spirits began to rise. After all, what did their plans for establishing a country club together mean but marriage? They couldn't keep their relationship secret in a country club as they did at the South Pacific, and Lance was too shrewd to let any personal scandal stand in the way of business. She fingered the letter in the pocket of her housecoat. Would now be a good time to tell him about the exciting place the agent had found?

L. F. looked up from his paper. "I see the Woman's Christian Temperance Union are on the warpath again," he said.

"What are they complaining about now?"

"Same old thing. The evil influence of the drink traffic on the morals of the young."

"Unfortunately, with the papers making such a fuss about drinking conditions, it's not the kind of thing you can afford to ignore. And that reminds me, I must see that there's a room kept for the deputation on Wednesday afternoon. Who's going to see them this time?"

L. F. laughed. "Allstone," he said. "It was H. V.'s idea — he's an old fox. Set the temperance women and Allstone with his community hotel bug onto each other, and the old hens'll tear him limb from limb because they'll say he wants to make drinking more pleasant. And he'll come back to the board with his tail between his legs and H. V.'ll sympathise with him on how difficult it is for the trade to help the public when the wowsers are so unreasonable!

"But quite seriously," L. F. went on, "we'll have to do something about the state of affairs in the foyer and the lounges. Once the Americans are out of this country — and it's only a question of weeks now — there'll be absolutely nothing to be gained by having the place overrun by the class of women we've had to put up with for the last couple of years. That's one clean-up Allstone can genuinely promise the WCTU deputation on Wednesday."

"But we'll still have the British fleet and there'll be a lot of Dutch around and they're great spenders."

"The Dutch may be, but the British haven't got it to spend and it'll only be the high rankers who'll come here. As a matter of fact that's what the directors' sub-committee meeting is for on Tuesday; they want to map out a new policy. So if you've got any ideas in the meantime, let me have them."

"I've got quite a number," Thelma said. "I'll jot them down as I think of them."

"Good. Let me have them as soon as you can. The plain, brutal fact we've got to get used to is that once the Yanks leave, the public bar'll have to depend on ordinary civilians and our own troops again, and they won't pay the prices the Yanks pay. They won't put up with what the Yanks put up with either and frankly, with the directors expecting me to keep up the inflated figures of the last two years, I don't like the prospect at all."

Thelma looked at his face to see if he had finished. It might be a good idea to show him the agent's letter now; it might make him feel better to remind him that they weren't going to be tied to the SP for life, and that at last they had a practical proposition for their country club.

Perhaps, though, she'd better wait until he'd had a rest and afternoon tea. Certainly it had been a bad week with the fuss over that wretched journalist and the publicity, and then the upset over Denise this morning. He'd seemed a bit edgy ever since he got up. Of course it might be that the westerly was starting another attack of hay fever — she hadn't thought of that, he'd been so free all September since the wattle was finished.

She scanned his face guardedly, but except for a slight frown he looked much as usual. She wondered if something had gone wrong that he hadn't told her about. Still, that would be most unlike him; it generally worked the other way and he took it out on her. Not that she minded, it seemed to soothe him and he really was highly strung.

Lance made the decision for her by getting up abruptly and pushing his chair back. "I think I'll go and have my rest now," he said, picking up an apple and biting into it. "You'll give me a call for afternoon tea?"

Thelma nodded and smiled at him. "Have a good rest, dear." She sighed, put the letter back in her pocket and began to peel a banana.

It was early afternoon when Deb and Angus came out of the Greengate Hotel, and the rising westerly blew hot and dusty against their faces. Angus mopped his forehead as he sank into the driver's seat beside her. "We'd have done better to go straight through to Palm Beach. This place is like an oven."

The sun burnt through a red haze and mirages flickered across the glistening surface of the Pacific Highway. It was no cooler when they turned off at Pymble for the run through French's Forest. The air was still acrid with the smell of burning bush and Deb closed her window against the blackened drift of leaves and smuts whipped up by the wind.

Angus smiled apologetically, "I seem to have made a bad choice, coming this way. We should have gone round by Manly, but every Tom, Dick and Harry seems to get out on that road on Sundays and you're so often held up in the queue at the Spit Bridge."

"Oh, I don't mind. It's such a relief to get out of the city, and it won't be long before we get a breeze off the sea."

"That's right. Besides, I always think it's worth coming this way for that excellent dinner they put on at the hotel."

Deb wondered what he'd think if he'd seen her yesterday bumping over this same road behind that impudent taxi driver and then looking like a drowned rat hosing Nolly's house half the afternoon. That'd surprise him. Well, it was quite true one half of the world never knew how the other half lived. She set her jaw grimly. Nolly and Tom could talk all the blah in the world, but she wasn't going to put herself deliberately in their half.

When they came out of the forest, the gleam of the sea, blue and still below them gave an illusion of coolness. But the following westerly and the blazing sun took all the freshness out of the coastal air. Angus gave her his brief intimate smile as he swung the car down the winding road.

"I'll be glad to cool off in the surf."

"So shall I."

"You look so cool now that it's better to look at you than the sea."

"Maybe, but not nearly so safe."

"Safe? I know this road by heart."

"I seem to have heard that before."

"Not from me, I'm sure."

"No...in the collection of famous last words."

Angus laughed with the sudden delight he always experienced when Deb came back at him with a remark like that. She hadn't much sense of humour — to be honest, he didn't like a woman with a sense of humour — but her sudden flashes had a salty quality and he loved the contrast with the deep femininity of her essential nature.

An unexpected creature, unlike the women he'd known. Poised, but natural. Lovely to look at, exhilarating to touch, stimulating without obvious effort. Deb had something more than any woman he had known intimately. Reserved — there was no clear term in his mind. It was not merely a quality of sex, though only he knew what her nearness did to him. Aloof, yes. Perhaps that was it. Even when they danced together, she was essentially aloof. Nothing easy about her. Perhaps that was why he wanted to marry her. He had known wittier women, more beautiful ones, women with more obvious sex charm, women whose smouldering desire had held him enchained till at last the chains were snapped in sharp revulsion of the body against its own thraldom.

That's how it had been with Liz. He'd been infatuated, but she had wanted too much. Grown possessive. Not that he wasn't fond of her; if he hadn't been, their affair would never have lasted so long. Eight years; it was a long time to remain more or less faithful to one woman. Without any strings, either. Liz had taken the break badly at the last, but it was really her own fault. If she hadn't begun to make demands on him he'd probably never have let it come to a showdown — as much from habit as anything else. Well, she had only herself to blame, he'd never made any promises.

Angus put his foot on the accelerator and swung out on to the Palm Beach road, taking so wide a curve that he forced a cream coupé coming in the opposite direction off the road. It skidded and righted itself.

"Whew!" Deb let out her breath in relief and turned as the coupé straightened out behind them. "For a moment I thought that was Dr Dallas MacIntyre's car, but it was a man at the wheel, wasn't it?"

"Yes, careless swine."

Won't admit he made a mistake, Deb thought. Aloud, she said: "Oh, Dallas is a wonderful driver, she'd never do a silly thing like that. She's a marvellous doctor too," she prattled on, giving him a chance to get over his discomfiture.

"If she's your doctor, I hope she is."

Deb laughed. "I'm one of those healthy people who never need a doctor. But Dallas is just like an elder sister, she lived with us practically all the time she was doing her medical course."

"Oh, did she?" Angus sounded surprised. "My sister-in-law speaks highly of her. She operated on her last year — very successfully too. Olive was telling me on Friday she's just been appointed the first woman honorary to the Harbour Hospital."

"That's right. We're all terribly proud of her. You know, she's my little daughter's godmother." Angus was silent. Touchy as the devil, Deb thought.

The wind caught them at the curve of the road. "The surf's very flat," she commented. "I hate it when there's a westerly, don't you?"

"Yes. It won't be so bad at Palm Beach, though. The hills behind break the force of the wind, and we'll be quite sheltered at my house afterwards."

Deb felt a little prickle of excitement. He had taken her to Palm Beach before, but she had never been invited to cross the sacred threshold of the stone house tucked away among the palms behind the beach. Angus had pointed it out to her several times, but always with some remark about the house-keeper being unprepared for guests.

His invitation today was a silent confirmation of their new relationship. She had felt a change, too subtle to define, in his whole attitude to her. It was as though a new intimacy and a sureness had been established. He no longer had the casual, bland, yet faintly patronising air of a wealthy man entertaining — on the most respectable basis, to be sure — a woman, whom he found attractive in spite of the social gulf between them.

Claire had told her a blistering story of his long established affair with Liz Destrange, that passé beauty with her daring clothes, her legendary furs and her specially blended perfume. Deb had seen her often at the Marie Antoinette, where she came to Claire for renovation when the hectic round of her "war work" got too much for her. SP bush wireless had it that Liz, faded survival of the gay twenties, had played Angus against a duller and less wealthy fiancé for years till the fiancé — in a moment of unforeseen rebellion — married the equally dull girl he'd known since childhood, and settled down to raising a family, while Liz grew more brittle and less brilliant in the frantic effort to keep up with a world into which the younger lovelies of the thirties had erupted with fresher charm and fewer inhibitions.

Liz must often have visited the Palm Beach house. And now she, Deb Forrest, was being admitted to its sacred hospitality — but on a very different basis. She was suffused with a pleasant feeling of her superior importance. Angus had asked her to be his wife, the mistress of his home. He had never married Liz. Well, she wasn't married to him either — yet. Suddenly she wondered, was he being too sure of her, taking her to his house like this?

And why shouldn't he be? Deb asked herself. Why not? If a man proposed to a married woman and she hedged but continued to see him and accept his attentions, surely he was justified in thinking that her hesitation was only feminine co-quetry. Was she a coquette? Guinea had a ruder and franker word for it than coquette. Was she like that? It was all so very difficult. With Jack now.... But Jack was returning in a week with a flat ultimatum for their future life, made without regard for her wishes or her plans. There was no coquetry between her and Jack. There never had been.

The rocky, broken coast spread out in front of them as they topped the hill above Newport Beach; the stone castle on its steep cliff stood out like a child's toy against the turquoise sea beyond; the headlands of Bilgola and Avalon and Whale Beach were ochre and dun under their rough native scrub. They rose out of a sea flattened under the westerly, giant sphinxes taking the force of the Pacific tides against their breasts, their paws submerged in the swirling waves that ran with a hiss of broken foam over the rocky ledges.

As the car curved across the isthmus at Palm Beach, leaving Pittwater behind, Angus commented angrily on the auto-tents crowded beside the golf links. "Look at that. Only October, and the place is already overrun with campers. Why the council permits it I don't know. Some of them are here all the year round — using the housing shortage as an excuse to stay. They've ruined the whole tone of the place. We've protested often enough but the council's more interested in collecting ground rents than keeping up decent standards."

Before Deb could think of a suitable reply, the beach burst on them with a glare of yellow sand, striped umbrellas and bright bathing suits. They turned slowly along the esplanade.

Angus's house stood halfway up the hill among a thick grove of palms, its sandstone walls mellow in the afternoon light. Deb had only seen it from the esplanade before, but now, as the car climbed up the narrow road from the beach and turned into the terraced garden, she realised how spacious and dignified it was. No mere weekender this, but a house of character and impressive solidity.

"Here we are at last." Angus got out of the driver's seat and stretched himself.

A dark-faced man, limping and spare, appeared from the garage and lifted a hand to his cap. "G'day, Mr McFarland."

"Hullo, Bert. Everything all right?"

Bert nodded.

"You've got the lawn in good condition. Did you get that hundred feet of new hose I ordered?"

Bert nodded again. "It came on Wednesday and I've been giving the place a good soaking every day."

"Oh good. You want to take care of it, it was hard enough to get even at a black market price. Here, take this first." Angus opened the boot and disclosed a portable ice chest. "Be careful," he warned, "and keep this end up. There are bottles in it."

Bert lifted it carefully, straining under the weight. Angus put a firm proprietary hand under Deb's elbow and guided her to the house.

The shaded coolness of the lounge, which opened on to a paved terrace, was restful after the dusty heat. The housekeeper, a small round woman with blank eyes, was at Angus's side almost as soon as he crossed the threshold. Her greeting just stopped short of a bob, and her acknowledgment of Deb as she was introduced was deferential and incurious — though knowledge of what went on behind such guarded faces at the SP made Deb wonder just what she was thinking.

"Would you care for a cool drink, after your long drive, Mr Angus?" she asked.

Angus smiled questioningly at Deb: "I think after we've changed, don't you?"

She nodded although her throat was parched.

"Show Mrs Forrest to her room then, Jean."

Deb turned to follow her along the wide corridor.

"Is there anything you require, Miss Forrest?" Jean asked, opening the door of the bedroom and standing back to let her pass.

An imp of malice pricked Deb to correct Angus's deliberately slurred introduction. "*Mrs* Forrest," she said, walking to the window and looking out on to the long stretch of sand that ran in a shallow curve to Barrenjoey headland.

"I'm sorry."

"That's quite all right. And I think I have everything, thank you."

The bedroom, with its low beamed ceiling and polished jarrah floors, was surprisingly unlike what she had expected.

No bachelor's room this! Her eyes went to the huge cedar double bed, to the antique candlesticks on the solid dressing table and the wide matching wardrobe. A room some woman had arranged with care. Great white sheepskin rugs were laid on the polished boards, and the curtains and covers were of cream and scarlet lacquered chintz. Startling and individual. The setting for a flamboyant brunette — a brunette like Liz Destrange.

Deb began to undress, an odd reluctance slowing her movements. She opened the wardrobe door to hang up her frock and a perfume drifted out that spoke of long and intimate use. It was unmistakably Liz's perfume; she knew it from the salon. She took the coathanger out and slammed the door. Her clothes would never hang there!

When she went into the adjoining bathroom she could hear Angus moving about in the room behind the further door. Convenient! The face that met her gaze in the mirror was flushed and the eyes glittered with anger. When she opened a cabinet to look for suntan oil, the same perfume floated out. She closed it and stood there, her hand still on the knob. No sense in going on like this. Liz Destrange was finished with — she should worry! But she'd have the place redecorated, by God she would, and fumigated too. It was her turn now.

As she buttoned the scanty shorts of her bathing suit and adjusted the brassière top, she had a rare moment of fantasy, and instead of herself she saw Liz Destrange standing before the long pier glass, her burning black eyes and high cheek bones catching the light. Had she loved Angus? Was that what had burned her out to a stringy forty? How did you feel when you loved a man who didn't care?

Her own reflection told her how Angus's eyes would light at her coming. As she put on her brief surf-coat over her bathing costume, she heard him padding softly along the passage. Slipping her feet into white sandals, she went to join him.

As Deb came into the lounge, Angus rose to greet her. He took both her hands in his and held them wide. "Perfect,

I'd forgotten how beautiful you are.''

His words and the look in his eyes banished her irritation. Liz's perfume might haunt the bedroom, but Liz's ghost had no more power.

Jean came in like a small grey automaton, placed a tray of frosted glasses before them and faded again with a rustle of her unfashionably long skirts.

"We've fixed a mint julep for you. I hope you'll like it.''

Deb had never tasted one, but she assured him she liked them.

"You wouldn't think it to look at her, but Jean's a great hand with the drinks.''

"Really. Has she been with you long?''

"She was with my mother, and her mother was with my grandmother. You can't get servants like her today. Bert's her son, and I wouldn't put up with him for five minutes only for that. He was boarded out of the army after Tobruk and came back quite a different fellow. Grown too big for his boots; nothing satisfies him now.''

Over the edge of her glass, Deb watched Angus with the sense of astonishment she was constantly experiencing with him. Family retainers! She'd only read about this kind of thing. Service in the blood, Tom would have said, only one step backwards to the bob of the knee and the pulling of the forelock. It was fantastic in Australia, but somehow right for Angus. And why not? You only complained about these things when you hadn't got them. It would be very nice to have family retainers to serve Mrs McFarland. Or would their shrewd eyes guess, without being told, what she was used to?

She pushed the glass away and stood up quickly. "Let's get down to the beach before it's too late, I'm dying for a dip.''

The sand was hot under their feet and sharp gusts of wind whipped the stinging grains against their bare legs as they stood ready to plunge into the uninviting surf. The westerly had flattened the breakers so that the open sea had no more movement than the sheltered bays across the isthmus.

A haze of heat suffused sea, sky and sand, but when they waded out the water was clear and bitingly cold. It fizzed around them like green soda water. As they plunged in, it struck chill against their bodies and they came up gasping. A man nearby grinned at Deb. "Cold current coming up the coast...it's like a blooming iceberg." She laughed in reply, exhilarated by the sting of the water.

Angus slid a hand under her arm, propelling her farther out. "A pity we're getting such a doubtful class of people down here," he said, frowning. "I hoped the petrol rationing would rid us of them."

She slipped her arm from his grasp and swam away, moving with an easy grace, and turning at last to float on her back with a feeling of utter relaxation. A flight of gulls swept down almost brushing the water, and far out three porpoises rolled in ebony curves round the headland.

The waves bore her on a light swell. She closed her eyes and the sun beat on her lids. There was a clop-clop on her ears as the water sucked at her cap.... This could be anywhere...Cronulla...Bateman's Bay.... This could be any time...five, ten years ago...

Angus's voice was beside her: "You're rather far out — the lifesavers say there's a dangerous undertow."

She opened her eyes and found him treading water beside her. She looked back at the beach and was surprised at the distance she had drifted.

"Silly of me," she murmured and began to swim back towards the crowd. Angus matched her pace with an obvious effort.

"Had enough?" he panted as he came up beside her in the shallows. She would have liked to swim out again, but when she saw the goose-pimples on his arms and the faint blue line round his mouth, she shivered sympathetically. "More than," she said and began to wade ashore with him.

The sun was just dropping behind the high ridge as they came out. The beach curved in a glowing pinkish crescent to the dark bulk of Barrenjoey; the low wooded hills were bathed in a faint, amethyst light and shadows lay purple and heavy in the narrow gully at the end of the beach where the palm grove caught the late sunshine on its fronds.

"I didn't realise I'd been in so long," she said in apology as they picked up their towels.

"You women seem to be able to stay in all day." Angus rubbed himself irritably.

Deb felt swift compunction. It wasn't fair to keep him in so long just because she enjoyed the water. "Let's run up to the house," she said, "I'm really freezing."

The annoyance went out of his eyes and together they ran across the sand to the track that led up to the house. He was panting before they reached it, and she stopped to lean against the rail as though in distress herself. "I'm absolutely winded," she called, "you'll have to go slower."

A gratified smile lit his face. "What a brute I am!"

They walked the rest of the way, Angus recovering his breath and Deb tingling with a sudden desire to run on and leave him puffing behind. He was really frightfully out of condition. She saw that the belt of his trunks was too tight and his belly bulged above it slightly, and pushed away from her as unworthy the thought that perhaps Elvira was right when she said he wore a girdle. Still, you couldn't get away from the fact that he was getting on, nearly fifty...seventeen years older than she was.

Deb walked up the road beside him with deliberate sedateness. A gramophone was blaring out from the house on the slope of the hill immediately behind Angus's, and couples were dancing on the broad balcony. A grey-haired man came to the railing and waved a glass to attract their attention.

"There's someone up there waving to you," she said.

Angus did not look up. His face took on its most aloof expression. "Take no notice of them. The fellow who's just bought the place is the chairman of directors of the South Pacific — Horatio Veale, and he brings all his flashy friends out from town. Fortunately it doesn't worry us in the front of the house, though Jean says they keep her awake half the night with their drinking parties. Personally I intend to have nothing whatever to do with them."

Angus opened the gate for her and they went across the lawn and up the broad stone steps. The housekeeper materialised silently and informed Deb that her bath was waiting.

The bathroom was heavy with steam and perfume. Deb threw off her bathing suit and stood naked, stretching her arms above her head and breathing in the scented air. She felt young and exultant. She was seventeen years younger than Angus — she'd never be in Liz Destrange's position. She slid into the deep roman bath and luxuriated in water, redolent of Liz's special bath salts.

She was still in the bath when she heard Angus go down the hall. But she took her time; he could wait. She dressed with leisurely care, knotting the blouse high to show her tanned midriff and putting on her new sharkskin slacks. The zipper caught and she tore her nail trying to fix it and thought despairingly that she'd have to put on her skirt after all, but a final tug released it and the teeth locked smoothly.

At last she was ready and Angus came swiftly across the lounge to meet her. "I thought you must have run away."

"Have I been terribly long? I'm so sorry."

His face cleared. "You must forgive me. I was too thirsty to wait." He poured a cocktail for her and another whisky for himself. The drink was strong and sent a pleasant glow through her body.

Angus lit her cigarette and leaned back in his chair. As she inhaled the smoke Deb gave herself up to a sense of well-being. The low-ceilinged lounge with its long glass doors and wide windows was cool and shadowy in the shelter of the hills. It was as though the house had gathered coolness to itself along with dignity and grace, and made an oasis in the world of blistering sun and hot winds. A smell of damp earth came from the terrace where Bert was hosing the scorched garden. The pleasant weariness of a day in the open relaxed her limbs. It was all so rich and safe.

Jean wheeled in a traymobile with enough food on it to feed a dozen hungry surfers. As her teeth bit into butter-soaked scones, Deb remembered Nolly's struggle with the butter ration. The tiny ham sandwiches were sharp with mustard which even the SP could not get, and she would have liked to wrap up the untouched asparagus rolls. What a morning tea party they would make for the Marie Antoinette staff! Most of them had forgotten what asparagus tasted like. And the cakes piled with forbidden cream. If this was Angus's domestic standard, it would soon swell his waistline — and hers too, if she wasn't careful.

Who was it said money couldn't buy everything? She would like to take the fool first to Nolly's on a hot Saturday afternoon and then bring him here. This was the kind of life a woman wanted. Gracious and dignified, no vulgar show; just life raised to its highest degree of satisfaction and security. Romance was all right when you were twenty-two, but at thirty-two you wanted something else. And above all you wanted it for your children.

Children...it came to her with a sense of shock: any other child she might have would be Angus's. Well...that could never injure Luen. They would be too far apart in age. Even if she had a son, it wouldn't affect Luen. How would Luen like all this? Her eyes rested on the heavily embossed silver tea service beside her, so old that the crest on the lids was almost obliterated. She had never seen one in use before, though she had admired them often enough in the windows of antique shops.

Jean wheeled out the traymobile as soundlessly as she had brought it in. As the door closed behind her, Angus rose abruptly. "We may as well finish our cigarettes on the settee."

She sank into the soft cushioned seat. For a moment he stood behind her and the grip of his hands on her shoulders startled her. "Sorry," he said as he came round and sat down beside her. "But you look so fascinating that I forgot myself."

His hand closed over hers as it lay on the cushion. A beautiful hand, she thought, examining it with the eye of a masseuse. A firm palm and long fingers with rounded well-kept nails. It was unlike the hand of any other man she had known well. Her father's, broad and rough, with enlarged knuckles; Jack's, brown and sinewy with square nails and a hard palm; Tom's, a mechanic's hand, the dirt ingrained in spite of scrubbing. All hands that had worked hard, with thumbs splayed out and roughened at the base.

Angus turned hers over and held it in his palm. Although the skin was softened with massage cream, it lay revealingly muscular against his. He raised it to his lips and kissed the hollowed palm. "You don't know how much it means to me to have you here."

"It's been a delightful day."

"So have others — but this, well, this is specially significant."

She was silent.

"I hope it is for you too."

"Of course."

"There'll be many more of them." And after a pause, he added questioningly: "I hope!"

Deb nodded. He got up and poured her another cocktail. "Let's drink to it. I can hardly live through another week."

Angus leaned towards her until their shoulders touched. She found herself adjusting the cushion so that it barred more intimate contact. He seemed not to notice, but she knew from the tightening of his mouth that he was sensitive to her slightest movement.

"It's time you met some of my family, I think," he said, stroking the back of her hand lightly. There was a harsh note in his voice as though he was secretly angry, and she realised that his gaze was fixed on her wedding ring. "Could you have dinner with my brother and his family tomorrow night?"

"I'm not sure if I'll be off in time."

"We can make it late. His wife and daughter are in town with him and I'd like them to meet you."

"Yes, but..."

"I don't think you'll find Olive and Helen very formidable."

"Oh, it's not that. I've seen them both in the Marie

Antoinette and they look awfully nice."

"Well, what is it then?"

Deb thought she heard the faintest shade of impatience in his voice. How tactless of her to mention the Marie Antoinette. Of course he'd hate the idea of his family seeing her there. She hastened to put him at his ease.

"I've never actually come in contact with either of them. They haven't the sort of figures that need my attention. It's just that it's so hard for me to set a time. Tomorrow's a holiday and most of the Marie Antoinette staff will be off."

"If that's the only difficulty, I think I can fix it."

Deb had a mental picture of L. F. bowing obsequiously to Angus's lordly request.... Oh, yes, he'd fix it! She felt resentful and amused at the same time.

"I thought we might go somewhere afterwards, so shall we say quarter to seven at the South Pacific? That will give us plenty of time."

"I'd be delighted."

Angus played abstractedly with her wedding ring, his brows contracted and his mouth set stubbornly. "I wish you wouldn't wear this."

"Why not?"

"That's an unnecessary question. You know, I got quite a shock on Friday night when you told me your husband was coming back next week. But now I'm glad."

"Are you?"

"Yes. I always prefer to take my hurdles quickly — and by this time next week the worst will be over."

"Well, hardly."

"I mean for me, and once you give me your decision, you won't have to worry about legal matters. My solicitor will go into all that." He pressed his lips to the inside of her elbow and she involuntarily drew back, yet so slight was her withdrawal that she was surprised when he sat upright as though at a rebuff.

He lit another cigarette and she saw that his hands were trembling. But he turned a face to her in which there was no shadow of emotion, and gave her his lopsided smile. "There are a number of things we shall have to sort out before then." He furrowed his brows. "It's not a subject I like to discuss but, after all, if you ask your husband for a divorce, you should have some financial security to see that you're not...shall we say, left high and dry?"

"Angus, please..." she protested.

"My dear, this is only commonsense. After all, while you probably know enough about me to realise that you can rely on me absolutely...there are other things. For instance, I might be run over by a tram."

"You are morbid..."

"No — merely practical. I might even drop dead from the strain of waiting for you."

She laughed, and with sudden tenderness put out a hand and pressed his. He held it in a grip so hard that her wedding ring cut into her finger.

"There's one thing I am going to ask you to do as soon as you allow me to tell my solicitor to go ahead and that is, to resign from the South Pacific staff. Just to please me."

"That sounds very pleasant, but you must remember it was the housing shortage which drove me to take the job in the first place. And things are even worse now than two years ago."

"If it's only a question of getting a flat, I can manage that easily enough. My sister Virginia is part owner of Martini Mansions — you know them, of course. Up near Wynyard. During the last couple of years they've been let chiefly to American officers, but they are always coming and going, and I could quite easily get a flat there for you."

Deb looked at him whimsically. "That's awfully kind of you, but...after all, I still have to have a job. You see, under such circumstances, I...couldn't go on taking an allowance from my husband."

"Of course not," he spoke jerkily. "Naturally, I should regard it as my responsibility as much as if we were actually married." He threw the half-smoked cigarette away. "The moment you give me the right I shall make a deed of settlement on you. The amount..."

She put a hand across his mouth. She did not want to hear the amount, she would not listen. This was no bargain — you do this, I pay you that. But Angus interpreted the touch of her palm against his lips as the sign he had been waiting for. He turned and took her in his arms. All the frustrations of the day found outlet in a kiss that bruised her mouth. His hand moved over her bare waist and burned against her breast through the thin silk of her blouse.

For a moment she was passive under his touch. He caressed her with the expertness of a man accustomed to wooing, and felt the answering wave of her desire. All the starved and disciplined months of loneliness rose up to defeat her, and she clung to him out of a desperate need. His fingers fumbled at the zipper of her slacks and tugged at it. It caught, as it had caught when she was dressing, and in that moment Deb came out of her madness. She gripped his hand fiercely: "No," she whispered. "No."

He was still at her touch. She could feel the thudding of his heart against hers, the trembling of his thighs. He held her without moving, trigger-tense. She lay still in his arms, hearing his heartbeats grow quieter, feeling the tension slacken and desire recede.

He bent and kissed her again with a laugh, half of joy, half of triumph, and smoothed back her hair. He kissed her lips again with tenderness, then he lifted her suddenly to her feet and held her closely. "I'd like to stay here forever," he whispered, "but now I know you feel the same as I do, waiting won't be so hard."

Angus slowed the car as they took the curve round Sunrise Hill on their way homewards. Below them was the narrow neck of the isthmus. The moon, like a great new penny halfway up the hazy sky, drenched the water with gold. In Pittwater, the anchored yachts swung in the race of the tide, behind them the surf broke with a dull booming on the ocean beach, and Barrenjoey light blinked its warning out to sea.

The glare of the headlights caught a flurry of black moths that thudded against the windscreen and fluttered heavily through the open window. Angus swore softly as he brushed them from the glass. One was tangled in Deb's hair and whirred frantically as she pulled it away, the furry body squashing between her fingers. "Bogongs!" she said, "ugh! Revolting."

He pressed the accelerator and the powerful engine of the car gathered speed. "We'll soon leave them behind," he murmured, slipping an arm round her shoulders and drawing her close to him.

Colonel Maddocks cruised slowly down Forbes Street and pulled up outside Guinea's place. It was the third time he had been round this afternoon. He craned out of the car to look up at her window — it was still shut. He lit a cigarette and noticed idly that another US Army car was parked in the narrow lane leading off the street.

What the devil was he going to do? Wait here till she came home? She might be hours. Go in and ask again? Somehow he felt that he couldn't face that landlady for the third time.

Goddam it all! He'd planned a wonderful day with Guinea. The sight of the harbour, blue and ruffled under the wind beyond the tangle of ships and docks at the end of the street, reminded him of how wonderful it might have been. What a glorious vital creature the girl was; brimming over with life; alluring, yet somehow untouched. This was what he'd been waiting for all his life. Imagine coming to a godforsaken dump down under and finding your fate waiting for you. He sighed, feeling hollow and a little depressed.

I will go in, he thought. Damn the landlady. He had just lifted the old-fashioned knocker when the door opened and Major Alfrickson stood in the doorway scowling at him. Colonel Maddocks felt as foolish as a small boy caught raiding the pantry. He made a snatch at his self-possession. "Oh hullo, Lew. I just dropped round to see if I could take the little girl for a run. It's been such a hot day."

Major Alfrickson slammed the door and came down the steps. "So I see," he said sourly. "The landlady says you've been dropping round all day at odd intervals."

"Well, not exactly. I did come round after lunch, but... well..."

"Well, she's not in. I've been sitting over there in the car with the sun frying me for the last hour and now the landlady tells me that when she goes out to see her family she never gets back till about ten o'clock at night."

Byron felt unaccountably cheerful. "Oh, is that where

she's gone?'' His heart warmed at the thought of that lovely girl going home on Sundays to see her family. Somehow it fitted in with his picture of her. "That's what I'd expect of her," he said fondly, "going home for Sunday dinner."

Lew scowled at him again. "Well, that's where she said she was going. Of course you never know." He stood beside the car, glaring at Byron settling himself in the driver's seat. "And if you want my opinion, I think it's a lousy trick to play, coming horning in on a feller — your oldest pal too, when I've got only a few more hours to spend with the girl before I'll be leaving for the States and home."

Byron offered him a cigarette and lit one for himself.

"You ruined my night too," Lew went on, "sneaking off with her like that and leaving me high and dry."

Byron looked at him, startled. "You don't mean you'd arranged to spend the night with her?" he asked in horrified tones.

Lew shook his head gloomily. "No, but I was hoping to. I've been trying get her round to the point for six months, but I never could bring her up to it. Then you had to come along and ruin everything."

Byron's face brightened and he looked positively happy again. "I'm awfully sorry, Lew," he said apologetically, his eyes belying his words, "but," he added severely, "I think you ought to be ashamed of yourself trying to seduce a girl like Guinea. After all, you're married."

"You don't have to remind me. I suppose it'll be flung in my teeth now that your second divorce has gone through. It's all right for you, you've got plenty of fun ahead. But what is there for me going back home to Sophie? That's all I've got to look forward to."

Byron threw his half-smoked cigarette away. "Cheer up. Sophie's ten thousand miles away. And why you don't divorce her, I'll never understand."

"She won't let me," Lew said gloomily, "you don't know Sophie."

"My God, I do! Listen. Go get your car and let's go back to the SP. I had a call from the Morgan twins today, and they're throwing a farewell party there. It won't be as good as being out with Guinea again, but it looks as though neither of us are going to have much chance of that."

"All right, I'll come. At least I'll be able to keep an eye on you."

Lew went across the street and got into his car, following Byron down the hill and back to the City. They parked the cars in Phillip Street behind the South Pacific and went up the side entrance into the hotel.

Blue lifted his fingers in salute as they stepped into the lift. "Corker day."

They both agreed.

"Just you wait till the real summer comes. Ever spent a summer here?"

They had not. The subject depressed Major Alfrickson. "By the time summer comes round here, I'll be back home freezing to death."

Byron clapped him on the shoulder: "Cheer up! You might even be dead by then, and I'll see they give you a slap-up funeral on the Equator with full military honours."

Major Alfrickson winked at Blue. "You haven't seen Miss Margaret Malone come in, have you?"

Blue looked puzzled.

"You know — upstairs, in the Salon."

His face cleared. "Oh, Guinea.... No, she doesn't come on Sundays, and I'm pretty certain she won't be in tomorrow either. She's got the weekend off."

Major Alfrickson sighed. Blue opened the door at the sixth floor and they went out, the Major stopping to hand Blue a cigarette and, after Byron had moved on, leaving him the whole packet.

"This is my number," he said, scribbling it on the side. "If she should turn up, call me up, will you?" He slipped a ten-shilling note across.

"Righto, major. I'll do my best." He grinned into Alfrickson's florid face and sent the lift downwards, disturbing the Sunday afternoon quiet with a piercing whistle.

As the two men went round the corner from the main

corridor, it became obvious to them that the Morgans' fare-well party was already on. Through the closed door of the suite at the far end came an appalling cacophony.

Byron raised his eyebrows: "The twins haven't changed, apparently."

"No. They never do."

The air throbbed with a native drum and a didgeridoo breathed monotonously on a low note.

"I wonder what they're up to," Lew muttered appre-hensively. "The last party of theirs I was at was in San Francisco when they turned their yacht over to the Little Ships. We'd have all ended up in the hoosegow if they hadn't found a cop who would listen to reason. I don't know what it cost them."

They stopped in front of a door on which a skull and crossbones was nailed above a Japanese flag, and banged on it for a couple of minutes before they were heard.

One of the Morgan twins waved them in. "Hiya fellas. I'm Murray."

"You look like Earle to me," Lew laughed.

Earle stopped thumping on his drum long enough to greet them with a piercing howl.

"Earle's a swell drummer!" Murray shouted, leading Byron into the middle of the room. "And listen to this." He picked up a long bassoon-like instrument and blew ear-splitting noises out of it. "It's a didjeridoo. We got 'em from the Abos up in the Northern Territory, and we're going to play 'em on top of the Washington Monument when we get home, aren't we, Earle?"

Earle stopped drumming and came over to Byron and Lew, taking their arms. "Sure. The guys in this country have got the right idea about what to do with niggers. Keep 'em in concentration camps. We'll do it ourselves back home after we've mopped up the Pacific."

"Sure thing," Murray agreed. "When Earle and I get back to the States, we're going to paint them red, white and blue and start a Ku Klux Klan of our own in the North. We'll show them all what to think of the USA and the

Four Freedoms."

"You see," Earle explained gravely, "we've been personally insulted. They didn't expect us to sit down under only four freedoms, did they? What about the fifth freedom? Free enterprise."

"To hell with that," Murray struck in. "What about free liquor, free love and free fun for the Morgan twins!

He struck a posture roughly resembling the Statue of Liberty and turned to the guests who were lolling drunkenly around the room. "Gentlemen, meet Colonel Maddocks, Byron C. Maddocks, alias Don Juan and Casanova. The only guy who beat 'em at their own game."

There was a roar of applause. Byron bowed and sat down.

"And you all know Lew Alfrickson, so let's get going. We've got to make such a party of this they'll remember it Down Under till we've smacked down Russia in World War Three."

Cheers went up again. Whisky and sandwiches were handed round. Murray solemnly brought out an iron tripod and stood it in the centre of the parquet floor, digging the pointed ends into the wood so that they would not slip. Earle opened up a duffle bag and took out a pile of kindling, arranging it under the tripod.

"What's that for?" Byron asked. "Getting in practice for the primitive life again?"

"Well, partly," Murray agreed.

"But not entirely," Earle added. "It's part of the farewell, you know. This dump's so dead on Sundays we had to organise a little brightness for ourselves."

"That's right." A boy looked up from banging a brass tray with a bottle opener. "It's like a one-hoss town back home, only here the hoss is dead."

"Damn right," Earle thumped his drum. "So we're going to have a barbecue. Nobody'll give you a decent meal in this godforsaken town on a Sunday evening, that's why we're going to cook our own."

"What — here?" Lew asked incredulously.

"Damn right. Here. We've got enough good steak to feed the bunch. Murray's got a barbecue contraption that goes over the top of this gadget and you can all hang your steak on it and watch it burn yourselves. Then we'll make a pot of real coffee and it'll be like we were up in the Adirondacks."

Murray examined the pile of kindling. "That won't do a proper barbecue, you need more kindling. And where's your charcoal?"

"I thought of that. Can't you trust your Uncle Earle?" He took charcoal out of the bag. "Lay violent hands on that radio table, Taffy."

"I'll sure lay." Taffy pushed the radio off with his arm, turned the table upside down and methodically began to wrench off the legs.

Lew looked at Byron apprehensively and, leaning over to fill up his glass, whispered: "Listen, I'm not staying for this. I don't want to be picked up by the provosts — I want to see Guinea before I go back."

Byron nodded. "Everything'll be OK for a while yet," he assured him softly. "We'll just have a few more drinks and then slip out and they won't even notice we've gone. Poppa Morgan's railroad shares might keep you out of trouble in San Fran, but here they don't know the guy."

"I'm not waiting to see."

Heavy blue cigarette smoke filled the room. Someone had knocked over a bottle of whisky and it was running unnoticed down the side of the lounge. There was a smouldering patch on one of the armchairs and holes on the polished table where cigarette butts had burned themselves out. In the bathroom they could see a young officer solemnly pouring beer into the bath, leaving varying amounts in each bottle. He brought them into the lounge, lined them up along the windowsill, wrenched a piece of wood off the side of the wireless and solemnly played a tune on the bottles.

"You're wasting good beer," a blond youth commented languidly.

"So what?" the xylophonist inquired and continued

his performance.

The phone rang and Murray went to answer it. He smashed a whisky bottle against the wall to command silence and his tanned face creased into a mocking smile as he spoke into the receiver. "Well now, is that you, Melva honey?" He winked broadly at Earle. "Forgotten you? Of course I haven't forgotten you. No. Now, what do you think of that? Party on tonight? I'm afraid we couldn't make it...no, not a hope in the world." He made regretful noises into the phone and leered at the others. "Unfortunately Earle and I are just going on duty...frightful, isn't it? If you'd only called us up before...sure...just at the last minute." He sighed deeply. "A yacht party in the moonlight — and you. No! Don't tell me any more, I can't bear it! Just a minute though, hold on, baby." He turned to the others. "Listen," he whispered, pressing the earphone into his chest, "any of you boys like to go on a yacht on a moonlight party that'll probably go on till tomorrow night?"

"Who's the doll?"

"Melva someone or other — I've forgotten her other name."

"Never heard of her," Earle said.

"Don't be crazy," his brother hissed, "you slept with her that weekend up at Babbatree."

"Did I?" Earle's face brightened. "That's right. She was a platinum blonde."

"You're nuts!" Murray whispered. "I slept with the blonde. Melva's a redhead. You remember, you fooled her you were me half the time and she thought she had us both on a string."

Earle clicked his fingers. "That's right, I remember. The Catto doll. And was she hot! Did I tell you that red hair wasn't natural?"

The crowd roared.

"I can recommend her. If any of you boys are staying on and haven't got a regular arrangement, I can guarantee Melva will give you the time of your life. Her father's got a yacht and a place like a country club at Babbatree — and

284

boy, is she good!"

Murray took his hand from the receiver and spoke soothingly into the phone: "Sorry to keep you waiting, honey, but the boys are just looking over the duty list. There's such a commotion in the stag line that I'm trying to draft out the best for you." He winked at his brother. "You trust the Morgans to find you something super-duper." He covered the mouthpiece again.

A thin boy levered himself up on his elbows from the settee. "I've got to be in this dump for a week," he drawled, "so maybe I'll take her over for you. Are you sure she's OK?"

"Positive."

"All right then." He swung his legs off the settee. "What time does she want me?"

"All the time." Earle picked up the receiver.

"Come as soon as you can, she says."

"Has she got a car?"

"Half a dozen."

"Tell her to send one round for me in an hour."

Earle spoke into the phone again. "Captain Alwyn Travers is just rarin' to go, honey, but he's got no way of getting out and he doesn't know the city well. He's always spent his leaves in Brisbane. You'll send a car? Well now, that's real nice of you, he'll be free in an hour. Tell the chauffeur to ring up to my suite when he comes. Sure, honey, I'll be seeing you again, when we come back. You won't forget me, will you, honey? G'bye now."

"Well, that's that," Murray said briskly as Earle put down the phone. "You'll have a swell time, Alwyn, and now, before you go, we'll have another round of drinks and I'll set a match to the fire and we'll play you a little farewell on the orchestra."

Earle poured out the drinks. Murray put a match to the kindling. The assorted instruments began to wail and throb.

Byron looked at Lew inquiringly. Lew nodded. They slipped quietly out.

In Thelma Molesworth's suite, Sunday afternoon and evening went through their unvarying routine. Every Sunday L. F. retired to his bedroom across the passage and slept for two hours, from half past one to half past three.

When Thelma got up from the lunch table she too went into her bedroom to rest. Today she glanced with pleasant anticipation at the red library bindings of a couple of new novels on her bedside table, took off her housecoat and put it carefully on a hanger, undid her corsets and breathed deeply several times, stretching her released muscles like a cat, before she slipped on a loose wrap, picked up her books and took them over to the day bed under the window.

She put her feet up, leant back pleasantly relaxed and opened the top book. *Sinner's Choice*... not her sort of title. Oh well, if Miss Hill had picked it out for her it was sure to be worth reading. Thelma bent back the stiff new binding and settled down to enjoy herself.

She read the first page, turned over and ran her eye down the next, a frown of annoyance deepening the two lines already marked between her brows. Whoever could enjoy this sort of stuff? And yet they sold. Look at *Grapes of Wrath*. It had had such a boom she'd simply had to make herself read it, but she never could understand what all the fuss was about.

She picked up the second book. Published in Sydney. Good heavens, what was Miss Hill thinking about? She knew she never read Australian books. Whoever wanted to read about the sort of people and places they had to live amongst? Not many of the SP guests would thank her for recommending a novel about Sydney. What they wanted was to know about London or Paris or New York, where their fashions came from, their wines, their visiting musicians and actors ... where they'd be going again as soon as the inconveniences of the war were over and they were free to escape from the dullness of home. She and Lance would manage it yet. It would be money and time well spent. If they could go after the war they'd be a jump ahead on exactly what the wealthy tourist would expect to find in a country club in Australia.

What a nuisance, she hadn't another thing to read. She tried the second book again, but it was no use. The young fellow in it was a bank clerk and spent his weekends on Coogee beach in the lifesaving team...a couple of chapters and he joined up with the AIF...good heavens, a war book into the bargain. War was bad enough without harrowing oneself with the details. She laid the second book on top of the first one and decided she might as well try and have a sleep now. It had been a hectic week, she was really desperately tired after the OBNOs Ball and, as if the whole Malone affair hadn't been bad enough last night, she'd had Denise's hysterics this morning!

She stretched her arms above her head and looked down with satisfaction at her breasts that were pulled high and round under the silk of her wrapper. She might be a little overweight, but at least she wasn't a skinny old thing like Mrs D'Arcy-Twyning. She held the thought in her mind, savouring it with pleasure. Of course the Twynings were only jumped up, she consoled herself. Rumour had it that Daniel's ambitious wife had made him get out of his chain of Kookaburra Cash and Carry shops and start his own investment business. That had flourished too. There was no doubt he was a clever businessman, and he had a reputation for honesty that made him a valuable front on the SP board. But the way they spoilt that girl...she wouldn't put up with Denise's tantrums if it wasn't for Dan's interest in Lance.

She closed her eyes and tried to sleep, but she couldn't. Her mind raced round and round. She would tell Lance her exciting news at teatime when he was rested. She'd show him the agent's letter and the exact spot where the place was on the big map of the mountains she had bought. They'd go over their plans again together. "Wentworth Falls Country Club"...she said the name aloud. No, it was too commonplace, they'd have to call it something really striking, she'd get hold of some of the American names. The house looked marvellous in the photograph, and there was a little wing that they could have for a private flat. Surely, surely Lance would want to be married then. A passion of tenderness flooded over her; she was sure he'd see that marriage wouldn't be an obstacle here. Of course he would see. He must see.

It was useless trying to sleep, she was too excited. She got up and began to dress. They'd been so busy this last week there hadn't been a moment to talk about their own affairs. But Lance had had a good morning with his starting prices and he'd had a good lunch. As a matter of fact he was in a better temper than he'd been for weeks, although he seemed to be preoccupied with something. Probably the directors' meeting on Tuesday and the new policy. . . . Well, he could put that out of his mind for a while and she'd show him the letter at afternoon tea.

She put on her housegown and felt the letter in its pocket again. She'd get out the map and note down a few things she must remember to tell Lance. First and most important, he simply must ask Mr Veale about building materials for the extensions they'd need. It wouldn't be easy to tell him they intended to leave the SP, she knew that, but it was no good putting it off, and anyway people didn't worry too much about things a long way off — she and Lance wouldn't be leaving till the end of the war. But they must get things going, and however good any place they got might be, it would still have to have a lot of alterations to make it the luxury country club they had planned.

Thelma smoothed her hair, touched up her makeup in front of the dressing table and went out into the lounge with a secret smile. She unlocked the drawer of her escritoire, took out a folded map, a file of correspondence and a sheaf of odd bits of paper pinned together.

A twenty-room private house would be the very thing to start with. If it was as expensively built as the agent said, it would give the air of a luxurious home that they wanted. Two thousand pounds for the carpets and furniture...oh well, they could all be sold, it would have to be stripped to the bone. And they could turn the house into the social centre of the club — that would mean most of the bedroom accommodation would have to be built. She liked the idea of cabins in the Californian style herself, though Lance was keen on wings connected with the main house, but whatever they wanted would have to be built. She couldn't see them getting a place they could take over complete. She looked through her letters again... Lance was rather keen on the south coast, developing the big game fishing. But she knew what that would mean; they'd have to run a fleet of launches and it would develop into a fishermen's club, and that wasn't her idea at all.

No, the Blue Mountains were ideal, and with the glorious view across the Jamieson Valley, there was nothing they couldn't do with 200 acres. And they really ought to start getting things organised now if they wanted to catch the first tourist flood after the war. Even with the manpower and material shortage you could get ahead if you knew the right people. It would take some wire pulling, of course, but Mr Veale was director of a building company and a brickworks and Dan Twyning was on the board of Cement Constructions and NSW Glass. If only Lance liked the place as much as she did and would start things going, they could get ahead with the swimming pool and the nine-hole golf course and tennis courts as well as the building.

Mr Veale was quite sure the war couldn't last much longer than six months now the Americans were leaving for the north. "The next thing we'll hear is that they've got back the Philippines," he'd said only last week, "and though things don't look very healthy in Holland at the moment, they know what they're doing. The terrific casualties are startling," he'd said, "but either it's a necessary diversion, or the War Office thinks the objective is worth the numbers."

Thelma could never get used to the way Horatio Veale talked about the war as though it was a giant sum in arithmetic, carried out quite regardless of human lives. He always calculated in figures and objectives and he'd been right so many times that she felt a sense of urgency ever since he had made the flat statement last week that he was basing his own plans on another twelve months of war at the most. "And," he'd added, "the money that'll be made the first year after the boys come back will go to the man who starts planning for the business right now."

Well, she and Lance had planned and now they'd get to work. A year was such a little time when there was so much to do. It was only when you wanted something at the end of it terribly badly that it seemed endless. They'd never get married while they were still at the SP, she knew that. But when they had their own place and Lance didn't have a board of directors to bother about any more, but just the two of them, then he'd see that there was nothing more to stop them. She read the agent's letter again. They'd go into the whole thing together as soon as tea was over.

There was a knock on the door and Lance came in. "Tea not up yet? I must be early."

"It'll be here in a few minutes, darling." She looked up, her eyes alight with her secret, her handsome head half-turned to him, and a welcoming smile on her lips. "Did you have a good sleep, my dear?"

"Not too good," he said rather plaintively, stretching out on the lounge. "I can't get rid of this head."

"You poor dear, I'll get you an aspirin."

"Oh, don't bother. It's just that I've had too much on my mind to go to sleep."

"Oh Lance darling, what is it? There's nothing happened you haven't told me about, is there?"

"Well, there is, really. I've been thinking over a proposition H.V. put up to me last week and I want your advice."

"Oh." Thelma looked at him doubtfully. When Lance asked her advice in that tone, he'd already made up his mind as a rule. "Veale? What does he want you to do?"

"Well, he's going to branch out just as soon as he can with the Empire Brewery, and he wants me to go in with him."

"Go in with him..." she began and stopped short, putting her hand defensively over the map and letter. "I never knew Mr Veale had anything to do with the Empire Brewery...and anyway Frith and Company squeezed it out of existence years ago, didn't they?"

"Yes, that was before the war. Now H.V.'s bought it for a song and his wife has a controlling share interest."

"What does that dried-up little mouse know about breweries?"

"She doesn't come into it, she's just a figurehead," L. F. said impatiently. "The point is that H.V. has great plans for developing it."

"Who are they going to sell to? I thought all the hotels in the district were tied to Frith and Company or Freney's, and they're not likely to let the Empire in."

"No, that's the trouble. H.V. thought he'd be able to swing Frith's board, but it didn't work that way and now he's on to a new scheme and, he thinks, a much better one."

"What's that?"

L. F. shot a glance at Thelma. She was sitting bolt upright at the desk, one hand flung across a collection of papers, her face clouded. His face brightened with relief at a knock on the door and he got up quickly to open it. "It's all very hush-hush," he said, patting her shoulder. "I'll tell you after tea."

Thelma watched him with growing uneasiness. So that was what was on his mind. When Lance put on that boyish, ingratiating manner, she always knew he was up to something. She turned back to her desk, folded up the agent's letter and the map and put them into the folder with the other correspondence.

The waiter shut the door silently behind him.

Thelma poured out the tea without speaking.

"I've been wanting to talk to you about this all the week," Lance began, wolfing a hot buttered scone. Thelma put down her cup and waited.

"H.V.'s letting me in on a pretty big thing."

"Yes?"

"Yes. He's decided that there's far more money to be made out of the bar trade alone on the capital investment than there ever will be in hotels, no matter how good or expensive they are."

"Nobody in their senses ever doubted that," Thelma said aggressively. "But hasn't he ever heard about the licensing laws?"

"If you're going to take that tone..." Lance looked injured.

Thelma took a grip of her rising temper. "Does he think he's powerful enough to change the law after all the fuss there's been lately about hotels that have closed up their accommodation?" she asked in a less truculent tone. "And how are Frith and Company going to stand for one of their directors playing fast and loose with the law, and doing a bit of brewing on his own?"

"This won't cut across Frith and Company anywhere. As a matter of fact, as things are now, they can't brew enough for their own hotels, so anything the Empire does isn't going to worry them."

"Well, how's he going to work it?"

"That's what I've been trying to tell you, if you'd give me a chance. H. V. is planning to work his scheme through the returned soldiers' clubs."

"But they can't get licences."

"H. V.'s got a watertight plan for supplying them without licences."

"Surely he's not going to join the sly grog racket."

"What do you take him for? Horatio Veale is one of the shrewdest businessmen in Sydney."

"Well, supplying liquor to places without a licence still sounds like sly grog to me."

"Look, do you want to hear about H. V.'s plan or not?"

"Of course I want to hear. That's what I've been waiting to hear the last half hour."

"Do you remember our wondering who was behind those articles in the paper a month or so ago — returned heroes stuff — full employment, proper housing, clubs for their leisure, you know, beer for the boys and all the rest?"

Thelma nodded.

"It was our old friend Horatio putting out a feeler to see

which way the wind was blowing over the liquor suggestions. And did it bring results! You know, the more I see of H. V., the more astonished I am at his flair for making things come his way. There were a few protests from the usual temperance cranks, of course, but hundreds of enthusiastic letters poured in from ex-servicemen.''

"But if they haven't got licences, whether they're returned soliders' clubs or not, they'll still be sly grog places to the police, and I can't see that even H. V. would get away with that.''

"What I'm trying to explain to you is that there's nothing to get away with. It's all perfectly legal. Before we go any farther, let me show you this.'' He unbuttoned his sports coat and took an official-looking document out of his breast pocket, walked round to her and laid it down on the table in front of her. "This is the Empire Brewery's agreement,'' he said, "drawn up by Macartney, and you know Macartney's reputation as a solicitor.''

"I know he never opens his mouth after the board meetings except to shovel the food in or agree with H. V.''

"Ah, but you don't see him at the meetings. H. V. never takes a step unless Macartney approves of it, and I've seen old Mac put a damper on what looked like brilliant projects to the rest of us. No, if he's drawn up this agreement, you can be quite certain it's absolutely watertight.''

He rested an arm on the back of her chair, leaning against her shoulder as he ran a finger down the document.

"I still can't see how a lot of mushroom clubs can be as profitable as hotels.''

"H. V. is certain they will be. He's been working for years behind the scenes to get an amendment to the liquor law to separate bars from hotel accommodation, and that's precisely what he's doing with this club idea without waiting for an act of Parliament.''

"Plenty of hotels do that already on one excuse or another, but with public opinion the way it is, I can't ever see it becoming law. And I think it'd be a scandal if it did. After all, a hotel ought to be something more than a grog shop.''

"My dear, you're pre-war. You want to catch up with yourself, we've got to move with the times or we'll get nowhere."

"Well I don't see how you can make plans to move in any direction until you know exactly what this liquor amendment is going to be."

"Oh, you don't want to worry about what the government's promising. They may tinker around with a few unimportant changes, but H. V. doesn't see the breweries letting any real alterations get through. There's too much money tied up, and you want to have a look at their share lists to see who'll be putting pressure on the government. Of course they may throw out a few sops like restaurant and community hotel licences, but you can take it from me there'll be no substantial alterations — except to our advantage, like late closing. As soon as the war's over, the breweries are going to put the pressure on to get ten o'clock closing."

"I don't see them getting it in our time. Every woman in the country will vote against it. Even the women who drink themselves are not going to give their husbands another excuse to work back."

"All the better for the clubs."

"How are Frith and Company going to take a number of their board launching out in competition?"

"H. V. says there's going to be room for all of us. You know yourself how this war has extended drinking habits in this country."

Thelma turned over the pages of the agreement and read it closely. The frown between her eyes deepened. L. F. watched her anxiously. She looked up and met his gaze. "What I want to know is, what's behind it all? Veale's got all the money he wants and his fingers in enough companies to keep him busy. Now, just what is making it worth his while to cut across Frith and Company?"

"Ah," L. F. sat down opposite her at the table, and leaned forward, speaking in a low tone. "You know, Thellie, you're wonderful the way you go to the root of things. It took me weeks to get round to that. . .and you've picked it up in a few minutes." He drew his lips back from his strong teeth in a conspiratorial smile. "You can take it from me he's playing for bigger fish with this scheme than he's ever played for before. He's made up his mind he's going to Canberra on the returned servicemen's vote the first federal election after the war. You mark my words, in another five years, you'll be calling him Sir Horatio."

Her face cleared. "Oh, so that's his plan, is it? Well, if he's made up his mind to that, we can take the Empire Brewery, the clubs and his seat at Canberra as foregone conclusions." She put the agreement back into its envelope and handed it over to him. "And where do you come into it? Are you going to Canberra too?"

"Don't be silly. You know I have no interest in politics."

"I'm not too sure after what you've been telling me that I know anything at all about your interests."

"Now, Thellie, don't be difficult. I want your advice."

"Huh!"

"H.V.'s offered me a parcel of shares in the Empire and I think I ought to take them instead of those Dan Twyning's been promising to wangle for me for the last six months. Personally, I don't think they'll ever come off, particularly after last night."

Thelma bridled. "I hope you're not still holding me responsible for that."

"Of course not, it was an unfortunate accident. I really am sorry for what I said to you last night, it was just that I was taken on the raw by what that wretched Mrs D'Arcy-Twyning had the nerve to say to me. But it's probably cooked my goose as far as the shares are concerned and that's why I'm thinking over H. V.'s offer so seriously."

"Veale's offered you shares in his new venture! Well, he hasn't done that for nothing. All the years you've been managing Frith and Company's hotels, helping to pile up the best part of a quarter of a million for him, he's never even so much as passed on a share tip to you." She looked at him, her lips thin and the corners of her mouth drawn down.

"And what does he expect you to do for it?"

Lance put the agreement back in his pocket deliberately and kept her waiting while he buttoned his jacket. "He wants me to go in with him."

The colour ran up Thelma's neck and spread in dull, ugly patches. "Go in with him!" she echoed. "How?"

"He needs someone he can trust to manage the club business." He went on quickly as she opened her mouth to speak. "There'll be the Returned Soldiers' organising end of it. Of course they'll do most of that themselves, but they'll need help with practical matters like advice on premises, layout of bar and clubrooms, etc., and H. V. thinks I'm the man for the job."

"Has he made you a definite offer?"

"He hasn't, but the Empire has. And the club business is only part of his scheme. We're going to get our stuff into all the free houses. H. V.'s got plans for making it a very big thing, and he wants me to take over sales and distribution."

Thelma gripped the sides of her chair under the table and tried to keep her voice from trembling. "It sounds a fulltime job to me."

"It is."

"How then are you going to combine it with running our country club?"

L. F. looked sheepish. "Well," he said, waving his hand vaguely, "that's what I wanted to discuss with you."

"Did you tell Mr Veale we were planning to run a country club together?"

L. F. studied his well-manicured nails. "Yes, I had a talk to him about that too. He has a place in mind down at Eden that would be first rate, he says. It's been shut up since 1940, but he's pretty sure he could get it for a song and he thinks you're just the person to run it as a country club. He was very enthusiastic about the idea."

Thelma bit her lip and it was a few seconds before she could trust herself to speak. "We weren't planning for me to run a country club. . .it was for us both."

"Oh yes, of course. But this is so much bigger for me

and you know you really are quite capable of doing the whole club scheme on your own, particularly with H. V. behind you. He's very keen, says he'll see you get any building done you want and he's even prepared to back you."

"He's prepared to back me!" Thelma's voice was icy. "You mean, he's prepared to buy you. What's he offering you?"

L. F. looked up sharply. "What do you mean, 'buy me'?"

Thelma choked back a spate of hot words. She never got anywhere with Lance if she lost her temper. Once she showed him how deeply she felt about anything, he always managed to put her in the wrong.

"I only meant," she said, and there was a quiver in her voice, "that he wants you so much he's prepared to buy me off so he can get you."

L. F. slewed his eyes round at her and saw that her chin was trembling. He spoke coldly. "Oh, well, it's a pity you have such an unfortunate way of putting things."

Her anger suddenly ebbed and she looked up at him pleadingly. "But don't you see what it will mean, darling? All the plans we've made together...our own place at last, run the way we want it run, and the schemes we had for making it absolutely famous so that we'd have people visit us from Europe and America...I couldn't do that without you."

"Oh, yes, you could. That's something H. V. wants to have a talk to you about. He thinks you should make a bid for quality, not quantity."

"What do you mean by that?"

"Well, not to start it on too big a scale. He reckons within a couple of years of the end of the war, there's going to be a depression. Business just isn't going to put up with the controls that have been clamped down on it during the war and as soon as things get back to normal there'll be a showdown with labour and they'll have to learn who's master."

"That doesn't seem to augur too well for your returned

soldiers' clubs."

"Ah, that's where you're wrong. There'll only be room for one good moderate-sized country club in this state, he says, to cater for the people who can afford to fly out here for the sunshine and surfing and the big game fishing, but there'll be room for thousands of small semi-private service clubs. And you know yourself, however bad things are, a chap'll always find sixpence for a beer and a get-together with his pals."

"But how are the men going to take a depression after all the promises that have been made to them?"

"They'll take just what they get, as they've always done. H. V.'s got his head screwed on the right way. This type of thing he's planning will flourish, and in addition to being profitable it'll be a safety valve. There's nothing like giving disgruntled chaps a place where they can get together over a few beers, air their grievances in private and let off steam. And I think he's probably right when he says it's a damn good way of counteracting red propaganda into the bargain; he reckons that Hyde Park corner and the English pub's the reason why Britain's never had a revolution."

Thelma's lip curled. "Quite the public benefactor!"

"Well, you know as well as I do, the big mouths who are always talking politics in the bar never do anything else about it," L. F. retorted hotly.

"What I do know is that you seem to have swallowed Mr Veale's propaganda hook, line and sinker."

"Oh, you women are all the same, you never can see anything from any angle but the personal one. If you are going to run a country club it's as much to your benefit as ours that there should be a proper government in the country. And talking of the club, we'd planned that it was to be the luxury and the quality of the service that was going to make it unique, and you could manage the whole thing easily with a good assistant. It really doesn't need my experience of large-scale organising at all."

Thelma turned away from him and blinked back the tears. When she had her voice under control, she began again. "But it wasn't only that, Lance darling, was it? Running it together, we were going to let up on the pace we've been going for the last few years and we were really going to have time to enjoy our work and each other." She couldn't go on. She bit her lip.

L. F. got up and went over to the photographs, fixing his eyes on the Pick-Pockettes. "Of course if you're going to take it like that, there's really no point in going on talking. But I'd have thought you'd have seen what a big thing it would be for both of us. Veale's offered me five hundred pounds a year more than I'm getting here and shares into the bargain."

"I know I'm silly," Thelma was struggling to keep her voice level, "and of course I want the best for you. It's only I've got a marvellous place to show you today and I thought we could begin almost at once if it's suitable...and, oh, I'm just being silly because I'm disappointed." She lifted her face to him with a tearful smile, but he wasn't looking.

"I'm sorry too," he conceded, his back to her still, "but I've thought it over very thoroughly and it seems to me to be far too good to miss."

"But Lance, we've...but, darling, we haven't been so badly off, and we've lived well...and you know you've been terribly proud of the reputation our hotels had...and a country club would be something of our very own. A home as well as a business, and I'm sure we'd make more than we'd ever need out of it."

"Certainly we get a good living out of this place but we make a damn sight better living for the shareholders. Now I've got a chance to get on that end of the stick myself and I'm going to take it, and after what I've been through the last two years in this place I don't mind if I never set foot inside a hotel again."

"How do you know you can trust Veale? Has he offered you any security? You can be quite sure he's not making a tempting offer like this unless it's to his advantage. He knows if you get these clubs going for him, he can forget about the whole business side of it while he rakes in the profits and makes himself a good fellow with the soldiers to get into the federal parliament. And anyway, when he's there and the seven-year agreement is working nicely for the Empire, where'll you be?''

Lance shrugged his shoulders and smiled whimsically at her. "Probably back with you, my dear, with a nice little nest egg tucked away so that you'll be able to start a chain of country clubs if you want to.''

Thelma pushed back her chair and got up. Her eyes were blazing. "If you do this to me, Lance, it's the finish. All our lives you've put business before happiness and I've been fool enough to let you do it. But this time, no. If you want to go in with Veale, nothing I can say will stop you. And when he's finished with you, if you want to come crawling back...''

A terrific clanging in the corridor cut across her words. They looked at each other in horror.

Fire!

L. F. was at the door, flinging it open. Thelma picked up the receiver and jiggled the phone furiously. "Where's the fire?'' she demanded.

"Fourth floor, madam. The Morgans' suite. I've rung the fire brigade.''

When Guinea and Kim came down the steps from the West Hills train, Central station was swarming with homegoing picnickers. Sunburned hikers jostled cheerfully through the crowd; harassed parents and crying children, servicemen and their girls streamed windblown and weary from the platform.

"Good to see the old crowd still at it. How'd you like a day down in National Park, Peg?"

She ran her eyes up and down his sturdy figure and then looked at him steadily. "Who, me?"

"Of course, you."

"What do you think?"

"Well, I hardly know what to think. Things seem to be rather different now you've moved up among the brass hats."

"It all depends on what you mean by different."

They stopped at the sound of marching feet and the crowd parted and stood back to form a laneway near the ramp to the main station. A company of men in jungle green, laden with full battle kit, marched four-deep from a chain of military trucks in Eddy Avenue, their heavy boots clanging on the concrete. Someone in the crowd started up the familiar battle cry, "Ho-ho-ho! Ho-ho-ho!" and the crowd took it up. A voice called derisively. "You'll be sorry!" Crooked smiles split the soldiers' faces, all so strangely alike under the slouch hats with their stained puggarees and leather chinstraps.

Kim slid his hand under her elbow and squeezed it. "Some more of the old gang going back."

Guinea was silent. It was damn silly, but she never saw a bunch of troops entraining for the north without remembering, as though it were only last week, how Mick had stepped it out just as these boys were doing.

Someone called from the crowd: "Give Tojo an extra one for me, mate," and a voice came back: "Gimme yer number and I'll ring you from Tokyo." Laughter welled up from the crowd and the pressure of Kim's hand tightened.

Someone started "Waltzing Matilda" in an uncertain voice too high, and stopped as laughter drowned the words. But the marching company took it up and moved more briskly with a swagger of white webbing belts riding lean hips. Soon they were all singing, and as the last laden figure disappeared a cheer followed them, ragged and mournful, and the full-throated roar of the marching company echoed back.

"Let go my arm, damn you." Guinea snatched her arm away and blew her nose vigorously. "I've got something in my eye."

"Yeah," said Kim, "it gives me something in the eye too."

She halted at the edge of the footpath. "Well, s'long now. Enjoy your leave."

Without waiting for his reply she ran across the road and jumped onto the platform of a crowded Bronte tram, deliberately keeping her back to him. That was the last of Master Kim Scott!

"Going my way, I see," he said pleasantly, behind her.

"What do you think you're doing? Haunting me?"

"I promised your mother I'd see you safely home. The city's no place for young girls with all these Yanks round... Ouch!" His face contorted.

She smiled sweetly. "In case you didn't know, that was my heel."

The crowded platform jammed them close together; his face was level with hers, their noses almost touching. "Dear, dear. Who's been teaching you those habits? I hope you don't do that to your admiral."

Guinea's brows were drawn angrily together. "I don't know what your game is tagging round like this after I've already told you what I think of you pushing yourself in up at home and starting all that fuss about a perfectly harmless picture."

"Shocking, isn't it?"

"It makes me damned mad."

"You usen't to be like this." He rubbed his nose against hers.

She strained her head backwards against the glass of the driver's compartment. "Do that again, Kim Scott, and I'll cripple you for the rest of your leave."

"You know, I think I like you best when you're mad."

"I'm not a bit interested when or how you like me."

"I've still got another ten days."

"You ought to have six months' CB."

"I thought we might get together. You can do a lot in ten days."

"Not with me you can't. This time you look out for somebody else, both for your loving and your leaving."

"Oh, so that's what's biting you, is it? I'm glad you told me. I thought you'd merely gone snooty on me."

In a rush of suffocating rage Guinea stepped off the foot-board on the wrong side. A tram coming downhill on the other line clanged loudly. She stopped dead, instinctively clutching her skirt around her. The driver shouted a warning, the tram went by in a jumble of light and shadow and Kim's arm closed round her waist as their own tram gathered speed behind them. For an eternity they stood rigid between the scything foot-boards and clanking wheels. The wind rushed through her hair and squeezed the breath out of her, conflicting currents of air tugged at her legs.

Kim's voice steadied her. "Whew! Caught in a slip-stream. Your mother was right, you're really not safe to be let out alone, you know."

They crossed to the footpath and she pushed his arm from her waist. "Take your hands off me, I'm not a cripple."

"But now I've saved your life, you can't very well object to me taking you home."

She glared at him under lowering brows.

"Well, I suppose now you're here, you might as well make yourself useful and help me find Monnie. But if you hadn't been chasing me I wouldn't have got off on the wrong side."

They turned into Campbell Street. Late diners were clattering down the steps of the Chinese cafés on either side of the road. Half a dozen lascars shuffled in single file across the footpath. A wrinkled old Chinaman watched them impassively from a doorway.

Guinea and Kim turned off into a side street, staring up at the house numbers. "I don't know where this place is," she said, taking Monnie's letter out of her pocket.

"It's on this side, anyway," Kim peered at a chipped number plate. "These are evens. It can't be far in a street this size."

A soft drawl came from the darkened veranda. "Say, what you lookin' for here, big boy?"

They started back. "Sorry," Kim said, "I didn't realise anyone was there."

The blurred shadow on the seat moved and a girl stood up; a tall figure uncoiled itself, black skin and drab uniform coming up from the dark. A faint gleam from a fanlight fell on the Negro's curly head as he leaned over the railing, sinuous and powerful. The girl's hair was a riot of straw around her pale face and her mouth a blur of smudged lipstick.

"Looking for a number?" she asked conversationally, nestling against her companion as his arm went round her shoulders.

"Yes," Kim said, "sorry we disturbed you."

"Oh, that's OK. What's the number?"

"One hundred and two."

"One hundred and two? I'm not too sure. Just half a mo and I'll ask." She pushed the hall door open and called into the house: "Say, any of you kids know where one hundred and two is along here?"

The strumming of a pianola stopped and two girls came out into the hall, their Negro companions looming behind them in the half-light.

"I think it's the last house in the terrace — right on the dead end," one of the girls pointed to the end of the lane.

The blonde looked from Guinea to Kim and smiled knowingly. "If it's a room you're wanting for half an hour," she said amiably, "they'd probably be able to fix you up two doors along. You can say Gloria sent you. We only have coloured boys here.''

The Negro snuggled her closer to him and laughed. ''That's right, honey child.''

Kim retreated stammering. ''Thanks...thanks very much...er...some other time...thanks, we'll be getting along.''

The soft drawl drifted after them. ''Goodnight, Aussie.''

''Bloody boong molls make me sick,'' Kim muttered under his breath.

''You've got a delicate stomach all of a sudden. The Negroes are only after the same thing as the whites — only I've heard they pay better.''

''Let's get a move on,'' he said tersely. ''Come on, we'll try the end house.''

They went down the narrow street. The air was stagnant and heavy with dust, the foetid smell of overflowing garbage tins rose from shop doorways. Slatternly women sat fanning themselves on the steps of cramped houses flush with the footpath and men loafed against the railings.

''If there were a few decent lights I'd like it better,'' Kim grunted. ''You ought to have more sense than to think of walking up here on your own. The place is lousy with bashers and thugs.''

''Nice of you to protect me.''

''Too right it is. I don't fancy having some of the talent round here putting the boot into me. Come on, let's find out if Monnie's here and get her out of the place. It stinks.''

''I thought after what you boys saw in the Middle East, Sydney'd seem quite tame.''

''Cut out the wisecracks and ring the bell. This is one hundred and two.'' A light shone through the stained-glass fanlight. Guinea pressed the bell-push beside the peeling door, but though they strained their ears they could not hear it ringing in the house. Kim knocked loudly on the door and after a time a window was pushed open upstairs and a man's voice asked surlily: ''What the hell do you mean battering the door in down there?''

They stepped back on the footpath and saw the outline of a bald head against the light.

"Sorry to disturb you," Kim's voice was placating. "But we're looking for a girl called Shirley McGovern. Could you tell us if she lives here?''

The man turned back into the room and they heard him growling a question, and a woman's voice replying.

"She did, but she doesn't now," he snapped. "Left here weeks ago. Bloody good riddance, if you ask me.''

"I suppose you couldn't give me her new address?'' Guinea inquired politely.

"I couldn't and I wouldn't if I could. After all we done for her she walked out of here without so much as kiss me foot." The man spat on the iron veranda roof. "Got above herself, she has. Stuck up in one of them flash joints round the Dirty Half Mile and for all I care, she can stay there and rot.''

He slammed the window violently. "Whew!" Kim turned to Guinea. "If you ask me anything, that Shirley wench showed damned good sense to get out of a place like this.''

"You're telling me. Jeepers, I'd have hated to find Monnie there.''

They turned and went quickly down the street and round the corner and back into Campbell Street. There was a sound of blows and shouting from a house that opened on to the footpath, and the sound of heavy footsteps. "Look out!" Kim called warningly, grabbing Guinea's arm.

They dodged quickly, just missing a soldier stumbling from a doorway. He stood on the footpath swaying, blinded by the blood that flowed from a cut on his forehead. There was a clatter of heavy boots down the wooden stair behind him. He moaned and staggered across to the kerb and stood there, his back against a light standard, his arms held defensively in front of his face. Two soldiers rushed out of the doorway and there was the sickening crash of a bottle on the man's bare head.

"Oh God," Guinea breathed, "they'll kill the poor devil."

Kim caught her hand and dragged her across the road. "Shut up, you mug. They'll kill us too. Beat it!"

They ran swiftly up the steep pinch of the hill, pausing only once to look back. Under the light they could see the man's body sprawled across the footpath between the two soldiers and hear the dull thud of their boots on his skull.

"No place for us. Let's keep going."

They ran a whole block before pausing breathless at the next crossroad. Guinea strained to look back again down the ill-lighted street. "We ought to do something. He'll be pulp."

"He is pulp by now, and nothing we can do will help him. I've seen what military boots can do in that line before this. The great Australian emblem — the boot and the bottle."

"But the ambulance..."

"They'll cart him to the morgue, not the hospital. And I don't want my leave ruined by being called in as a police witness in an affair like this, any more than you do. Come on, unless you want to go back and pick up the pieces."

Guinea turned and went silently up the hill beside him. They reached the top of Taylor Square. Kim took her arm. "Come on, Peg, we've earned a drink, and here's a milk bar."

Guinea drank a raspberry milkshake in silence. Who'd have thought last night that in twenty-four hours she'd be trapesing round Surry Hills with Kim Scott as though the last two years hadn't existed — and glad to have him? Hell! life was a muddle! She refused a second drink.

"Brawl ruined your appetite?" Kim asked, ordering another for himself.

"Well, it's not my favourite sport." She shuddered at the memory of the man's bleeding face and the sound of the dull crunch of boots against bone. "It's awful. They're beasts."

Kim shrugged. "I don't like it myself. But it's hard for

coves to remember that what gets you a medal in the jungle will get you gaol at home." He put down his glass. "Not worried about Monnie, are you?"

"I am rather. I wonder if I rang the Mill could I get on to Shirley."

"Well, you can't do anything in that line till Tuesday morning, and in the meantime she'll be OK. After all, you were younger than her when you first started going places."

"Yeah," she looked up at him, her eyes hard and mocking. "But don't forget I had you to look after me."

"And that," said Kim, "seems to be my cue to take you home."

They walked in silence down the long stretch of Forbes Street leading towards the tangle of the Woolloomooloo docks and the harbour, now silvered under a full moon. When they reached her doorway she stood for a moment looking at him.

"What about surf tomorrow?" he coaxed.

"Nothing doing. I'm going to look Monnie up."

"I'll help you. Call for you at nine. We can have a look at the procession first."

She hesitated. "No, I don't trust you."

"What better guide than me?" He put his foot in the door as she tried to shut it. "I'm the kind of fellow you need. Knows all the lurks."

"And how!"

"Lidey, you ain't seen nothing yet. I've learned a lot since I went north."

"So've I."

"What a woman!"

"Woman enough to give you one hell of a kick in the shin if you don't get your foot out of that door. You'll wake the house bellowing there like that."

"That's an idea. I wake the house or you meet me at nine." He raised his head and let out a wailing wolf call.

"Shut up," Guinea looked anxiously back into the hall.

"I'll give 'em Tarzan next. That'll fetch 'em."

Guinea clapped a hand across his mouth. "OK. OK. I'll

be here," she whispered desperately.

Kim kissed her hand and she drew it away as though his lips stung her. He ran down the steps and saluted smartly.

"I'm not going all the same," she whispered piercingly. "I only said that to get rid of you."

"OK," he called back. "I'll be here."

"Don't waste your time."

"I won't."

She closed the door firmly, and heard him go whistling down the street.

MONDAY
I

At half past nine, Claire hung up the receiver, wrote another name in the appointments book and turned to Deb. "Well, that's the last one I'm going to book in for this morning. I wouldn't have given Guinea and Val the whole day off if I'd known we were going to be so rushed." She scanned the closely pencilled morning section. "Looks like everyone's going to the races — only two bookings this afternoon so far."

"It's hardly worth keeping open after lunch, is it?"

"If I had my way we wouldn't be open at all on a public holiday. Six-Hour Day. Nice way to celebrate it. Trust old Mole."

"Let me see, who's next for me?" Deb examined the book.

Claire looked at her watch. "What on earth can be keeping Alice?" Her lips tightened as she ran her pencil down the page. "Six shampoos and sets, and she knows Guinea's off. If that girl doesn't turn up..."

"That's ridiculous." Deb's voice was hostile. "She must turn up."

"Must," Claire repeated dryly. "How do you make that out? That little chiseller'd get out of anything. Look at the song and dance she put on to get out of staying back on Friday when it was her turn. I'm sorry, Deb, but I'm afraid you'll have to start on Mrs Stather, she's due any minute — shampoo and gold rinse. I've got a facial waiting, I'll start on that. If Alice hasn't turned up I can leave my old girl with the eyepads on and fit Stather's set in. Blast that girl." Claire got up from the desk and went to a cubicle at the far end of the corridor.

As Claire disapppered, Deb heard the outer door open and looked up. Alice came in.

"You're pretty late," Deb began sharply, and stopped when she saw her puffy face and tear-reddened eyes. "Why, what's the matter?"

"I can't tell you here." Alice went swiftly through the boudoir and along the corridor to the dressing-room. Deb was just about to follow her when a tall, elegant woman opened the door.

"Good morning, Mrs Stather."

"Good morning, Miss Forrest," she smiled pleasantly.

"Will you come this way, please." Deb showed her into a cubicle and went on to the dressing-room where she found Alice slumped on a chair.

"Mrs Stather's here," she told her. "I say, what is the matter?"

"Oh Deb, it's something awful. I just couldn't go in yet."

"Nothing wrong with Ross?"

"No...Ross is all right," Alice blew her nose.

Deb waited a few seconds. "Oh, well, I'll do the shampoo for you and that'll give you five minutes. Try and pull yourself together," she added kindly.

"Thank you so much." There was an unusual note of gratitude in Alice's voice.

Deb gave her a quick glance and went out.

By the time Mrs Stather was ready for her set, Alice had appeared. Her nose was freshly powdered and she apologised for her cold. Mrs Stather made a little flutter about infection and then settled down to have her hair wound in tight little snails for the dryer.

Deb was in the massage room changing the sheet and pillow case for her next appointment, when Alice came in. "Mrs Stather's under the dryer now," she began, and went on hesitantly, "I wanted to ask you something when you've got a few minutes."

"I've got about ten minutes now. Let's go along and make

a cup of tea, shall we?"

"I'd rather talk to you here. Do you mind? I don't want Claire to hear."

"Of course, if you'd rather."

Alice's eyes met Deb's and the tears welled up in them.

"My dear, what's wrong? Here, sit down." Deb pulled a chair over for her; Alice sank into it gratefully. She bit her lip.

"It's...it's my sister Mary. Oh, I don't know how to tell you..."

"What's the matter with Mary?"

"She's...she's...in trouble," Alice sobbed out.

"You mean...she's going to have a baby?"

"Yes."

"Oh dear, that's awful. Poor kid. Won't the fellow marry her?"

"He's...married," Alice gulped.

The old story, Deb thought. Another of these service girls out to catch someone else's husband. Aloud she said, "That certainly does complicate things."

"He did want to marry her, only his wife won't divorce him."

"Well, I suppose you can't exactly blame her for that. After all, it's not a very nice position for her."

Alice mopped her eyes and looked up, trying to control her voice. "But the most awful part about it is that Mary really wants to go through with it."

"You mean have the baby?" Deb asked, incredulous.

Alice nodded.

"She can't realise what it'll mean...and what about your family?"

"That's what I said to her. I think she must be out of her mind. I told her the shame of it would kill father and mother, but she said she could go away somewhere and nobody need know."

"But you can't keep that sort of thing secret."

"I told her that, but nothing I say has the slightest effect, even when I said the least she could do was to consider Ross and me. She just said he wasn't worth marrying if it would make all that difference. I don't know what's come over her since she's gone into the Army. Ross is so honourable, he'd never get over it." Alice's tears flowed in a fresh gush.

Deb patted her shoulder. "You wait here and I'll slip along and put on the jug. A cup of tea will do you the world of good."

She switched on the electric jug. What a thing to happen to the Parkers, of all people! Even if Alice did madden you, you couldn't help feeling sorry for her being in a jam like this. Getting a glory box together for five years for that prig of a Ross who was too honourable to marry her till he got a promotion because it was against bank rules, but not too honourable to keep her hanging on for the best years of her life. She'd like to see herself waiting for any man if he didn't have the guts to marry her on the quiet like the other bank chaps did, and be damned to their rules. Other girls could go on working, why not Alice? Still it was pretty tough to have all your plans wrecked because your sister got herself into a mess with a married man and didn't care if she involved everybody else.

Deb took a cup of tea back to Alice. Mrs Stather was growing restless and she soothed her by taking her a cup too. Alice had washed her face and put on fresh makeup.

"I really told you about it, because I thought you might be able to help . . ." Alice began, keeping her eyes on her cup.

Deb looked at her in alarm. "Me help? How do you mean?"

"Well, when I talked to her all Saturday night, she wouldn't listen to reason, but yesterday she went to see his wife and when she came back she was different, sort of broken, and she wouldn't talk any more. But she did ask me if I knew anyone . . . and I've got a feeling that if I could find somebody to help she'd do something about it now. And I thought you might know of someone." She spoke the last words in a little rush.

"Good heavens! How should I know anyone?"

"Well, you're such great friends with Dr Dallas MacIntyre, I thought you might ask her if she'd help. We can pay."

Deb looked at her indignantly. "Dallas wouldn't touch

anything like that."

"Yes, but she might know someone..."

"I couldn't even mention it to her."

"Oh, I'm sorry." Alice sank back into her chair. "I only asked because you've always said she was just like a sister and I thought...well, since you said you knew her so well, you could ask her in a friendly way."

Alice's tears began to flow quietly again. She tried to choke them back and looked at Deb with appealing eyes. "It was only your saying she grew up with you and was just like a sister that made me ask. I'd never have thought of it otherwise."

"She did grow up with us," Deb said sharply, "but after all, that doesn't give me the right to approach her about a thing like this...You must know as well as I do, it's illegal." She went over to her cupboard and began a wholesale tidy-up.

Alice's eyes followed her imploringly. "But if she's like a sister...Mary didn't mind telling me."

Blast her and her sister, Deb said to herself furiously. She simply couldn't go to Dallas with a thing like this. Besides, she hadn't even seen her for months. She turned to Alice. "You must realise, my dear, that a reputable doctor would regard a question like that as an absolute insult."

"Oh, I know that; that's why I didn't mean Mary going to her as a patient. If she'd tell us something Mary could take...They do that sometimes, don't they?"

"I don't know anything about it."

Alice clasped and unclasped her hands. "I don't know what we'll do," she wailed. "I couldn't sleep last night for thinking Mary might do something desperate. If she did anything to herself..."

Deb spread a clean sheet on the massage table with unnecessary vigour. Why on earth should she be dragged into this?

Alice began again. "But I'm so terrified of Mary getting into the hands of one of those awful old women...You know, like that one in Brisbane where Val's friend was done — the one who died."

"She wasn't Val's friend," Deb snapped. "Whatever made you think that?"

"Oh, wasn't she? Not that I've ever discussed it with her, of course...I just thought...hearing her and Guinea talking about it on Saturday when it was all in the paper. What I really mean to say is I don't want Mary done by one of those old women and I thought..."

Alice blew her nose and sat up.

"I can understand you not wanting to be mixed up in a thing like this, Deb; after all it's nothing to do with you if my young sister gets into trouble. And I understand how you feel about Dr MacIntyre, I couldn't go to our family doctor..."

Deb looked up at her sharply. Good heavens, the girl didn't believe she really did know Dallas.

"But please, Deb, would you do just one thing for me?" Alice went on. "You know how terribly difficult it is to get appointments with doctors for weeks and weeks unless they know you, and Mary's only on leave till Saturday, then she has to go back to Queensland. She's right up north on Atherton Tableland and she doesn't know a soul there she could tell, and she couldn't get another long leave for ages and it's over two months since it happened. If she goes back and they find out, she'll be dishonourably discharged and everyone will know. I've just simply got to find someone to help straight away. That's why I was going to ask you to ring up Dr MacIntyre and ask her if she'd see me...just as a patient. It wouldn't be anything to do with you, just an introduction and as she knows you..." Alice made her appeal almost in a single breath. Her voice tailed off.

Deb closed the cupboard door with a slam. Make an appointment for her! Heaven alone knew what Alice would say about her and her affairs if she ever got to Dallas. No, better go herself if the girl was absolutely determined. There must be someone else... "Haven't you got any friends who might know someone?"

"Oh, Deb, I simply couldn't ask them. If they knew at the church club..."

"Well, let's ask Claire."

"Oh, no. I couldn't bear Claire to know, she'd tell Guinea."

"No, she wouldn't."

"Deb, you're the only one I could bear to talk to about it — you're so different from the others. Besides, you're married; and with Dr MacIntyre being like your own sister..."

"Now listen," Deb made one last effort. "I'm pretty sure Dr MacIntyre won't be able to give you the slightest help, but Claire might. If she doesn't know anyone...then I'll see what I can do."

"Well...if you really think Claire might be able to help?"

"I think she's the most likely person next to Guinea."

"Oh, I'd never raise my head again if Guinea knew. But perhaps Claire..."

"The sooner we ask her the sooner we'll know. I'll go in and get her now."

Alice raised a woebegone face as Claire followed Deb into the office.

"Hullo. Have you got a cold?"

Alice shook her head, biting her lip to keep back the tears.

"No, she's upset," Deb explained briefly. "She wants your advice. Her sister's got into trouble and we thought you might know somebody."

Claire whistled softly. "That's tough all right." She frowned, tapping lacquered nails on the desk.

"Do you know anyone, Claire?" Alice whispered.

"No, I'm afraid I don't."

"I thought there were lots of people."

"If there are I don't know them, my dear. There was a nurse at Croydon, but she got enough money out of it to buy a private hospital and she's been going straight for over a year now."

Alice wept silently and hopelessly.

"Oh, it's not so bad as all that. Guinea will be in tomorrow and we can ask her."

Alice lifted an agonised face. "Not Guinea. She's so common."

"So is pregnancy, my dear. Common to the whole female

sex. And frankly, I don't know who else could help you."

Alice looked across at Deb. "Well, Deb promised if you didn't know anyone she'd ask Dr MacIntyre."

"Did she?" Claire's eyebrows went up.

"Of course, it's quite hopeless." Deb saw a loophole. "She'd never have anything to do with that sort of thing."

"Oh, but you did promise, Deb."

"If Deb's promised to try her, that's the best thing you can do then." Claire handed the matter back to Deb. "And I hope Dr MacIntyre will be able to help you. I'm sorry, but I can't leave my facial pack any longer."

Alice looked at Deb imploringly. "When will you see her?"

"I'll have to give her a ring and find out when she can see me. She's a very busy person."

"Yes, I'm sure she is. I often see her name in the paper. But today's a holiday, perhaps she wouldn't be so busy today."

"My dear, public holidays mean nothing to an honorary at a big hospital." Deb smiled at her patronisingly from Dallas's bigger world.

"I didn't mean that," Alice was immediately apologetic, "but there's only till Saturday."

"Yes, I know. I'll definitely ring her this morning. Will that satisfy you?"

"Oh yes, thank you, Deb. I'll try and get the number if you like."

"You go back to Mrs Stather. I'll ring Dallas, don't worry."

Alice gave her a sickly smile and went out. Deb went into the boudoir, took up the receiver and dialled. She was in for it now.

Deb sank back on an outside seat of the Mosman ferry and sighed with relief. The holiday rush in the Marie Antoinette that morning had worn her out completely.

Above the squat little ferry a hospital ship loomed white and enormous at No 2 wharf. Next to it was a battered tramp with patches of rust staining the grey hull, its blue and yellow flag fluttering stiffly in the westerly. Beyond the protection of Sydney Cove the harbour shimmered like polished pewter under the wind, and the waves chopped against the side of the little boat as it chuffed its way across to Old Cremorne.

Deb began to wonder what she'd say to Dallas about Mary. Doctors were inclined to be touchy where their profession was concerned. Besides, it was so long since she and Dallas had really discussed anything that mattered, and it wasn't going to be at all easy to bring up the subject. She realised with a feeling of shame that it was months since she'd been to see Dallas, but with the perpetual rush at the salon, she never got a minute for herself. Still, she was ashamed of herself for neglecting Dallas. Dallas was so much a part of her past — it was twenty years now that they'd known each other. . . Her mind went back to her schooldays at St George High School when they'd all fallen for the new science teacher, and Deb was back there again on that speech night when she was only sixteen.

It wasn't till long afterwards that she had realised that that was probably the proudest night in her father's life, a kind of peak to which all his labour and his loyalty had slowly carried him, and from which the rest of his life dropped sharply away like a landslide. She could see him now, tall and angular, her mother's arm linked in his. Nolly too, her face full of pride and excitement at seeing her older sister invested with a prefect's badge. She could see her father, when the speeches were over, rather gawkily topping the crowd and shaking hands with teachers and mothers and fathers and girls — and waiting to meet this Miss MacIntyre Deb was so keen about.

He'd confessed afterwards he'd been rather surprised to find her so young and good-looking. Somehow you didn't expect to find teachers either young or good-looking, particularly if they were specialists in science — but this one was a beauty. Black curly hair, clear grey eyes, and an infectious laugh as she shook his hand warmly and congratulated him on his daughter. Damn fine woman, he'd said. Waste to have a woman like that wearing herself out teaching when she ought to be making some good man happy and bringing up a family of her own. Not that she didn't have plenty of time still. . .she couldn't be a day over twenty-five. A fine girl; Deb was lucky to have her for a friend. Teachers certainly had changed. Now in his day, they kept themselves to themselves as though they were creatures of another world.

Odd, the friendship that had grown up between Dallas and her father. Jim Penfold had risen the hard way, first as a carpenter, then a builder, then a contractor on a bigger scale, and he was Dallas's strongest champion when she decided to give up her well-paid job as a high school teacher for six thin years as a medical student. "Don't worry," he'd said, "there's always a bed and meal here for you. It'll be useful to have a doctor in the family." The country needed builders, he'd said to Deb and Nolly, and Dallas was building too. They'd felt something deep under his words, something glowing and staunch like the fire in the bowl of his old pipe that blazed to life only when it was puffed. His pride in Dallas was like that of a man for his son. Dallas's family were in West Australia and she fitted into the Penfold home as though she was one of themselves.

They had lived on the top of the hill in a rambling, comfortable bungalow with a view over the whole sweep of Cronulla beach from the southern headland to the far sandhills of Kurnell. In summer, the winds swept the house all day with their long sustained aerial tides out of the nor'east, and the southerlies came up with gusty roars bringing a cool change in the evening.

It was a solid house, Dad used to say, nothing fancy about it, but it would outlive him and outlive his children. No mortgage on it, either. A married man with a family had no right to mortgage his house. That was his theory and he stuck by it. Whenever he walked out onto his veranda and looked over the curve of the beach, lying like a silver crescent between sandhills and sea, to the wooded cliffs of Cape Sutherland, his heart swelled with a pride he never admitted to anyone except Dallas.

Jim Penfold had been an institution in Cronulla, a man whose word was his bond. He used to say, when people brought get-rich schemes to interest him, "I'd never lift my head up,

Mum, if I did a thing like that." He'd had a hand in building the place; that was where his roots were. Every street had a meaning for him, every park was a matter of personal pride; he'd had a say in every improvement on the beach front.

That was what a man should aim at when the first flight of youth was over. You'd wasted your time if, when your forties came, you hadn't a house of your own, a growing family to put in it, a bit of money in the bank so that the wife wouldn't have to look at every penny twice before she spent it, and enough to be able to give your kids a decent education and a chance to do what they wanted in the world.

Deb sighed. How out of date it all seemed now.

The ferry chugged its way around Cremorne Point and across to Musgrave Street wharf, then back across the bay to Old Cremorne. Deb could see Dallas's place now, the windowboxes bright with flowers against the weathered grey stone. She'd had the old house converted, keeping a flat for herself.

Dallas was standing on the balcony as the boat drew alongside the little wharf and Deb waved to her. That was the way Dallas used to wave, welcoming and reassuring her, from the veranda at Cronulla in those awful days before Mum died. If it hadn't been for Dallas they could never have kept her at home till the end and there would have been nothing for it but a public hospital — the depression had seen to that. If Dad hadn't been so worried about the business and all of them so disappointed about her own failure to get a scholarship to the teachers' college — that was the year the government had economised on training scholarships — they'd have noticed what was happening to Mum. All the year she had become thinner and yellower; there were dark rings under her eyes and a dragging pain in her back, but she wouldn't go to a doctor.

Dallas had taken a job in the country for the long vacation because she needed the cash, and it wasn't until she came back and took charge of things at home that they had realised how ill Mum was.

The ferry drew in at the ramshackle wharf and Deb went up the sloping tree-lined path to the gate at the bottom of Dallas's lawn. Dallas was at the top of the garden steps to greet her and kissed her warmly.

"It was lucky I was in when you rang. It's the first afternoon I've had at home in months. Come on in and we'll have a cup of tea straight away. I put the jug on when I saw you come off the ferry."

A golden voice was filling the flat with unendurable grief.

"It's Marjorie Lawrence in the *Liebestod*; she's singing it at the concert tonight," Dallas said. "Isn't she glorious?"

The record finished and Dallas switched off the gramophone.

"She's singing some marvellous stuff...and singing from that wheelchair! Her courage is an inspiration in itself."

Dallas made the tea and carried the tray through to the balcony. It was cool and sheltered and gay with cane furniture and bright cushions.

"Put your feet up," Dallas said, motioning her to the lounge. "You must be run to death in that glamour factory of yours."

She sat down and her strong, capable hands moved lightly among the tea things.

"Get it over straight away," Deb said to herself, trying to pluck up her courage. But the opening that had seemed so easy on the ferry was not at all easy now she had Dallas in front of her. After all, she hadn't seen Dallas for months... perhaps she'd better lead into it naturally after they'd had a chat...

Dallas handed her a cup of tea and passed a plate of scones. "Mrs Blake's scones are death on the figure," she laughed, "but after all it's a holiday." She bit into one herself with relish.

"You don't have to worry about your figure." Deb looked at her with a professional eye. Really, she thought, Dallas is still quite beautiful judged by any standards. She must be at least forty-three or four, and her figure's as good as mine and the way she wears her hair cut close to show the shape of her head gives her a distinguished look.

"I let hard work solve my beauty problems." Dallas took another scone. "I'm afraid your salon wouldn't get much of a living out of me.''

Deb wondered again why she had never married. Of course she had her profession and she was terribly successful, and she had lots of men friends. But Deb could not imagine herself being satisfied with a profession, however successful. And Dallas had had to fight hard enough before she got her appointment to the Harbour Hospital. "That's one thing the war has done," she had said when she got the news. "Only for the shortage of men they'd never have appointed a woman honorary."

Yes, Deb thought, whichever way you take it, whether we're married or unmarried, the going's harder for women — and no one knows that better than Dallas. Her mind went back to Mary Parker. It's ridiculous, she told herself, the way I'm putting it off. After all I'm only asking her advice to help someone; the whole thing really has nothing to do with me.

She finished her cup of tea and put it down deliberately, but as she looked up to begin, Dallas was already speaking.

"I dropped in at Nolly's yesterday afternoon expecting to find you there. I had a long letter from Jack to show you.''

Deb winced. "I did stay over Saturday night, but I simply had to come back to the SP yesterday. The Marie Antoinette is on tap all the weekend for the hotel guests, you know.'' She hoped she sounded convincing.

"Wonderful service," Dallas raised her eyebrows. "And to think we've just had to close down a maternity ward for lack of staff!''

Deb was silent and Dallas went on, "Isn't there any chance of your being able to go up to the Vineyard at all?''

Deb found herself making a long and involved explanation which petered out lamely. As she took up her cup, she met Dallas's steady grey eyes set deep under level brows. "It's all most unfortunate." She felt like a schoolgirl, stammering through some clumsy excuse.

"What are you going to do about Nolly then? She's doing far too much, you know.''

Deb recovered and her voice rose a tone in virtuous indignation. "Of course I wouldn't think of letting Nolly down.

By going on working the first fortnight of Jack's leave while he's up at the Vineyard, we can all be together at Nolly's when she's in hospital. I'm looking forward to getting some sewing done for the kiddies then, too."

"That's splendid." Dallas's smile was warm. "Nolly's so generous she never knows where to draw the line. When she comes home after this baby she must have a chance to take a thorough rest. What about you taking Debby and Jack with Lu up to the Vineyard till Christmas? Jack's quite a little man and Lu manages Debby as well as Nolly does."

Deb drank her second cup of tea in a scalding gulp. "I'll have to think it over," she said with an air of genuinely considering the suggestion. "It's just a question of whether we can really afford it. When Jack comes back we're going to need every penny I can earn."

Dallas's eyes ran from the expensive brown-and-white shoes to the simple tailored suit. "You're looking very smart today," she commented. "Did you make the suit yourself?"

Deb flushed and flicked an imaginary smut off the yellow linen. "You've got to have a few decent clothes in my job," she said defensively.

"Don't you wear uniforms?"

"In the salon, of course, but I mean, coming in and out."

"You've got a wonderful suntan for this time of the year. I thought you had stockings on at first. Have you been doing much surfing?"

"On no." Deb ran a hand over her tanned leg. "We've got a new sunlamp in the salon and we've all been getting up a good tan."

"Sunlamp! Somebody at the SP must have a lot of influence somewhere — or is it the black market? Our physiotherapy department has been held up for months waiting for a lamp, among other things."

"Lots of people attribute things to the black market that's really only good management," Deb made an effort to make up the ground she had lost. "After all, if you know how to go about getting things that are in short supply and you're prepared to spend the money, I don't see why you shouldn't have them. And the regulations are so silly that people have to get round them to live at all.''

"What you mean is, of course, that ten per cent of the people with cash and no conscience get round them at the expense of the other ninety per cent. Which doesn't seem very different to me from plain gangster tactics.''

"Well, I can tell you quite frankly that if I'd known a bit more when I was looking for a flat two years ago, I'd have probably got one. But I was a complete innocent; I didn't know then that you only had to put down fifty or a hundred pounds for the key and the flat was yours.''

"I didn't realise that you had fifty or a hundred pounds at the time.''

"I hadn't.''

"That's what I'm saying. People who could afford it got the flats, whether they needed one as badly as you or not. In any case, I'd have found it hard to blame you, whatever racket you got into. It must be awful being separated from Luen and cooped up in that dingy little cupboard of a room at the SP after your own home.''

"I was very lucky to get a job that included accommodation.'' There was a defensive note in Deb's voice again.

"Yes, that's true. Housing conditions are frightful. It's simply heartbreaking the number of women with babies we've got to send back from hospital to overcrowded little rooms. No wonder marriages break up. They may be made in heaven but they're unmade in cramped surroundings among bickering relatives.''

"The government seems to be trying to do everything to obstruct building,'' Deb parroted Angus.

"Oh, nonsense. I'm prepared to admit that we've got to win the war and that there's a shortage of manpower and materials, but anyone who blames it all on this government is talking through his hat. What about the ten years before the war when we had piles of material and hundreds of thousands of unemployed and we let them rot on the dole rather than organise an intelligent housing programme, because it might interfere with private profits? Look what happened to your own father.''

"But surely," Deb began hesitantly, "if you don't allow people a fair profit on their work, there'll be no incentive to work at all."

Dallas put down the teapot and raised her hands in a gesture of helplessness. "I give up. When I hear women like you talk like that, knowing what your father and your husband and your sister went through in the depression, it makes me despair of knocking any sense into human beings at all. If you wanted any disproof of that cant about the profit motive, you've just got to look at the war. The people who do the fighting and endure the worst of wartime conditions are not the people who make the profit out of it."

Deb was silent. She knew there were a lot of answers she could have made. They sounded so convincing when Angus made them, but looking into Dallas's grey eyes, sparkling now with an impersonal sort of anger, they seemed feeble.

"If I had my way," Dallas said firmly, pouring herself a third cup of tea, "I'd confiscate all these big half-empty houses and let them out under a housing committee to homeless families."

Deb thought of Angus's house at Palm Beach. "You dare not let people in," he had explained to her. "However much you feel you'd like to do something, with the law as it is, you simply can't be sure of getting them out again if you want it for a holiday yourself."

"I think you're right up to a point," Deb agreed, trying to bring the conversation on to easier ground. "But the trouble is you can't get them out when you want to, and the way they knock places around! Some people would make a slum of anything."

"That's only too true, unfortunately. Our system breeds irresponsibles at both ends of the social scale. I see by this morning's paper that a couple of playboys held a barbecue in one of the SP suites yesterday."

"Yes, that was absolutely disgusting. But at least they can afford to pay for the damage."

"That only makes it worse. I can forgive people who have

326

never had the opportunity to learn decent behaviour, but I can't forgive wealthy playboys who imagine that being able to pay for things justifies every sort of vandalism."

"Of course, half the trouble with the housing here is due to the Americans," Deb said placatingly. "When I think what I went through after we were turned out of the flat so that it could be let to some Yank serviceman for about ten times what I was paying, and dragging Luen round from suburb to suburb for weeks on end, trying to find a place..."

Dallas nodded sympathetically: "Poor kid, you've had your bad time, and then, in the end, you had to let Lu go to Nolly to get a roof over your head. From what I see of conditions, except for the men in the front line, it's the women and children who take the brunt of the war."

Deb seized the opportunity: "That's really what I wanted to talk to you about, Dallas. I...want some advice."

Dallas looked at her questioningly.

"It's about a girl I know. Well...I don't exactly know her, but her sister works with me, and she's got into trouble, and" — the words came out with a rush — "I thought you might be able to tell me the name of some doctor who did that sort of thing."

A professional mask slid over Dallas's face. "I presume you mean an abortion?"

Deb nodded. She felt her face flush under Dallas's keen glance.

"When did this happen?"

"I...I can't tell you exactly."

Dallas looked at her professionally. "Deb, if you want me to help you, it's no good beating about the bush."

Deb looked at her blankly. It took a few seconds before Dallas's meaning penetrated her mind. "Good heavens," she gasped, "why Dallas, surely you don't think...whatever could put such an idea into your head?"

"You mean that it is not for yourself?"

"Of course it's not. Why...how could you think such a thing."

Dallas shrugged her shoulders. "Have a cigarette and we'll

get this business clear.''

Deb puffed furiously, virtuous indignation mounting. She felt like walking straight out of the place. That Dallas should think that of her. Dallas of all people!

Dallas went on with infuriating calm: ''You'd better tell me what you know.''

Deb controlled her indignation. ''It's an AWAS, Mary Parker's the name — her sister's the hairdresser at the salon.''

''Won't the man marry her?''

''He can't. He's already married and his wife refuses to divorce him. Mary and he have been on the same station for two years, and then he was sent to the Islands. It was his final leave.''

Dallas sighed. '' 'Final leave'. How often I've heard that.''

''But you can't help being sorry for her.''

''You'd be less than human if you weren't. In the ridiculous social set-up we have, it's always the girl who's penalised. Nobody worries about the man.''

''He seems to be a decent enough fellow.''

''But he hasn't got to take the consequences. He'll go on serenely to promotion while the girl gets a dishonourable discharge, and when the war's over he'll return to the bosom of his wife. I can never see why, when they regard VD as an occupational disease for men in the army, they shouldn't regard pregnancy in servicewomen in the same light.''

Deb felt more and more depressed.

''What do you expect me to do?'' Dallas asked briskly.

''Well. . .I thought maybe. . .you might. . .you could suggest something.''

''If you mean you hoped I might do something, I'm sorry, my dear, that's quite out of the question. I'm not afflicted with the particular brand of sentimentality that regards it as murder to remove an unwanted fœtus and at the same time applauds mass slaughter in war, but I can't afford to risk my future in a profession for which I have worked very hard, for the sake of one or even one hundred little AWAS, however sorry I feel for them.''

Deb was silent, fidgeting with the spoon on her saucer.

Dallas got up and leaned on the railing. "I'm so sorry for women. Whichever way they turn, most of them are caught. It doesn't matter whether they're driven by love or lust, they're the ones who fall in. If I had a daughter...as I won't, because society says unless I'm prepared to tie myself up to some man legally, I have no right to bear a child — but if I did have a daughter, I'd teach her very early that the only real salvation for women is work."

"It's all very well for you to talk like that, you've got brains and ability and you can stand on your own feet. You don't seem to need a man permanently, though goodness knows you always have plenty of them around. But what is there for the average woman if she doesn't get married? Only an underpaid job and a back room in some cheap boarding-house. And anyway most women are romantic and if you gave them their choice they'd rather have love than a career any day of the week."

"You misunderstand me. I have nothing against marriage or love, but love as we know it is too wild and unpredictable a passion on which to build a whole life. And even marriage, unless love develops into something more lasting than the most thrilling romance — for instance, into a partnership such as Tom and Nolly have — destroys itself and usually the woman with it. Only a romantic philanderer like Byron could have uttered that nonsense about love being of man's life a thing apart and woman's whole existence. He never stayed long enough with one woman to find out that she was a human being as well as a romantic thrill, and even if he had, he belonged to the class that never has its comfort interfered with by babies' feeding times or nappies drying round the kitchen fire."

"Good heavens, Dallas, you reduce everything to such a material basis."

"I don't exactly know what you mean by material, but if you mean the solid things like eating and working and loving and bearing babies and building a life together and taking equal responsibility, then I agree. My complaint about human relationships, as the films and the cheap magazines present them, is that they destroy the real material basis and substitute a cash arrangement by which the larger the fortune Cinderella manages to snare into matrimony, the higher the romance. Of course it's all part of the harem tradition. Wealth is power and it buys beauty and youth.''

"If you had your way," Deb broke in, "there wouldn't be any romance in the world at all.''

"You can call it romance if you like, but to me it's a degradation of a once lovely word. And, as a matter of fact, it is only in the last century or so that romance has been degraded to mere sex titillation. For the women of pre-industrial days, the domestic arts were a fulltime job, as they were for our grandmothers.''

"Surely you don't want to put the clock back and make us all domestic drudges again.''

"Certainly not. I want to see all the benefits of science used to give women fuller lives, less drudgery and more leisure. Time to enjoy their families. What I resent is eighty per cent of the women being drudges whether they're married or unmarried, and the other twenty per cent kept for display. It took the wealthy class to reduce women to fine ladies and parasites. On the whole, the man with money today uses his wife as an advertisement for his assets, since it's no longer fashionable for him to go round in cloth of gold and diamonds himself.''

"The society women I come in contact with work pretty hard one way and another keeping up their position, and if their husbands like to buy them furs and jewels and model frocks, why shouldn't they? It seems to me to be much better than what Tom has reduced Nolly to,'' Deb replied with heat.

Dallas smiled and looked round at her. "It may surprise you, Deb,'' she said, "but do you know, if I weren't so very fond of being myself, I'd choose to be Nolly. She's that person so rare in the world today — a fulfilled woman.''

"Well, if that's your idea of fulfilment, it certainly isn't mine, and so far as I'm concerned, you can have it on your own.''

Dallas went on without answering her: "When I see a happy woman, I generally find that she is good at something outside romantic love. How I've come to loathe those words, romantic love! Boiled down all they mean is that women have let themselves be sold the idea that sex is a substitute for life, instead of seeing it in its right proportion as only one part of living. There comes a time for everyone when sex, merely as sex, fails you. And then, when your heart's shattered into little bits, there's no better cement for putting it in usable shape again than the knowledge that you're really crackerjack at something else besides love, whether it's ballet dancing or playing the piano or running a home expertly, or teaching a class or flying a plane.''

She stood silent for a few minutes looking out over the harbour, her eyes the same sparkling grey as the water under the western sun.

"And now," she said, turning back to Deb, "what are we going to do about your little AWAS? Has she got any money?"

"Her sister and she can rake up twenty-five pounds between them."

"Hasn't the man sent her any?"

"He doesn't know yet."

"I'm afraid there's not a reliable doctor about town who'll do it under forty these days."

"Forty pounds!" gasped Deb. "Someone said twenty-five.''

Dallas shrugged her shoulders. "Supply and demand, my dear. The price has gone up — wartime inflation, like everything else. But even then the only man I really could have guaranteed has retired and bought a property somewhere in the wilds!"

"Isn't there anyone else at all you could recommend?"

"I'm afraid there isn't. Is it urgent?"

"Yes, I'm afraid it is. She's got less than a week's leave left in Sydney."

"That certainly complicates things. I'll tell you what I'll do, Deb. I'll make a few discreet inquiries tomorrow, but for goodness sake don't raise her hopes. And don't mention my name to a soul." Dallas looked at her watch. "And now, my dear, I shall have to go. I'm having dinner in town with Colonel Gisborne and I want to drop into the hospital to see a patient first.''

"Is he a new one on your list?"

Dallas laughed. ''Not exactly, I met him right at the beginning of the war. He'd had a pretty bad time at Dunkirk, and they gave him a job as MO on the ship when they sent the German prisoners out here — really to give him a chance to pick up. Now he's advance medical service for the British Navy.''

"Quite one of the brass hats," Deb said dryly.

"He wouldn't recognise the description. He's merely interested in doing a good job — and I might add, he's a fine fellow all round. We're going on to the Marjorie Lawrence concert afterwards.''

Deb stood up. "I'll have to be getting back too."

"If you wait ten minutes while I change my frock, I'll run you over."

"Thanks. I'll wash up then while you're getting ready."

"Good. Mrs Blake won't be in till late and I hate leaving her a pile of dirty things. And by the way," she called from her room, "you and Jack can come over here any time you like, and Mrs Blake'll fix you up in the spare room. I know how difficult it is for you to make any arrangements at the hotel.''

"Oh thanks," Deb called. Jack could come here and that would let her out of sharing her room again, she thought with relief as she took the tray into the kitchen.

Dallas came out just as she was putting the things away.

"You look awfully nice in that get-up," Deb said, frankly admiring her severe black frock.

"Glad you like it."

"I haven't seen those earrings before, have I?"

"No. There's a bracelet too. Like it?" She held out her wrist with a heavy hand-wrought silver band.

"It's lovely."

"Adrian picked up the set somewhere in the Middle East." She put on a tiny black hat and adjusted her silver fox cape.

She's clever, Deb thought as they went out to the car, the

way she plays up to her hair, silver and black like the cape. Distinction, charm and brains — it's hardly fair that any woman should have so much.

They drove in silence until they came up the broad approach to the Bridge.

"I hope you didn't mind me dragging you in on a beastly sordid affair like this," Deb said in an apologetic tone at last, feeling that she must re-establish herself. "And I do appreciate your trying to find..."

"Sordid?" Dallas broke in. "Sordid is a word I hesitate to use. Things I find sordid, other people find eminently respectable."

Deb went on hastily: "Naturally, one's sorry for a girl in a jam like this, but after all when they play around with married men they only get what they deserve."

"Pay every man according to his deserts and which of us shall escape whipping?" Dallas quoted.

"Well, anyway you must admit that the promiscuity among young people nowadays is absolutely revolting," Deb said virtuously. "Girls don't seem to have any regard for other women's husbands at all."

"Lots of married women I know seem to have very little regard for their own husbands."

Deb felt a prickling of anxiety. Was it only her imagination, or was there another meaning in Dallas's voice? She glanced at her anxiously, but her profile conveyed nothing. "I don't know what you mean, but if it's just because I'm not going up to the Vineyard with Jack..."

"Why aren't you going to the Vineyard with Jack?"

"I've told you. I'm needed at the SP."

"Professionally or personally?"

"Really..."

"My dear," Dallas's voice was cool and brisk, "I have no right to pry into your affairs, but when you deliberately lie to me about why you didn't stay at Nolly's yesterday..."

"What do you mean — lie?"

"Oh, don't be a fool, Deb. Your escort's magnificent limousine nearly skittled my partner yesterday on the Palm

Beach road.''

Deb felt her face flaming. ''If I can't go for a run on a hot Sunday...''

''I hear the gentleman's been squiring you round the high spots rather constantly of late.''

''Did your partner tell you that, too? He must have a very dirty mind. And while we're on the subject, I think it's most extraordinary of you to take a refugee into partnership with you — and a Jew at that. Surely you could have got an Australian.''

Dallas's nostrils flared.

Oh Lord, now I've done it, Deb thought anxiously.

The car slowed down at the toll-gate and Dallas handed out the coins. When they picked up speed she spoke again and her voice was cold. ''I've been astonished at the tone of a good deal of your conversation this afternoon, Deb, but when you say a thing like that I'm positively shocked. It shouldn't be necessary for me to remind you that Karl Rosenberg was not only one of Vienna's leading specialists, but willing to suffer for his political principles as well. When I hear you repeating such ignorant and dangerous prejudices, I wonder what on earth's coming over you.''

''I've a right to my own views,'' Deb retorted feebly.

''If they were your own, it wouldn't be so bad. But it's positively sickening to have to sit down and hear you parrot a lot of undigested opinions you've picked up.''

''Well, anyway, plenty of other people think the same thing.''

''I am not interested, and in this case, I'll ask you not to make that remark again anywhere. Karl has had a difficult enough time as it is without his name being dragged round by someone who ought to know better.''

Dallas drove along Bridge Street in silence, and ran the car into the circular drive in front of the Conservatorium, shut off the engine, and half-turned in her seat. ''Listen, Deb, you can tell me to mind my own business if you like, but I'd feel that I had failed our whole friendship if I didn't tell you how what you're doing looks to me. I probably wouldn't have got to the point only for your being so smug about that poor little AWAS. 'Sordid and ugly', you said. You know, I don't see any difference between a girl having an affair with a married man and a bachelor having an affair with a married woman.''

"If you're alluding to me," Deb said hotly, "there's absolutely nothing wrong in what I'm doing."

"By which I suppose you mean you haven't slept with him."

"Of course I haven't. You should know me better than that."

"I'm afraid I don't know you at all, after today."

"You seem to expect me to behave as though I was still a schoolgirl."

"On the contrary, I expect you to behave like a grown-up woman. You've got a decent husband, he's away fighting and he trusts you, but you're so caught up in that luxury life at the South Pacific that you're prepared to ditch him on his first leave in eighteen months."

"Surely I have some right to my own life and happiness."

"Not on those terms. Your right to happiness is in the life you've built together with Jack and Lu."

"Even when Jack doesn't consider me in the slightest?"

"What do you mean by that?"

"You and Nolly seem to take it for granted that my life should be run entirely to suit Jack's whims. Did I want to leave the Vineyard and come into town when he got the craze for being a motor salesman? No, I hated the idea. Did that matter to him? Not in the slightest. And then just when I got myself adjusted to that way of living, he had to rush off into uniform the moment the war came. Did he even so much as tell me until after he'd enlisted?" She broke off shakily, tears choking her voice.

Dallas's eyes softened as she watched her. "Go on," she said gently.

"Don't talk to me about patriotism. From what I saw of Jack and his pals it was just excitement and adventure. But what do you care about all this?"

"I care a lot. I'm very fond of the three of you."

"You tell me you're shocked at me. Well, I'll tell you, Dallas, that I'm surprised at you. You ought to have seen enough of the hardships that the women left behind have to put up with, to try to understand their problems instead of condemning them. When men get into the Services they just shelve all their personal responsibilities and women have to take them on. We've got to manage on less money, bring up our kids without any help, and we're expected to put up with loneliness and having no social life and all the rest of it. You complain about me going out with other men, but I'd take a bet on it that if I ever discovered that Jack had been out with other women, you'd advise me to overlook it — even if he'd been unfaithful — because he's a soldier. I've managed on my own for nearly five years and Jack hasn't given me a scrap of help and now, without so much as by-your-leave, he wants to dump us all on that rundown Vineyard just because he's got some mad idea into his head about not going back into business. Does he even ask me what I'd like to do? Does he consider what's best for Luen? Not him. Well, I'll tell you, and I'll tell him as soon as he arrives, that I'm not going to do it. I had enough of living from hand to mouth when we were first married, and as for pigging it in that rural slum again, I'm not going to do it. One thing living at the South Pacific has done for me, it's shown me the way I want to live."

"I'm glad you told me that, Deb," Dallas's voice was very quiet. "I understand things a lot better now. But you're making an awful mistake. You think you're seeing life with a capital L at the SP. Luxury, glamour, expensive entertainment...Oh, I know how it is. I've been taken in that way myself, but believe me, it doesn't mean a thing."

"That's a matter of opinion."

"True, my dear, but it's still not life in the round. The reverse side of the enticing picture is exploitation and servility. Women reduced to the level of slaves whose very existence depends upon their pandering to men's passing whims."

"Angus McFarland isn't that type. You couldn't find anyone more honourable."

"Meaning?"

"Well, he's asked me to marry him."

"He knows you're married?"

"Of course he does."

"Strictly honourable!"

Deb put her hand on the door. "If you've nothing more to say, Dallas, I'll get out and walk up to the hotel."

"Oh, don't be childish. Anyway, I've got a lot more to say."

Deb stayed where she was.

"I'm sure all you tell me about Mr McFarland is quite true, and I've no doubt he considers he's being very honourable. My point is simply that men like that, middle-aged bachelors of private means living on money they've never earned and with a string of mistresses behind them, just don't take women seriously."

"Even if what you're saying was true," Deb retorted, "and I'd like to know what evidence you have, I can't see any greater proof of a man's seriousness than a proposal of marriage."

"That's not what I mean. What I'm trying to say is, they think the whole function of women is to be decorative and entertaining."

"I don't think you really know anything about it."

"Don't I? I know only too well what men like that expect from a woman. They expect her to be a kind of magnifying mirror, reflecting an image of themselves so much larger than life that they never have to face the truth. That's why King David gat him a young virgin, my dear."

Deb moved impatiently. "That's revolting."

"Yes. I quite agree. That's what I call sordid — old men buying young women."

"You speak as though I were a common pick-up girl."

"You really have very moral attitudes, haven't you? 'Sordid' and 'pick-up' and 'affairs with married men'."

"I suppose you realise just how offensive you're being?"

"Oh quite. But I'm trying to be honest."

"I don't know if it's honest to practically accuse me of being immoral."

"You know, Deb, to hear you, one would think that morality is merely a matter of sex. Unless it cuts across other loyalties I think people's sex lives are their own affair. Virginity for its own sake has never impressed me. When people impose the discipline of chastity on themselves it's usually because they regard it as an important part of a larger loyalty, the basis on which two people can plan a life together — like having a joint bank account and trusting each other. But neither self-discipline nor a bank book are any good unless you are going to have a future. I don't blame the young people you criticise so harshly; I blame a world that takes away their hope of security and gives them little prospect of life. Marriage is part of the social pattern, and when that pattern is broken, marriages crack up — like gardens in an earthquake. But you have no such excuse, your marriage had time to send down deep roots. It was a partnership."

"Well, it's not a partnership any more. And don't blame me for that either. When Jack went overseas I had all the romantic ideas about keeping our marriage alive on paper, but it takes two people to do that. His letters were bad enough when he first went away, but they got steadily worse. Why, now he can't even write to Luen regularly and he knows what his letters mean to her."

"Deb, don't think I don't understand how hard it's been, but you know that for one faithful husband there are a hundred men who can pour out all the blarney in the world on paper. I've watched you and Jack for a long time, and the way you two faced the depression and the dole raised my opinion of human nature. Mind you, I expected it. I'd seen your father's courage with all his world sliding into ruins around him, and I'd had the privilege of helping to nurse your mother. My God, what courage she had! Never a complaint out of her. It wasn't till I'd seen a lot more cases like hers that I realised just how gallant she was."

Deb's face was turned away and her voice came muffled and stubborn: "I don't see what any of this has got to do with what I decide to do with my life in the future."

"If you don't, then nothing I say can show you." Dallas

pressed the self-starter and took the car back into Macquarie Street.

"I mightn't be seeing life in the round, as you suggest," Deb said stiffly, "but what I have seen is enough to make me determined that I'm not going to let my daughter grow up without security."

Dallas sighed and pulled the car up at the service lane beside the hotel. "Goodbye," she said, "this is where you get off, isn't it?"

Deb slammed the door and the car gathered speed along Macquarie Street.

Guinea had just put away her breakfast things and was sitting in the sun that poured through her window, reading a note from Byron. He said he would call round early. Not too early, she hoped, with the room in this mess! There was a knock on the door. Holy mackerel! Don't say this was Byron already!

"Hold on!" she called, pulling a housecoat on over her pyjamas and dragging the spread over the unmade bed. She threw her scattered clothes higgledy-piggledy into the lowboy, ran a comb through her hair and opened the door.

"Good morning! I'm here!"

"Oh Jeepers, it's you!"

Kim followed her into the room. "Would I be intruding to inquire who else you would be expecting at nine am?"

She went on fixing her bed without answering.

"Don't tell me your admirals drop in for breakfast? Or maybe they drop out?"

"What do your lady generals do?"

"I wouldn't know. I've never met anything in the Women's Services higher than a captain. Not socially, that is, they keep 'em on ice for the brass hats."

He handed Guinea a jar in a brown paper bag. "Here's some of Aunt Annie's special fig jam. She sent it to you when she heard I was coming in. With love. The old man said to tell you you're his favourite pin-up girl; he's got the photo out of yesterday's paper over the head of his bed. Good for his arthritis, he says."

"They're darlings. I don't know how you come to have such nice relations."

"Heredity works funny ways. You've got a pretty fine bunch yourself if it comes to that."

"I suppose Aunt Annie hasn't heard from Monnie?"

"No, she hasn't. I told her about the letter and your mother being anxious."

"What did she say?"

"Well, you know Aunt Annie, Monnie's the white-haired girl where she's concerned. Your mother doesn't understand her, your family don't appreciate her, and altogether none of you deserve to have a wonder child like that, but she gave me a message for you. She said what about coming out next weekend, and bringing the kid with you?''

"I only hope to God we've found her by then.''

"Of course we'll have found her. I bet she pops up bright and smiling at work when we ring there tomorrow morning.''

"I'm not too happy about the whole business.''

"Aw, she'll be all right. If it'll make you any happier I'll go out to the mill and see her myself in the morning. Now, let's think about us for a change.''

"OK. Now you've done your messages, what do you want this hour of the morning, anyway?''

"If you look closely you'll see I have swimming trunks and a towel. I thought — first, just for old time's sake, we'd go and take a peek at the Six-Hour procession, and second, we'd hop out to Bondi and have a surf, and in between times scout round for young Monnie.''

"Do you expect just to whistle her and see her come galloping up to you out of the blue, with half Sydney on holiday?''

"That's my idea. I've been told I have a magnetic personality.''

"You ought to collect old scrap iron then. I can introduce you to a bit of it.''

"I don't doubt it, with the Yanks leaving.'' He glanced at his watch. "Shake a leg, or we'll miss the procession.''

Guinea thought rapidly. Shirley McGovern and her crowd always used to go to Bondi on the weekends. There was just a chance she and Kim might be able to get a line on Monnie there, and she certainly wouldn't take Byron on the hunt for a young sister. Besides, she'd like to see the procession. She could tell Dad about it, and she could easily be back in time for Byron. She'd leave a message for him. "Get outside,'' she said, "till I put some clothes on.''

Kim picked up Sherwood's photo from the mantelpiece. "Who's the joker?''

"General Eisenhower,'' she snapped and pushed him out

of the door.

In ten minutes she joined him on the landing.

Kim let out a long whistle. "A-a-aha! Is she any good? I like that nood tummy of yours."

"Tummy me foot. That's my midriff. Don't you know your anatomy?" She went ahead of him down the stairs.

"Not very well. But I could learn." He played a tattoo on the expanse of browned bare back between the brief green top and dirndl skirt.

"Do that again," she warned him, "and it'll be your funeral procession I'm watching."

"OK, OK. Look, no hands." He tucked them behind him and smiled at her angelically as they came out on to the footpath.

"Just so long as you remember." She pulled on an enormous green cartwheel hat and tied the matching ribbons under her chin. "Holy mackerel! We'll be grilled in this westerly."

Kim gazed at her with frank admiration. "You look good-oh. Surprising what clothes — or lack of them — can do for a girl."

"Baloney! Keep that for your lady captains."

He tucked a hand under her arm, feeling the skin of her waist satin-smooth against his wrist.

She pulled away sharply. "And remember those hands."

"What do you expect me to do with them all day? Sit on them?"

"You can do anything you like with them, except put them on me."

They came up the long hill of Forbes Street in the bright sunshine, past the convict-built walls of the old gaol and out into Taylor Square. The crowds were straining against the barriers in Oxford Street and the air throbbed with the drumming of approaching bands.

All the traffic was stopped along the route and a mounted policeman kept back the good-humoured crowd. A raucous voice barracked from a window of the corner hotel: "Where did you get your nag, sergeant?" The policeman grinned, drawing the reins tighter so that his white horse curvetted proudly.

"Understudying Hirohito?" someone else chiacked. The policeman lifted a hand in acknowledgment. A roar of laughter went up.

"Hang on to my belt," Kim instructed, worming his way through the crowd till they came out on the little island under the tramway signal box. "Hop up," he said, and she climbed a couple of rungs of the iron ladder.

From her perch she could see the white horse of the marshal leading a detachment of mounted police up Oxford Street. Behind them, trade union banners fluttered in the dancing air. As far as she could see, the procession flowed in an unbroken stream of colour and movement. The mounted police turned into Flinders Street, horses stepping high to the beat of the band, their satin coats gleaming. One by one the floats moved past.

Pity Sher was missing this, Guinea thought. He'd been looking forward to it. "It's gonna be fine to watch a union march without thinking that at any moment a cop'll give you a push in the nose," he'd said. "First time I ever marched with the union they turned out the cops, the militia and the steam hoses. You ought to have seen my old man, they did him up like a bit of raw beefsteak. You do this sort of thing better Down Under than we do in the States, though maybe it'll be different when us guys get back. Somehow I just don't see us lettin' them pull that kind of rough stuff any more. We'll let 'em know we know the score."

The banners of her father's old union came up the hill. Kim looked up to her. "Remember when your dad and my dad used to step it out with the big banner? And we used to hang over the barriers and barrack our heads off?" Sure, she remembered.

They watched the two-mile procession slowly mount the slope from the city and stream down Flinders Street towards the sports ground. As the last detachment passed, Kim looked up. "Let's hop it down to the Bellevue Hill tram now, and we'll be out catching the first breaker before the crowd knows the show's over."

They clung precariously to the straps on a tram jammed

to the footboards with holidaymakers. The westerly whipped the dust up from the crowded streets. Though it was still early, the sun beat down fiercely on the unshaded walls of the old terraces. Crowds poured out of the narrow streets and the cramped houses with their mean slices of backyard; cheeky boys intent on dodging their fares jumped on and off the tram; family parties hauled along overflowing picnic baskets and bouncing babies. At each stopping place young couples in bright sports clothes clambered aboard the already overcrowded tram and clung to the footboards.

The conductor's voice rose, brisk and good-natured: "Get inside there, get inside there...for Gawd's sake, get along in there, mate."

Kim put his head out of the door, "What d'yer know?" he said, "If that's not old Andrew McCracken. Used to be our tail gunner. Hiya there, Andy," he called.

Andy swung himself onto the footboard near their compartment as the tram gathered speed. "For cryin' out loud, if it's not me old pal Kim!"

"How d'yer like being back in civvy street?" Kim inquired.

"I'll give it away," said Andy. "Sitting in the tail of a bomber with the Nips taking pot shots at you is home from home compared with hanging on by your teeth on these death-plank trams. How long are yer down for?"

"Got another week."

"Gimme a ring," said Andy, "the same old joint, and we'll toss over a pot or two together."

"That'll be fine," Kim agreed.

Andy moved off along the footboard, from stanchion to stanchion, calling "Fez please" in a brisk voice.

"Great chap, Andy," Kim remarked to Guinea, "whitest bloody Pommy in Australia."

The tram hummed out like a moving beehive into the wide tree-lined streets of Woollahra and Bellevue Hill, clanging its way past magnificent houses set back in their formal gardens. The undulating green of the golf links spread below them, studded with dark shrubs and the camouflaged ack-ack guns.

"I suppose you do a round there now and again," Kim said.

"Oh sure, I got some injections of blue blood so I could join."

"Bright idea. Did you get some shots into the bank balance too?"

She laughed, "I need them."

Guinea craned out of the tram at the close zoom of a plane and Kim's arm slid round her waist. Together they watched a flying boat circle overhead and out above Rose Bay, then turn and sweep up the laneway of signal boats to the flying base in a flurry of feathered spray. The tram turned and clattered down to Bondi Beach along the narrow neck between harbour and ocean.

Kim leaned against the railing on the Esplanade and watched Guinea come out of the surf pavilion. She was a wow all right, he had to admit, and what a bathing suit! A wisp of green brassière and the briefest trunks. Bet she got that from a Yank. She swung a green bathing cap in her hand and her gold hair streamed in the wind.

She walked across the Esplanade through an admiring chorus of wolf calls and whistling. Crikey, Kim thought between anger and pride, what a girl! She doesn't bat an eyelid.

A photographer came running up. "Just hold it a minute," he pleaded. Guinea stopped and turned to him, amiably posing at his direction while he took snap after snap. The hell thought Kim. Thinks she's a film star? She thanked the photographer with a beaming smile when he handed her a sheaf of tickets.

"If you'll give me the tickets I'll get them done for you — that's if you'll autograph one for me," a young soldier offered.

Before she could answer, Kim snatched the tickets out of her hand. "Lay off," he growled, "what do you think she is, a circus?"

Guinea shrugged her shoulders and smilingly dismissed the soldier. "Jealous," she whispered loudly. "Carries a tommy-gun under his towel. You'd better hop it."

"Bloody hide they've got," Kim muttered bitterly. "A bloke'd need to carry something with all these pirates around. If this sort of thing goes on I'll be giving someone a poke in the eye before the day's finished. Your Yank friends seem to have infected the talent with their bad habits."

"You want to keep up with the times."

"Don't tell me you like it."

"Why not? A girl might as well be laid away on ice if nobody pays any attention to her."

"I don't know what's come over the place," he said sourly, as they walked across the beach together. "I hardly recognise it since I came back."

"You and the Vice Squad," she mocked, "when does the big clean-up begin?"

The rising wind flicked the sand against their bare limbs and Kim looked across at the wind-flattened surf. "Even the surf's gone off," he complained, kicking at the sodden bodies of the bogong moths that marked the high-tide line. "Beach lousy with moths, too."

"You're not blaming that on the Yanks, are you? There've been swarms of bogongs as long as I can remember. Come on in and get wet, sourpuss, you need your liver tickling up." She raced ahead of him.

He caught her up and together they splashed through the shallows and dived into the deepening water in the channel. They came up gasping at the chill and swam out towards the sandbank, pacing each other in a steady crawl.

"Crikey, it's freezing." Kim shivered in the wind that struck cold against his wet flesh.

"Garn, you're a sis," Guinea taunted and plunged into the deeper water beyond the sandbank where usually the big combers curled. Today, under the westerly, they only rose and subsided in an endless swell.

Guinea grew tired first and puffed and splashed her way back to the sandbank. She could see Kim swimming through the green water out to where the buoys marked the turning point for the surf race. Reckless surfers floated on surf skis and boards, a sunbronzed frieze rising and falling with each wave, waiting hopefully for a breaker they could ride to the shore. He drew into line with them, his dark head bobbing against the shimmering water. Beyond, the ocean curled listlessly against the cliffs of Ben Buckler, and far out on the horizon two grey corvettes mustered a gathering convoy for its long voyage north.

Guinea watched the surfers turn to catch a curling wave, the surfboard riders paddling frantically for position. The breaker lifted them on to its crest and she saw Kim flailing his way in the foam, suspended a moment between the glass-green sea and the pale sky. The wave brought him almost to her feet on the sandbank.

"Why didn't you come out with me?"

"Not me. I've given up shark-baiting. Mug's game."

"Gone soft, eh? Too much high living."

"Sez you. If I had your easy open-air life, I'd beat you hollow."

He dived and swam underwater and she could see his swirling shadow dart towards her. She braced herself to duck him, but his arms closed round her knees and they went down together in a tangle of arms and legs. When she came up spluttering he was beside her, mocking and exultant.

"You cow," she gasped, coughing up water. "Why don't you grow up?"

He turned on his back and his feet beat the water, sending it splashing into her face. She made a quick lunge and pushed his head under water and held him there. He came up spluttering and calling for mercy. "Quits," he pleaded. "My God, you're strong. It's like playing tip with an elephant."

"And don't you forget it."

They splashed idly on the sandbank while they watched a lifesaver swim out to the buoys, turn and raise his arm to the rescue team waiting on the beach for his signal.

"It's a filthy surf," Kim said, as the beltman swam out to his "patient" with long steady strokes. "Waste of time practising, I'd say."

"Oh, sure. You're one of the champs who doesn't take

the belt out until the waves are thirty foot high."

"Oh, come off it! Let's get back and have a sunbake while there's still room on the sand to stretch out."

They waded through the shallows, watching the rescue team paying out the line to the beltman with arms raised stiffly above their heads.

By now the holiday crowd had swarmed over the beach and striped umbrellas and wigwam shelters made a brilliant colour pattern against the bleached sand. They found their towels where they had parked them close beside the reel, and watched the precise routine of the lifesavers. The wheelman wound the line slowly back onto the wheel; the linesmen, bodies bowed to the weight of the beltman and his "patient", drew in the line hand over hand.

"Nice job," Kim commented, when at last they laid the "patient" on the sand and began the long resuscitation drill. "Good to think these kids are keeping it up. I'll be back with my old team the day I'm out of the RAAF."

"That'll be the day for the girls," Guinea murmured, pillowing her head on her arms and stretching lazily on the hot sand. "You want to advertise it."

Kim stretched out beside her. "I'll rescue you if you can wait that long."

"Thanks, but I'll take a man-eating shark for preference if you don't mind. I'd feel safer."

Kim laid his chin on her arm. "You're not very encouraging."

She sat up, pushing his head away. "Listen. You don't want to sleep, and you won't let me sleep. OK, we get going. I was going to take half an hour off and then look for Monnie, but we look for her now. And what's more, we'll need all that magnetic personality of yours if we're going to find anyone in this crowd."

Kim leaped to his feet. "Just you watch!" He put his two fingers between his teeth and emitted a long-drawn piercing wail that turned every head within a hundred yards. "What did I tell you?"

"Garn. They just think you're a wolf on the loose. And

anyway it hasn't brought Monnie."

"Then we'll comb the beach," Kim announced. "Better bring your towel. You've got a route march ahead."

Between sunbaking and surfing and sunbaking again they searched haphazardly, growing less and less enthusiastic as the morning wore on. When Guinea, remembering Byron's note, insisted that she simply had to get back, Kim pointed out that they had not covered half the beach yet, and nobody but mad dogs, lifesavers and themselves started surfing till the afternoon on a holiday anyway.

For lunch they carried sandwiches and fruit and lukewarm cordial to the shelter of the sea wall. A strong wind drove the sand in stinging showers across the beach, the sun was a brazen ball in a dusty sky, and the reddish dust haze hung low over the water, but the crowd still poured down the Esplanade looking for space to picnic.

By four o'clock they were burnt with wind and sun, their eyelids were stiff with salt and their eyes reddened with flying sand. They had trudged stubbornly from one end of the long beach to the other without finding any trace of Monnie or Shirley, and at last they turned up the steps at the north end. Guinea took a last look back at the thinning crowd on the beach.

"I wouldn't worry if I were you," Kim said comfortingly.

"Neither would I — if I were you. But after all, she is my sister." She paused, suddenly brightening. "Y'know, I wouldn't be a bit surprised if Monnie's rung the SP and left a message explaining just where she is. I think I'll hop in and ask."

"Fine," Kim agreed, "I'll hop in with you."

"Don't bother. I'll have to go home and make a quick change to be presentable at the SP."

"OK. Let's go."

Deb seethed with anger as she came down the service lane and went up the staff steps. A nice afternoon she'd had. The hide of Dallas. Not even an apology for that insulting suspicion.

In the service lift, Deb took off her hat and ran her fingers through her hair. All she'd got for her pains was a raging head, and the afternoon wasn't over yet...she still had to face Alice. Oh hell, why did people have to push their troubles onto her?

When she opened the door of the salon, a white-faced Alice met her. "Ssssh," she whispered, with a warning glance over her shoulder. "Elvira's in there."

A familiar cackle came from one of the cubicles.

"I've just finished setting her hair — it's frightful. Claire is doing her face up now." Alice's eyes searched Deb's face. "Any luck?"

Deb shook her head. "Come into the office."

"Doesn't she know anybody at all?" Alice asked anxiously, as she shut the door.

"Sorry. I'm afraid you'll have to ask Guinea."

Alice flopped into a chair. "I can't tell Guinea...I simply can't."

Deb looked at her unsympathetically. "If you can think of anyone else..."

Alice burst into tears.

"Well, the sooner we can get rid of Elvira, the sooner we can clear up. I'll go in and give Claire a hand," Deb said briskly.

As she went into the cubicle Elvira met Deb's eyes in the mirror. "'Ullo luvvie," she greeted her. "'Ad a nice run?"

"I've had a most trying afternoon, I've been out on business," Deb firmly dismissed the implication. "You've got a new hairstyle, I see."

"Yeah. Cut the style out of a movie mag. Gives me 'eight, don't yer think?"

"Very smart."

Claire gave Deb a questioning look. Deb shook her head in answer.

"I got a new 'at too, one of them 'aloes."

Claire shrugged behind Elvira's back. "Wait till I've finished giving her this new makeup. That'll pep hubby up."

"Oh, go on with yer. Mr Beauchamp likes me to look smart, but 'e don't need no peppin' up for 'is marital rights, I can tell yer. 'E's a one 'e is." She cackled happily.

Claire pencilled her sparse eyebrows and mascaraed the motheaten eyelashes.

"I could be getting on with your nails." Deb suggested.

"Now I call that real nice," Elvira cooed, extending a bony hand. "I believe you 'ad mornin' tea up with L. F. and 'is lady friend yesterday."

"Yes," Deb replied coolly. How the devil did the old harridan find these things out?

"They must 'ave 'ad you up to soothe 'em down. They'd just 'ad a 'ell of a time with D.D.T. after she saw Guin's pitcher in the paper." Elvira rolled her eyes.

Deb began to gouge out the dirt from under her bitten-down nails.

"Ouch! Ooo, you 'urt."

"Sorry. I was trying to get the black from under your nails before I put the varnish on. What colour would you like?"

"Somepin nice and bright. Mr Beauchamp loves my nails bright."

Deb selected a vivid scarlet. Elvira continued, "I seen Mr McFarland's brother goin' up to 'is suite as I was comin' along."

"Did you?" Deb hoped she sounded non-committal.

"Not the figure of a man Mr Angus is. 'E's got style. Proper gentleman too. Always gives yer a whackin' good tip, and besides that I make a couple of quid every week sellin' 'is empty Scotch bottles. Not that yer ever see a sign of liquor on 'im. Marvellous 'ow some men can carry it, ain't it?"

Claire interrupted. "Take a look at yourself in the mirror. How do you like that?"

Elvira grimaced at the thick makeup covering her tiny wrinkled face. "Cor lumme," she said, "Mr Beauchamp'll just lap that up. Don't me eyelashes look nice with that stuff on 'em?''

"Positively Hollywood. Now keep your mouth still and I'll put on your lips.''

"Gimme a cupid's bow, luvvie,'' Elvira pleaded, "Mr Beauchamp loves a cupid's bow. I used to have one nacheral till I got me false teeth.''

"OK,'' said Claire, "I'll paint it on you.'' She tilted her face and outlined a cupid's bow above the thin, upper lip. Deb shuddered. She doubted whether Claire's policy of appeasing Elvira was worth it. The old hag couldn't do you any more harm than she did already.

Elvira was gazing admiringly at her painted mouth. "Indelible, ain't it?'' she asked anxiously.

"Stand anything but a steam hose,'' Claire assured her.

Elvira screamed with laughter.

Deb could hear Alice moving about restlessly in the office. "What time are you meeting your husband?'' she asked Elvira.

"Aw, got plenty of time yet. I didn't 'urt meself on the work this afternoon — beat it before the Randwick crowd come back. Gawd, you ought to see some of the rolls them bookies 'ave got in their cases. And do they mind you seein' them lockin' it away? Not them. I 'eard one feller and his clerk countin' out a cool seven thou on Satdy. And the ways they think up to dodge the taxation! Gives you a 'eadache listenin' to them. And me with me wages tax took off me every week, makes me fair ropable it does. Not that they ain't generous with their tips, they are, and they don't make 'alf the work the women do. No, I won't be goin' up again this afternoon.''

"Well, we're going to skip it the moment we've finished, so you'll have to wait somewhere else, my pet,'' Claire said firmly, and added, "The Marie Antoinette's practically been kept open for your benefit this afternoon. Damn nonsense on a public holiday, we could have finished at half past twelve.''

"Me too. The only bell that's rung since lunchtime was D.D.T. to press her blouse and the honourable gent from Canberra to see if I could get 'im any black market petrol tickets. Just as well too, I was wore out after yesterday. I always says to Mr Beauchamp when 'e's done his settlin' on Sunday, 'Mr B., you earn your money.', I says, 'dashin' from one phone to the other the 'ole bloomin' Satdy afternoon.' Them that says SP bookies gits easy money don't know what they're talkin' about.''

''By the way,'' Claire cut in, ''you haven't given me that new phone number yet and several people have complained to me that the old one's always engaged.''

''I'll write 'em both down for yer,'' Elvira said obligingly, ''we only got the noo phone in on Thursday, 'ad to wait three months for it.''

''I don't know why you don't put one of them in the phone book,'' Claire said, ''it'd save people a lot of trouble.''

''Oh Gawd, no, we'd never 'ave any peace. I says to Mr Beauchamp, 'You and yer two silent numbers Mr B.,' I says, 'you'd think you was the CIB.' And don't 'e think 'imself someone! 'Well,' he said to me, 'there's a lot of people at the SP wouldn't spit on the likes of you and me, Elvie luv, but 'ave they got two silent numbers? Can they even get a phone on? Not them.'''

''Do well Saturday?'' Claire enquired.

''Real good. Only one favourite come in the 'ole day and that at odds on. And my, didn't we rake in a pile on Stormcloud; come in fifteen to one and only Blue's bet to pay out on it. Stable musta kep' it dead secret.''

''Well, not exactly,'' Claire's voice was a little patronising, ''my boyfriend had a fiver on her. Just think of it, seventy-five lovely smackers!''

''Waddyerknow! 'Ow did 'e get the good oil?''

''My dear, he knows the owner well. He often runs Nigel home from baccarat. He's got a filthy big car.''

''Mr B. pointed 'im out to me once. Sport 'e called 'im. Bit of a lair, ain't 'e, with a chassy kind a walk?''

''Yes. That'd be him. Nice enough fellow, but no breeding at all.''

''Well fancy that. I'd 'ave thought from the look of 'im, 'e was real masculine.''

Claire laughed. ''Well, that wasn't quite what I meant.

He's come up the hard way, I'd say. Nigel's been showing him the ropes. His taste in clothes was absolutely appalling until Nigel took him in hand. He's frightfully grateful for any little social tips. And he's simply crackers about Stormcloud. No wonder, she's absolutely sweet; the prettiest grey. And you should have seen her come in on Saturday. She made a marvellous finish."

"Me see 'er come in! Gawd, I got no time to go to the races, our phone's that busy on race days it takes the two of us goin' 'ammer and tongs takin' the bets the 'ole afternoon. What the perlice 'ave got against startin' price bookies I don't know, we work as 'ard as anyone. 'Ow would all of them as don't go to the races get a bet on if it weren't for us? A public convenience, that's wot we are, as I always says to Mr Beauchamp."

"That's right," Claire agreed. She stood back. "I don't think I could improve on that."

"Mind the nail varnish," Deb cried warningly. "Here, I'll put your hat on." She pressed the wide lacy straw halo onto the black curls. Elvira stood up to get her full reflection.

"Come out to the big mirror," Claire suggested.

Elvira minced out to the boudoir on her high-heeled ankle-strap sandals and postured before the long mirror, her arms held out, fingers extended.

The outer door opened and Guinea came in. "Gawd," she ex-claimed, as she saw the grotesque reflection. "If it's not me old friend Virus getting up steam for the marital rights."

Elvira jerked round and made a sweeping curtsey. "Miss Margaret Malon, I perzoom."

Guinea bowed low in reply. "At your service, madame."

"Cor lumme. Did you rock the place on Satdy night, Guin! When D.D.T. saw that pitcher of you yesterday, she threw a sixer. 'Ad to get 'er mother in and Ole Mole bust 'alf a dozen blood vessels."

"Oh, hullo, Guin," Claire came in and greeted her. "And might I ask Miss Malone if this is your private telephone? I've done nothing but answer the phone for you the whole day, and if you can wait till I've finished Elvira, I'll give you all the messages."

"Don't mind me, luvvie," Elvira said hopefully.

"Oh, I'm not in such a hurry as all that. Did Monnie ring, though? That's what I really dropped in for."

"No, she didn't, but that four-star general of yours, Byron G. Maddocks, has spent the day on the phone, and he sent you some flowers as well. There's the box, just behind you."

Guinea reached for the small florist's box, opened it and took a glance at the spray of golden orchids inside, then put it down again without bothering to read the card.

Claire watched her out of the corner of her eye. "Well, the General's flowers don't seem to cause much of a flutter. But what about Who's Who? My dear, I'm simply dying to hear about the Saturday night do."

Guinea closed her eyes ecstatically. "Girls, it was a wow. You'd have fainted if you'd seen me. Me doing the sweet young innocent stuff — and how! And all those guys with more ribbons on them than horses in the Six-Hour procession, hanging round with their tongues out and their teeth bared. Do they like 'em virgin? Not that they leave 'em long that way if they get half a chance."

"If you 'eard what D.D.T. 'ad to say about yer..." Elvira gave her a lascivious wink.

"I can guess, but go ahead."

Elvira launched happily into obscene mimicry. "Cor lumme, did she lay 'er tongue round you...and the langwidge...'Mr B.,' I said, when I told 'im, 'if you'd ever soiled your tongue with langwidge like that in front of me, I'd 'ave walked out on yer, marriage lines or no marriage lines.' Do you know what she called yer?" She bent over and whispered in Guinea's ear. Guinea flung herself back on the brocade lounge and hooted with laughter.

Deb frowned. The whole scene made her uncomfortable; it was so indescribably vulgar. She beckoned surreptitiously to Claire, who followed her into the office and shut the door.

Alice raised a woebegone face.

Claire turned to Deb. "How did you get on with Dr

MacIntyre?"

"Just as I told Alice from the start. No help there," Deb said flatly.

Claire shrugged. "Great help to their suffering sisters, these women doctors."

Deb wished Dallas could have heard her.

Guinea's laughter came to them loud and ringing, breaking the tension.

"Well there's still Guinea you can ask, and frankly she's the most likely person to know."

Alice sighed despairingly.

"Well, it's up to you. If you want to help Mary, now's your chance. It's lucky for you Guinea dropped in."

Alice took a deep breath, blew her nose again and almost whispered, "If you think there's no other way..."

"Frankly I don't, if time's important. Of course there are lots of doctors who'd do a curette for a married woman without asking too many questions, that's quite legal." Claire reached for the phone book. "Let's go through the Pink Pages, some of the names might ring a bell."

Back in the boudoir Guinea had collapsed in a gale of laughter. "Gawd, Virus, you're a wonder."

Elvira took a bow. "That's D.D.T.'s plan anyway. She's gonna marry Tickety-Boo come 'ell or 'igh water."

"She's welcome to him. His whiskers tickled me the whole time I was dancing with him. God only knows why the Navy wants to disfigure themselves with facial jungles like that. The only naval bloke I ever had nearly took the skin off me every time I got into a clinch. It was like kissing an Airedale."

"Yeah," said Elvira, "makes 'em look so effeminate too."

Guinea hooted again.

"D.D.T.'s 'avin' a party Satdy night to announce it...son of a lord, 'e is."

"He'll have a hard job to make a lady of D.D.T."

"I'll say. Throwin' a real big party for them *Hincorruptible* officers. Arst me to come out and 'elp, Mrs D.D.T. did. But I'm not 'avin' any, I been there before. Cost three hundred quid one party did larst year — and they give me ten bob for the night.''

"You've got no social ambitions, Virus. They won't ask you to the wedding now.''

"I know them parties, cocktails and booffey — standin' room only at the beginnin' and lyin' two deep at the end. Oh well,'' she picked up her handbag and gloves, "now I must be getting along or Mr B.'ll be that het up waitin' for me it'll ruin 'is night. How do I look, Guin?'' Elvira turned with a flounce of her skinny hips.

"Out of this world, Virus. But you'd better take a taxi home or the wolves'll rape you before you've gone a block.''

"I can 'andle them,'' Elvira smirked complacently.

"Where did you get your Yank-snatchers?''

Elvira held out a skinny foot displaying black patent ankle-strap high heel sandals. "Mr Beauchamp brought 'em 'ome for me. Got 'em in a payoff for some liquor. Ain't they smart?''

"Terrific.''

"Oh well luvvie, I'm afraid I'll really 'ave to be leavin' yer.'' She swung double red fox furs over her shoulders, tested a nail to see if the lacquer was dry and pulled on elbow-length cyclamen gloves. "You ain't got one of them orchids you wore on Satdy night to go with me gloves, 'ave you dear?''

"Get along with you,'' Guinea laughed, smacking her bony bottom. "Add an orchid to that get-up and none of us girls'll have a bloke left.''

"Like the ennsembly?'' Elvira enquired, as Claire came in.

"You look ravishing,'' she said.

Elvira smirked, "I'm not that kind of a girl.'' She minced to the door. "Thanks a lot, girls. I won't fergit yer.''

The door swung shut behind her.

"Too bloody right, you won't,'' Guinea remarked. "An elephant's memory's got nothing on Virus's, specially when it comes to the dirt.''

Claire came straight to the point. "Guin, Alice wants to see you before you go. She's in a spot. Her sister Mary's pregnant.''

Guinea's face lighted with unholy glee. "A Parker prego? Did I hear right?"

"You heard."

"Holy mackerel! I didn't think they had it in them."

"Cut the cackle. You can imagine how much use Alice is to her."

Guinea's face sobered. "The poor kid. Fancy having to rely on that drip."

"We're all at our wit's end about getting hold of somebody. Do you know anyone?"

"Yes."

"Well, let's go into the office and tell Alice."

"I've asked Guinea," Claire explained to a stricken Alice. "She says she knows someone."

"That's right. He's quite a decent bloke, and the kid'll be as safe as the bank with him. What the devil is his name again? You remember, Claire — he used to wear a monocle."

"Oh, I know him, but I thought he was in Brisbane."

"So he was while the Yanks were there. Now's he's back to help out with the British, I expect. Here, sling me over the phone book." Guinea dialled a number. The bell pealed continously; eventually an angry voice answered.

"Mrs Albert told me to ring," Guinea explained. "Is the doctor home?"

"No, he's not. He'll be away for a week." The phone clicked in her ear.

"Away for a week," Guinea explained.

Alice lifted swollen eyes. "But Mary can't wait for a week."

Guinea sighed. "Bad luck. I'm afraid I don't know anyone else at the moment."

"I'm so frightened that something'll happen to Mary."

"There's nothing to be frightened about, if it's done properly," Claire comforted her.

"But look at that girl in Brisbane," Alice's voice quavered. "And all that awful publicity." Tears splashed down on her folded hands.

"That was quite different. These doctor fellows take every

precaution — for their own sake as well as yours. You're as safe as if you were in hospital. The trouble about that Brisbane girl was that she got into the hands of one of those dirty old women.''

"They're not all like that," Guinea said defensively. "There was a woman where I lived and she was a real trimmer. Used to do it for five quid, and if you were really down on your uppers, she'd do it for nothing."

"What about her?" Alice said hopefully.

"She's in quod. Some girl she'd done got windy and spilled the beans. I reckon that's the lousiest thing anyone can do."

Alice relapsed into tears.

"I'm afraid I'll simply have to hop it," Guinea said apologetically. "Kim's waiting for me down below. Cheer up, kid. Between us we'll think up something." She pinned Byron's orchid to her suit. "So long."

There was a tapping on the outer door. Guinea came back: "It's Mrs Cavendish."

"Tell her to come right in," Claire called. "Your luck's certainly in, Alice, she's sure to know someone."

"Am I intruding?" Mrs Cavendish put a stylish head round the door.

"No, come in, Cynthia. My word, you look stunning in that rigout."

"I ought to, my dear. If you knew what it cost! I hadn't a coupon to my name and I had to get it black market. I'll simply never get over it."

"You should worry!"

Cynthia preened herself. "My dear, I feel a hag. You simply must touch up my hair. I've got a new man."

"What's he like?"

"Oh, my dears, he's a darling type."

The phone shrilled. "Half a minute," Claire lifted the receiver. "It's for you, Deb," she called through to the massage room.

Deb came out and spoke briefly. She hung up and turned to Claire. "I'm sorry," she said, "Mrs Molesworth wants me. Can you manage without me? I don't think I'll be back."

"We'll have to, I suppose, if Old Mole wants you. She's got a hide calling you upstairs when she's asked us to stay back specially in case of a last-minute rush after the races."

Deb looked uncomfortable and went out.

"That's old McFarland's girl friend, isn't it?" Cynthia inquired.

Claire nodded. "Did you want to see me particularly?"

"Just to tell you that Coddy's moved the school again tonight. He asked me to let you know. We've got the duckiest little flat at Point Piper."

"Oh darling, you know I'd love to go, but Nigel specially wants to have a quiet evening at home."

"The way you always do what he wants!" Cynthia's voice was petulant. "You make me sick. Give him a ring."

"All right," Claire sat down at the desk. "Listen," she said while she dialled, "go along to the office, Cynthia, will you, like an angel? Alice Parker's there, and she wants to talk to you."

Cynthia drifted into the office. "Hello," she said, "Claire told me you wanted to ask me something."

Alice dropped her eyes. "I'd rather wait till she came in."

"Oh, she won't be a minute, she's just ringing that boyfriend of hers. My dear, the way she waits on him simply slays me!"

"I suppose she's very fond of him."

Cynthia shrugged her shoulders lazily. "And he's very fond of himself." She peeped through the glass partition to see that Claire was still at the phone. "Have you ever met him?"

"No. I've only seen his photos in the ads. There's one of him in tonight." She picked up a paper from the desk and glanced through it.

"Let me have a look." Cynthia took the paper from her. "Don't tell me Nigel's modelling safari jackets! What a scream! The only place he'll ever wear one is hunting lizards in the lounges."

"He looks very refined," Alice said uncomfortably.

"Refined! My sweet innocent, you don't want to be taken

in by that. His type's two-a-penny round our way."

Claire appeared in the doorway. "Sorry, I can't raise Nigel; he can't be home yet."

"Oh, too bad, darling. We've just been admiring this photo of him."

"He does look well in that sort of thing." Claire glanced fondly at the advertisement.

"Super," Cynthia agreed. "Well, just in case you can persuade him to change his mind, here's our new phone number." She scribbled it on a scrap of paper and handed it to Claire. "Just ring up if you want the car sent along."

"Thanks, we will." Claire pocketed the number. "Did you ask her, Alice?"

Alice shook her head. "I was waiting for you."

Claire turned to Cynthia. "Her sister's got herself in trouble."

"Oh, has she?" Cynthia ran her eye up and down Alice's slender figure curiously. "Hm — too bad."

"Do you know anyone?"

"Why yes, of course. 'The Doc', Claire. You must have met him at the game. Madly distinguished-looking."

"Oh him, of course. But I thought he'd given it up altogether."

"He did for a while, but he lost so much at baccarat he's started again." She tittered. "Lucky for us girls."

"He's supposed to be very good, isn't he?"

"Super, my dear, service-de-luxe. But he's awfully pricey."

"What does he charge?" Alice asked weakly.

"Forty pounds. But he's wonderful, he does all the best people."

"Forty pounds?" Alice's jaw dropped, "but we haven't got that much."

"Well, darling, you'll just have to find it. He's not in the game for love, you know."

"Could I go and see him?"

"Not tonight," Cynthia said hastily. "I happen to know he's going to a party tonight. But I'll tell you what I'll do.

361

I'll get all the details and ring you first thing in the morning."

"My sister's only got a week."

"Don't worry about that. It's easier than getting a dentist's appointment when you're in the know. If I don't see Claire tonight I'll ring you the minute I get up tomorrow."

"Oh thank you. I am grateful. It's so awful."

"Don't be such a silly little girl. It's absolutely nothing. I could show you hundreds of women...out to a party the next night. Now, I really must get along. Buck up, dear, time enough to cry when your turn comes." She squeezed Alice's hand, and went out chatting brightly.

Kim lounged against the wall of the lift while he travelled up and down with Blue, waiting for Guinea. "Christ!" he said, "could I do with a beer! I've got a thirst on me as long as me arm."

Blue was sympathetic. "Not a hope in this joint, not unless you're one of Uncle Sam's boys, a British admiral or a blacketeer — in a big way, you understand."

"And that's what you fight for," Kim said morosely.

"Looks like it," said Blue. "My missus works in the public bar downstairs and I had it from her that as soon as the Yanks hit this country, the management told the staff not to waste time on us Aussies. Not enough dough, we haven't got, for their liking."

"What the government ought to do is take over the whole beer racket and run it properly."

Blue looked up at the ceiling. Kim followed his gaze with an enquiring look.

"Whew!" Blue let out all his breath. "I expected the roof to fall in on us. That's high treason in here, mate."

"High treason or not, from what I can see they'll have to do it. A bloke's stuck up in the jungle for eighteen months and you come back and you can't get a beer in your own country unless a Yank shouts you. Nationalise the breweries tomorrow, I would if I had my way."

"They'll never do it," Blue said morosely. "I saw in the paper the other day it'd cost the country a hundred million to buy the breweries and their pubs out."

"A hundred million!" Kim stared at him incredulously.

"That's right. A hundred million of the best."

"Christ almighty! Sounds like the figures in a Yank air communique."

"That's right," Blue agreed, "only difference is that it's true."

"Bloody Yanks," Kim muttered bitterly. "I'll be glad to see the last of them."

"Aw, you can't blame them. Pretty decent coves one way and another. Even their brass hats aren't as high and mighty as our blokes. Got a couple of millionaires from the Little Ships staying here — the Morgan twins — and you couldn't meet a couple of nicer kids."

"Yeah?"

"Too right. Wild as they're made, though. Nearly gave the manager and his girlfriend heart failure yesterday. The twins threw a farewell party in their suite and lit a campfire to have a barbecue. The place was full of smoke and everybody rushing round with fire extinguishers, half a dozen fire engines clanging outside, and when they broke in the door, 'ere was one of the twins putting out the conflagration with a soda siphon. Suite looked as if a couple of liberatin' armies'd been through it. Broke up the chairs and the table for the fire, they did, liquor everywhere. And 'ere's old L. F. nearly havin' apoplexy between 'orror at the way the place looked and rememberin' who the Morgans were! 'What's the damage?' the young pup says, calm as you like. 'I'll write you a cheque.' L. F. gives a sickly sort of smile, bows himself out and goes off to explain to the fire brigade."

"Yeah," said Kim bitterly. "I know the sort. Kinda thing you get away with if you're a millionaire or a university student, and get stuck into Long Bay for as a dead-end kid if you're not."

"Same in the last war," Blue said. "We was the Army of occupation then, and you ought've seen some of the things we got up to in England and France. Good old Paree." He sighed reminiscently.

"You a retread?" Kim inquired.

"Yeah. Though if you ask me privately what I am, I'd say just a plain, bloody mug. Sniped at by Jerries in France through one war and chased out of Greece by them in this." He cast a glance at the ribbon on Kim's tunic. "See you've been in the Middle East yourself."

"That's right. Our squadron was brought out from England."

"How'd you find England?"

"As I was there in 'forty and 'forty-one, I spent most of my time dropping bombs on other people or dodging the ones being dropped on me. But what I saw of the people looked good to me."

"What were you flying in?"

"Bombers. Fairy Battles. Bloody deathtraps they were, too."

"We had a lot of crook stuff, if you ask me."

"I'll say we did. Crikey, I still get goose pimples on me goose pimples when I think about flyin' over the North Sea in that open cockpit with nothing between me and the drink but a monkey strap attached to my harness."

"I dunno how you blokes take it up there."

"Well, I never know how you blokes take it down below, so we're even. I'll never forget those ops. A cove my size was more or less standing up all the time. We had one bloody little gun on a swivel and when the coast of Norway came up all hell'd break loose and all you needed was the pilot to go into an extra fancy bit of weaving when he was doing a spot of evasive action, and the flaming gunner was shot out. Crikey, did I have the wind up."

"Whew!" Blue closed his eyes and shuddered. "You give me the creeps."

"Well, you coves didn't exactly have a party in Greece, from what I've heard."

Blue's face sobered. "No. Bloody massacre, that's what it was. Stuck us in there, they did, with no guns, no ammunition and no air cover. Christ! Were we a lot of prize mugs! When did you come out to the Middle East?"

"End of 'forty-one. They had us flying round in Wimpies till the Nips got going properly in the Pacific and we landed back here about the middle of 'forty-two."

"Well, nobody can say you haven't seen the world, mate."

"I've seen enough of it to last me for the rest of my life. Here's one cove they won't get back for World War Three. I've had it."

"O-o-oh, I dunno. Kinda gets in your blood. No feelin' in the world like bein' up against things with a lot of mates y'know y'can trust. When I read in this morning's paper we was going to Greece again, well, I'd have given something to be there with the old gang meself."

"You can have it for mine," Kim commented. "A lot of sentimentality amongst you retreads, I think. Fought your battles in Returned Soldiers' Leagues for twenty years and then rarin' to go when you smelt powder again."

Blue chuckled. "What sort of powder do you mean? Gunpowder or face powder?"

"Whichever way you like," Kim laughed.

"We had our good times too, I'll hand it to you."

"I'll say you did. When we reached the Middle East more than twenty years after you, the Aussie reputation was still so hot that fathers clamped their wives and daughters in the safe deposit the minute we were sighted."

Blue slapped his thigh and roared with laughter. "Tasty little bits they were too, though they didn't look as good to me in this shindy as they did in the last — too streamlined and modernised. But the first time! Boy, did we paint the town red. They were the goods."

"Not any better than the bunch of skirts parading in the Cockpit downstairs."

"You'd be wasting your time there. They're on the lay-by for Yanks."

"After their rolls," sneered Kim.

"That's what the Tommies used to say about us."

"Oh well, the Yanks'll be gone altogether soon and then we'll see. The girls'll come crawling back, but there won't be many Aussies'll want the Yank leftovers."

"Aw, I dunno, can't blame the girls. One thing, the Yanks know how to treat 'em. You boys'll have to put on your running boots to catch up to them, and from what I can see there'll be a hell of a lot of them going to the States anyway."

"Huh!" Kim mocked derisively, "there'll be a hell of a lot more staying here."

"You know, just quietly, I wouldn't be surprised to see Guin going off with one of them brass hats."

"From what I've seen, brass hats don't marry working girls."

"Ah, she's different, good sort, Guin." Blue took a breather at the top floor and switched off the call bells. He lit a cigarette Kim offered him, "Smart as paint too."

Kim pursed his lips. "Not too dusty," he said carelessly, puffing smoke rings towards the ceiling, "but have you seen 'em at Tel Aviv?" He clicked his tongue against his teeth.

"She's got that Colonel Maddocks by the wool, and he's not the only one," Blue went on. "You should see the wolves with their tongues hanging out when she comes out after work."

"Remarkable!"

"The belle of the ball the other night too. Wasn't one of them silvertails in the same street. She's got style, that kid — and brains."

"D'you reckon?"

"My colonial oath I do," Blue took his finger off the bell silencer and released an angry buzz. "Keep your hair on," he remarked to the air, as he carefully extinguished his cigarette and put the butt in a half empty tobacco tin.

"I suppose I've known her too long," Kim remarked as casually as he could, "to think she's anything out of the bag. Nice enough kid of course, but . . . boy, you should see 'em in Cairo."

"I have," said Blue, and laughed. "Paris for me, though. But if I was twenty years younger I'd trade 'em all in from the Equator to the North Pole for one Guinea Malone."

"Peg," corrected Kim. "I don't know how she got that fancy monicker."

"Pinup girl," Blue informed him, "and did they fall for it!"

"You don't say."

"Just as well you're not struck on her," Blue said as he slowed down at the ground floor, "you'd have to put in a hell of a lot of hard graft to get anywhere with her, I'm afraid."

Kim drew himself from the wall and straightened up. "I've met competition before. I should worry."

"Bit of a hit with the sheilas, eh?"

"Climbing trees to get away from it." He stepped towards the door. "I think I'll wait down here," he said, throwing Blue a dirty look.

"That's right," said Blue encouragingly, "keep your eye skinned for a nice bit in case one of Guin's field marshals butts in on you." The door slid open, Kim stepped out and shouldered his way through the bunch of people impatient to get in. "Let the bastard try," he said to himself.

Kim stood where he could watch the doors of the lift and relit his cigarette which had gone out. Damn her, she'd been up at the Marie Antoinette almost a quarter of an hour already. What the hell could be keeping her? He seethed with mounting impatience. If she stood him up. . . She was spoiled, that's what she was, not the girl she had been when he first knew her. Swelled head, that's what the damned Yanks did. He'd let her know where she got off, he'd wait another five minutes and not a second longer. He'd let her see that he wasn't the type to come crawling around with orchids. He'd be a doormat for no woman.

He brooded with sudden melancholy deflation as he watched the crowds in the foyer. He didn't mind the chaps in uniform, Yanks or otherwise, they'd earned their fun and so long as they didn't cut across his tracks they could have it for him. But he felt a slow sour anger at the civilians, well fed and perfectly tailored, streaming into the lounges. A bookmaker he recognised stood near him with his clerk waiting for the lift, and their conversation was larded with betting figures as big as the war debt. They were flying to Melbourne for the Cup next month. They'd fly to Melbourne for the Cup!

But let any serviceman's wife try to get across the border to her husband and there was hell to pay. Imagine Peg trying to join him somewhere — not that Peg'd be any good for a poor man's wife now.

A bloke was a mug to go to the war at all. Get tucked away in some nice safe, soft reserved job — nothing strenuous or dirty, of course. That was the idea. Not that you'd be much better, though, when the government grabbed half your money in taxes. Ride the rackets — that was the lurk. Nobody could keep a tab on you there. But do it in a big way, none of these small time blacketeers that got pinched for selling three bottles of beer. Up with the big shots, that was the place if you weren't lucky enough to have the dough rolling in in respectable war dividends. OK, he was a mug.

He was suddenly aware of his desolation. He wished to hell Peg would come, it was nearly half an hour. Jumping Jeepers, if she'd given him the brush off with one of those damn Yanks he'd slit her throat next time he saw her. He wished he was back with his mates again. He'd had Sydney and he'd had girls. On the nose, the whole damn place.

Guinea stepped out of the lift. His heart soared and he was suddenly himself again. "You've been a hell of a long time. I nearly went off with a bushfire blonde I pirated."

"Why didn't you?" Guinea adjusted the orchid pinned on her lapel. Kim's eyes glistened and his fingers itched to tear it off. She went on without looking up, "If you'd like to run along now, it's OK with me. The guy who sent this left a message to say he'd be waiting on me for dinner."

"A pity for the poor bloke to starve," he murmured savagely, steering her through the crowd. "Any news of Monnie?"

"No. Kim, I'm worried. It's not like her at all."

He squeezed her arm, "We'll find her, don't you worry, Peg. It'll all come out in the wash."

They went down the hotel steps. The westerly had dropped with the sun and the sky above Martin Place was lilac with the high dust haze.

"Are you going out with your brass hat?"

"What about your bushfire blonde?"

"I told her I was on duty."

"OK, so'm I."

They grinned at each other. "That's fine. Let's queue up for a bite of supper then we'll start the rounds. Where do girls go to get seduced nowadays?"

Guinea flashed him a glance. "You should know."

In the next block they joined the dinner queue at the top of the steps that led down to Cahill's. It moved slowly and there was much laughing and banter as men and girls, burnt from the long holiday in the sun, waited with good-humoured patience their turn to go in. That was one of the things she liked about Kim. Where other men did their block over being held up, he always took it as part of the fun.

There was a large florist's box on the table when Deb came into her room, and as she opened it, the perfume of lilac was released in a heady gust. There were masses of it, mauve and white and pink and deepest purple. She buried her face in the flowers; the dewy spray on the petals was cold. Lovely, lovely. It was wonderful to think that if she married Angus she wouldn't have to worry about anything any more. What Dallas said about the cards being stacked against women was true, but it was no use trying to beat the system; life was too short for that. It was all right for Dallas to be sentimental about Tom and Nolly; she'd never been caught in that sort of life.

Deb lifted out the heavy sheaf. She'd really have to buy some more vases; there was nowhere to put it except the basin. A pity, but after all she wasn't in the room during the day, only the rest of this holiday afternoon, and now she was going to have a gorgeous rest until it was time to get dressed.

She kicked her shoes off, lay down, closed her eyes, and immediately fell into a deep sleep.

The first thing she wakened to was the heady scent of lilac, the second a feeling of urgency. A glance at her bedside clock showed she had just half an hour to dress for this important family dinner. She swung her legs off the bed and sat up. She felt wonderful. Ready to tackle the whole McFarland clan. Half the women in Sydney would give their eyes to be marrying Angus.

By the time she sat down at her dressing table to put on her light makeup, she was excited and she felt daring. Her mind switched back to Dallas. Service lane indeed! If she had her here now, she'd tell her exactly what she thought of her interference...

She took down the plain black suit from her wardrobe. Claire had helped her to choose it and it hung perfectly. She scanned herself in the long mirror. The tailored lamé blouse lifted the suit into the dinner-dance class and her tiny toque of crimson feathers gave to the essentially severe ensemble a note of daring and excitement. She touched her ears and her chin and the hollow of her throat with the Chanel 5 and gave a last glance at herself in the mirror. She could dine with the king tonight and not turn a hair, Angus's brother would be chickenfeed.

When she stepped out of the lift, Angus came to meet her. His eyes were warmly admiring. "What an enchanting little bonnet," he said pressing her arm as he led her to the Refectory.

She smiled up at him, her lips parted. "I must thank you for that lovely lilac I found waiting in my room."

"I had it flown down specially for you from the garden at Burramaronga."

"Oh Angus, that was lovely of you."

"I'm afraid the little party I arranged for tonight hasn't come off. My sister-in-law has gone down with influenza and it seems that Helen has some engagement she could not put off, so there will be only Ian at dinner."

Deb detected a faint rasp under the smoothness of his voice. "I'm so sorry Mrs McFarland's ill," she said.

"It's probably just a cold. Women make too much of these little ailments." He spoke irritably, as though Olive had taken to her bed just to spite him.

At his tone a doubt crossed Deb's mind. The two women wouldn't be refusing to meet her, would they? But no, they weren't snobs. The girls at the Marie Antoinette could pick that type in a minute and both Claire and Val liked Mrs Ian McFarland and her daughter. "Shy kind of kid," Guinea had said, "but the real goods. You can tell the pure merinos in a minute after jumped-up bitches like D.D.T. and her crowd."

"But to make up, I've got a surprise for you," he smiled down at her, the irritability smoothed out of his voice.

"What a wizard you are!" A drive out to Palm Beach, she thought hopefully.

"I rather fancied I'd like to hear the Marjorie Lawrence programme tonight, so I rang down half an hour ago and I was lucky enough to get two good seats."

Deb's heart sank. Dallas! "That will be nice," she said, searching for an excuse, "but I'm not dressed."

"I don't mind, and you look perfect."

Ian McFarland watched them from the table in the corner as they came down the long room. He was a weatherbeaten edition of Angus, sparser, even taller, and with the reddened skin and startlingly white forehead of the land man who is accustomed to pull his broad-brimmed hat low over his eyes. His manner was non-committal when he rose and acknowledged Angus's introduction, and the expression in his deep-set grey eyes was as coldly appraising as if he had been judging a horse. Whatever else might be implied in his scrutiny, Deb thought, it certainly wasn't approval.

"My wife and daughter have asked me to apologise for them," he said shortly. "Wife's down with flu and Helen's got an appointment." He turned to Angus. "It's a confounded nuisance Olive getting ill. I must go back tomorrow night. Shearing starts next week."

"There's probably nothing much wrong with her: she'll be about in a day or two." Angus tried to dispose of Ian's grievance. It did not promise well for a pleasant dinner.

But it's genuine all right, Deb told herself. Ian McFarland isn't the sort of man to embroider a polite lie.

From the beginning Deb was aware of tension between the two men, Angus self-consciously anxious to impress his brother, Ian politely determined to perform his family duty and no more. It gave her a feeling of power to sit between them and feel the cross-currents of emotion. Ian ate his oysters in a silence she felt was as much a matter of policy as of habit; Angus kept up a flow of conversation to which she replied with a look or a laugh and only a rare word, but she returned the pressure of his knee against hers under the table and was aware of his gaze enfolding her with secret understanding.

If Mr Ian McFarland wanted silence, he could have silence while she and Angus were absorbed in the wordless converse of touch and glance; if he wanted non-committal conversation he could have that too. She was busy enough with eating, and hungry enough to appreciate the rich food the waiter placed before them. The meal was so perfect that one would never guess it was past scheduled dining time in the Refectory. Elvira said Angus tipped the cook two pounds a week and his special waiter a pound, so that the problems of rationing and the restrictions of austerity meals never affected him. He looked urbane and handsome beside Ian, and much younger, though she knew Angus was the eldest of the family. They sipped their sherry in silence.

"Did you go out to Randwick on Saturday?" Ian asked abruptly.

She shook her head, smiling.

"You're not interested in horses then?" The question was a challenge.

"In horses — yes. But not in racing."

"I can hardly imagine a horse-lover not being interested in racing."

"But most people don't really go to the races for the sake of the horses, do you think?"

"I do."

"But you are hardly typical, are you?"

"I'd call myself a typical countryman."

"I wouldn't know about that. I only know that the majority of people from the South Pacific go for the betting if they're men, and for the fashion parade if they're women."

"And neither of them interested you sufficiently to take you out to the spring meeting?"

Deb looked up and caught his eyes on her across the table. To hell with your impertinence, she said to herself, and aloud, with a smile of calculated charm, "I always spend Saturday afternoon with my daughter."

Angus caught his breath sharply and turned it into a cough. So that's out, Angus thought. He'd given Ian no indication of how young Deb was, nor that she had a daughter. Well, he'd have to get used to the idea some time or other that there'd probably be an heir for Burramaronga. Everyone in the family had got into the habit of taking for granted that it would go to young Angus. He looked at Deb fondly. My God, he thought, she's got spirit. I've never seen Ian behave so badly and it hasn't even put her out of her stride.

Deb returned his glance. It wasn't going to be all plain

sailing with the family. A bachelor brother was one thing, kept the money and the property in the family, whatever his affairs might be. But an elder brother marrying, and marrying a woman with a child, and still young enough to have more children. . . . In a flash, the root of Ian's hostility was clear to her. So that was it. These people! Enough money to last them till Doomsday and terrified that someone else might get a bit.

"You didn't miss much not going to Randwick," Angus broke in. "There was a vile wind and the place was smothered in dust. It's absolutely ruined since the military took it over. There was only one bright spot in the day and that was that I backed Stormcloud. She came home at fifteen to one. Rank outsider."

"How clever of you."

His eyes lingered on her. "Well, even though she is one of the prettiest little mares I've seen for a long time, I really can't claim the credit for picking her. I happened to run into her owner last week and he gave me the tip. Ian was too cautious so I had it all to myself."

Obviously the brothers didn't hit it off too well, Deb thought. She watched Ian's freckled, red hands, hard-working hands like her father's, and thought that their different ways of life were probably at the root of the trouble.

Angus went on eating, apparently unperturbed, while Ian started angrily on the petrol shortage. "So far as I can see, the only people who go without petrol are the people in the country. I don't see any shortage in the city," he said.

Angus grimaced. "You're right up to a point, but we pay through the nose for it. I work it out that it costs me ten shillings a gallon to get enough to be of any use. My ration is four gallons a month and with a heavy car that's useless."

A picture of Tom slid across Deb's mind, his face heavy with anxiety as he patched the tyres on the utility truck. He got four gallons a month, too. And out of that he'd built up a reserve to take Nolly to hospital. Irritation at Angus's complacency broke through her guard and she said impetuously, "As a woman, I naturally feel there's more need for petrol

374

in essential services like maternity ambulances.''

Angus lifted an eyebrow in surprise.

"My sister is expecting a baby," she went on, "and my brother-in-law has to keep enough petrol out of four gallons a month to get her to hospital because there's no ambulance in their district."

Angus smiled at her and said, "I think perhaps I could let him have a few coupons."

Deb gave him a smile warm with promise. What a fool you were to let people talk you down, she thought. In future, she'd say just what she felt. The way she felt now she wouldn't care two hoots if she did run bang into Dallas and her English colonel at the concert.

"And I could let you have a few coupons too, Ian, if you're stuck," Angus was saying.

"Petrol's no good to me without some new tyres."

"Do you know what it cost me to put new tyres on my car?"

"I don't see what you want a car for at all in the city."

"We're not discussing that. But it may interest you to know I paid fifty pounds for a pair of tyres, ordinarily worth seven each. And when I had to get a new universal joint that should have cost a pound, I had to pay eight for it."

"Why don't you take it to the Prices Commissioner?"

Angus laughed out loud. "My dear Ian," he said, "you don't think these little transactions are the kind one wants to draw the Prices Commissioner's attention to."

Ian looked at him. "You mean you got them on the black market?"

"That's exactly what I do mean. And if you really want petrol and new tyres, I can get you fixed up too."

"I wouldn't touch it with a forty-foot pole." Ian's lips clamped together uncompromisingly.

"That's your own affair, of course, but the way things are, to live at all, the best of us are obliged to do things we don't consider particularly admirable."

"You want to come into the country for a while and see how the man on the land lives without the black market." Ian turned to Deb. "Do you know the country at all?"

"No unfortunately, though my brother-in-law, who's an engineer, has a farm he runs as a hobby."

"Hobby! Huh! If you came up to our place for a while and saw what shortage of labour and interfering governments are doing to the people who make their living off the land, you'd get a different picture. I'd like to know how places like this hotel keep a full staff when there's no manpower or woman power for primary production up our way. My wife and daughter have had to do all the cooking, in addition to everything else, for the last six months. If they made some of these refugees come onto the land and do a bit of honest work instead of letting them batten on the cities, there'd be some sense in it."

"I certainly agree with you there," Angus said. "It's deplorable to see these Jews buying up property all round the best suburbs. It's the same everywhere — when they come to a country you never find them doing any of the hard work."

"I dunno about that. Young Ian wrote back that he was very much impressed by their land settlement in Palestine. And from what I've seen of racketeering this last week in the city, the Jews can't teach our own people anything."

Angus put down his coffee cup and looked at his watch. "I'm very much afraid that if we don't leave now we'll miss the beginning of the concert."

"Then you'd better be off," Ian said. "I'm meeting George Dalrymple at the club any time after eight, so don't worry about me. I'll just finish my coffee and walk round."

Deb picked up her bag and gloves. Ian rose. "Goodnight," he said, bowing to her with the same cold formality with which he had greeted her. "I hope you enjoy the concert."

Deb smiled. "I'm sure I shall, goodnight."

The oppressive heat still lingered and the air was stifling with the powdery dust brought down by a two-day westerly from the drought-parched plains. The full moon swung so low and close in the heavy air that it seemed tethered to the black tracery of the trees beside the old mint. Val looked up at the gilded hands of the clock on the old barracks. Half past seven...No use calling for Bessie yet, she wouldn't be off duty till nine. Between the rattle of the trams, faint gusts of music came to her from the band playing in Hyde Park. She and Ven had listened to the band on his last evening. "Oh, darling," she whispered, "'come back and wake my winter heart'...Come back, come back," and he was with her again.

She made her way across the broad intersection above St James's Church where five roads meet and the holiday traffic shuttled swiftly to and from the city. Three Indonesians loitered by disconsolately, their voices a low, liquid gabble. Two young English sailors watched her with heartsick eyes. So pitifully young, she thought. All these people so lonely, so far from home. The city is full of them, adrift on the tide of war, talking of home in alien tongues...servicemen and women, refugees, evacuees who have lost all the dear, familiar things — all those to whom this city is a refuge without sanctuary.

"I am lucky," she told herself, "for here, at least, I am at home. This is *your* city, Val Blaski, every point of light, whichever way you look, means something to you. Down there where the lights end and there is a pool of darkness, your eye knows even in the dark that the waters of the Harbour are moving as the tide runs out to sea. If you were to come back from Ven's northern mountains or the South Pole, these city towers against the sky would knock on your heart. This is *your* country ...even the hot smell of the western dust, borne by winds across the earth your great-grandparents ploughed to make a home out of a wilderness, is yours. You are at home."

A young GI and his girl sauntered hand in hand up the steps to the park and stood a moment by a blossoming peach tree, their lips joined in a long kiss. It was as though a hand

squeezed her heart and she stumbled past them along the concrete path between the lawns, her face so lost and withdrawn
that the solitary serviceman who stepped out to accost her
hesitated and drew back.

In front of her an avenue of frosted light globes stretched through the park, leading her eye to the towering bulk of
the War Memorial, now silver-grey under the moon. "It's not
shrines to the dead we should build," Ven had said once when
they stood together watching its reflection in the Pool of
Memory. "The dead are safe, they've gone out with their illusions still upon them and we can't hurt them any more. It's
shrines to the living we should be building, to remind them of
what they fought for, so they can't be fobbed off when they
don't get it, and to remind the others back home that a block
of marble and a wreath on Remembrance Day won't pay their
debt."

She walked through the lighted park, where each shining
globe was a magnet for the blundering bogong moths that the
hot wind had blown in a cloud over the city. Dance music and
laughter floated out from the Anzac Buffet and she stood a
while watching the dancers as they moved across the lighted
windows.

Surely...no, it couldn't be. But that girl looked like
someone she knew. She racked her brains, but the girl had passed the window. Val moved forward a few steps and waited
for her to come into view again. Yes, there she was, and as
she passed her partner swung her round so that Val saw her
full face.

The girl was extraordinarily like Helen McFarland...but
she must be mistaken. The McFarland girl was so shy and quiet,
she could not imagine her looking like that, gay and...Val
searched for the right word. It was not "abandoned" in the
free-and-easy sense; but as though she had left her old self
behind. There was a shining look about her as though there
was nothing else in the world but this moment of happiness.

When the couple came round for the third time, Val knew
it was Helen. They were not so near the window, but had moved into the floor a little and were dancing slower and talking.

Val caught a glimpse of the man's face, rapt and happy. "It's Helen McFarland, and she's in love," Val said softly under her breath. "And he's in love too...like Ven and me."

She turned away from the lighted window and walked slowly back into the shadows. Night and the heavy trees softened the sound of the band to a windy sigh and touched familiar melodies with unbearable poignancy.

I've seen Ven look at me like that when we've danced together...and perhaps I looked like her, because that was how I felt — as though nothing else in the world mattered but Ven and our love. But it was Ven who taught me that love isn't enough for happiness; you have to understand other people too. Here, in the park, where Ven and I walked so often as other lovers are walking tonight, here where every path, every shadowy retreat, the garden seats, the trampled lawns, are like old and known things to me, here he taught me to understand.

Her lips moved. "Darling, I understand it all now, you made me see it. It isn't ugly any more. This endless procession walking aimlessly up and down, these girls and men, their arms around each other's waists, these couples sprawling on the grass, embracing in the shadows, lost in a world of their own."

"Oh you poor lovers!" she cried soundlessly. "Ven knew. The old and the wise, all those whose lives and houses are safe and solid round them and whose future stretches like a broad high road out of their past, they may say you're tawdry and vulgar because you lie unmoving cheek to cheek, lost to the old shame. It's easy for them to condemn you meeting casually, loving briefly; laughter and lust a shield against the black shadow that hangs over us all. He made poetry of you, sailor clasping your girl in the shadow of a tree, abandoned and lost. For you there is no yesterday and no tomorrow; the only reality a girl's lips soft against yours, her breast round under your hand, body cleaving to body as though all the passion in the world must be gathered and used before the moon goes down."

"This is happening back at home too," Ven had said, "it's happening all over the world wherever people are uprooted.

And the old and the safe will never understand."

She stood a while under the big tree overhanging the foot-path near the underground station; above her in the thick foliage a colony of sparrows still chattered like men in a bar at closing time. Across the street she could see the lighted windows of the American Centre and the stream of khaki figures drifting in and out, pausing on the edge of the footpath, laughing and talking with the shoeshine boys, moving on again, crossing in twos and threes the broad street to the park.

In all the restless crowd, only she was alone. There was nothing so terrible and so terrifying as being alone. All these people were trying to push loneliness away for an hour, for a night...

That was why the girls stood in pairs on the steps near the station entrance, their young faces hard, their voices raucous, brazen and enticing, waiting for hungry men, some man, any man, so long as his need matched their own. Live while there is yet time, before the young men's bodies are broken and the young girl's flesh stale from too much lusting without time for love.

We were lucky, Ven and I. "We are invulnerable," he had exulted, holding her close that last night....

> We are invulnerable, you and I.
> Twin worlds spun to a star
> Between dark and dark...

"For these others," he had said, "there is no time for love, no time for the shy flowering from glance to speech, from speech to touch, and from touch to ecstasy. Why should they wait," he asked, "when tomorrow their ship may be among the missing, their plane go down in the mad spiral to death? These bodies steeled to perfection, these minds trained to watch, to observe and to kill, maybe to slow and die instead. The enemy is mortal. Yes, but we are mortal, too. And when the old rules were made, the old customs set, the old patterns designed, mortality had a biblical span before it. Three score years and ten. But today, the life of a flier in the air is twenty-four hours.... Shut it out, shut it out — the past and the future. There's only tonight.''

Somewhere a clock was striking eight.

It was dark when Guinea and Kim came out again after dinner. At the top of Martin Place the bulk of Sydney Hospital was black against a luminous haze and the full moon floated, an enormous red-gold ball, just above the roof.

They wandered down the hill through the evening crowds and stopped at the corner of Pitt Street to wait for the traffic. Kim looked across at a railway tram. "Listen, Peg," he said. "What about giving the hunt a miss tonight and hopping up to the Tiv to have a look at Mo? I haven't seen Mo for years."

Guinea shook her head. "Not on your life. It's looking for Monnie or nothing, so just keep your mind on the job."

"OK. If you say so."

Men and girls were loitering on the steps of the GPO, leaning against the pillars and waiting in shadowed corners. There was a little knot of people gathered at the Cenotaph; the men with sparse, greying hair, the women with patient faces. They stood watching as one of the men placed a home-made wreath of laurel leaves and crimson poppies against the base of the memorial.

"Christ," Kim muttered, "still at it. You'd think people'd have had their bellyfull of war memorials, wouldn't you?"

"Oh, I dunno. If you care about somebody and they're killed, I suppose it gives you some comfort."

"Listen," Kim said, "those old geezers are still celebrating World War One — take a dekko at their medals. You can't go on feeling sorry for somebody who stopped one thirty years ago — it's just a habit."

"Well, it's a habit that gives a lot of people comfort."

"There's no comfort for death. When your best cobber doesn't come back from an op, you drink his health in the mess that night, smash his glass and forget him. When you're standing by waiting for his plane to come in, you've got a hollow feeling — butterflies in your belly, like before you take off. And when he doesn't come, you feel all sort of flat, so you get on it that night, and next morning when you're going out you try not to think of him. And then in a couple of mornings you just don't think of him any more.''

"My God, you've got hard.''

"If you went drooling round the place with a face like a kangaroo pup with distemper whenever one of your cobbers went for a burton, well...there just wouldn't be any flying, that's all.''

"That's how you feel now, but wait till the war's over. Dad wouldn't miss a single one of the old Thirteenth Battalion reunions.''

"To hell with reunions,'' Kim said harshly. "Maybe if you come through a war you've got time to moan about your cobbers who don't. But right now, when you're in the middle of it the only union you're interested in is what these blokes hanging round the post office steps waiting for a pick-up want. When I come back I'm going to start a campaign against Returned Soldiers' Leagues.''

"I don't see they do any harm. They keep the old boys out of mischief.''

"Yeah, that's just what they're meant to do. From what I can see of returned men between the two wars — my own Dad and yours among them — they joined up these clubs just to get a chance of drinking their beer and fighting their battles over again. While they had enough money to buy any beer, that was. But once the depression hit them, it was a bloody fat lot the League did for returned men. You want to hear my dad on it. The clubs were only an excuse to keep the men legroped with their baloney about Lone Pines and mam'selles. Keep the boys out of politics, that was the big idea, so they wouldn't get in the way of the shrewdies who made a packet out of the last war and were determined that none of it would be filched from them by any repat policies that might really do any good for the blokes who needed a helping hand.''

"Quite the budding politician, aren't you?'' Guinea looked at him in surprise.

"OK, you can sling off. But I've learnt a few things in this war and one of them is that politics isn't merely soap boxing and flag flapping.''

"Well, my dad never kept out of politics."

"He was the exception. And I'm just beginning to see the point of the things he used to say. Everything that affects life is politics, and when they've run the numbers up at the end of this war, if we don't keep our eyes peeled the big bosses'll make politics mean bombs in the backyard again, your best cobber going down into the drink, and dole queues for heroes, the moment they think it's time to put in the boot."

"From what I've seen of the brass hats, you've only got to mention politics for them to go off like a blockbuster."

"That's their lurk. The military mind hates politics, and last time the big shots put it over the poor mugs in the name of king and country, I remember Dad saying, 'The League must keep out of politics.' Keep out of politics, hell. They let themselves become just a lot of stooges for big business. If we're not going to have a repetition of what happened after the last war, believe you me, returned servicemen and women'll have to get into politics right up to the neck as soon as they call off this dogfight. I bet you in this burg, right now, some hardhead is planning how he'll fob off the boys with free beer and Friday night smokes to keep 'em from making nuisances of themselves. Well you can take it from me, when I get back here, I'm going to be one hell of a nuisance — and how!"

"Why don't you hop up onto the Cenotaph," Guinea gibed, "they need an airman to make it complete."

Kim grabbed her arm roughly. "Let's get out of here." He turned his back on the Cenotaph and pulled her across to the footpath. "If I had my way, I'd drop a bomb on every bloody war memorial in the country. And I'd stick up in their place what's left of a cove when his kite's gone up in flames, and a few footsloggers with their guts hanging out, and a coupla torpedoed sailors after they've floated round in the water for a week, and just for luck I'd chuck in a few bombed babies and the woman I saw being dug out from under a blitzed house in London. I'd give 'em war memorials, and they'd get such a bloody kick out of it that this time they'd really do something to make certain that there'd never be a World War Three."

Guinea slipped an arm through his. "It's not eight yet," she said glancing up at the clock jutting out from the George Street face of the GPO, "the Glaci won't be open yet so what about hopping down to the Fun Parlour near Wynyard?"

He patted her hand resting on his sleeve. "Okey-doke. Little ray of sunshine, aren't I?" he said self-consciously.

"I know. I feel that way myself sometimes. Let's hop across and put a penny in the jukebox."

The Fun Parlour was crowded and the air was crashing with the din of hot music. American sailors with their gob caps stuck on at every angle clutched their cuties tightly to them and leaned over the jukeboxes, their faces mournful and absorbed. Kim stopped at a row of slot machines.

"Let's have a look at what Uncle Henry saw in Paris. I'll go first to see if it's fit for you." He dropped a coin in and put his eye to the peephole. "Hell," he said disgustedly, "I've seen better on Bondi Beach. Here, take a squint."

"Jeepers," Guinea snorted, "she needs a week in a sweat-box. She bulges like old Ma Dalgety."

"Garn," Kim said, "you don't know what beauty is. Let's have a peep at Mabel in the Bath." He dropped a coin in the next machine. "No go," he said disgustedly, "there must be something wrong with me glands."

"Probably worn out," Guinea suggested. "You great lovers are usually played out before you're twenty-five."

"Nonsense," Kim retorted, "the doctor told me I'm still as good as any man of fifty."

"Sez you! Let's have our fortunes told anyway."

Kim craned at the machine. "You're officially Virgo, aren't you?"

Guinea kicked his ankle.

"Ouch!" he dropped a penny into the slot and handed her a card.

"Now another one for the sign of the Bull," she insisted, "I want to know all the dirt about you as well."

Kim looked at her card. "Fame and Fortune will befriend you this year if you have the courage to take the bull by the horns." He gave a yelp. "Yippee!" he cried. "What have I been telling you?"

Guinea read the rest to him with malicious delight. "Listen to this. 'A sea voyage will come your way, watch out for a tall, dark stranger from over the sea.'"

"Does it say anything about four-star generals?"

"Not in so many words, but I'm sure that's what it means. What's on yours anyway?"

"'Those born under Taurus should be circumspect this year. Venus smiles on you but there are malignant forces at work.' Just what I thought," he said, "nothing for it but to shoot that brass hat."

"Quick, look. There's Monnie." Guinea grabbed his arm and pushed her way through the groups of men and girls crowded round the games tables and the slot machines. Two GIs let out loud wolf calls as she brushed past them.

"Lay off, pal," Kim said coming up beside her and slipping his arm round her waist.

"Just admirin' her," a GI explained.

"No offence. Platonic," another said, staring after her hungrily.

"Where's Monnie?" Kim asked.

Guinea stopped in front of the archery range. "Gosh," she said, "I was sure that was her."

Kim looked over to where she pointed. An American sailor was helping a small brown-haired girl to draw back the string of a huge bow, his arms encircled her. "Well, if that was Monnie in a clinch with a guy like that, she'd have come a long way since I last saw her."

"She hasn't changed. She'd faint if a strange man looked at her." Guinea turned away. "Let's get out of here, I've had it."

"Have it your own way." Kim turned to follow her out. Girls brushed against him provocatively, tossing shoulder length curls in his face, smiling at him.

"What's your hurry, big boy?" a redhead asked, blocking his way.

Kim tickled her under the chin. "Got to see a man about a dog," he whispered, "I'll be right back."

"Whacko," he said as he joined Guinea on the pavement. "Plenty of little red riding hoods waiting in there to kidnap the big bad wolf tonight. You'd better look after me better or one of those sheilas'll tuck me under her arm and gallop home with me, and then where'll you be?"

"I'll risk it."

"Well that's one place we know Monnie's not, anyway."

"They'll have to put you on the Vice Squad. Come on, let's run for this tram."

They scrambled onto a packed Leichhardt tram and stood jammed together in the crowded compartment among the evening holiday crowd.

"Shall we go straight out to the Glaci?" Kim asked, his mouth close to her ear.

"That's a good idea," she agreed, "lots of these kids go there."

The tram jogged its way up George Street to Central station.

"Funny," Kim grinned, leaning backwards to let picturegoers get out, then bending forward to let other passengers get in, "the way half the city wants to get to one place and the other half wants to get away from it."

At Railway Square they pushed their way out and breathed with relief as they joined the crowd streaming down the Glaciarium ramp. The ice was already crowded. Kim looked at the skaters gliding past, turned and looked at Guinea and shrugged his shoulders.

"Napoo," he said, "no tinkee findee. We might as well give them an exhibition ourselves."

Guinea looked round doubtfully. "I dunno. I think we ought to have a good look from here first."

"We could skate round. We'd be more likely to see her that way."

"Not if she's not skating, we wouldn't," Guinea said firmly.

"Well, we'll do both, have a look round the seats first and then put some skates on."

They made their way round the rows of seats, scanning

387

each group and every solitary girl.

"No go," Kim said at last, "now let's get our skates."

As Guinea laced up the hired boots, she remembered the last time she had been on the ice had been with Sherwood; they'd done a lot of skating on his leaves. Poor Sher, he was sweet. None of Kim's cockiness, not even Colonel Maddocks took as much for granted as Kim. Still, Kim had his uses. She couldn't imagine herself trekking round Sydney after a runaway sister with Sher or Byron. You didn't have to put on any dog with Kim either, he knew the worst about you and you knew the worst about him. She tugged savagely at a knotted lace. All that the war was doing for him was to make him more and more bumptious, so far as she could see. He might be a hell of a good flier but when the war was over and you were back to hard facts again, being a good flier wouldn't get you far. Probably it was lucky they hadn't got married when she'd gone off the deep end with him four years ago.

When Guinea came out of the ladies' skate room Kim was standing with shoulders and head leaning against a pillar, his hands locked behind him and profile uplifted. Hell, she thought, I must watch my step. They say you never get over your first man — well, I'm not going to be that kind of sucker. She came up behind him and jogged his elbow. "Speed it up, sourpuss!"

He grinned at her and they walked clumsily over the matting to the ice, where she glided ahead of him, then slowed down till he caught up.

"Been getting a bit of practice, I see."

"Just comes natural."

She put on the pace again and left him behind. When he caught up with her she was leaning against the railing and watching the crowd stream by.

"I can't see Monnie anywhere."

"Neither can I." He frowned and looked searchingly around as though no other thought had been in his mind. "And I think I've had a peek at everyone on the ice."

"From their back view anyway!"

"Come on," he said, grasping her hand in a hard grip

and drawing her up beside him, "you can give me a lesson now."

They skated hand in hand with long rhythmic sweeps until the music stopped.

"That was great," he said, "let's have a drink before they start up again."

In companionable silence they sucked the icy synthetic orange drink through thin straws and moved back to the ice when the music began again.

An instructor came up to Guinea. "Hullo, Guinea," he said, "dancing tonight?"

"Sure," she said.

"Not with me," Kim said firmly, "I'm not in the exhibition class."

"D'you mind then?" the instructor asked.

Guinea placed her hand in his and floated off before Kim could answer.

No wonder that flash bastard wanted her to dance, he thought grudgingly, watching the pair of them moving in perfect unison to the slow beat of the waltz. He hated the way the fellow smirked at her. Damned hide, picking up another fellow's girl, though she seemed matey enough with him. She certainly hadn't wasted her time in these last two years he'd been away.

They glided back to him, Guinea flushed and radiant. "Gee, that was bonzer," she said laughing at the instructor.

"The pleasure was all mine." He bowed in what Kim considered a pansy fashion. "We must do it more often."

The hell you will, Kim thought, taking her arm and drawing her off the ice. "If we're going to find the kid we'll have to get cracking," he said severely. "We're not just here for fun, you know."

Guinea had the grace to look apologetic.

"Get your skates off," he ordered, "and we'll hop it. I've got the kid on my mind, if you haven't."

It was five minutes to ten by the railway clock when Kim and Guinea came out into the street again.

"Good old Sydney," he said sentimentally, looking down the slope of the broad, busy street. "It's the best damn city in the world. Nice girls too."

"You ought to be a judge by now, though I'm told anything in skirts looks good after six months in the jungle."

"Not to me. I have my standards. Not but what I won't like the place a lot better when your Yankee friends have finished using it as first base."

"Snaky?" she asked, looking at him judicially, "or just gone troppo?"

"Who, me? Nothing wrong with me. I'm like Hitler, that's all — I just want living room." He cast a sidelong glance into a shop doorway where a sailor and a girl were clasped together. "Wonderful! I don't know how they do it. I'm not good at perpendicular lovemaking myself, but these coots all seem to be fitted with a gyroscope. And take a look at those."

Guinea slid her eyes to an island window and looked hastily away. "If you don't want to buy a fight, you'd better keep your eyes in front of you."

"It beats me, all this public lovemaking. Hand in hand, arms glued round each other and hop into the nearest doorway for a clinch. It's not my taste."

"No? But you can't expect them all to bring their own haystacks."

"Maybe not," Kim countered, "but what are parks for?"

"Not for me," she said, "and step on it. The way you're sticking your nose into other people's business you'll end up with such a poke in it you'll be no use to anyone for the rest of the evening. Come on."

They went laughing down the broad footpath to the bottom of the hill and up the short rise beyond Goulburn Street to the Coconut Grove. The usual groups were clustered together in the entrance, the usual men stood solitary, watching the girls flaunting their way in pairs across the foyer.

Kim looked at Guinea and winked elaborately. "Say, honey," he mimicked, "what heaven did you drop down from?"

Guinea prodded him in the ribs. "None you're ever likely to see, buddy. Come along, let's get this thing over."

"God," Kim gasped as she towed him through the wide doors, "what a woman!" He took a glance into the crowded ballroom and clung to her in mock terror. "Whew!" he whistled, "the gathering of the wolf clans."

The music of the orchestra sobbed out to meet them; a woman's husky voice was crooning: "I had a wonderful dream last night."

"We might as well dance this," Kim said, "plenty of time to look round after."

"Not when we're looking for Monnie. Have you forgotten we're not here just for fun?"

Kim shrugged his shoulders. "I asked for it. Come on, then, let's stand here and watch the crowd and we can go round among the tables when they sit down. Say, look at that corner." He had caught sight of the jitterbugs flinging themselves through their fantastic contortions. "Whacko-the-diddle-oh! The Yanks certainly have pepped up this town."

"Why not? We needed shaking up a bit. The place was dull as ditchwater till they came."

"Well, I don't see any improvement. Do you know what I really think of Uncle Sam and his glamour boys?"

"I haven't the faintest idea, and I couldn't care less."

"No?" He offered her a cigarette. "One thing, we don't go flinging our rolls around like they do to catch the girls."

"You're telling me. The Yanks know how to spend. They're gentlemen. Not like you guys. You come down with fifty quid in your pay book and splash forty-five of it on beer and nags and keep a fiver to make a big man of yourself showing your girl friend the world. You're wonders, you are."

"All I can say is, it makes me and my cobbers pretty sick to come back and see what the girls have been up to with the Yanks. Haven't they got any decency at all?"

"Aw, go bag your head. It makes me want to puke when I hear you fellows going on with all this purity bunk, after putting the hard word on all the girls from Sydney to London. And then you come back squealing because there aren't enough virgins left to go round."

"Break it down, Peg, you've turned into a regular prickly pear since I've been away."

"Well, I'm sick of the way you Aussies go on. So long as you don't give a girl twins or VD you think you're just it."

"Aw, come off it, Peg."

"You just lay off the Yanks then. Any brawls that have been started round Sydney in the last couple of years have been started by you chaps coming back from overseas too big for your boots. The Yanks don't go looking for trouble."

"You want to see some of the blues up round Brisbane and Townsville."

"Well, I'd give ten to one on who started them. If you Aussies were as well behaved as the Yanks, we wouldn't have anything to complain about. Holy mackerel! just think of a quarter of a million Aussies let loose in a strange country. Before they'd been there a week the place'd look as though it had been through a blitz and all the female inhabitants between sixteen and sixty'd be living underground."

Kim grinned at her. "Maybe you're right. Wonderful personality us boys have."

"Personality? You haven't even got started in the personality stakes. You want to get a few lessons from the Yanks!"

"You seem to know a hell of a lot about them." Kim's eyes met hers levelly. "You're not by any chance on their propaganda staff, are you?"

"What's it got to do with you if I am, anyway?" Guinea began to thread her way among the tables as the dancers came from the floor. "You're not my keeper, are you?" she flung over her shoulder.

Kim followed her in and out among the chattering crowd, the laughter quenched in his face and his eyes puzzled. A heavy thwack on the shoulder nearly laid him face downwards. He turned with a snarl to be wrapped in a giant arm and find a glass of beer frothing under his nose.

"Kimmy, old boy!"

"Jerry!" he cried, recognising one of the pilots from his squadron. "Cripes, am I glad to see you!"

"Me too," Jerry boomed, bringing an enormous hand

down on his shoulder again so that his teeth rattled on the glass. "Come and meet the talent." He turned to his table. "Say, folks, this is Kim Scott, gamest bloody gunner in the squadron."

Kim was greeted with loud hooroos, and it warmed his heart to see the familiar faces. He'd met some of the girls before, too. "Have another," Jerry urged him, "this is better than jungle juice."

"I'd better get me girlfriend." He looked over to where Guinea was tapping a foot impatiently.

"Whew!" whistled Jerry, "what a looker! Bet you didn't get her in your Christmas stocking. Has she got what it takes?"

Kim brought Guinea over to the table, smiling with pride. Introductions were made all round, the girls gave her a swift appraising glance, the men's eyes lingered. The orchestra struck up, and before Kim could put his glass down Jerry had swept her onto the floor. The others moved off, and Kim, disconsolate and polite, invited Jerry's little brunette to dance.

Trust Jerry to do the dirty on you like that! Well, he was the mug, he should have had more sense than to bring Peg over. He smiled with an effort at his partner's chatter. Over her shoulder he could see Peg, laughing face upturned to Jerry. If he knew Jerry he was shooting a line, the bastard, and no doubt like all the rest of her sex she was falling for it. Cripes, you couldn't trust a woman as far as you could see her; the sooner he got back to the jungle the better.

Back at the table they all raised their glasses together, clinking them to each other. With the first note of the orchestra, Kim was on his feet, his hand firm on Guinea's arm.

"You're in a hell of a hurry, aren't you?"

"Too right," he said tersely, drawing her to him. They moved off to the familiar rhythm. Nobody could dance like Peg really; probably that was because they'd learned their first steps together in the local hall when they were only bits of kids. It was two years since they had danced together, that was just after he got back from the Middle East. The two years slid away.

Cripes, what a mug he'd been, just another one of those

big mouths he secretly despised. Her face so close to his was cold and withdrawn. What was she thinking about? Was she remembering that night too? Or was her mind off somewhere with Jerry or some of those fancy Yanks of hers? He remembered, with the pang of something irretrievably lost, the weekend back in 'forty on his grandfather's farm. His final leave. He could see her as though it was yesterday, her head in the crook of his arm as they lay together in the old haystack, her hair bright against the bleached hay. She'd clung to him and they had kissed again and again and he swore he'd be faithful to her for ever. They had lain close together a long time and she had cried because he was going so far away.

Well, he'd meant it all then, hadn't he, and it would never have happened only he was sailing in a few days. He'd always seen himself and Peg in a hazy sort of way going on just being friendly until they were old enough to get married. But the war and being in camps speeded things up and they couldn't wait. They were both only kids, and he didn't know what life was then, and that there'd come a time when the urge of his body would be more compelling than any vow, and he'd need a girl's flesh to lie between him and the frightening future. Even that wouldn't have mattered when he came back, if he'd been man enough to do the decent thing by her. No one else had ever really got under his skin like Peg. And when he'd come back she'd leapt to meet him like a flame.

He didn't know why he'd given her that knock-back; probably listening to too much talk among the shrewdies in camp about how cunning a bloke had to be not to get caught with all the girls around who'd jump at the chance of being an allotment wife. Not that Peg was like that, he'd never really thought she was that sort; but when she'd snuggled against him in the narrow bed in her tiny flat and whispered: "Let's get married before you go north. It won't be so bad waiting when we really belong," something old and wary wakened in him. He'd panicked and boasted about all the girls he'd had. "Love 'em and leave 'em," he'd said, only half meaning it and making himself a devil of a big fellow. But she'd drawn away from him and he'd had only one glimpse of her face puckered like a child's with horror, before the fury broke and he went sprawling on the floor under the impact of two hard feet against his thighs and her strong hands thrusting against his chest.

Well, that had been the end of it. There had been a lot of girls since, but none like her. She had been his first girl and she was the only person in the world who knew what he was really like. Kim tightened his grip and rested his cheek against Guinea's. She did not draw away and they moved in a tranced silence till the music throbbed out its last gluey bars. This was more than heaven. He had made a comeback after all.

Kim stood below Guinea on the step, tense and expectant, as she slid her latchkey into the outer door. She turned and looked down at him. "Well, g'bye now."

He stepped up beside her and slipped an arm persuasively round her shoulders. "Aw gee, Peg, aren't you going to give a bloke a break?"

"What kind of a break?" her voice was low and ominous.

"Aren't you going to let me...come up with you?"

"What do you want to come up for at this hour of the night?"

He touched the hollow at the base of her throat with gentle fingers. "What do you think?" he said, with half-hearted bravado.

She brushed his hand away. "What do you think I am?"

"You know what I think about you, Peg. You're not going to hold a few words spoken in fun against a bloke forever, are you?" He tightened his arm round her shoulder.

She shook it off roughly. "Our ideas of fun don't seem to be the same."

"Well...you'll admit we've had pretty good fun tonight."

"And now you expect me to pay for it?"

He stiffened. His jaw was out-thrust and his mouth had an ugly twist. "You mistake me, lady. I'm not one of the Yanks. If I like a girl well enough I sleep with her, but I don't feel obliged to buy her. I keep that for whores."

He went down the steps, turned and lifted two fingers to his cap in ironical salute. "Goodnight."

She closed the door quietly behind her and leaned against it, shaking with rage and humiliation. The stamp of his footsteps down the road grew fainter and fainter.

The Town Hall clock struck eight as the taxi driver pulled up sharply at Beberfalds' corner beside a couple of American airmen and their girls. One of the Americans opened the door and stood there politely waiting for Deb and Angus to alight.

Angus pulled the door shut again. "This won't do, driver," he said sharply, "take me across to the Druitt Street entrance."

The taxi driver cocked an insolent eye at him. "Nothing doing. Can't you see I've got other passengers waiting?"

"I'll report you for this," Angus snapped, "I've got your number." He opened the door and stepped out, turning to help Deb.

"OK," the driver called after him, "but you'd better pay me first or it'll be me that's doing the reporting. It's half a dollar," he said holding out a grimy hand.

Angus dropped two shillings into it. "And that's more than your fare," he said turning away.

"Hey!" the taxi driver called after him, "would you like sixpence back so your girlfriend hasn't got to walk home?"

The girls tittered loudly as they got into the taxi.

"I'll certainly report that insolent fellow. Wait till the Americans have gone, these drivers will find a difference."

Angus piloted Deb across the street to the crowded footpath where men in uniform lolled against the stone railings and clustered round the top of the subway watching the girls who stood giggling in pairs and swaggered up and down on stilt heels, their short skirts swinging impudently, pert breasts outlined under their thin frocks.

"I cannot understand why the Town Hall authorities allow their main entrance to be used as a pick-up place," Angus continued in the same sour voice, as though this was another personal affront. "Sydney has become a disgrace in the last couple of years. If the police did something about this sort of thing instead of wasting their time on traffic offences, the city would have a better name."

When they were ushered to their seats the members of the

orchestra were already in their places and the air was full of the wailing of tuning strings. Angus had secured a perfect position two rows behind the vice-regal party and Deb wondered again how he managed always to get what he wanted.

When the prelude to the *Meistersingers* was over, he turned to her and commented quietly: "Very prosaic."

She nodded in silence. She had rather liked it, but she did not know much about music and would never have risked an opinion of her own.

"Wagner requires magnificence," he told her. "Australian orchestras just don't seem able to bring it off. I am interested to see what Marjorie Lawrence will make of him."

"She looks magnificent enough herself," Deb said, craning to watch the singer as she was wheeled to the centre of the stage, her red-gold hair shining under the strong spotlight, her face so bright and exalted that you forgot she was a cripple and saw only her radiance among the black-clad figures of the orchestra.

The audience met her with wave upon wave of cheers and clapping. Deb felt a lump rise in her throat. "She's marvellous, isn't she?" she whispered.

Angus smiled at her. "We'll soon know."

The orchestra sighed out the opening bars of the *Liebestod*, infinitely mournful and far away, and the singer's voice rose in the first soft tones of Isolde's lament.

"She's glorious," Deb burst out, when at last the wheeled chair had finally disappeared after the singer's last tumultuous recall.

"Very fine," Angus agreed, "I'm glad you're liking it. Shall we go out and have a cigarette?"

The huge chandelier in the vestibule glittered above a chattering crowd. Angus led Deb across to the outer door, acknowledging friendly greetings without stopping. She was keenly aware of the eyes watching her, noting every detail and commenting after she had passed. Well, let them talk! She had the laugh on them.

They had just reached the entrance hall when the grasp of a hand on her arm and a familiar voice froze her. "Why

Deb," Dallas cried, "you didn't tell me you were coming tonight."

"I didn't know, then," Deb stammered self-consciously.

"Antony..." Dallas spoke to the English officer beside her, "this is my friend, Deb Forrest. You must meet her. Colonel Gisborne, Mrs Forrest. And you've never met my partner, have you, Deb? Dr Karl Rosenberg."

Deb bowed. "How do you do." She put a hand on Angus's arm and introduced him.

Angus smiled his most charming smile at Dallas and inclined his head deferentially as she spoke of the concert.

You wouldn't think she was a day over thirty-five, Deb thought resentfully, and squired by two such distinguished men. Gisborne was taller than Angus, sinewy and brown, and as for Rosenberg, you would pick him out anywhere with those deep set brown eyes and his young face under the shock of startlingly white hair. Looking at Dallas, brilliant and animated, with the three men hanging on her words, Deb thought with a pang of what Claire had said when she picked up the photograph in her room. She had never thought of Dallas like that before, but it was quite obvious she could charm any man when she wanted to.

"British Army?" Angus was saying. "Very nice to see you here. As an Englishman, tonight's news of the taking of Calais must make you feel very proud."

"You will probably be disappointed to hear that it only makes me depressed," Colonel Gisborne said. "I was at Dunkirk, where I alternated between pride in the almost unbelievable courage of the men and anger at the stupidity that had let them in for it. Now when I read about the capture of Calais, I'm afraid I think only of the number of men it's cost."

"I see you're not military-minded," Angus said.

"No doctor can be military-minded, especially after five years of war. And I confess that the spectacle of one army escaping from France with heavy losses in 1940 and another one fighting its way back with heavy losses four years later, only fills me with a sense of futility."

"But the courage," Angus said, "that unbreakable

English courage...What they must have endured..."

"Do you know I've come to the conclusion that people can have too much courage. It makes them endure a whole lot of things, in peace, as well as in war, that they've got no right to endure and that they'd be much better not to endure. If I had my way, I'd wipe out all this poet laureate stuff about courage and endurance as national virtues, and substitute commonsense."

"Hear, hear," Dallas cried. "I always say that about women. They put up with all kinds of things they should refuse to put up with, and so long as they do, there'll always be someone to write a lot of blah-blah about it as though it were a virtue instead of their worst vice."

"Exactly," Colonel Gisborne agreed.

"You medical people do like to pretend you're cynics." Angus smiled at them benevolently. "And am I to understand that you're a forerunner of the British Army in Australia, Colonel Gisborne?"

"Not exclusively, I'm really amphibious," Colonel Gisborne smiled. "It's mainly our Naval forces that will be based here, but there's other medical organisation needed as well, and that's my end of the job."

"You're finding Sydney strange, I suppose?"

"It's like heaven! Sunshine and fruit and all the food I can eat. I tell Dr MacIntyre she'll have to keep an eye on my waistline."

"That's what Karl always says," Dallas turned to him.

"It is heaven, I assure you," Dr Rosenberg spoke quietly. "I came here from Vienna five years ago and every year I am more and more convinced."

"Oh come," Angus demurred, "you don't have to flatter us like that, you know. I know Vienna well, and I can assure you it was my idea of heaven. The music...the graciousness...even the air seemed different in Vienna. You must find Sydney unbearably crude by contrast."

Dr Rosenberg smiled politely. "What you say is true, but it is not the whole picture, and I have come to think, as I do my work here, that graciousness and culture are not enough.

It may shock you, but, apart from my old friends, the one thing I really miss from Vienna is the coffee."

Dallas shook her head. "Poor Karl, he tries so hard to be polite about our coffee."

"I'm inclined to agree with him," Colonel Gisborne said. "I haven't yet solved the mystery of what exactly you do to it, but as I'm not a coffee specialist like Dr Rosenberg, I'd be just as happy with tea — if I could get it. Can someone tell me why you close up all your cafés in this city as soon as the sun goes down?"

Angus looked triumphant. "I tell you, we're a barbarous people."

"I don't know about that, but I do know that after the concert on Saturday night Dallas and I wandered round the streets for an hour looking for somewhere to have supper, and we couldn't even get a hot drink."

Angus looked at Deb. "Perhaps I can solve that problem tonight if Mrs Forrest isn't in too great a hurry. Could you all come round to my suite at the Hotel South Pacific and have supper with me?"

"That would be lovely," Dallas agreed, "but how do you manage it? Don't tell me you have a black market restaurant of your own?"

"You'll see," Angus smiled. "It's a trade secret. Would that suit you two gentlemen?"

"Splendid, provided we're not keeping Mrs Forrest out too late."

"Oh no, I'd love it."

"Then that's settled. If you'll excuse me one moment, I'll get one of the attendants to ring through to the hotel for me so that everything will be ready when we get back."

The bell marking the end of the interval sounded.

When Angus ushered them into his suite after the concert, supper was already set out, and within a few minutes a waiter came in with silver jugs of steaming coffee and dishes of hot savouries.

Dallas lifted the lid on an entrée dish. "Oyster patties!

I insist on knowing that secret, Mr McFarland!''

Deb lifted the other lid. "Ooh, bacon and prunes, my favourite.''

"I remembered that,'' Angus smiled at her.

"I don't believe it,'' Gisborne exclaimed. "At any moment it will all disappear.''

Angus beamed. "Will you pour for me, my dear?''

Deb seated herself in front of the coffee tray. "Of course. Now, how do you like your coffee?''

"Half and half for me,'' Dallas smiled wickedly.

"I'll have nearly all milk,'' the Colonel said, "if you've got it to spare.''

"And you, Dr Rosenberg?''

"Black, if you please.''

"Oh, the same as Angus,'' Deb shot a glance at Dallas and turned to pour out. Angus handed the cups round.

"Only one lump for you, Angus,'' Deb insisted with mock firmness.

"You're very cruel,'' he complained, "you let Colonel Gisborne have four.'' They laughed together.

"How is your coffee, Dr Rosenberg?'' Deb asked him graciously.

"I might be in Vienna.''

He really is charming, Deb thought, watching his aquiline profile as he listened attentively while Angus and Dallas talked about the concert. It was not surprising that Dallas had taken him into partnership.... She wondered if there was anything more to it. Dallas was deep. They were all chattering nineteen to the dozen about music and orchestras and singers. She really felt rather out of it. Between the four of them, they seemed to know all the operas that had ever been sung.

Angus was talking to Dallas with an animation she had never seen him show before. He was obviously quite taken with her and to look at Dallas's vivacious face you'd think butter wouldn't melt in her mouth. Angus would feel rather differently toward her if he'd heard what she said about him this afternoon. At any rate, this would show her that her suspicions were wrong and his intentions were really honourable.

Dallas flashed a glance at Deb. "I was playing Marjorie Lawrence's Brunnhilde record when Deb came to see me this afternoon, and I felt then she'd recorded larger than life size. But I take it back, she's better than any of her records."

"Very fine," Angus agreed, "though I'd like to hear her with a first-class orchestra before I really made up my mind. Bernard Heinze of course is local and lacks that wider experience."

Colonel Gisborne looked up from his third cup of coffee. "Really," he said, "you surprise me. I thought he was very good."

"By local standards, yes," Angus agreed, "and while the quality of Marjorie Lawrence's voice is superb, I always feel that Australians lack the cultural background that would make them first-class artists."

"Well," Dallas laughed, "I'm no connoisseur, but if that's the case it's fortunate for the home-grown product that the big world doesn't seem to know about our limitations. From what I've heard, Melba and Judith Anderson...Constant Lambert, Robert Helpmann and of course John Brownlee, to name only a few, seem to have put it over quite successfully."

Colonel Gisborne leaned forward in his chair. "I think you're inclined to rather underrate your own standards here," he said. "I'd say that Heinze, allowing for all the limitations of a concert platform instead of an opera house, conducted that colossal scene with a drive, judgment and grandeur that would compel admiration anywhere."

"The last few years in Europe have caused a good many people to revise their ideas of culture," he went on.

"I can't say that gives me any degree of comfort," Angus countered. "Sometimes I wonder whether I could ever bear to go back. You were in France after the liberation, were you not, Colonel Gisborne?"

"Yes."

"Was there a great amount of damage done? I mean anything like the destruction in England?"

Colonel Gisborne took his cigarette from his lips and looked at its burning tip, frowning: "It all depends on what you mean by damage. If you mean the destruction of old buildings, there was remarkably little in France. England's a different matter, and of course we don't know what these V-2 bombs are going to do. But it all seems to me profoundly unimportant, compared with the damage that has been done to human beings."

"Ah, but those glorious cathedrals, those old castles, the enchanting medieval cities; they stood for something unique in our culture."

"Well, McFarland, you may regard me as a Philistine, but to me, the world's greatest cathedral is not so important as a good human being, and I'd exchange all the medieval cities of Europe for one well-planned town where people could live decent, comfortable lives. And as for the castles, they're anachronisms, and the only function they fulfil in this age is that of a monument to the bad old feudal days."

"Some of us learned that after the last war, and there were many people in Vienna who would have. . .what do you call it? — swapped all the castles of the Hapsburgs for such projects as our workers' flats, our new schools, our children's playgrounds; all the things that make for the living future against the dying past."

"You surprise me. I should say your extreme views are hardly those of my English and Continental friends, who respect and love their traditions."

"You're probably right," Colonel Gisborne agreed, "but I can assure you our views are typical of an increasing number of Europeans today. There's nothing so fatal to tradition as blitzes and starvation. People are beginning to question whether it isn't time we started a new kind of tradition."

"You frighten me. I was looking forward to going back when things had settled down a little more."

"Then I hope you'll look me up. I shall be delighted to give you a line into the new tradition."

"Thank you. It would be most interesting. I think we might drink to that." Angus took a bottle of champagne from the silver bucket on a side table, filled the glasses and handed them round.

Dallas sipped the champagne and looked up at him. "I'm not a connoisseur of wines, but please tell me, where did you get this? You'll never convince me you haven't got a special black market."

"Much worse," he said. "I inherited it in the family cellar."

"Horrifying! Did you hear that, Antony? Mr McFarland has a family cellar."

"Astonishing! I thought they went out with the supertax."

Angus smiled and refilled their glasses.

"Enjoying yourself, my dear?" he whispered as he handed Deb hers.

"Lovely," she whispered back.

Dallas raised her glass. "I'm already drunk with the music, so now I'm going to drink to the local lass come good. If she couldn't sing a note, I'd still admire a woman who had the courage to come out onto a concert platform in a wheelchair."

Angus sat down beside her. "I'll drink with you, but it will be to my memories of the great days of Bayreuth. One thing I'll never forgive Hitler for is that he made it impossible for us to enjoy the musical feasts of Salzburg and Bayreuth. One wonders how so high a culture on the one hand could be accompanied by such barbarism on the other."

"That is what I was saying, culture of that sort is not enough." Dr Rosenberg leaned forward, his fragile glass held delicately in a strong square-tipped hand. "It is not enough for people to be lovers of great music — you will remember Hitler poses as a worshipper of Wagner, and there are many like him who are connoisseurs of the arts."

"I hardly feel that love of music explains all the dictators. We have a great number of petty ones in this country who don't know 'Waltzing Matilda' from 'Pop goes the Weasel'."

Colonel Gisborne looked at him thoughtfully. "I find you Australians a remarkable people and I've heard a lot about your national inferiority complex, but, do you know, this is the first time I've met it."

Dr Rosenberg nodded gravely. "I think it is that they have

been told so often that Europe is the seat of culture that they believe it and undervalue what they have made in this new country."

"I'm afraid you're too kind and I can assure you here's one Australian who will be back in the seats of culture just as soon as the war is over."

"Good." Colonel Gisborne put down his glass. "By then we might be able to take a run over to Bayreuth and Salzburg together. Up till Munich I rarely missed a festival, and as soon as they reopen I shall be there again. It will be interesting to hear how they compare with what we've heard tonight. I can only say I've been most impressed by the quality of the music and the size of the audience."

"I hate to disillusion you on that ground," Dallas broke in, "but when Marjorie Lawrence came out here five years ago, the poor girl got such a poor reception that she had to sing in picture shows. But she's become a celebrity since; so there's as much snobbery about the audience as there is love of music." She got up. "And now, I'm terribly sorry, I hate to break up the party, but I have to operate at eight tomorrow morning, so I really must be getting home."

She offered her competent hand to Angus and turned to go, slipping her arm through Deb's. "About your little AWAS friend," she said softly, as they walked towards the lift.

"She's not my friend," Deb spoke irritably. "I thought I explained that."

"Oh, well, that doesn't matter. But I spoke to one of my friends at the hospital this afternoon and he said he can get me the address of a good man, so if you ring me at eleven tomorrow..."

"Thanks very much," Deb's voice was cold, "but the girl is already fixed up."

She withdrew her arm from Dallas's adroitly.

Dallas smiled at her with a crinkling of the fine lines at the corner of her eyes.

"How clever of you!" Her voice flicked Deb to anger. "But then, living at a place like this one makes such useful contacts."

She turned to Angus. "Thank you so much for a really delicious supper."

Angus was still assuring her that he hoped they would have the pleasure of repeating it, when the lift took them down.

The sound of voices seeped into Monnie's mind, stirring her out of sleep. A streak of moonlight filtered through the curtains and across the bed. She stared round her, bewildered for a moment, her head heavy and aching; then she felt the satin coverlet and smelled the magnolia, thick in the stale air of the room, and memory came flooding back. Grace's flat...She crept quietly out of bed, her heart thudding at the nearness of the voices. Perhaps she could climb down the tree. Perhaps there was a way out of the walled yard. She pulled back the pink curtains and looked out. The magnolia tree rustled softly, the giant flowers gleaming unearthly in the moonlight, the heavy perfume sickly sweet on the night air. In the flats behind someone was singing.

There was the sound of a key turning in the bedroom door. She flattened herself against the wall, pulled the curtain in front of her and stood there, with her heart thumping. The door opened and the light went on.

At the sight of the empty bed, Grace's motherly smile was switched off. "Where the flaming hell...?" she began, then her eyes fell on the shrinking girl and the smile fixed itself again on her face and her voice was thick and sweet like honey. "Oh, there you are, darling. Time for supper now." She came over and took Monnie's hand in hers, drawing her out of the bedroom and along the hall to the lounge-room with a grip like steel.

Sport looked up from the settee on which he was stretched, reading the evening paper. "Hullo," he said pleasantly, "you look a ball of muscle tonight. Don't she, Fay?"

Fay came in with a tray in her hands. She looked at Monnie with hostile eyes and said flatly, "Looks a million dollars to me."

Monnie turned from her in repulsion and pulled her hand away from Grace.

Sport smiled at her cheerfully. Monnie stared into his round, unlined face and saw grey eyes under thick, dark brows, hair sleeked back, powerful shoulders in his silk sports shirt.

He went on admiringly, "Real pretty kid, ain't she, when she's got a bit of makeup on."

"Yes, and when we've bought some pretty clothes for her tomorrow you won't know her," Grace agreed.

"Going to splash your dough on some pretties, eh? That's a good idea."

"I've got no coupons," Monnie protested weakly.

"Well, we won't let that stand in your way. Gracie here and me, we've got a way of gettin' round that."

"That's right. It'll cost a bit more, but she deserves it."

"Too right. Coupla them fellers last night told me she was a wow. Just wait till she gets into her routine. You other girls'll have to pull your socks up then."

"D'yer reckon?" Fay said sourly.

"I must say," Grace went on, "that you did very well for an inexperienced girl."

"Really, Sport, you're absolutely ridiculous about that horse."

"Mare," Sport corrected.

"There's nothing special on tomorrow, is there?"

"No. Smiler's takin' over for a while and I'm gonna have a bit of a breather."

"Oh, did he get out of his call-up again?"

"Yeah. The army took one look at his police record and hoofed him out on his ear."

"How's he shaping?"

"Top-notch. Got a head on him, Smiler has. He's got hold of a bunch of school kids that've been shoe-shining outside the American Centre. That gives 'em a taste for the money. And now he's got 'em deliverin' for him and collectin' labelled empties. They're smart kids all right; he'll be able to make something of 'em."

"A very good idea!"

"Smiler's making a bloody good thing out of it. I have to cough up two ten a dozen for the stuff and so long as he doubles it for me I don't ask any questions, though I know the bastard often turns it over for twice as much to the Yanks. With Christmas only a coupla months off now, the sky's the limit. He's tuckin' it away all right."

"I reckon he earns it," Fay said.

"Whaddaya mean?"

"Well, Mack's in the boob, isn't he?"

"So what?"

"Well, he took all the risks, didn't he?"

"Who said?"

"I said, and I'll also say you left him to it when the cops got on to him."

Sport stared at her. "I wouldn't say it again if I was you, even if he was your boyfriend. He was nothing but a bloody stoush merchant anyway."

"At least he wasn't a bludger." Fay flung the words at him furiously. "And it's the truth about the cops, isn't it?"

Sport leaned his elbows on the table and picked his teeth with a match, still staring at her. Fay moved uncomfortably and dropped her eyes.

"You ought to've learned by now that truth don't always pay, sister."

There was a long, bristling silence.

"Jesus!" Fay gave a strained laugh. "Can't you take a joke?"

"Yeah," said Sport, "but I don't have to."

"Fay, dear," Grace broke in, "take Monnie into the bedroom and see she gets tidied up properly and dressed, will you? I left fresh clothes for her — you'll find everything you want."

"OK, OK," Fay snapped. She got up, pulling Monnie after her, and stamped into the bedroom, slamming the door.

"She's so impulsive," Grace murmured soothingly.

"Yeah, so'm I. Remind her sometime, will you?"

Grace drew her lips back in a forced smile and changed the subject. "Just exactly when are you going to Brisbane?"

"I can't give you a definite date yet, it all depends on how Stormcloud's runing and when I can get a seat on a plane."

"Really, I'm sick of the sound of Stormcloud. You haven't had your mind on your business ever since you picked him up."

"Her," Sport corrected, "and don't you have any doubts about me havin' me mind on me business. Havin' contacts on the course is the best way I've found yet of dodging the taxation."

Grace looked at him with new interest. "Really?" she inquired.

"Yeah," Sport said. "I went around all last week with five thousand smackers I'd just got in from Smiler and Cec burning a hole in me trousers pocket. Jesus, did I have the wind up? And then out at Randwick on Saturday, I give the wink to a bookie I met at Joe's and he pencilled in a phoney bet for me about whatever horse won the second race, and there I was all fair and square with the books showing me winning five thousand quid to five hundred and all I got to do tomorrow mornin' is to drop into the bank and stick me winnin's in. Bloody bookmaker makes a cool five hundred quid out of it and shows a losin' bet on the race. Christ, some fellers make their money easy."

"That's an idea," Grace looked more cheerful. "I'll get you to introduce me to him."

"Whacko! Come along to Joe's one night."

"I will when I get that money from Brisbane. There should be a good amount coming to me from there?" She looked at him questioningly.

Sport laughed, avoiding her eyes. "Oh sure, you did a nice job up there, I'll hand you that."

"What do you think it'll pan out at?"

"O-oh..." he paused to consider. "Roughly, I'd say we'll clear up about the same as we did in Townsville."

Grace's face darkened and a harsh note came into her lowered voice. "Same as Townsville? Not on your bloody life, Sport! Keep that one for the Taxation Department. You know perfectly well my expenses were practically double in Townsville, what with the cost of getting plane priorities for fresh girls to come up and the losses we had through not being able to keep their health checked up properly. Don't try to put that one over me. I have a good idea what we made in Brisbane and I know who did the work, too."

"OK, OK, keep your wool on. None of us'll know for sure what's coming till things are wound up."

"All I know is that we made a damn good thing out of Brisbane, and don't you forget it, or I'll have a thing or two to say you won't exactly like to hear."

"Aw, get off your bike."

"It's all right for you, you can afford to talk like that, but who has to do the work and take the risks?"

"You should worry. You could retire tomorrow and live in luxury for the rest of your life on what you've raked in since the Yanks came."

Grace flashed him a calculating glance. "I don't know so much about that. After all, I've worked hard enough for it. Don't I have all the responsibility for getting the right type of girls and keeping them in decent condition?"

"I'll hand it to you there, Grace. This place has the rep for being one of the safest drums in the town."

"I can assure you, it costs me a lot of extra trouble keeping it that way. I'm absolutely worn out."

"You women are never satisfied." Sport lit another cigarette. "Think I don't know what that house you bought at Leura cost you?"

"You don't expect me to work for nothing, do you?"

"No bloody fear of that! I know you've got enough tucked away to keep you sittin' pretty for the rest of your life. But just stick it out a bit longer and we'll see how things go when the Limeys settle in. That's my advice to you. And if it's no go, we'll both get out of it." He stopped short as the bedroom door opened and Fay brought Monnie out, her hair combed and a fresh ribbon tied round it, a childish blue frock patterned in daisies flirting round her knees.

"M-m-m." Grace held out a welcoming hand to her. "You do look pretty, darling. Come over here and sit down and I'll pour you out a nice hot cup of coffee, and while you drink it I'll explain to you some of the things you'll have to know. Fay will tell you how well we look after our girls, don't we, Fay?"

"Sure!" Fay flung herself sulkily into a chair.

"And you can stay with me for a while, darling, out at my own home at Vaucluse," Grace murmured silkily. "I have the duckiest little spare room. It looks right over the harbour. It's my daughter's — the one who is at boarding school, you know. You will be happy there as the day is long."

Monnie pushed her cup away. A passion of protest swept over her; it set the blood throbbing in her head and rose in a scream in her throat. She dug her nails into her palms and opened her mouth. No sound came. She looked with frantic eyes from one face to another. They smiled back at her, persuasive and evil.

With an enormous effort she blurted out, "I'm not going to stay."

Sport put down his glass with a bang. Fay got up and started for the kitchenette.

Grace folded her heavy white hands with their lacquered nails and sighed. "You're being very foolish, my dear." Her voice was low and throaty like the cooing of doves. "How would you feel if we reported you to the police for breaking in here?"

"They wouldn't believe you."

"Oh, wouldn't they? Well, it might interest you to know that your parents have reported you as an uncontrollable child. When you were asleep this afternoon, a police call came over the air asking anyone who has seen you to report to the police."

Monnie went deathly white. "You wouldn't tell them."

"What makes you think that?" Grace tapped the table with her fingertips.

"I'm not going to stay."

"Aw Jeez, kid," Sport broke in, "don't let's start this business over again. You gimme a headache. Go along with Gracie here, that's a good kid. You're on a damn good wicket. Do you know how much you made last night? Twelve quid, after expenses are off. That's a hell of a lot more than you'll make in any other job."

"No," she whispered vehemently. "No."

Sport rested his elbows on the table and leaned towards her. He was smiling still but his eyes were like cold steel.

"Listen, kid," he said very softly. "I like you, so does Gracie here."

Monnie stared it him and shook her head.

Grace sighed. "Such a pity," she said, getting up from the chair and moving to the telephone. "I do so hate to give a young girl up to the police. Just imagine how your poor mother will feel when she hears the whole story." She lifted the receiver and dialled slowly.

Monnie watched each movement of her fingers with the shining pink nails.

"Hullo," Grace said softly, smiling into the receiver, "will you please put me through to Detective-Sergeant Bettington."

Monnie leapt up with a cry and clutched her arm. "Don't do it...don't...don't!"

Grace laid down the receiver slowly. Monnie threw herself onto the lounge, covered her face with her hands and broke into loud, wild sobbing.

Grace pulled her to her feet and shook her angrily. "Now stop that nonsense this very minute. Fay, take her into the bedroom, give her a dose of sal volatile and make her lie down till we're ready for her. Really, my nerves won't stand any more."

Fay took Monnie roughly by the arm and pushed her into the bedroom. "Come on, you snivelling rat!"

Grace sighed and leaned her forehead on her hands as though she was exhausted. "I'd like to flay the hide off the little bitches when they go on like that. Really, my nerves are just in shreds."

Sport got up and put on his jacket. "She'll come round," he said easily. "Them ones with a bit of kick in them are the best, particularly when they're young. Blokes like 'em that way."

Monnie lay watching the shadows on the ceiling, the magnolia tree rustled against the window. Grace bustled in and out of the room between clients, persuasive and domineering. She made up Monnie's face and helped her to put her clothes on, touching her breasts with perfume and spraying it on her hair.

"A gentleman has been ringing me up all the evening and he's just arrived. I want you to be specially nice. He'll be with you an hour and it'll be worth ten pounds."

Almost immediately she brought in a civilian, lean and tall, with black eyes burning in an ascetic face. He folded his clothes meticulously and placed them on the chair. But it was just the same. He dressed with the same care, counted out notes from a wallet and put them on the mantelpiece. "Thank you. Goodnight," he said, and was gone.

The sailor who came next was gay and a little drunk. He talked and sang to her in a cracked half-whisper with his mouth buried in her hair. "Stardust, that's what you're like, and a little new moon. Do you love me?" She lay there a long time, his hands warm and intimate on her body. "I don't want to go to sleep," he murmured drowsily, "you're too lovely. But you'll wake me, sweety-pie, won't you, if I do? We're sailing tomorrow and I got to be on board by seven. This is my last night."

She promised, praying for sleep to shut him away from her. He snuggled her closer, nuzzling her soft throat. "Next time we're in port, I'll look you up again; that's if the crabs aren't nibbling my toes somewhere up round the Islands." After a little while he murmured, drowsy and gentle. "I'd like you for my girl, only I don't get enough pay for that."

She grew sleepy herself and dozed till she was no longer aware of his breathing or the weight of his hand on her breast.

She woke suddenly to the noise of doors flung sharply open and banged again, the thudding of heavy feet on the stairs and corridor, the shouting of rough commands, and a voice screaming hysterically in the next room.

The door of her own room was flung back and she lay blinking in the sudden glare. Two men loomed enormous by the side of the bed. She dragged the bedclothes around her chin but they pulled the covers off roughly. She hunched herself into a ball, covering her breasts with her hands.

"Jeez," exclaimed the sailor indignantly, sitting up, "what's going on in here?"

"Get up," one of the men commanded. "Get your clothes on and get out."

"OK, sergeant, keep your hair on. I'm not doing anything I shouldn't, am I?"

"I'm not too sure," he said, measuring Monnie's childlike body with an expert eye. "How old are you?"

"Eighteen."

"You don't look it. Get your clothes on and come along with us."

The sailor scuttled into his uniform. Monnie crawled from the bed, hiding her nakedness as well as she could. She put on her brassière and scanties with trembling hands and slipped the blue frock over her head. The policeman stooped, lifted up the coverlet and picked up something from under the bed.

Betty was still laughing hysterically next door. Monnie heard the murmur of Grace's voice and the sound of a sharp slap. The laughter stopped and the air was filled with loud sobbing.

Monnie went down the stairs, the plainclothes policeman treading heavily behind. Shirley was already in the hall with two other girls, and a policeman brought Fay from a back room. "You keep a quiet tongue in your head, my girl," he warned her, "or you'll get more than you bargain for."

"To hell with the lot of you!" Fay flared back. "Why don't you spend your time picking up some of the bitches round the SP and those toney joints for a change and give girls like us a break?"

"I warn you that anything you say may be used in evidence against you."

"Too bloody right it will, and anything I don't say as well! You cops make me sick, you haven't got the guts to tackle any of the big shots."

He put a hand on her shoulder and pushed her into line with the others.

"And keep your hands off me, too. When men paw me they pay for it."

Monnie flattened herself against the wall as far away from them as she could. She saw their faces floating disembodied in the soft glow of the hall light: the policemen, detached and unruffled; the girls defiant, tense and frightened; and Grace, stalking grimly down the stairs dragging Betty behind her.

TUESDAY
I

A heavy knocking on her door woke Guinea out of a deep sleep. Gosh, I must have overslept, she thought. The knocking sounded again and she sat up. "Coming!" she shouted.

Who the devil could it be? Her landlady would have stuck her head round the door and yelled if she'd noticed she wasn't up. She stood, her housecoat half on, every movement suddenly still at the thought that it must be Kim. He'd come crawling back like this yesterday, the louse. Who did he think he was? She'd show him. She buttoned her coat, dragged up the covers on her bed fiercely, and ran to the door, her heart rising at the thought of battle. She paused to make certain her face was set in the proper mask before she flung open the door and stared belligerently.

The policeman at the door seemed to fill the tiny landing. "Sorry to disturb you, Miss," he said, and then added inquiringly: "Miss Margaret Malone?"

Guinea nodded. Her mind was racing. What was he here for? She looked at him suspiciously, then had a sudden moment of panic. What if Dad. . .? There was a sound of someone stirring in the hall below, the constable looked over the railing and coughed, and they heard doors closing one after the other. "What I have to say is private," he said quietly. "I think I'd better come inside."

She opened the door wide, and he came in and she was grateful then that she'd been so furious with Kim when she got home last night that she couldn't go to sleep and had spring-cleaned the whole room. It looked bright and fresh in the morning sun with the green-and-white cover on the bed and the lacquered chairs. She pulled one forward.

"Will you sit down?"

The policeman looked around. H'mm, clean as a new pin, and the girl a good type. A decent house too. He sat down and took off his cap, putting it carefully on the floor beside him, and slowly unbuttoned the breast pocket of his tunic. He took out a black-covered notebook, unclipped a silver pencil and slowly adjusted the lead.

My God, why didn't he hurry up, she thought frantically. She leaned against the table, her hands gripping the edge tightly, and said nothing. Let him get what he had to say off his chest first. That'd give her time to get her story ready, whatever it was he wanted.

He opened his book and held the pencil poised. "You have a sister?" he began slowly.

"Yes."

"Monica Bernadette Malone, aged sixteen?"

The colour drained out of her face. "Is she hurt?"

The constable drew up another chair. "No, she's not hurt," he said deliberately, "but I think you'd better sit down, there's quite a bit more yet. Residing at No 78A Elm Lane, Kings Cross?" he asked.

So that's where Monnie was!

She nodded. Whatever had happened to her, she'd better back her up.

The policeman scratched the top of his head with the pencil. "Well, Miss Malone," he said apologetically, "I have some information for you. It's not exactly a nice story but, well. . ." he paused.

I'll crown him if he doesn't hurry up, Guinea said to herself. She stared at him imploringly.

He shuffled uncomfortably under her clear gaze. "I don't know how much you know about your sister's life, or the girls she was sharing a flat with, but I've come round to advise you that a girl purporting to be Monica Bernadette Malone, aged sixteen, was arrested by the Vice Squad this morning in bed with a sailor in a brothel."

Guinea jumped to her feet, pushing the chair back so

violently that it overturned. "I don't believe it! It couldn't be Monnie! Monnie's not like that, you must have made a mistake."

"We don't make that sort of mistake." He stood up. "Your sister Monica Bernadette Malone was picked up in a house of ill fame at three o'clock this morning. She was taken to Central Police Court because she falsely gave her age as eighteen. The policewoman there discovered when she was interviewing her that she was only sixteen and she is to come up before the magistrate at the Children's Court this morning."

"But it must be a mistake," Guinea blurted out.

"You can tell all that to the magistrate, miss. What I want is your parents' address." He stood looking at her sternly.

Guinea's mind leapt as though it was trapped. If Monnie hadn't given their address she would stick by her. "We have no home," she lied, looking up into his face.

He met her gaze suspiciously, closed his book and put it back with the pencil in his breast pocket. "Well, you have to be down at the Children's Court at half past nine," he said, turning to go out. "Don't be late either. And I wouldn't try to deceive them down there if I was you. Anything you say can mean a lot to your young sister."

She heard his feet clump down the staircase and along the front passage. The door banged behind him.

Monnie! How in God's name could Monnie have got herself into a jam like this? Guinea pushed the thought away from her with horror. Get dressed, you mug, think about it later. She put a saucepan on the gas ring. Better get a cup of tea before you go out. Oh God, what am I going to do? Ring up the Marie Antoinette first? No, better get Claire before she leaves her flat. I might strike that nosey Ursula if I ring the salon.

She opened her lowboy and took out her best frock and the high-heeled Yank-snatchers that went with it. She stood, holding the frock in one hand and the shoes in the other. Holy mackerel! she couldn't wear those, the police'd stick

Monnie in for life if she appeared in those. She put them back and looked over her frocks. What did you wear to the Children's Court? She knew those policemen, let them see a bit of neck and a bit of knee and they'd run you in as soon as look at you. But one thing she did know, she'd have to get a move on. She took an old black frock from its hanger.

It was plain and neat, right up to the throat. Thank God she'd kept it, and the white Peter Pan collar was clean; that was a miracle. It must be two years since she'd had the damn thing on.

It was the kind of thing Monnie still wore. Trust Mum for that. In the name of heaven, how could Monnie ever have got mixed up with such a crowd? Oh, stop thinking and get dressed or you'll never catch Claire. There was a hat that went with the dress somewhere too. Where the hell could it be? She rummaged under the bed and found it in a dilapidated hatbox. God, what a stinker! Flat crown and shiny black straw with a sailor brim. Mum must have thought she was going to a funeral when she bought it for her. She unpinned the bunch of artificial field flowers she'd bought to brighten it up. It was years since she'd worn a hat. She put it on the back of her head and looked at herself in the glass. That wouldn't do, they'd run her in as well. She tipped it over one eye and hastily straightened it. She'd have to wear it dead straight even if it made her look like the whole Salvation Army.

Jeepers, she thought, examining herself in the mirror when she was dressed, I look like a morgue. Half past eight. No time for a cup of tea if she was going to catch Claire before she left home. She picked up her bag and clattered down the stairs.

The little shop next door was just opening. The grocer looked at her with astonishment and stopped smiling.

"Gee, Guinea," he said anxiously, "nothing wrong, I hope? Nobody dead?"

Guinea flickered her eyes and looked down soberly. Let them all think that, the old hens next door would tell him about the policeman as soon as they got the chance. "A great friend of the family," she said huskily. "I'm going to the funeral."

She dialled Claire's number and a voice came impatient and sharp. "Sorry, Claire," Guinea mumbled, "but I can't possibly get in till after lunch."

"Oh," Claire snapped, "we're frightfully busy. What's the matter?"

Guinea saw the grocer listening as he dusted the counter. "I got to go to a funeral," she lied.

"Oh, sorry," Claire's voice was softer, "it's not...one of the family..."

"An old friend of my father's and I've got to take Dad."

"Bad luck," Claire said sympathetically, "but don't worry, I'll fix things. Just get back as early as you can."

Guinea went out of the shop and breathed deeply with relief. That was over.

Twenty to nine. She'd just about pass out if she didn't have something to eat. There was a place on the corner opposite St Vincent's Hospital that was always open. She walked up Forbes Street, the westerly had dropped and the morning was radiant. The sky was clear and pure and a little wind stirred the camphor laurels across the street. Gosh, didn't spring make you feel good. Only yesterday morning she'd walked up here with Kim and they'd joked about finding Monnie. A hell of a fine joke.

She wished to God he was here now so she could have talked things over with him, but after last night she'd finished with Kim for good and all. Dammit, this was the kind of jam where he'd be so useful. She wanted to talk to someone, but who was there? You couldn't tell Bridie, she was as smug as a cat with two tails, just because she'd been lucky enough to marry the first man she fell in love with. You couldn't tell anyone at the Marie Antoinette, they moved in a different world. They'd been decent enough about Mary Parker but that was the sort of thing that could have happened to any of them. She went over them each in turn: Claire, Val, Deb, Alice, Ursula — you couldn't tell any of them about this sort of thing. Bessie...the thought of Bessie gave her a sudden hope. But no, Bessie had a heart as big as a pumpkin but she'd be no use to Monnie, she'd be just as scared of the police as she was herself.

It was twenty minutes past nine when Guinea came down the last steep pinch of Albion Street. The Children's Court stood gloomy and menacing on the corner of two dingy streets. She looked up at the drab brick walls, at the lower windows with their iron bars and the upper ones covered with a pattern of strong wire, and stood hesitating at the foot of the steps leading up to the forbidding porch. She felt the whole building was a trap that would close on her if she once went in the door. She knew them, they were out to catch you the moment you made a false step. She'd heard about lots of girls being picked up under the Vag, some of them the wrong girls too, like Monnie. But did the police ever go for the Pick-Pockette crowd? Not them. From what she could see at the SP, it wasn't vice they picked you for, it was for being poor and not having influential friends. You could get away with anything so long as you were rich. Look at that D.D.T., you couldn't imagine the Vice Squad breaking into her private suite and picking her up with Tickety-Boo. But he was a sailor, wasn't he? And D.D.T. wasn't fit to clean Monnie's shoes.

At the thought of Monnie, her throat went dry with fear. How in God's name could she ever have got into a place like that? Monnie was so shy, a bit of a sook really. Just the kind those mug policemen would pick on. She'd have to keep her wits about her to see she didn't get pooled herself.

She stood looking at the swinging frosted glass door beneath the notice GENERAL OFFICE, and peered down the narrow, twisted passage that led to the boys' shelter. She felt again the same panic that had gripped her in her room when she saw the policeman standing at her door. This was the drawing in of the net that was flung out to catch anyone who was out for a bit of fun. Unless you had cash behind you, the police and the Manpower had traps for you whichever way you turned.

She pushed open one of the doors and went through. Typewriters were pounding in the glassed-in offices on one side and a dispirited queue of men and women leaned against the wall waiting for their turn at the counter. Poor devils, having to pour out their stories in public with not a bit of privacy for anyone. She passed them and went out into the concrete courtyard where more people sat on wooden seats waiting. A half-obliterated notice informed her that No 2 Court was for offenders under eighteen. She hesitated a moment at the foot of the shabby staircase running up from the yard, and looked back at the men and women in the courtyard. They all looked strained and worried, they were probably in the same boat as she was. Perhaps their daughters or sisters had been picked up with Monnie.

The thought of Monnie set her mind off again on its treadmill. What was going to happen to her? How could they hide it from Mum and Dad? Dad'd never stand a shock like this. He thought the sun, moon and stars shone out of Monnie. You could trust him to try and understand, but Mum'd never forgive the kid. How could it have happened? She came back at each question to the unbelievable fact that Monnie was somewhere in this hideous building waiting her turn to come before the court. If she could only see her and talk it over and find out what had gone wrong!

In desperation she ventured up the inner staircase, hoping to find someone who could tell her something. But when she met the grey-haired matron, she was told to wait her turn downstairs and she would be called when she was wanted. She went down again, her feet dragging on the threadbare drugget. The red border on the carpet and the red stars in the mosaic shield at the entrance were the only bits of colour in the whole damn place. Why the hell couldn't they paint it up and make it a bit more cheerful? Just waiting here made you feel like a criminal. It was the bloodiest luck, getting hauled into a thing like this. If she didn't watch her step, the Manpower might get their claws into her and turf her out of her job at the SP and stick her into some damned mill like Monnie where you didn't get enough to keep body and soul together. Damn the lot of them!

Her short flare of rage petered out and she felt suddenly forlorn. A sob tightened her chest and she bit her lips to keep it back. She fled to a lavatory and shut the door behind her, and there, in the smell of stale urine and carbolic, the sobs broke from her uncontrollably. She was afraid, desperately, horribly afraid, for herself as well as Monnie, and alone with no one to turn to as she had never been alone before. She hadn't cried like this since Kim went away the first time, and her weeping left her spent and uncomforted.

She wiped her eyes and tried to powder over the marks of her tears, mechanically reading the scribbled obscenities on the yellow walls. Through the grimy glass louvres came the sound of voices from the prison yard of the boys' shelter. The thought of the high walls closing them in filled her with terror again and when she went out, her feet took her across the courtyard and half way down the entrance steps in a senseless panic.

She'd go to Byron now, she had his phone number. It was in the letter she'd got that morning. And from the way he was chasing her it was perfectly obvious she'd only have to play her cards carefully to bring him up to scratch. If she married him she'd be out of all this. Safe. She'd be rich too, and if she was rich she could send money to help Monnie, even if she was in America. The temptation took her down Commonwealth Street to a narrow, sunless lane running between a huddle of crowded houses.

Just ahead of her, a black-haired toddler staggered out from a door and went sprawling headlong on the dusty asphalt. She picked her up. The tiny brown face puckered and tears rolled out of the slant eyes. A young Chinese woman rushed out of the door and took the child in her arms, soothing her in a soft sing-song. She was lovely, Guinea thought, as together they coaxed the child and dusted her bruised knees. The woman thanked her and went in again with the child cuddled close. Guinea watched them go down the shabby hallway and through a dangling screen of beads.

She drew a long breath and turned and went slowly

back. There was no choice, she'd have to go through with it. Monnie had no one else.

Monnie waited her turn to go before the magistrate with the rest of the girls. The room was hot and stuffy, and the sun poured in a dusty beam through the wired window. The matron had warned them not to talk, but the air was full of low-pitched chattering. On one side of her, Betty was sprawled along the form with her head in Shirley's lap.

Monnie looked at the other girls sitting dejectedly round the walls and turned her face away from them with loathing. If they'd only keep quiet! What use was there in going over it all again? She leant her face against the wall and closed her eyes. If she could only get away somewhere on her own! From the time the policeman had pushed them into the Black Maria she'd never been alone for a minute. They'd been bustled into the police station and the policewoman had come and asked them questions. Somehow they got her to tell her right age but she didn't let on about home. She had a feeble sense of triumph. All she'd given was Peg's address and she knew Peg would never split on her.

Shirley stirred restlessly and yawned. "Why don't they bloody well get a move on?" she asked no one in particular.

A tall girl with silver-blonde hair swivelled round in her chair. "Why the hurry?" she asked in a soft, educated voice. "They'll come for you soon enough. Haven't you been here before?"

"No, I haven't," Shirley snapped.

"Well, if you had, I assure you you wouldn't be in such a hurry. When the magistrate's finished preaching to you, it all boils down to a choice of two evils — Parramatta or the Manpower."

"Aw, can it, Duchess," a brassy blonde beside her broke in. "You think you know all the ropes just because you been to a ladies' college."

"Manpower!" Shirley spat out of the side of her mouth. "They think they're Godalmighty, them Manpower bastards."

"Yeah!" a tall girl whispered, nervously pushing back her dark curls. "Look what they done to me. I been in a florist's shop ever since I left school and I was real happy; then along comes the Manpower and drags me out and sticks me in a flaming shirt factory in Redfern."

"Aw, you don't know you're alive," Shirley waved her aside. "I started at the mill before I was fourteen, I did, and I had to get a special permit to leave school because Dad was out of work. Started on fourteen-and-six a week, and that's a fact. Two-and-six a year rise, s'welp me God! and then when the war started and I had the chance of a job I could live on, there was the Manpower waitin' to shove me back."

"Live?" The tall girl laughed harshly. "I'd like to know how they expect you to live on the few lousy bob you get. I couldn't even afford to keep me old room on when they man-powered me and I had to doss in a stinkin' little back room down in Redfern to save fares. This here dump's a palace to it. The only view I had was out on the dunnikan. I'd like some of them Manpower fellers to try lookin' out on a dun-nikan week in and week out. And cold! Not so much as a gas jet you could make a cuppa tea over. Christ, could I do with a cuppa now!"

"Cuppa!" Duchess ran a comb through her long pale hair. "What could I do with a double Scotch!"

"That goes for me too," moaned the brassy blonde. "Gawd, am I dry! But I'd settle for just one cigarette."

There was a chorus of groans.

"If they try to stick me back in that flamin' shirt fac-tory," the tall girl went on passionately, "I'll cut me throat."

"Shirt factory? Huh! You don't know what work is till you've worked in a woollen mill," Shirley shivered in the hot room. "Freeze the backside off a brass monkey, it would, them winter mornings. Stuck there in front of the machine till your feet freeze off of you and your fingers are that numb you can't help making mistakes."

"You don't have to tell me," the tall girl interrupted. "I used to go to bed with me feet like lumps of ice, and then I couldn't sleep all night."

"Jeez," Betty roused herself, "you was lucky to have a bed at all. I come in from the country to get a job. I got the job all right, but could I get anywhere to live? I slept round all the ladies' rooms of all the stations in Sydney till they chucked me out. I even tried sleeping in railway carriages. Gawd, what a mug I was! All kinds of blokes offered to take me home. But not me. I wasn't that sort."

Monnie looked across at her with a flicker of interest. This was a new Betty. .

"Sure, it's tough," the tall girl took the floor again. "But what do they expect? I had to go and get all me meals out, and after paying ten bob a week for that rathole, I had a hell of a lot over to buy them with."

"You was lucky to have even a rathole to yourself," Betty took up her own story in the first pause. "One night when I was down in the ladies' room at Museum station, a real nice-looking woman offered to take me home with her. She said she could put me up..."

There was a burst of derisive laughter from the rest of the girls. "Aw Jesus," muttered one, "have we gotta hear how another good girl went wrong?"

"I was a good girl," Betty went on with monotonous vehemence.

"Yeah, we know. And before you knew where you was, in come a great big buck nigger!"

"No," she said soberly, "he was white and an Aussie."

"Oh, can it!" croaked a skinny redhead, picking at a sore at the corner of her mouth, "they're all the same in the dark, only the niggers pay you better. A girl I know's makin' a hundred quid a week in a place just a coupla streets up from this joint."

"Whew!" another whistled, "lead me to it!"

"OK. It's the fifth house in Chelmsford Lane — on the right from Campbell Street. Ask for Cissie and tell her Maisie sent you. I can't stick niggers meself, not at any price."

"They stink," a dreary voice murmured.

"All men stink. So what? You don't expect a Frankie Sinatra served up to you with a hundred smackers a week, do you?"

"Niggers?" a girl with a bleached fuzz of hair broke in. "What's wrong with them? Negroes are gents compared to a lot of white men I know."

One girl who had been silent looked up from the handkerchief she was twisting and untwisting between thin fingers with long scarlet nails. "You're just in the kindergarten," she jerked out. "You ought to try pervs."

"Hell," said the flashy blonde, "save me from pervs."

"Why not, they pay well and it's fun."

"Fun," groaned the tall dark girl. "Oh, Christ."

The nervy girl lifted her stringy handkerchief. "Have you tried them?" she asked. "Easy work and regular when they get to know you. I got a feller pays me ten quid and brings along a pigeon and all I got to do is wring its neck till he comes."

"Aw, shut up," hissed the blonde, "you make me vomit. Wringing a harmless bird's neck! Gawd, niggers are gentlemen to that."

The nervous girl spat contemptuously. "You don't know nothing," she said. "Why, there's a place down in Elizabeth Bay..."

Monnie tried to shut her ears against them but she could not, and her mind went down into depths so dark and filthy that her stomach heaved.

There was a peremptory knock on the door and Duchess shooshed them to silence.

After a moment's quiet the tall, dark girl took up her monotonous recital again. "What I'd like to know is, what do they expect a girl to do when she only gets a bit over a quid a week and pays ten bob for her room and can't even make a cuppa tea in it?"

"Aw, go and bag yer head! We've had all that."

"Hasn't anyone got a butt?" Duchess looked round with feverish, glittering eyes. "I'll give anyone this ring for a butt." She held out a thin hand weighed down with a heavy silver fraternity ring.

"Give you a butt for junk like that?" sneered the brassy

blonde. "Why, if you melted down all I've got at home you could make a jeep."

The dark girl went on in a rapid monologue. "I had to go out on the streets for meals, and the only people who offered me anything were Yanks. They fed me and took me to the flicks and to parties. They were swell guys."

"Too right, they're swell guys," snapped the brassy blonde. "I dunno what we're going to do without them."

"I wasn't doin' no wrong to nobody, was I?" the dark girl went on muttering. "If it was wrong, why didn't the police pick up the Yanks as well as me?" She looked round the room, glaring at each in turn.

"Aw, bullsh!" Betty snapped, "ain't yer learned yet men can't do no wrong? Has any one of yer ever had the man you was with pinched when you was picked up?"

"Jesus," murmured the redhead, getting up and stretching, "there'd be something to it if they locked the men up with you." She pressed her heavily painted mouth against the wall, leaving its scarlet imprint, and taking a lipstick out of her pocket she scrawled above it "To Huck from his Honey."

"Really, you should write a poem to him with a name like that," Duchess whispered in her soft, embittered voice.

"That's an idea," the redhead went on scribbling. Monnie stole a guilty glance at the writing and looked away quickly. The bleached fuzz got up laughing. She took out her lipstick and scrawled across the opposite wall "To Danny from Dakota! Come back quick you big gorgeous he-man!" She added a crude sketch that started a burst of laughter. It was quickly hushed when they heard footsteps outside in the corridor.

"You're telling me the Yanks are swell guys!" a little brown-haired girl said acidly. "The first guy I ever had was a Yank. He picked me up in Hyde Park and called me his little dream-girl and promised me the State Building if I'd sleep with him. So I beat it from home. That was easy, with Dad in the army and Mum back in a job and me with me own key, and I was three bloody weeks with him in his flat and he give me a pile of money and I just left it lyin' round in a drawer thinkin' he was on the level, and the day after the stinkin' louse went north, I find he's pinched all me dough. Oh yeah, them Yanks is swell guys all right." She rocked herself to and fro.

The tall, dark girl sighed. "I like them, I nearly married a Yank once."

The brassy blonde tossed her head and laughed. "Sez you?" she jeered. "I bet there ain't a girl in our game in Sydney today who didn't nearly marry a Yank one time or another. I nearly married a bloody squadron."

Betty laughed. "Sounds like Fay, don't she, Shirl? She was a Unit girl till the Unit beat it."

"Who's Fay?" the brassy blonde demanded.

"A pal of ours. Probably out in Long Bay by now. She's nineteen."

"Oh, well, she'll tell you the fun we had. Cripes, was I in the money then! And fun! Jeez, we was out every night dancin' and drinkin' at the kind of places I thought once I'd never get me foot inside." She stared dreamily into the beam of sunshine that had now dropped from the wall and lay in a pool on the shabby, scratched linoleum. Her grey eyes widened at the memory and showed the whites streaked with little red veins. "Four of us girls there was, and the squadron had a real nice house down there in Rose Bay near the water. Swell furniture and everything. The owners beat it to Blackheath when the Jap war started. If we hadn't of got evicted I wouldn't be here. If you kids are working on your own don't never go to the Meldrum in Liverpool Street. When the bloody Vice Squad come last night, the landlord stuck 'is 'ead out of the window, dropped them down a key, and told him the numbers of the rooms there was couples in. Charged yer a packet fer half an hour, too!"

"You want to try the Gem down in George Street," Duchess advised.

"I say," a little baby-faced girl broke in urgently, her eyes wide with fear. "What do they do to yer in there in the court if you're not sixteen?"

The others looked at her. "Tell 'em y'are," one said, "one lie more or less don't matter."

"I did, but they'll soon find out."

"Sixteen me fanny," the bleached-blonde scoffed, "what do they expect you to do? Wait till you're an old woman? This your first time?"

"Yeah."

"Who did they pick you up with?" another asked.

"My boyfriend," she whispered.

"A Yank?"

"Oh, no. An Aussie. We used to work at the same place till he got his call-up. He's goin' north any time now and we've only been sharing a room for two weeks."

"Well, if you want to keep him out of clink you'd better stick to your story you're over sixteen. They don't treat the Aussies like they treat the Yanks. The Yanks can get away with murder. Their MPs don't care a hoot if they've kidnapped you out of a perambulator. All they're interested in is that you haven't given 'em prickly heat or thrush. You take my advice and stick to the Yanks when they let you out on probation to your family."

"I haven't got a family."

"Then it's Parramatta for you, kiddo."

"But they won't do anything to him, will they?"

"Gawd," one of the girls laughed, "you're a sucker! It's yourself you ought to be thinkin' about. You don't look as though he paid you too well."

"Paid me!" The girl shook her head vehemently. "Oh no. I was working and shared expenses. He didn't pay me. I wouldn't of took it."

"What did you do it for?" the redhead said with a puzzled look.

"He's on final leave and my boyfriend, and I love him."

There was a complete silence, then the redhead's voice went up in a cracked, hysterical laugh. The bleached blonde bent over and slapped her face hard. "Shut up, you goon." The laugh stopped and the redhead looked at her, tears spilling down her cheeks. "Jeez," she whispered, "it was that funny.''

Baby-face shrank back in her chair. "I do love him," she whispered sullenly.

"Well, whether you done it for love or cash, you'll end up in Parramatta just the same."

"Parramatta," the redhead picked it up. "I made a break last time for all their stone walls and the bitches of wardresses, and I'll do it again. That bloody place gives me the pip. It's that old and dirty..."

"Parra!" Betty gave a loud raspberry. "If they stick me back in Parra, I swear I'll beat it again." She groaned and sat up, running her tongue round her teeth. "Ugh! Jeez! Hasn't anybody got a drink?"

"You'll get plenty to drink when they pop you back in Parra. Milk laid on," someone jeered.

"Milk!" Betty puked and shut her eyes again.

While they were chatting together, Monnie sat with her face turned to the wall, but although she kept her hands pressed to her ears scraps of their conversation filtered through until she felt that her mind was like a spider's web with all kinds of evil things caught buzzing in it. She remembered against her will loathsome words that she had tried not to hear but could not forget; words she had seen written on lavatory walls, words she'd overheard at the factory. Here they leapt into life as the girls mouthed filthy oaths, boasted of ugly encounters, and defied God and life and the Children's Court to do anything to make them change their ways.

There were footsteps in the corridor. The door opened and the matron came in. "Maisie Maxwell," she called. The skinny redhead got up sullenly and went out. As soon as the door shut behind her the chattering started again.

Monnie put her fingers in her ears under her loose falling hair and tried to shut out what they were saying. But it was no good, she could not keep her ears blocked, she had to listen for the matron's footsteps and each time the door was opened she sat up with quivering nerves, half hoping and half afraid that it would be her turn next.

The matron opened the door and led Monnie into the court-room. "That's the magistrate over there," she whispered.

Monnie dragged back and tried to hide behind her; she hung her head, imagining that everyone was staring at her. But no one seemed to notice she was there. The officials at the long table continued to talk among themselves, turning over papers and writing notes. The magistrate sat at a desk apart with another man beside him, pointing out something on a paper, and she watched him with growing interest until she realised that they were talking about her.

She looked away quickly and across the room the flutter of a raised hand caught her eye. It was Peg. Relief flooded through her. Peg was smiling at her, her chin thrust out as though there was nothing to be ashamed of. She was by her-self. So she hadn't told Mum. Monnie shook back her hair and smiled at her wanly and then had to bite her lips to stop herself from crying.

The two men at the desk were watching them. Suddenly both girls felt their glance, and dropped their eyes, the smiles fading from their faces. Although Monnie did not dare to look up again, the thought that Peg was there comforted her as much as if she had been able to put out a hand and touch her. Peg would not believe that she was bad.

The door opened and two men came in. Monnie shriv-elled in a flush of shame as she recognised the plain-clothes policemen who had picked her up last night. They would tell everyone how they'd found her...

When her name was called, the matron had to touch her arm and whisper: "Answer the court officer," before she realised they were speaking to her.

Yes, she was Monica Bernadette Malone. Yes, sixteen last March. Her answers were scarcely audible and the magis-trate asked her to come closer. The court officer standing beside him read from a paper. "You are charged with being a neglected young person exposed to moral danger."

She looked at him blankly, the words sliding off the sur-face of her mind.

"Do you know what that means?" he asked kindly.

"Yes," she whispered. Oh yes, she knew what moral danger was.

They'd arrested her at No 78A Elm Lane?

"Yes."

She listened while one of the policemen gave evidence in a flat voice. When he spoke of the upstairs back bedroom, all the blood in her body burned with shame. She saw the room again full of pink light, and the overpowering smell of the magnolia was in her nostrils, and rank sweat and the fumes of stale drink. She was naked again and cowering beside the sailor.... The policeman's voice went on monotonously.

"Yes," she whispered, when he'd finished. Yes, it was the truth, but it wasn't all the truth. She looked round wildly. If there was someone she could tell how it really happened, if they would only let her talk to Peg. If she could explain how they'd kept her there...

The court officer began to ask her questions quietly as though he really wanted to know the answers. How long had she been at No 78A Elm Lane? How had she come there? How long had she known these girls? Who had introduced her? How long had she shared a flat with them? Why hadn't she left them when she discovered what they were? Oh, they had actually locked her up, had they? Why had they done that?

Her voice grew lower and shakier. The story of the party and Calvin was dragged out of her in broken phrases. Then, how had she come to share a flat with these girls in the first place? What was she doing at that time of night on Central station? Where had she lived before?

Monnie hesitated and he asked the question again. She blundered, lying feebly. The eyes of the two men were watching her. She knew they knew she was lying. She looked from them across to Peg sitting taut and nervous. Her eyes came back to the magistrate, frantic with fear.

"Well, my dear?" he probed gently. She burst into a wild flood of weeping. To his further questions she only shook her head.

They called Guinea over to the magistrate's desk. Monnie listened in agony while the officer questioned her. Where did their parents live? She saw her hesitate and flush. He asked again, and she gave the address almost inaudibly and explained about Dad.

He turned back to Monnie. "I think we'd better wait until we have your mother here."

"Oh no," she whispered, "not Mum."

He arranged the papers in front of him with careful hands. "You have nothing to worry about. I'll talk to her first myself."

Monnie looked round wildly, she could never face Mum. The matron put an arm round her shoulders and the court officer beckoned her nearer the desk, but she was beyond caring what anyone thought and she struggled to break free. "I don't want to go home. Please don't send me home. I don't care what you do to me, but I can't go home." The matron held her arms, speaking soothingly. She broke into noisy sobbing.

When her sobs grew quieter she heard Peg's voice, uncertain and trembling, answering the questions the officer put to her. From a long way off she heard Peg telling about Mum's temper and the munitions job and Dad's wound from the last war and the dole and how wonderful he was at home, and Bridie and Jim and Mick and the twins and the row about Bob and the dance. And what a good girl Monnie had always been and how she had to leave school before she got the Intermediate because Dad had been sick and they wanted the extra money. And how the Manpower had sent her to the woollen mills though it was not the kind of job she wanted at all. They were clever, these men, they could get anything out of you, but it was all so ordinary that she wondered why they wanted to know.

The magistrate's voice, speaking to her, dragged Monnie back. "So you don't want to go back home?" She shook her head vehemently and whispered, "I can't go back."

"Have you any other relative you can go to?"

"She could come home with me," Guinea said eagerly.

The two men exchanged glances and spoke together in low tones. The magistrate looked up. "I'm afraid you're not old enough to take such responsibility and you live in the same locality where your sister was found. She'll have to go back to the shelter tonight until her parents are informed, and then we'll talk about it again when we're all here together tomorrow."

Monnie looked at him desperately. Surely, they'd never bring Mum here, she couldn't bear Mum to hear that dreadful evidence. She'd rather they sent her to Parramatta or even to gaol. . . . If they had to tell anyone, why couldn't it be Aunt Annie? Perhaps if she asked him. . . . She took a step towards the magistrate, but she could not get the words out.

The magistrate made a gesture of dismissal and the matron touched her arm and led her out of the room.

It was a few minutes to nine when Alice cautiously opened the door of the powder room and gave a quick glance around. She looked back to Mary. "It's all right," she said reassuringly. "Come along, there's no one here."

They slipped through the half-opened door and Alice drew a sigh of relief. "I was terrified Elvira would see us, she's down on this floor in the morning. But it looks as if she's finished here."

She looked round the powder room. Full-length mirrors in frosted silver frames were set in the pale blue walls, reflecting the easy chairs upholstered in blue brocaded velvet. A shaft of morning sun slanted down from between the drawn curtains and made a pool of light on the rich blue carpet. Mary stood just inside the closed door, one hand still on the knob behind her, the other hand gripping the handle of a little suitcase so tightly that her knuckles showed white. Her drab AWAS uniform looked out of place in the luxurious room.

"I'd rather not wait here, Alice," she said. "I'd rather not, someone's sure to come in."

Alice gave her a swift glance. She was so pale that the freckles stood out and there were deep blue rings under her eyes. "This isn't the place," she said impatiently. "You'll be quite alone in Bessie's little cubicle. Come and see."

She led the way through a curtained archway into a tiled room with elegant pedestal hand basins of soft blue, toilet tables and mirrors, and along one side, three discreet lavatory doors. At the end of the room, tucked between the wall and a lavatory, was a curtained cubicle. It was a gloomy little cavern, just large enough to hold a cupboard and small table and a couple of wicker chairs.

Alice switched the light on and drew the curtains together. "You'll be quite all right here. And anyway, you won't be long. Mrs Cavendish promised to ring through the address first thing this morning. And as soon as Claire gets the message I'll slip out to the Gloucester Room and ring you. I wouldn't dare ring you from the salon with Miss Cronin on the desk. And for heaven's sake be careful what you say, because it goes through the switch and in this place you never know who's listening in.''

"What if the woman in charge here comes in?''

"Oh, Bessie. You don't want to worry about Bessie, she doesn't open up here till eleven and you'll be away long before that. It's quite likely the doctor'll take you today. Mrs Cavendish said it was much easier to get an appointment with that sort of doctor than to get one with a dentist nowadays.''

Alice saw Mary wince and tried to give her some of the confidence of Cynthia's breezy assurance. "You really are silly to take it like that. I know it's horrible, but you should have heard Mrs Cavendish talking about people she knows who've had it done, and they're back at work next day, she says.''

Mary didn't answer.

Alice saw the tears well up into her blue eyes. Alice felt injured. After all, she'd had all the beastly business of trying to find out about somebody and everyone sniggering at her in the Marie Antoinette.

"You sit down here,'' she said, trying to infuse some warmth into her voice.

Mary sat down on the edge of the chair.

Really, she did look awful. She had never been pretty, but usually with that mop of short cut curly red hair and her pretty white teeth and blue eyes, people found her attractive. But now with her hair tucked up under her pork-pie AWAS hat and all those freckles she'd got since she'd gone north, she looked absolutely ghastly. Alice hoped to heaven she wasn't going to faint. That'd just about advertise everything to the whole SP.

Something in Mary's attitude sitting bolt upright on the edge of her chair with both hands gripping her suitcase on her knee, made Alice suddenly anxious.

"You're going to wait, aren't you?'' she insisted.

"Yes, I'll wait,'' Mary put the suitcase on the floor beside her.

"Well, I must fly now," Alice said as breezily as she could. "I'm sure it won't be long before I ring you."

She went out through the curtains and Mary heard the click of the outer door.

Alice needn't worry, she wouldn't go back on it now. It was just the big room that had frightened her, she couldn't have borne to wait where people were coming in and out. But here in this tiny cubicle with the drawn curtains, she was hidden. Whenever she was alone she had a strange awareness of her body as though its secret life was something quite apart from the tossing misery in her mind and the despair that clutched at her heart.

She was tired, tired to death. It was no good thinking about things any more, she'd done nothing else ever since she'd come down on Friday. Nothing could make any difference now. She had made up her mind, and though her body rebelled and her whole being shrank from what she must do, she knew she would go through with it. If only she could sleep...just for a few minutes until the phone rang and she had to start on all the practical details that would be necessary. The very thought of action appalled her. Her head reeled and her stomach heaved. She mustn't be sick. If she started being sick she would give everything away. She brought all her will to bear and forced down the rising nausea.

She took off her hat and lay back in the chair, resting her head against the high back. Her face in the frame of her red hair with the pale dropped lids was a mask of desolation.

Under her closed lids, her mind burned with a bright flame and the past leapt to life again. She was back in Townsville two years ago when she had first gone up there, a shy rookie in the filing department at headquarters. She had only been there a week when she met Frank at a Saturday night hop in the canteen. He'd just been posted there too and he didn't know any of the girls and they danced together most of the evening.

He teased her about her freckles and she laughed and asked what he'd advise a redhead to do who liked swimming, and he'd said he liked swimming too and he'd think it was worth it if he got like a cooked prawn every time he went in. He didn't of course, with his dark hair and olive skin, he just went a lovely tan. He came from Sydney too, and he'd told her all about the tidal pool he had helped his father to make at the bottom of the garden when he was only a kid. They lived up the Lane Cove River and he and the other boys around had made a fleet of corrugated iron canoes in which they used to go exploring round the foreshores.

"But weren't you frightened of sharks?" she'd asked.

"We weren't but Mum was."

Frank was never frightened of anything. That was one of the things she loved him for. "Don't be a 'fraidy cat," he used to say when she was frightened of the captain in her office and the AWAS lieutenant who was always nagging them in barracks. "You only make things worse for yourself if you're afraid."

She must try to remember that now. There wasn't really anything to be afraid of. Other girls had had to do it too and they'd been all right. There'd been that poor little Sergeant Wallace, her boy had just gone off and left her. But she'd come through all right.

She went back and savoured the joy of those early meetings with Frank. She'd told him all about her home at Croydon; he was easy to talk to and it had made her feel less homesick. He was a bit of a gardener himself, he said, when she told him about Dad's prize dahlias, and he loved the story of her wire-haired terrier Snub finding the brown snake under the house.

That was when he told her he was married. It was the second Saturday they'd danced together. He lived at Beecroft now because the sea air didn't suit his wife, but he missed the swimming.

It wasn't till they had been going together to the Saturday hops regularly for a couple of months that he said any more about Barbara. And then not much. Barbara and he had married when they weren't much more than kids. It was a mistake to marry young, one didn't know enough important things then — like him and Barbara. They'd drifted somehow, it wasn't really anybody's fault, but now that she was back at work since he joined up and had a girlfriend living with her in the house, she seemed to have found the solution for herself. But that didn't fix things for him. He was dead lonely.

They were walking along the beach in the moonlight when he told her. She was so sorry for him that she'd touched his sleeve and he took her hand and drew it through his arm. They had walked together a long way without speaking. How could any girl married to Frank make a life without him, she'd thought then. He was so gentle and considerate; not like so many of the fellows who thought they were just in the Army to have a good time and they didn't care who they had it with.

Frank wasn't like that. He said he liked her companionship and she made him forget he was lonely. She understood him so well and Barbara didn't understand him, that was the root of the trouble. And all the time he was talking, she wondered how any girl married to Frank could become so selfish in a few years. It wasn't that Frank was the complaining sort, he'd told her what a fine person his wife was and that what had happened wasn't anyone's fault, really. It was just one of those things.

It wasn't until he went home on leave at the end of six months that she really knew how she felt herself. She nearly died of loneliness. And when he came back and told her what a flop his leave had been, she burned with love and pity for him. He told her that Barbara hadn't even got leave from her job, and her girlfriend Phyllis was always round the place. She could hardly bear it for him. If he had been her husband, how differently she would have welcomed him!

Mary came back to the present with the sound of footsteps on the tiled floor outside. She heard a door shut and a bolt shoot, and opened her eyes in the bright electric light, blinking for a second, then looked at the telephone and down at her wristwatch.

It was ten o'clock. Goodness, she'd been waiting an

hour. What could have happened to Alice? Her throat contracted at the thought that something might have gone wrong. But she mustn't let her mind run away with her like that, she'd just have to go on waiting and try and concentrate her thoughts on something else. She picked up a magazine from the table and opened it. There was no sense in remembering. She was only torturing herself and nothing could come of it.

She turned over the advertisement pages deliberately, looking at the pictures and carefully reading the captions. But she didn't know the words she was reading.

Ever since Sunday afternoon when she knew she couldn't have her baby, it had been as though there were two Marys: one secret and real, the other a shadow that lived in the world of other people. Every moment, she was aware of her baby with one part of her mind; it was as though her nerves and muscles were braced to defend it against the decision that the other part of her mind had taken.

All last night and all Sunday night she had lain awake going over and over what Barbara had told her. But still she couldn't understand...How could Frank have lied to her? No, he hadn't lied, she was sure he hadn't lied to her. But then how could he have told her all those things about Barbara? Not that he said anything horrible, but only that Barbara didn't understand him and she didn't really care about her home or having children or any of the things you wanted if you loved a man. Oh, it was all like a horrible nightmare...

Had she been the one to blame? Had she just read into the things he said what she wanted to believe because she loved him? No, she knew she hadn't. But then why had Frank...?

She mopped at the tears that were running down her face and wiped a splash off her uniform. She held her closed fist against her mouth and bit into her knuckles to choke back the sobs. She mustn't cry. She mustn't. Crying would do nobody any good.

Nothing made any sense any way she looked at it. Going

to see Barbara.... She'd expected everything to be so different. It wouldn't be easy, but it had seemed simple. All she had to do was go to Frank's wife and tell her about their love and their baby and she'd divorce him. She wouldn't try to keep him when she didn't love him any more and he loved someone else.

It had all turned out so differently. When she got to the flat there were friends there, the girl who lived with Barbara and another girl on leave from the WRANS. She'd never thought of that happening. And when Barbara had welcomed her warmly when she heard she came from Townsville and knew Frank, and had taken her in to the others and they had asked for news of him, there was nothing she could do but try to play the part they expected of her.

"What rotten luck to have his final leave cancelled," Phyllis began. "It was just about the meanest thing I could imagine a superior officer doing."

"Probably just showing off his own importance," the WRAN spoke passionately. "I know these officers. Most of them never got more than six pounds a week in a clerk's job before the war, and when they jump up to a bit of rank in the Services they all try to show they're great men by throwing their weight around."

"I expect there really was some good reason for it," Barbara said quietly. "After all, the Army has to fight, and if the men are needed urgently, wives don't matter very much."

"It was damn bad luck, anyway," the WRAN said.

"Oh well, as Frank would say, 'It's just one of those things.'" Barbara turned to Mary. "He wrote that he was quite over his dengue. I do hope he really was better before he went away."

"Y-yes," Mary stumbled over the words, "yes, he was quite well."

She'd sat there staring from one face to another. How pretty Barbara was, and so sweet. Frank had never told her that he'd had to lie to Barbara about that leave. When he'd suggested their spending it together, she'd just taken it for granted that his wife and he had drifted so far apart that she wouldn't expect him to go home. She felt her hands were clammy and realised that she was holding them tightly clasped together.

"It was awfully bad luck getting dengue that leave before. I haven't seen him for nearly a year now, so you can just imagine how grateful I am for you coming to see me."

Barbara smiled at Mary and insisted on getting her a cup of tea in spite of her protests, because she said she looked tired. Had she had the dengue too? Barbara asked. No, she'd said, it was just the sudden heat wave and the uniform was awfully hot.

Barbara had made her take off her coat and she'd sat there in her khaki skirt and shirt, feeling as though a defence had been stripped from her. Then Barbara had gone from the room to get some snaps to show the WRAN and Phyllis had turned to Mary.

"I'm so glad you came, Barbara was awfully in the dumps about Frank going away without leave and now it won't seem so bad with you giving her news of him. Did he have dengue badly?"

"He was pretty sick, but he was all right when he left." They chattered on. Oh, would they never go and give her a chance to say what she'd come to say? She couldn't bear it much longer, every word made things harder for her.

"That accounts for his letters," Phyllis was saying. "He sounded awfully blue." She turned to the WRAN. "I think I'll walk to the railway station with you when you've seen the snaps and that'll give Barbara a chance to ask Corporal Parker all the questions about Frank she wants to."

"They're a couple of lovebirds, aren't they?" the WRAN laughed. "I always say I won't get married until I get someone as dotty about me as Frank is about Barbara. It was pretty tough him not being able to get down here."

"Rotten. And you should have seen all the preparations that last month, my dear! I needed a rest cure. We spent every night after we got home from work refurbishing this place. I personally kalsomined the kitchen, and Barbara recovered all the cushions in here and made the new curtains.

Pretty, aren't they?''

Mary couldn't help looking at them. "Lovely." She'd hardly been able to speak.

"And the poor darling spent all her lunch hours queuing up for records. She managed to get a Schubert trio Frank's been wanting for years. And she got the car registered again and managed to get hold of some extra petrol tickets... Yes, it certainly was tough. And just to make everything as bad as possible mother got ill and I had to go home. From the look of Barbara when I came back she must have cried herself to sleep every night.''

Barbara came in with an envelope in her hand. "I suppose you've seen them," she said to Mary, taking out some prints and handing them to the WRAN.

Yes, she had seen them. He must have sorted out the snaps of himself alone and sent them down to Barbara, and he must have written to her before he left then. That was the film she took of him on that last leave "so we can tell our children all about how their brave Daddy went off to the wars," he had said. She reminded him of that when she wrote to tell him that they were going to have a baby. He had taken a film of her too and there were several of them together. She had the photographer's wallet with all the snaps in the satchel on her lap.

The WRAN handed them back. "Well, I'd say you had nothing to worry about, Barb. He may have lost a bit of weight but he looks awfully well.''

"He does, doesn't he?" Barbara had smiled fondly at the snaps before she put them back in the envelope. "That was the last time I heard from him," she said. "Has anyone on the station had any news?''

"No. No one's heard from his unit at all," Mary's hands were trembling. She clasped them together tighter. She was afraid she was going to break down and cry in front of them all.

"Oh well," Barbara said, "I just keep on writing and hope my letters will catch him up somewhere.''

The two girls had gone at last and Barbara came over

and sat beside her on the lounge and smiled at her and said, "Now we can really talk. It was nice of you to come out and see me. Have you been up there long?"

"Two years."

"The same as Frank. Well, I expect you know each other quite well."

"Yes."

Barbara glanced up at her. "Are you sure you're all right?" she asked. "You look terribly pale."

Mary couldn't answer. She could feel Barbara staring at her. She put her hand on Mary's and when she spoke again, her voice was different. "Please, my dear, you haven't come to tell me there's something wrong with Frank, have you?"

Mary shook her head. She tried to speak but her lips were quivering and her eyes filled with tears. She fumbled in her pocket for a handkerchief.

"Well, what is it then?"

"I...I...didn't know you loved him." The words came out at last. She felt Barbara draw back, but she couldn't look at her.

"You...you mean you didn't know I loved Frank?" Barbara's voice was incredulous. It seemed a long time to Mary before she spoke again and there was a new harsh note. "I really think you'd better tell me what you came here for."

"I...I...Frank and I..." Mary could get no further.

Barbara took her hand away and looked at her in horror. "Are you trying to tell me you're in love with Frank?"

"I...I...I didn't know about you."

"You're not trying to tell me you didn't know he was married."

"Yes. But...I thought it was all over between you. I didn't know what you were really like." Mary buried her face in her hands.

Barbara had dragged the whole story out of her, and as she told it, it was no longer the same. It was stupid and ugly like something that had happened to someone else. The leave when he was supposed to have had dengue, he and Mary had gone with a party to Magnetic Island.... And the final leave when he'd borrowed a friend's car and they'd gone up to a little village beyond Ayr and they had been lovers and he'd promised her that they would be married as soon as Barbara would divorce him.

"How do I know all this is true?" Barbara asked.

Mary had fumbled in her satchel for the snaps and handed them over to her without a word. She'd looked for a long time at one of them both with their arms round each other's waists that the bus driver had taken.

"Then he didn't have dengue?"

"No."

"And his final leave wasn't cancelled?"

"No."

"I suppose you suggested he should make those excuses to me."

"I never knew he'd made them until I came here today. He just said you would be glad if he stayed away."

When Mary looked up, Barbara's face was white and she was biting her lips, but she went on asking questions in a level voice.

"I didn't know about you, really I didn't. And I know Frank thought you didn't love him any more. He said you were quite content here with your little flat and your job and your girlfriend and he didn't have any part in your life any more."

"And you believed him?"

"Oh yes. I love him. . . and he wants to marry me."

"He wants to marry you, does he? Are you sure it isn't you who want to marry him?" Barbara's voice was scornful.

"You've told me your story, now I'll tell you what I think really happened." Barbara fixed Mary with her brown eyes. "You took advantage of a lonely man. You Service girls are all the same, you rush madly into uniform and leave the dull jobs at home for people like me. All you're out for is the glamour and a good time. And it doesn't matter to you who's hurt."

Mary tried to protest, but she brushed her aside. "I know how it is. I've seen it happen too often. If you want a man you go all out after him; you've got nothing to lose and you think you might gain something...you might even get someone else's husband if a man's too soft to see through your game. Well, don't come asking me for sympathy, because you'll get none. If you think I'm going to divorce my husband because you got round him when I couldn't be with him and he's got himself tangled up with you, you're making a big mistake.''

Mary had flared out at that. "I didn't need to get round him. He loves me and I love him and if you're as good a wife as you pretend to be, why did you go on with your job when he came down that first leave from Townsville, and why did you keep your girlfriend in the house?''

"Are you sure he didn't tell you as well, that my boss was ill and he'd been so good to both of us that I couldn't let him down, and that Phyllis came here after her own job to cook for us and look after the flat and went and slept up the road at a friend's so that he and I could be together every minute we could get? Didn't he tell you that, too?''

Mary shook her head. "He said he thought that having a job was more important to you than keeping house for him.''

"I suppose, then, he didn't explain that I wanted to join up, but I didn't because it would have meant giving up our home and he got so down in the dumps at the thought of losing it and his precious garden, that I went back to the office job? And he didn't tell you as well that I live on my salary and bank every penny of my allotment so that he'll have that to add to his deferred pay when he comes back?''

"No...no, he didn't tell me those things, but they don't count when a man would rather have children.''

"He didn't tell you then..." Barbara's voice broke, but she forced herself to go on speaking. "He didn't tell you that when we first got married I wanted a baby more than anything in the world, but he wanted a car and we couldn't afford both...so he had his car and I had to wait for my baby? Did he tell you that?''

"He said...you'd put off having a baby...''

"Oh." Barbara stared at her for a moment, then she got up abruptly and went over to the window. She had stood there with her back to Mary and her shoulders were shaking. Mary watched her. She wished she could do something, but there was nothing anyone could do.

At last Barbara turned round and came over and sat beside her again. Her lashes were still wet and her voice was unsteady. "I'm sorry for what I said about Service girls, I don't really think you're like that at all, it was just you took me off my balance."

"I'm sorry a...about everything."

"I can't understand it. It's not like Frank, he's always been so gentle. I've never known him to do anything cruel in his life before. And now to hurt us both like this..."

"I'm sure he never meant to hurt either of us."

"But he has, and he's hurt you more than he's hurt me, because when he comes back he and I will take up our lives together again...but yours is just another wartime romance."

She stared at Barbara without taking her words in. But it couldn't be just another wartime romance. Not when they were going to have a baby. Then something in her mind had suddenly clicked. No...it was she who was going to have a baby. Barbara didn't know. Barbara didn't even guess and however much he wanted to, Frank couldn't come to her.

"Do you mean you still want him?" she said. "Even though you know about him and me?"

"Yes. I still want him. You see, I love him and our lives have been bound up together for a long time. We were married three years before he went away and we were happy, and whatever he's done when he's been lonely, I know he still loves me."

"But if you were making a mistake and he...didn't. Wouldn't you divorce him?"

"I can't answer that until I know whether I am making a mistake. Even if he told me himself that he wanted a divorce I would have to wait till the end of the war to make sure it wasn't just the loneliness and us being apart and him having no home. You must see that."

While Barbara was speaking Mary's tears had dried. She had suddenly seen what she must do. But she couldn't speak yet.

Barbara leaned over to her and said gently. "I know you didn't do this to me deliberately and I am so sorry for you." She put her hand on Mary's. "I'm sorry for both of us. And there's nothing I can say that will help you, and you can't help me. We've just each of us got to face up to it in our own way."

Mary got up. "I'm going now," she said.

"What are you going to do?"

"I know what I'm going to do." She walked over to the door and half turned. "You won't have to worry about me any more."

She went out of the house without looking back, almost running down the neat little path between the garden beds. All she thought about was getting away from Frank's wife, and she turned down the street neither remembering or caring which way she was going.

Yes, she knew what she must do. She couldn't have her baby. No matter how much she wanted it, she could never have a baby of Frank's. She could never see Frank again. He loved her, she knew he loved her, but you couldn't have a baby just because you loved a man...you couldn't do that to his wife who loved him too. You couldn't do that to your baby...

She walked until it was dusk and the first stars were coming out. It was only when the lights came on in the streets that she remembered where she was and caught the train for home. The family was at church and she went straight to the bedroom that she shared with Alice and went to bed, pretending to be asleep when Alice came in.

But she didn't sleep all that night. Her mind circled round and round and she went over and over again her talk with Barbara, and when she was lying still wakeful in the dawn she had a half-sleeping, half-waking fantasy in which she told Barbara about the baby, and the divorce was all arranged so that she and Frank could marry when he got his next leave.

When Alice got up to get ready for work, Mary woke sluggish and weary. In the morning all the fantasy of the night slid away and she only knew that she must ask Alice to help her. She could see Alice's face now when she had told her. At first it was immensely relieved, then full of anxiety. She was more frightened than Mary herself and she'd been awfully good offering her that money she'd saved for her trousseau and to try and find somebody.

Alice! Mary came back to the present with a start. Alice hadn't rung...she couldn't have got the address yet. What could have happened? It was nearly eleven o'clock — if she didn't ring soon Bessie would be in and catch her there. She couldn't stay much longer, but where could she go so that Alice could get hold of her? Perhaps she really ought to ring the Marie Antoinette and find out what had happened. She stretched out her hand to the phone...No. She couldn't do that. She'd just have to go on waiting.

Mary started when she heard footsteps coming across the tiled floor towards the cubicles. She sat perfectly still holding her breath. The curtains parted and a short, stout woman looked in. "Oh," she smiled pleasantly. "Were you waiting for me?"

"I...I...You're Bessie aren't you?"

"Yes, I'm Bessie."

She came in and put a bunch of flowers down on the table.

"I'm Mary Parker, Alice's sister. She said you wouldn't mind me waiting here a while."

"That's all right, dearie. You wait here as long as you like. I'll be glad of a bit of company."

"I thought I'd be gone before you came. Alice was going to ring a message through that I have to wait for, but she hasn't yet."

Bessie glanced at the girl's swollen eyes and pale face.

"You're quite welcome to stay." She got out her overall and low-heeled shoes from the cupboard and began to change. "Don't take any notice of me, dearie."

Mary turned over the pages of the magazine on her lap in embarrassment. It was awful of Alice, leaving her here till Bessie came...but probably she hadn't got the address yet. Supposing Mrs Cavendish hadn't been able to get it...then what would she do? Who else could she ask? There was no one; she had been all over that on Sunday night before she had finally asked Alice to help her. Panic began to rise in her and her head felt light and dizzy.

Bessie finished lacing up her flat-heeled shoes. "Me feet hurt something awful in me best shoes," she remarked cheerfully as she straightened up. She stopped dead as she caught sight of Mary's white face. "What is it, dearie? Don't you feel well?"

"It's nothing. I'm quite all right."

"But you're as white as a sheet. Do you feel faint?"

"I do...a little, but I'll be all right in a minute. Please don't worry."

"You put your head between your knees while I get you a glass of water," Bessie ordered kindly.

Mary bent forward and let her head hang. It was so much easier to do as she was told.

Bessie was back with the water immediately. She raised Mary's head and saw that the colour was coming back to her face. "Here, drink this." She held the glass to her lips.

"Thank you, I feel much better now. That was silly of me."

"Are you sure you're quite all right? Do you often have fainting attacks like this?" Bessie was looking at her with shrewd eyes.

Mary drew several deep breaths and felt better. "I don't know what could have come over me, I've never fainted in my life. It must be that I'm very tired."

"Poor lamb, you look it too, with those big blue rings under your eyes. Now you just sit back and rest while I arrange these flowers. Pretty, aren't they?" She held out the bunch to Mary.

"They're lovely. Where did you get these sun orchids?"

she asked.

"Up Middle Harbour. I took my two little grandchildren for a picnic in the bush yesterday and they picked this bunch of flowers, so I just had to bring them in. We went over by bus to the Roseville Bridge and there were lots of them in the bush there."

"My grandfather used to live over there, right on the edge of Kuring-gai Chase and he loved the bush flowers. Alice and I used to spend our holidays there and we used to got out with him looking for swarms of bees and come back with simply armfuls of flowers for Granny."

"You were a lucky girl. That's what I'd like for Carry and Jean, my boy's little girls. They're seven and five, and they just love the bush, but they never get a chance to get into it unless I can take them like yesterday."

The strident ring of the telephone interrupted her and she reached for it at the same time as Mary put out her hand. They both hesitated.

"You take it," Bessie said. "It's sure to be for you." She slipped out of the cubicle as Mary lifted the receiver.

"Yes, yes it's me, Alice. What did you say? Not till tomorrow. What? Me ring? Oh! no I couldn't. . . . All right then. Forty-five pounds? Oh dear, that's a terrible price. Just a minute." With shaking fingers she undid her satchel and got out a pencil and piece of paper. "Yes, I've got a pencil." She wrote down a telephone number. "I'll ring. Thanks awfully." She heard the phone click in her ear and put the receiver back mechanically, while her eyes fastened on the number scrawled on the scrap of paper.

She was to ring between twelve and twelve-thirty. There was nearly an hour to put in. Oh, dear, why couldn't the doctor take her today? They'd said it was so easy to get an appointment and now she'd have to hang round till tomorrow. . .another twenty-four hours.

Bessie put her head round the curtains. "All serene?"

"Yes, thank you, I'll be going now. Thank you for being so kind." Mary got up, but her knees were unsteady and she had to hold on to the side of the chair.

"Just you sit right down again." Bessie put a firm hand on her shoulder and pushed her gently back. "You're in no fit state to go yet. Now I'll tell you what I'll do. I'll make us both a cup of tea. It's just my morning tea time and if you'll have a cup with me that'll be real nice." She did not wait for Mary to answer, but opened her cupboard and got out two cups and saucers and a tin of biscuits. "There's nothing like a cup of tea when you're feeling a bit peaky. How do you like it?"

"Weak please, and no sugar."

"My boy always says the tea they get in the army's so stewed he doesn't recognise it for the same drink when I make him a cup at home."

Bessie poured the tea, put a cup on the table beside Mary and sat down in the other chair, taking some knitting out of her bag. "It's a pullover for my little granddaughter," she explained. "I get quite a bit done here, especially in the mornings when there aren't many people about."

Mary picked up her cup, but the hot smell of the tea made her stomach heave. She put it down again.

Bessie pushed the biscuits towards her. "Too hot? Some people can't drink it hot. Now, I like mine just as it comes out of the pot. Real scalding."

Mary felt Bessie's eyes on her and raised her cup again, but her throat contracted and she shuddered. "I'm afraid I am a bit off colour. I think I must be bilious."

Bessie let her knitting fall into her lap and looked at the girl anxiously. "Would you like a drop of soda now? Might settle your stomach."

Mary shook her head and pushed the cup away jerkily, so that the tea slopped over. At the smell of it, the retching that she had been holding down all the morning burst its way up. She clapped her hand over her mouth and ran out to the basin.

Bessie followed her and stood beside her while she vomited, then wiped her face gently with a damp towel and led her back to the cubicle and sat her down in the chair. She poured out a glass of water without speaking and handed it

454

to her. Mary drank a little.

"You poor little kid," Bessie smoothed back her hair tenderly. "It's not my place to poke my nose into your business, but it's more than a bilious attack you've got, isn't it?"

Mary averted her face.

"If it'd be any help to you to talk to someone who's old enough to be your mother, well, dearie, Bessie's had a lot of knocks from the world and she'd understand. I know just how you feel. You think you're the only one this has happened to — don't you? But if it's any comfort to you, I've been through it too."

Tears splashed down the girl's cheeks. Bessie put an arm round her shoulders and felt Mary relax against her.

When the first burst of weeping was over Mary straightened up and looked at her shamefacedly. "I...I didn't mean to do that. I'm...I'm sorry."

"Of course you didn't. But there are times when we can't help ourselves and no matter how much we cry the tears never seem to dry up." Bessie leaned forward and patted her hand. "You don't have to tell me what's wrong with you, dearie, not after having two babies of my own and half my friends' in a manner of speaking. That's what's worrying you, isn't it?"

Mary nodded.

"Well, there's many a girl thought the world'd come to an end just because she got into trouble, but it hasn't and in good time she's had a home of her own and a good man and all the babies she wanted."

"But it's worse than that. He'll never be able to marry me."

"Mine couldn't either. It was one of the fellows in the boarding-house where I was working and I didn't know he was married."

Mary looked at her with swollen eyes.

"I was keeping myself and sending money back home, so I just had to get rid of it so I could go on working."

"Was it very bad?"

"Bad enough. I didn't have anyone to turn to except a

girlfriend that put me on to the woman who done it — and a horrible dirty old thing she was too. And when it was over — well, we won't talk about that. Then I had to go back to me room at the boarding-house that night and be up at six next morning as if nothing had happened! But they do things much better nowadays, everything nice and clean. I've known a lot of girls who've had it done and been back on the job next morning and not one bit the worse for it."

"Oh, it's all so horrible."

"Well, I suppose you're right. Lots of people think it's wicked as well, but what's a girl to do? The man goes scot free and the girl gets all the blame and loses her job, so how could she look after the baby even if she had it? I didn't like doing it, but there wasn't any other way out."

"I don't know how men can be so cruel."

"Well, they're not all like that. It was only a year after that I met my old man and we got married and Ken and Nance came along and there wasn't a happier woman in the world, even if Dad did take a drop too much at times. And after what he'd been through in the last war you couldn't blame him for that either."

"But didn't he mind about the other?"

"I didn't tell him. Why should I? It don't do nobody any good telling them that sort of thing."

"Oh...I'd...feel I had to."

"Get along with you," Bessie said, smiling at her. "I knew he'd had other girls and I didn't ask him about them — not that he was the kind to leave any girl in the lurch — so why should I tell him about me?"

"I hadn't thought of it that way."

"But we don't want to talk about me. What about you, dearie? What are you going to do?"

"I'm going tomorrow."

"Tomorrow. Have you got hold of someone good to do it?"

"Yes. I've got the address of a doctor."

"That's fine. Have you told your mother?"

Mary shook her head. "I couldn't do that."

"Well, where are you going to afterwards?"

"I'm going back to the Women's Service Club."

Bessie drew in her breath disapprovingly. "That don't seem right. Who's going with you when you have it done?"

"Alice."

Bessie rolled up her knitting and put it firmly on the table, then she leant over and took Mary's hands in hers. "I'll tell you what you're going to do. You're going to get Alice to bring you over to my place when it's all over and you can stay the night with me."

"Oh, I couldn't do that."

"Why couldn't you?"

"I couldn't put you to that trouble."

"It'd be no trouble, my dear. I'd feel as though I was looking after a daughter of my own. Nance is just about your age, and I've got a bed she always uses when she's on leave, and I'd take it as a real kindness if you'd come over tomorrow and spend the night in Nance's bed."

"You are kind, Bessie." Her tears started to flow again.

"Nothing of the sort. I'll love to have you. Now dry your eyes and no more crying."

Mary looked at her watch. "I'll really have to be going now. I've got to ring the doctor between twelve and twelve-thirty, and I'd better go down to the GPO and do it from a public phone."

Bessie looked at her anxiously. "Are you sure you're all right to go out?"

"I'm still a bit shaky, but I'll be all right when I get out in the air."

"Well, I'll give you a towel and you go and wash your face. I just want to slip out a moment and I'll be back by the time you're ready."

Bessie peered cautiously along the corridor, then slipped across to the door of the Madrid Lounge. What that poor little thing needed more than anything was a nip of brandy to settle her stomach. Tubby came on duty at twelve and if she could have a word with him he'd get it for her, but she would have to keep her eyes skinned for Old Mole. At the

457

door of the Lounge she almost collided with Blue, who was just coming out. He gave her a cheerful hail.

"How're yer doin', Bess?"

"Oh, Blue," she whispered urgently, "is Tubby in there?"

"No. He's round serving a hen party in a private room. Old Mole's in there, she's having a nerve war this morning. Anything I can do for you?"

"Well," Bessie hesitated, "there's a little girl in the powder room, Alice Parker's sister. You know, up in the salon."

"Oh, the snooty one?"

"That's right, but Mary's not a bit like her. She's got a touch of food poisoning, I think, and she's been terribly sick. I thought if I could get a nip of brandy for her it'd settle her stomach and she'd be able to get home. That's why I'm looking for Tubby."

"I'll fix it. You hop back to the powder room and I'll be along in two ticks."

When Bessie got back to the cubicle Mary was powdering her face.

"My!" Bessie exclaimed, "you do look different. Wonderful what a bit of lipstick does for a girl. Now turn round and I'll just give your uniform a good brush down and you won't know yourself."

Mary turned obediently and Bessie brushed her khaki jacket and skirt, standing off to admire her as she put on her hat. "Gee, you've got pretty-coloured hair," she said. "Just wait a minute, there's a curl loose here at the back." She slipped in a bobby pin and patted the curl into place.

A soft whistle came from the door of the powder room.

"That'll be Blue." Bessie hurried out.

Blue took a small flask out of his pocket. "Here y'are. Tubby gave me a couple of nips. Everything all right?"

"Blue, you are a darling. How much is it?"

"You don't have to worry about that, Bess. Tubby says it's on the house. It won't break them. Anything else I can do for you? I got a few minutes yet before I take over."

Bessie looked anxiously back towards the cubicle and dropped her voice. "She's been crying, Blue, and she looks an awful mess, and I don't want her to risk running into anyone. If you wouldn't mind taking her out the service way ...I can't leave this floor now the lunch people are beginning to come."

"Righto! I'll just wait round the corner out of sight. I don't want to turn the popsies off when they come cantering along to put their faces on."

Bessie went back to the cubicle and poured some brandy into a cup. "Blue got this for me. Drink it up and put the rest in your bag, and if you feel faint you take a nip. Blue's going to show you the back way out so you won't run into anyone. And don't you worry about tomorrow. I'll send a message up to Alice to come and see me and I'll fix everything with her so she can bring you straight round to my place after it's all over."

"I don't know how I can ever thank you enough."

"Well, don't you try. Just think I'm a selfish old woman that loves a bit o' company. Now come along."

Blue was waiting in a side corridor.

"This is Mary Parker, Blue, and this is Blue Johnson, Mary. You go along with him and he'll look after you." She pressed Mary's arm affectionately. "See you tomorrow."

Blue took Mary's case from her and smiled down into her red-rimmed eyes.

"It's awfully good of you."

"The pleasure's all mine." He looked at her bright curls under the brim of her Service hat. "I bet they call you Blue too."

"They do, as a matter of fact."

"I knew it. Never leave us redheads alone. Jealous of our personality, that's it." He opened the door of the service lift for her. "This way. I'll take you out by the staff entrance, then you'll be sure not to run into any of the Gestapo. There's always somebody snooping round to see what you're doing and tell you not to. It's worse than the army. I suppose it's the same with you women soldiers?"

"It is rather. I can never quite understand why they have so many regulations. Nobody could possibly keep them all."

Blue laughed. "Good old AR! We always reckoned the blokes at base made 'em up just so as they could keep themselves in cushy jobs. When you're in the front line nobody takes any more notice of them, but the closer you get to headquarters, the more there are, till when you hit base proper the regulations are thicker than barbed wire entanglements and just as much nuisance."

He opened the door of the lift at the ground floor and stood aside to let her step out. "This way, corporal, I was a two-striper meself once." He took her arm and led her down the steep narrow staircase to the top of the service steps.

Mary put out her hand to him. "Thanks awfully."

"That's all right." Blue held her hand. "Anything I can do for you at any time just call on me. Any friend of Bessie's is a friend of mine — particularly another Blue."

Mary smiled, blinking back the tears.

"Chin up," he said, "and remember, 'old soldiers never die'."

She turned away and hurried down the steps.

Blue watched her go down the laneway. At the corner she turned and looked back. He raised his hand in a salute and saw the quick lift of hers in reply.

Claire jammed the receiver down on the telephone and snatched the appointment book out of Ursula's hand. "Damn that D.D.T. bitch!" she said furiously. "Who does she think she is?"

Ursula shrugged her shoulders. "Well, she is the daughter of one of the hotel directors," she said in a superior manner, "and while you mightn't have any respect for me or my feelings, I do think you ought to be careful what you say about her. One day someone will report you, and then where will you be?"

"Don't tell me you're joining old Mother Molesworth's Gestapo, because otherwise I fail to see how anything that's said here is ever likely to get back to D.D.T."

Ursula sat down at the desk and began to rearrange the flowers. "Just because you happen to be in charge of the salon, there's no need to be offensive."

"And just because you happen to be in Mrs Molesworth's pocket there's no need for you to suck up to every guest in the SP. After all, we have to do the work, not you. So please try to remember that in future, will you?"

Claire went down the corridor, stopping to call Val from a cubicle. "Listen, Val, I'm awfully sorry, but D.D.T.'s just rung down again and insists on having her hair set up in her room. Old Mole says someone has to go immediately. Guinea's not in and I can't send Alice — it's quite obvious to anyone that she's been howling her eyes out, and anyway, she's planted Mary down in the powder room so she can let her know the doctor's phone number as soon as Cynthia rings. So I'm afraid it will have to be you."

Val's eyes flashed and her mouth set stubbornly. "I won't go, Claire. That's flat. I had all I'm ever going to have of D.D.T. on Saturday morning. Why can't Deb go up? She can do a hairset and she always seems to miss out on the dirty jobs."

Clare tried to control her irritation. "This place is getting like a madhouse. Half of the staff moping round like wet hens — Guinea away, and Deb can't go, she's absolutely flat out." She tried to speak persuasively. "It'll be different this morning, Val, and it won't take any time." She watched Val's face.

"I'm sorry," Val said briefly, "but I'm not going. If you like to give me an order, OK. You're in charge of the salon. But if you do, I'll leave here and now."

Oh, God, thought Claire savagely, I'll have to go myself. No use getting Val het up and losing her. She's too good for that.

"If that's the way you feel I suppose I'll just have to go myself." She handed Val the appointment book. "Put that back on Cronin's desk, will you? You'll have to share my appointments between you while I'm up there. I'll fix it up with Deb and Alice to do Mrs Harvey and Mrs Menzies."

Val took the book. "I don't like doing this to you, Claire," she said apologetically, "you're always so decent, but I just couldn't take it, and that's the truth. I'd rather leave than go near D.D.T. again."

"All right, all right, only the three of you will have to work like flaming hell down here. I'll see the others and get along. Get me a hand dryer, will you, and all the things I'll need."

She went into her office and unlocked the side cupboard of her desk. She'd have a brandy before she went up. No, better not — too risky. If D.D.T. smelled it on her, she'd be as likely to report her as not.

Claire stopped at the desk on her way out. "Miss Cronin, I'm expecting an urgent phone call from Mrs Cavendish. If it comes through while I'm upstairs, please call Miss Parker to take it. It's rather complicated and anyone else will make a mess of it, so don't forget, will you?"

Ursula murmured something unintelligible and stared after her suspiciously.

Claire stood outside the door of Denise D'Arcy-Twyning's suite and knocked twice. Nobody answered. Probably nobody had heard, judging by the laughter and the squeals that were coming from inside. Nice to belong to the class where you could hold parties in your suite at 11 am and send orders down for personal attendance. She balanced the tray on her left arm and knocked loudly a third time. The laughter and chattering stopped for a minute and she heard a faint "Come in."

She turned the handle and went in.

Denise's voice floated to her from the bathroom. "You'll just have to wait a teeny-weeny minute, I'm afraid, I'm still in the bath."

A burst of giggling followed this, as though she'd said something witty. A head of burnished red curls came round the bathroom door. Claire recognised another of the Pick-Pockettes.

"Oh, it's you, Miss Jeffries," the girl said. "Denise didn't expect you yet. She won't be frightfully long."

"Not a minute longer than I can help," Denise called, provoking more giggles. "Just get the things ready, will you, while I'm rubbing myself down, so you won't keep me waiting." Then she added, as an afterthought: "Oh, just come in here a minute, will you?"

Claire went to the bathroom door. Denise floated like a pale flower in the green bath. The steamy air was full of the scent of pine needles and cigarette smoke.

"Take my glass, will you, Melva," Denise held up a half-filled glass of sherry, "while I explain to Miss Jeffries just how I want my hair done."

Melva leaned over from the edge of the bath where she was sitting and took the glass. Claire's mouth watered at the sight of it. What a fool I was not to have had that brandy, they'd never have smelled it on me in this reek.

"Take a good look how the Marquise's hair is done, Miss Jeffries," Denise ordered.

The Marquise de Chesne blew a smoke ring and pivoted slowly on the lid of the water closet, turning her head from side to side. Claire recognised her as Colonel Parmetter's daughter Cheryl, who had dazzled Sydney with the splendour of her marriage to a broken down Free French Marquis a year before, and whose engagement to a wealthy American was now being featured in the more lurid weeklies, side by side with reports of her divorce. She could afford to look like something out of *Vogue*! Poppa must have made a packet out of those war contracts in the Middle East, though the inquiry never succeeded in sheeting anything home to him. Too many big shots involved, they said.

"Cheryl's just come back from America," Denise explained, "and I want my hair done like that. She's flying to Melbourne tonight, so she doesn't mind, do you, Chel?"

The Marquise assured Denise, in her newly acquired drawl, that she didn't mind in the least.

It'll take hours to do, Claire thought angrily. I'll be up here till lunchtime, damn her. "Very smart and most attractive," she agreed sweetly, "and it suits the Marquise's classic profile perfectly, but yours is such a different type of beauty, Miss D'Arcy-Twyning, it may be a little too severe, don't you think?"

Denise's flower-like face looked murderous. "That's for me to decide," she retorted haughtily. "I want it done like that just to see how it will look. How can I tell if it'll suit me until you've done it?"

Denise pulled herself up out of the bath and called for a towel. She stood there slim and pink and childishly flat-chested, wrapping the big towel round her and waving the others out imperiously.

"You go on into the lounge, Miss Jeffries, and wheel the long mirror out of the bedroom."

She turned to Cheryl. "Angel-pie, let her have a good look at you so she'll be all ready when I come out."

Claire set out a tray on the side table and plugged the hand dryer in the reading-lamp. No wonder Val refused to come, she thought. My God, what a bunch they are! All of them lousy with money and doing nothing but lounge round other people's suites all day. Does the Manpower ever get hold of them? Not they. Half tiddly the lot of them already. If you have the money you can get away with anything.

Denise drifted out from the bathroom in a floating pale pink negligée. "I'm absolutely exhausted," she groaned.

"Do pour me out another drink, treasure-bud."

Melva poured them all another drink and Denise sank into a chair with a dramatic sigh. "Now I'm going to watch every single thing you do in the mirror, Miss Jeffries," she said warningly, "and I'm going to have the Marquise sitting right there near me so I can see her all the time. Light me a cigarette, Chel, there's a cherub."

Claire combed out Denise's wet hair and began to set it.

"That's roughly the idea," Cheryl said patronisingly, as Claire wound the first curls, "though you mustn't be disappointed, Denny darling, if it doesn't turn out exactly like mine. The hair stylist who created mine in New York was absolutely tops and it's too much to expect that you should get the same standard out here."

Melva chimed in disconsolately, "It's utterly ghastly what we have to put up with just because we're in Australia. Goldie says in India you get the most wonderful service." She sank onto the lounge and stretched out languidly, cigarette in one hand and sherry glass in the other. "Am I worn out," she yawned and waved her glass about feebly. "Do you know I had to spend three whole afternoons last week driving Dinkie round."

"My dear, don't tell me the ridiculous Manpower is still worrying you here! Why in the States..."

"It's absolutely revolting," Audette broke in. "In spite of the way I've slaved with the Pick-Pockettes, Daddles had to put me on the factory payroll as his private secretary or heaven knows where I'd have found myself."

Cheryl looked her over lazily. "Honey child, I just can't see you as secretary to a pickle factory."

"Oh, can't you, darling? Surely you haven't forgotten that it was only your marriage to the Marquis that saved you from being cashier in an army canteen."

Melva sighed dramatically. "Well, three afternoons in one week dodging the Manpower is too much for me, on top of everything else. I'm absolutely fagged out, and I've got to drive Dinkie to golf this afternoon."

"No wonder you're worn out, from what I can hear of

that party on the yacht," Audette broke in acidly.

Melva opened reproachful eyes. "Treasurekins," she pleaded, "I don't think you really believe that I did try to ring you. I wanted you to come most frightfully. Girls, it was terrific. Wasn't it, Cheryl?"

"Definitely super — for Sydney, that is; but I must tell you about our farewell party on Long Island . . ."

Melva quickly cut in. "Dinkie was furious when we brought the yacht back. He said it'll cost him hundreds to repair things, but Mumsie dealt with him. She manages him wonderfully. You should have seen the American captain I had."

"Darling, how too terribly desolating for you," Denise cooed. "Down to an itsy-bitsy captain! Why, even in the worst days of the war I never had to make out with anything less than a major."

"But, Denise sweet, I never was rank-happy like you. I like my men male. And Alwyn, cutie-pie, he was simply the berries, wasn't he, Chel?"

"Definitely tops."

Melva sighed rapturously. "He fell for me on sight. I haven't had anything quite so thrilling since we had the Morgan twins down at Babbatree."

"I believe they're frightfully wild," Denise said disapprovingly, "they practically burnt the hotel down on Sunday."

"They should worry," Melva dismissed it with a laugh. "They're simply mad with the money; their father could buy half a dozen South Pacifics. God, that weekend at Babbatree! They were both crazy about me and honestly, I never knew which one it was. My dears, there were times when it was terribly embarrassing." She giggled. "They had to go on duty on Sunday, so they sent Alwyn along."

"Fancy risking a blind date," Denise said reprovingly. "I've never come to that."

"Oh, live dangerously, that's always been my motto. And did the twins give me a write-up! The moment Alwyn hit the deck he was raring to go. God, how am I ever going to settle down with Dougie?''

Audette emptied the sherry bottle into Denise's glass and examined her new hairdo. "Denny-pet, I think that uplifted line is going to do wonders for you, don't you, Chel?"

"But definitely."

"Just stand aside, Miss Jeffries, till I get a real look." Audette walked round the chair. "Yes," she said, "it has something."

"But I'm going to need an entirely different type of clothes with it, aren't I?" Denise pouted.

Cheryl looked her over critically. "I'm afraid you are, darl, but what's that to you, with your father prepared to give you the world?"

"That sounds all right. But he can't give me a good dressmaker, and there's not a rag in the shops you'd put on your back."

"My dear," Audette began, "Goldie told me that she'd found an absolutely super dressmaker down in Double Bay. I met her wearing the most stunning suit and she's getting those saris made up. Goldie's a bitch, you know. I simply had to drag the name out of her. The woman's a Viennese."

"Oh, a reffo?" inquired Denise.

"I suppose so — but can she make! Goldie's suit looked every inch a model. And my dear, she's just been down at Buffalo with the ski club and she's most gloriously snow-tanned."

Denise twisted her head to look round. "But the dressmaker," she added impatiently, "she's really good, is she?"

Audette nodded. "Crackerjack. And not terribly expensive. Eighteen guineas for the making. When I went round town last week there wasn't anyone worthwhile who'd touch my material under twenty-two." She rolled her eyes and collapsed on the cushion, waving her glass in Cheryl's direction. Cheryl opened a new bottle.

"Daddles says it's positively scandalous about these refugees," Audette agreed. "He says the government should do something about them."

Denise jerked her head round. "Daddy says the Jews'll

overrun the place like rabbits if we're not careful. He was trying to buy some flats at Bondi and one of those beastly reffos got at the owner first."

"That's right," Cheryl agreed. "Poppa says if we're not terribly careful they'll be running the country yet. Always cashing in on other people's misfortunes."

"Did Goldie give you the woman's address?" Melva asked.

Audette lifted her head again, her eyes wide with indignation. "She did, but only after I'd absolutely wrung it out of her."

"What is it?" Denise demanded. "I simply must get some new clothes."

Audette lay back in her chair, closing her eyes as though in painful thought. "Let me see...somewhere down in Double Bay. Afraid I've forgotten it."

"Well then, ring up and find out," Denise snapped, "there's the phone beside you."

Audette shrugged her shoulders. "OK," she gave in, "it may be in my bag. What about having lunch with me down at Prince's and we'll drop out to see her afterwards?"

Denise turned an astonished glance on her. "Lunch with you!" she gasped. "Why Audette, my sweetest, you must be losing your punch. You know I never go out in public with just another girl, it ruins you socially."

"She's right," Cheryl swept over Audette's protests. "Thirteen Pick-Pockettes lunching together is good publicity, but two just advertises your manless condition."

"Well, I'll have a look in my bag when I'm strong enough to get up. Pass me a cigarette, will you, Chel? At any rate, I don't see that you really want any new clothes, Denise. The clothes you got from that fiancé of yours in America were just too divine. Why, you could dress all of us Pick-Pockettes and not miss them."

"I hear Dwight's on his way back."

"Yes," Denise sighed and pouted. "And I'm in a frightful jam, because, you see, I'm not going to marry him now."

Cheryl groaned. "You're crackers, absolutely crackers.

Fancy missing a chance to go and live in the States — my dear, the clothes, the food, the nightclubs — we don't know we're alive out here. And the service! Why in the South the Negroes still practically crawl to you. I'm going back just as soon as my divorce is through! I don't intend to live in Australia a minute longer than I need.''

Denise dropped her eyes demurely, then looked up at her with a malicious sparkle. ''I'm not intending to live in Australia either. You see, I asked you girls up this morning to tell you I'm going to marry Commander Derek Ermington.''

Melva sat up with a start, splashing her drink over the carpet. ''Derek Ermington,'' she exclaimed, ''why he's the son of a lord, isn't he?''

Denise smiled patronisingly. ''Yes.''

Cheryl looked at her admiringly. ''I'll hand it to you, you're a quick worker, Denny.''

''But what about your American fiancé?'' Audette asked.

Denise fluttered her hands helplessly. ''Too wearing,'' she murmured, ''but well, it's just one of those things.''

''But definitely,'' Melva agreed.

Audette came over beside her. ''When are you going to be married?''

''Oh darling, he's in the most frightful hurry, he said he simply can't wait, so it's going to be in ten days. The most dreadful rush. That's why I was so interested about the Viennese woman. She might be able to help out with clothes because I want to have the most absolutely knockout wedding. Everything tops. I want the whole twelve of you Pick-Pockettes to be my bridesmaids.''

''This calls for a celebration,'' Cheryl declared. ''I must have a real drink on it.''

''Let's all get high,'' Melva sparkled.

''It's the most exciting news I've heard in months,'' Audette cried.

Denise gurgled. ''I suppose it is quite a thing,'' she said. ''What would you like?''

''Whisky for me.''

"Me too."

"I'll have a gin and lime."

"It's a gin for me too. Audette angel, ring down, will you, and tell them to send up a bottle of Scotch, a bottle of gin and a tray of savouries — say savouries for six. That'll deal with their silly old austerity. Oh. . .and tell them to send some lime too and not to be long about it. . .and make sure it's real Scotch. Chel, darling, how does my hair look? Is it too utterly stinking?"

Claire fixed a curl into place and resisted the temptation to jab the bobby pin into Denise's scalp.

Cheryl got up and examined the set critically. "Not bad," she said at last, "not at all bad considering. But darling, you mustn't be too disappointed. After all, this isn't New York."

Claire pushed open the door of the Marie Antoinette and brushed past Ursula's desk without even looking at her. She put the tray down in her own office, slammed the door, sat down and unlocked her cupboard. She poured a stiff brandy into a cup and gulped it down. What a morning! That was the last time she'd go up to do D.D.T. even if old Mother Molesworth went down on her knees to her.

There was a knock at her door. She put the bottle away quickly and called, "Come in."

Val put her head round. "I've made you a cup of tea," she said placing it on her desk. "Here drink it up, I know how you're feeling."

"Thanks." Claire drank the tea thirstily. "After what I've been through this morning, I don't blame you for refusing to go. How someone hasn't murdered the girl before this, I'll never understand."

"Was she very bad?"

"Bad! She was revolting, and I had three of her Pick-Pockettes into the bargain giving a ball-to-ball description of their filthy love lives in their phoney Darling Point accents."

"I can believe it. Look, I'll have to fly back. I'm just in the middle of Mrs Slowman and I'm going to give her a cup of tea. The poor old duck's got word that that son of hers who's been missing since Crete is officially reported killed.''

"Poor devil. I'll go in and see her when I've got through this. It's always the decent people things like that happen to.''

"Well, don't hurry. Guinea's back and going like the devil and we're well on.'' Val went out.

Claire had just finished her cup of tea when the door opened again and Alice's woebegone face peered round. "I thought you'd never get back,'' she whispered. "She rang.''

"Who rang?'' Claire looked puzzled.

"Mrs Cavendish, with the message she promised first thing this morning. She didn't ring till after eleven.''

"Well I suppose she rang as soon as she woke up. What did she say?''

"I didn't speak to her. Miss Cronin took the message, she wrote it down and gave it to me.''

Alice took a neatly folded piece of paper out of her pocket and handed it over.

"One day I'll slit Cronin's throat for taking my messages.'' Claire snapped. "I told her to call you.''

She read the pencilled note. "Ring YT5591 between 12 and 12.30 today for an appointment on Wednesday. Say Mrs Peterson recommended you. The damage will be 45.''

Claire laughed dryly when she saw Ursula's pencilled initials. "She'd throw a willy if she knew what she was signing her name to!''

Alice looked pained.

Claire whistled. "Forty-five! She said forty yesterday, didn't she?''

"Yes. That's the trouble, we've only just managed to rake up forty quid between us with me not paying my laybys this month, and Mary won't get any more pay for another fortnight.''

Claire unlocked the top drawer of her desk and clipped the note on a file. "Someone else might need this,'' she remarked.

Alice shuddered.

"You get back to your job," Claire said curtly, "and send Val to me."

"Want me?" Val asked.

"Yes? You know the Parker kid I told you about this morning? Well, it's going to cost forty-five pounds and she and Alice have only got forty between them. Would you stand by me if I started a collection for a wedding present for D.D.T. from the staff here?"

Val looked at her in astonishment. "For D.D.T.? Oh, I see what you mean. My dear, I'll head the list with a quid."

"Good," said Claire. "I'll chuck in a quid myself and Deb and Guinea'll give something and Cronin can cough up the rest. I'll teach her to take my messages."

"Lovely! I'll give you the money at lunchtime."

"Just a minute and sign this before you go."

Claire took a sheet of paper and wrote in her scrawling hand across the top: "CONTRIBUTIONS FOR WEDDING GIFT FOR MISS DENISE D'ARCY-TWYNING FROM THE MARIE ANTOINETTE STAFF."

She passed it over to Val who wrote, "V. Blaski...£1." Claire added her own name.

"Listen," Claire said when Deb came in a few minutes later, "you'll be relieved to know everything's been fixed up for the Parker kid to be done tomorrow."

"I certainly am relieved." Deb's voice was edgy.

"I know Alice is impossible, but you can't help feeling sorry for the kid."

"I never want to hear the name Parker again. These Service girls who think every man they meet is fair game..."

"I really don't think you're being quite fair. Mary Parker's not like that."

"Well I hope it will teach her to leave other women's husbands alone."

Claire's eyes dropped to the paper in front of her. Deb followed her gaze.

"Good heavens," she said, "you don't really mean..."

"No. But the job's going to cost five pounds more than the Parkers bargained for and they haven't got the money, so I thought I'd take up a subscription and get Cronin in on it."

Deb frowned. "Personally, I think it's a bit hot. I had to waste all yesterday afternoon and humiliate myself going over to ask Dallas."

"All right," Claire said, "forget it. We'll make it up some other way."

"Don't be ridiculous. If you and Val are giving a pound, I'll give a pound, but I'm not doing it for those Parkers. It's just because you're helping out."

"Thanks," Claire smiled at her. "I really do think it was pretty tough asking you to go over to Dr MacIntyre. Just give Guinea a call as you pass, will you?"

Guinea appeared at the door.

"Christ, you look like death warmed up," said Claire. "Is everything all right now?"

Guinea dropped her eyes and nodded.

"A funeral's a hell of a strain, I know. Guin, have you got a quid to spare?"

Guinea flashed her a look of surprise. "Why, of course I can let you have it."

"Oh it's not for me." Claire pointed to the list beside her which now had Deb's name on it.

"What! You don't really mean that you expect the staff to go sucking up to that bitch?"

"Don't panic," Claire laughed. "Mary Parker's job's going to cost forty-five smackers and they've only got forty."

Guinea's face cleared. "Oh, that's different. But haven't they got a bank behind them?"

"Yes, but I can't see boyfriend Ross embezzling the funds for this kind of thing."

"Neither can I. But why this camouflage?"

Claire chuckled. "I'm going to ask Cronin to throw in."

"No! Crikey, that's the best I've heard in years."

"Well, is it all right with you?"

"Yes. Do you want it now?"

"No. Lunchtime'll do."

Guinea wrote down her name.

Claire got up. "I'll take it along to Cronin now. She'll have kittens if ever she finds out."

"What are you going to tell her we're buying? A tar and feathering set?"

"No, something slower and more painful."

Ursula looked up coldly as Claire approached her desk and laid the list beside her. She goggled at the heading.

"I thought you might like to give something towards this, Miss Cronin," Claire said sweetly. "You've always been so fond of Miss D'Arcy-Twyning. She and her mother have been such an advertisement for the salon," Claire explained, "that the rest of us feel it's rather a good idea."

"Well, er. . .er. . ." Ursula began.

"You know I think it pays to be well in with the directors, don't you? Manpower and all that."

"I wouldn't give it for that reason," Ursula said self-righteously. "When I give a present it means something."

"Naturally, but for the rest of us it's just a matter of business. You've always got on so well with the D'Arcy-Twynings."

Ursula looked down the list. "Isn't Alice Parker giving anything?"

"Yes. She promised the same as the rest of us."

Ursula took out her purse from the top drawer and fumbled with the clasp. "A pound does seem rather a lot."

"But Miss Cronin, you know you can get nothing worth giving under a fiver today and you wouldn't like to give her anything cheap."

Ursula looked doubtful. "What were you thinking of giving her?"

Claire lied spontaneously. "We had thought one of those silver charm bangles DJ's have got in — with the flags of all nations in coloured enamel. They're quite the newest thing, and she's got practically everything else."

Ursula frowned. "It doesn't seem very dignified." She took a pound note out of her bag and handed it over reluctantly.

Claire pocketed it. "Well what would you suggest?" she asked.

"I think perhaps a good etching."

"An etching! Oh, my dear," Claire laughed. "I'm sure that Miss D'Arcy-Twyning has been asked up to see all the private collections of etchings in Sydney at one time or another."

"I don't see that that matters."

Claire pushed the paper over to her.

"Here, write your name under Guinea's. If we'd have had more time we could have had a miniature of the Bouncing Belle struck for her as a souvenir."

She picked up the paper and went cheerfully down the corridor.

Ursula looked after her. It was certainly very odd, but she couldn't afford to be left out.

Angus towelled himself vigorously after his surf, then stretched out on the sand beside Ian. "Invigorating," he said.

Ian grunted.

"Marvellous how the surf braces you," Angus continued amiably. "Cigarette?"

Ian took one and they smoked together in silence.

A cool southerly had sprung up and Maroubra beach was almost deserted, except for a few toddlers splashing in the rock pool and their mothers sitting on the beach waiting to take them home.

Judging by the sun, it must be after three o'clock, Angus thought. There was a good surf running and the breakers rose and crashed a long way out, rolling into the beach in long lines of foam. The northern cliffs gleamed pale against the blue sea and southwards the afternoon sun cast long shadows up the rifle range. Angus was so full of wellbeing that not even Ian's morose silence could dampen him.

"Astonishing how different you feel when a cool change comes after a heatwave," he went on.

Ian lifted his lined face, reddened by western suns. "You people in the city don't know you're alive," he said. "Call that a heatwave? Like to push you all west for a while and let you find out what a heatwave really is, with no surf to flock to, and no pubs to hang round either."

Angus shrugged his shoulders. "You can hardly blame people for choosing to live in the city. After all you chose the country, and you don't do too badly out of it, I might say."

"I'd like to see how you fellows in the city would get on if it weren't for us," Ian retorted contemptuously. "Just a lot of parasites."

"Oh come," Angus tried to mollify him. "You're a bit touchy because it's so long since you had a holiday."

"Holiday!" Ian snorted. "What's the use of a holiday to us when it means working twice as hard when we get back? I was going to ask you if you couldn't come up for a few months. There's a hell of a lot to be done between now and Christmas. We're short-handed and I don't see a chance of getting any more labour. I don't mind working from sunup to sundown myself, but it doesn't seem fair to Helen, and I don't propose to take Donald from school. He's done the work of a man in the holidays ever since the war began and I'm not going to have him sacrificed in his last year."

Angus threw a half-smoked cigarette away. "Good heavens, Ian, now just what use would I be up there? I haven't been in the country, except for a holiday, for twenty-five years. I never was much of a hand at the practical side of it anyway."

"I know you wouldn't be worth your salt as far as the outside work goes," Ian replied, "but there's a devil of a lot of work you could do. Clerical work. We've got all behind with the stud reports...Helen's been doing her best but it's a fulltime job keeping the records up to date. Since it's the Burramaronga stud that makes most of the money you spend down here, I don't see that it would hurt you to come up for a couple of months. And there's the hand feeding. We've been hand feeding stock all the winter and there's no prospect of being able to let up. That bit of scattered rain in the Riverina this week won't do us any good, and it's too late, anyway. That's something you could give us a hand with. Take some of the weight off you too — getting a regular paunch."

Angus ignored the personal remark and lit another cigarette. God, he said to himself, leave Sydney just now with Deborah's husband coming home! He gazed reflectively out to sea as though giving the matter mature thought. "I don't see how I can possibly manage it, old man," he said at last. "Not now at any rate," he added, "but maybe later. After all, I may be wanting to open up the old home at Burramaronga myself shortly."

Ian sat up. "What do you mean? Opening up Burramaronga?"

"Surely that would be obvious. Naturally when I'm married I'll have a certain sentimental interest in the old place.''

"Sentimental be buggered," Ian exploded. "I've been wondering ever since you told me you were thinking of getting married whether you'd be wanting to do anything about the property. It wasn't until I met Mrs Forrest last night that I realised she was just about half your age."

"Really, Ian."

"Well, she's a damned sight younger than you, anyway. Quite young enough to have a family."

Angus met his brother's eyes stonily.

"I think we ought to have a clear statement on the matter now," Ian went on.

"I fail to see what you mean by a clear statement. After all, Burramaronga is my property and if I choose to marry and have a family, I can't see what that has got to do with you."

"Good God, Angus, I sometimes wonder if you're quite human. You know as well as I do that it's been an understood thing that young Angus would have Burramaronga eventually."

"You mean when I'm dead, I presume?" Angus gave a short laugh. "Let me remind you that, as I am only in the prime of my life and perfectly healthy, so far as young Angus is concerned it might be deferred for a very long time."

"Bunkum," Ian said. "Long before he left school, Angus was the brain of that place, and when he took over the management he put everything he had into it. He's worked like a nigger there and it's a credit to him."

"It is a credit to him, and he's been well paid for it," Angus said icily. 'I've never had any complaints from him on that score."

"Paid! You can't pay anyone for what he's done. If you ask my opinion, I think it's a damned dirty trick, especially now he's a prisoner-of-war up in Malaya and depending on coming back to Burramaronga."

"Naturally I'd keep him on as manager. He's done a first-class job," Angus said in a more conciliatory tone. "I would have no intention of doing anything else."

Ian looked at him, his eyes full of hostility. "You know, Angus, sometimes I wonder how our family managed to produce anyone like you. You've never done a day's hard work in your life. If it weren't that you look so much like the old man I'd swear you were a ring-in. Whatever the McFarlands have got has been built on hard graft. We've all been grafters, except you. Grandfather and Dad and Grandmother and Mother, and if it comes to that, Olive and me and our kids. And not only the boys, but Helen too. She's worked a damn sight harder than a lot of men."

"Well I'm not content to throw my lot in with your hard grafters, and I never was. I made that perfectly clear to you over twenty years ago when I came back from Cambridge. You know I've never felt at home here. I suppose I could sum it up by saying that England is where I really feel I belong."

"If that's the case, I can't understand why you didn't stay there and try to do something to help when the war broke out."

"My dear fellow, you know as well as I that I'm over age for military service."

"A matter of opinion, that. No wonder there's all this talk about absentee landlords living on the other fellow's labour. You and the overseas investor — you're the curse of Australia. You put nothing into the country, and take everything you can out. All you're interested in is fat dividends, and you don't care if the country's ruined by overstocking to provide them for you."

"Aren't you being rather melodramatic? After all, this country would never have developed without overseas capital."

"Bunk. This country has been developed like any other country by the men and women who've worked in it. Australia's never been a place for loafers, there's always been too much to do and too few of us to do it. And now with half the world depending on us to feed and clothe them, there's less room for loafers than ever. It beats me how you've been able to sit down on your backside in a city pub and do nothing, with the war practically on your own doorstep."

Angus tried to divert him. "Well, judging by what I've been reading today about the Red Army pouring into Yugoslavia, we'll probably all be waving the Red Flag before we've finished."

"It'd serve you bloody well right if they put you up against the wall and shot you," Ian snapped. "I don't blame these coal miners for striking when they see your kind, living on the fat of the land and not doing a hand's turn to justify your existence."

"Look, Ian," Angus said placatingly, "there's no use trying to make me responsible for the state of the country, you'll be blaming me for the drought next."

"Well, if men like you who get the money from the land without doing anything for it spent their time trying to make the government give the man on the land a decent deal, there'd be something to it. But does it worry you that we're short of labour and we can't get proper drought relief measures? Not a bit of it. First time you'll wake up to what's happening is when the government decides to nationalise everything and then you and your friends sitting round on your backsides in city clubs'll go running round squealing like stuck pigs, and begging us chaps from the country to come and save your skins like you did in the General Strike in 1917."

"That sounds to me mighty like you're advocating Communism."

"Bunk. I believe in the right of every man to own what he's worked for, but you're the kind of chap who makes Communists, and I can tell you, there's one thing I do approve of in their policy, and that's their idea that if you don't work you don't eat."

"You'll be advocating the nationalisation of land next."

"No I won't, but I would be prepared to advocate that men who own land and don't look after it should have it taken away from them. After all, you can dismiss an inefficient employee so why shouldn't we be able to dismiss an inefficient landowner? Why should he be allowed to ruin a valuable national asset when there are plenty of people only too willing to work it properly?"

"I suppose you know you're being thoroughly offensive," Angus said coldly.

"It's the truth, and if it's offensive then I can't help it. You inherited Burramaronga, you've lived off it and lived damned well, let me remind you. Money that ought to have gone back into improvements you've tucked away into steel shares and it's been at the expense of me and my family. And I tell you now plainly, I think it's damned unjust and practically dishonest."

Angus' nostrils flared and his mouth set hard.

Hanging on to his temper, Ian thought furiously. Why the hell doesn't he come out into the open and say what he really thinks? Planning to keep young Angus on to manage the place...like his hide. And talking about starting a family at his age. A nice welcome it will be for the boy when he comes back. It's always been understood that he'd have Burramaronga and young Ian would get our place. Well, he wouldn't get it now and Helen would get a third of whatever the stud made.

Ian stared at Angus's stony face. Patronising bastard, he thought, spending his life running round all the lounge lizards' haunts in the world with nothing else to do but collect the fat cheques that we've sweated blood to make for him. Well, we'll teach him. He can have Burramaronga. We don't need to toady to him — we'll find some other way of making out. Buy the property on the other side for young Angus when he comes back, set him up there. Brother Angus will soon find the difference when he starts putting in outside managers. Not that the money out of the place matters too much to him now; those BHP shares he got for a song after the last war must be bringing him a packet. All he wants Burramaronga for is to make it a damned showplace where he and his city wife can entertain their city friends. Before he finishes with it, it'll be like a bloody tourist resort.

Ian got up and shook the sand out of his bathing costume, wincing as he pulled up the shoulder straps onto his burnt shoulders. "We'd better get along now," he said.

"I've still got a lot of things to do and I don't want to be late meeting Olive."

He turned and stamped up to the surf pavilion. Angus got up slowly and followed him.

As soon as Deb put down the receiver, she regretted that she'd agreed to meet Angus in the Bull Ring. But she'd been so swept off her feet by his ringing her at the Marie Antoinette — something he'd never done before — and begging her to come down to the Madrid Lounge at once, that she'd agreed without thinking.

She looked at the clock. Heavens, it was only quarter past five. It was true she had no more appointments, but there was still a terrific lot to be done. She'd have to pretend it was Mrs Molesworth ringing for her to do a facial pack and makeup for one of the guests in her own room.

Claire took the announcement explosively. "The old bitch!" she said. "Who's she to give orders over my head? All this service in private rooms...you called off now, and me having to fit D.D.T. in this morning. It's absolutely the limit. I'll have to have a showdown with her. I was here till after seven last night and this means I won't be able to get away again."

"I'll tell you what," Deb suggested. "You leave all the cleaning up here to me and get away as soon as the last job's done."

"That's jolly decent of you, but it means you being late. It really is the limit."

Deb began to get her makeup box together.

Claire called Guinea from a cubicle. "Old Mole's sent for Deb and you'll have to give me a hand as soon as you're through, I'm afraid."

"Gawd, I've got as much as I can get through as it is."

"I know. I'm sorry, Guin, but it's Mrs Archer and she's always so decent I can't cut down her treatment."

"OK, I'll do my best."

Guinea eyed Deb distrustfully. "Going to do a make-up?" she inquired.

"Yes," said Deb and went out with as much poise as she could manage.

She ran round to the service lift and went up to her room. It took her only a few minutes to slip out of her uniform and into her yellow suit and put on a hat.

Angus was waiting for her on the first floor. His hand closed on her elbow and he piloted her into the Bull Ring to a table reserved for him by a long window in a far corner. A waiter pulled out a chair for her. Angus seated himself opposite her and smiled the sudden slight smile that lifted his face from aloofness to intimacy. He smiled as though he were bestowing a favour, she thought, as royalty smiles. But it no longer irritated her. She knew that there was uncertainty and tension behind his apparent assurance.

Angus looked up at the heavy tapestries round the walls with amusement. "I was examining these while I was waiting for you. I always wonder where they got such horrors from."

"Mrs Molesworth told me they're practically priceless," Deb laughed.

"I can believe her. I've seen bullfights in Spain and Mexico, but never a bull quite so skittish nor a toreador so unconcerned. And calling a lounge Old Madrid, so pretentious."

"The staff call it the Bull Ring."

"It's inevitable," he said.

Deb was glad she hadn't called it by its nickname to him. She supposed it was vulgar but she rather liked it — and anyway, the place was vulgar. She looked from the furniture covered with dark red leather and studded everywhere with brass nail heads to the heavily gilded ceiling with the mock beams, and back to the crowded tables.

A white-coated waiter, balancing his full tray high in one hand, made his way to them past the queue that waited near the door in the hope of getting a drink before six o'clock. Poor old Tubby, she thought, looking at the waiter's flushed face as he swerved round to their table. That look means his feet are playing up on him. Claire's veins were giving her gyp to. . . . She had a pang of guilt at the thought of Claire and the others still up in the Marie Antoinette while she sipped iced beer down here like a lady of leisure. It really was mean of her to sneak out on them like that. She hoped to heaven Old Mole didn't pay one of her visits to the salon; it would only need Claire to complain about appointments in private rooms during salon hours and the fat would be in the fire.

"Phew! Hasn't it been hot!" Deb breathed, sipping her ice-cold beer while the waiting crowd eyed them thirstily.

"Very trying," Angus agreed, finishing his drink swiftly and signalling the harassed waiter for another.

One thing with Angus, you always got service and that gave you a sense of power, too. The confusion, the uncertainty, she felt when she was with Dallas, and with Nolly and Tom, left her when she was with Angus. This must be what people meant by saying that you had the world at your feet — a sense of elation, of being removed from other people's problems and oh, so safe.

"I took a run out to Maroubra with my brother before lunch and we cooled off in the surf." Angus went on with a monologue about this weather and its effects on him. "The only place on a day like this. A slight southerly came up while we were there. We're in for a cool change, I think."

"It hasn't reached the city yet, or at least not the Marie Antoinette. It's been like an oven there all the afternoon."

"You poor little girl," his smile caressed her. "I wish you could have been with us. Ordinarily, my brother doesn't get much chance to loaf, so I like to lead him astray when I can."

Deb lifted her glass and the chill against her hand, the tang of icy beer on her tongue and the cold trickle down her throat were delicious.

Angus looked at her meaningly. "It's fun leading people astray."

"How I envy you," she hedged, "we've simply sweltered here."

"My dear," he murmured, "you won't have to put up with it much longer. You don't know how I long to sweep you away from that wretched job."

"Oh, it's not so bad, as jobs go."

"But not for you. It's all wrong for you. Just think of it — next spring! If the gods are kind to me," he laughed softly, "we'll be deciding our activities by the mercury and not by the Marie Antoinette."

Deb sighed. If only it could be now. Oh, to be free to enjoy the leisure of luxury, all the things that marriage to Angus could give her! Oh, to be rid of all the wretched explaining and arguing she'd have to cope with in the next few weeks, the resentment and the criticism! Jack and Tom, and Dallas, too, for that matter, seemed to think she was still a child, the way they tried to run her life for her. Next spring! She wished the time would go quickly just as much as Angus did. It was hard to understand now how she could have kept him at arm's length all these months. But then, of course, she'd never dreamed that he'd want to marry her. It was strange what a difference that had made to her feelings. It gave sanction to his kisses, privilege to his touch; it warmed her, and she needed that as a defence against Jack. When a girl married very young and never even had a flirtation with another man, much less let him touch her, she was absurdly at a disadvantage with her husband. She might just as well be in a harem! She smiled at the extravagance of her thought and, looking up to meet his smile, saw his eyes travel beyond her and a frown cross his face.

"What is it?" she glanced round. "Oh!" She turned back quickly and lowered her face over her glass.

"My dear, it's only Sharlton."

"But I shouldn't be here," she whispered, keeping her head lowered.

"Why not? If Sharlton dares to say a word to you afterwards, just let me know. I'll soon make it clear to him why you're here."

"Please, Angus. Don't draw attention to us."

"Good heavens, Deborah, what's wrong with you? It's ridiculous for you to be sitting there cowering like a naughty child. Anyway, he's just taking some of the directors round."

Deb peered at him from under the brim of her hat. "Are you sure?"

"Of course I'm sure." He looked towards the door again and inclined his head in a faintly patronising nod. "He's got Horatio Veale with him."

Deb half turned and stole a glance. "Which one?"

"The one with the mop of greying ginger hair. From the look of him you'd never take him for the financial wizard he is, would you?"

"You certainly wouldn't. He looks...well, rather soft."

"Soft?" Angus smiled ironically. "I can assure you that is merely the fact that he has let himself run to seed in a disgusting fashion. Mind you, he's not a young man, but that soft genial manner covers a mind like a rapier and a heart as hard as a rock. Made his money buying up bank books when the Government Savings Bank failed in the depression. It's common talk that he drove a harder bargain with the poor devils who couldn't afford to wait till the bank reopened than any other man in Sydney."

"Oh." Deb looked at Veale in repulsion and she saw again her father's face the night he'd sat up and stared at his bank book and wondered whether he should sell. She pushed the thought away from her.

"Who's that enormous man with him?"

"That's Macartney. Shrewdest company solicitor in Sydney."

"He looks half asleep to me."

"Lots of people have made that mistake. He and Veale have been hand-in-glove ever since I've known him. And the little chicken-boned fellow with the greasy hair is Dan Twyning. Made his money in chain-stores."

"Twyning," she said, stealing another glance, "that'll be Denise's father."

"Do you know her?"

"Unfortunately, we know her only too well in the Marie Antoinette."

He frowned and signalled the waiter again. "Deborah, I

don't know if you realise how repellent it is to me to think of your having to wait on a little upstart like Twyning's daughter. You must let me get you out of that place soon. It's not fair on me."

She looked up at him. His face was flushed and his mouth drawn down at the corners. His expression softened under her glance, and he smiled whimsically. "Do I seem terribly possessive to you?"

She stared at him without answering. I wish you were more possessive, she thought. I wish you'd snatch me away by force. Give me no time to think. Oh God, how am I ever going to tell Jack?

His eyes met hers. "You look such a child when you look up at me like that. I want the right to protect you. You know I adore you, don't you?"

"Do you really?" she said softly.

"I used to think I was a well-balanced man."

"You seem very well-balanced to me."

"Now I know I was only deceiving myself."

"How did you discover that?"

"Need you ask?"

She smiled at him and went on sipping her beer.

"When I left you last night and said I was afraid I wouldn't be able to see you until Wednesday evening, I overestimated my powers of restraint."

"I think you are very strong."

"If you say things like that...I warn you, I'll kiss you right here and now in the Madrid Lounge."

"I'm sure Mr Sharlton wouldn't like it."

"It's not him I'm going to kiss."

Deb laughed gaily, her spirits soaring suddenly.

"I simply couldn't spend a whole day without seeing you, my darling. That's why I rang. I hope I wasn't too importunate."

"Oh no," Deb lied, remembering the expression on Claire's face when she had put down the phone and told her it was another summons from Mrs Molesworth.

He sighed deeply. "To think that I might have been

spending this evening with you and I have to go to a family dinner instead. You just can't imagine what our family dinners are like.''

Deb thought she could, but she didn't say so.

Angus looked at the clock and groaned. "My sweet, I simply must be going. I've got to be up at Wahroonga for seven-thirty dinner and the world goes to pieces for Virginia if dinner's a minute late.''

Deb glanced at the clock, it was five to six. There was an anxious shuffle near the door as the queue pressed forward. Angus followed her glance. "I have to call at Graythwaite on the way,'' he explained, "my old batman's there. He was badly knocked on the Somme and has been on his back ever since. When I'm in Sydney, I always drop in to see him on Tuesday night and I don't like to make it a rush visit. You won't mind if I get away by ten past?''

"Of course I won't. I think it's perfectly lovely of you.''

"To be perfectly honest, it's very little compared with what he did for me. But before I do go, would you like to know how I spent my morning?''

"I'd love to hear.''

"I spent it looking at rings.''

"Oh!''

"And do you know, although I went to four different jeweller's shops, I couldn't find a single ring I thought worthy of you. So I've decided to have something very special made. My mother had some lovely stones, they've been in safe deposit for years, but they're mine to do as I like with, and I got them out and took them round to the jeweller's. We picked you out a solitaire emerald; it's a flawless stone, square cut. He says it will make a unique ring.''

Deb looked at him without speaking, and managed a weak little smile. An emerald... And she hated green! Fancy him deciding on her engagement ring without even asking her what she liked. All the implications were suddenly frightening.

"Are you pleased?'' Angus was smiling in anticipation of her answer.

"It sounds lovely," she heard herself saying.

The voice of a waiter paging the lounges interrupted them. "Paging Mr McFarland. Paging Mr McFarland," he chanted monotonously.

"I'm so sorry, my dear, I'm afraid I shall have to go. May I see you to the lift?"

He took her elbow in the cup of his hand. The disappointed queue, still peering thirstily into the lounge, opened to let them pass.

A shaggy head in a dilapidated slouch hat was poked cautiously round the door of the side lift and a hoarse voice whispered: "'Ow yer doin', Dig?"

"Lofty!" Blue grabbed his hand and pumped it up and down enthusiastically. "Well, for cryin' out loud! Hop in." He slammed the door and took the lift express to the roof. "Where did you spring from, you old sinner?"

Lofty propped his lanky frame against the wall, pushing his hat still farther back on his mop of hair, cream and crinkly as a merino fleece. "Got in on a troop train coupla hours ago after a fortnight comin' down from Broome across the Transcontibloodynental; I been pub-crawlin' round this bloody city ever since, tryin' to get a bloody drink, and the larst 'arf-hour I been dodgin' round that bloody Bouncing Belle lookin' for you and tryin' to give them blokes in the lion-tamer uniform a miss, till somebody worded me you was round here in the side lift."

"It's a wonder the Bouncing Belle didn't fall off her perch at the sight of an Aussie uniform in this pub."

Lofty grinned. "Not 'er. She was the only sheila around that didn't look as though she 'ad a bad smell under 'er nose when she got 'er lamps on to me."

"Aw, yer don't want to take any notice. Lot of tarts, most of 'em. All be out of jobs when the Yanks leave the place."

"They're welcome to 'em for mine. Funny kind of shape the sheilas give themselves today, Blue. All look as though they got a coupla ack-ack guns stuck on their chest. Knock yer eye out if yer wasn't careful."

"Ah!" Blue said confidentially. "That's glammer."

"I don't care what it is. I ain't interested in wimmen," Lofty dismissed glamour dourly. "All I'm after's a beer. I got a thirst on me like a sunstruck bone and I'm dead motherless broke. Coupla bastards come the raw prawn over me on the last lap up from Melbourne and I done me last bob at swy."

"Don't panic, brother," Blue consoled him. "I'm in the money this week. I come the raw prawn meself over a coupla Yanks the other day. Hop out."

He switched the lift over to automatic, followed Lofty out onto the top floor and closed the door. "Let's beat it round to the service lift. You're in luck's way, they got the beer on today from five to six and I'll take yer down to the bar."

"Five to six! What do they do with it the rest of the time?"

"Serve the Yanks and their babies up in the lounges at twice the price. Pretty tough I call it, all these kids getting in on a man's beer. Illegal too!"

"Whaddayamean — illegal?"

"No drink to be served in hotel lounges to girls under twenty-one. That's the law these days."

"Well, ain't they copped it?"

"Copped it? The SP?" Blue said in a disgusted voice. "Didn't yer know when the SP comes up against the law, the law moves over to make room."

"Jumping Jesus," Lofty observed morosely. "Seems like the bloody Yanks've bought the place."

"You'll see. The bar'll be lousy with 'em, and we'll probably have to fight our way in, and I tell you I'd just as soon walk into a dugout full of Jerries meself, with the little old trouble-and-strife down there pullin' the beer, but I'm not the bloke to see an old pal what pulled me out of the mud at Passchendaele do a perish for the want of a drink." Blue gave him a cheerful grin.

"A fat lot of gratitude I got too. Kickin' like a bloody mule, you was. Nearly kicked me guts out. Crikey, Blue, that hard old dial of yours is a sight for sore eyes. How yer feeling yerself, anyway?"

Not too dusty. I had nine months in the Hundred-and-Thirteenth, and they patched me up goodo. Where've you been in the last coupla years?"

"Me?" Lofty groaned. "I been pissantin' round the Northern Territory most of the time. Reckon I must 'ave swallowed 'alf a ton of dust. Gawd only knows why they think the Nips'd want to take a place like that. All I got against the politicians and their flamin' Brisbane Line is that they didn't give the bloody place away. 'Ave you seen anything of Billo lately?"

"Yeah. He's put his deferred pay into a taxi and he's makin' a real good thing of it. If you stick around you'll see him about seven. He always comes into the parkin' area down below and has his tea with the caretaker."

Lofty sighed. "Nothin' as good as this 'as 'appened ter me for donkey's years. Gawd, it's good to hit the old Steak-and-Kid again."

"Wait till you've been here a bit longer," Blue advised him. "It ain't the same old Steak-and-Kid any more. What with the Yanks blewing their cheques and the home-front Aussies takin' 'em down, you'd think you was back with the Froggies in the last war."

"Christ," muttered Lofty, "and did they clean us out!"

"Remember that leave we had in Paree in 1917?"

"Do I?" Lofty sighed dreamily. "I reckon I practically bought the Eiffel Tower."

"Well, that's what's happening to the Yanks here today — poor mugs. We ought to give 'em the Harbour Bridge to take home with them."

"D'you reckon?"

"Too bloody right. And are they booze artists! Boy, we thought we could put it away, but they beat us hollow. Ever seen 'em send down their beer chasers after a whisky?"

"I ain't seen no beer nor whisky neither since the last war," Lofty mourned.

Blue opened the lift door at the lower ground floor. "Stick yer head out and take a dekko, will yer, Dig? See if yer can spot anything prowlin' round that looks like the manager."

Lofty put his head out. "What's he like?"

"He's got striped pants and looks like a hungry kangaroo dog. There's a panic party on today — directors doin' an inspection, that's why they got the beer on. And they might take a dim view of me hopping down for one."

Lofty peered up and down. "All clear," he whispered.

Blue stepped out. "Crikey," he said, "ten to six. Just half a mo till I get this off." He opened the door of the men's staff room. "I don't dare show me face in the bar in this get-up," he explained, slipping off his maroon jacket and taking a faded khaki tunic and stained slouch hat from a hook.

"Ah, that's more like it," Lofty said approvingly. "Seeing you in that lion-tamer's uniform give me the willies."

"Between you and me and the gatepost, mate, it gives me the willies too. I only took the job on because the wife wanted me to, and she's been working that hard all the war tryin' to get enough together so as we could get a little country pub, I hadn't the heart to knock it back."

"'*Service Our Watchword*'," Lofty read out from a notice over the washbasins. "Huh! Fat lot of service I got."

"That ain't meant for you, old timer." Blue slapped him affectionately on the shoulder. "That's meant for them overfed blokes yer see around the foyer who are so swole up with their black market profits that they can't even tote their own bags round. And when they slip yer a coupla bob they think they've bought yer. It don't suit me at all."

Blue pushed open the house entrance of the public bar and the hot smell of crowded bodies struck them in the face. American servicemen were packed deep back to the wall, and the air was full of clamouring voices. Heavy shoes scraped on the tiled floor, glasses clinked and the cash registers tinkled incessantly.

"What-oh she bumps!" Blue edged along the wall towards the end of the bar. "Infiltration, them's the tactics."

"A bloke feels like a bloody foreigner in his own country," Lofty remarked loudly, shouldering his way after Blue.

"Shut yer mouth and keep down this end," Blue warned. "Me wife's on the other side and she'll raise a hell of a stink if she sees me."

Two fresh-faced American airmen were trying to get a companion through the swing doors to the lavatory, their hands clamping a handkerchief over his mouth; they had to step over a splather of vomit over which the useful was shovelling sawdust.

"Bunch of flamin' sissies. Why don't they learn to hold their booze?" Lofty rumbled, gazing contemptuously after them.

"Fer Chrissake, Lofty, lay off the Yanks, if you want to come out alive. Besides, they're winnin' the war for us, don't fergit."

"Balls!" Lofty put a boot like a steam shovel on the brass rail and leaned an elbow on the bar as he'd leaned it on innumerable bars from Ypres to Milne Bay. He spat with deliberation and mumbled under his breath that he could run a bloody war with one hand tied behind him better than the whole of this flash-tailored bunch with their fancy buckled shoes, bent on doing an honest digger in for his beer.

A hard-faced barmaid with a hennaed pompadour and a permanent smile was pulling beer rapidly.

"Pass us over a couple," Blue whispered persuasively.

Lofty commented adversely upon the collar that foamed over the top.

"Cripes," Blue whispered at him, "you been stuck up there in the jungle that long you don't know there's a war on. If you're not careful she won't serve you at all."

The barmaid continued to fill glasses and slide them across the counter.

"Here you are, gentlemen," she said, directing her smile over Blue's shoulder.

A hand reached out, passed over a ten-shilling note, and took a middy from her. "Keep the change, sister." She rang up the sale on her register and pocketed the change.

Blue repeated his order. She ignored him again.

Lofty glared over his shoulder. "Whaddaya expect," he muttered bitterly to Blue, "from the coves what murdered Phar Lap as soon as they got him to the States?"

There was a rustle along the counter. The barmaid's smile lost some of its brilliance.

"Lay off the Yanks," Blue warned, "and keep your

494

mind on the beer.''

"Listen, lady,'' Lofty said, resting two arms on the counter and sticking out his bony jaw, "we asked for two beers.''

The girl darted her eyes over his faded green uniform, flashed her smile at two GIs who breasted the bar beside him, and slid the next glasses to the newcomers.

"What the flamin'...." Lofty began.

"Take it easy,'' Blue pleaded, putting a hand on Lofty's arm as he began to unwind himself with a deliberation Blue knew only too well. "Pass 'em over, girlie,'' he begged, "we got here before them other blokes.''

"You wait your turn!'' she snapped as though hearing him for the first time, "like the others.''

"Christallbloodymighty!'' Lofty bellowed, bringing his fist down on the counter with a thump that set the glasses rattling. "Has a bloke got to stand here and be insulted in his own country, while a bunch of refugees from Pearl Harbor mop up all the beer?''

There was an ugly murmur behind them and a clank of glasses along the counter. The barmaid retreated; the girl next to her cast a startled eye in the direction of the disturbance and whispered to the useful, who disappeared round the corner of the bar.

Blue shut his teeth and groaned. "I suppose you know them's fightin' words?''

He picked up an empty bottle by the neck and slid it down beside him, turning his back to the counter and calculating with the expertness of long experience the distance and the opposition between them and the door. He looked sideways at Lofty, who had also turned and was leaning with his back against the bar, one heel on the rail, fists slowly clenching, while a smile spread across his face.

"Fightin' words?'' he drawled. The murmur died down. "What's wrong with sayin' they beat it from Pearl Harbor?''

The murmur swelled to a roar, the crowd pressed forward. A rangy young GI shaped up to him. "If you don't take that back,'' he shouted, "I'll, I'll...'' Lofty stuck a knobbly fist under his nose. "Take a Captain Cook at that, buddy. One more squeak out of you and I'll knock yer bloody block off."

The boy lashed out at him. Lofty's open hand caught him in the chest and sent him staggering back against his mates. A stocky airman made a swipe at Blue.

"Job him one, Blue," Lofty called encouragingly.

"Go easy, pal." A tall, wiry sergeant pushed his way through to Lofty, a smile creasing his atebrined face. "Say, buddy, weren't you at Milne Bay?"

Lofty glared at him from under lowered brows. "What's that gotta do with you?"

"Well, if you were," he laughed, "I reckon you're the guy that sold me a phoney Nip flag."

Lofty stared at him hard. "Christ Almighty," he shouted, "so y'are. I didn't know y' at first, yer lost that much weight."

The young GI made another lunge.

"Lay off, kid," Lofty said in a lordly fashion. He slid an arm round the American sergeant's shoulders. "Listen, youse blokes," he shouted, "it was all a mistake. It was some other blokes I meant. Yer serg here and me was pals at Milne Bay, and any Yank what's been at Milne Bay with me can 'ave all the beer in Sydney, for all I care."

"It's OK, buddies," the sergeant called, "he's a white guy. It's just he don't speak English too good."

A ripple of laughter went up from the crowd as the tension subsided.

"You bloody beaut," Lofty clapped him on the back. They turned to the bar together.

Blue looked up and saw a group of faces framed in the house door. L. F. and the directors! Jumping Jesus! He hurriedly faced the counter. The clatter at the bar had begun again.

"You can't blame us," the sergeant was saying, "if these dames've got their minds set on the tips instead of the taps. Have a drink on me." He turned to the barmaid. "Speed it up, sister," he said in a slow drawl. "Three, and make it snappy."

Lofty's rumbling subsided. "My bloody oath," he said, clapping him on the back again, "and if it don't make an appearance p.d.q., I'll wreck the whole bloody joint." He thumped the counter, bellowing cheerfully.

"Starve the crows!" Blue moaned as a plump figure came rapidly round the corner to them. "Wouldn't it?"

Doss flashed him a withering glance and switched on a smile of professional amiability for the American and Lofty. "What can I get you boys?"

Lofty leaned forward with the confidential leer that had once laid the mam'selles low in the *estaminets*. Doss smiled back, ignoring Blue. This means an earbashing for me tonight, he thought dismally.

"Three schooners," Lofty ordered with the lordly amiability of the host in his own country.

"And there'll be three more on me," added the American.

Doss took three glasses with a flick of her fingers and turned on the beer tap, filling them quickly and working the glasses so that there was only a narrow rim of froth on the top.

"There you are, boys," she said, "put it down. You'd better be quick if you want another. It's just on closing time."

The three men lifted their glasses and the beer went down smoothly.

"Never touched the sides," sighed Lofty.

"Fill 'em up again," said the American.

Doss beamed on him warmly.

Turning on the personality for them, Blue thought to himself sourly, but just wait till she gets on to me.

As the beer rose to the top of the glasses, Lofty threw out a commanding hand. "Take a look at this, you froth-blowers," he called to the other barmaids. "The bloody top weight's got you all stitched."

A male voice came through the burst of laughter. "Time, gentlemen, please!"

Doss gathered the three empty glasses again.

The voice was calling out monotonously. "All out gentlemen, six o'clock. All out, gentlemen, please."

The bar counter packed tighter as the unsatisfied mob surged forward frantically. Doss fixed Blue with a cold grey eye. "Your shout, I presume? The same again?"

"That's right," said Blue in a subdued voice.

She slid the glasses back to them and picked up the pound note he pushed across the counter, her eyes widening with surprise. She pocketed the change from the cash register and leaned her arms on the counter, smiling up at the three men sweetly.

"That's the last," she said in a soft voice, "and I hope it bloody well chokes you."

She was gone before Blue's companions had finished gaping. He stumbled through his explanation.

"Your wife?" they shouted, clapping him on the shoulder. "Gawd, what a woman."

Blue agreed, sighed deeply and finished his beer.

"Humph!" Horatio Veale grunted, turning away from the house entrance of the public bar and walking towards the service lift with the little knot of men at his heels. "Nearly had a nasty situation on your hands, Sharlton," he remarked unpleasantly.

L. F. pressed the lift button. "That's something we can't always guard against. The barmaids have their orders to give preference to the Americans and generally there are enough of them to discourage the few others who try to push their way in. But if you get a big fellow like that who's looking for a fight..."

"Yes," Veale took him up, "and there'll be more of them pushing their way in as the Americans thin out, and more of them out to fight for what they want. That simply bears out my point, gentlemen. The time has come when we must provide better drinking accommodation for our own servicemen."

"I quite agree with you." A spare, middle-aged man with deep clefts in his thin cheeks looked at Veale through rimless pince-nez perched on a high-bridged nose. "That's what I've been saying all this year — ever since I was appointed to the board. It's not only a question of profits. As a hotel, we owe decent service to our own boys."

The lift came down and L. F. opened the door, allowing the four directors to enter. He followed them in.

"Quite, quite, Allstone." Veale turned impatiently to L. F. "Stop at the second floor," he ordered. "I want these gentlemen to see the Gloucester and Windsor rooms. If we do away with the private rooms on the first floor and enlarge the lounge accommodation, the Gloucester and Windsor rooms will still be available for private tea parties and charity committees."

"I don't know if the ladies are going to like that at all," Daniel D'Arcy-Twyning put in in a high, thin voice. "My wife tells me it's getting very difficult to book a room for her committees at reasonable times, since we turned Milady's tea room into a drinking lounge."

"Well, old man," Veale said heartily, "you'll just have to explain to your wife that we feel we owe it to the boys. You saw for yourself ten minutes ago, that queue waiting at the Madrid Lounge...Yes, I'm afraid the ladies will have to adapt themselves a little so that we can give our men a fair deal."

"What I can't understand," Allstone's face had a puzzled look, "is why you're so keen about our own boys at this late date when the Americans are going anyway and I've been advocating the whole year..."

Veale turned to the big man at his side. "You know, Macartney, I think we'd have done the right thing if we'd listened to Allstone earlier."

Macartney answered with an agreeable rumble that started in his throat and seemed to travel down into his huge paunch.

"After all," Veale went on, turning to Allstone, "we did feel we had a duty to the American boys who were so far from home and gallant allies at that. And if we haven't given our own boys the deal we should have, we're going to make up for it now."

L. F. opened the door at the second floor. Allstone stepped out with a springy step and glanced up and down the corridor like a bird. Two women came out of the Marie Antoinette Salon and passed them. The men turned a corner and paused in front of a door labelled WINDSOR in elegant gilt lettering.

L. F. opened the door slightly. Veale motioned Allstone to look in. The large, panelled room was packed with bridge tables around which women of all ages were seated, intent on their game. A fashionably dressed woman near the door glanced up. L. F. gave her a reassuring smile, Allstone withdrew his head.

"Lady Lucy Govett's monthly bridge party for the starving Greek children," L. F. explained.

"By the way, Sharlton," Dan Twyning put in, "my wife tells me there's been a good deal of criticism about the catering for these afternoon functions. She says it's gone off badly."

"I don't think she'll have any further cause for worry," L. F. said confidentially. "Mrs Molesworth is giving her personal attention to it this afternoon. She even managed to get some cream."

Veale gave a short laugh. "Queer cattle, women, aren't they? It doesn't matter how much they eat at home, they're never happy unless they can gorge themselves in the middle of the afternoon."

"Well, if they pay for it," Twyning said truculently, "they've got a right to get it."

Veale clapped him on the shoulder. "That's right, old man, that's right. And the more they eat the easier they are to live with, eh?" He dug L. F. in the ribs. "If Mrs Molesworth's taking over, everything'll be all right."

The little procession walked along the corridor to the next door where GLOUCESTER was lettered on the grained wood.

"I don't know if Mrs D'Arcy-Twyning has finished her meeting," L. F. hesitated with his hand on the chrome knob.

"I should like Allstone to see the room," Veale said in a smooth voice. "Will you ask Mrs D'Arcy-Twyning if she would excuse us looking in for a minute, Sharlton?"

L. F. turned the knob resolutely and went in. Almost immediately he was back, holding the door open for Mrs D'Arcy-Twyning. She fluttered up to Horatio Veale, greeting him effusively.

"Why of course, Mr Veale, please come in. And how do you do, Mr Macartney? I'm just having our winding-up committee meeting for the OBNOs Ball...such a success...I'm so glad you came, I'm sure my ladies would like to have the opportunity of meeting you." She paused and turned to her husband. "I'm afraid I haven't had the pleasure of meeting all the gentlemen, Daniel."

"Oh I'm sorry, my dear. This is Mr Allstone, the newest member of our board. My wife, Mr Allstone."

Mrs D'Arcy-Twyning inclined her head and gave

Allstone a gracious smile. She ushered the gentlemen into the room and the buzz of conversation died down.

Mrs D'Arcy-Twyning went to her place at the head of the table and confronted her committee with an air of importance. "Ladies," she began, "I did not think I should have the pleasure of introducing the gentlemen to whom we owe such grateful thanks for allowing us to use Who's Who for our OBNOs Ball on Saturday night. Mr Horatio Veale, Chairman of Directors of the South Pacific Hotel, has brought two of his fellow directors down specially to meet you." She waved a beringed hand in the direction of Veale, who bowed courteously. "Mr Macartney and Mr Allstone. And you know my husband. And, oh yes of course, Mr Sharlton the manager," she finished without looking in L. F.'s direction.

The five men stood uncomfortably with the smiles pinned to their faces.

"And now let me introduce my ladies: Mrs Anstruther on my right, the honorary secretary, and on my left Mrs Catto, a wonderful treasurer...she's just told us we've made a clear profit of three hundred pounds, nine shillings and five pence after all expenses are paid. Wonderful, don't you think? If I'm not careful, you'll be stealing her to do your hotel accounts."

Veale bowed again. "You're very fortunate in having such a good treasurer," he said, and added hastily before she could start introducing the dozen or so ladies of the committee, "We are delighted that you had such a successful ball. And now, if you will excuse us, we must continue on our inspection of this floor. I do hope we haven't disturbed you!"

But before he could get out, Mrs D'Arcy-Twyning's voice rose again, shrill and insistent. "And we do hope, Mr Veale, that you're going to do something about the way this naughty Mr Sharlton is crowding us poor committee women right out of the hotel. We do hope now the Americans are beginning to go that you'll give us back our rooms again."

"Of course, of course," Veale agreed heartily. "Can't

have the ladies upset. We'll have to go into the matter, Sharlton."

He bowed again, the men all murmured amiably, took the smiles off their faces and followed him briskly, treading on each other's heels.

L. F. ushered the directors out of the lift at the sixth floor and followed them down the corridor to the board room, where Thelma was waiting with whisky and siphons set out on a side table.

"Well, well," Veale greeted her, "I hear you've been supplying illicit cream to the starving Greeks, Mrs Molesworth."

Thelma flashed him her brilliant smile. He could afford to be pleasant after what he'd put over Lance.

"I hope you're not going to fob us off with an austerity dinner to make up for it," he quirked an eyebrow at her.

"I've done my best within the five-shilling limit, Mr Veale. National Security price fixing, you know," she said archly. "You wouldn't have me break the law, would you?"

He laughed and sat down at the head of the board table.

Macartney took the seat on his right and rumbled amiably. "Have to send my cook up to get a few lessons from the chef here, Mrs Molesworth. Best meal I get in these days of rationing is the one you put on for us."

Thelma poured his glass half full of whisky. "I appreciate that compliment coming from you, Mr Macartney."

Mr Allstone wished her good afternoon courteously, and Dan Twyning sat down without a word. So he had his knife into her over Saturday still. Well, let him. Him and his bitch of a daughter. She poured out his whisky and handed L. F. a glass of lemon squash.

Veale raised his glass and held it to the light. "You know, it always gives me a twinge when I see you hand Sharlton his lemon squash after pouring out whiskies for the rest of us. Lucrezia Borgia touch. How do I know you haven't put a spot of cyanide in mine?" he said jovially.

"How indeed?" Thelma laughed. If the old fox only realised, there was nothing she'd like to do better. She set two bottles of Scotch with a jug of water and a siphon on the table within reach, placed a box of cigars at Veale's elbow and a box of cigarettes beside the drinks.

"Now, is there anything else I can get you?" she asked, including them all in a gracious smile.

"Nothing at all thanks," Veale assured her, "you anticipate our every need."

"You see my point about the new policy," Veale took up his theme again as soon as the door was closed. "We all know that the British fleet is on its way to the Pacific and you've seen for yourselves that the drinking accommodation, both of the public bar and private lounges, is completely inadequate."

L. F. nodded his head and took out his pen to take the minutes.

"I put it to you," Veale continued, "that the Princess Elizabeth and Margaret Rose and the Duchess of Kent rooms on the first floor should be turned into further drinking lounge accommodation — have to change the names of course, *lèse majesté* and all that. What do you say to that, Allstone?"

"Yes, that seems all right to me, but more lounge accommodation won't really benefit the average Australian serviceman, will it?"

"I'm coming to that," Veale continued. "What I had in mind was converting the men's staff room on the lower ground floor into an extension of the public bar. With the width of the passage thrown in, that will give us roughly another twenty feet of bar and should accommodate quite a few of our lads."

Allstone put his pince-nez back on his nose and spoke judicially. "I support the extension of lounge and bar facilities in principle, but before agreeing to your proposals, I should like to hear what alternative accommodation you propose to give to the male staff."

Before Veale could answer, Twyning cut in. "Talking about male staff, what's been done about that liftman? My wife and daughter had to listen to that game of two-up going on for twenty minutes while they waited for the lift. The language was disgusting, they said." He glared at L. F.

Veale leaned forward and put on his most persuasive manner. "Now look here, Dan, you know as well as we do that liftman is a returned soldier of two wars and we can't afford at this moment to pick a fight with the RSL with the *Daily Sketch* watching our every move and the rest of the journalists panting to be in at the kill. Apart from returned war correspondents, too many of their general reporters are ex-servicemen themselves."

Twyning thrust out his jaw. "Well, I'm damned if I'm going to have my wife and daughter insulted by a larrikin like that fellow Blue, as he calls himself, Returned Soldiers' League or no Returned Soldiers' League."

Allstone turned on Twyning a politely inquiring face. "Was there actual discourtesy on Friday?"

Dan shuffled his feet angrily. "The whole thing was discourteous. Keeping them waiting."

"Oh," Allstone's face cleared. "That was due to mechanical failure. I presume there was nothing in the words or actions the liftman directed to the ladies to which they could take exception."

Veale attempted to close the argument. "There's nothing against him except that when the lift stuck he played two-up with some American officers. That's the plain fact, and apart from a tongue-bashing from Sharlton, nothing else would have been heard of it if it hadn't been for that *Daily Sketch* fellow snooping around on the lookout for something he could make capital out of."

"Well, that's not my wife's opinion." Dan stared sulkily into his glass.

Veale exchanged glances with L. F. "Look here, Dan," he said placatingly, "we don't like keeping him on any more than you do, but the fellow's only here temporarily and you just imagine how the RSL would rush to take up the case of a veteran of two wars who's trying to turn over an honest penny in between coming out of hospital and waiting for his discharge, and how the *Daily Sketch* would love to get their teeth into the story."

"Why don't you put him somewhere where he won't be able to insult the guests and give the place a bad name?" Twyning demanded.

L. F. made a helpless gesture. "I'm afraid that's impossible. I did think of putting him on the goods lift but his war injuries won't permit him to do heavy work."

"I'm sorry, Dan," Veale said soothingly. "I'm afraid there's nothing for it but to put up with him for a while at least, and I for one feel that it would be an absolutely fatal policy to run our heads up against the Returned Soldiers. What do you say, Allstone?"

"I think you're right."

"Well, that's settled." Veale heaved a sigh of relief. "Now, let's get on with our business."

"Mr Sharlton was going to tell us where he intended to put the displaced male staff," Allstone prompted.

"There's a room coming vacant," L. F. explained. "It is at present used as a bedroom by the masseuse of the Marie Antoinette, but Mrs Molesworth has informed me that Miss Forrest will be leaving shortly. The room is dark and on the service lift and quite unsuitable for a guest room, so that it would serve very well as a second staff room."

Allstone straightened his pince-nez. "I quite see the desirability of extending the lounges in the present congestion, but I'm not at all sure that we have the right to do so at the expense of staff conditions," he said with quiet obstinacy.

Veale cut in. "I'm in complete agreement with Allstone. Nothing but the best working conditions for the employees."

"I have a suggestion, Mr Chairman," Macartney began in his rich, lazy voice. "I propose that Mr Allstone and Mr Twyning should make a joint inspection of the proposed new staff rooms and report fully with any recommendations they may see fit to make, to the full board."

"Very good idea, very good idea indeed," Veale agreed quickly. "If you two gentlemen would be good enough to undertake a joint inspection and report to the board next

Tuesday, we can close this meeting."

The two men signified their agreement.

"Well, I think we've all earned a drink," Veale poured out half a tumbler for Macartney and helped himself. "How about you?" he said, passing the bottle to Allstone.

"Thanks," Allstone poured himself a nip and filled his glass with soda water.

L. F. poured out a drink from the jug of iced squash.

"Allstone, just take a look at that fellow," Veale said jocularly. "I've known him twenty years and I've never seen him take anything stronger than a glass of squash. Bad advertisement for a hotel, don't you think?"

Allstone smiled. "I think you should arrange for him to receive this Woman's Temperance deputation instead of me."

"It's your turn to be delivered to the lions this time," Macartney rumbled amiably, "but I always say we should hold him up as an example of resisting temptation. What do you think of yourself in that role, Sharlton?"

L. F. gave the sickly smile of one who has smiled too often at the same joke. He half rose. "Shall I order the dinner to be sent up now?"

"Just one moment, if you please," Allstone held up his hand to L. F. "There is another matter I'd like to bring forward before you break up the meeting, Mr Chairman. Frankly I can't get out of my mind that scene we witnessed in the public bar downstairs half an hour ago. I can tell you I'm not proud of it."

"None of us are," Veale's voice was brusque. "But show me any hotel in the city that's any better."

"That doesn't seem to me to be the point," Allstone drew a newspaper cutting out of his wallet. "Personally," he said, "I don't see that we can ignore any longer such outspoken comments as appeared in this morning's paper. And when the papers talk of 'pig-trough drinking', 'the six o'clock guzzle' and the general hoggishness of our drinking conditions, they're absolutely right."

"That's exactly why I'm proposing to open up further

accommodation," Veale said with asperity.

"I appreciate that, Mr Veale, but it will still mean perpendicular drinking with more opportunity for more people to join in the six o'clock swill."

"If that's the way people like to drink, what do you expect us to do about it?" Dan Twyning said belligerently. "You don't expect us to run the bar like a ladies' parlour, do you?"

"No," Allstone turned to Veale. "If the chairman will permit me, I have a practical proposition to make which I would like to discuss with you gentlemen before bringing it up at the full board meeting."

Veale looked at his watch impatiently. "All right, all right," he said, "we haven't much time, so let's have it."

"Gentlemen," Allstone began, "there's a magnificent public room on the seventh floor of this hotel which is fully equipped to seat three hundred people. Why can't we lead the way and turn it into a friendly drinking lounge on the lines advocated by the community hotel movement?"

"Who's Who!" Dan Twyning put his glass down and stared at Allstone as if to reassure himself that the man was still in his senses.

"A community drinking lounge," H. V. repeated, as if he hadn't heard correctly.

Macartney kept his eyes down and took a gulp of neat whisky. L. F. blanched and looked quickly from one face to the other.

"That's the idea," Allstone went on, unconscious of the sensation he had created. "Friendly drinking in the afternoon with light refreshments, tea or coffee if they prefer it, and dine and dance in the evening."

"I presume you don't mean the same people to stay on and take advantage of the dual arrangement," Veale said acidly.

"Oh, I don't think that's necessary," Allstone replied with careful consideration. "Although I do advocate the provision in suburban hotels of facilities for family parties, recreation and other club amenities, there isn't the same need in the city."

"So you would leave Mr Sharlton his Who's Who for the evening," Veale sighed in mock relief.

Allstone went on earnestly. "Sooner or later Australia will have to come into line with other countries. As our boys return from overseas, they're going to be less willing to put up with the scrimmaging and shoving that goes on at the pig troughs we call public bars."

Veale tapped impatiently on the table. "Come, come, those are strong words."

Allstone looked at him mildly. "I feel very strongly about it. So strongly that I consider it our duty as one of the most important hotels in the state to take the lead in establishing civilised drinking conditions."

"But you've already heard our plans for improvement," Veale said testily.

"Pardon me, I've heard only plans for increasing drinking facilities. What I'm advocating is a reversal of policy. I want to see this hotel run for the benefit of the customers and not merely to provide bigger profits for the shareholders."

Veale poured himself another drink and shook his glass in Allstone's direction, his little bloodshot eyes snapping. "Really, Allstone, I've sat at many board meetings but I've never had to listen to bunk like this before."

"Balmy," Twyning spat out.

"You're a sound enough businessman," Veale went on, "to know that what you're suggesting simply couldn't be done."

"Why not? It's been done before."

"Look Allstone, I warn you, I can't take another word about German beer gardens or Paris cafés."

Allstone was unruffled. "I had no intention of mentioning beer gardens or cafés." He opened his wallet again and unfolded a typewritten document. "With your permission, I'd like to read you some figures of a venture much nearer home." He cleared his throat. "When I was in South Australia recently, I had a chance of going over the Renmark Community Hotel, and I can tell you gentlemen I've rarely been so impressed. It's not only the excellent manner in which the place is run, but the hotel is an integral part of the community, not a parasite on it as ours unfortunately tends to be."

Veale looked at Macartney speechless.

"To be brief, just let me give you these figures. In the fifty years since it has been established, it has built up hotel assets valued at approximately one hundred thousand pounds and has donated a further hundred thousand to the community. This has been shared out between the local hospital, council, sporting bodies and benevolent institutions, as well as providing substantial encouragement to science and the arts. When you consider that Renmark's quite a small town, it's a magnificent record. Think of what they've been able to do with one hundred thousand pounds! Why, our net profit over the last two years only has been more than that."

There was a deathly silence round the table. Macartney opened his eyes lazily. "Make a full report on it to the next board meeting," he boomed.

"Yes, yes. Give us time to think it over." Veale grasped at the suggestion. "Now for that dinner, Sharlton."

L. F. sprang to the telephone.

Allstone stood up. "If you'll excuse me, Veale, I'm expected at home."

"Of course, of course," Veale agreed heartily.

"Well, good evening, gentlemen. I'll have the report along to you before the end of the week."

"You won't forget that you're meeting the ladies here at two thirty tomorrow," L. F. reminded him.

"No, I won't forget, although I can assure you I feel decidedly nervous. This will be the first time I have ever received a deputation of ladies."

"Don't worry about that," Macartney reassured him. "They're used to it even if you aren't. Annual affair. We've all been through it. Quite simple."

"Don't you go giving them any of the community hotel stuff," Twyning warned.

"Oh no, of course not. I shouldn't think of making any public statement until the matter has been before the full board." Allstone picked up his hat. "Please make my apologies to Mrs Molesworth, Mr Sharlton."

He went out.

"Mad!" Veale exploded.

"Damn dangerous." Twyning threw out his hands expressively.

"Disgruntled," Macartney boomed. "Better get some more shares for him."

"It's not as simple as that," Veale said. "When he didn't agree with the board over our policy of preference for the Americans, he approached me about resigning and offered to sell the shares he's already got."

"Damn pity you didn't let him," Twyning slumped morosely in his chair.

"And where would we have been with Manpower if I had? Answer me that. No, keep him so long as we need him. Better we should have to listen to him once a month than that he should go spreading that nonsense abroad."

Macartney agreed.

"I'm not too sure he hasn't already been doing just that," Twyning suggested. "He's probably the fellow behind all this newspaper stink."

Veale set up with a startled expression. "By God, if I thought that..."

L. F. looked at Veale's set mouth. Allstone's brand of publicity wouldn't do H. V. any good in politics, he thought.

A knock came at the door and Mrs Molesworth entered, followed by a waiter pushing a traymobile. There was dead silence while he moved a small table out into the room and set it under her direction.

Evidently things hadn't gone too well, she thought, taking a glance at the grim faces of the four men as they went on drinking. Allstone must have gone. She wondered if there'd been a row, he was always dropping bricks. All she hoped was he'd dropped one on Veale, good and heavy.

"Everything is ready, gentlemen," she announced.

The men rose and moved over to the dining table. The waiter came in with the hors d'oeuvres. Thelma dismissed him and served them herself.

Dan Twyning stabbed an oyster with his fork. "Community hotels! The fellow's crackbrained! Do away with perpendicular drinking!" Dan went on aggressively. "Reckons a man has three drinks standing up to every one he'd have sitting down."

Veale agreed. "With his community drinking the overhead'd be three times as heavy for one drink as it is for three now. Of course the fellow's a crackpot — all reformers are the same... When he offered to sell me his three hundred South Pacific shares, he told me then he wanted to put the money into a central community hotel scheme for Sydney. Even if they get it going there won't be a penny out of it for years — if ever. They've got a haywire plan of not having shareholders in the ordinary sense and putting the profits back into clubs and entertainments and playgrounds for kids. He saw you about it, didn't he, Mac?"

Macartney nodded. "Consulted me about floating a company under the Co-operative Societies and Community Settlement Act."

"What did you advise?" Veale cocked a humorous, inquiring eye.

"Told him to wait for the amendment to the Liquor Act and his committee'd probably get a licence handed to them." Macartney returned to his soup.

"You sly old dog," Veale leaned over and clapped him on the shoulder.

Dan looked up in alarm. "Where did you hear that?"

"Don't get excited, we're attending to that. I'll bet you ten to one if there's any provision for community hotels at all they'll have to be established by municipal or shire councils. That'll hamstring them, eh Mac?" Veale said jovially.

Macartney nodded.

"We'll show 'em community hotels and doing away with bar drinking! Eh, Sharlton?" Veale exchanged smiles with L. F.

Thelma turned abruptly to the serving table. It was sickening to hear the way they went on. She wondered how she could ever have been such a fool as to fall for Veale's geniality. He was even foxier than Macartney.

The waiter came in with the next course. She lifted the silver lids, set her lips in their customary smile and moved over to serve the gentlemen.

"Nice bit of fish," Veale remarked to her amiably as he savoured his first mouthful of grilled flounder.

She inclined her head graciously, poured out his chablis and hoped he'd choke on it.

"That brings me to something that I think you gentlemen will find interesting," Veale went on, as though there had been no interruption. "I have here a copy of a circular letter directed to the ALP Leagues. Pretty little document," he said grimly, spreading the foolscap sheets on the table beside him. "Starts off like this. 'The hotel-keepers of this state are perturbed and alarmed that in the proposed Liquor Act amendments no mention is made by the government about looking into the activities of the breweries.'"

"Hotel-keepers of this state," Dan Twyning echoed, "they wouldn't dare."

"Of course they wouldn't dare openly," Veale agreed, "but apparently there's a bunch of them have got together and they've concocted this circular. It's an anonymous document — at present! Now, just listen to this. 'We strongly urge a Royal Commission to inquire into the following matters'. And the matter for the first inquiry is tied houses."

"Tied houses. I'd give them tied houses if I found out any of them were Frith and Company managers or licensees. They wouldn't be 'tied' for long," Twyning said viciously.

"As a matter of fact, I have reason to suspect that a number of them are. There's one fellow I know for certain has a free house, but he's working on a loan from Frith and Company and selling our beer — he won't be difficult to bring to heel. If the others are whom I suspect, they're all on short leases. We'll put the rents up, that'll get rid of them."

The door opened and the waiter came in with a heavily laden tray. Veale turned the papers over.

When he had sampled his chicken Maryland and found it good and Thelma had refilled his wine glass, he went on reading between mouthfuls. "Second item suggested for inquiry is bonuses and increased rents demanded by the breweries, and third...just listen to this, they want the Royal Commission to inquire into 'the real capital involved in the breweries and the payment of thousands of pounds into the funds of the political parties'."

"Royal Commission!" Twyning spluttered. "Whoever drew that up ought to go back to the kindergarten. Do they think any political party is going to hand over a set of figures all neatly audited for the convenience of a Royal Commission?" He cut up his chicken with vicious jabs. "It's like all this damned agitation for nationalisation. They don't know what they're talking about. If the public only realised it would cost a hundred million to buy out the breweries' interest and then work out what that'd do to their taxes, they'd soon call the cranks off."

Veale stabbed the paper with his forefinger. "This is the kind of thing the ULVA ought to prevent. Getting slack."

"Anything else they'd like enquired into?"

"Plenty. You can have a look for yourself." He pushed the paper across the table.

Twyning picked it up. "Do you think there's a chance of the sub-committee taking any notice?"

"What's your opinion, Mac?"

Macartney wiped his mouth. "Forget it," he said. "That document might look like dynamite, but it's only a squib. There's no one strong enough in this state to even begin talking like that. We've got 'em all sewn up."

"But what about the amendment? Do you think that'll have any influence?" Twyning demanded irritably.

"You can take my word for it, all the amendment'll do is deal with the sale of liquor. It won't touch the breweries. There'll be a referendum on hours and a few concessions, like restaurant licences and registered clubs. The wowsers'll spend hundreds of pounds on yelling 'Down with the drink evil' and we'll spend hundreds of thousands reminding the public that temperance means moderation, not prohibition.''

"They can knock back the late closing referendum," Twyning said morosely.

Macartney moved his huge head slowly from side to side. "What harm can that do whichever way it goes? If it stays at six o'clock they can still drink in the lounges as late as they did in every pub in the country till the liquor got short — and we can charge 'em twice as much. And if the hours are extended, the breweries will put up the rent of the hotels for every extra hour they're open."

Dan Twyning looked relieved. "I'm quite sure you're right," he said, "but you never know how much fuss there's going to be in the meantime. It only wants the papers to get hold of documents like that and they can be an infernal nuisance, beside stirring up a whole lot of nosey parkers who'd be better looking after their own business."

"Don't let it spoil your dinner, Dan. Look at Sharlton, it isn't upsetting his appetite."

Veale gave L. F. a conspirator's smile.

"I shall begin to worry when you gentlemen do. I have implicit faith in your judgment," L. F. murmured silkily.

"And we in yours — and in Mrs Molesworth." Veale lifted his glass to her.

"Hear, hear," Macartney rumbled.

L. F. looked at Thelma anxiously; she inclined her head like a queen.

Veale picked up the document. "Now, what have you got for dessert?" he inquired as Thelma removed his plate. He shook the paper at her playfully. "Something nice, I hope, to take the bad taste of this out of our mouths."

Ursula took a small florist's box from the messenger. *Miss Margaret Mallon* indeed! She put it down distastefully on the edge of her desk and stared at it, wondering who it came from. Then she picked it up and looked at it carefully, turning it over in her hands. Of course the card would be inside! Probably from that Colonel Maddocks who had been ringing up all the morning and left the message. He'd be waiting at five-thirty, would he! She glanced at the clock. Well, he could wait, for all she cared. That would teach Guinea to come in with a high and mighty air half way through the morning and walk past her without so much as a word. Ursula put the box down on the far end of the desk. Let her find it for herself.

The rest of the staff had left when Claire called Guinea and showed her the box. "Didn't you know it was here?"

"Hadn't the faintest."

"That's Cronin up to her usual tricks and I'm perfectly certain she doesn't deliver all our phone messages. What's he sent you this time?"

Guinea opened the box and looked at the card. "I'll be waiting. Byron", was all it said. She threw it down irritably. "What's he mean, he'll be waiting? He must be nuts." She fingered the orchids gloomily. "Jeepers! More orchids!"

"You're getting blasé, my girl." Claire lifted up the exquisite creamy-gold spray. "I wish I had half your luck."

"You take them, then," Guinea thrust them impulsively into her hand. "I'm fed up to the teeth with them."

Claire was incredulous and delighted. "My horoscope says this is my lucky day, and it must be right." She held them against her shoulder. "They'll look perfect with my brown suit tonight. We're going to the game."

"I hope they bring you luck, then." Guinea lingered disconsolately watching Claire wrap up the orchids again.

"I'm sure they will." Claire took a swift look at Guinea's gloomy face. "Say, Guin, there's nothing wrong, is there?"

Guinea shook her head. "I'm OK. Just got the pip."

"You're missing Sherwood, I suppose. You should worry, with Maddocks tailing you up like this. And didn't I see you with that nice Air Force lad of yours in tow again yesterday?"

"That skunk."

"Well, anyway, you've got more men than a film star."

"Men!" Guinea kicked the wastepaper basket passionately. "Men! Crikey, how I hate men!"

"You've got the willies after going to that funeral this morning. That's what's the matter with you."

Guinea hesitated and then looked at her. "Listen, Claire," she began hesitantly, "I'm awfully sorry, but I've simply got to get off tomorrow morning."

Claire flipped open the appointments book. "I don't see how it can possibly be managed," she said shortly. "You know Alice has to get away at one o'clock to go with Mary and I really do think it's a bit over the odds even asking me when you were off this morning. The rest of us have been running our feet off all day."

Guinea flushed scarlet and kept her eyes down. "I'm sorry, but I've got to go, that's all there is to it."

Claire slammed the book back on the desk. "If you ask my opinion, I think it's the limit and it's absolutely unfair to everyone. I suppose it's another funeral," she added sarcastically, and looked up to see that Guinea was crying. "Good Lord, Guin, there is something wrong and you'd better tell me. You're not in the same jam as Mary Parker, are you?"

"No, it's much worse than that. It's...it's Monnie, and I've got to go."

"Come on into my office." Claire took her arm. "We don't want anyone walking in on us here."

In the office she took out the brandy and poured out two stiff drinks. "Now come along, what's the trouble?"

Guinea told her. Claire gave a long-drawn whistle. "My God, you're in a hell of a hole all right. Was she really in a brothel?"

"Yes, the poor little devil. I don't know how she didn't

517

pass out; the evidence nearly made me sick and I'm tough enough. Oh Claire, you just can't imagine how utterly revolting it was. If I could get my hands on those girls who dragged her into it, I'd slit their throats. You couldn't believe such rotten little bitches existed.''

"Couldn't I?'' Claire poured herself another drink. "My girl, there's nothing you can tell me after spending half the morning up in D.D.T.'s suite with her Pick-Pockettes. They make me vomit. But what are you going to do?''

"That's the awful part, I haven't got the faintest idea. The kid's that frightened of Mum she says she won't go home.''

"God spare me from good women!''

"But Claire, they won't let me have her and unless she goes home there's nowhere else for her to go but that awful Parramatta reformatory. And she simply mustn't go there.''

"Haven't you got any relations in the country?''

"Mum's got a sister up at Orange. But she's even stricter than Mum, and Dad's people are in Victoria and we don't really know them.''

"What about your Aunt Annie you used to talk so much about? Who's she?''

"She's not a real aunt, she's Kim's aunt, and I'm not asking favours from his family.''

"But if Monnie won't go home you've got to clutch at any straw to keep her out of Parramatta.''

Guinea's face suddenly lit up. "Holy mackerel, you're right! Why didn't I realise that before? Of course, Aunt Annie's the one. Monnie's been her white-haired baby ever since they lived next door to us. I'll go out and see her tonight.''

"Why don't you ring her up now?''

"I will,'' Guinea rushed to the phone. She had a moment's misgiving — what if Kim answered? Oh, to hell with Kim, she'd finished with him. What was going to happen to Monnie was more important.

After a long wait, Aunt Annie's voice came, monosyllabic and cautious. Kim reckoned when Aunt Annie answered the phone she sounded as though she expected you to put in the nips for a fiver. Her voice brightened when she discovered who it was. Could Guinea come out? Why, of course, come to tea. Guinea hastily said she would have to work a while yet. The thought of sitting down to tea with the Scotts was more than she could bear. Besides, if she got out there a bit later Kim would probably have gone out. Well, after tea then, Aunt Annie's cheerful voice agreed, as early as she could manage. It would be wonderful to see her.

Guinea put the receiver down with a sigh of relief. "It's all right," she told Claire. "I'll get a bite to eat and then I'm going straight out."

"Well, that's fine. And don't worry about tomorrow at all. I'll fix things somehow or other."

Guinea gave her a bear's hug. "Thanks for everything, Claire. You don't know what you've done for me." She grabbed her bag and went out.

At the top of the staff steps Guinea stopped and groaned. Below her in the service lane stood Colonel Maddocks, his face creased into a broad smile.

Wouldn't it! Just the man she had wanted to see earlier and now she'd have to put him off. "Well, this is a surprise," she said, trying to sound welcoming and warning at the same time.

"I called you up and left a message I'd be waiting here at five-thirty. Didn't you get it?"

"No."

"But you're glad to see me all the same, aren't you." He slid an arm through hers persuasively. "What about a spot of dinner? I've got the car here."

Guinea got in beside him and his hand closed over hers.

"If I hadn't caught up with you tonight I was going to call out the kidnapping squad."

She shuddered. Fine joke, that was!

"Why have you been eludin' me, honey?"

"I haven't. I've been busy."'

"It amounts to the same thing. Did you get my

flowers?"

"Yeah. I gave 'em away." He smiled wryly, and she added, relenting. "One of the girls at the salon was going to a special do and she's never had orchids before."

"You're a sweet child," he said, kissing her fingertips.

Crikey, what suckers men are, she thought. If Aunt Annie takes Monnie I'll marry him. I've had Sydney, I've been here too long. That'll teach Kim Scott a lesson too.

"You're going to have dinner with me," he said masterfully.

"If you like."

"And maybe dancing afterwards? It seems years since we danced."

"Two nights," Guinea corrected, "but I've got to go out to my aunt's after dinner."

He started up the car. "We'll eat first anyway. Where'll we go?"

"Somewhere quiet. I feel like a funeral in this dress."

"You're just perfect. You look like a black lily with a golden crown."

"I don't feel like it."

"What about the Coq d'Or?"

They walked down the narrow lane of Angel Place with the setting sun throwing their shadows grotesquely ahead of them and falling radiantly over Guinea's hair.

"You've sure got a wonderful halo," Byron said, "they'll be thinking I abducted an angel."

She smiled faintly at him, and his heart missed a beat. She was enchanting and childlike in the plain black suit with the little white collar. He had never seen anyone like her.

The restaurant was crowded and Byron greeted friends on all sides. The proprietor came up to them. "I have two seats for you, Colonel Maddocks." He led them to a table in a quiet corner. Guinea knew that heads turned to watch them, and she moved with ladylike steps and downcast eyes. Byron must be an important old gink, she thought as she sat down on the cushioned wall seat, to get service in a place already lousy with Yanks.

"This place has an air," he said, seating himself beside her, "it reminds me of Greenwich Village with those cute murals."

Guinea looked up at the gaily-coloured peasants cavorting primly round the walls in their fairytale farm. Cripes, Guinea thought, haystacks!

"I'd like to have a day with you in the country," Byron murmured.

Not a hope, she thought, but she murmured back: "It'd be lovely." Holy mackerel, men had only one thought in their minds. She gave him a side glance and wondered if she could stick him if she married him. From all the symptoms, it wouldn't take much to bring him up to scratch, especially as he'd taken the trouble to tell her he was divorced. She dropped her eyes demurely, calculating how long she had to work on him, and raised them again in a slow confiding glance.

"You look awfully sweet tonight." He moved closer to her. "I like you in black and that little-girl collar does something."

Yeah, nearly cuts my throat, she thought, smiling up at him with appealing wistfulness. Love was blind all right, waste of time buying clothes for men; when they got to that state all they knew was whether you were dressed or undressed.

He opened the menu out for her. "What would you like?"

"Just whatever you think," she said demurely. He chose omelettes, the place was renowned for them.

Golly, how she'd like to get her teeth into a good underdone steak. She was starving, she'd had practically nothing to eat all day. She sipped her soup delicately and crumbled the roll, disguising her hunger, but she need not have worried, Byron was so absorbed in what he had to say that he didn't notice when she spread the last of the butter on his roll and ate it as well as her own.

"You'll maybe think I'm crazy," he was saying, "but I haven't been able to get you out of my mind since

Saturday night."

She fluttered her eyelashes at him tremulously.

"Did you see that big hole in the sidewalk outside your house? If my friends back in the States could see Byron Maddocks wearing the sidewalk out for a little dream girl he'd only seen once, they'd laugh their heads off."

She curled her fingers trustfully in his hand lying on the padded seat beside her. They won't laugh their heads off when you bring that same little dream girl home with you, brother, she thought, I'll see to that.

"Did your landlady tell you I called Sunday?"

She nodded. "I was awfully sorry I was out, but I had to go home. It was Daddy's birthday."

Byron loved her for that and his eyes told her so. "I'll bet you're your Daddy's little sweetheart," he said tenderly, "but I'd have driven you out, if you'd only asked me."

Guinea smiled and a cold shiver ran up her spine at the thought of her mother's face if she had arrived with Byron. "It would have been lovely." Her lips were parted and her eyes had a faraway look.

Byron drew a deep breath. "I came round yesterday, too, and they told me you'd gone surfing."

"My cousin's on leave," she murmured.

"He's an Air Force guy, isn't he?" Byron's voice was accusing.

"That's right. He's down on leave from Borneo. He came out to see Mummy and Daddy on Sunday too. I hadn't seen him for ages."

Byron started on his omelette. Family affection was very touching in its place, but this seemed carrying it a bit too far. "I called the SP too in case you'd drop in and get my message. But it just didn't seem to be my lucky day."

Nor mine, thought Guinea, wishing her omelette was twice the size.

"Is it the same cousin you're going out to see tonight?"

"No. His aunt."

Byron felt the family relationships were unnecessarily involved. "I could drive you then?"

"It's an awfully long way," she said half-heartedly. But if he did drive her out it'd mean she'd have an excuse to get away as soon as she'd told her Aunt Annie about Monnie.

He lit two cigarettes between his lips and handed her one. "I'd take you to the moon if you wanted me to."

"I may take you up on that one of these nights."

"Yes, I hope it's one of these nights."

She watched him critically through half-closed eyes. He had quite a lot of grey hairs, and his skin was leathery and wrinkled. But he was lean and tall and his uniform was splendidly tailored. Probably runs away in the shoulders, she thought. Alfalfa was forty-seven and they'd been boys together, so he'd be somewhere about there too. My God, nearly as old as Deb's McFarland. He'd been divorced twice, Alfalfa had told her. Heavens, he might be a grandfather — the thought struck her with horror. But Byron was sweet really and only for the grey hairs you wouldn't have known he was so old, not like Alfalfa, who'd started to run to fat round the middle and had jowls and a bald spot on his crown.

"A penny for that one," Byron murmured.

"I was just wondering why you're being so terribly kind to me."

He drooped over her with an infatuated smile. "Can't you guess?"

Too right I can. She picked up his hand and glanced at his watch. "What's the time?"

His lean fingers closed over hers and her hair brushed his face as they both bent their heads to look at the watch.

"I'm afraid I'll have to be going."

"You'll let me drive you?"

"OK, but you'll have to stop outside, it's family business."

"I won't mind that, so long as you're not too long."

"You can depend on that," she said with a fervour he misunderstood.

They went out into the darkened street. The car soon carried them out of the city traffic and Byron put on a burst of speed along Parramatta Road. He drove with one arm around Guinea's shoulder and she wished they could go on like this forever, shut off from her own problems as well as Monnie's.

When they turned into Liverpool Road and she sat up to direct him to the Scotts' turnoff, the world rushed in on her again, and she had a hollow feeling in the pit of her stomach at the thought of having to tell Aunt Annie about Monnie. She wondered with something approaching horror if she would have the job of telling her mother, too.

They drew up at last in front of the Scotts' old-fashioned brick cottage, set back from the road among shrubs. It was on a corner, and Kim's father had built the garage at the side of the house to face the main road, so that the garden and the cottage still kept their old seclusion behind the high hedge. The wisteria was out and rioted over the arch above the gate in masses of heavy bloom that the streetlight turned to silver.

"Your uncle's a gardener, I see," Byron remarked, as he opened the door for her.

"Yes," Guinea agreed. It was all too complicated and there wasn't time to explain that it wasn't her uncle. But if it came to that, it wasn't her Aunt Annie either. She felt that it was all better left where it was, since eventually it would work out that Kim wasn't her cousin.

"You wait here," she said firmly, pressing his hand to soften her words.

"You won't be long?"

"I can promise you I won't be a minute longer than I can help."

Guinea's knees were shaking as she walked slowly up the path. Only for Byron watching her she'd have turned and fled. Get along with you, Peg, she said to herself, you're yaller, my girl.

Any further hesitation was ended by Aunt Annie appearing at the gauze door and drawing her in. Her welcome was so warm and her kiss so loving that the knotted tangle in Guinea's chest began to unravel.

"Did I hear a car, Peg?"

"Yes, and I can't stay long, it's waiting for me."

"Are you sure you wouldn't like to ask him in?"

"No, Aunt Annie. I've got something terribly serious to talk to you about."

"Something wrong at home?"

"In a way." She looked around nervously as though they might be overheard. "Is there anyone else about?"

"No, not a soul. Kim's over in the garage with his father. I didn't tell them you were coming, but I'll give him a call if you like."

"No, don't do that. It's you I want to see."

Aunt Annie's face clouded with disappointment. She was romantic and she'd hoped...She sighed. Well, young people had to find their own feet. "Come into the kitchen," she invited, "I'm just having a cup of tea." She poured out a second cup and they sat down at each side of the table. "You'd better tell me without any beating about the bush," she said.

"It's about Monnie."

Aunt Annie sat up in alarm and her voice was sharp. "Monnie? Good gracious, what's happened to Monnie?"

"She's in an awful mess."

"Is she ill?"

"No."

"I suppose she's had another row with your mother, is that what it is?"

Guinea passed her hand wearily over her eyes. "This is something worse than anything you could possibly imagine."

Aunt Annie's eyes widened. "She's not going to have a baby, is she?" she asked in mounting alarm.

Guinea shook her head.

"That's a relief anyway. Well, get on with your story, though it seems to me if she's not in trouble you're making a mountain out of a molehill."

Guinea sat staring down at the cup she held cradled between her hands. "Listen, Aunt Annie. Last night Monnie was picked up by the police...in a brothel...in town...and I've been down at the Children's Court all the morning trying to find out what's going to be done about her.''

The little fat woman put down her cup very quietly. She took off her glasses and polished them with her handkerchief. She put her glasses back again with hands that shook, blew her nose, then looked at Guinea and said in a voice that she had never heard before, "Now, whoever could have taken my little Monnie to a place like that?''

"It wasn't her fault," Guinea began.

"Who's saying it was her fault?" Aunt Annie's colour was returning and she sat with her hands clasped tightly together. "Does your mother know?"

"She will by now. Monnie wouldn't give the police her home address at first, but I had to tell them this morning.''

"Where have they got the poor lamb now?"

"She's in the girls' shelter at Glebe.''

"And why, pray, have they taken her there, if the child's done nobody any harm?"

"You don't understand, Aunt. When the police found her, she was in bed with a man.''

"A man!" Aunt Annie gave a snort of contempt. "I hope they horsewhipped him.''

"Oh, they don't do anything to the men.''

"Isn't he locked up too?"

"The Vice Squad don't arrest the men.''

"Why not? There wouldn't be any girls in brothels unless the men went there, would there?"

"Well, that's how it is, anyway...unless the girls are under sixteen.''

"Under sixteen!" Aunt Annie's voice was full of scorn for all men and their laws. "Next thing they'll be arresting baby girls in their cradles for ogling the men. What we want is a few women making the laws. Then the men wouldn't get off scot free.''

"Well, they get off now and all that matters to us is that Monnie's in the Glebe shelter till we find somewhere for her to go.''

"Somewhere for her to go? What do you mean? And us with an empty bedroom here!"

526

"Look, Aunt, I don't think you really understand. Do you know what a brothel is?"

"Of course I do. You girls today seem to think you're the only ones who know anything about the facts of life. But what I do know is that Monnie isn't the kind of girl who'd have gone there of her own choice."

"She didn't."

"Well, how did she get there?"

"That's what I'm trying to tell you."

"Well, aren't I waiting?"

Guinea took a deep breath and poured out the whole story. "So now you see, since she absolutely refuses to go home, there's nowhere for her to go but the girls' home at Parramatta."

"Not if I know anything about it. Herding innocent little girls in with the scum of the streets. That's how they make girls bad."

"Maybe you can find some other way out," Guinea said wearily. "I'm stumped."

"Some other way out? Certainly I'll find some other way out." Aunt Annie went to the back door and called Kim in a high piercing voice. "I'll get him to run me across to your mother's tonight," she said, coming back to the table. "I know how she'll be feeling and I want to be in at the court myself tomorrow morning to give those policemen a bit of my mind. They can't have a brain among the lot of them not to know that a girl like Monnie is a good girl, the moment they set eyes on her."

Guinea was saved from answering by the sound of Kim coming up the back steps, two at a time. "Here I am," he began, and stopped short when he saw Guinea. "Oh, hullo. I didn't expect to see you here."

"I didn't expect to be here."

Aunt Annie swept through the explanations and embarrassment. "Kim, get the car out, I'm going straight over to the Malones' place and I'll be stopping the night."

"Nothing wrong, is there?"

"There is something very wrong. While you two were

gallivanting round town supposed to be looking for her last night, little Monnie was kidnapped and taken to a brothel."

Kim went sickly yellow under his tan. "Crikey, is that right, Peg?"

"Yes. She got in with a bunch of girls the night she ran away from home and...oh, it's all so awful, I can't go over it again."

"We've got to be at the Children's Court, wherever that is, at half past nine tomorrow morning," Aunt Annie called from the bedroom where she was bustling into her best frock. "Go and tell your father I won't be back tonight and bring the car round."

Guinea got up. "I'll have to be going now, Aunt Annie."

"Aren't you coming with us?" Kim inquired.

"No. I've got to go back and work." She went to the bedroom door. "Goodbye, Aunt Annie. I'll see you at the court in the morning." She kissed the soft plump face, hugged her gratefully and went down the hall.

Kim came after her, picked up his cap from the hallstand and set it at a rakish angle. "I'm awfully sorry, Peg. Gee, I feel it like Monnie was my own sister."

"You wouldn't recognise her, Kim, she looked awful. Sort of...half dead."

He took her arm comfortingly. "Don't you worry. Once Aunt Annie gets on the trail, Monnie'll be OK."

When they reached the gate he took her hand and held it a moment and their heads were close together. "I'm sorry," he began, "about...aw...lots of things...."

Byron tooted impatiently from the car. Kim looked up and stiffened. His hand dropped. "Pardon me. I didn't know you were working for the military!" He lifted his hand in an ironical salute and turned away abruptly. She heard his footsteps go up the path and his voice raised to call his father.

Byron opened the door for her and they moved off city-wards in silence. Relief about Monnie was mingled with anger at Kim. It was a dead, hurt anger, quite different from the fury she had felt when he'd left her the night before. The hide of him — who was he to dictate to her? She hated him, how she hated him; but when she tried to use her hatred to whip her anger up all the fire went out of her. The grip of his hand on her arm and his nearness as he stammered out a few halting words were more vivid and real to her than Byron close beside her in the car.

"Is that the Air Force cousin who took you surfing?" His voice startled her.

"Who, Kim?" and then remembering, "Oh yes, yes of course."

"Your family affection is certainly a credit to you. Have you any more cousins?"

"Dozens."

"All male?"

"Not all."

"That's something to be grateful for."

She was silent and he turned to look at her. Her dark frock was lost in the depths of the car, and her face and golden hair faded and gleamed in the passing light and shadow. That is how he had seen her standing a few minutes before under the silver waterfall of the wisteria; her hair a pale flame in the green street light, her face unearthly, the boy's head bent close to hers, urgent and pleading.

What did that boy mean to her? What could a boy give her that could match what he had to offer? Such golden youth as hers was for the connoisseur; only a man of experience could savour it to the full. He would marry her and be damned to that young cub!

Everything was clear. His divorce was through. What a bit of luck he hadn't been free before he left New York or he'd have been tied up to Geraldine. At the thought of Geraldine he squirmed uneasily, but she'd get over it. She had probably been having a damn good time while he was away, in any event. He dismissed Geraldine. There wasn't much time, but he was a specialist in lightning tactics and he began to formulate his plan of campaign with the thoroughness of a military strategist. He wanted Guinea, and when he wanted a thing he got it.

"It's half past nine," he said as they came back down the long sweep of Parramatta Road, "let's go dancing."

"Let's," Guinea smiled up at him, eager and bewitching. She'd marry him and to hell with Kim.

"Ten minutes to your place, ten minutes for you to dress, and ten minutes later — heaven."

He put an arm around her shoulder and she nestled against him. He trod on the accelerator and they went along the broad road in a scurry of startled pedestrians.

Claire slipped two thick T-bone steaks under the griller and examined the vegetables steaming on the hotplate. Everything was going nicely. She set out cream lace mats on the dark polished gate-legged table and golden-brown wallflowers in a horseshoe centrepiece of translucent green. Nigel had given her the heavy sterling silver spoons and forks with the old crest almost obliterated from generations of use; the two Queen Anne candlesticks were his too, they had been sent out to him from his great-aunt's home in Devon. She straightened the wick of each green candle. Time enough to light them when he came in. She stood back and admired the table. Everything was perfect.

Nigel always said the room, with its thick cream carpet and deep, luxurious green chairs, was a perfect setting for her. He really said the sweetest things. She looked up at the large portrait on the wall; it was quite the best thing the studio had done of him. His sensitive face was strongly highlighted, his beautifully shaped hand curved round the bowl of his pipe. There was no doubt he was marvellously photogenic; she could never understand why they had not snapped him up for films. Of course local stuff was so crude and they were probably jealous of him, but if only he could get overseas she was sure he would be rushed for the *Esquire* type of modelling, and he was simply made for English films.

She turned to the long mirror and looked at her own reflection with satisfaction, admiring again the green housecoat floating around her. It made her look taller than her five feet two, and concealed how skinny she was. She really would have to try and put some weight on, she was getting positively scraggy. But even so, she consoled herself, I am much pleasanter to look at at thirty-eight than I was at twenty-eight...well, perhaps not pleasanter...but more striking, more distinctive.

She smiled experimentally into the mirror and smoothed the wings of chestnut hair that swept up gleaming from her temples. She did hope Nigel would like her new hairstyle; he was so proud of her when she looked her best. The light threw faint shadows under her too-prominent cheekbones, caught the clean line of her jaw and showed the droop of her small mouth. She'd have to do something about those lines at the corners, Nigel was so fussy about these little things. She bent forward and examined her lipstick anxiously. Yes, the line was right, it made her lips look fuller and it wasn't overdone. Your mouth really is too small, my girl, she told herself, you should never be seen without lipstick.

She turned away from the mirror. God, she was tired and her veins were giving her hell. That climb up the stairs with all the parcels always finished her. It wasn't that Nigel was thoughtless, but he so hated carrying parcels that she hadn't the heart to ask him to pick up anything on his way home. He wasn't used to that kind of thing.

She turned to the sideboard; she'd have a quick one before he came in. She poured out a glassful of sherry and drank it eagerly. Ah, that was good! Better have a mouthwash; Nigel hated her to smell of drink or cigarette smoke. He was so fastidious.

From the bathroom she went back to the kitchenette to turn the grill, whistling softly to herself; she never felt happier than when she was preparing for an intimate meal with Nigel. They had been terribly lucky to get two adjoining penthouses in the Cross — the whole roof to themselves; you could make a home of it. That was one of the good things that had come from the war. The tenants had fled to some inland hideout when the Pacific war started and luxury flats on the top of any building in the eastern suburbs went for two a penny. Even if you could get flats like this today, you'd have to pay through the nose for them with landlords cashing in on the housing shortage everywhere. Thank God rents were pegged and their old shark could do nothing about it, no matter how much he grumbled about what he ought to have been making out of the flats while the Yanks were in Sydney.

She wandered out onto the roof. The roar of planes going back to Richmond blotted out the sound of the city traffic, and searchlights raked the sky with inquisitive fingers. The sliding pencils of light silvered the planes high up, then glided down the sky to rest, leaving the night darker than before. Below her the city fell away from the foot of Victoria Street to the trough of Woolloomooloo in a sea of twinkling electric lights, and rose again in a glittering wave to the broken skyline beyond Hyde Park. The narrow street below was bright and busy and three slender poplars beside the Minerva Theatre were bathed in silver light from a passing car. The rattle of trams, the tooting of taxis, the grumble of buses and the distant roar of an electric train crossing the Harbour Bridge rose to her in a muffled throbbing.

The sherry had given her a pleasant glow; she was certain they were going to be lucky tonight. With that seventy-five pound win on Stormcloud to play with, they simply couldn't lose. She rested her arms on the parapet and began to calculate just how much they had to win to get that thousand in the bank. "I wouldn't ask any woman to marry me with less," Nigel always said, no matter how much she protested that it wasn't necessary. Until they'd got into the game she couldn't see any way they'd ever land a thousand. Poor darling, he was so honourable, other men wouldn't care. There was no doubt about it, breeding did count. There was nothing crude about Nigel; she adored his clear-cut profile and his tall, slender body. But for all his exquisite delicacy there was nothing effeminate about him either, that's why he modelled men's fashions so perfectly. There was an innate refinement about him too. To be married to him would be all her dreams come true...

She heard the outer door open, and turned to go back. "Hello, darling," she called gaily.

"God," Nigel sighed, bending to kiss her. "I've had a madly exhausting afternoon. My head's simply splitting."

"You poor darling, you must be terribly tired. Take off your things while I bring your lounge coat. Now sit down and rest, while I get you a sherry. The dinner's practically ready."

He sank into a deep chair and closed his eyes. She

smoothed his fair straight hair with a gentle hand. "Sure you wouldn't like an APC?"

He shook his head. "I'll be all right after a drink."

She took two crystal glasses, filled them with sherry, and sat down close to him on the wide arm of the chair.

"Clever sweet," he said, holding his glass to the light. "Where did you get it?"

"My faithful Blue — we're like that." She held up two fingers tightly crossed. "Doss gets it for him."

"That virago!" he shuddered. "Look out she doesn't tear your eyes out."

She dropped a kiss on his ear. "I'll risk it for you, darling. But you haven't told me how your screen test went."

"It didn't. I waited round simply hours at the studio and then nothing happened. I'm sure it's all a fake."

"I think that's the limit," she said indignantly, "when they promised to call you."

"My sweet," he made a gesture of utter fatigue, "they really don't want men of my type for Australian films. A decent accent is a handicap in this country."

"Never mind, darling. When we get our thousand we'll go abroad and then you'll get your chance."

He lifted her hand and pressed it against his cheek. "*Ma petite*," he murmured, "what would I do without you?"

She scanned his face anxiously. He did look exhausted. The corners of his mouth drooped pathetically and the slight puffiness under his eyes was discoloured. Poor darling, having to rub shoulders with all sorts in the business world was a perpetual torture to him with his background and upbringing. She clinked her glass to his. "I'm sure it's going to be a lucky night for us, darling. Both our stars say so. Now take your time and I'll serve."

Nigel uncoiled himself slowly from the big chair when she brought in the dinner.

"Everything looks perfect," he murmured as he pushed her chair in for her and sat down opposite.

"I hope it's as nice as it looks." Claire gave a little nervous laugh and looked at his plate with the creamed potatoes between the fresh green peas and grilled tomatoes.

He began to cut the steak and took a mouthful, then looked up at her, drawing his brows together. "Not so tender as usual."

She tasted her own. "Mine seems all right. Would you like to change?"

"Oh, it doesn't matter. Where did you get it?"

"With the meat strike on I had the greatest difficulty in getting any steak at all. I had to go to five butchers and I was just lucky that Teddy up in Darlinghurst Road had this put away for someone else and gave it to me. I only got it because I passed on to him that Stormcloud tip."

"Well, you'd better tell him if he wants any more tips like that in future, he'll have to see that we get tender meat."

Claire's chin quivered and she put down her knife and fork distastefully. Really, she wasn't terribly hungry after all.

The telephone rang as they were drinking their coffee. Claire got up to answer it. "It's for you, darling," she handed him the receiver.

When he'd finished, he turned to her. "That was Coddy. The school moved again last night, they're at Point Piper. He said they'd send a car for us. What do you think?"

"Just as you like, darling. But the big money's at Joe's."

"That's what I think. Better call him back and say not to bother."

"Mind you," Claire dialled as she spoke, "Coddy's is much nicer if you want a social evening and I must hand it to him, that blonde pick-up of his can put on a supper. We'll go another time; I want to keep in with Cynthia. But if it's real baccarat you're after, you can't beat Joe's, and while our luck's in..."

"I feel that way, too. He seems to bring me luck. Besides, you haven't got the threat of being raided constantly hanging over you down there. It's as safe as if you were dining at Government House."

"Nothing will happen for a few weeks anyway after last night's raid."

"What's the time?"

"Just on nine."

"Good." He stretched out in the lounge. "I'll have forty winks while you're fixing up. There's no hurry, they never start to warm up till about half past ten at Joe's."

Claire closed the door of the kitchenette and did the washing up as quietly as she could, methodically setting out her own breakfast things and a morning tray for Nigel. Oh, she felt happy tonight! The run of luck they'd had last Friday and again at the races was surely a sign they'd moved into a lucky cycle. If only her veins didn't ache so...

She was almost gay as she dressed, putting on the new cocoa-brown suit that she was keeping as a surprise for Nigel. It represented a nice spot of commission from Madame Renoir on the Marie Antoinette patrons she'd sent round, and when Deb married McFarland she'd put the nips into the old girl again. That introduction would be worth hundreds to any frock shop.

The brown suit was just her cup of tea, she thought, simple and tailored, yet essentially feminine. So was the bit of velvet nonsense — brown and ochre flowers in a mist of tulle — that served as a hat. It was gay and ridiculous. Thank heaven for Cynthia, who could discard hats according to whim without considering either coupons or cash and pass them on to her friends for next to nothing. My God, what a rakeoff she must get from Coddy! Well, she earned it. She'd made his school. They said that whatever school she was at was absolutely safe from the police. How on earth did she do it?

When she'd finished dressing she tiptoed into the lounge where Nigel was still sleeping. She bent and dropped a kiss on the end of his nose. "Time to go, darling."

He opened his eyes and blinked at her. "What a vision," he murmured. "I haven't seen that bonnet before — or the suit. Let me look at you." He scanned the details of her outfit. "Perfect! You grow lovelier every day. Now turn round. Yes, I couldn't have chosen anything for you myself that I liked better. Give me a kiss before we go." He sat up and pulled her down beside him.

"Do be careful, darling. You'll ruin my makeup."

"You'd be just as lovely without." He pressed his lips gently onto her closed eyelids as she lay still a moment, her head against his shoulder. Then he drew her up. "Come along," he said with mock firmness, "much more of this nonsense and we'll never get to the game." He took a wallet out of his inside pocket. Claire whistled at the neatly folded notes. "Seventy-five lovely smackers!"

"Minus twenty-five pounds," he corrected as he put it back. "I simply had to pay the tailor for this suit."

"Oh Nigel, what a snag!"

"I wouldn't have, only the swine was hanging round the studio and practically asked me straight out. That's gratitude for you, after all the custom I've brought him."

"Oh, never mind, he makes wonderfully, and it's my favourite suit. Now, quite sure you've got rid of all your brown money?"

Nigel went through each pocket carefully and made two little piles of pennies and halfpennies on the table. "That's the last," he said, "you haven't any in your purse, I hope."

"Not a bean. Think I'd risk our lucky star for a brownie?"

"Well, that's everything then, so let's be on our way. Ring for a car, will you, sweet."

Claire dialled for several minutes. "No one answering."

"Give them another tinkle."

Claire tried again. "Nothing doing, I'm afraid."

"Oh, darn it all. We'll have to go down and try for a taxi. Private hire service has gone to pot these days like everything else. Will I be glad to see the end of the Yanks!"

They came out from the flats and went up to the corner of Macleay Street, where Nigel hailed a cruising taxi. It drew up.

"This is a miracle." Claire cried.

"It ain't yours," the taxi driver snarled at them. "These coves called me before you."

Two American privates sauntered to the edge of the

537

pavement. He opened the door and they stepped in.

"This," said Nigel bitterly, "is what you have to put up with when you have an army of occupation. Once they're gone the taxis'll be glad enough to come crawling round."

An empty cab circled beside them ignoring their signal, drew up in front of the American Naval Hostel on the opposite side of the street and took on a quartet of sailors who had just come out of the canteen.

Claire sighed resignedly. "We'll stand here waving all night at this rate. Better get a trolleybus; there ought to be one leaving Wylde Street about now. Oh, here it is — our luck is certainly in!"

WEDNESDAY
I

Claire looked out of the tram as it hummed up the slope between the little island parks where the new green leaves glistened in the sunshine. It's a perfect morning, she thought, far too lovely to be inside. On a sudden impulse, she got out at the next stop. I'll walk to the SP. Who cares if I am late this morning!

She ran up the steps into Hyde Park whistling to herself. Pigeons were strutting around the lawns, their feathers iridescent in the sun, and the air was full of their soft cooing. A gardener nodded to her. "Nice mornin', miss." She smiled back gaily. Good heavens, I must look as happy as I feel!

It must be years since she had been in the park, one had so little time these days. . . When she first came to work in the city she used to bring her lunch here every day with the other girls, but that seemed a very long time ago now.

The trees were enchanting in their spring green, and the drifts of pink and white blossom made your heart sing . . . She'd see if she could buy some blossom for the Marie Antoinette. She stood for a moment at the top of the steps going down into Queen's Square. The bronze spire of St James's Church was luminous green against the morning sky. Lovely, she thought, old and dignified. I'd like to be married in St James's. It would be just right for Nigel and me. Mrs Nigel Carstairs. . . she savoured the name slowly. A distinguished name — like Nigel himself. She could still see him as she had seen him that morning when she took his breakfast tray in before she left for work — his profile pale and handsome against the monogrammed linen pillow, the shadows dark beneath his eyes. But she'd soon fix them; she must remember to take home a pot of anti-shadow cream.

Ursula Cronin came out of the underground entrance just ahead of her. Claire retreated to the park hurriedly; she simply could not walk down to the SP with Ursula this morning, it would put a damper on everything. She watched her cross the tramline and disappear into Macquarie Street. I'll dodge down Phillip Street, Claire said to herself. I'm not even going to think about that woman a minute before I have to.

Her mind went back to Nigel. . . They had sat together in her lounge after the game last night when she had tried on the jade clips and earrings he'd won for her. She had coveted them so often on Mrs Gartred that she couldn't believe her eyes when they were thrown in as a stake. Winning them seemed to set the seal on their luck; they couldn't go wrong now.

She had been so wild with excitement when they got home that she couldn't keep still, but Nigel was quiet. He had kissed her and thrown a handful of banknotes on the carpet. "For you, Claire, *ma petite*. 'Tread softly, for you tread on my dreams.'" He said such sweet things. "It's our nest-egg, and with our luck the way it is, tomorrow night we'll have our thousand. And then we'll go along to some quiet little church and get married and live happily ever after. With a thousand behind us we'll never need to worry, and I swear that I'll never put my food inside a baccarat school again."

She had to wait near the end of Phillip Street while a lorry, laden with bottles, backed out from the lane behind the Continental Gym. Good heavens, she thought, the grog they must get through at Down Under! Every morning as she came to work she saw the same lorry pulling into Phillip Street full of empties. Absolutely brazen! None of these nightclubs had liquor licences, yet they did this sort of thing in broad daylight under the very nose of the police. Oh well, everybody did it, and if you were not in one racket it seemed you had to be in another if you wanted to live at all these days.

Her mind went back to Nigel and their winnings. With a thousand pounds to play around with, she would start her own salon and market her own stuff. Give her a couple of good girls and the contacts she already had, and the thing would be a gold mine. Why should she go on working like a galley slave to pep up SP dividends? With what she'd make out of the business, and Nigel managed to pick up from occasional modelling, they would be able to live really well. They could get the penthouse done up.... He'd be so much more comfortable in her larger flat, and he could keep his small bedsitter for a den. He'd never regret marrying her, she would make sure of that. Poor pet, he was so frightfully scrupulous about always contributing his share of the expenses that she never let him know really how much things cost. He was just a babe in the wood where money was concerned, and so honourable that it would have killed him to think he wasn't paying his full share. It was lucky he was so vague about financial matters, because that made it easier for her to overcome his horror of taking money from a woman, by giving him expensive presents of things he simply must have in the modelling game, but which he could never have afforded to buy.

She saw Ursula disappear round the corner of the SP on the way to the service entrance. To hell with the service entrance, she said to herself, and ran up the side steps. If it came to that, to hell with the whole SP!

Blue greeted her in the lift. "Forgettin' your place, Miss Jeffries?"

She laughed. "Sure, it's spring. Didn't you know?"

"I'm not sure if I ought to take you up," he winked at her. "You know this lift's for the nobs only."

"Blue, my angel, just between you and me, I nearly moved into the nob class myself last night."

"Well, for cryin' out loud!"

"Yes, we had a win. Blue, I really believe we've struck a break at last. It's my lucky star."

"I'm glad to hear that."

Blue closed the lift door and looked at her admiringly.

"Baby," he said with a mock American accent, "you sure look like all the spring days rolled into one in that white dress and them green thingummebobs."

She put her hand up to her ear and touched a jade clip. "You're a flatterer," she laughed, "I'll tell Doss on you." She blew him a kiss as she got out.

Blue caught it in midair and collapsed on the stool.

"Honey," he called after her, "what a mouthful!"

Claire waltzed into the little office, tossed her hat onto a peg and threw her arms round Deb's neck. "Darling, look what I've got!" She fingered her jade earrings lovingly.

"Where did they come from?"

"Nigel. He won them for me last night. They're practically priceless, just look at the carving." She slipped them off and put them into Deb's hand while she took off her frock.

"Exquisite," Deb said. Green! But of course, Claire didn't mind green. Still, she hoped it wouldn't break her luck.

Claire whistled rapturously as she buttoned up her uniform. Oh boy! Oh boy! who would have thought she'd ever feel like this again? She wouldn't change places with Deb or the queen! This was her lucky star all right. Oh lucky, lucky star! I must remember to give Nigel a ring about eleven o'clock, she thought. He should be awake by then. Just to tell him how I adore him.

The sound of the outer door opening brought her back to earth. She bent over Deb's shoulder to look at the appointments. "What a list! We'll have to do some reorganising, with Alice having to get off at one and Guinea not coming in this morning."

"That's pretty tough, isn't it?" Deb said disapprovingly. "Two days in succession."

"It just can't be helped, I'm afraid. Family troubles. Guin's not the kind to try to get out of anything."

Deb looked up sharply. For one awful moment she thought someone must have told Claire about the Madrid Lounge yesterday, but there was no hint of hidden meaning in her face.

Alice came in, looking pale and tearful.

"Oh, hullo," Claire gave her a warm smile, "we're just fixing up the appointments so that you can get off sharp at one o'clock."

"I don't know how I'm going to get through the morning at all. I feel absolutely awful."

"You won't have any time to worry. We'll all have to go like seven devils to get through with Guinea away."

"Oh," Alice sniffed, "that's a bit over the odds, isn't it, after being away yesterday morning?"

"Well, you know, other people have family troubles too, my dear," Claire said, and added hastily as she saw a light come into Alice's eyes. "A death in the family. Just give Val a call, will you, and we'll get these appointments straightened out. And answer that phone, on your way. I wonder where the devil Cronin's got to?" She turned back to Deb. "Mrs Dalgety's the biggest problem. She's down for the whole works."

"Look, I'll do Mrs Dalgety myself," Deb offered impulsively. "I can manage her." She felt better about yesterday afternoon after she had made the offer.

"I call that definitely heroic of you. You really are an angel."

Ursula came in at twenty minutes past nine, long-faced and superior.

"You're very late," Claire snapped. "The phone's been ringing its head off."

"I've been with Mrs Molesworth," Ursula said importantly.

"What's biting her now?"

"All this absenteeism in the salon."

"Any complaints about the work?"

"No."

"Then go jump in the lake. So long as the work's done, the staff's my business."

Ursula retreated sniffily to her desk. If it were not for the salary she was getting, she told herself, she'd leave the place and get a job somewhere else where one did not have to be in constant contact with such a common lot of girls.

Claire followed her to the reception desk and had just begun to explain the alterations when Elvira pushed open the outer door.

"Busy, luvvie?" she asked Claire.

"Madly. Is it important?"

"Terrible."

"Go along to my office and I'll be with you in a minute."

Ursula watched them go down the corridor. Thick as thieves, those two. Thank heaven she had Mrs Molesworth to turn to; she didn't know how she would put up with the job if it wasn't for her being so friendly. Look at the way she had invited her into her office this morning and talked to her — quite as though they were equals. And they were going to have coffee together just as soon as Mrs Molesworth could make time. That would give her a chance to get some of her own back.

Claire shut the office door behind her.

"Something wrong with Guin?" Elvira asked hopefully.

"Death of a relative," Claire explained, "and she has a lot of business to fix up for her father."

"Oh, is that all. Well, I've got a message for her anyway. That Colonel Maddocks caught me at the service entrance when I was comin' in and arst me to tell her 'e'd like to see 'er immejitly. You don't think...it wouldn't be..." She did some mental arithmetic. "Oh, no, 'e ain't been 'ere long enough." She paused, leering expectantly at Claire. "I seen her comin' in yesterday lunchtime and she looked that upset, and she'd been cryin' and there's only one thing I could imagine Guin crying about...And anyway," she lowered her voice to a whisper, "you take my tip, there's somethink wrong there. Nobody can put nothin' over me. I can spot trouble a mile off."

"Well, you keep your spotting to yourself, my good girl. We're hellishly busy, so let's get on with the business. Now what have you managed to do about that stuff?"

Elvira came back to business reluctantly. "I got a load of nail lacquer if yer want it."

"Good. I'll take anything I can get."

"The price 'as gone up."

"Oh, has it? Why?"

"They was raided. National Security. They got a lot of the stuff away 'cos they was warned. Ain't it a terrible shame?"

"Oh well," Claire shrugged, resignedly, "the price of manicures will just have to go up, too."

Elvira raised her voice as Alice went past. "Lovely weather we're 'avin' for this time o' year, ain't we?" She drew her face into a doleful mockery of Alice's expression. "What's wrong with 'er? The bank gone bung?"

"Just a cold."

"Seems to be a real 'indoo on the place, don't there?"

Val came to the door with a manicure tray.

"'Ullo, luvvie." Elvira greeted her with delight. "Goin' up to do 'er Royal 'Ighness's toenails?"

"I'll cut them right off if I ever get my hands on them again."

"Did you 'ear she's leavin' today?"

"Not really?"

"Cross me 'eart." Elvira made an extravagant gesture over her skinny bosom. "I was takin' a tray up to 'er this mornin' and I 'eard 'er on the telephone talkin' to 'er mother. I didn't like to interrupt, so I waited outside till she'd finished."

"Naturally," Claire murmured.

"Goin' 'ome she is, to git ready for the weddin', and they're spendin' their 'oneymoon in Melbourne for the Cup, and then she's going to join 'im in England."

"God help the English!" Claire rolled her eyes upwards, "as though the poor devils haven't had enough to put up with."

"It's the best news I've heard for a long time," Val remarked fervently.

"Me too. I nerely said to 'er: 'I'll be glad to see the larst of yer.'"

Elvira looked up at the clock. "'oly Moses," she squealed, "I 'ad to take coffee to old Ma Dalgety at nine — black and strong. Well, I'll tell 'er it's nine. She's that pie-eyed, she don't know whether it's Pitt Street or Christmas, and 'er diamond watch don't go since she dropped it into a glass of gin with 'er false teeth the other night."

"Is she on it again?"

"Paralytic! That kep' feller of 'ers went back to the 'ome front last night."

"Good," Claire said. "Then she won't be down here this morning."

"Not 'er. A stummick pump's more in 'er line. Whew!" Elvira fanned herself and got up to go.

"All right. You'll let me have the stuff as soon as you can, won't you?"

"Righteo! Mr B.'ll pick it up some time ternight."

She scuttled down the corridor and smiled ingratiatingly at Ursula as she went out. Ursula's lip curled in disgust. She took a diary out of her handbag and made a note in it, smiling to herself as she wrote.

Guinea stood at the entrance to the Children's Court and watched Aunt Annie towing her mother across Albion Street like a fussy tug. Kim trailed sheepishly behind them, looking younger and less confident than she had seen him look for a long time. Mrs Malone's face was grim under a stiff black hat and her gaunt shoulders were squared. She met Guinea's mumbled words of greeting with silence.

Aunt Annie pecked Guinea's cheek.

"It's all right, Peg, I explained it all to your mother. I've been explaining to her all night."

"Facts are facts," Mrs Malone said. "You can't explain facts away."

"Aw gee, Mum," Guinea pleaded, "it wasn't Monnie's fault. Don't be too hard on her. She's that broken-up you wouldn't know her."

Mrs Malone stiffened her already straight figure. "Hard? Have I ever been hard on my children?" She turned abruptly to mount the steps. "This is a judgment on me. If I'd been harder on you all, this would never have happened. Let it be a warning to you too, my girl."

Guinea's heart sank and the courage oozed out of her. Kim held the swing door open and gave her an understanding smile. "Don't worry," he whispered, "Aunt Annie will fix things." In spite of herself, Guinea warmed to him.

In the court officer's room they sat side by side in stiff-blacked chairs pushed against the wall, while the officer questioned Mrs Malone at the desk. Her bleak replies laid out before him the whole of their family life, its poverty, its struggle, its decency, its hardness and its failure. The tears pricked Guinea's eyes. Poor Mum, it seemed so unfair that out of them all it should be Monnie and Mum who had to go through this.

When Aunt Annie got a chance to speak she was voluble in her opinion of policemen who, instead of catching the real criminals, had nothing better to do than arrest little bits of girls like her Monnie. Her round face reddened, her eyes snapped and her short, plump figure swelled with indignation. She'd like to know whose idea this was, calling Monnie a neglected child? She'd never been neglected in her life. And whose fault was it that she was exposed to moral danger? If the police did their work properly it would never have happened. And why didn't they arrest the man too? There wouldn't be any brothels if men didn't go to them. She fixed the court officer with her snapping eyes. Did he think Monnie was a bad girl?

He shook his head. No, the situation was unfortunate, but so far as he could judge there was no vice at all in the child.

Aunt Annie snorted. "I'm glad somebody has sense enough to see that. Now, what are you going to do about her?"

The court officer hesitated. "Well...er...in cases like these, we usually let a girl go back to her parents on probation, unless there is some strong reason against it."

Mrs Malone stared at him defiantly. "There's no reason at all why Monnie should not come home. Her father and I have always done the best we could for our children, and we'll continue to do it, whatever the disgrace she's brought on the family."

The officer scribbled on the blotting-paper in front of him. At last he looked up at her. "I'm afraid it's not quite so simple as that, Mrs Malone. You know how difficult it is to move young girls when they get an idea into their heads, and the trouble about this case is that the girl herself, for some reason or other, is most unwilling to go back to her home."

Mrs Malone met his gaze stonily. "I don't see what the girl's fancies have to do with the matter at all," she said at last. "Surely a mother has the right to decide what's best for her own daughter."

"Of course," he agreed hastily, "and who better? But I thought that the best thing for this little girl might be a complete change, away from her own home and the mill she was working in. I don't really feel that she is suited to that type of work at all.''

"The Manpower sent her there. I didn't want her to go to a mill.''

The officer made a gesture of sympathy. "Unfortunately, in the pressure of war, Manpower officials have to make a lot of decisions without regard to the individual likes and dislikes of the young people they are handling, and they have no time — and I'm afraid in some cases, they have no training — to judge their capacity or incapacity to do particular jobs. You're quite right, Monnie is capable of doing a different type of work from what she was doing in the mill, and therefore, I think that the wisest thing to do would be to give her a complete change — to an office, perhaps.''

"After what's happened, I intend to keep her at home altogether,'' Mrs Malone announced with finality. "With me and her sister in munitions there's plenty of work for her to do at home, and we don't need her money. I wouldn't trust her out of my sight again.''

Guinea was sitting forward in her chair, holding on to the seat tightly with both hands. If they sent Monnie back home it would be the stone end of everything for her. But you'd never make Mum see that. Well, she'd have to speak up herself if nobody else would tell them just why Monnie couldn't go home. She made a movement as though to get up.

Kim put a hand on hers and held her back. They watched the genial, sympathetic face of the court officer change. Kim looked at Guinea. She held her breath.

"I think perhaps, Mrs Malone, that you don't quite understand,'' the officer was saying. "The decision does not rest entirely with you. We feel that it is only asking for a repetition of trouble to send a girl anywhere against her will, and unless some other suitable arrangement can be made, there is no alternative for her but to go to the Parramatta Industrial School.''

"Nonsense,'' Aunt Annie exploded, thumping her umbrella on the floor. "Why can't she come to me? I've been begging and praying her mother all night to let me have her.

Why, I practically brought that girl up, and I can tell you I'm not ashamed of Monnie Malone, whatever anyone else has to say about her." She glared belligerently at the officer.

"Are you a relation then, Miss Scott?" he asked.

"What's that got to do with it?" Aunt Annie demanded. "If I can bring good references and I want to have the girl, isn't that enough?"

Kim stood up and cleared his throat to attract attention. "Excuse me, sir..." The officer looked up with penetrating grey eyes. "I don't know if it will make any difference, sir, but you see we are practically related. Miss Scott is my aunt, and Monnie's sister here and I have been engaged since I went overseas." He felt his face flush as the keen eyes bored into his, and moved with searching, impersonal scrutiny from his face to Guinea's.

Kim put his hand on Guinea's shoulder. She looked up, the warm colour suffusing her face, and nodded. If it was going to do Monnie any good, she would stand by his story till they got out of there.

The officer was looking at Kim again. "You live with Miss Scott?"

"Yes, sir. She's looked after my father and me as long as I can remember."

"And your father and you would also be willing to accept responsibility for the girl?"

"Yes, sir. Dad and I talked it over this morning."

The officer turned to Aunt Annie. "You realise, Miss Scott, that if the girl is put in your charge she will be on probation and regular reports will have to be made to the court on her behaviour?"

"I'll have no trouble in answering for her behaviour." Aunt Annie was still truculent.

The court officer linked his fingers together and leaned forward. "It's not an easy thing you're offering to do, you know. From our medical officer's report, this girl is quite healthy, but what injury this experience has done to her in other ways, you will have to find out for yourself. She thinks she's a bad girl." Aunt Annie snorted and the officer went on hastily. "She's not, of course. She's been through a terrible experience, but from what I have seen of her myself and from what you tell me of her, she is essentially a good girl. And I want you all to remember, too, that she would never have got into difficulties in the first place only that she was a victim of one of the oldest tricks; they got her drunk without her realising what she was taking, and even after that she had the strength to resist the threats and promises of a strong-minded woman with a most unsavoury record."

He looked from Aunt Annie to Guinea and Kim, and last of all to Mrs Malone, and met her eyes, fixed and implacable. "I would plead with you all in her interest to put away every conventional idea of shame and disgrace, and regard her as you would regard a child who had been knocked down in a street accident and temporarily crippled. If this young man here, who is engaged to her sister, came back to you from his war service with an injury, you would feel only pity and love for him. Well, in another way, little Monnie is a war casualty too."

He looked at each one of them in turn again, his eyes burning with the intensity of his feeling. Mrs Malone stared ahead of her, Aunt Annie blew her nose, the tears ran down Guinea's face and dripped unchecked onto her dress. Kim put his hand on hers and squeezed it tightly.

The officer went on, "It's the same in peacetime. I've been watching the boys and girls who pass through this court for more than twenty years, and I never cease to be touched by the fact that so few of them are bad at heart, and to be angry that most of them have had no chance to grow into the decent citizens they could have been. It's all so stupid and wasteful and, of course, wartime is more wasteful than peace. The children who are passing through here now — boys and girls — are as much victims of war as if they'd been hit in an air raid."

He paused and turned to Aunt Annie. "Whatever happens to this child in the next few months will decide the whole of the rest of her life. She has had the benefits of a sound and decent upbringing in circumstances that would have daunted a woman less courageous than her mother has shown herself to be; but now, I think, everyone's interest can best be served by the court giving her into the care of Miss Scott, who not only has much more time to devote to her than her mother, but what is even more important, can give her an entirely new set of suroundings and an opportunity to make a new life."

He stood up, gathering his papers together. "If it is of any comfort to you, in all my years here I have rarely felt more hopeful of a child making a new life than I do today."

Aunt Annie beamed at him from overflowing eyes. She leaned forward, clasping her small fat hands together imploringly. "Oh sir, if you give her to me, I promise you I'll do everything I can to make her happy so that she'll forget this awful business. I couldn't love her more if she was my own child. How soon can I have her?"

He smiled at her. "If Mrs Malone is satisfied, I see nothing in the way of your taking her home with you today. I shall arrange for one of our social workers to go out and see you later in the week, and I think you will find her very helpful. Now I'll get the little lass in."

When Monnie came in through the door with the matron, Mrs Malone turned her gaunt face to look at her. Her throat was working and when she spoke her voice came out cracked and unrecognisable. "Come here, child."

Monnie took one frightened glance at her mother and turned away.

Aunt Annie jumped up and went towards her, clucking soothing and broken phrases. "There, there," she said. "There, there, pet," and Monnie came to her plump arms like a frightened chicken to its mother's wing.

Mary Parker looked round the comfortable lounge of the Women's Service Club. A group of AAMWAs near her were looking through a guide to Sydney and planning a day's sightseeing; they had evidently just arrived down from New Guinea, by their yellowed faces.

She put down the magazine she was trying to read. She couldn't concentrate, and anyway nothing in magazine stories happened like real life, only the way you wished things would happen... What on earth could she do with herself until she had to meet Alice at a quarter past one for the doctor's appointment?

It was too early to go to the movies. Besides, she was sick of the movies after one yesterday afternoon and two sessions on Monday. When you went to the movies you hoped they'd keep your mind occupied, but they didn't. You went on thinking just the same. What on earth could she do with herself all the morning?

Better go out. At least she could walk somewhere and that would help to take her mind off things. She booked out of the club and the woman at the desk was very nice. "Yes, thank you," Mary replied in answer to her inquiries about the rest of her leave. "Yes, I'll be staying with friends."

What a darling Bessie was, Mary thought as she went out to the lift. If it hadn't been for her kindness, she'd have had to come back here alone tonight — she could never have gone home.

She came out into George Street and stood for a moment in the club entrance with her suitcase in her hand. If she hadn't been in uniform, she might have been back four years ago hurrying to work with the office crowds herself.

The clock jutting out from the face of the GPO opposite showed just on nine. She had an inspiration. She would go and buy something for Bessie's grandchildren. She dodged through the double line of traffic and began to search the windows of a stationer's shop. Carry and Jean were seven and five, Bessie had told her. Inside the shop she browsed for half an hour, reading snatches of fairytales and turning over the pictures of bush creatures. She fell in love with a baby platypus and a pair of kangaroo joeys and came out with the two books in her suitcase.

She turned into Martin Place and walked along the colonnades of the GPO in a blaze of sunshine, the only dawdling figure in the hurrying crowds.

The flower stalls were nearly all looked after by women now. They wore sacking aprons over their thick coats, some had heavy gloves on and one wore a pair of gumboots reaching half way up her navy blue slacks. The woman called out to her, "Flowers, miss? All fresh this morning."

Mary shook her head smiling and walked on to the next stall where the woman was sorting flowers out of big bundles and putting them into green-painted jam tins. There were masses of sweet peas on the stall, sweet peas of every colour, and behind them were carnations and roses and snapdragons and big flaunting crimson poppies. They were all dewy fresh and she longed to put her face against them.

Beside the next stall was a bucket of tall crimson waratahs. So they were still allowed to pick them for sale. When she'd been quite a little girl she remembered her grandfather thumping the table one day and blazing out that if the law didn't take a hand and stop people from selling wildflowers, they'd have all the bush round Sydney stripped to the bone and it'd never recover. Well, people had gone on picking wildflowers; there was never a spring when the stalls weren't crowded with them and at Christmas, everywhere you looked there were Christmas bells and great masses of feathery Christmas bush.

She walked slowly on past the Cenotaph. The spring leaves on the two poplars at either end were dancing in the wind and the steps at the foot of the memorial were covered with wreaths. They must have been sent from a funeral, she thought.

She paused beside the news stand at the corner, waiting for the policeman on point duty to stop the Pitt Street traffic. At the next corner, a street photographer motioned to her to pause and put his camera to his eye. She hurried on up the hill and pressed the pedestrian traffic button to cross Macquarie Street.

She wondered if she'd spend the morning in the Public Library, but the warmth of the sun, the green of the gardens and the glint of blue water beyond made her feel it was too lovely a day to waste indoors. She imagined herself an office girl again coming up from the city with the lunchtime crowds. But all that seemed so terribly long ago now; it was hard to believe that you could change so much and everything else remain the same. The same palms rippled down the length of Macquarie Street, the same peanut seller stood on the corner and they might even be the same pigeons that swished over her head to alight on the statue of Matthew Flinders.

She crossed over the Domain Drive to the little grassy island with the Shakespeare statue, pausing a moment while her eyes wandered idly over the quotation engraved on its marble base. They lingered on the last lines: "We are such stuff as dreams are made on and our little life is rounded with a sleep."

"Our little life..." Yes, that was all it was, she supposed, if you got things in proportion. Whatever you did, even if it seemed the end of the world for you, life still went on for other people. But if what you did really mattered so little, why couldn't you live in your own way and be happy? Her thoughts flashed back to Barbara. But then if everyone lived in their own way, that still wouldn't solve the problem because there'd always be someone who got hurt.

She went through the ornate iron gates into the Gardens where the smell of the newly cut grass came to her in a wave ...everything was so fresh and lovely.

People were already strolling along the paths and the terraced lawns, children were sliding down the grassy banks and turning somersaults. Mary walked down the pathway between the rose beds and over the broad stretch of grass to the sea wall.

As she leaned on the warm stone and looked down on

the rippled shadows in the shallow water, all the things she had pushed away rushed back into her mind and she was with Frank again in that precious week of final leave when the days swung between the miracle of present happiness and the enchantment of the dream future that they planned together. Of course Barbara would divorce him, he'd said. There wouldn't be any difficulty about that, they'd grown so far apart during their separation. And although Barbara didn't understand him, she was really fine and she would never stand in the way of his happiness. And Mary had believed him because she wanted to and because she loved him.

When they'd lain close together in the double bed in the little cottage, they'd talked of the children they would have. She wouldn't be like Barbara. As soon as the war was over and they were able to get married, she would make a home for him and they would have children.

"I will give you babies," she had whispered shyly as she lay in the dark with his arms around her.

"Not just yet, my darling. I'm taking good care of that." Then he'd laughed. "Just imagine a little Corporal Mary coming along before her time. A nice example you'd be to the Australian Women's Army Service."

She'd snuggled closer into the curve of his arm. "All the others'd get themselves babies out of pure envy."

"Silly little sweet. But wait till the war's over, then we'll be together for always, Mary, my darling."

"For always, Mary, my darling." That was their secret code. Whenever he'd written her a note, even about the silliest things, it always finished like that: "For always, Mary, my darling." But there hadn't even been a letter since she'd written a month ago when she'd first been anxious.

The tears ran down her face before she knew she was crying. She wiped them away angrily. She was a fool to cry, it couldn't do anyone any good.

Could it be only four weeks since she'd known? The slow procession of those anxious days chased out all other memories and she felt her chest tighten with fear as it had tightened that night when she'd wakened up and known without need of a doctor's word that she was going to have a baby.

Oh, it was no good going on like this. She wasn't going to have a baby, even though her breasts were tender under the light pressure of her shirt. She'd been over everything a thousand times and it was all decided now. She wouldn't think about it and she wouldn't cry. She blew her nose vigorously and put her handkerchief back in her pocket.

She looked at her watch. She had to change, and that meant she ought to go to the ladies' room by the kiosk where children were lining up for ice creams. Here she locked herself in a lavatory and, opening her suitcase on the seat, she began to change swiftly out of her uniform and into her blue floral frock. It was all she could do not to vomit at the faint smell of urine that underlay the strong carbolic.

She took in great gulps of fresh air when she came out and felt better. Gripping her suitcase, she walked briskly down the path, over the lawns and up the steps to the back of the Conservatorium where the air was full of the strumming of pianos and the squeak of strings.

By the time she got back to the gates, the one o'clock crowd had begun to stream in and the ice cream seller was dipping swiftly into containers in his huge green canvas bag and handing out little buckets to the queue lined up along the fence.

Mary walked down to the corner, the rising southerly whipping her thin frock around her legs while she waited for a break in the traffic that streamed endlessly up and down Macquarie Street. She slipped across and sheltered from the wind in the entrance of the old Public Library.

All the morning, Alice had worked with a swiftness and skill that seemed something apart from herself. All she could think of was that Mary's appointment with the doctor was for quarter past one.

She waved and curled, pinned and set blonde heads and brown, she made suitable answers to pleasant remarks, held the back mirror up for final approval with just the right touch of flattery, sped the departing client graciously, welcomed another head to be shampooed and set.

Quarter past one, quarter past one, quarter past one... She must be ready to leave at one. Even if Mrs Molesworth came rampaging in again, if it meant losing her job, she still had to meet Mary at the old Public Library corner not later than ten minutes past one.

By one o'clock Alice was ready to leave. With this cool change it was lucky she'd remembered to bring in Mary's coat, she'd need it to put on over the floral frock she was going to wear to the doctor instead of her uniform. She didn't want to go getting a chill on top of everything else.

When Alice put her head round the corner of Claire's office, Guinea had come in. "Claire, I'm...going now."

"Oh, good." Claire opened her drawer and took out some notes. "Here's the extra five pounds." Alice took it without looking up and pushed it into her bag, mumbling her thanks.

Claire cut her short. "That's all right. Don't worry too much, everything'll be all right."

"I...I suppose so."

"Got a new coat?" Guinea said pleasantly, looking at the navy coat over her arm. "What do you use for coupons?"

"It's not mine, it's Mary's. I was frightened she might catch a chill."

"Isn't she in uniform?"

"Yes...that's...no. She was going to change into a floral frock for the...appointment."

"Crikey," Guinea looked at Claire. "Wouldn't it! Do the boys have to change out of uniform when they hop along to the blue light joint for treatment?" Claire shot her a warning glance. "I don't know what that has to do with it, my pet."

"Well, I do. If VD's an occupational disease for male troops, pregnancy ought to be for the women. They make me sick."

Alice turned away with a shudder. "Well I'll have to go.

And thank you for all your help."

"Goodbye, then," Claire smiled at her. "Give Mary our cheers, and don't forget to ring up and tell us when it's all over." Alice nodded and hurried out.

Mary was waiting for her inside the entrance to the old Public Library.

"I've brought your coat," Alice said.

Mary slipped it on gratefully. "Thanks awfully. I've been nearly frozen. I'm awfully sorry to have had to drag you away like this."

"Oh, that's all right. We've had a hectic morning, the Malone girl was away again and that meant extra for all of us, but we got through. Now we'll have to hurry."

They turned down Macquarie Street, past tall narrow buildings with ladders of brass plates framing the doorways.

"This is it," Alice said, leading the way up wide steps into an impressive hall. Mary stepped over the snake outlined in the mosaic floor and shivered.

The lift took them up and they trod softly on the fine carpet that stretched down the corridor between closed doors, each with polished brass plates flanked by shining bells. At the last door they stopped. Alice put her finger firmly on the button and the door was opened immediately by a smart young woman in a spotless overall, who ushered them into what was obviously the vestibule to a suite of rooms.

"You had an appointment with Doctor?" she inquired briskly, going to a desk.

"Yes. A quarter past one." It was Mary who spoke.

The receptionist ran her finger down the pencil entries in her book. "What name did you say?"

"Mrs McDonald," Mary spoke low.

"It was made for you by telephone?" she asked.

"Yes. Yesterday morning," Mary answered. Her throat was dry and her knees were shaking.

"Will you come this way, please."

They went into a little waiting room just large enough to hold four chairs and a low table with magazines. The window looked out into a light well and was discreetly veiled with heavy net curtains. An electric light burned from a centre pendant, garish and yellow in the filtered daylight. Alice and Mary sat down.

For the first time, they looked at each other. "Feeling all right?" Alice asked, anxious to reassure herself as well as Mary.

Alice opened her bag and handed over five one-pound notes. "Here's the money I told you about last night."

Mary took the money and put it into her wallet. "Really, those girls are wonderful. They must think a terrible lot of you to do this for me. I'll write and thank them."

"Oh, for goodness sake don't do that," Alice was dismayed and added quickly when she saw Mary's surprised expression. "You don't want to worry. I'll fix all that up."

"Well, if you're sure it'll be all right." Mary picked up a magazine. She tried to make her mind focus on the pictures and turned over the pages resolutely. Alice clasped and unclasped the buckle on her bag with nervous fingers. The receptionist returned. "Will you come with me, Mrs McDonald? Your friend can wait here."

The receptionist ushered Mary into an office where a youngish man, dressed in a well-cut grey lounge suit, was sitting behind an imposing desk.

"Will you sit down," he invited pleasantly, leaning back in his chair. "You wanted to see the doctor?"

"Yes," she said with parched lips, "I have an appointment."

"Did you make it yourself?"

"Yes. By telephone yesterday morning. Mrs Peterson recommended me."

"Yes, yes, of course. That's quite all right." The young man became businesslike. "You know the fee?"

"Forty-five pounds."

"That's right. I'll take it now."

She opened her handbag and took out a bundle of notes neatly folded in half.

He flicked them through, took out his wallet and put

them in, returning it to an inside pocket. "Now, let me see. When did you have your last period?" he asked with professional crispness.

"On the third of August," she replied without waiting to think. That was something she was only too certain about.

"Hmm. Ten weeks," he calculated from the desk calendar in front of him. "Why did you leave it so long?"

"I couldn't get to Sydney."

"Have you ever been pregnant before, Mrs McDonald?"

Mrs McDonald... of course, that was her. "No... no, I haven't," she answered without looking at him.

He looked at his watch. "Half past one, we'd better get along. I've got a car outside." He took his hat from a stand in the corner.

She got up. "My... my sister is with me," she said hesitatingly.

"Yes, yes of course." He went to the door. "We're ready Miss Jackson, if you'll tell the lady in the waiting room." The man led the way to the lift and out to the street where a closed car was waiting twenty yards down from the building.

He opened the door for the girls to get in the back and stepped into the driver's seat. The car turned in the wide street, joining the line of cars that streamed through the avenue of Moreton Bay figs between the Gardens and the Domain.

Alice put her hand on Mary's, it was cold and clammy. Her fingers closed tightly giving warmth and reassurance. She tried to make her voice sound natural.

"Look, there's the Art Gallery," she said. "Ross and I went there to see the Archibald Prize this year. My dear, the one that won it was the ugliest thing I'd ever seen. What they make all the fuss over that Dobell for, I can't think."

Mary looked at the columned entrance without interest. "I read about it," she said.

"Ross said it was absolutely disgusting. Someone ought to do something about a picture like that getting the prize. It gives such a bad impression of us overseas."

The car turned down behind St Mary's Cathedral and through the maze of Woolloomooloo, slowing down in the bottleneck of King's Cross. In another five minutes they drew up outside an imposing block of flats set back among lawns. The man led them up to the second floor and opened a door with a latchkey. They came into a pleasant, sunny room where a slim young woman was lying on a settee under the casement window. A magazine lay open on her lap and hot dance music blared out from a tiny radio on the window sill. She turned it off and got up languidly.

"This is Mrs McDonald and her sister, Terry," the man introduced them.

"Hullo Len, I didn't expect you for a while yet."

"Doctor ought to be here any time. He rang the surgery and said he'd be here before two."

There was a noticeable quickening of the young woman's interest. She put up her hand to smooth her blonde hair which she wore in an exaggerated pompadour. "Which is Mrs McDonald?" she said, regarding her lacquered finger-nails.

"I am," Mary spoke so low that the woman turned to look at her.

"Come along this way, then," she said, walking across the room. Mary followed her. The man went into an adjoining room. It was all so casual that it was a few minutes before Alice realised that Mary had gone for more than another interview.

The girl led Mary into a bedroom, opened a drawer in the dressing table and took out a nightdress. "Put this on and get into bed," she said, negligently putting the garment down on the double bed and opening the wardrobe from which she took a white overall. She went out with it over her arm, leaving the door ajar.

There was a coat hanger on a hook behind the door. Mary hung her dress and coat on it carefully, took off her slip and brassière and stepped out of her scanties. She folded her underclothes neatly over the back of the chair and placed her shoes side by side beneath it. These were familiar movements and she made them without thinking. It was only when she put on the strange nightdress that the significance of what she was doing suddenly penetrated her mind.

She stared at the bed neatly folded back with the sheet a white triangle against the soft bedspread. Two white pillows lay side by side. It was not her bed, not her room, this expensive bedroom with cream walls and the thick carpet under her bare feet. This was not Mary Parker, this girl in the wispy pink nightdress sprigged with tiny flowers.

It was as if she were watching another girl lift the sheet. It was someone else who noted an extra undersheet running across the width of the bed, someone else's fingers that felt beneath the edge and touched the smooth chill of a rubber drawsheet.

This was a bed prepared for an operation...for her operation. Her knees shook and she sat down on the bed weakly. Her stomach felt hollow and there was a choking feeling in her throat. Almost without knowing what she was doing, she slipped her feet between the cool sheets and felt the chill of the under rubber. She let her head sink into the soft pillow and drew the covers up over her bare arms. Through the closed door the voices of the man and the girl came to her in a low hum. If only they'd get it over. If only they'd be quick. The words on the Shakespeare statue floated through her mind: "We are such stuff as dreams are made on." Yes, that was it. She'd thought Frank loved her, but that was only a dream too. "We are such stuff as dreams are made on and our little life is rounded with a sleep." Oh please God, make them be quick...

At the sound of the doorbell Mary was alert again with every nerve quivering.

"Hullo, Doc." The girl's voice was warm and welcoming.

"Nice to see you, Terry. Did you enjoy your swim?"

"Bit chilly. How did the game go last night?"

"Rotten, my luck's out. How's things here?"

"Everything's tied up. Have you had any lunch?"

"Not a bite, I've just come straight round from the hospital."

"Pretty busy morning?"

"Terrific list. One of them took three hours."

"You poor dear. Like a cup of coffee first?"

"No, thanks. I'll have it when I've finished. This won't take long, we'll get straight into it. I'll scrub up now."

Mary strained her ears to listen, her nails dug into the palms of her hands. The voices were casual and intimate. There was no note of anxiety in them, no hint that this was a day different from any other. She heard a tap running in the bathroom opposite her room and the tinkle of metal and brisk footsteps passing her door. For her, every sound was full of menace. She and the unseen doctor and the man and the girl were alone together in a little island of time where there was neither past nor future.

The door of the room opened and the girl came in in a white overall. She had a pile of towels folded over one arm, in the other hand she held a white enamel pail which she put down beside the bed. The man in the grey suit followed her carrying the doctor's bag. He placed it on a table which he pulled up to the bed, and closed the windows. The nurse spread some newspapers on the floor, undid the doctor's bag and took out a white bundle which she unrolled carefully onto a tray without touching the gleaming instruments it contained. They both smiled at Mary and went about their preparations with swift, practised movements.

The door opened again and a tall figure in a white overall came in. So this was the doctor. Mary stared up at him as he came to the side of the bed. His face was kind under his greying hair, but his eyes were tired and there were lines in the loose skin under them and deep clefts from nostril to mouth.

He greeted her cheerfully. "So this is the patient. Feeling quite at home? Nice comfortable bed, isn't it?"

He went on as though her low-spoken "yes" matched his own cheerfulness. "Well, it won't be long before it's all over now.'

She watched him adjust his mask, take a pair of rubber gloves from a basin and begin to pull them on. The nurse drew down the covers and threw them over the foot of the bed. Mary felt naked in her skimpy nightdress and held it close against her legs. The nurse untucked the waterproof sheet and let it fall down the side of the bed with a rustle.

"Now would you mind lying across the bed, Mrs McDonald?" the nurse said. "And bring your buttocks as far over to the edge as you can. A bit further...that's right."

She covered her with a sheet, rolled her nightdress up to the waist, then placed her hands by her sides and tucked the sheet firmly round them.

The young man went round behind her with something white in his hand which he placed over her nose and mouth. There was a hissing sound.

"Now I want you to count with me," he said. "One... two..." he began.

"One...two..." she repeated obediently after him.

She heard the hissing sound again, it came in spurts. "Five...six..." She spoke from a long way off. Her hands and feet began to tingle, her head was floating, her voice came slower...slower...more and more distant. "El-e-v-e-n ...t-w-e-l-..." and she slid out.

Alice got up from her chair and looked out the window. She couldn't sit still. The sound of the muffled voices coming through the closed door kept her ears straining, but she could pick out nothing. The nurse seemed to be an old friend of the doctor the way they talked when he came in. It would have to be someone he could trust. Mrs Cavendish said he never used the same flat for more than a week or so at a time. She wondered how he got the flats. Her mind flew to all the people she knew who couldn't find a home, husbands who had to live apart from their families and children who lived with grandparents. Even if she and Ross had enough money to get married, they still couldn't find anywhere to live. But it was like the SP she supposed, anything was possible when you were on the inside of the racket and had money enough to pay.

This flat, for instance. What a perfect flat if you were just married. Her mind recoiled from the thought. This flat ...no, never. How horrible, to start your married life in a flat where this sort of thing had been going on. But if you took a furnished flat, how did you know what had gone on in it before?

In a way, what was happening to Mary was like this flat. If Mary had never told her and had got it done without her knowing, it would never have touched her and Ross, just as this flat wouldn't hurt people who didn't know about it.

Alice heard the voices again, muffled at first then louder. The door opened, someone was coming out.

Mary struggled back to consciousness out of a great void. The world came to her like the throb of a giant piston, formless and terrifying. Light filtered through her lids as the enveloping blackness slid away. Someone was making sounds, disconnected, incoherent and a long way off. Beside her, a voice said distinctly, "Not so much noise, Mrs McDonald. You're quite all right." Slowly she opened her eyes and saw the blonde nurse bending over her holding a basin beside her face. "That's a good girl," she said heartily, "it's all over now."

Consciousness came back to Mary in a flood. It was really over.

The nurse smoothed the sheet under her head. "Now, you rest for a while and hold the bowl yourself. I'm just going into the next room for a few minutes."

Mary heard the clatter of cups and murmur of voices. The girl laughed and the man's voice came to her. "Here it is, doc. Thirty-five, all singles. I've given Terry her five and I've got mine."

"Thanks."

"What are the arrangements, Len?" The doctor's voice was tired.

"There's another at four o'clock. Will you do it here?"

"Better make it at Number Seven, I think. We'll move for good next week. Been making the pace a bit too hot here lately."

"OK, Doc. I'll be getting back to the surgery."

Mary opened her eyes and saw the doctor smiling down at her. He'd taken off his gown and was in a dark suit. "Feeling all right?" he asked.

"Yes, thank you."

He patted her cheek, "It wasn't so bad, was it?"

She shook her head, and tried to smile.

"Well, you're well rid of that." He dismissed the whole matter airily and went out. She heard him speak to the nurse in a low voice. The outer door slammed.

The door of the bathroom across the passage was open and Mary saw the nurse pick up the pail that had stood beside the bed. She heard the clink of its iron handle and a heavy splash. The cistern gushed...Oh, she was well rid of that.

Colonel Byron Maddocks stretched out on the lounge and relaxed happily after his Turkish bath. A waiter placed a teatray beside him, took the proffered ten-shilling note and fumbled for the change. Byron waved him away and poured himself a cup of milkless tea, sugaring it heavily. It was a vile drink, he didn't know what Australians could see in it, but the coffee they made was even viler. However, there wasn't any choice, he'd decided to go on the water wagon. He always went off Scotch when he fell in love — marvellous how it toned a man up. It wasn't easy, though, but somehow even thinking of that sweet kid made going prohibition worthwhile.

The prospect of going north again shook him. He couldn't possibly string things out in Sydney beyond the end of the week. By now, poor old Lew would be frying on the Equator. Do him good, take a bit of weight off him, and really a fellow like him with a wife and family back home in the States ought to be ashamed of himself hanging around a girl like Guinea.

What a lucky fellow he was to have found such a girl. She was unique; he'd never met a girl like her before. She had everything — beauty, brains and that childlike candour you didn't find in women today. He lit a cigarette and drew the smoke deep into his lungs, exhaling slowly. He felt a hundred per cent after his treatment; he should have started these baths and massage earlier. Of course what he really needed to keep him in form were his regular visits to the gym, but the war interfered with so many of a man's habits. The last complete course he'd had was in January after he met Geraldine, and as soon as he got back to New York he would go to Reilly's and get them to put him in first-class shape again.

He hadn't felt like this for years. This is what love did to you. Yes, he'd ask Guinea to marry him tonight. There would be time to get a special licence through before he left. That would at least give him peace of mind while he was away — make certain nobody else'd snap her up.

Boz Spreckles'd be moving out of the penthouse he had in Macleay Street at any moment and he was sure to let him have it. It'd be cosy for her there till he came back. Or perhaps he could persuade her to come up to Brisbane; he could easily set her up in a flat there and it would be much more convenient when he came back to HQ instead of having to bother coming down to Sydney.

He stretched again and closed his eyes. Yes, he'd ask her tonight on the trip up to Lapstone — there was nothing like a long drive through the dark to work up the right atmosphere.

Angus stirred uneasily on the scrubbed wooden bench in the hot room. It was damned hot; he wondered if his blood pressure was up again. The last couple of times he had come in for his weekly Turkish bath he had found the steaming heat almost unbearably oppressive. Perhaps he should get himself checked over again. He would ring Mathews for an appointment early next week, though probably all that was wrong with him was his uncertainty about Deborah.

He looked at Ian lying relaxed in a deckchair, his eyes shut and his mouth slightly open. The heat did not seem to be worrying him, though the sweat was pouring out. Probably do his rheumatism good. He was glad he'd persuaded him to come for a Turkish bath on his last day in town. No use being on the wrong side of Ian or it would make the whole business of opening up Burramaronga extremely difficult.

Ian looks old, Angus thought. Put the two of us side by side and you'd say I could give him at least ten years, although I'm two years older. There was no doubt about it, the land was a hard life; he didn't know why Ian stuck to it. If he sold the place or even put a manager in, he had plenty to live on in comfort.

Angus looked down at his own body, pulling in his abdominal muscles and admiring his even tan. I've got the body of a young man, he said to himself complacently. He watched the sweat gather and run down through the mat of hair on his chest, noticing with a sense of shock how much more grey there was in it lately. A feeling of depression settled on him, and he slumped back against the seat, relaxing his muscles. Damn it, Ian was right, it was no good deceiving himself; he'd have to get a few inches off his waistline. He looked quite all right when he was dressed — what his elastic belt didn't control, his tailor disguised. But that wouldn't do when he was married; it would put a man at a disadvantage for his wife to know he wore a belt. He would have a talk to the masseur about it.

He looked at the other men seated round the hot room, their heavy flesh glistening with sweat and their mouths gaping in the heat. Disgusting job, massage, he thought. Somehow it was impossible to associate Deborah with such work. He stirred again uneasily. Perhaps he ought to cut down his time in the hot room and have some extra massage to make up. He caught the eye of Horatio Veale, who was sitting on a bench at the far end of the room. Veale smiled genially; Angus nodded and coughed, averting his face to discourage any approach.

Ian opened his eyes. "What did you say?" he asked drowsily.

"I didn't say anything."

Ian sat up and looked around, yawning. "Isn't that Horatio Veale over there?"

"Yes, and D'Arcy-Twyning with him. Birds of a feather."

Ian scrutinised the two men from under his lids — Veale, with his bland, unlined face under a mop of greying hair, his tallow-coloured skin and sagging paunch; D'Arcy-Twyning, short and chicken-boned, with his ribs sticking out and hairy spindle-shanks, his bony fingers gesticulating as he talked.

Angus smiled ironically. "Twyning — good old English name!"

Ian cocked an eyebrow at him.

"Jew, of coure," Angus explained. "Trust them to be in where the money is."

Ian surveyed the two men. "Not any more than the Gentiles, so far as I can see. All city middlemen are just a lot of bloody parasites anyway...ruining the country." He closed his eyes again. "Parasites."

Angus wondered whether it was the hot room sending Ian's blood pressure up or just natural bad temper. He'd be glad to see the last of him when he went home tonight; he couldn't stand much more of his bigoted provincialism. He looked at Ian's trim waistline with growing irritation. That was one thing hard work did for you, he thought enviously, kept your muscles firm. Perhaps he ought to take up riding again, but the thought of cantering around Centennial Park alone every morning filled him with boredom. He wondered if Deborah could ride. She ought to look magnificent on horseback. He would talk to her about it. It would be a way of killing two birds with one stone — spending time with her and getting his waistline down. He stole another glance at Veale; the fellow was getting grosser every time he saw him. No doubt about it, once a man was over fifty, he had to watch himself.

Ian looked up as a youngish thickset man came in and padded across the hot room, walking slow-footed and light like a cat. He went unobtrusively to a chair in the far corner, opened his legs wide and relaxed to give himself up to the heat.

"That fellow walks like a burglar."

"He may be, for all I know, but I think it's improbable," Angus retorted dryly. "He's Stormcloud's owner."

"Oh, is he?" Ian studied him with interest. "Got a fine little mare there. What's his name?"

"Walters. I don't know very much about him. Bit of a rough diamond, but seems a decent enough fellow."

"I'd like to have a look at her before I go back," Ian brightened up. "Do you think he'd take me out to see her?"

"He'd probably jump at the chance."

Sport rippled the powerful muscles in his shoulders and yawned. He was bloody tired. What with being out at the tracks at four o'clock this morning, and all the worry about Grace and Elm Street and having to move his flat in a hurry, he hadn't had a wink of sleep for the last two nights.

He caught Angus's eyes upon him and nodded amiably. McFarland had tickets on himself all right. That must be his brother with him, had the same snooty look. What was it he'd heard about him? Ah! now he remembered. That stud they were running him on to buy was practically next door to the McFarland place up Bathurst way somewhere. Bit of luck he'd given the old boy that tip on Saturday; knowing him might come in useful. He'd been lucky to come out of that affair with that bastard of a Doc Smethers the way he had. Stormcloud wasn't only the sweetest little mare a man could have come by, but she was turning out a bloody good introduction as well. All he needed now was a few decent clothes and a few more points on how to wear them properly, and he could go anywhere among the bloody nobs.

He rubbed his upper lip reflectively. He'd grow a moustache too and get his hair cut shorter and part it on the side like old McFarland. Then he wouldn't mind being photographed in the saddling-paddock: "Mr Cyril Walters, owner of Stormcloud". It would look well. It was a bit of luck to have that bitch of a Grace out of the way just now too. He didn't need her any more and by the time she came out of the Bay he'd be finished with the girl racket for good. Someone else could run it for the British; the pickings on their pay weren't worth the risk. There was a packet to be made out of liquor for a hell of a long time yet. . . . He looked up startled at a sudden noise.

Horatio Veale slapped his pale, dimpled knee again and laughed. "By God, that's good, Dan, bloody good. Where did you hear it?"

Twyning looked round to make sure the men on either side of them could not hear. "Denise has been staying at the South Pacific the last couple of weeks and that old housemaid on her floor told her that McFarland is carrying on with the masseuse in the Marie Antoinette."

"I wouldn't have believed it of him. A masseuse! And married, did you say?"

"Yes. Husband's at the war."

Veale looked across at Angus with malice. "Sly old dog.

Fancy the squattocracy getting mixed up with a masseuse —
and at the South Pacific too.'' He dug a finger into Dan's
bony ribs. Dan doubled up with a gasp and they went into
silent laughter together. ''They say he's always been a gay
dog,'' Veale chuckled, ''but stuck to his own class. You
know the line those fellows out of the top drawer have —
always sleep with your best friends' wives.''

''Disgusting!'' Dan said virtuously.

''Wonder how she caught him? She's evidently got her
head screwed on the right way.''

''Yes, Denise said this maid told her the masseuse is
dressing up to the nines. Got a wardrobe full of new clothes,
and she doesn't do that on her wages — or tips either.''

''Apparently going the whole hog.''

''No doubt about that,'' Dan agreed. ''He had her down
at his Palm Beach house last weekend.''

Veale sat up. ''Oh, so that was her I saw coming up from
the surf with him on Sunday. I had a party on at my place
so I didn't take much notice, except to think she was a fine
figure of a wench and that McFarland had better look to his
waistline.'' Veale ran his eyes critically over Angus. ''Putting
on weight. You don't notice so much when he's dressed.
I wonder who his tailor is? Probably got a stock of clothes
he brought from London.''

Dan grunted.

''What I'd really like to know is how he managed to
shake off that Destrange woman. He kept her dangling long
enough. I always thought she'd get him in the end, with the
family she has behind her and the pull they've got.''

''Huh, disgusting business.''

Veale pursed his lips. ''He's well out of that, from what
I hear lately. She's been in for a cure. Drugs.''

''Serve her right, the way she's gone on for years. Public
disgrace. You'd think women would have learnt by now that
men never marry the girls they play around with. And you'd
think a man of McFarland's position would have something
better to do with his time.''

Veale controlled his face and cast a malicious eye over

Dan's figure. Sour grapes, he thought. Dried up. A man was mad to let himself run down nowadays when there was no need for it. Look what Oscar's platinum pills had done for him. And if the worst came to the worst, look how old Warwick Dalgety had got himself pepped up abroad, and still going strong at eighty if you could believe all you heard. Oh well, perhaps you couldn't expect Dan to show much enthusiasm with that wife of his. Like going to bed with a clothes horse. Now that juicy piece of McFarland's, there was something worth having. Sharlton said she was leaving, so he must be going to set her up in a flat. Veale leaned back and chuckled again. That was rich.

Dan felt Veale's body shaking with silent laughter beside him. H. V.'s a dirty old devil, he thought sourly. Kind of man no woman's safe with. It's disgusting the way he boasts there's no woman he can't get if he wants her. Bet it costs him a pretty penny. . . . He looked across at Angus and back to Veale. Personally, he couldn't understand what men got out of that sort of thing. And the way they poured money out on women. Now, if it was your own family, that was a different matter. It was as good a way as any of showing just what you were worth. But pouring it out on a lot of trollops and expensive trollops at that. . . . Well, he thought philosophically, thank God women don't worry me.

"How do you like your prospective son-in-law?" Veale cut across his thoughts. "Son of a lord, isn't he?"

"Yes, younger son of Lord Weffolk."

"Well, you never know your luck," Veale said cheerfully. "V-bombs or hæmophilia might bump the others off. These old families are usually pretty dicky. Hope you're going to invite me to the wedding."

"Of course, of course," Dan assured him. "Pretty packet it's going to cost me, too, but the wife and I have never stinted the little girl and we're not going to start now — particularly when it's something she's really set her heart on."

Veale moved his position in the chair and looked up to see Sport picking his way carefully across the floor. Angus waved him to a seat beside Ian, who leaned over and began to speak rapidly.

"My God, look at the McFarlands sucking up to that fellow Walters. They must be after a tip."

"Huh! If you own a racehorse you can get anywhere in this country," Dan sneered. He wasn't interested in racing.

Veale watched Sport with interest. "Bit of a mystery about Walters. I believe he's in the sly grog racket up to the neck."

"I've heard he supplies half the nightclubs in Sydney." Dan looked at him disapprovingly.

"I bet he's socked a pretty packet away. No worry with the Taxation either." Veale brooded enviously over Sport's carefree life.

"All I know is he's come a long way in a short time. Nobody's got the full strength of him. Slippery customer, I'd say."

"It'd give the McFarlands a shock if they knew who they were talking to."

"Sure," Sport was saying genially, "come along and welcome, Mr McFarland. How'd yer like to see her on the tracks termorrer mornin'? I could pick you up at the SP across the way about 'ar-past four." He turned to Angus. "How about you taggin' along too?"

"No, thank you. I expect to have a very late night. Some other time perhaps."

"Okay, just give me the word," Sport said easily and turned back to Ian. "By the way, me trainer has been tellin' me about a nice little place that's up for sale somewhere round your way. Bungaloo or something. He thought I ought to hop in and grab it while the goin's good, in case I want to put Stormcloud out to stud."

"Oh, that'll be Bundalong — Cameron's place. Very nice little place too. Are you going in for horse-breeding seriously, then?"

"Well, I haven't thought a lot about it, but I'd like a foal out of Stormcloud, she's that pretty. You've got a stud of your own, ain't you, Mr McFarland?"

"Ours is a Corriedale stud," Ian explained, smiling.

"Aw...draught horses, ain't they?"

Angus laughed tolerantly. "It's Clydesdales you're thinking of. My brother has a sheep stud."

"Oh, my mistake. Anyway, I'll be hoppin' up to give that place the once-over soon. I'll probably look you up."

Angus rose abruptly. "It's too hot," he said. "I think I'll move next door. Coming, Ian?"

Sport nodded sympathetically. "Find it a bit hard on the ticker with your weight, eh?"

Angus drew his towel around him and went out like a Roman senator.

Sport raised a hand in friendly farewell. "I'll be seeing you."

Ian got up. "Four-thirty tomorrow morning, then."

"It's a date."

In the massage room Oscar pummelled Sport vigorously. "You'll have to get some of this weight off, pal," he said, speaking out of the corner of his mouth.

"Yes, but I don't seem to have no time for exercise nowadys. I'm kept that busy with one thing and another."

"Well, it's no flamin' good to yer. Take a look at them fat old bozos out in the other room and see what high livin' and drinkin' and no exercise does to yer. I'm warnin' yer, and I know."

"OK, OK. I heard you the first time."

"Well, you're not takin' any notice." Oscar grabbed a handful of fat on Sport's belly and held it up in a ridge. "Two years ago you didn't have a bit of spare flesh on you — and now, look at that."

"I'll get it off," Sport snapped. "Once I get a bit of time to get some exercise, I'll be back in me old form in a month."

"Yeah? I've heard that one before. Every sixteen-stoner out in that hot room thought that once. Just you give old Veale the once-over and be warned in time."

"He's twice my age." Sport's voice was indignant.

"But he's not twice your weight. Before you know where y'are, with all the likker you're puttin' away and all the fat you're puttin' on, you'll be the same."

"Oh, fer Chrissake, lay off, Oscar! I promise yer I'll get a stone off before Christmas. Will that satisfy yer?"

"If you don't, I'm warnin' yer, it won't be many more years before you're in the same state he is and you'll have to come sneakin' around for some of them platinum pills I get him, before you can take a girl away for the weekend."

"Well whaddayaknow!" Sport chuckled. "Is that a fact?"

"'S a fact and plenty others like him."

"I reckon, judging by the look of Dan Twyning, he could do with a course of treatment."

"Him! Nothing short of a complete set of monkey glands'd do anything for him." Oscar grunted as he kneaded the slack muscles. "Trouble about you is since yer got hold of that flamin' little filly, you ain't had no time fer business at all."

"Fair go, Oscar," Sport snorted indignantly. "You know that ain't true."

Oscar stopped massaging and went to the curtained doorway, looked out, then came back, making his soft whispers even softer. "Gotta keep me eyes skinned for Ted next door, he's just been put on and if you ask me he's a dark horse. I've a feeling he might be in with the dicks."

Sport's eyes narrowed. "Don't he know it's dangerous?"

"He'll find out soon enough. I hear you had a spot of bother at Elm Street."

"Yeah."

"What are yer gonna do about the joint?"

"Give it away."

"No." Oscar's voice was incredulous.

"I've had it. Stickin' to grog in future."

"Oh, then you wouldn't be interested in a proposition I was arst to pass onter yer."

"What sort of proposition?"

Oscar's eyes lit up with enthusiasm. "It's a cinch, Sport. You couldn't miss."

"Spit it out."

"Feller got a residential, top of George Street. You must know it — called the Gem. He's made a pile out of the Yanks, and now he wants to get out."

"I'm not buyin' any more trouble."

"There won't be no trouble about this place. The bloke he's got in as manager has got a certificate of good character from the police and the place runs itself."

Sport shook his head. "With the Yanks goin' the game's finished as far as the big money's concerned."

"Yeah, you're right. For pricey joints like Elm Street with a touch of home about 'em, I agree. What you want now is a kinda cash-and-carry joint. Low profits and quick turnover, and this is the glassy marble. The bloke's had it all divided into cubicles — looks a bit like the horse stalls out at the showground, only wire-netted over to stop any gingerin'. The girls bring their own trade and all the manager has to do is provide a room by the half-hour and collect the dough. If there's a police raid the girls are picked up under the Vag. and that's all there is to it. The feller who owns it gets his rent and his rakeoff and he don't ever need to see the place."

"What's he askin' for it?"

"Ten grand."

"That's a helluva lot."

"Think it over. I'd come in with yer fifty-fifty if you'd give it a fly. So that tells yer what I think of it as a payin' proposition."

Sport sat up and swung his legs off the table. "Well, get his figures checked by the time I get back from Brisbane."

"I'll be waitin' for you," Oscar assured him. "It's easy money and no risk."

"Now what about tonight?"

"I've got about three hundred bottles of scotch you could pick up. Bloke off one of the Yanks' little ships got 'em in to me."

"Good, I'll be round just after midnight."

"Another thing. Before you go to Brisbane you'll have to do something about Down Under. They're complainin' about the hooch you're supplyin' to them.''

"Who's complainin'?'' Sport fixed him with a cold eye.

"Listen. They're complainin' — it's nothin' to do with me.''

"Let 'em complain to me, then. They sell it, don't they?''

"Well, they reckon the last lot of grog practically blew the lid off the joint and they don't want the police in, not after what happened to that club in Gloucester Street last week.''

"The day they'll have to start worryin' is the day when nightclubs get licences and they have to sell their stuff at a fixed price.''

"Well, they got the wind up, anyway.''

"They got nothin' to worry about even if they get fined. Can't they read? That joint in Gloucester Street got the maximum fine of a hundred smackers for at least ten thousand quid's worth of trade they done under the lap.''

"You talk to them, then.''

"OK.'' Sport gave a short laugh. "I'll talk to them.''

Blue rapped on the door of Denise D'Arcy-Twyning's suite. Elvira opened it and gave him a warning wink. "The lift-man's 'ere, mad'm."

Denise came to the door. "Oh, there you are. I've been waiting simply ages for you."

"Fair go, lady. I come up as soon as I could."

"Well, get this luggage out as soon as you can, porter."

"I think somebody's made a mistake, lady. I'm the lift-man. You better ring for a porter. This stuff ought to go down in the goods lift."

Denise waved his protest aside. "I don't care whose mistake it is," she said. "Now you're here, get this stuff out into the lift as quickly as you can. I can't wait here all day."

Blue shook his head. "Not my job, lady," he said firmly.

Denise ran her eyes over him contemptuously. "Oh," she said, curling her lip, "can't you lift anything heavier than a double-headed penny?"

Blue coloured under his tan. "I'm not supposed to do this, it's the porter's job."

"Good heavens," Denise gave a tinkling laugh, "don't tell me you're a cripple in addition to not being able to work a lift properly."

Blue gritted his teeth and drew a deep breath.

"I'll give it a go," he said curtly, "but next time ring for a porter."

"Well get on with the job, then."

Blue looked grimly over the innumerable suitcases, hat-boxes and cardboard boxes, picked up a hatbox and a heavy suitcase and staggered out, bending sideways to take the strain.

Denise turned to Elvira. "If you hadn't taken so long over the packing, there wouldn't have been all this delay."

Elvira sagged pathetically. "I'm sorry, mad'm. I done me best."

One of the housemaids peeped cautiously round the

door. "Excuse me, madam. I'm very sorry, but Mrs Dalgety particularly wants Elvira." She cast an agonised and imploring look towards Elvira. Elvira went out into the corridor.

"She wants some more gin," the maid whispered.

"Did you tell 'er the manager said she wasn't to 'ave any more?"

"No. She threw the empty bottle at me and I got out."

"She must've got the DTs again."

"What'll I do?"

"I'll be along in two shakes of a dead lamb's tail." She went into the room again.

"I'm so sorry, mad'm, I just 'ave to go. Mrs Molesworth asked me to keep an eye on 'er pertikler. She ain't very well."

Denise kicked the wastepaper basket petulantly. Elvira picked it up quickly. "Oh, mad'm," she said reproachfully. "Fancy ruinin' them lovely grey shoes! Why yer got a foot like Cinderella in them."

Denise smoothed the scuffed kid with her finger. "Well, you'd better get along to Mrs Dalgety," she said. "Apparently it doesn't matter about me."

Elvira lingered. Her eyes travelled to Denise's scarlet shoulder bag, thrown over the end of the bed. "Oh, mad'm," she said, "you know I'm always only too 'appy to do what I can, it's a pleasure I'm sure."

Denise's eyes followed Elvira's. She gave her tinkling laugh. "Oh, of course. Pass me over my bag, will you?" She pulled out a bunch of crumpled notes, selected a ten-shilling note and flipped it into Elvira's hand.

"Thank you, mad'm," Elvira tucked the note into her pocket under her apron. "Though I don't want you to think that anything I do for you is for this." She scuttled out with the wastepaper basket in her hand.

Blue returned whistling. He undid the neck of his tunic, picked up another suitcase and got it to the lift, resting several times on the way. There were beads of sweat around his mouth. Crikey, that'd tickled up the old back. He was a bloody mug to have started on the job. Sharlton knew he couldn't touch heavy stuff, but a bloke hated bellyachin' in front of that tart.

When he came back, Denise was standing in front of the long mirror, adjusting the belt of her suit. Its woven silkiness clung to her slender hips and outlined her flat little bottom provocatively. She examined herself from all angles to see the contour of her bosom. The smart jacket fitted like another skin. There was no doubt what those cheaters did for a girl's bust, no one would ever guess it wasn't her own.

Blue whistled low through his teeth. She turned sharply, but he was busy collecting boxes and parcels. She turned back to the mirror, ran a comb through her silver-blonde hair, set a perky grey beanie on the back of her head and clipped a diamond initial onto it.

When Blue brought his next load along, the lift bell was buzzing persistently. "Keep it up brother," he said with a half salute to the bell, "you'll get tired first."

Two more trips disposed of the luggage. He drew a long, sighing breath. Crikey, he'd have to get Doss onto the old liniment tonight. His back felt as though somebody had stuck a red-hot needle into his spine.

"Oh, porter!" Denise's voice came down the corridor, "you haven't taken everything, you know."

Men of Blue's old company would have wisely taken themselves off when they saw the particular look that came over his face at her call, but Denise merely leaned against the jamb of the door and pointed to her golfbag leaning against the wall near the window.

She watched him cross the floor slowly. She'd show him where he got off, she thought, her eyes bright with anger.

Blue picked up the bag, slipped the strap over his shoulder, buttoned his tunic and turned. He walked across to the door and stopped.

Denise leaned against the jamb, half blocking his way. Under the smart tight jacket her breasts were uplifted in impudent challenge.

Blue looked down on her delicate face in its frame of silver-blonde hair, his eyes dropped and lingered on her pointed breasts. Then he looked her straight in the eyes with an engaging grin. "Come clean, lady," he pleaded in a half whisper, "are they dinkum?" He brushed past her with the bags.

"You...you..." she spluttered after him.

He heard her at the phone, rattling the receiver frantically and demanding the manager, the hostess, the house manager.

"Better call out the Navy," he suggested, putting his head round the door.

Blue whistled his way back to the lift; he felt better. He seated himself and waited patiently for his passenger to join her luggage.

Thelma panted in from one lift, L. F. stalked from another. Denise threw herself on the bed and beat a tattoo with her high heels. L. F. rang for brandy, Thelma wet her own handkerchief and damped Denise's forehead. They both paled before the recital of her injuries. L. F. strode down the corridor to Blue. The bell was buzzing furiously.

"Listen Mr Sharlton," said Blue virtuously, "have I got to wait here all day for Miss D'Arcy-Twyning to come out? Guests're waiting down below for this lift."

L. F. choked. Thelma's voice came down the corridor in a piercing whisper. "Lance...er, Mr Sharlton, they've rung to say the Temperance deputation is waiting downstairs."

"Go down immediately, Albert, and take the ladies up to Milady's Room," L. F. commanded with a gesture of dismissal. "I'll deal with you later."

"Where'll I pack 'em?" said Blue, "on top of this junk?"

"Put it out at the ground floor."

"OK. Every care but no responsibility." Blue closed the door and whistled his way downwards.

L. F. gazed down the lift well and wished that the cables would break. He'd deal with the fellow this time, if he was a veteran of fifty wars, no matter what H. V. wanted from the returned soldiers.

Blue opened the door at the ground floor where he was

met by a group of middle-aged women of such obvious respectability that he almost suggested that they'd come to the wrong address.

The leader, grey-haired and distinguished, stepped forward. "We have an appointment with the manager."

"Won't keep you a minute, lady. Just wait till I get this gear out."

"Certainly," she answered, smiling.

Blue piled the luggage beside the lift. "All aboard now, ladies."

"You're a returned man, I see," said one of them, noting his badge.

"That's right. Just waiting for me discharge to come through. See you got a boy there yourself." His eyes rested on her mother's badge.

She touched it gently. "Yes," she said, "he's been up in the islands for nearly eighteen months and I'm expecting him home on leave any day now. He's in the commandos."

"Well, you've certainly got something to be proud of there, lady. I seen them boys in action up near Markham Valley and I hand it to them. They're bobbydazzlers."

The woman smiled gratefully.

"Do you like working here?" one of the others asked.

"Lady," he said, pulling up at the first floor. "You can take my tip for it, a jungle full of yeller bellies is a home from home compared with this pub."

The deputation gasped.

"We're a Temperance deputation, you know," the commando's mother said softly, "so I must warn you that anything you tell us will be used in evidence."

Blue gave her his friendliest smile. "It'd be a pleasure. What do you want to ask me?"

"Well, we're very anxious to find out whether the regulation is being observed about girls under twenty-one not being permitted to drink in lounges. You know about that of course?"

"Too right," said Blue, "I'm all for it. Pretty tough, all these kids getting in on a man's beer."

"Oh...well...perhaps you'd tell us if they observe the rule here."

"Observe it! Huh! You come in about five o'clock, lady, when the Bull Ring begins to get steamed up. The Yanks practically wheel 'em in, in prams. They like 'em young and tender, you know."

The deputation spoke together in low voices. "But we never see any actual prosecutions for the South Pacific. Perhaps you could tell us how they get round the law."

Blue turned with his hand on the lift door. "Lady, the day the SP gets on the wrong side of the law, the law'll move to make room for it."

The door slid open.

"Bull Ring on your left. Straight ahead for Mother's Ruin — you can't miss it — and order anything you like on the house, the manager said. He's on his way down."

The deputation stood close together, taking their bearings in the unfamiliar surroundings. Blue lifted his hand in a salute, closed the door and whistled his way back to the foyer.

Mrs Molesworth had given orders that guests desiring to use Milady's Room after three o'clock should be directed to the general lounges, but Mrs Dalgety was beyond warning. The night before, Alistair had left her to go south to the Victorian border to improve his soldiering, travelling, alas, second class in his private's uniform.

Ever since the Melbourne express had pulled out, Mrs Dalgety had been drowning her loneliness at his departure and her misery at the hardships he was enduring. By two o'clock the next afternoon, she had forgotten the origin of her sorrow and had reached the stage where she was making up for her enforced spell on the water wagon since her darling's unexpected arrival on the previous Friday.

She had wakened to find her lunch tray beside her untouched and the supply of gin in her bedroom exhausted. She rang for Elvira, but Elvira didn't come, and she threw an empty bottle after the housemaid who answered her ring.

She picked up the telephone and rang through her complaints to the manager's office, but the manager had been called upstairs urgently. Milady's Room presented itself to her as the haven her thirsty soul required. She put on her shoes and stockings, half struggled into her corsets then discarded them with happy abandon. What the hell, she could screw the tops of her stockings up just as well. She donned her black suit from Hartnell — black suited her mood, she was a woman in mourning, though whether for the departed Alistair or the departed gin she wasn't sure. Her black hat sat rakishly on her tousled curls, her skirt gaped. Never mind, her coat would cover that. But her coat strained at the buttons and she'd forgotten her blouse. Never mind, her scarf would cover that.

The door opened noiselessly and Elvira's face appeared. "Sorry I been delayed, mad'm," she apologised.

Mrs Dalgety focused on her groggily. "Get out," she shouted. "I ring for service an' I can't get service. Might as well be stayin' at the People's Palace instead of spending a fortune in this dump."

Elvira came cautiously around the door. "Don't take on like that, mad'm," she said soothingly. "You just let me help you back into bed and I'll have a nice new bottle of gin up before you can say Jack Robinson." She took Mrs Dalgety by the arm.

Mrs Dalgety shook her off. "Dunno any Jack Robinson." She fixed her eye on the door and set a wavering course for it.

Elvira seized her arm again and began pulling her towards the bed, making soothing noises. Mrs Dalgety swung round and planted an open hand on her chest. With a powerful shove, she pushed her backwards onto the unmade bed and threw the bedclothes over her. While Elvira was still struggling to free herself, Mrs Dalgety staggered out of the door and slammed it behind her.

A reluctant liftman helped her off at the first floor, noted the general direction of her zigzag progress and reported to the floor supervisor. By the time Faulkiner arrived, Mrs Dalgety had intercepted a drink waitress bearing a bottle of gin to a private suite and was firmly entrenched in Milady's Room at her favourite table by the window, through which the afternoon sun poured in a blaze of pitiless light.

By the time L. F. arrived, accompanied by Mr Allstone, she was telling a fascinated deputation the story of her life and love and calling for glasses all round. L. F., stricken, shepherded the deputation to Mrs Molesworth's suite, leaving directions with the floor supervisor to persuade Mrs Dalgety to return to her own room immediately.

Mrs Dalgety was not open to persuasion.

The supervisor returned with reinforcements. She was not amenable to force.

He sent for a full bottle of gin, locked the door carefully behind him and for the rest of the afternoon Milady's Room bore a printed notice, CLOSED FOR REPAIRS.

The taxi drew up at a shabby terrace house, indistinguishable from the twenty others that stretched in a solid facade from end to end of the block.

"This is number fifty-seven," the driver said.

The girls got out, Alice paid him and pushed open the spiked iron gate. The palm in the centre of the pocket handkerchief lawn was bedraggled and dusty, the cement path was cracked. Alice took the key out of her handbag. "I feel like a burglar...just walking into someone else's house."

"I know," Mary agreed. "It's funny you've never been here before. But then you don't know Bessie very well, do you?"

Alice shrugged. "We just hadn't anything in common."

They went in like conspirators, treading softly on the worn linoleum, skirting the hallstand with the flourishing aspidistra and climbed up the narrow staircase without meeting anyone. Alice opened Bessie's door with a second key and they went into a bed sitting room that led onto a diminutive balcony. The western sun was streaming through the half-glassed doors, lighting an enormous bowl of pink hydrangeas on a table in the middle of the room.

There were flowers everywhere, yellow Iceland poppies on the top of a cupboard, delphiniums thrusting their blue spikes up from mantelpiece to ceiling. A great jar of frosted ruby gum tips was set in the hearth and beside the divan bed on a little table was a bowl of sweet peas which scented the whole room.

Alice picked up a note from the table. "Dear Girls, I hope you find everything nice and comfy. There's tea and sugar and milk in the safe on the balcony and biscuits in the tin. Just put the kettle on and make yourselves at home until I come. The bed in the room is all ready and Mary must go to bed at once. Val's coming on duty for me early so I'll be home soon after five. With love, Bessie."

"She's a darling," Mary said warmly.

"She's right, Mary. You'd better get straight into bed

and I'll make a cup of tea."

Mary opened the suitcase, took out a nightdress and began to undress. As she folded her clothes and placed them on a little chair, she remembered without emotion that she had done exactly the same thing less than three hours before. But that was all over and done with now. All she wanted to do was get into bed and rest.

When Alice brought her a cup of tea she sat up and drank it thirstily, then she lay back on her pillow with her eyes closed, her body relaxed and her mind empty.

There was a light rapping on the door.

"Open the door, will you, dear?" It was Bessie's voice.

Alice jumped up to let her in. They exchanged a glance of question and answer and Bessie went straight over to the bed and beamed at Mary over her armful of parcels.

"Well, now, isn't it nice to see you," she said. "You look real comfortable there. Feeling all right?"

"Quite all right, thank you," Mary smiled at her. "I couldn't be anything else with all these lovely flowers." She put out her hand and touched the vase beside her. "Sweet peas. My favourites."

Bessie dumped her parcels in the kitchenette at the end of the balcony and came in again. She took Mary's hand between her own and patted it. "We'll be all right together, won't we? A good long night's rest, that's what you need. No one'll worry you tomorrow and you'll feel as right as a trivet by the weekend."

"You're very good to me, Bessie."

"Go on, it's nothing. I just feel as though I've got Nance home again."

"Well, now you've come," Alice said, "I'd better be going if you think everything will be all right. I've got to pick up some dry cleaning for mother before the shops shut."

"You get a move on then. And you won't forget to slip up to the Marie Antoinette, will you? I promised you'd ring the girls before they left, but Cronin's got a nose as long as your arm and she seems to think there's something in the wind, so you'd better go up to be on the safe side. They're not anxious of course, but you know how it is, they'd all like to know Mary's quite all right."

"Yes," Alice hesitated, "I suppose they would."

Bessie went out to the balcony and beckoned Alice after her. "Everything go all right?"

"Yes. The nurse said there was nothing to worry about, though she did keep her quite a while after it was over. She said to see she rests for a few days."

"I'll see to that. She can stay here as long as she likes. Now, you get along home and see you have a good sleep yourself tonight, or your mother'll be asking questions about your pale face."

Alice picked up her bag and went over to the bed and kissed Mary. "Goodbye now," she said cheerfully. "I'll be over tomorrow afternoon, and don't worry. And thanks awfully, Bessie. I do appreciate your kindness."

Bessie closed the door softly and came back to Mary.

"Now, what would you like for your tea? Do you like oysters? They're grand for getting back your strength — I got a bottle at Fernandez, real beauties. And some breast of chicken, and what do you know? A tin of real asparagus Elvira got for me. She thinks I'm having a party with a boyfriend." Bessie gave a rich chuckle.

"Oh Bessie, you are a darling, and it all sounds lovely. But could we keep it for tomorrow? I just don't feel like eating."

"Just as you say, dearie. I'll pop the oysters and the chicken down in Mrs Jones's ice chest and it'll all keep till tomorrow. Now, you have a good rest while I fix up these parcels and make my bed up."

"Oh, Bessie, you shouldn't have given me your bed."

"Nonsense. I've got a fine little stretcher on the balcony. I always sleep there when Nance comes. I'd have left it made up from last weekend when I had Val if I'd known you were coming. Now, just you shut your eyes and don't take any notice of me."

Bessie went out onto the balcony, closing the door softly behind her. She went into the boarded-in corner of the balcony that served for a kitchenette, filled the kettle out of a big enamel jug and lit the tiny gas stove that stood on top of a cupboard made of butter boxes. The rest of the furniture consisted of a safe with high legs standing in jam tins of water and an enamel washing-up dish underneath, a little table with a wooden chair tucked under it and a bucket in the corner for the slops.

Bessie spread some thin bread and butter and made a pot of tea. She opened the door a crack and stood, accustoming her eyes to the dim light.

Mary smiled at her from the bed. "I'm awake, do come in."

Bessie brought the tea on a tray and put it down on the bedside table, drawing up a chair to pour out.

"You mustn't shut yourself out on the balcony, Bessie. I'm really not a bit sleepy."

"Well, you ought to be. You've been through a big ordeal today and sleep's the very best thing for you."

Mary drank her tea thirstily. "This is lovely tea."

Bessie poured her another cup.

"I've been wondering if those are your little grandchildren on the mantelpiece," Mary said, looking over at a group photograph in a silver frame.

"Yes. That's Carry and Jean when they were little." Bessie brought the photograph over to her. "And that's my boy Ken and his wife, Jess."

"They're lovely children, aren't they? What a happy family they look."

"They were a happy family when that was taken but that was three years ago. Things are different now."

"Oh Bessie, nothing's happened to your boy has it?"

"No it's not him, he's all right. It's Jess, she's sick."

"Not serious, is it?" Mary asked.

"Bad enough." Bessie stopped short and looked over at Mary. "But I'm not going to tell you my troubles. You've got plenty of your own."

Mary put out a hand to her. "I told you my troubles and I'd like to hear about your family."

Bessie squeezed her hand. "I believe you would. You see, now I haven't got Nance to talk to and Ken's away, I do get a bit bottled up over things. But it'll all be over soon. Ken's on his way down from the Islands and going to get his discharge and then I'm leaving the SP and he's going back into business and I'm going to look after him and the children."

"Oh, Bessie, that will be lovely. What lucky little girls they are to have a granny like you."

"You see, dearie, they're in a home now, and that's what's so bad. Jess had a nervous breakdown over the shop. She tried to keep the business on when Ken went away and with two babies and the grocer down the street that had the wine and spirit licence and was dealing black market, getting all the business away from her, she just went to pieces."

"Oh Bessie, that was awful."

"Yes," Bessie nodded her head, "that was last year, and they had to put her away in the end. Poor girl, she tried to kill herself and the children. If it hadn't been for me going along to see her after work that day, she would have. I smelt the gas and I got the man next door to break in. The children got better but she went out of her mind and that's how it is the children had to go to a home. I couldn't have them here because the landlady won't have children and Nance was just married and she couldn't get out of the WAAF and Ken was away, so I had to put them in a home."

"My dear, I'm so sorry."

"Oh well, every cloud has a silver lining," Bessie looked up and smiled. "And now Ken's on his way back, and just as soon as he gets his discharge he's going to put his deferred pay into another business, and I'm going to look after him and the children."

"That will be lovely. Much better than looking after the SP powder room."

"Oh, that. That wouldn't last longer than the war. All of us over forty-fives'll be the first to go when they lift the Manpower restrictions. But it shouldn't be long before Ken gets fixed up. He's due back in a couple of weeks and there are quite a lot of little grocery businesses to be picked up now. When the war's over and all the boys are coming home, they'll be a lot scarcer and more expensive. So we can't grumble. And next time you come down to Sydney on leave, you'll be coming out to see me and then you can see the kiddies too and tell them all about those bush flowers you know so much about."

"I'd love to."

"And now I'm not going to talk any more. What you need is to go to sleep."

"I believe I will, Bessie. I feel so much better since you've been talking to me."

Bessie came over and tucked her in. "I'm going to have a lie down and read on my bed on the balcony," she said, "and if you go to sleep I'll slip into bed without waking you."

"You are sweet to me."

"Well, and who wouldn't be?" Bessie bent down and kissed her cheek. "There now, goodnight, dearie."

Deb snapped off the ribbon from the florist's box irritably. Roses! They were glorious, deep velvety red ones on long stalks. But her room was already full of flowers and she had absolutely nothing to put them in. The basin was still crammed with wilted lilac and the vases she had got from the housemaid yesterday were full of carnations. Well, the roses would just have to stay in the basin overnight and she would take them down to the salon in the morning. Really, her room was beginning to smell like a funeral parlour. She threw the lilac into the wastepaper basket, fished out the slimy face washer she'd had to put round the plug to stop the water from leaking away, and dumped the roses into the basin. An envelope slipped to the floor from among the flowers. She picked it up with a sigh; she didn't feel she could take romance tonight. But this wasn't merely a card, it was too heavy.

She slit the envelope and took out Angus's card. A carved jade fob was clipped to it. *"Perfection to Perfection"* the card read. Oh God, she thought, more green! And nobody wore fobs now. It was probably priceless, but she wished that just once for a change he would ask her what kind of things she liked. But not Angus. His taste was perfect, and if she didn't like it then she'd just have to learn to. She would have to learn lots of things to keep up with Angus's standard, she thought with a sigh. Marriage to him wouldn't be all plain sailing.

The phone rang. It was Mrs Triggs from Suite 79, and she was hysterical. She had been trying to get a spot off her dinner frock and the cleaning fluid had ruined her nail lacquer. Would it be possible for Miss Forrest to come up and re-lacquer her nails? Miss Forrest was sorry but the salon was closed and Miss Jeffries had the key. She slammed the receiver back. If Mrs Triggs didn't like it she could lump it. And that went for old Molesworth too. She was sick of being at everybody's beck and call. And anyway she had to get ready to meet Angus and that was more important than any

SP guest who wanted private service.

If she lay down straight away she could relax for ten minutes and that was better than nothing. She closed her eyes, put on the eyepads and tried to relax, but she couldn't. Jade! Emeralds! Didn't Angus notice she never wore green? Not that she was superstitious, not really. But she just didn't like it and anyway, any time she'd ever had anything green she'd had bad luck. She saw herself with an emerald engagement ring the size of a traffic light.

She wondered what she would wear. It all depended on where Angus had decided to take her to dine. She hoped he'd have the sense to take her out of the city. What she'd like was a quiet dinner somewhere without an orchestra banging in her ears, and then a long restful drive afterwards. She would put on her blue frock. It was simple and cool.

She had a moment of misgiving when she took a last look at herself in the mirror. She usually dressed more formally for her dinner dates with Angus. Oh, bother formality, she thought, slamming the door behind her. Let him dress and dine to suit me for a change. I'm always trying to think a jump ahead of him, so that he'll be pleased with me. I've always done whatever he's arranged. It's stupid. I'll tell him I want to go for a run round the harbour this evening. She found herself searching for just the right words, with just the right mixture of coquetry and insistence. "I adore you when you're stubborn," Angus always said when she reluctantly gave in to something he took for granted she would agree to. "That little moue...fascinating!" "My God!" Jack would have said, "you're as obstinate as a mule!"

A pain shot through her temple as she stepped into the lift and she felt rebellious. What a strain life was going to be with Angus...always on the alert, always schooling yourself in case you might do or say the wrong thing. Still, she supposed you could get used to anything and in the long run it'd be worth it. Better than being a wornout drudge like Nolly. She shuddered at the thought.

Blue greeted her with a friendly grin.

"Hullo," she said in mock surprise, "still with us?"

"Not much longer to live, I'm afraid. Just seen that little runt of a Dan Twyning poppin' into the office lookin' like a shyster bookie in 'is peewee hat."

"Don't tell me you're in trouble with D.D.T. again?"

Blue was virtuously indignant. "Don't blame me, blame her. Whew, is she hot stuff!"

"You haven't been making passes at her, have you?"

"Her!" he said in a tone of disgust. "Not my type, though it'd serve her damn well right if a bloke did."

"I've booked for us at Prince's," Angus greeted Deb, and her hope of a cool, quiet evening was shattered in a flash of irritation. Bodies, she thought, more hot bodies.... I've been pummelling bodies all day in the Marie Antoinette... I don't want to go dancing tonight.

"Oh," she murmured flatly, "that will be nice... though I wish you'd rung me and I'd have put on something more suitable. I thought we'd probably be running out to a beach on a night like this."

"You look perfect," Angus assured her.

"You don't think it's too hot for dancing?" she tried again.

"Not a bit of it. There's quite a cool change, a southerly has come up."

"How nice," she said aloud, congratulating herself on the agility with which she was learning the art of saying one thing while thinking another.

"You see, it really is quite cool," Angus insisted, as they stood on the hotel steps and felt the breeze that swept along Macquarie Street. "We'll walk down, shall we? It's only a step."

They turned into Martin Place. Taxis were setting down a laughing crowd at the lighted entrance of Down Under.

"I wonder the police don't do something about that place," Angus remarked. "They tell me it's practically a sly grog shop."

She felt a wave of irritation at his smugness. "None of the nightclubs ever seem to be short of liquor, from what I can see."

"True, but it's a very different matter with reputable places that are well conducted. Our liquor laws are so ridiculous they simply ask to be broken."

"I suppose that's what the people at Down Under think." She gave a little forced laugh to soften her words. Oh damn! she thought, I am behaving badly. And I haven't thanked him for the flowers or the jade.

"Your roses were lovely," she said, trying to infuse some enthusiasm into her voice.

"They reminded me of you."

"And that exquisite fob!" She hoped she sounded enthusiastic. "You really shouldn't, you know."

"Now just tell me why I shouldn't?"

She gave him a long smile for answer.

"Come along, tell me. I insist. You mightn't realise it, but I'm a very masterful man."

"You surprise me," she said feelingly, "I'd never have guessed it."

The banter went out of his voice, and he gripped her arm firmly. "Only three more days and I hope I shall have the right to give you everything I want to give you. I hoped you might wear that jade tonight. You've never worn anything of mine."

"I couldn't wear it with this colour," she explained lamely.

"No . . . no . . . I suppose not. It's rather a rare little piece I picked up in Peking. I had it made into a fob especially for you."

"Oh Angus, you do the sweetest things!" She put a hand on his arm in a moment of compunction.

They turned into Prince's, and Henri hastened to meet them at the foot of the stairs. Coming out of the cool air the room seemed stuffy, and her head started to throb again before they had even sat down.

"How do you feel about grilled steak and mushrooms?" Angus inquired.

"I'd like something cold."

He pursed his lips. "Lobster mayonnaise . . ."

"That'd be delicious."

"I really think you should have a steak. You little girls don't eat enough, you know. I'm going to have one myself. I had lobster for lunch."

The waiter was desolated. The droop of his head, the curve of his shoulders, his outflung despairing hands all bespoke his desolation. "But m'sieur — Mr McFarland, sir... the steak. We have no steak."

Angus's brow clouded.

"It is not us that is to blame. You will not find steak in Sydney. We are the victims. It is the meat strike." The waiter hesitated while the full iniquity of the situation sank in.

"Monstrous. In wartime too. These fellows have no sense of responsibility." Angus picked up the double menu card and put it down again impatiently. He never put his glasses on in public. "Is there anything you can suggest that's fit to eat?"

The waiter was voluble. They compromised on turkey. A wonder bird, second only to the goose that laid the golden egg, if the waiter was to be believed; bred, reared, transported from the Middle West for just such an occasion.

"I think you'd better have it too," Angus said, "there's nothing in a salad."

An excellent dinner restored his good humour in some degree but he still felt aggrieved. "If we don't take a firm hand with these strikers, we deserve all we get. Australia's going to rack and ruin. We're frightening away all foreign capital."

Deb, who was not fond of turkey, took up the theme out of pure contrariness. "But it's not only here that there are strikes, is it? The coal miners in England...America, and the steel strikes too."

"That's what makes it so dangerous, it's symptomatic. It's the typical irresponsibility of the fellow without any stake in the country."

Deb restrained a giggle. At first she had thought he meant s-t-e-a-k. She buried her twitching mouth in her table napkin.

"If we gaoled all the strikers we might really get somewhere."

"But who'd do the work then?"

He ignored her interruption. "A few prosperous years have gone to the workers' heads. They'll be brought to their senses when the war's over and there aren't enough jobs to go round."

The laughter drained out of Deb. "You don't mean there might be another depression?"

"The experiences of two wars have taught me that our only hope of restoring industrial efficiency is another depression."

"It's horrible."

"I agree with you entirely," Angus's voice was crisp. "But I am afraid there is no alternative."

"You can't realise what people suffered when you say a thing like that. The hopelessness — the misery."

"I realise it perfectly. But serious economists everywhere are agreed that all that is more than compensated for by the stimulus to prosperity a depression gives."

Angus smiled across at Deb. He felt better after his dinner and the steaming coffee restored his good humour.

"I think it's absolutely awful when you remember that half the men who are fighting in this war — in England and in America, as well as here — were on the dole for years because there was no money to do anything for them...." She broke off and stirred her coffee defiantly.

Angus smiled at her. How sweet she was when she was stubborn! "Go on. I like to hear you."

Deb felt her anger rising. Really, he was treating her like a child. "What I'd like to know is why, when there was no money then for anything useful, governments can find millions and billions of money to fight the war, and even before it's over they're talking about another depression."

"My dear little girl," Angus said with affectionate forbearance, "you can't treat matters like this sentimentally. Wars are inevitable and so are depressions."

"I don't believe it." Deb's voice was shaking.

"My dear Deborah, it's not a matter of belief, it's a matter of economic law that cannot be altered merely because a number of young men now fighting in the front line were once on the dole."

Deb felt the sense of helplessness that always engulfed her when Angus launched into one of his dissertations on economics and war. She felt that she was walking on the edge of a precipice and it terrified her. She just could not go through again what they had all suffered then — the insecurity, the poverty.

He leaned across and covered her hand with his. "Little one, you're too lovely to bother your pretty head about such dull things. Let us talk about you — and me."

She ignored the tone in his voice. She was not going to be talked down. "Well, I think it would be awful if there was another depression after this war, and I wouldn't blame anyone for wanting to start a revolution if there was."

He laughed fondly and turned her hand over, curling the fingers into the palm one by one, as though he was playing this little pig went to market with a child. "A twentieth-century Joan of Arc, eh? I should like to see you on a white horse riding up Macquarie Street to Parliament House. You'd look adorable."

She withdrew her hand. "What would you do if it did come?"

"What came?"

"A revolution."

He smiled patronisingly. "All that would be needed would be to tighten the purse strings as they did in 1931 — and you'd see the revolution fizzle out in a few noisy speeches in the Domain. A general withdrawal of credit would paralyse the country and the rebels would soon come crawling back and be glad to take the dole."

"That's awful."

"But you'd have nothing to worry about, I assure you. Even if there was a revolution, we'd be quite safe.... I'd spirit you off to an impregnable castle and we'd live on our income and let the rebels stew in their own juice."

The orchestra was playing softly, the crooner began to sing:

The southern stars are bright above. . . .

"Our tune," Angus smiled across at her. "Shall we dance? I never want to spend any of my precious time with you on anything but loving you."

Deb rose reluctantly.

He drew her close and they danced without speaking. Words were unnecessary when her nearness worked magic in his nerves and blood.

She wished she had an aspirin. Her head was aching and her feet were sore and she hated the tune anyway. Every messenger boy in town was whistling it. Angus's words still echoed in her ears.

They'd be safe, would they? Earthquake, war, revolution. . . Angus would be safe. But would he really? Her father had thought that too. Perhaps it wasn't a fair comparison. He was small fry by Angus's standards, but he was quite a big fish in his own little pool, and look what happened to him.

He'd thought he was safe enough, then the depression had caught him like a landslide. It was a landslide all right — no less real because you couldn't see the rocks and the earth breaking away and bringing down the hillside that had seemed so permanent.

The papers called it a world slump; the banks called it a withdrawal of credit; Angus called it a stimulus to prosperity. She'd like to know just how stimulating he'd find it to walk up to his bank one morning, as Dad and she had done, and find the door closed and a printed notice tacked up: PAYMENT SUSPENDED.

She could remember every detail of that day — even the date. It had been in 1931, two days before Anzac Day. Dad never missed an Anzac march and he'd gone to draw out a bit for the day's expenses. They'd all had to bully him into doing it. He hadn't wanted to go with Mum so sick, but Mum had insisted most strongly of all. It was Mum who'd made her go to the bank with him to see that he really did get the money so that he'd have no excuse to stay at home when the day came.

She remembered as if it was yesterday the southerly whipping the sand over the Esplanade and hurling the rain in a clatter against Dad's oilskin cape. As they walked up the street towards the bank, they wondered why people were standing outside in the rain. Then she and Dad had read the sodden notice with the ink already smudged on it.

They hadn't believed it. Neither did the other people who were there. Some of them pounded frantically on the double wooden doors. Others stood by with stunned looks on their faces. There were some who cried; others who, like Dad, insisted that there must be an explanation. This sort of thing didn't happen these days. Not in this country. You read about it in New York, just as you read about bankers and stockbrokers throwing themselves out of skyscraper windows. But that was America. They had blizzards and hurricanes and wood alcohol in America, but not here in New South Wales. This was the Government Savings Bank! He'd heard rumours, of course. If he hadn't been so worried about Mum he might have taken more notice of them. But it was unthinkable. He wasn't a Labor man himself and he didn't hold with Jack Lang, but not even Lang would dare touch the people's money.

Yet there it was: PAYMENT SUSPENDED. "By God," he'd said, "I helped to build this bank, helped to put up those walls. I helped to set that door so you could only open it with a battering ram, and here it is closed in my face with a notice on it: PAYMENT SUSPENDED!" A man near him suddenly began to curse. He cursed the bank, he cursed the government, he cursed Jack Lang.

"Lang's all right," called another man who had hoisted himself up on a ledge to look through the windows, "Lang's right enough. It's those bastards Stevens and Bevin with their whispering campaign. They've been trying to do this for months and now they've brought it off, the swine!"

She remembered it all, though then she'd hardly known

what it meant.

An old man held up a work-worn fist and shook it in the air. "To hell with the bloody government. What's it doing except feathering its own nest, while we rot on the dole and the bank closes down on the bit of savings we've got?"

A little old woman ran over to the door and began to pummel on it with frail blue-veined hands. "Let me in, let me in," she kept calling in a cracked, high voice.

Dad had gone over and held her hands in his. They were tiny and bony. "There, there, mother," he had said soothingly, "don't take on. It'll all come right."

Deb came back with a jerk when the orchestra stopped. Thank God she could sit down now. Angus clapped with the rest of the crowd and smiled warmly down at her as the pianist went into the opening chords of the encore. He put his arm round her. She smiled at him with her lips and her feet moved round the floor while her mind went back again.

"It'll all come right!" How often Dad had said that, but with less and less conviction as the months went on. She could see him sitting with his head in his hands the day he and the constable had been out looking for Arthur Hollis. Arthur was one of Dad's tenants — safe as the bank, her father had always said, but that hadn't stopped him from being put off at Brace's when they closed a whole department down.

Then Arthur had shocked the whole of Cronulla by taking his skiff out into the middle of Burraneer Bay — he was after blackfish, he said — and going overboard with the kellick rope wound round his neck. It might have been an accident; the coroner said it probably was, and everybody pretended they believed it. But not Dad. He remembered how Arthur had looked when he came into the office to tell him that he'd been put off. Dad had tried to cheer him up: "Just hang on a bit and it'll come right." But it hadn't come right and Dad had gone out in the police launch and helped to drag in what was left of Arthur after leatherjackets and the crabs had had a go at him.

Dad had gone down to the bank day after day, and every day the notice was still there, only shabbier and dirtier. But it never said anything else, only PAYMENT SUSPENDED. You didn't know who to blame. Certainly not the poor devils working in the bank; they were in as bad a way as anyone, working one day on and one day off. That meant half-pay, and a bank clerk's pay didn't allow anything to play round with at any time.

The day came at last when the doors were opened. The same men were behind the counter, all looking as miserable as bandicoots themselves. Some of the people shouted and abused them as though they were to blame.

No, he couldn't get his money out. They told Dad not more than £3 a week and that only when he'd given all kinds of family details and sworn to their truth. The bank manager didn't like what he had to do, but he had no choice. £3 a week and Mum, who knew nothing whatever about what had happened, Mum having to have another operation.

Lots of people were selling their bank books. Every day there had been advertisements in the papers. Dad spoke to one of the men at the bank. He told him to hang on if he could manage it, sellers were only getting 10s and 12s in the pound. Dad had looked at his passbook for a long time that night. That money had been accumulated slowly and honestly and now it was going to be taken from him in some dirty thieving way he didn't understand, and he had no choice. No choice at all.

Deb looked up at Angus and a sudden intimate smile illumined his face. "Happy?" he whispered.

She nodded and dropped her eyes. He pressed her hand gently. She wondered what Angus had done during the depression. Certainly he'd never had to sit up all night staring at his passbook, trying to make up his mind to sell it for little more than half it was worth because he simply had to have the money.

Poor Dad, she could remember his face when he sold it finally — through an advertisement in the *Sydney Morning Herald*, which he vaguely felt made the transaction more honourable — for twelve shillings in the pound. And when Mum came home for the second time, there wasn't much left of the money he'd got. Everyone had been wonderful, Jack, Tom and Dallas, particularly Dallas. She was halfway through her medical course then and she'd nursed Mum to the end.

Deb could see Mum still, like a little yellow ghost, her face shrunken and her hair quite white, lying in her big bed by the window overlooking the beach. The doctor had said it couldn't be much longer. Only constant needles could dull the pain.

They had tried to keep it away from her about the bank book but she knew nearly everything. What she didn't know was that Dad had mortgaged the house. He hadn't even told Deb or Nolly. Only Dallas. Mum had died without knowing.

It had taught Deb a lesson she would never forget. If depressions were inevitable she was going to make quite certain that next time one occurred she was safe. She would never go through again what she and Jack and Nolly and Dad had gone through. Never. Dallas could talk about hardships building your character and all the rest of it, cementing partnerships, teaching you wisdom. Well, she was wise now as she had never been wise before. She knew that if you didn't look after number one nobody would do it for you.

The music throbbed away into silence. Angus released her and drew her hand through his arm possessively, leading her back to their table. She did not sit down, but stood looking up at him in appeal. "I'm awfully sorry, but I've got a frightful head. I'm afraid you'll simply have to take me home."

"My poor darling. Perhaps if you had a bromo-seltzer you'd feel better. I'll get the waiter to bring you one."

"I'm afraid it wouldn't do the least bit of good. When I get neuralgia like this I simply have to lie down."

Angus glanced at his watch. "It's very early," he pleaded. "You don't want to rob me of the rest of the evening, do you?"

"I'm sorry," she pressed her hand to her forehead. "I'm afraid if I stayed I'd be very poor company."

"Just to be with you is enough for me. I have an idea.

I'll get them to ring through and have my car sent round and we'll go for a good long run by the sea and the fresh air will blow the cobwebs away.''

Oh God, Deb thought, how silly men can be! If he'd taken me for a drive when I wanted to go I'd never have got this head. "All right," she conceded reluctantly and gathered up her bag and gloves.

But in the car, with the cool wind blowing on her face, the dark road sliding beneath them in the glare of the head-lights, Angus's arm around her shoulders, some of the tension went out of her. She pushed back into the recesses of her mind the thoughts his casual words had stirred. What was the sense of thinking about them? Foolish to let old memories wound you, old grief waken. Her father's loss, his suffering — all that was so long ago. Unreal now, for her, just as the happiness of her early marriage was unreal. You couldn't let them decide your future. Perhaps it was true that you changed every seven years — became a different person. It was nearly seven years since Jack had left the Vineyard and come to town — the end of a cycle, the beginning of a new one.

Angus's arm tightened, drawing her closer to him. "Feeling better now?" he whispered, rubbing his chin against her temple.

"Much. It was the heat, I think, after such a stuffy day."

"My poor little darling."

The car turned away from the road and the white walls of South Head lighthouse glared for a moment before the lights were dimmed. Below them they could hear the sound of the surf thudding against the cliffs and a sea-mist swept across the windscreen.

"Poor little darling!" Angus repeated, drawing her closer. "We'll sit here for a little while till the wind blows your headache away and then I'll take you home so that you can get to bed early."

Deb sighed, snuggling against him. Sitting like this, with his lips against her cheek, made her feel safe. It was funny, she didn't feel so guilty about Jack now that she had found out that she didn't mind Angus touching her. There was a lot of nonsense talked about this one-man business. Just because you were brought up that way, there was no need to go on all your life. Not that she would ever have let Angus kiss her if he hadn't asked her to marry him. She wasn't cheap.

"You know, Deborah," he said, a stern note creeping into his voice, "this indecision isn't any better for you than it is for me." He squeezed her hand, his fingers roughly twisting her wedding ring.

She was silent. There did not seem to be anything she could say.

"I specially wanted to discuss something with you to-night — what I started to say to you on Sunday. You didn't misunderstand me when I said that I could get a flat for you when you left the South Pacific, did you?"

"Why — no — at least I don't think so."

Angus laughed. "What a little innocent you are! I was rather afraid..." he hesitated.

"Afraid of what?"

"Well, to be perfectly frank, that my talk of finding a flat and making a settlement might lead you to think that I wasn't really serious about marriage."

"Oh Angus!" Deb drew away from him.

"I couldn't have blamed you. After all, some men do those things."

She remembered the wardrobe saturated with Liz Destrange's perfume and pushed the thought away. She wasn't Liz.

"I'm pressing things now because — apart altogether from my own feelings and yours — all kinds of technicalities will be involved if you re-establish any relationship with your husband when he returns. I feel that if you could present him with an ultimatum — say you want a divorce — and then let me put the matter in my solicitor's hands."

An ultimatum! Why shouldn't she? Jack had presented her with an ultimatum. But at the thought of telling Jack she wanted a divorce, she had a feeling of panic. She could see him shoot out his jaw, his grey eyes narrowed. "What rot!" he would say, or "What put that idea into your head?" the way he always overrode what she said when it didn't suit him. She gave in to him too easily, that was the trouble. The only thing she'd ever stuck out against him about was staying on at the South Pacific last time he was down on leave.

Angus was right, she must make everything plain from the beginning. If once she established a relationship with Jack again there would be more than technicalities. Jack was unpredictable, life with him was a series of mad leaps from one thing to another. Marriage with Angus would be peaceful, pleasant, civilised. With Jack — she pushed the thought away from her; it was too disturbing, even after all these years of marriage. Yes, there would be more than technicalities.

"All my suggestions, of course, are based on the assumption that your husband will naturally do the gentlemanly thing when you ask him for a divorce. But, till that is through and we can be married, I want you to believe me when I say that in no way do I desire our relationship to be altered except that I shall have the privilege of arranging for your welfare and taking you away from that wretched job. You realise that there will be gossip when this is known, Deborah, and I want no taint of scandal to mar our marriage." He switched on the dashboard lights, his face was set and frowning. "If you could make a decision before your husband's return..."

Deb listened to the silky purring of the engine. She could not think of any answer. She laid her hand on his as though to seek in his touch some solution of her own perplexity.

It seemed to Val that she had been in bed for hours, but still she could not sleep. It was funny how you noticed things when you couldn't get to sleep, sounds that you didn't hear in the daytime, or ordinarily at night — like the branch of a gum tree scratching against the guttering and the lions roaring across the water in Taronga Zoo. They had a wild, lonely sound.

She wondered how Bessie was getting on with Mary Parker. Dear Bessie, she only had to get a whisper of someone being ill or in trouble and there she was, on the spot in a jiffy, ready to give you her home or her heart. There was absolutely no need at all for her to take Mary Parker; it was just sheer goodness of heart. The Parkers were nothing to her — as a matter of fact, that little snob of an Alice didn't even deign to see her half the time. But Bessie didn't seem to notice things like that, she was always so overflowing with kindness herself that she never realised that other people weren't the same.

Val pulled the clothes up tighter around her neck, trying to shut out the chill southerly that had begun to blow the curtains about. She would have to get up and put on some more bedclothes, her feet were freezing. If she didn't look out, with this sudden cold change she'd get another dose of malaria.

She slipped out of bed and put down the window. Heavy clouds blowing up from the south were scudding across the moon. Well, now she was up, she'd heat some milk and get herself a hot bottle and another blanket. That ought to help her get to sleep. Ah, this is better, she thought, snuggling down. I think I'll take an APC too, just to make sure. But even with the warmth stealing through her and the powder quietening her restless nerves, she still couldn't go to sleep.

She couldn't get Mary Parker out of her mind. Poor little devil. She looked such a quiet, simple kind of kid; nothing rackety about her at all. How awful it must be to fall in love with a man who was married, and now, to have to go through all that to get rid of his baby...

Quite suddenly, all the stupidity and futility of life over-whelmed her. There was no sense in anything at all. Why did things always have to turn out like this? Why couldn't she have been the one to have a baby, instead of Mary? She and Ven had wanted a baby so much. If she'd had a baby, she'd never have been lonely, even when he was away.

It made her sick when she read what those fools wrote to the papers about why women didn't have babies. Let them ask her and she'd tell them soon enough. "How can I have a baby?" she'd say, "when you've snatched my husband from me and sent him up into the jungle fighting, instead of doing his own work at home? When you turn him to killing instead of to living, just because the people who make wars are greedy and old and selfish and have forgotten what it means to be young?"

She switched on the light and lay looking at Ven's photograph on the bedside table. His eyes were tender and there was a half smile on his lips. "It will be different after-wards when we've finished this scrap," he had said. "Oh, it will be different." Then he had laughed. "I warn you, when I come back next time I expect you to meet me down at the boat with nothing less than twins!" And though her throat was tight and she could hardly keep back the tears, she'd laughed too. "I'll make it triplets."

"I'll settle for twins, and we must make a very special pair of babies. A girl like you and a boy like me, only much, much better because loving you has made me feel a larger than life-sized kind of guy. And when we're sitting holding hands on our silver wedding day, I want to see a girl like you come dancing in, the way you came in that first evening at the hospital, when all the stars rushed together and sang."

"We'll tell the world when our babies are born," Ven had said. "Announce it by radio, send out the town crier, splash it across the newspapers — 'To Mr and Mrs Stephen Joseph Blaski — twins! A boy and a girl. Specially created and destined by their makers to inherit the new world.'"
And then he had taken her in his arms again and whispered:

"Don't worry. I'll come back. If a new world's worth fighting for, it's worth waiting for."

Well, she had waited — and there hadn't been any twins. It didn't seem possible that you could want a thing so badly and that it shouldn't happen. Suddenly, the tears were running down her face again and she was weeping with her head buried in the pillow and Ven's photograph pressed against her cheek. "If he's killed, I won't go on living. Why should I live? What do I owe to life or to God if they don't bring Ven back to me?"

She checked her sobs and held her breath for a long time, trying, as she often tried, to send her love and her thoughts to him wherever he might be. "Wherever you are, my darling," she was saying soundlessly, rigid with the effort to project her love to him. "Wherever you are, my husband, I am with you."

As they came through the turnstile onto the McMahon's Point wharf, Alec and Helen heard the clatter of the gang-plank being pulled off the ferry. They raced down the ramp and the gap between the wharf and the deck was already widening when he grabbed her hand and shouted: "Jump!" The deckhand steadied Helen as she landed and slid the rail into place behind them. "Serve you right if I'd of let you fall in, young lady."

She smiled into his tanned old face. "I'm used to jumping."

"She can run all right, too," Alec panted in mock distress.

"She nearly caught it without me."

Still holding her hand, he led her across to the far side of the boat and they stood leaning against the rail, watching the moonlight break into silver fragments in the widening ripples made by the ferry's bow. Someone was playing a banjo on the deck of a cargo boat tied up on the opposite side of the cove and the sound floated alien and melancholy across the water.

Alec spoke first. "The harbour's different by moonlight

somehow..." He was groping for words that would not sound too sloppy. "It's sort of strange and unreal...a bit like a kid's fairytale."

Helen had a breathless feeling of excitement. Anything was possible in this white radiance. "Perhaps it is a fairytale. Perhaps Fort Macquarie over there really is an enchanted tower..."

He followed her glance to where the battlemented tower of the old fort cut sharply into the luminous sky and the round, trimmed trees in Bennelong Park had the look of a fairytale garden.

A fairytale! Yes that's what it had been, she thought. An enchanted week that would end tomorrow. Back to Gunyawaraldi and shearers...out of fairyland and back to reality. But she would not think of it tonight. She was conscious of Alec's sleeve touching her bare arm, and a sense of his warmth and nearness flooded through her and mingled with the beauty of the night. There was no tomorrow...it was enough just to be alive...to be young...to be happy. Tonight was forever...

It was not until the ferry curved out of the moonlight into the shadow of the Harbour Bridge, bringing into view the lights of the park, that Alec broke the silence.

"I thought I was never going to get near you tonight with all that crowd."

"And here we are, after one dance, running away to Luna Park like a couple of children playing the wag."

"Sorry, eh?"

"Not a bit."

The huge grotesque face of the park entrance grinned across the water. A thousand coruscating lights flickered a welcome.

"I haven't been to Luna Park since I was a kid," he said reminiscently.

"I've never been."

"No? Well, you've got something ahead of you tonight. Do you get seasick?"

"Never."

"Good. Then we'll go on everything that whirls and whizzes until you cry for mercy."

"I won't."

"We'll see."

They climbed the little hill from the wharf and stepped through the giant's gaping grin straight into a noisy, swirling crowd. Down both sides of the park the sideshows beckoned in brilliant electric lights; mechanical cars raced thrillingly up and down miniature hills and valleys; the mermaid lay languorously on her seashell inviting you to throw balls at her; the octopus swung squealing couples on the ends of its giant arms into the darkness above the harbour; crowds of young men in uniform pressed round the rifle ranges and coconut shies, handing back their prizes to their girlfriends with self-conscious laughter; girls carrying dolls on sticks and hideous china vases clutched the arms of servicemen and turned on them eyes full of promise. Everywhere there was laughter and harsh lights and a moving kaleidoscope of colour.

It was a bit like Sydney Royal, was Helen's first thought. Ever since she could remember, the whole family had come to Sydney at Easter for the Royal Agricultural Show, and it had been one of her greatest thrills as a small child to visit the sideshows and slide down the slippery slide. And yet there was a difference. At first she thought it was the uniforms, but it was something more, something undefinable, a feverishness, a snatching at pleasure, rather than the way one enjoyed the Show with time to pause and laugh and saunter on. Here, everyone seemed greedy. She watched the couples coming out of the Magic Cave, flushed with their kisses in the darkness. A sailor had his arm round a slip of a girl with her brown hair fuzzed up into an exaggerated pompadour and her lipstick all smudged. He had lipstick round his lips and a hungry look in his eyes. She turned away involuntarily.

Alec felt her movement. "Come on," he said, "this is the place to do things, and here we are dawdling round watching other people. What shall it be first? Have you got a good enough stomach for the cars?"

They climbed into a little car for two, and gripped the

bar in front of them with both hands. She had a perfect inside for topsy-turvy thrills and laughed aloud with childlike enjoyment as the car went spinning round. Suddenly she felt Alec lurch heavily against her and she saw that his stiff hand had slipped. She caught her breath with a little gasp of fear.

"I'm terribly sorry," he shouted above the noise, locking his thumb round the bar again.

"You'd better hang on to me for safety," she shouted back. It was really dangerous if you didn't hang on properly and they couldn't get off until the thing stopped.

"Thanks, I will." Alec slid his arm round her waist and clung tight as the car started whirling again. She gripped the bar in front of her with all her strength and felt the pull of his weight.

When at last they got out onto solid ground he pulled out a handkerchief and wiped his forehead, grinning shame-facedly. "That's one of the things I won't try again. Silly, isn't it, how your imagination just doesn't serve you. You have to be humiliated by experience every time."

"I don't think it's humiliating to try things — that's the only way you can find out what you can do as well as what you can't. If you let your imagination loose, well...maybe it would stop you trying anything at all."

He took her arm and drew her into the crowd making its way towards the Katzenjammer Castle. "This'll shake off the cobwebs," he promised, then turned to her, serious again. "If I'd let my imagination put me off, I'd never have got up the courage to dance with you that first night, and then look what I'd have missed. I'd have spent five whole nights haunting the Buffet and perpetually screwing up my courage in case you turned me down flat, without ever getting round to asking you. As it was, I only spent two miserable ones wondering if you'd ever come again, and three...well, three pretty good ones. That is, when I could push through the clamouring hordes and get an occasional dance for myself."

Helen looked at him and smiled. She wanted to cry out, "Oh, Alec, did you really want to dance with me so much? Did you think of me in the daytime and wonder if you would see me again at night? And when we danced, did you feel as though nothing else mattered but us dancing and laughing together? Because if you did, we both felt the same." But there was nothing she could say.

A noisy couple lurched against them in passing.

"Come on," Alec cried, "our turn for the shake-up," and they were swallowed in the doorway of the castle.

For two hours they made a hilarious round of thrills and horrors, with Alec leading the way. It was as if he was determined to show her that although he might have to cling to her for support on the Krazy Kars there was nothing else he could not do. And Helen let herself be spun off revolving platforms and slide down the steepest of the slippery dips with her heart in her mouth and her eyes dancing.

They ate steaming fish and chips from greasy brown paper and bought fairy floss and laughed themselves sick in front of the distorting mirrors, their noses buried in the pink spun sugar that melted to nothing in their mouths.

She rode on the Big Dipper with Alec's arm tight around her waist and hers round his, their outside hands grasping the bar firmly, and rushed down the giant switchback in delirious laughter with the wind tearing through their hair and stopping their breath.

"I think I left my stomach behind on that one," he gasped.

"Me too. But I've got it again for the next."

"So've I."

They went up again, up, up to the highest point and were poised a moment like gods above the world. Far away the city lights twinkled, and below them was the harbour with the glittering fun fair like a bright island in the immensity of the night. They went down again in a rush of moonlight and wind.

It was just before midnight when they came out of the park and found a seat at the stern of the little ferry boat. Alec took her hand in his and she left it there with a sense of comfort and deep happiness. In silence, they watched the silver wake widen between them and the shore.

"It's not just tonight..." he began rather haltingly. "I mean, what I want to say..." He stopped and tried another tack. "I say, must you really go back tomorrow?"

"Yes, I really must."

"Helen," he tried again. "There's something I must say." His hand tightened round hers. "I...I want to tell you that...well, I don't want you to think that these evenings we've spent together have been just...a pleasant way of passing the time while I'm tied up at the hospital. It's been something more than that..."

Helen hung on his words, happiness running through her like a sparkling tide. But she had no words of her own to answer him.

"I know I'm clumsy at making speeches, but what I want to say is that I don't want you to go back home and forget me."

"I won't forget you, Alec." Her voice was low and she kept her eyes on the water.

"I say, do you really mean that? I mean, it hasn't been for you just another chap to dance with for a few days in town?"

"No, Alec."

"You wouldn't mind if I wrote to you, then?"

She looked up at him. "I'd like you to."

"And perhaps you'll be coming back again before Christmas."

"I'm afraid not. Once I get home there's so much to do, I simply won't be able to get away."

"Then tonight is goodbye."

A feeling of chill touched her heart. "Oh no, Alec. Not goodbye!" she cried out, and stopped short, hearing the urgency in her own voice.

"Not really goodbye," he said quickly, reassuring himself as much as her, and added in his more ordinary voice: "But I shan't be here after Christmas. I expect to be boarded out then, whether Algy's learnt to behave or not. I just can't go on doing nothing round Sydney waiting for him, so it's probably civvies and back to Grafton to look for a job in the

New Year."

"But why need it be? Susan says the doctor is sure your fingers will learn to work again if you only put your heart into the treatment."

"Put my heart into it! I've been doing my best for the last three months and I've got my thumb working. That'll have to be enough. I'm bored to death going to the hospital five days a week and tinkering round weaving eternal scarves and making toys for kids. However well I make two fingers work they'll never get me into vet science."

"But they will make all the difference to a job on the land, and the carpentering will be awfully useful."

"Who's going on the land? Not me."

"Who said you're not?"

"I did. I expect I'll go back to that pot-bellied old accountant I used to work for. 'There's always a job waiting for you here, my boy'," he mimicked in a gruff voice. "'Always plenty of auditing of other people's books to be done. I'd think twice before throwing up a job with a future, my boy.'" Alec's voice stopped on a defiant note.

"Don't talk like that, Alec." She turned and faced him. "It's not really you speaking. That's the man who's giving up at the hospital. So easily, without a fight."

"Well, what is there to fight for? I can't do the work I want to and that's that."

"There's nothing to fight for if you can't see it for yourself. But I didn't think you were that sort. I thought you'd make your fingers work like you've made your thumb work. I thought you'd scorn to go back to a job you hate; I thought you'd fight every inch of the way to go back to work you do care about even if you can't be a vet. What's happened to you tonight?"

"Nothing's happened to me tonight more than happened on Friday and Monday and Tuesday...I'm sorry, Helen, I expect it's because I feel so utterly futile. This is our last night and I'm behaving badly. Forgive me." The bitterness had gone out of his voice now and he went on, "I was jogging along more or less resigned last week, and then I danced with you and...well, I've been fed up with myself ever since. Funny how a chap can change in just a few days."

Funny how a girl can too, she wanted to say.

The ferry was already half way up the Cove, the moon had sunk behind the hill and the water was black now. In a few minutes they would be at the wharf. Helen took hold of her courage.

"If you can do any more good with Algy," she said, "there might be a job going for you."

"What do you mean?"

"I mean, two fingers and a thumb that work are all Dad would care about if you'd like to come and give us a hand over Christmas. Not just jackerooing, but a real job."

"Are you suggesting that your old man would take me on?"

"I don't see why not. We're so short-handed he's been talking about cutting down stock again if we can't get more help."

"But..."

"Wouldn't you like to come?"

"Like to! There's nothing I'd like better."

"Well, you could give it a try," she said in as matter-of-fact a voice as she could. "No harm in that. And then if you'd rather go back to your old ledgers, well, that'll be for you to say. But there's a condition attached, don't forget."

"I know. Algy's got to be a going concern by Christmas."

"That's it. You've got over two months. Do you think you can do it?"

"Think? I know I can. I'll show that doctor."

"I knew you would."

"Bribery and corruption, that's what it is." He dropped the light, bantering note. "There's something else I wanted to say too. I've been a mug, I suppose, but that's really why I haven't danced. I didn't think any girl would want to touch my hand, but you never seemed to mind. Does it sound silly?"

"No, it doesn't. I understand how you feel, but of

course, I don't mind." She tried to bring back the bantering note. "I've got quite a motherly feeling towards Algy. That's why I want to see him getting on in the world."

The ferry drew into the wharf and the gangplank clattered down. They got up from the seat and stood hesitating, turned towards each other.

A voice shouted raucous and insistent: "All ashore! All ashore! Last trip!"

"We...we'll get left behind if we don't hurry," Helen said.

"Yes. Yes we'd better go."

The deckhand grinned amiably as they got off at the tailend of the crowd. "Want to come and tie up with us for the night?"

"Not tonight." Helen gave him a radiant smile.

He watched the tall young soldier with the red hospital tie tuck a hand under her arm and draw her close as they walked up the ramp.

The deckhand heaved the gangplank onto the wharf with a flourish.

Claire and Nigel walked up the narrow concrete staircase leading to Joe's and knocked at a green baize door. The pot-bellied doorkeeper opened it cautiously a few inches, grunted in recognition and let them in. They went through a swing door on the left into a large bare room.

The game had already started and the faces round the long narrow table were raised only for a moment; the croupier's hands scarcely paused in their deft shuffling; then play went on again without any sign of recognition or welcome. Every chair was occupied and the low-hanging, brilliant lights lit the players' faces to ghastly radiance and spotlighted their hands against the baize.

"A fair crowd already," Claire whispered. It was odd the way everybody whispered at Joe's.

"I think I'll get straight into it," Nigel whispered back, "as soon as there's a chair vacant opposite Freddy. Stand behind me for luck."

"We're going to have it, darling."

Claire nodded to two youngish women she'd come to know by sight. Their absorbed faces split into mechanical smiles. Joe's wasn't a place for personal contacts; it was a place where you staked all you had and more if you could borrow it. Joe never minded staking you when you were broke, provided you came often enough, like Freddy, the croupier, who sat in the centre of the long side of the table, and Cec, the tally clerk opposite him. That's how they had started here. Poor mugs, Claire thought pityingly, why didn't they get out while the going was good? Everyone knew that now they were so deep in, they had no choice but to stay there working for Joe and getting deeper in every week on the handouts he so generously gave them to keep their heads above water.

The tally clerk looked up at them, his face flickered into the semblance of a smile. "'Night, Mr Carstairs, are you taking a bank?"

Nigel nodded.

Before long, a dark Slav-faced man with a Merchant Navy badge in his lapel rose from the chair beside Cec. He made a gesture of hopelessness to his companion behind him and another to show that his pockets were empty. The mugs, Claire thought, the poor bloody mugs. They come here from their ships knowing next to nothing about the game, with great fat rolls they've earned carting munitions through all the danger zones of the world, and do them in in a night. Well, if your luck was out, you just had to take it. Luck was something you couldn't do anything about. But when your luck was in and you had a system you'd proved, the sky was the limit.

Nigel seated himself slowly. She looked down across his superbly tailored shoulders to his pale, tapering hands lying negligently folded on the baize. She squeezed his shoulder, trying to convey to him something of her own confidence. He put up a hand and touched hers and she heard him murmur: "My guardian angel."

Her heart overflowed with tenderness and hope. She gripped the back of his chair until it cut into her hands. Always, at this moment, she felt as though she was watching him wade out into a surf full of treacherous channels where she could no longer protect him. He never played for the first few rounds, but during that time, while he was being drawn into the solitary absorption in which each one played, she could feel him being swept away from her as surely as if he was caught in an undertow.

Count the people at the table, she said to herself. See if it's a lucky number. She counted round the feverish, greedy faces — how different they looked from Nigel. Forty seated. Marvellous! Forty was divisible by five. Five was his lucky number — five letters in his name. Now count the standing ones. Her eyes rested a second on each shadowy figure standing behind the players, brooding over them like the ghosts of their own decadence; each one a second self in its shared absorption. Forty-five. Lucky again.

If the woman in the silver fox cape wins, we'll win, she told herself. Watch the broad-faced Greek calling "Back-it-in, back-it-in.'' She had watched him often. Whenever he lost, they won. It was as though the tide of luck ebbed and flowed between them. His fleshy lips were drawn in a strained smile that always indicated he was losing. Confidence mounted in her.

A tall man with a lined, ascetic face sat down opposite them. It was the Doc; Cynthia said he was going regularly to Coddy's now — probably he'd come on from there. It was only last week she'd heard him swear he would give up the game. He could afford to, with his practice. But not many ever gave it up once it got into their blood. She and Nigel would, they were quite determined on that. Just let them get that thousand behind them! But the Doc was different, everything about him was a gamble, including his practice. He used to own a couple of racehorses too, but something had gone wrong there. Looking at his drawn face and shaking hands, she hoped they had been steadier than that for Mary Parker this afternoon. Probably he had just dropped a packet at Coddy's; he always went to pieces like that when he was losing.

The fat man beside him chewing a cigar was John Greenott, KC. She wondered how he'd get on in the unlikely chance of their being raided! It would be a mixed bag tonight, the kind of people you'd never meet outside this room, yet you got to know them by their first names here. It was a world of its own. Once the door swung behind you, you were a different person with different values. When she and Nigel had first started, she used to be shocked and horrified; now she just took it all for granted, just as she took for granted the fact that tonight she was wearing the jade clips and earrings they had won last night from the plump woman with the bejewelled hands at the end of the table who gambled frantically and endlessly. Every afternoon, every night you could find Mrs Gartred at one of the schools. She had gone through several fortunes, it was said, made out of brewery shares — easy come, easy go. And when the fever really rose, she threw in furs and jewels, anything that could be settled for cash. Well, she had thrown in the famous jade clips and earrings for the last time.

Claire started as the tally clerk called out in his monotonous, nasal voice: "Mr C, your bank." She drew in her breath as though to call up all her strength for Nigel.

"All right," Nigel said quietly, "I'll have twenty-five pounds in it."

He unfolded his hands with leisurely grace and threw down two tens and a five-pound note.

"It's on," she said. "We can't lose."

"Thank you." The banker added the notes to the money already in his hand, his voice was flat and impersonal. "All right, I'll back the bank for a hundred. I'll have any part of a hundred."

The money started to flutter towards him and the hum of voices died down as the croupier announced with his air of authority: "That'll be ten for J. G. and fifteen for the Doc. That ten's yours, Captain. That's right, Mrs Gartred: thirty for you. Five from P. D. and five from Larry. OK."

He gathered the notes swiftly, packing them neatly together: "All right. Now, have you all set your bets?"

A furtive mutter of acquiescence rose from the end of the table. Joe did not encourage side bets except to keep people coming back when they'd been cleaned out.

Freddy gave a sharp glance round the table. "All right then. The cards are out. Silence, please."

Silence fell deeper than in a church; a ripple of excitement ran round the table. Two cards were thrown face downwards to Mrs Gartred, and two to Nigel. Mrs Gartred's plump hand glittered as she turned over the first. Five. Her hand hovered above the second as though she could not bear the moment of revelation. It was a two. "Seven," she sighed.

"Seven," called the croupier, leading a chorus that sighed "Seven" again.

Nigel quickly turned over the cards: "Eight." His voice was as cool and impersonal as the croupier's.

"Eight," called the croupier, "and the bank wins. That's fifty pounds to you, Mr C. Do you wish to take it out?"

"Yes, but I'll leave the stake." Nigel gathered the notes that were thrown to him and stacked them neatly to one side.

Soon there was only the blaze of light beating down on the green baize: men's faces, women's faces, blonde hair, grey hair, black hair, brown, all merged, all the same, as though greed had slipped a mask over each one blotting out their features so that they became only voices and hands.

Among them all Nigel remained unruffled and aloof. His sensitive fingers turned the cards and folded the notes tidily beside him. Again and again he won. Claire could have laughed, it was so easy. Oh, the stars were right!

She relaxed her tension as a powerful-looking man, with a broad-brimmed hat pulled low on his forehead, slouched into the garish light. It was Joe's bodyguard, Curly — stand-over man as well, they said. Rumour credited him with a fantastic retainer. Knuckleman and thug to the life, Claire thought. He looked more Hollywood than any Hollywood gangster, with his enormous sloped shoulders, his tie hanging loose over his silk shirt, and his expensive suit that fitted him nowhere — like trying to tailor a baboon!

Curly stood watching the game, his thumbs in his belt and his stumpy fingers beating time on his belly. Joe's chauffeur, a thin, effeminate youth, passed behind her, trailing a faint perfume. He looked over in her direction and whispered something to Curly. They both laughed. She looked away in revulsion. It was Nigel's bank again. His low voice dropped into the pool of silence: "I want fifty in."

He was playing surely and coldly with the genius for grasping chance at the right moment that occasionally illumined him. His bank won again. He was only backing them in tonight. His hunch was right.

A sharp-faced redhead near her was laying side bets. She's nearly hysterical, Claire thought. The fool! why doesn't she keep calm? A chair was vacated, and a sea captain with a quiet, weary face under a thatch of grey hair slumped into it. He watched the betting closely, his eyes following the voices. He was plunging again. He had done two thousand last week. Poor devil, he earned it hard enough.

"I want sixty pounds. Thirty's a half," Freddy was chanting in his singsong voice. A damned good croupier, Freddy, she thought. He works up the excitement, gets them betting.

Nigel rolled the pile of notes beside him, slipped a rubber band over them and handed them to Claire over his shoulder. There must be three hundred. She took them without a sound. She must not break the spell.

The baize door swung open and she glanced up. A short, stocky man entered. Her heart leaped with excitement. It was Stormcloud's owner — Walters. There was a lucky omen if you needed it. Here they were, playing with Stormcloud's winnings and the owner turned up. She saw the Doc glance at him, scowling. If you could believe all you heard, it was more than luck that Walters had ever got his hand on Stormcloud. They said he had been chucker-out for the Doc when he owned the Bandwagon nightclub before the war. He had slipped a bit these last few years, while Walters had gone up. . . . Well, that was luck.

It was the Doc's bank and he threw over four ten-pound notes. "Forty for the Doc," the croupier called. He gets it easily enough, Claire thought.

Joe came out from the mysterious office in which he lurked between his rare appearances at the table, and stood in the shadow, small and inconspicuous in his navy-blue suit with the white shirt and spotted bow tie. She saw him greet Walters with his tight little smile and they strolled over to the table and stood watching the betting. She wondered if they were going to lay a bet: she had never seen Walters bet and she knew that Joe never did. Joe's retainers betted occasionally; it was said he only encouraged them to bet when he didn't want to lose them. Then it was useful. They rarely won.

Joe patrolled the table quietly and gave Claire his thin smile. It struck chill through her exultation. His eyes were as cold as a fish. After tonight, she and Nigel would never set foot in the place again.

There was a sudden commotion at the table. The sea

captain leapt to his feet with a cry like an air-raid siren. "Jesus," he shouted in a cracked foreign voice, "can't I get any more money?" He pounded the table till it vibrated. "I ask you — is it fair? I haf lost plenty money here and now they will not gif me any lousy money."

The players looked up at him dispassionately. The croupier eyed him with boredom. Claire watched him with distaste and uneasiness. He had begun to sob and was mouthing incoherent phrases, stretching out his hands appealingly. Revolting! He'd be foaming at the mouth next. A superstitious shiver went through her. Thank God, Nigel never lost his head.

The captain screamed again, louder. Curly was at his side, soundless and swift as a ballet dancer; he took his arm gently. Joe strolled up and smiled. The captain stopped struggling, he did not scream any more. The three men, with arms linked, went towards the office as though for a friendly drink. Those round the table watched them briefly and dropped their eyes again.

From time to time players got up abruptly and backed from the table, pushing their chairs away with movements so similar that they seemed part of a routine. Others took their seats. Curly watched them lazily as they made their way to the door and the paunchy doorman let them out with an expressionless face.

Joe and the captain came back arm-in-arm; his seat was occupied and Joe brought him round near Nigel. He touched the shoulder of a pasty-faced woman who wasn't playing and she relinquished her seat without a word. The captain placed a neat bundle of notes beside him. So they have accepted his cheque, Claire thought. Poor mug, they'd pluck him feather by feather until he hadn't a farthing left.

The croupier was preparing for a new "shoe". The players relaxed for a moment and watched him shuffling the cards with deft, controlled movements. It was always like that when the pack was being reshuffled. All eyes were fixed on him as the cards flickered through his hands, white and strong in the bright light. The eyes round the table watched as though hypnotised, absorbed in every movement, happy that for a moment they were only spectators of a fascinating ritual, relieved however briefly of the agony of decision and suspense. Freddy held out the shuffled pack and invited Mrs Gartred.

She smiled, flattered. "Four, Freddy."

He scattered the four cards, then packed the rest neatly in front of him.

It's funny how everyone trusts Freddy, Claire thought. If Joe laid so much as a finger on that pack there'd be a riot.

A sigh went up when he spoke. "We're off! Quiet, everybody."

It was Nigel's turn for the bank again. She knew he would take it. She knew every step before he made it. It was as though their minds were one. As if he were answering her thoughts, he looked up at her and said: "I'll let it run."

"Mr C, your bank." Nigel nodded and passed over fifty pounds.

"That's fifty for Mr C."

So he was really going to play his hunch. Fifty pounds. Why, it would only have to run four banks and they'd be holding four hundred. Add four hundred to what they had already won tonight and they'd be home on the pig's back.

"Silence please. The cards are out."

Nigel waited for the out-bettor to turn up his cards.

"Six." The whisper swelled round the table.

"Eight," Nigel said, turning his cards over.

"Eight," called the croupier, "and the bank wins."

"That's fifty for you, Mr C," the tally clerk called. "Will you leave it?"

"Yes."

The table settled down and betting started again. Once again the cards were out. Claire drew in her breath. This was the test of Nigel's hunch. He turned over the cards methodically. He was right.

"The bank wins again."

Oh the darling! From his quiet manner, you would never guess that the rest of their lives was hanging on this. They were on the crest of the wave and she had seen enough to know that luck like this might never come again.

Excitement simmered. Faces craned forward as the bets were laid. The croupier was still calling bets. "I want fifty pounds, ladies and gentlemen, then I'll let her go."

Mrs Gartred was whimpering. Nobody took any notice. Mrs Gartred always whimpered when she was losing; she probably wasn't even aware of it herself. She rummaged in her jewelled handbag and spilled the untidy contents on the table. She was obviously cleaned out. Her dark face puckered like a hurt child's. Then she took the sable cape from her shoulders with shaking hands. "It's worth hundreds," she croaked, pushing it into the centre of the table.

"Will you settle for fifty?" Freddy was unmoved.

She whimpered. "Yes, who'll give me fifty?"

Quick as a whiplash a sharp-faced blonde beside Nigel threw her the notes and she pushed the cape across the table.

"All right, ladies and gentlemen," Freddy called. "Silence, please, while the cards are out."

He threw two cards to Mrs Gartred and two to Nigel.

She fumbled hers over with shaking hands. . . . "Seven."

Nigel turned his slowly. "Nine!"

Claire's heart leaped. Four hundred! They had done it!

The tally clerk's flat voice rose through the murmur of envious comment.

"Well, four hundred, Mr C."

"I'll take it."

He addressed the croupier. "Four hundred for Mr C."

"Here you are, Mr C, three hundred and sixty pounds for you." He folded the remaining forty pounds neatly and slipped the notes through the slit in the box that stood in the centre of the table, between Freddy and Cec. God, they got a wonderful rake-off, Claire thought. Ten per cent of all in-winnings to the house. That was the rule. No matter who lost, the house won.

Nigel took the notes and counted them. He stood up with a casual air, almost as though he were merely stretching his legs, backed away from the table and dropped the notes into Claire's hand.

She could have laughed for joy, but no one ever laughed at Joe's. She could have danced a wild jig round the bare floor, she could have smothered Nigel's calm face with kisses.

Joe smiled at them in his fatherly way. "You'll stay for supper?" he invited.

Nigel shook his head. "No, I think I'll have an early night for a change."

"What about the little lady? She must be worn out standing up there all the evening. Regular little lucky charm, ain't she? Come in for a few minutes anyway," he said, motioning to the office. "I won't have a car right away and you can have a snack while you wait."

Nigel smiled down at Claire. "In that case, I suppose it won't hurt us."

Joe piloted Claire and Nigel to the office. "You haven't met Mr Walters, have you?" he said to Claire.

"Pleased to meet yer." Sport continued to swing one leg over the end of the table on which he was sitting, and went on cleaning his nails with a silver toothpick.

Joe took a bottle of whisky from a cupboard. "Genuine scotch, and I can guarantee it."

Sport gave a short, explosive laugh. "D'yer reckon? What's the bettin' on it?"

"I never bet," said Joe.

Claire turned to Sport gaily. "Well, we do, I'm glad to say, and I must thank you, Mr Walters, for that marvellous tip you gave us on Saturday."

"Pleased to oblige." Sport offered her a cigarette.

"And isn't she the sweetest little mare?" Claire gushed. "We went round to see her in the enclosure and I fell in love with her."

Sport's face lit up. "Did you, really?" he asked, with real enthusiasm. "Here, you might as well take the packet. Plenty more where they come from."

Claire thanked him and slipped the cigarettes into her handbag. Joe handed round the drinks and they took up their glasses. Joe raised his to them. "Well, here's to three lucky people. I wish you could pass a bit of it over to me." They all laughed dutifully at his joke.

A knock came on an inner door and a pert little blonde came in with a tray.

"Good," Joe said, taking it from her. "Now beat it, kid, and tell Billee to speed up the rest of the eats. Freddy's needin' a breather."

He closed the door and motioned them to the tray. "Bog in, it's all on the house. 'The satisfied customer always comes back' is our motter."

They laughed again, and Claire smiled at Joe gaily as he took the lid off the entrée dish. That's what you think, Joey, she said to herself, but I swear to God it's the last time you'll ever set eyes on us.

"Will you have some of this lobster stuff?"

"Thanks...lobster mornay...I adore it." She broke the crisp browned surface with her fork. "I really am starving, you know. I was so excited before I came that I couldn't eat my dinner."

"Then you mustn't miss these," Sport spoke with his mouth full, pushing a plate of asparagus rolls towards her. "These are the goods."

"'Scuse me, won't you?" Joe said. "I won't be a minute. Coupla things I've got to give an eye to." He went out.

Nigel helped himself to the lobster again.

Claire turned to Sport. "I suppose you'll be going down to Melbourne for the Cup?"

"Too right. Got to keep an eye on the little filly, y'know. Lucky she don't need no fancy clothes like a woman. Though I'll have to get a few duds meself to do her proud." He looked at Nigel's suit admiringly. "I bet that never come off the peg."

"You must let me take you to my tailor," Nigel offered. "I'm sure he could fix you up even though the time is so short."

"That'd be real nice of you."

"He's very pricey," Nigel explained, "charged me a

cool thirty guineas for this, but I feel it was worth it.''

"Phew!" Sport whistled. "Sounds like racketeering to me, but if he turns me out like that I'll be happy to cough up the ante without squealing.''

Joe put his head round the door. "No hurry, but Curly tells me there's a car back — that's if you really want to go.''

"Thanks, we do," Nigel accepted the offer. "I'm going to have that early night." He turned to Sport. "Will twelve o'clock tomorrow at the SP suit you? I'll take you straight round to my tailor.''

"OK by me. Maybe we'll have a spot of lunch together afterwards." Sport gave him a parting wink.

Nigel looked doubtful. "I'll try to make it," he said. "Columbia are trying to persuade me to have a film test for the *Smithy* show and the director wants me to lunch with him, but between you and me I'm not keen about it, and if I can put him off, I will. But I'll see you at twelve anyway.''

"Goodnight," Claire smiled at him, "and give my love to Stormcloud.''

"Sure, I will.''

"Well, goodnight," Joe said genially. "Be seeing you again soon, I suppose?''

Not us, Claire said to herself. She flashed him a brilliant smile. "Thanks for everything.''

They turned and went out and the doorkeeper closed the outer door carefully behind them.

Joe turned to Sport. "Think they're not going to play any more," he said contemptuously. "Poor mugs! We'll have all that dough back within a week.''

"What are you sucking up to that tailor's dummy for?" Sport inquired.

"I'm thinking of opening a new club, and if I do I can use him. That Pommy line of his'll fetch the suckers.''

"Pommy be blowed. His father was a remittance man, used to drink himself silly on his quarterly cheque down at the old SP before it went toney and moved up town. I used to keep nit for 'em down there when they were sly groggin' and I was only a bit of a kid; so there's nothing you can tell me.''

"Well, what are you wasting your time on his nibs for, anyway?"

"I need some real slap-up clothes for Melbourne, that's why."

Joe gave him a sharp look. "I hope Smiler don't let me down while you're away. Mack made a hell of a muck of things last time you was up in Brisbane. I only got half the quantity of liquor I should of got. We don't want that to happen again."

"You don't have to worry about Smiler."

"Well, anyway keep your eyes peeled for the Doc. He's been goin' round threatenin' to do you in ever since Storm-cloud won last Saturday."

"I should worry. The Doc never did have no guts. Anyway, I got the horse from him all fair and square, didn't I?"

"He don't think so, so just keep your eyes skinned. And about those clothes. You know you'll have to pay through the nose for them, that feller gets a rakeoff on everyone he introduces."

"That won't worry me so long as I get the class."

"Well, I'll hand it to him, clothes is the one thing he does know something about," Joe conceded, finishing the asparagus rolls.

"And films," Sport gave a broad wink, "don't forget about films."

"Him in films!" Joe spluttered with his mouth full. "He ain't an actor's toerag. Give him enough rope to hang himself though, and we'll have him where we want him like Freddy and Cec. Yes," he added thoughtfully, "he'll make a damn good runner for the new club."

THURSDAY
I

When Claire opened the door of the office, Deb was already sitting there poring over the appointment book. Claire greeted her gaily. "Darling, we've done it!"

"You mean you've had another win?"

"The thousand's ours!"

"Oh Claire, how wonderful. Your jade brought you luck, after all."

"It certainly did." She caressed the earrings tenderly and bent over to whisper, "And now, well, darling, they're my wedding present!" Claire's eyes were misty and Deb pressed her arm warmly in response.

"Oh Claire, I'm so glad."

They heard the outer door open and footsteps along the corridor.

"Don't say a word to the others," Claire warned. "Oh God, to think I'll soon be able to get out of this and have a place of my own." She brushed a kiss on Deb's cheek. "I'm relying on you to give me your patronage, Mrs McFarland."

Deb laughed self-consciously and went out.

Claire sat down at her desk, whistling under her breath. I must remember to give Nigel a ring about eleven o'clock, she thought. He should be awake by then. Just to tell him how I adore him. To think of it — only two days more and I'll be Mrs Carstairs!

Guinea put her head round the door. "The top of the mornin' to you, me darlin'," she called cheerfully.

"Hullo, Guin. You're looking very bright his morning in spite of the weather. How did the trip to Lapstone go last night?''

Guinea sighed and closed her eyes. ''Out of this world. I felt like a princess. You ought to have seen me sitting there like Jacky wrapped up in an ermine cape Byron brought back from Yalta!''

''Ermine?''

''Dinky-di ermine! And when I walked into the hotel with the damn thing flogging my heels, everybody in sight fell flat on their pusses — me, that's always had to keep out the winter draughts up till now with bunny.''

''Don't tell me he gave it to you?''

''As good as. I take it, it goes with his heart and his hand.''

''Did he really ask you to marry him?''

''Nothing less.''

Claire sat on the edge of the desk and gazed at her with shining eyes. ''Aren't you the lucky girl! Why, I believe he's quite one of *the* nobs.''

''That's right. All upper crust, Long Island and the deep, deep South, whatever that may mean.''

''When are you going to be married?''

''His idea is a rush 'do' before he goes north next week — it seems the war won't wait for him any longer and he wants to leave me in a penthouse down in Macleay Street. Me! What's never paid more than fifteen bob for a room in my life!'' She laughed. ''But I said it's Brisbane or nowhere for me. He thinks that's because it's six hundred miles nearer to him, and I didn't have the heart to tell him it was being six hundred miles further from Sydney I was interested in. I've had this place.''

''How's your Air Force hero going to take it?''

''Kim Scott? What's he got to do with it?''

''Oh, I don't know. It's just that I've always had an idea you two'd make it up in the end. You've turned down so many other good offers.''

''I wouldn't marry Kim if he was the last man on earth.'' Guinea kicked off her rainboots passionately and threw them across the room. ''That's what I think of him.''

"Well, you know best, my pet."

"Just think of it, Claire! For the last two and a half years, practically all the forty-eight States have made some proposition or other to me, mainly dishonourable. But up to this, nobody ever wanted to marry me that had more than two bucks to rub together in peace time. And it's not as though he was a wornout old wolf like Alfalfa. He's a really decent stick."

"Then you really are going to get married this time."

"Well," Guinea frowned, "I am and I'm not, if you know what I mean. I told him I can't give an answer till I've seen my family. Gawd! Imagine me telling Mum! But it sounds good. And if he still insists on us getting spliced before he goes, I'll make it the very last minute. I just couldn't come at a honeymoon."

"No. I can understand that with Sher just gone, but you'll soon get over it. I take it then that the colonel's as attractive as he looks."

"My dear, he's a wow. And what a line! He calls me his little dreamdust and kisses me as though I was made of glass. You'd swear I was marked 'Fragile! This end up with care. Never so much as a pass!'"

"It sounds like true love to me."

"Looks like it. He's even gone on the water wagon. Only trouble about that is that I have to go on it too, and I swilled so much ginger ale last night it gave me the hiccups. But I judge from his normal form that he'll only lay off the liquor till we're married. And are we coy about the facts of life! He takes it for modesty."

"They say it does men no harm to keep them guessing."

"I've never been much good at that line before. I don't know how you can if you're in love with someone. But this time your old friend Guin has everything taped. I've had love — and how! Now it's whacko-the-diddle-oh and me for the States. Oh gee, Claire, will I be glad to get out of this country! This last week has just fed me up to the back teeth. I don't care if I never see Australia again."

"Well, I've got a bit of news for you myself.... Oh

blast! here's Elvira. I'll tell you after.''

They could hear her greeting Ursula. ''You're looking like the cat that ate the canary this mornin', luvvie. Won the lottery?''

Ursula replied coldly, ''I never gamble!''

''Cor! What you do miss!'' Elvira scuttled down the corridor.

Ursula picked up the phone and asked for Mrs Molesworth in a low voice. This was just the chance she had been waiting for. She'd show her how lax things were in the Marie Antoinette with people coming in any old time and skipping off whenever they felt like it.

Thelma's ''Hullo'' was curt. ''Oh, it's you, Miss Cronin.''

Ursula strained over the desk to see that no one was coming. ''It's what we were talking about last evening,'' she whispered. ''Elvira's just come in again.''

''Ah. I'm glad you rang. I shall come up immediately.''

Ursula smiled at the satisfaction in Thelma's voice.

Elvira put her head round the door of Claire's office. ''Ullo, luvvie,'' she bared her false teeth amiably. ''Got a minnit?''

''What do you want?'' Claire asked impatiently. ''I'm frightfully busy.''

Elvira put a box on the desk beside her. '''Ave a look in there.''

Claire opened it and lifted up a pair of gossamer-fine stockings. ''Nylons! Whew!'' she whistled, ''where did you get these?''

''D.D.T. musta chucked 'em into the wastepaper basket when she had me up there packin' yest'd'y afternoon.''

''Oh, did she? Very careless of her.''

''Yeah, wasn't it? And this pair of scanties too. I washed and ironed them. Ain't they real dainty?''

Claire fingered the delicate sheer. ''Part of a trousseau set, I imagine. You want to be careful.''

''Aw, 'er. I wouldn't worry about that. She'd need a private detective to keep track of all the scanties she leaves layin' round.''

Claire unlocked her top drawer, slipped the box in and relocked it. ''I'll let you know what I can do with them tomorrow. I think I know where I can place them.''

Elvira sighed. ''Well, I'm afraid that's the last for a while from 'er.''

''Too bad.''

''Though I'm real glad to see the back of 'er, that I am. 'Er kind of goin's on is anathemia ter me. And all I gets is a lousy ten-bob tip out of her. After all I done for 'er too. Still an' all, the larst time she was 'ere she sneaked out without tippin' me at all. So you could 'ardly expect me to take back the stockings and scanties when I found 'em in the waste-paper basket, now, could yer? I got to get paid for me trouble one way or the other.''

''Hardly. But I really do think you'd better get back upstairs now. If Old Mole catches you here, there'll be hell to pay.''

''Gawd, you're right about that, and me with old Ma Dalgety on me 'ands. She's been as full as a goog ever since 'er boy friend went back Toosd'y.''

She scuttled up the corridor, stopping to put her head in a cubicle. '''Ow yer doin', Guin?''

''Hi ya, Virus.''

''Feelin' OK?''

''Fine and dandy, why?''

''Oh, I just thought you been off the last coupla mornin's, you mightn't be too good, like.''

Guinea poked her in the ribs. ''Pointing the bone at me, are you, you old witch?''

Elvira cackled and stopped sharply, turning a startled face as the outer door opened and Ursula's voice rose in unctuous greeting.

'''Oly Moses!'' Elvira went pale. ''It's Old Mole.''

Thelma swept into the corridor, blocking Elvira's way. ''Pray, what are you doing down here at this time of the morning, Elvira?'' Her voice was resonant and commanding.

Claire came to the door of her office.

Elvira was gazing up at Thelma like a frightened rabbit. "I just come in to give Miss Jeffries a message from Mrs Dalgety," she lied glibly. "She was to 'ave 'ad a massage but she don't feel up to it."

Thelma turned inquiring eyes on Claire. "Is that so, Miss Jeffries?"

"Quite right, Mrs Molesworth," Claire's voice was smooth.

"Oh," Thelma looked from one to the other doubtfully. "I still don't see why you had to come down from your own floor, Elvira. There are house telephones, aren't there?"

"Yes, mad'm." Elvira's voice was meek and her mouth had a pathetic droop.

"Well, don't let it happen again, and get back to your work immediately."

"Yes, mad'm." Elvira made washing movements with her bony little hands.

"And before I forget. Miss D'Arcy-Twyning rang up to say that a pair of nylon stockings is missing. Did you find them?"

Elvira looked up at her as though she was going to cry. "No, mad'm."

"Who cleaned the room out this morning?"

"Me, mad'm. It was in an awful mess after 'er packin' yest'd'y, papers and rubbish everywhere and I put the lot down the incinerator." Elvira sniffed.

"Oh well, I know Miss D'Arcy-Twyning is sometimes inclined to be thoughtless and we can't be held responsible if she's careless with her things."

"Thank you, mad'm." Elvira scuttled out.

Thelma turned to Claire. "I want a word with you, Miss Jeffries."

"Will you come into my office, please?" Claire closed the door behind her.

"It's about all this absenteeism in the salon."

"Yes?"

"I understand Miss Malone was away yesterday morning and on Tuesday morning as well."

"That is so. There was a death in the family."

Thelma murmured conventional sympathy in an irritated voice. "And Miss Parker went off at lunchtime yesterday?"

"Yes, she was sick."

"Oh." Thelma looked baffled. "It's all very unsatisfactory, you know."

"Have you had any complaints from the patrons, Mrs Molesworth?"

"No. Not exactly. But that has nothing to do with the principle of the thing. And if you can afford to have the girls running in and out like this, then perhaps the place is overstaffed."

"Considering how often we have to work overtime," Claire retorted, "I feel that an hour or so off duty here and there when we're not busy is only their due. I'll be grateful if you'll tell Miss Cronin not to take any further after-hours bookings in future. Last Friday, Miss Malone, Miss Forrest and I were not able to leave here until nearly half past seven, owing to a last-minute booking which Miss Cronin took for Mrs Dalgety."

Thelma dismissed her complaint with a wave of her hand. "I'm afraid you do not clearly understand the hotel's policy, Miss Jeffries. The Marie Antoinette exists for the convenience of the guests." She broke off. "Where are the rest of the staff? I may as well take this opportunity of saying a few things to you all that have been in my mind for some time."

"Certainly. I'll call them in."

Claire put her head round the first cubicle, clicked her tongue and winked at Val and Guinea. "Miss Blaski and Miss Malone. Would you mind coming into the office, please?"

Guinea ran her finger across her throat significantly. "Allee same slittee," she whispered.

Claire moved on to the massage room. "Mrs Molesworth wishes to speak to the staff in my office, Miss Forrest," she made a grimace to Deb.

Deb swallowed nervously.

"Don't let that old bitch put the wind up you," Claire whispered, "and find Alice, will you?"

"She's just come in. I haven't had a chance to give her Bessie's message yet."

"That'll have to wait." Claire went to the reception desk. "Will you come into the office please, Miss Cronin."

Ursula rose with a smug smile and smoothed her uniform importantly. She walked across the boudoir with her head held high. Claire followed her back to the office.

Thelma looked at each girl in turn as she came in. "Good morning. I wish to take this opportunity of speaking to you all," she began. "There has been far too much absence here in the salon lately..."

The phone rang at the reception desk and Ursula got up to answer it with a murmured apology. She was back in a minute. "It's a private call for Miss Parker," she announced triumphantly.

Alice's pale face flushed. Thelma turned an accusing eye on her. "Really, I'm surprised at you, Miss Parker. Private calls at this hour of the morning."

Alice opened her mouth feebly and closed it again; she looked imploringly at Claire.

Thelma turned to Ursula. "I'm sorry, Miss Cronin, but will you please say that Miss Parker is engaged and cannot come to the phone."

Ursula was back again, her eyes snapping with excitement. "It's Bessie Napier from the powder room, Mrs Molesworth, and she says it's most urgent and she's got to speak to Miss Parker."

"*Got* to speak to Miss Parker?" Thelma's voice rose. "I don't understand." She turned to Alice, glaring suspiciously at her white face. The rest of the girls stood silent with their eyes downcast and their faces blank.

Alice spoke unsteadily. "I'm sorry. I'll have to speak to her." She pushed her way out of the office.

In a few minutes she came back.

"Well?" Thelma demanded.

"I'm very sorry, Mrs Molesworth. . .but. . .my sister's been recalled suddenly and she's leaving immediately."

"Leaving immediately?"

"She's in the AWAS and she's going back to Queensland. I. . .I'll have to go and see her."

"But this is most irregular."

Alice looked round at the others frantically. "I'm sorry, Mrs Molesworth. . ." Her mouth was working and she could hardly hold back the tears. She turned with a sob and bolted out of the room.

"Well, I declare," Thelma exploded. "Miss Jeffries!"

Claire ignored her and followed Alice into the cloak-room. "Did Bessie say what's wrong?" she asked, helping her into her raincoat.

Alice nodded. "Mary's been bleeding and Bessie's terribly worried. She wants me to go there at once."

"Has she got a doctor?"

"She's trying to get one."

"You'd better take a taxi. Ask Blue to get one for you. Have you got enough money?"

"Only. . .only a couple of shillings."

"Here's a quid till tomorrow. You never know what you might need to get."

"Thanks awfully." Alice pulled on her hat and looked at Claire with panic-stricken eyes. "Oh Claire, I'm so frightened."

"Well, that won't help anyone. Take a pull on yourself and get along as quickly as you can and see how she really is."

Thelma was making a speech to the girls when Claire went back to the office. She broke off in the middle of a sentence and turned accusing eyes on her. "Really, Miss Jeffries. I shall expect Miss Parker to give me a very good explanation of her extraordinary behaviour."

"I apologise for her, Mrs Molesworth. Miss Parker is usually most careful in such matters, but her only sister has been suddenly recalled to Queensland and there's simply no one else to fix up some important business for her."

Thelma glared at her suspiciously. "Then I think she might at least have done me the courtesy of an explanation instead of rushing out in that hysterical fashion. As I have just been saying to these girls, courtesy has always been our watchword at the South Pacific, courtesy and service, and I must say that I'm very far from satisfied with the standard of either in the Marie Antoinette."

"I'd be glad if you'd state exactly what you mean, Mrs Molesworth."

"What I mean, Miss Jeffries, is that there are certain things that we have been obliged to put up with on account of Manpower problems and other difficulties inseparable from the war, but that is not to say that we will tolerate a slackness among the staff that practically amounts to dishonesty."

Claire interrupted her with heat. "If you are meaning to imply, Mrs Molesworth, that there is any withholding of moneys from the salon to the hotel, then I can only take it as a grave reflection on me as the person in charge, and offer you my immediate resignation."

Thelma looked startled. The colour ran up her throat and ebbed unevenly, leaving ugly blotches on the white skin. "You misunderstand me, Miss Jeffries. I was speaking — er — figuratively. There is no question whatever about the accuracy of your accounts."

"I'm very glad to hear that. You realise, of course, Mrs Molesworth, that a remark of that sort is very close to slander."

"Really, Miss Jeffries." Thelma's voice rose in alarm. "You're reading into my words meanings that are not there at all."

"Your choice of words then is singularly unfortunate, Mrs Molesworth. And in view of what you have said I feel it is impossible for me to continue here. Of course, you realise the trade mark of the Marie Antoinette products is registered in my name."

Thelma licked her lips. "Now, that's very hasty of you, Miss Jeffries. You know very well that we've never had any complaints about you personally or your work."

There was a note of triumph in Claire's voice. "I shall hand in my resignation formally to Mr Sharlton this evening. In any case, I've been considering opening my own salon for some time with a manageress, as I'm going to be married and it would be impossible to carry on my own home with the long and irregular hours you expect us to work in the Marie Antoinette."

Thelma drew in a deep breath. The hate in her eyes deepened. "Going to be married," she gushed. "You must let me be the first to congratulate you." Her lips set in a strained smile. "We will have to talk with Mr Sharlton about that, but promise me you won't do anything foolish until we've seen him, won't you. I'm sure we shall find a way of relieving you of some of the heavy responsibility you carry here."

"Just as you like," Claire's voice was cold and impersonal. "And before you go, I should be grateful if you would please say a few words to Miss Cronin about her taking bookings in private suites without consulting me. It's utterly impossible for me to keep things running smoothly here while she repeatedly takes it upon herself to do this."

Ursula drew herself up with an air of pained virtue.

Thelma frowned at her. "Dear, dear, Miss Cronin, I am surprised to hear that. You really must be more considerate of Miss Jeffries."

Ursula brought her head up indignantly. "Oh, but Mrs Molesworth . . ."

Thelma swept her protest aside. "After all, she is in charge of the salon, you know, and you must always consult her first. Now personally, I would never dream of sending for one of the salon staff myself without asking Miss Jeffries' permission."

Claire looked at Deb meaningly. Deb avoided her gaze, blushing up to her hair.

"Now, is there anything else I can do to make you feel happier, Miss Jeffries?"

"All I require is your assurance that I am in full charge, Mrs Molesworth. If I have that, I think we may be able to manage things more satisfactorily.''

Thelma shed her flashing smile upon the staff. ''Now I'm sure we all understand each other. I know that everything will go on quite happily. And before you do anything rash, Miss Jeffries, you will have a talk with me, won't you?''

Claire bowed without speaking. Thelma swept up the corridor with Ursula trailing behind her.

''The crawling old bitch,'' Guinea burst out. ''Crikey, Claire, are you really going to be married?''

Claire nodded. ''On Saturday. I was just going to tell you when Elvira barged in.''

Guinea gave her a bear's hug. ''Gee, I'm glad. Jeepers! was that one for her ladyship! You could have knocked her down with a feather when you told her that. I bet she'll rush straight upstairs and put the acid on L. F.''

''I must give you a kiss for luck, Claire,'' Val's eyes were full of tears, ''and I think you deserve the VC for the way you towelled Old Mole up.''

There was a knock at the outer door. They heard Ursula's voice. Guinea put her head out. ''A messenger,'' she said, ''asking for Mallon. Crikey, that's me. Here, give me a bob to tip him, Claire.'' She loped up the corridor and came back half hidden under an enormous florist's box. ''Holy mackerel! Byron must have shares in a hothouse.''

They untied the ribbon and revealed a riot of orchids, cream and green and brown and mauve and pink and purple, sprays of them, single perfect blooms, resting on a bed of roses and water-lilies, carnations and lily of the valley.

''Whew!'' Claire whistled, ''it must have cost him a fortune. I've never seen anything like it.''

''I'll tell you what, Claire,'' Guinea said impulsively. ''We'll go halves in the lot and you can have a bouquet of orchids for your wedding on Saturday and there'll be enough over to do up your flat.''

''Oh Guin. . .'' Claire touched the flowers gently. There was a lump in her throat. ''You're too generous.''

The outer door opened and two women came in. Guinea looked out. ''The invasion's started. Just stick the lid on and we'll sort 'em out at lunchtime. I only want enough to wear tonight. Byron's giving a do to some of his brass hat friends to introduce me and I'll want a bit of advice from you on the rigout I ought to wear."

"Of course. We'll have to see you look your best." She squeezed Guinea's arm. "Really, Guin, I don't know what to say. You're just the most generous kid in the world."

"Aw shucks. And anyway, what's this lend-lease for except to give us Aussies a taste of civilisation?"

Bessie had a broken night. The wind came up and rattled the windows and a sudden shower pattered against the glass. Several times she woke and heard the creak of Mary's bed, but she seemed to be asleep, although she moved restlessly.

At last, just before dawn, Bessie went off into a deep sleep from which neither the familiar clatter of the milkman nor the early Bellevue Hill trams disturbed her. When she opened her eyes she saw with a shock that the hands of the alarm clock pointed to eight. She bounced out of bed with one movement of her bulky body, wrapped an old dressing gown over her nightdress and tiptoed into the room. Mary was lying on a tumbled bed, her bright hair dishevelled on the pillow. She turned at the footsteps and Bessie saw the grey pallor of her face with a catch of fear.

"I'm a nice one," she said with her friendly smile. "Give me a visitor and I think it's Sunday. Fancy me sleeping till eight o'clock. Now I'll just get the kettle on and it won't be a minute before there's a nice cup of tea. How'd that go down?"

"Lovely." Mary smiled at her.

"Did you have a good night, dearie? Tossed about a bit, didn't you?" she said smoothing the bedclothes.

"I'm...I'm afraid I've got a confession to make." Mary was embarrassed. "I...must have bled a bit in my sleep and...it's on the sheet. I had to take it off and...I put a towel on the bed instead. I'm so sorry."

Bessie hid her alarm and dismissed the confession breezily.

"Don't worry about that. Soon change a sheet. I'll get one out of the cupboard now and we'll sit you up on this chair while I make up the bed."

"I had to take my nightdress off too and I put on my slip." Mary smiled rather wanly as Bessie turned the covers back and she got out of bed in a short white slip.

"You poor lamb. Why didn't you call me?" Bessie re-made the bed and handed Mary a clean nightdress of her own out of a drawer. Mary put it over her head and let her slip slide to the floor. She stood for a moment, a slight figure in a pale blue Milanese nightdress that reached halfway down her calves and sagged round her in voluminous folds. The bosom was decorated with elaborate coffee-coloured lace.

"My goodness," Bessie laughed. "Fits you all over and touches you nowhere."

"It must look lovely on you," Mary said kindly.

"All I can say, it fits me a bit better. Now, you hide in bed or you'll be getting vain. And you'll be getting a chill too, it's turned quite cold. Are you sure you've got enough blankets?"

"Yes, quite. Thank you."

"Well it looks like being an awful day so the best place for you is in bed."

Bessie picked up the soiled sheet and nightdress and took them with her to the balcony where she unrolled them with an anxious frown. She saw with relief that the stains were not big.

She put the kettle on the gas ring and dressed quickly in the little enclosure, sluicing her face in a basin of cold water. I've a good mind to ring that doctor, she thought as she cut thin slices of bread and butter, poured out two cups of tea, and went back to Mary.

"This'll make you feel better. We'll have some tea first and I'll slip round to the shop and get some nice fresh eggs for breakfast."

"Don't bother for me. I'm not hungry. Tea's all I want, really."

"Well if you don't want any breakfast, I do." Bessie said decidedly, pouring her out another cup. "There's a break in the rain now and I think I'll nick out straight away. I'll be back in five minutes."

She stood on the front veranda buttoning her old rain-coat round her and watching the rain splash up from the asphalt footpath. My, it was a downpour, she'd get soaked out there in that phone box, but it wasn't the sort of thing you could go to the grocer's to ring up about. It must be

647

about quarter to nine. Dr Smithers wouldn't be at his surgery yet. Well, there was nothing for it, he'd just have to put up with being disturbed at home. He'd been paid well enough.

When the rain eased a little she hurried out of the gate and down the road to the telephone box on the corner. Beastly things they were, just a box to put your head and shoulders in and the rest of you got soaked. Her plump finger ran down the columns of physicians in the Pink Pages of the telephone book...Smithers. There were five of them. Ah, here he was — Dr Mark Smithers, Macquarie Street, and his home number as well.

She dialled and a woman's voice answered. "Dr Smithers. No, I'm sorry, he can't be disturbed. If you'll ring his surgery after ten o'clock...."

"I have to speak to him now," Bessie insisted. "It's about a patient of his."

"A patient of his? Well, you can ring the surgery...No. I'm very sorry."

"Will you please ask the doctor to speak on this telephone or I won't answer for the consequences." There was steel in Bessie's voice.

"Oh. If it's as urgent as that...I'll see if doctor can come."

"Yes. What is it?" a man's voice came gruffly.

"Is that Dr Smithers?"

"Yes."

"You operated on a Mrs McDonald yesterday."

"Well, what about it?"

"I'm a bit worried, doctor. She's bleeding still and I just want to know if it's all right."

"Is she losing much?"

"Not very much but it was on the bed this morning."

"Well that's nothing. Just keep her in bed and give her plenty of fluids to drink."

"But what do I have to do if it goes on? She looks awfully pale."

"Ring your local doctor if you're worried and tell him she had a miscarriage yesterday." He hung up.

Bessie stood there with the receiver in her hand. Who did he think he was? God? She put the receiver back.

He did say there was nothing to worry about, but still she didn't feel satisfied. She'd like a doctor to look at Mary, just to make certain. She wondered who she could get. It was so difficult nowadays with doctors so busy you had to make appointments weeks in advance unless you were practically dying. The Parkers might have a family doctor. Perhaps she'd better ring Alice and see if she knew anyone. Anyway, she'd feel happier in her mind if Alice was round.

Bessie dialled the South Pacific and asked for the Marie Antoinette. Ursula's voice came unctuously sweet and sharpened noticeably to answer that Miss Parker wasn't in yet, she'd gone home sick yesterday lunchtime and hadn't been in since. Miss Forrest? She'd see.

Deb's voice was guarded. "You wanted me?"

"I wanted Alice Parker."

"She isn't in yet. Could I take a message?"

"Didn't she come back yesterday?"

"No."

"Well tell her to come round here as soon as she can get away. I'm not too pleased with Mary and I think I ought to get a doctor."

"Oh," Deb said anxiously. "Things not too bright?"

"Bright!" Bessie almost snorted in her frustration. "Listen. Does anyone there know a doctor I could get hold of?"

"Just wait a minute and I'll ask."

Bessie's legs ached with the strain of standing on her toes to reach the mouthpiece set too high for her. She fumbled in her purse with her free hand and found she had run out of pennies.

"Are you there?" Deb's cool voice came again. "Miss Jeffries suggests that you try these numbers. Have you got a pencil to write them down?"

Bessie fished the stub of a pencil out of her pocket and scribbled on the telephone book. "Thanks, I'll ring straight away. And the moment that Alice Parker comes in, tell her

649

to come round here to me."

While she was getting change at a nearby shop, a man took over the telephone box. Bessie moved round where he could see her waiting. He turned his back. She tapped impatiently on the glass. He ignored her. The rain streamed down. Bessie could bear it no longer. She put her arm in and grabbed his shoulder. "Please, please, I've got to get a doctor," and her voice was so urgent he hung up.

It was not until the fourth call that she got hold of a doctor, who said she'd be round as soon as possible — about twelve. By this time Bessie was in such a state that she rang back the Marie Antoinette and demanded to speak to Alice.

She was wet to the waist when she let herself into her room nearly an hour after she had left Mary, and she was trembling with cold and anxiety. She forced a smile as Mary opened her eyes. "It's all right, dearie. I rung up the pub and they gave me the day off."

"You've been a long time," Mary murmured. "It seemed ages."

"Lord," said Bessie, "you know what it's like getting the SP. Alice is going to drop round to see you. The girls will arrange it for her."

"They're sweet." Mary's eyes drooped wearily. "But I wish she wouldn't. She gets so het up about things and she feels it's such an awful disgrace."

"Disgrace me foot," Bessie said indignantly. "Just let me hear her talking like that! Now, you try and have another sleep."

"Could I have a drink first?"

Bessie lifted Mary's head to sip the water. Was it only imagination, or had her lips got paler? And she seemed to be breathing queerly, quick and shallow. Bessie plumped up her pillow and smoothed back her hair. "You try to have a sleep now till Alice comes."

"I'll try." Mary turned to the wall and closed her eyes.

Mary was asleep when Bessie let Alice in. They tiptoed through the room to the balcony.

"How is she?" Alice asked fearfully.

"She's asleep now, thank goodness, but I don't like the look of her at all."

"Oh, dear."

"Now, don't you go fainting on me. I've got enough on my hands. And why didn't you go and tell the girls last night like you promised?"

"I remembered I'd gone off sick and I thought it wouldn't be wise."

"Well you could have rung them."

"Did you get a doctor?"

"Yes. I managed to get hold of a woman doctor in the end."

"When's she coming?"

"She said she'd be here as soon after twelve as she could, but they're all that busy. Here, you get out of your wet coat and I'll make you a cup of tea."

The two women sat down on the balcony to wait. At the sound of every car swishing on the wet road they looked out through the glass panes. Time stretched out. Eleven o'clock. Half past. Twelve o'clock. Half past. One o'clock. Half past one... The rain came down unceasingly. Mary slept restlessly.

Two o'clock.

"I can't stand it any longer," Alice got up. "I'm going to ring that doctor again. Something must have happened."

She put on her coat and went out.

Bessie tiptoed in to look at Mary. Her closed eyelids gave her face a waxy pallor against her red hair. She looked frail in the grey light. Bessie's heart contracted with pity.

She racked her brains. What did you do in a case like this? There must be something you could do. She whispered softly: "Would you like anything, dearie?"

Mary opened her eyes and gave her a little smile. "You are so good to me," she murmured as if from a dream. "I only want to sleep." Her eyelids closed again.

"Sleep. That's fine. That's the way to get your strength back." Bessie touched her shoulder reassuringly and lingered watching the still face. There was nothing more she could do.

She went back to her vigil on the balcony.

Mary lay wide awake behind her closed lids. Ever since she had wakened in the morning she had been filled with depression. The sense of freedom she'd had after the operation had left her. Last night she had been Corporal Mary Parker, ready to go back to her job, ready to take up her life again as it had been before this had happened to her. But this morning she had wakened up to desolation. They had taken her baby. They had taken away a part of herself and all she had left of Frank, and she had let them do it. How could she ever have believed that life would be the same again? She was a monster, a woman who had destroyed her own child. All the morning between her fitful dozing, this vision of herself had tossed in her brain and danced in ghoulish shapes under her closed lids. Her breathing came quick and shallow. She felt a choking in her throat and a tightening of her chest when she tried to get her breath. There was a strange feeling of lightness in her head, a sudden release in her body that terrified her. "Bessie, Bessie..." she called out.

Bessie was at her side. "Bessie, I'm bleeding," she gasped.

Bessie threw back the clothes and saw the quickly spreading crimson stain.

"It's all right, dearie," her mind cast round wildly. "I'll fix you up in just a minute." Haemorrhage. She must stop it, she must stop it at all costs. "Lie quite still," she said urgently and grabbed a towel to try and stop the flow. Mary was lying back on the pillow as if she had fainted. She couldn't leave her. She must do something or the girl would bleed to death.

She went to the press and got another towel and threw the soaked one down. "You must lie quite still, dearie. Don't move. It's just till the doctor comes. She'll be here any minute. Alice has gone out to fetch her."

At last she heard footsteps on the stairs and along the passage. The door opened and Alice came in with a fresh-faced competent looking woman.

"Bessie, this is Dr Cookson."

"Oh, thank God you've come, doctor."

The doctor went straight over to the bed and put down her bag. She picked up Mary's wrist and felt her rapid, feeble pulse. She pulled aside the bedclothes and removed the towel.

Bessie watched her from the foot of the bed.

The doctor quickly replaced the towel and pulled up the bedclothes again. She turned to Bessie and Alice. "I'll want both of you," she said. "One of you get me some more blankets and the other get me a hot water bottle and some hot coffee, just as soon as you can."

She looked round the room, saw the row of books on the mantelpiece, and picked out the four fattest ones. "Help me lift the foot of the bed," she said to Bessie, "and we'll put the books under it."

Bessie raised the bed with her and Alice fumbled with the books, putting them under the legs with shaking hands.

"Now get me a glass of water and a teaspoon, will you?" the doctor said.

Bessie hurried out onto the veranda. The doctor opened her bag, took out a syringe and filled it then she swabbed a patch on Mary's upper arm.

Mary's eyes followed her movements.

"Just a prick," she said soothingly as she inserted the needle of the syringe.

Bessie was beside her with the blankets, and together they spread them over the bed. "Is there a phone in the building?" the doctor asked.

Bessie shook her head. "No. The nearest one's on the corner. That's where I rang from this morning."

The doctor beckoned Bessie out onto the balcony. Alice turned to them with terrified eyes. "Is she very bad?"

"She must go to hospital immediately." The doctor's voice was urgent. "There's nothing more I can do now."

"Oh!" Alice gasped, leaning back against the table.

"I'll go and ring the nearest hospital and send an ambulance as soon as I can."

She turned to Alice. "From what you told me about your sister and from her present condition she may need a blood transfusion. You'd better go to the hospital with her."

She turned to Bessie. "Are you a relation?"

"No, I was just looking after her."

The doctor frowned. "Well just see that she drinks plenty of hot coffee and keep her warm. That's all you can do till the ambulance comes."

She turned and walked briskly back into the room and over to the bed. "I'm going to get you into hospital," she said, "so don't worry. Just drink up all you can like a good girl and it won't be long before the ambulance comes."

She picked up her bag and went out the door.

Deb poured herself out a cup of tea and sat down on the edge of the desk.

Claire pushed the tin of biscuits across to her. "It only needs Old Mole to walk in again and catch us sipping afternoon tea together like ladies of leisure and she'll be absolutely convinced that we're overstaffed. And it's just on closing time anyway."

"Well, you certainly told her off this morning. It took the wind out of her sails all right."

"Oh those bullies, they're all the same. But at least I did some good for myself, losing my temper. Evidently she doesn't want to lose the Marie Antoinette products, so in future I'll take nothing from her, because where I go they go."

"She certainly climbed down pretty quickly."

"That kind of thing makes me sick. And turning on Cronin. I loathe the woman myself but at least I didn't expect her to turn on her pimp like that. It's wonderful what a bit of money does for you, isn't it? You know, I'd never have had the guts to say those things if Nigel and I hadn't won that money. It just shows you, doesn't it?"

She picked up another biscuit and nibbled it thoughtfully. Yes, with the Marie Antoinette products and that thousand, she and Nigel were set for life. She'd open up her own place — she might as well get the profits as the SP.

"I'd better go in and see how Mrs Montgomery is doing," she said. "You stay here and finish your tea in peace."

Deb watched Claire go up the corridor and sipped her tea thoughtfully. Claire was right, it was wonderful what a sense of independence a bit of money gave you. If she had a thousand pounds she wouldn't let anybody put anything over her. Well there was another way she could get her independence and security. Really, Angus was a dear, ringing her up this morning after the way she'd behaved last night. She'd have to keep a watch on herself. You couldn't expect a man to put up with that kind of thing too often. He'd been consideration itself on the phone, inquiring after her headache, and then telling her that he'd arranged a real celebration for this evening. And would she dress, just to please him? She'd wear her black again. He liked that. She'd better go now and see if Mrs Marble had finished dressing and tell Guinea there was a cup of tea. The girl was going round like a dog with two tails with her American colonel and that unbelievable box of flowers.

Deb heard the telephone ringing. It was to be hoped that was another cancellation, they certainly all needed a break after the hectic week. Overstaffed indeed. She'd like Old Mole to come down and try working at their pace for a while.

Ursula picked up the receiver and heard someone faint and a long way off. Good grief, it was Bessie again. She glanced furtively down the corridor; thank goodness all the girls were busy. Well, this time she would really find out what Alice Parker's rushing in and out meant. She sank her voice into a whisper. "Yes, Miss Cronin speaking."

"Wait a minute," Bessie's voice was almost inaudible. "I can't hear, there's a tram going by."

Ursula waited, her ear glued to the phone; she heard the noise of a tram swell and fade.

"Could I speak to Miss Jeffries?"

"I'm afraid not, she's very busy."

"Then...would you mind getting one of the others?"

Ursula cast another glance down the corridor. "No, I'm sorry I can't do that. Mrs Molesworth's given special orders about no private calls."

"Oh," Bessie's voice faded. She was obviously very upset.

"It's quite all right, Bessie, you can give me the message," Ursula cooed in her most sympathetic voice. "Miss Jeffries said she was expecting you to ring."

"Oh," Bessie hesitated. "It's just..." her voice broke, "tell her that...that...Mary Parker's dead."

Ursula recoiled. "Oh...how awful..." Somewhere in her mind a red light flared. Keep out of this, it warned. But she had to know. "Are there any details you want me to give her?'' She cuddled the phone to her ear, her hand cupping the mouthpiece.

"Just that they took her to hospital and she died."

She could hear Bessie crying, and the receiver clanked down in her ear.

She put her own receiver down very slowly. Panic caught her. What a fool she'd been, why hadn't she called Claire? There was something fishy about the whole thing. How was Bessie mixed up in it? You never knew with these common old women.

Claire came into the boudoir. "Was that call for me?"

Ursula stared at her without speaking.

"What's wrong with you? You look as though you've seen a ghost."

"It was...Bessie. She said to tell you...Mary Parker's ...dead."

The colour drained out of Claire's face leaving her painted lips grotesque in an ashy mask. "Dead?" she repeated incredulously.

"It's awful, isn't it? Was it an accident?"

"Yes, it was an accident." Claire's face set hard. She went down the corridor to her office.

Ursula, leaning over her desk, strained her ears to catch every syllable and every movement, but she only heard her say: "Could you spare a few minutes, Deb, and ask Val to come to my office as soon as possible." She saw her draw Guinea after her into the office. Val and Deb followed and the door closed behind them all.

Ursula gnawed the top of her pencil. She couldn't bear not to know what was going on. If it wasn't for Mrs Molesworth being so horrible to her this morning she'd give her a ring. All of them cooped up in there like a lot of conspirators! She lifted the receiver and hesitated as the switch-girl's voice answered, murmured an apology and put the receiver down. Better not. Better not know too much, just in case.

The four women stared at each other in Claire's tiny office.

Mary Parker was dead.

Pity welled up and united them for a brief moment, then their minds jumped back like springs released, and each became the centre of her own world again. Mary Parker was dead, but they were alive.

Guinea broke the silence. "It's awful. She was such a nice kind of kid."

"Poor Bessie, oh poor old Bessie." The words burst out of Val. "She must be nearly frantic. I'm going down to get a taxi straight away."

Claire pulled her up sharply. "Don't be such a fool," she said. "You don't want to get mixed up in it."

Val looked at her puzzled. "Mixed up in it? What do you mean?"

"You're just being a fool. You know damn well what'll happen. The police will be at Bessie and Alice as soon as the report goes in about Mary's death, and heaven only knows what they'll say. They'll probably tell everything they know in sheer panic, and if you're there as well, that'll be enough to bring a policeman round here questioning the lot of us before we know where we are. And what good will that do anyone?"

"That's right," Deb agreed. "It would be a different matter if we could do any good, but the poor girl's beyond our help and there's absolutely nothing we can do except keep out of it for everyone's sake."

"Take my advice and don't go, Val." Claire took charge. "As the thing stands it'll probably pass over with just a few lines in the paper. They won't be interested in an obscure little AWAS and an old woman like Bessie, unless they get some line on it that's going to make a sensation."

"But look at the fuss they made about that AWAS in Brisbane," Deb said nervously. "Everybody that had even spoken to the girl in the last month had their names dragged through the papers."

"My God!" Guinea exclaimed, "that'd be awful." A sudden picture of her mother's ravaged face rose in her mind. That would just about kill her after Monnie.

"It would be awful, all right." Deb tried to organise her thoughts which were spinning like a piece of crazy film in a broken projector. Angus...Luen...she could not possibly have her name in the paper in connection with a thing like this. It would be the end of everything with Angus. She must have been mad to go rushing over to Dallas like that. What on earth was she to do?

Claire's mind was racing. I'm deeper in than any of them, she thought; after all, I got the number. Once let them get hold of my name and find out that I'm going to marry Nigel and it will be splashed all over the place. Nigel couldn't stand that. It would finish him. I won't let them spoil things for Nigel and me now. I've worked hard and waited long enough, and besides it can't do anybody any good.

I ought to go with Val, Guinea was thinking. I'm the two ends and middle of a louse if I don't go. But I can't risk it, it might upset everything for Monnie if I was dragged into a thing like that. After all, she's only on probation.

Claire turned to Val persuasively. "Look, my dear, there's no sense in any of us sticking out our necks unnecessarily. Of course if there is any trouble — and I very much doubt if there will be if we lie low — after all, Bessie's got a clear alibi and no paper in the city would risk mentioning the SP in a case like this even if they hate L.F.'s guts. But if there should be any trouble we'll all throw in to help Bessie, and that will be quite the most practical thing we can do."

Val got up without answering and started to take off her uniform. "I'm going to get a taxi now."

"It's plain madness, Val. It's not even as though there were only yourself to be considered, but you're involving us as well, and you've got no right to do that. If you really want to help Bessie, my advice is to wait until she gets in touch with us and we know exactly what's happening. Then, if she needs any money, I'm quite sure everyone would be willing to throw in. What do you say, girls?"

Deb was fervent in her agreement.

Val looked back from the door. "You're a generous bunch, I must say," and was gone before they realised what she was doing.

Claire spoke first. "We should have locked her up. Running off like a harebrained Joan of Arc."

"I've always thought she was a bit unbalanced, living like a hermit the way she does," Deb said harshly.

"She's cuckoo." Guinea's voice was savage.

"If you ask me," Deb added indignantly, "Bessie will be able to look after herself, and I'm quite sure she won't be grateful for anyone rushing up and giving the whole show away. What business is it of Val's, anyway?"

Claire looked at Deb, new understanding lighting her face. "Of course, that's it. Yes, what business is it of hers? She wasn't here when we were arranging things."

"Gawd," said Guinea, "is that right?"

"Too bloody right. Come on, we'd better get back to work."

Deb made a last protest. "I think it's absolutely the limit Val making a heroine of herself and all the time knowing she's the only one of us who wasn't involved."

"Aw gee, I don't think she thought of that," Guinea defended her. "Val's not that kind."

"No?" Claire's voice was grim. "We'll know about that soon enough. All I can say is, if anyone comes here asking questions keep your mouths shut."

As they came out of the office Ursula peered down the corridor. Ever since Val had rushed out without a word of explanation her curiosity had been raised to agony. She knew that whatever the trouble was, they were all in it up to the neck. Well, serve them right! When perfectly healthy girls like Mary Parker died suddenly and mysteriously there was usually something very odd about it. Judging from their conversation and the kind of lives they led it was a wonder something hadn't happened to one of them long ago.

I give up, she thought. As soon as we close I'll go and tell Mrs Molesworth myself. That'll show her I was right all the time. I'll teach her to humiliate me in front of the others. Obviously, the whole Marie Antoinette staff are mixed up in this as well as that old Bessie — probably she's been doing it as a sideline for years. It's my duty to warn Mrs Molesworth that something's wrong. One can't be too careful.

After the last appointment was finished, Claire went out to the reception desk to check up the day's takings. Ursula watched her silently. They both looked up when Elvira sidled in, her eyes bright and restless as a monkey's.

"''Ave you 'eard the news?'' she whispered dramatically.

"What news?'' Claire's eyes were guarded.

"About Mary Parker. Died in 'orspital this afternoon.''

"Yes, we heard. Terribly sad, isn't it?''

Elvira looked from one to the other searchingly.

"Awful. Gimme a real shock, it did. And 'er so young.'' She clasped her bony fingers to her chest, closed her eyes, then opened them suddenly. Her whole body was tense with curiosity. "What 'appened?''

"I haven't the faintest idea,'' Claire replied coolly, checking the notes Ursula handed to her, "but it's all very sad.''

"I was that shook up I nearly fainted when Trissie told me. 'I don't believe it,' I said, flat like that. 'Someone's 'avin' you on, me girl.' Why, only last Tuesday I seen 'er with me own eyes goin' inter the powder room early in the morning with 'er sister, and lookin' as well as Miss Cronin 'ere. Yer never can tell, can yer?''

Ursula shuffled indignantly.

"''It must be a mistake,' I says to Trissie. But she said 'No' she 'eard it from Daphne and she got it straight from the 'orse's mouth, as you might say, meanin' Gwennie down on the switch.''

Claire's heart shrivelled with foreboding. You couldn't beat the grapevine. "It's true enough, unfortunately. They rang here and Miss Cronin took the message.''

"Purely by accident,'' Ursula explained hastily. "They asked for you.''

"Oh, did they? Why didn't you call me, then? I was just next door.''

Ursula's eyes snapped and her mouth curled into an

ugly line. "If I had known you were personally concerned, I would have called you."

Elvira gnawed her nails in rapture.

"There's nothing personal about it at all. It's merely that I like to run my salon efficiently and I can't possibly hope to do that if you persistently interfere, as Mrs Molesworth was obliged to remind you this morning." Claire turned and stalked down the corridor and into her office.

"Cor lumme," Elvira breathed, "you 'ave put yer foot in it proper, 'aven't you, luvvie?"

"I've done nothing of the sort. And I'll be grateful if you'll mind your own business." Ursula got up. She'd show them who had put their foot in it. Her conscience was clear. She'd go straight down to Mrs Molesworth.

"What's the row about?" Guinea asked Claire as she came into the office.

"The news is all over the whole bloody pub. That bitch of a Gwennie has broadcast it to everyone."

"Oh," Deb put a tremulous hand to her mouth. "That's awful."

"And God only knows what the police have got out of Bessie by now."

There was a knocking on the outer door of the salon. Deb drew her breath sharply.

"Jeepers," Guinea breathed, "who's that?"

Claire slammed the drawer of her desk, turned the key and pocketed it. "Probably the police. Come on and remember you know nothing."

Guinea sped along the corridor to open the door, but Elvira beat her to it.

"It's a cable," she said, peering at the envelope the messenger handed her, "for Miss Alice Parker."

"I'll take it." Ursula came swiftly round her desk.

Claire snapped it out of her hand. "Not while I'm in charge of the salon." She signed the messenger's book and tipped him.

Ursula was trembling. "You've no right to do that. Making a fool of me in front of a telegraph boy."

Claire put the envelope into her pocket. "My dear Miss Cronin, nobody needs to make a fool of you, you've only got to be natural."

"I wonder what's inside it," Elvira asked in an awed voice. "Think we ought to open it?"

"No, I don't."

There was a faint rap on the door.

"Hell!" Guinea breathed. "Who's that"

Deb opened the door a couple of inches and drew it wider to admit Val. They stared at her in silence. She had obviously been crying.

"Cor lumme," Elvira exclaimed hopefully, "you look real upset, luvvie. 'Ave you heard the news?"

Claire put a firm hand on her shoulder and pushed her towards the door. "I'm awfully sorry, my dear, but I can't possibly fix up that business this afternoon."

"But...but..." Elvira wriggled protestingly.

Guinea took her other arm and opened the door.

"Come up and see me first thing in the morning," Claire said sweetly.

"Oh, but..." Elvira's voice rose to a wail.

"Amscray." Guinea pushed her out of the door. She shut it behind her and slipped down the latch.

"Come along into the office, all of you," Claire ordered, "we don't want anyone listening in."

Ursula drew herself up. "I'm going straight down to Mrs Molesworth to tell her everything I know."

Guinea took her by the shoulders and ran her down the corridor. "Get in there, you pimp, before I dong you one."

Val slumped into a chair.

"What happened?" Claire demanded.

"The police came for Bessie just after I got there."

"What did they do?"

"They took her to the station for questioning."

"My God!"

Ursula turned to make for the door, panic-stricken and shrill. "I'm not going to stay here. I'm not going to stay here. This has got nothing to do with me."

"Shut up." Guinea pushed her back into the room. "You're in it right up to the neck like the rest of us."

Ursula sobbed hysterically. "It's not true, you're just making it up. You all hate me. That's why you're doing it."

Guinea blocked the doorway. "I warned you your stickybeaking'd get you into trouble one of these days."

"There's no harm in taking a message. Bessie was on a public telephone and she was afraid of being cut off."

"And just exactly what did Bessie say to you?" Claire asked quietly.

"She said Mary Parker was dead."

"You don't think we murdered her, do you?"

Ursula's voice rose shrilly. "Just because I don't live the kind of life you girls live you needn't think I don't know anything. All the mystery and the whispering this week... I bet from the way you're going on Mary Parker's had an... an illegal operation and you all had something to do with it, and that's why you're so frightened. You think you'll all be dragged in as witnesses like that case in Brisbane."

"And you're not frightened?"

"I haven't got anything to be frightened about."

"No? Of course you didn't take the message giving the doctor's phone number, did you?"

"I didn't, I swear I didn't."

"Well, it's in your handwriting — time and price and all — with your initials on it. I put it away carefully."

"Whacko!" Guinea slapped Ursula on the shoulder. "Copped!"

"I did nothing of the sort."

"Not on Tuesday morning when Mrs Cavendish rang and asked for me and I had left express instructions with you for Alice to take the call?"

Ursula put the back of her hand against her mouth, recollection dawning in her eyes. "But... oh no..."

"Oh yes, Miss Cronin. Up to your old game of trying to find out other people's business instead of calling them to the phone. Well, this time you got your fingers good and properly burnt. And it might also interest you to know that if there's any nonsense from you about telling Mrs Molesworth what you know, or shooting off your mouth to the police, you're in this too. If we go to court as witnesses, you come too. If our names get into the press reports, so does yours. And if our faces are splashed all over the Sunday papers, they'll splash yours too. We'll see to that, won't we, girls?''

"Too right," Guinea said darkly. "I reckon with that note in her handwriting they'll say she's practically an accomplice."

"But...it's murder," Ursula gasped.

"Sure," Guinea agreed, "and if you don't keep your trap shut you'll swing with the rest of us."

Ursula gathered up her handbag and gloves and stumbled from the room. They breathed a sigh of relief when the outer door slammed behind her.

Guinea slipped down the safety catch again. "I reckon she's safe."

Claire gathered herself together with an effort. "Did you have a chance to talk to Bessie at all?" she asked Val.

"Only for a few minutes."

Claire fiddled with the nail file. Deb and Guinea stared at Val. Claire spoke without looking at her. "Did she...give you any message?"

Val lifted her reddened eyes and looked at each in turn. "She said to tell you all not to worry. And if anyone asked you any questions to say you didn't know anything about it. She and Alice decided that at the hospital when they knew the way it was going."

Claire lifted a face illumined by relief. Deb straightened herself as though a burden had slid off her shoulders. Guinea shuffled uncomfortably.

Val went on tonelessly. "She said to tell you that she was in it, anyway, and there was no sense in any of you being dragged in and not to be silly and think you had to do anything about her."

Claire got up. "Thanks for bringing the message, Val."

Val looked up at her. "Don't think I'm trying to put the blame onto you people. I know really that Bessie's right, and there's no sense in you being dragged into it, but I think you all ought to know just what taking the rap really means to Bessie. She's only been staying at the SP to get a bit of money together till her son comes down from the Islands. He's got his discharge because his wife has gone out of her mind with worry, trying to run a business and look after the children as well, and they've had to put the kids in a home because Bessie's landlady wouldn't let her have them there. Well, her son's due back next week and Bessie was going to make a home for them all. So what she's doing and all the awful publicity she'll get, even if nothing worse happens, is just about going to bust everything wide open for her."

"Christ," said Guinea, "what a lot of gutless wonders we are."

"I agree with you," Claire said.

Deb met her eyes a moment and turned away. "Oughtn't we to open that cable?" she suggested, "it might be important."

Claire drew it out of her pocket and slit the top of the envelope with a nail file. She stared at it.

"What's it say?" Guinea looked over her shoulder. She read aloud: "CABLED FIFTY POUNDS GPO TODAY. GIVE MARY ALL MY LOVE. FRANK."

They were silent. Claire folded the form and put it back in her pocket.

"We ought to post it to Alice tonight," Guinea said.

"I'll fix it up if you like," Val offered. "I'm going straight back to Bessie now. I can drop it in a postbox."

"Thanks, Val." Claire handed it to her. "Not that it's any good now, but still it's all we can do. That poor little wretch of an Alice must be going through hell."

Guinea kicked a hassock across the room. "Wouldn't it!" she muttered furiously, "wouldn't it!"

Claire slipped down the latch of the outer door after Val. "Well, that's that. Come on into the office, both of you. What we all need is a good stiff drink."

"And how!" Guinea followed her.

Claire unlocked her cupboard and took out a bottle of brandy, pouring a stiff nip into three cups.

"Not too much for me, Claire," Deb said, "I'm going out tonight."

"Do you want any water, Guin?"

"Just a drop. What I'd like to do is to get real stinking high and not wake up till tomorrow morning."

Claire drank hers neat and poured herself another. "There's no use moping about it, my pet. It's just one of those things."

Guinea shuddered, frowned into her cup and gulped the brandy down. "It gives me gooseflesh when I think of that cable. It's all so damn silly."

"Well, that's how life is and there doesn't seem to be anything we can do about it." Claire tried to be matter-of-fact. "Now, if we get a move on and tidy the place up a bit we can all get away just as soon as it's done."

Guinea laughed suddenly. "I bet Old Crow's had kittens by now. If a traffic cop so much as looks at her she'll probably die of fright."

"Serve her right. It's not often pimps get paid in their own coin. Now, let's tear into things and get away. I want to get home to that man of mine. What time's your appointment, Deb?"

"Not till half past eight. But I have to dress."

"Jeepers, so've I."

"Oh well, you'll both have plenty of time, it's only just after six."

Deb stripped the massage table and threw the sheets into the laundry basket viciously. She really must stop going over and over the whole thing. All she'd do would be to ruin her evening with Angus again. He'd been pretty decent about it last night, but you couldn't expect a man to put up with tantrums twice running.

Hell, Guinea said to herself, putting away a permanent-wave machine. She wished to God she didn't have to go to a party and be shown off to Byron's brass hats. She felt so down in the mouth she would never be able to put on the show he expected of her. What she'd really like to do would be to go out and see how Monnie was getting on and have a talk with Aunt Annie. But if she did that she'd most likely run into Kim, and the way she was feeling she couldn't take that either. The sooner she put half the world between that bloke and herself the better. Though she had to hand it to him, he'd behaved pretty decently about Monnie. That was typical of him — behave like a louse when things were going well, and then when you were all set to slit his throat, he turned up trumps when you were in a jam.

Claire collected the jars and bottles of cosmetics and took them to the showcase under the big mirror. The soft lights burnished her upswept hair. "You don't look too bad, my girl," she said to her reflection. Her eyes were brilliant and the dark smudges that had been so noticeable the week before had practically gone. "That's what happiness does for you. I believe you've put on a bit of weight too."

She sighed. Poor little Mary Parker! Plain, shy, uncertain of herself, born to marry some equally shy, uncertain young man and have two or three children and scrape along on a small salary somewhere in the suburbs. And war and love had brought her to this. Mary wasn't made for tragedy. She pushed the thought of her away. They were damned lucky that Bessie and Alice had turned out the kind who could hold their tongues. That was something you wouldn't have expected of Alice. But then, you never really knew what people were like inside or how they'd behave when the pressure was put on them. There would be no fuss now. And, although the police could make it damned unpleasant, there was nothing at all they could pin on Bessie. These things were only a nine-days' wonder anyway. No, there was absolutely nothing more she could have done than she had done, and the fact that Deb and Guinea agreed with her showed she was right. She simply couldn't let anything interfere with her marriage to Nigel. He was so terribly fastidious about sex himself that he simply wouldn't understand this sort of thing...and he'd never get over a public scandal.

The phone bell cut across her thoughts. "It's all right," she called to Guinea, "I'll answer it."

She felt a bit light-headed as she crossed to the reception desk. She really shouldn't have taken all that neat brandy on an empty stomach, but she was feeling fine. Even if it was Mother Molesworth ringing, or L. F. himself, she could manage them. She lifted the receiver and said in her crispest voice: "Marie Antoinette Salon."

Nigel's voice came to her, unfamiliar and distraught.

"Yes, yes, it's Claire. Oh darling! But Nigel, are you all right? You sound ill.... Where have you been all the afternoon, darling?...Not at Joe's?" She gripped the side of the desk. "Our money! You mean you didn't bank it after all?.... Oh no..."

The telephone receiver fell from her hand and clattered on the desk. Guinea came rushing in as she fell.

Deb got a wet cloth for Claire's forehead and chafed her limp hands. Guinea dipped her finger into the brandy and rubbed it on her lips.

"Do you think she's all right, Deb?"

"Her heart feels all right, but she's an awful colour."

"She went down as though someone had donged her."

Deb wiped the wet cloth over Claire's face. "What on earth could have happened?"

"I dunno. She just called out to me she'd answer the phone and the next thing I heard was a bang and I tore in and just caught her as she flopped."

"Do you think it's something about Bessie?" Deb's voice took on a new note.

"What else could it be? Oo — er look, I think she's coming round."

Claire's lids fluttered, she raised them, looked up into the girls' faces and lowered them again.

Guinea slid an arm under her shoulders and raised her a little. Deb held the cup to her lips and Claire sipped the brandy weakly.

"She's a better colour," Deb said hopefully.

"Hold on, Claire, and I'll take you over to the lounge." Guinea gathered her up in her arms and laid her gently on the elaborate Louis Quinze settee.

Claire opened her eyes slowly. "I'm all right now." She put her hands to her head and pushed her fingers through her hair. "I'm awfully sorry. This isn't a bit like me. I must have given you an awful fright."

"Oh my dear, don't worry about us," Guinea fanned her gently with a magazine.

"Did you get some news about Bessie?" Deb was tense with anxiety.

Claire shook her head. Deb relaxed with a faint sigh.

Guinea clasped Claire's hand tightly. "It's not Nigel, is it, kid?"

"Yes," she whispered, "it's Nigel."

"Oh Claire! There hasn't been an accident, has there?"

Claire shook her head. "No. It's just he went to Joe's this afternoon and lost all our money." She closed her eyes again and turned her face away. "I'll be all right if you'll just leave me alone for a minute."

They looked at each other helplessly and went out.

"If I could only get my hands round the neck of that flabby little squirt for a few minutes," Guinea murmured passionately.

"It's awful." Deb's eyes were full of tears. "She's been so happy...and now this. To think that a man you are in love with could do a thing like that to you."

"Love! There's nothing men won't do to you if you give 'em a chance. And the more you love them, the more you're at their mercy. Gimme another drink." Guinea poured herself out a brandy. "Hell, there's a hindoo on this place all right."

"I'll have one too." Deb choked over the strong spirit. "Claire had better come up to my room for a while, she's not fit to go home yet."

"OK. I'll help you up with her. And when she's a bit better I'll ask Blue to get a taxi and I can take her back to her flat on my way home. Byron's not picking me up till eight, so I've got plenty of time."

"That'll suit me too. I've simply got to be ready by eight myself. Let's go and see how she's feeling now."

Claire opened her eyes. "I'm keeping you," she said apologetically. "There's absolutely no need for you two to wait. I'll be quite all right. You get along now and I'll go home later."

"No," Deb insisted. "You're coming up to my room till you feel a bit better and then Guinea's going to take you home. Do you feel well enough to move yet?"

Claire stood up shakily. "Yes, I'm fine, and I don't want to muck up the evening for you and Guin."

"Nonsense, here are your things." Guinea helped her on with her coat.

"Anything else you want?"

"Would you mind wrapping up what's left of the brandy, like an angel."

Deb went into the office and wrapped the bottle up, disguising it as well as she could. Byron's enormous box of flowers was in a corner. She picked it up, took down Guinea's raincoat and carried them out into the boudoir.

Guinea looked at the box in dismay. "Holy mackerel! Have I got to take that florist's shop with me?"

"You can't leave it here. Now come along, Claire." Deb put an arm round her waist and they went to the door, Guinea following with the huge box and the bottle of brandy.

Deb tucked the eiderdown round Claire. "Now, how does that feel?"

"Marvellous, thank you. I'll be absolutely all right in no time."

"There's no hurry, so stay there till you feel quite fit. I'll go and have my bath and get on with my dressing if you don't mind, and you'd better have a bath here too, Guin. It'll save you time when you get home."

"Whacko! If old Mother Molesworth finds me dipping in an SP tub she'll probably call for the water police."

Claire tried to laugh. "That'll be a break for them."

The phone rang. Deb stared at it crossly. It couldn't be Angus, it wasn't even seven yet.

She picked up the receiver.

Val's voice came to her. "Oh Deb, thank heavens I've got you. I've been ringing and ringing the salon and I thought I'd never get on to anyone."

"What's wrong now?" Deb asked sharply.

Val's voice faded. The sound of a tram roared, dim and far off, through the phone.

"Speak up, I can't hear." Deb's voice was full of impatience.

"It's about Bessie."

"Oh." Why on earth did the fool of a girl have to go shouting Bessie's name for the whole switch to hear? "What about her?"

"The landlady's turned her out of her flat and now she won't let me in to get her things because she says she owes her rent."

"What on earth are you ringing me for? I can't do anything about it." Damn her, Deb thought, the whole SP will be listening in by now.

Val's voice was stubborn. "I can't manage by myself, Deb. You'll have to come out and help me."

"Good heavens, girl, I can't come out and help you."

"Oh Deb, I can't manage by myself."

There was a silence. Val's voice came again, faint and full of distress. "I can't hear you, Deb. Wait a minute, there's a tram coming."

Deb heard the sound of the tram swelling through the telephone. She replaced the receiver gently. Let her think they'd been cut off.

Claire was sitting up, her face full of alarm. "Is anything wrong?"

"Nothing we can help. That was Val."

"Val?" Guinea started up. "What did she want?"

Deb picked up her spongebag and shower cap. "The little fool," she said furiously, "shouting Bessie's name all over my phone. She's got no more sense than a two-year-old."

"But she wouldn't ring unless there was something really wrong," Guinea persisted.

"It seems the landlady's turned Bessie out of her flat and now she refuses to let Val in to collect her things because she says Bessie owes her rent."

"Oh, but that's plain robbery."

"Well, there's nothing we can do about it tonight and I told her so. I've been through enough with this business one way and another, and I'm not going to have my evening ruined. After all, I hardly even knew Mary Parker."

The phone began to ring again.

"Let it ring," Deb said. "She'll get tired before we do."

Guinea went to the phone, her mouth set in a stubborn line. "Yes Val, it's Guinea here. . . . Yes. You must have been cut off. . . . What? . . . You're going to take her over to your place. . . . OK, kid, don't worry. I'll be out there just as soon as I can get a taxi. Keep your chin up."

Val's voice was full of relief. "Oh Guin. You're marvellous. The landlady's performing like a lunatic and I simply can't manage by myself."

"Don't you worry," Guinea comforted her. "I'll push the old bitch over the balcony if she starts any nonsense with me." She hung up.

Deb looked at her coldly. "Well, you are a fool."

"You're not really going out there, are you, Guin?" Claire asked anxiously.

"What else can I do? Bessie's taking the rap for something she didn't do, and the least I can do is to see that she's not robbed of her few bits and pieces as well."

"Oh nonsense," Deb snapped angrily. "Val has only got to wait till the morning and get the police. All this melodrama . . ."

"Who's going to drag the police into this?"

"But it's ridiculous, Guin," Claire pleaded. "It's nearly seven now and you'll never be ready for Byron at eight."

"He'll have to wait."

"You ought to have more sense," Deb threw at her angrily. "How's Byron going to like your being mixed up in an affair like this?"

"I have no idea, but I'll soon find out." Guinea began to put on her raincoat. "I'm terribly sorry, Claire, but I'm afraid you'll have to manage by yourself."

"It doesn't matter about me, Guin. It's you I'm worried about. You've got the chance of your life with Byron, everything you could want, and you're mad to risk it. You'll never get back by eight. And besides, you haven't any idea how he'll take a thing like this if it gets into the papers. Men can't bear a scandal."

"No? Well, that's just too bad."

Deb looked at her bitterly. "No decent man would like his fiancée being mixed up in a thing like this."

"Listen," Guinea said, tying a scarf round her head, "if Byron doesn't like me the way I am, he can lump it."

She slammed the door behind her.

Blue opened the lift door and Guinea stepped in.

"Hullo," he said, making no attempt to start the lift. His face was solemn. "Bad news about that little redhead. You could have knocked me down when I heard she'd passed out. You know Bessie got me to take her out the back way on Tuesday. Been crying her eyes out all the morning from the look of her. Crikey! It's a helluva mess for poor old Bessie to be landed into, isn't it?"

Guinea saw a sudden ray of hope. "I bet Doss is pretty upset."

"She will be when she hears. It's her afternoon off and she's out visiting some friend or other. If I could have got hold of her she'd've been up at Bessie's long ago telling them John Hops where they got off."

No help there. "That's where I'm going, to Bessie's. She's been taken to the police station for questioning and Val's in strife with that old shark of a landlady over Bessie's bits and pieces. She just can't cope. Be a pal and get me a taxi.''

"Some hope on a night like this."

"Oh, Blue, I've got to get there."

"Tell you what. A mate of mine, Billo Bennett from me old unit, has brought his taxi round and he's in the bar now with Lofty waiting for me to come off duty. I'll get hold of them."

The lift stopped at the ground floor. Blue set it for HOLD and shot off to the bar for Billo.

Deb pushed her fringe back from her forehead with shaking hands. "Really! The place is like a madhouse and Guinea's the maddest of the lot."

Claire sighed and lay back on the pillow. "I suppose she feels she has to do it," adding uncertainly, "Some queer idea of loyalty."

Deb swung round with blazing eyes. "Loyalty?" she spat out the word venomously. "More like exhibitionism, if you ask me. Rushing off like that when there's not the slightest need for it. I don't call that loyalty."

Claire looked up at her in surprise. Deb's face was flushed, her mouth drawn down at the corners. She's furious, Claire thought. I've never seen her so angry before. It makes her look old.

"Oh, Guin's just an impulsive kid. You can't blame her..."

"Well, I do blame her. It's time that girl grew up. Hasn't she any loyalty to Byron at all? No — off she goes rushing wildly into God knows what trouble..." She caught the look of surprise on Claire's face and pulled herself up. "Oh, well," she said, dismissing it with a shrug. "I suppose it's none of my business, but it's time Guinea learnt that if you don't look out for Number One in this world, no one will do it for you."

Claire pressed her hand to her head. Deb was at her side in compunction. "Oh, you poor darling. You're all upset."

Claire tried to control herself, but tears ran down her

cheeks and sobs racked her thin body. Deb sat by her solicitously bathing her temples. "You look absolutely knocked up. You simply can't go home tonight — not feeling the way you are."

"But I must," Claire protested. "I couldn't take your bed."

"Nonsense, I won't be home till late, and I can easily fix up a bed. That chair pulls right out. No, I insist on your staying here the night."

"But Deb," Claire dropped her eyes. "You see — Nigel —"

"Oh, damn Nigel! Don't tell me you care two hoots what happens to Nigel, after what he's done to you."

"I'm afraid I haven't quite taken it in yet."

"You'll take it in only too soon. All your future smashed just because he hadn't the guts to keep away from gambling."

"It's my fault...in a way. I shouldn't have left the money with him."

"But you can't go on with a man like that — someone you've got to treat like a child because you can't rely on him."

Claire nodded drearily. "No, I suppose you're right. But he's never done anything like this before." She choked, and the tears overflowed again.

Deb soothed her. "Lie back and rest now, and when you feel a bit better get right into bed."

"You're awfully kind, and I'm ashamed of myself to be going on like this but well, I banked so much on the win and now...it just seems like the end of everything."

"It's not, my dear. You're well rid of him, and you're so attractive, in no time there'll be someone else. And this time it'll be someone you can depend on instead of his depending on you."

Claire put her hands behind her head and stared into space. No, there'll never be anyone for me but Nigel. Aloud, she said: "This time I'm finished with him," and her words rang hollow in her own ears.

Deb patted her hand affectionately. "That's the most sensible thing I've heard you say. Absolutely the most sensible." She got up and went to the wardrobe.

Claire watched her enviously, a fountain of pain welling up within her. You're lucky, she thought. You don't know how lucky. Two men mad about you — a child — security and luxury waiting for you to take them; and now, with the anger washed out of your face and excitement warming it, you're young and lovely. Of course you'll marry Angus.

Watching Deb's absorbed face as she hung her suit up in the breeze from the window, Claire wondered what she was really feeling. Would she find perhaps that Jack was part of her fibre so that cutting him out of her life would be like cutting part of herself away without an anæsthetic? They had anæsthetics for everything today, but not for love. Why didn't they find an anæsthetic for love?

Deb came over to the bed. "Is there anything else I can get you before I have my bath?"

"I could do with a brandy. Very large."

Guinea pressed her finger on the old-fashioned bell-push and heard the bell jangle in the depths of the house. No one answered, but she saw the curtain on one of the front windows move slightly. She pressed the bell again; still no one came. She stepped over to the window and rapped on it. There was no answer.

"Want any 'elp?" A voice bawled from the taxi drawn up at the kerb.

"Not just yet, Lofty," Guinea called back, "but if somebody doesn't get a move on pretty quickly, I may have to call on you and Billo to kick this damn door down."

There was a rustle inside the window, and she rapped sharply again. "Would you come and open the door for me, please, and step on it."

There was a smothered sound from inside the room, then the slapping of slippers on the hall linoleum and the front door was opened a crack. A man's bald head gleamed in the hall light. "What is it you're after?" he asked nervously.

"I want to go up to Mrs Napier's room."

He hesitated. She gave the door a push and brushed past him. He retreated, holding the evening paper up against his waistcost as though to defend himself, his adam's apple working up and down above the brass stud that fastened the neckband of his collarless shirt.

"Would you please tell me where her room is?" Guinea demanded.

"Er...er..." he seemed unable to speak.

"Then, will you please tell me where I can find the landlady?"

"Oh! just a minute." He peered at her owlishly over half-moon glasses, then shuffled along to the foot of the stairs and stood there looking like a little black elephant in his baggy pants.

"Mrs Bondfield," he called in a quavering voice.

"What d'yer want?" came from the upper hall.

"There's a lady here askin' for Mrs Napier."

Guinea walked to the foot of the stairs. A face peered over the banisters.

"Who let her in?"

"I did."

"What did you do that for?"

"She made me." The little man blinked apologetically.

A heavy, sallow face glared down at Guinea. "A lady, huh! I'd like to know what any lady'd be doing coming asking for Bessie Napier."

Guinea ran swiftly up the stairs and paused when her face was level with the landlady's. Black eyes snapped at her under a mass of dyed black hair.

"Would you please tell me which is Mrs Napier's room?" Guinea asked in her best Marie Antoinette voice.

A door opened at the end of the hall and Val's voice called, "Along here, Guin."

The woman moved to the head of the stairs and barred the way. "Who gave you permission to come into my house?"

"I didn't need anyone to give me permission. This is not a private house." Guinea was now level with the woman, who stood in front of her, broad and powerful, with her feet apart, one strong hand holding the knob of the balustrade, the other flat against the wall.

"Well, you've had your trouble for nothing and now get out."

"What are you afriad of? The police?"

"Me frightened of the police!" the landlady screamed. "It's not me that's done anything to be frightened of the police. I'm a respectable woman, I am, and I run a respectable house. And what's more I don't have nobody in it the police are after, neither."

"Listen, I came here to get the things out of Mrs Napier's room and I'm going to get them out. Are you going to move out of my way or have I got to make you?"

"It's not Mrs Napier's room any more. Do you think I'd have a woman like that living in my house again? Besides, she owes me rent, she does, and so long as she owes me money I'm the one to take charge of her things.''

"Bessie doesn't owe her any rent." Val's voice came loud and indignant.

"Call me a liar, would you?" The landlady bellowed threateningly.

"I'll call you a lot worse than that if you don't get out of my way." Guinea put a foot on the next step.

The landlady stood firm. "The old woman's stuff's staying where it is and so are you."

"That's what you think." Guinea leaped up the last step and pushed her arm off the wall. The woman staggered, clutching at the balustrade for support, and sat down with a thump while Guinea darted up the hall to Val.

"I'll have you up for assault!" the woman screamed after her as the door banged.

"Oh Guin, you were wonderful," Val looked at her with admiring eyes. "You can't imagine what she's been like. When I came back from the phone, she wouldn't let me in at all, although Bessie had given me her keys. I sneaked in when I thought she'd be having her tea, but she heard me coming up the stairs and came after me roaring like a bull. I just managed to get in here and slam the door and she's been standing out there threatening me with the most dreadful things. She says Bessie owes her money and I know she doesn't because I saw her pay last Sunday morning and the receipts are in this old vase. Look, she's paid up till next Sunday."

"That's an old game. What she wants is to get her hands onto the stuff and Bessie'll never see it again. It's a furnished room, isn't it?"

"Yes. But all the blankets and the linen and crockery and these vases are Bessie's. I know exactly, because we talked over just what things she'd have when she set up house for her son."

"What on earth are you going to do with them if you do get them out?"

Val flashed her a glance. "I'm taking them over to my

flat," she announced, removing Bessie's clothes from the wardrobe and beginning to fold them. "I'll store everything there, and as soon as the police let Bessie go I'm going to take her over to stay with me for as long as she likes."

Guinea looked at her in astonishment. "But I thought there wasn't enough room. I mean...you didn't..."

"I know what you mean, that I didn't want anybody to stay with me. That's perfectly true, I didn't. But this is different. Bessie's been good to me and now I've got to see her through. She can have my room and there's a divan in the lounge that'll do me, and with what I earn and my allotment I've got enough for us both."

"I think you're a brick."

Val looked up at her, one hand on the lid of the open suitcase. "It's what Ven would want me to do; I know that now. Even if he does come home while she's there, he won't mind. He'd hate to think of me living there alone just wrapped up in myself. That's not his idea of things at all. I see that now."

"If he's the kind of bloke you say he is, I'm sure you're right."

"I know I'm right."

"Well, where do we go from here?"

"That's just the trouble. How on earth are we going to get the things to my place? That awful old woman'll never let us out with them."

"Give me the front door key."

Guinea went onto the balcony, pushed back the sliding window and whistled. Lofty's head peered out of the taxi waiting below.

"Listen, Lofty," she called, "we're in a spot. Do you think you could give us a hand?"

Lofty opened the taxi door, unfolded himself, and stretched up to his full height. He looked enormous and menacing in the street light with his greatcoat flapping in the rain and his slouch hat shoved onto the back of his head. A slow smile split his face. "Could I what!"

A short man emerged from the other side of the taxi,

flexed his knees, settled his belt and walked round beside Lofty.

"Catch," Guinea called, "here's the key of the front door. Come right up the stairs."

Lofty jerked his thumb at the door. "Come on, Billo. Over the top!"

Val looked at Guinea in astonishment. "Well, you certainly know how to pick your boyfriends."

"They're Blue's cobbers. I'd never have got out here but for them."

They heard the front door slam and the measured tread of heavy feet up the stairs and along the upper hall. Guinea opened the door to let them in. Lofty beamed, Billo grinned toothlessly.

"This is Lofty and Billo, Val. Meet Val Blaski, boys."

They both raised two fingers in solemn salute.

"Who's makin' the trouble?" Lofty demanded. "The bloomin' house is deserted as far as we can see."

"I'll bet it is," Guinea said grimly. "But it was a different story with us. That old hag of a landlady says she won't let us take anything because Bessie's behind with the rent, although Val has the receipts here up to next Sunday."

"She won't, won't she?" Lofty's voice was smooth. "Well, you girls just go ahead and start to get things packed up."

"We haven't got anything to pack them in, except a couple of suitcases. We'll just have to wrap them up in blankets."

"Oh," Lofty stroked his nose. "Well, you get things started anyway, and we'll go along and have a bit of a chinwag with the old girl. She'll probably come round. Billo 'ere 'as a wonderful personality. Come on, mate."

"We'll leave it to you boys." Guinea and Val watched them tramp heavily down the hallway. Lofty's great fist hammered on every door in turn as he roared: "Where's the landlady? Won't somebody tell me where the landlady is?"

They traversed the top hall and returned, stamping down the stairs and chanting a rhythmic: "Ho-ho-ho, ho-ho-

ho." Doors slammed downstairs. The search for the landlady continued. At last there was silence.

"My God," Val breathed, closing the door. "I hope they don't murder her."

"My God," Guinea said fervently, "I hope they do. Now, let's start sorting."

They had finished clearing out the cupboards on the balcony when Lofty and Billo returned and put down two large packing cases in the middle of the floor.

"You're a nice pair, you are." Lofty looked at the girls and shook his head reproachfully.

"Why, what did she say?"

"It was all a mistake. You misunderstood her, that's what you did. She's just a poor little widder woman with an 'eart of gold."

"Lofty," Guinea clapped him on the back, "you're a marvel."

Lofty jerked his thumb at the grinning Billo. "It's Billo 'as done it, 'e's a wonder, Billo is. Specially with the wimmen."

Billo grinned.

Val stared at the cases. "How on earth did you get those?"

"Souvenired 'em," said Lofty with a broad wink, "off of that cupboard outside the landlady's door. That kind of thing's right up Billo's alley."

"Is it really all right?" Val asked.

"Right as pie. Now you can really get on with your packing, girls, and as soon as there's something to take, Billo and me'll start carting it down."

Guinea glanced at her watch. Heavens, she'd forgotten all about Byron and it was twenty to eight. But she couldn't leave Val to cope with everything, even with Lofty and Billo, not with all Bessie's personal things to go through. Well, if Byron didn't understand that she wasn't the kind to stand him up and that only something terribly serious would keep her, then there was nothing she could do about it. She turned to the others. "Let's get cracking, there's a hell of a lot to be done."

"Righto!" Lofty agreed, "but before we get stuck into it, I reckon we could all do with a drop of pig's ear after what we been through. Billo's got a coupla bottles in the boot. What do you say, girls?"

Val looked at Guinea, who nodded. "Whacko! It'll save me life."

"'Op down and fetch it up, will yer, Billo?"

Billo grinned and departed.

"Now," said Lofty, looking around the room. "Where do we start?"

Two hours later Billo pulled the taxi up at the foot of Forbes Street. Lofty waved a lordly hand. "Miss Malone's mansion up the steps on yer left, Woolloomooloo on yer right, and Kings Cross behind yer. Take yer pick."

"I'll take the lot," Guinea laughed, "if I can only get out from under this pile of bedding."

Billo pushed the sliding bundle back onto the packing cases.

"Wait a minute," said Lofty. "Now then, little lady, get up orf of me lap till I get out and let Miss Guinea Malone unwrap herself from the gears. It's stopped rainin' so you won't get wet."

"I can't move," Val groaned, "your knees are up around my neck."

"You're mistaken," Lofty corrected her, "they're your knees. Anyway, peel yourself orf of the door 'andle and I'll open up and we'll all sort ourselves out."

The door swung open and Lofty put his legs out onto the kerb. Val straightened herself with difficulty. "O-o-oh, I'll never be the same again."

Guinea dropped a kiss on Billo's cheek. "Thanks a lot, Billo. I don't know what we'd have done without you."

Billo grinned.

She slid her legs out onto the footboard. Lofty put a hand under her arm and hoisted her onto the pavement. "There y'are," he said, "everybody got the same set of limbs they started with?"

"I think so," Guinea laughed, "but I won't be really sure till the morning."

"Nothin' left in the back?" Lofty inquired.

Billo peered over his shoulder at the luggage piled up to the roof.

"Nothing. I only brought myself."

Val got into the car and sank onto the seat with a sigh of relief. "That's better. Lofty, you've got knees like a praying mantis."

Lofty tucked himself in beside her and looked down with condescension. "I'd 'ave you know, young lady, them knees 'as been admired over two 'emispheres and through two wars."

Guinea leaned her arm on the window. "I hope you'll be safe with these two, Val. Keep a special eye on Billo."

"I 'ave everything under control, includin' Billo," Lofty informed her with dignity.

Guinea put her arms round his neck and gave him a warm kiss. "Goodnight, Lofty. You've both been marvellous."

"Jumping Jehosophat!" Lofty looked down at her in delight. "I'd do it all over again for that."

The taxi moved off. Lofty thrust his head through the window and waved. "Hoorroo!" His voice came back to her as they gathered speed down William Street.

Guinea turned towards the steps and pulled her coat closer as a flurry of rain caught her. She wondered if there would be any message from Byron or if he'd just gone off in a huff. You couldn't blame him if he had; it was pretty hard on a man when he'd got up a party specially to show his future wife off to his brass hat friends. She wouldn't have done a thing like this to him deliberately, for the world. He was such a nice bloke.

The rain drove against her face as she went up the hill. What a muddle life was! Well, there was no use worrying now. What she had better do was get a good sleep, and it would all sort itself out in the morning.

FRIDAY

I

Mary Parker's death rated one inch at the foot of a column on a back page of the morning papers, but the SP bush telegraph, which carried important and unimportant news alike from basement to Who's Who, had spread a highly coloured version of the story throughout the whole hotel by ten o'clock on Friday morning.

To Mr Sharlton and Mrs Molesworth it seemed that the whole building around them was humming like telegraph wires on a windy day. They had read and reread the few obscure lines in the paper and drawn comfort from the shortness of the notice and anonymity of the statement: "A woman has been held for questioning."

"If this is all there is, we've got nothing to worry about," Thelma reassured L. F. "It's not as though the girl was anything but a nonentity, and I can't imagine anyone being remotely interested in what happens to Bessie."

L. F. shot her a malignant glance. "Not even the Town Crier? What I can't understand is how you didn't know long ago what sort of game that Napier woman was up to."

"Oh Lance, that's quite unjust. After all, I can't be held responsible for the private lives of the staff."

"I still think you ought to be able to pick that sort by now, after all your experience."

She crossed over and put a hand round his shoulder. "Whatever happens to Bessie Napier, there's not a paper in town would dare to mention the South Pacific in connection with a case like this. Not even the Town Crier column. Don't worry so much, darling."

"You'd worry if you'd heard what Veale said when I rang him. He and Twyning will be round any minute now."

"I don't know why you rang him at all."

"And what would Veale have to say if I didn't ring him and by some stroke of bad luck the South Pacific was dragged in? I hope you've warned the Marie Antoinette staff to keep their mouths shut. And for God's sake, if any reporters do turn up, keep yours shut too. You always talk too much."

Thelma looked at him stricken. "Oh, Lance."

There was a knock at the door and the commissionaire put his head round; his eyes were popping. "Mr Sharlton, sir," he whispered breathlessly, "the reporters are here."

L. F.'s distinguished pallor took on a sickly tinge.

"What do they want?" Thelma demanded.

"I...I didn't ask them."

"Tell them to wait."

The commissionaire retired. L. F. turned and snarled accusingly. "There you are, what did I tell you?"

The door opened and a young man looked in. "Can you spare a couple of minutes, Mr Sharlton?"

He came in, followed by a flaxen-haired girl, whom Thelma disliked on sight. L. F. waved them graciously to chairs, seated himself behind the desk, cleared his throat and looked from one to the other with funereal gravity. "And what is it you want?" he asked.

"We're trying to trace a US sergeant," the young fellow explained cheerfully. "The lucky cove has just got third prize in the lottery and we thought it might make a story."

L. F.'s skin returned to its natural pallor. Thelma poured over the reporters the smile usually reserved for guests in the ten-thousand-a-year class. "I think the reception desk might be able to give us some information," she purred, picking up the house telephone. "What name is it?"

"Homer P. Alcorn. They said at the desk that he booked out last Friday and we thought you'd be the most likely ones to know where he'd gone."

L. F. beamed on them. "Homer P. Alcorn, of course,

of course. A most distinguished and charming young fellow. His father is a millionaire."

"Well, what do you know!" The young reporter looked at his companion in disgust. "The cove's lousy with money already and he goes and wins three thousand quid in the lottery!"

L. F. got up. "If you'd care to come up with me to the office on the first floor, we shall see if he left a forwarding address."

He opened the door, motioning to the girl to precede him, bowed her out with his far-famed courtesy and followed her, leaving Thelma and the young man to look after themselves. He rang for the lift with an imperial gesture and chatted affably to the girl.

When Blue opened the lift door, L. F. ceremoniously ushered the party in. "First floor," he commanded.

The reporter took out his notebook. "We do appreciate all the trouble you're taking for us, Mr Sharlton. Now, perhaps there are some personal details you could give us about this Homer P. Alcorn?"

"Crikey," Blue blurted out. "Did you say Alcorn?"

"Alcorn's right. Homer P."

"Strike me pink! Don't say anything's happened to him on top of everything else!"

"Only winning three thousand pounds in the lottery this morning. Ticket number 9571."

Blue gaped. "Say that again."

"Why, do you know anything about him?"

Blue stopped the lift with such suddenness that Thelma staggered against the side. "Really!" she exploded wrathfully.

He began to examine the varied contents of a shabby wallet with complete disregard for the fact that they were marooned between floors, and that the lift bell had begun to buzz insistently.

"Know him?" he said. "Why, we was real cobbers. Take a dekko at this."

The reporters read the inscription on the lottery ticket he

held out to them.

"To my old pal Blue Johnson from Homer P. Alcorn in settlement of a debt of honour."

"What a story!" they exclaimed together. "What about coming out somewhere to give us the strong of it?"

Blue laid the ticket carefully in his wallet, put the wallet back in the pocket of his faded jungle green shirt and buttoned up his tunic. The reporters began to question him with breathless excitement. He swung the handle with great deliberation and the lift started downwards. Before Thelma and L. F. realised what was happening the door slid open at the ground floor.

Horatio Veale and Dan D'Arcy-Twyning were standing there. L. F. stepped out.

"Good morning, Mr Veale, Mr D'Arcy-Twyning."

"Good morning." Veale cast a suspicious glance at the reporters standing in the lift with their notebooks open. "We had better go up to the boardoom, I think."

"Certainly." L. F. stood aside and the reporters stepped out. He waved the two directors into the lift. "Sixth floor," he ordered.

Blue turned and looked at Thelma and the three men. They were all staring straight ahead, studiously ignoring him.

He stepped out of the lift. "Just hang on half a minute, kids," he said, putting his hands on the shoulders of the journalists, "and then we'll hop downstairs and break the news to the little old cheese-and-kisses in the bar. She may be able to rustle up something for us on the strength of it."

"Albert," L. F. snapped impatiently, "we're waiting."

Blue turned and smiled at him. "And you can wait!" He bowed to Thelma in cruel caricature of L. F. "Lady!" He turned to the three men and bowed again even more deeply "Gentlemen!" He waved his hand in an expansive gesture. "Your lift," he said, "all yours. And you know where you can put it."

Deb tidied up the massage room and pushed the towels into the linen-basket with unnecessary violence. Guinea was going out to lunch — probably with Colonel Maddocks. He'd been ringing all the morning, though you'd have thought the way she treated him last night would have finished that affair. Some girls seemed to be able to get away with anything.

Val leaned against the wall watching Guinea run a comb through her hair. They were talking about Bessie. "Are you sure they'll let her out on bail?" Guinea asked.

Val nodded, her eyes were sparkling. "Yes, it's all fixed up. Wasn't it lucky I've been putting away Ven's allotment money? He'd be thrilled to think it came in so useful."

"I bet Bessie's thrilled to be going home with you."

"She was so happy she cried. You know, it makes you a bit ashamed, Guin, when you think of all the people Bessie's done a good turn for. After all, that's what got her into this jam — and yet she doesn't expect anything from anyone."

Deb watched the two girls go down the corridor and muttered a grudging answer to their goodbyes. She went into the office.

"You'd think Val had won a lottery," she commented acidly to Claire, "the way she's going on. She's like a hen with chickens."

"She's sweet," Claire said, looking after them wistfully.

She sighed. Her head was aching frightfully and there was a dead, heavy lump in her chest. God, she'd be glad to get home. Home? Home without Nigel. He'd rung three times during the morning but she hadn't spoken to him. Each time Deb had answered for her. She was sorry now that she hadn't spoken herself. Better to tell him straight out that she didn't want to talk to him, didn't want to see him — ever, that so far as she was concerned, she was finished with him. Deb was right — you were better rid of a man you couldn't trust. And if it came to that, she would have a lot more money to spend on herself now that she was rid of Nigel. Less work at home, more freedom. Her heart grew heavy at the thought of all the freedom she would have now that she had finished with Nigel. She sat down at her desk and rested her head on her hands. She should be glad to have found out just what Nigel really was. Better now than when it was too late.

Deb's voice roused her. "Head aching?"

"It is rather. I think I'll get a cuppa." She got up and paused with her hand on the switch, debating with herself whether she couldn't take the afternoon off. She'd be no good to anyone with this head and the bookings weren't heavy. Anyway, let them double up for her for a change. But the thought of facing the flat alone was unendurable. "Deb," she spoke impulsively, "are you going out tonight?"

"I'm not quite sure."

"If you're not, what about having dinner with me? We could go somewhere quiet."

"I'd like that, and I didn't exactly promise Angus..." Deb looked suddenly tired and bewildered. "You see, with Jack coming this weekend.... Oh, it's all so complicated."

"Just when is he arriving?"

"I'm not sure. I've been expecting a telegram all morning."

"Have you told Angus you'll marry him?"

Deb shook her head, a frown of uncertainty darkening her face. "It didn't seem quite fair to say anything definite till I'd seen Jack and told him just how things stand. If only I knew when to expect him. I just couldn't bear him to turn up unexpectedly and find me with Angus. It would look so bad — not that there's any harm in it," she added hastily.

There was a knock at the outer door. "That'll probably be a telegram boy now. I'll go."

Claire's heart leaped and thudded when she heard the voice. Nigel! She took a step and stopped.

"Oh yes, she's still here," Deb was saying in her coldest manner, "but I'm not sure that she wants to see you."

Nigel's voice came to her, pleading, urgent. No longer calm and detached. She started up the corridor. Better see him here, with Deb to back her up, instead of having to go through a scene at home.

He turned to meet her. Claire felt that her heart had stopped beating when she saw his dishevelled hair and ravaged face.

"Oh, Claire —" his voice broke. "I thought, when you didn't come home last night..." He sat down in Ursula's chair and hid his face in his hands. "Not being able to get you all day on the phone. I've been nearly insane."

"Oh, darling," Claire's voice softened. Warmth flowed through her. She hesitated and looked apologetically at Deb, who made no effort to go but stood there looking accusingly at Nigel.

Claire swallowed. "I — I think I'd better talk to him."

Deb shrugged and turned to go down the corridor. "I'll be in the office when you want me."

"Why did you come here?" Claire tried to make her voice cold and accusing.

Nigel looked up at her, his mouth twitching. "I nearly went mad with anxiety last night waiting for you. And then all today. I couldn't bear it any longer."

He got up abruptly and came to her and lifted her two hands in his and pressed his face against them. "Claire my sweet." She felt his tears wet against her palms.

"No," she said sharply, drawing away. "No. This time it's too late."

"Don't say that," he implored. "Oh, my sweet, if you'd only believe I did it for you. I thought — it's our lucky star and if I follow my hunch we'll be safe forever. My little Claire will never have to work again."

He was searching her face for some sign. Her lips were trembling and she tried to choke back the tears.

"Sweet," he pleaded, confidence growing in him again as he took her hands gently and pressed them to his lips. "Oh, my sweet, if you only knew how much I wanted to make things perfect for you."

Claire felt the life flow back into her. She slipped a comb out of her pocket and smoothed back his disordered hair.

His face brightened hopefully. "It was hell without you,

Claire," he whispered. "When I went into the empty flat, there all alone...." He turned her face up to his. "Take me back this time, *ma petite chérie*, and I swear —"

Claire pulled his face down to hers and pressed her lips to his so that she would not hear whatever he was going to promise.

She faced Deb defiantly in the office. "I'm awfully sorry, Deb, but I'm going to take the afternoon off. This head.... Will you arrange things for me?"

"You don't mean...? Surely you're not?"

Claire nodded.

"You don't really mean to say you're going back to him?"

Claire began to take off her uniform. She didn't want to look at Deb, who was standing with one hand on the desk, the other pressed to her throat in a ridiculously theatrical gesture.

Claire pulled up the zipper of her skirt, tied the collar of her blouse and put her coat on. Deb stood watching her in silence, her eyes blazing, two red spots flaring in her cheeks. I don't care what she thinks, Claire said to herself. I'm not going to let her influence me. She turned half apologetically. "Darling, I'm awfully sorry about letting you down for dinner tonight, but you see...."

"Dinner!" Deb exploded. Then a pleading note came into her voice. "Oh Claire, you know it's not the dinner. To think of you letting Nigel talk you over after what he did."

"He's explained," Claire mumbled, setting her hat on her curls carefully. "And he's promised...."

"Promised! You know just how much his promises mean." She seized Claire's arm. "Oh, my dear, you know it simply means you'll have all this over again."

Claire drew her arm away sharply. "I don't care. Nigel needs me."

"Look, Claire, I can help you. I didn't like to tell you before but Angus is going to make a settlement on me as soon as I make up my mind. I could set you up in your own business. That's what you've always wanted, isn't it? Well, I give you my word — now — I'll set you up in business. You can be free." Deb was astonished at the urgency in her own voice. Suddenly it had become desperately necessary to her that Claire should not take Nigel back. Somehow, in a confused way, her own decision to leave Jack was mixed up in it and she passionately wanted Angus's money to be a way out for Claire too.

But Claire was too deeply caught in her own emotion to be aware of Deb's. She was pulling on her gloves with feverish haste while Deb was speaking and heard her offer only as a threat to separate her from Nigel. "It's awfully good of you, darling, and I can't tell you how much I appreciate your offer, but..."

You poor dumb fool, Deb thought savagely, watching her. You've got more glamour than any woman who comes in here. With my money behind you, you could build up a business that would make you safe for life.

Nigel's voice called plaintively from the boudoir. "You haven't forgotten I'm waiting, have you, my sweet?"

Colour suffused Claire's pale face. Magically, it seemed, the strain disappeared. "I'm coming now, darling."

She put out a hand impulsively and squeezed Deb's arm. "I can't tell you how grateful I am for all your kindness, Deb. And now I simply must be going."

Deb listened to her footsteps, light and eager, and Nigel's welcoming voice.

"Claire, *ma petite*, shall we have dinner out? You must be tired."

"No, oh no, darling. Let's go home."

The door closed softly behind them. The Marie Antoinette was silent.

Deb sat down at the desk. Fatigue engulfed her and depression settled down on her like a dark cloud. When a knocking came on the outer door she went to open it mechanically, taking the telegram from the boy and closing the door again. She sat at Ursula's desk and slit open the envelope. It was from Jack.

EXPECT REACH SYDNEY MONDAY AM. SUGGEST ALL

CATCH MIDDAY TRAIN TO VINEYARD. WIRE ME SERVICE
CLUB BRISBANE. LOVE JACK.

Monday! And this was Friday. If she sent a wire now
he'd be certain to get it. Midday Monday? She wasn't going,
of course. She'd wire and arrange to meet him somewhere in
town. He must not come to the SP. Then she would explain
that she couldn't go to the Vineyard with him because she
had promised Nolly to go to her for the last fortnight. She
wouldn't tell him about Angus. Not yet. Not till she had
delivered her ultimatum. But one thing was clear. She wasn't
going to agree to any plan of Jack's about taking over the
Vineyard and living there. She'd explain all that. Her head
was whirling. When would she explain all that? Over lunch in
a café? It seemed a cruel way to meet a man on his first leave
in seventeen months! In the weekend? Jack would expect her
to take Luen up for the weekend whatever else she did.

Deb sat staring at the telegram. The Vineyard with the
red dust swirling between the neat rows of vines was vivid
before the eye of her memory: the creeper spilling onto the
veranda, throwing shadows on the hollowed flagstones; night
falling, swift and full of stars, with the old house on its hill
like an island in a dark sea full of the scent of the orange trees
in bloom; the large shabby bedroom opening on to the garden, the old iron bedstead with chipped paint; faint rustlings
in the vines and a willy-wagtail calling sleepily: "Sweet pretty
creature."

For a moment the picture was so real that she came back
to the present — Ursula's polished desk, the mushroom carpet, the air redolent of the Marie Antoinette perfumes —
with a sense of shock. She got up and walked slowly into the
boudoir, stooping to pick up the petals that had drifted from
a bowl of pink cherry blossom. She liked the elegance of the
boudoir. Somehow it symbolised all that she had learnt in the
two and a half years she had been there. The things Claire
had shown her to be so important for a woman; how to
capitalise your looks and your youth so that when they were
gone you weren't left stranded — left high and dry
somewhere like the Vineyard or Nolly's place, or doomed,

like Claire, to a life of insecurity with a shiftless man who would use — and lose — every penny you made.

The thought of Claire stuck in her throat. In some way her going back to Nigel seemed like a betrayal. She had as good as told Claire, when she offered to set her up in business, that she was going to marry Angus. And married to Angus she would never have dropped her friendship with Claire. But Claire had let *her* down by giving in so weakly to Nigel. It wasn't that she couldn't understand the force of his pleading. She could. The very thought of Jack shook her, stirred old memories, woke old desires. Even now, by some trick of the brain, it was not the cloying sweetness of the Marie Antoinette air through which she moved, but the smell of wet earth, the tang of ripening grapes. And she knew with absolute certainty that once let her sit again at evening in the old-fashioned kitchen with the light shining down on Jack's head and Luen cuddled against him, solitude and love binding them inseparably within the circle of the lamp, she was lost as Claire was lost.

"Nigel needs me." Claire had said in defence of her weakness. But what she really meant was that she needed Nigel. "Well, I don't need Jack," Deb spoke aloud to an invisible opponent, "and he doesn't need Luen or me." A sob rose in her throat. "He's become self-sufficient. He thinks only of himself and what he wants. He doesn't care about me or about Luen any more." She saw Luen as she had seen her at Nolly's — hoydenish, shabby, undisciplined. What had life with Jack to offer Luen? Nothing. Nothing but what she and Nolly had had. It wasn't enough.

Married to Angus, she could give Luen everything a girl had a right to expect from life. Everything she had missed herself. At first the child might resent what she was doing. But that would only be because she was too young to understand. Later, when she had learnt a sense of values, she would realise that her mother had acted for the best for both of them. She found herself framing the words: "You see, darling, Mummy wanted you to have all the wonderful things she never had when she was young. She didn't want you to suffer as she did when she was first married and when you were born." Then she would tell her the true story of the camp by the sea, the primitive shack, and their poverty and isolation. No fairytale, this, of a magic Christmas tree turning the fruit on its branches to gold and jewels. She tried to fan her indignation to flame at the memory of those threadbare days when they were completely down-and-out. She tried to conjure up the misery of their wrecked shack and themselves crouching in the lee of the cave from the winter gale that roared out of the south. But the picture would not come. She saw instead a sickle of sun-drenched sand against a dancing blue sea and Jack, his naked body tanned to leather, silhouetted against the light, a string of silver schnapper in his hand.

She pressed her palms against her eyes to shut out the picture. Fool, she cried angrily to the girl who stared at her out of the past. Fool! What future is there for you and Luen at the Vineyard? Only interminable drudgery and terrifying uncertainty. Living from precarious season to season ...always worrying, always insecure. "No. No!" she cried aloud, crumpling the telegram fiercely. Not back to the Vineyard for her and Luen. He could have that on his own. What was left of their young love was an overbearing husband and a rebellious wife, who couldn't even talk to each other now. She had a right to have a say in how she would live, and it wasn't on the thin edge of sixpence in a rural slum. No! I'll wire him now.

"An urgent telegram," she said to the telegraphist. She'd send it urgent. Make absolutely certain he got it. She had finished with shilly-shallying. She gave the address firmly. And the message. Make it clear. Final. No danger of being misunderstood. If she didn't do it now she might never do it. "I'll read it back to you," the operator said in her crisp voice. Deb checked the number and address with part of her mind, and the message: NOT GOING TO VINEYARD AGAIN EVER. RING ME HOTEL TO MAKE OTHER APPOINTMENT. DEB. A formal, rather ridiculous message when she thought about it. Well, that would make it quite clear to Jack that from now on their relationship would be formal.

When she put down the receiver she felt exhausted, like the time when she had been caught in the undertow and carried out beyond the surf. She had fought her way back, fear growing in her as the breakers crashed down on her and the pull of the current dragged her back into the churning sea. At last a dumper had caught her and flung her up the beach in a smother of sand and foam and she had lain there a long time without either thought or feeling. And now, as she sat at the desk, she was drained of all strength and her heart was pounding and her throat was tight as though, once more, she had escaped a great danger.

After a long time she picked up the receiver again and asked for Angus's suite. She could hear the change in his voice when he realised who was speaking.

"You're not going to tell me that you can see me this evening, after all?"

"Yes, darling." She had never called him darling before. Had he noticed?

He had. "Oh, Deborah..." there was a new note of tenderness.

"Would you like me to dress?"

"Yes, yes, my dear. I'd like to make this a very special celebration."

"That will be lovely."

"Shall we say at eight then?"

"Yes."

Deb's mind was racing. Would she ask him to make an appointment with his solicitor? No, better wait. Let him suggest it. She would lead round to it after dinner. And once she had seen the solicitor, Jack would have no power over her. Never...any more.

Guinea looked cautiously up and down the service lane. Thank God, Byron wasn't waiting for her. He had rung up and begged her to have lunch with him, and though she'd told him she had to work through the lunch hour, she wasn't sure he believed her.

He was being awfully sweet after the way she'd let him down last night. Not many men would have taken it as decently as he had. But what with Claire going round the salon like a ghost and trying to carry on as usual, and Mary Parker being buried this afternoon, she just couldn't take the thought of lunch with Byron. Time enough tonight to listen to him being all tender and romantic. Personally, she was prepared to give romance away.

Well, she thought gloomily, she supposed she was a very lucky girl to have the chance of marrying a man like Byron — Deb and Claire didn't hesitate to tell her so, anyway. But the trouble was he had stuck her up on a pedestal where she didn't belong, and it was going to be damned uncomfortable trying to live up to his idea of her.

She lingered at the top of the steps and wondered where she'd go for a snack. It was almost impossible to get in anywhere after one o'clock, and she would just as soon have stayed in the salon, but the Marie Antoinette had been like a madhouse the whole morning, and she couldn't stand it another minute with Alice's absence a constant reminder of what had happened to Mary, Ursula as jittery as hell, Deb behaving like the Lady of the Manor, and Val so taken up with her plans for Bessie that you couldn't get a word in edgeways about anything else. Oh well, she'd get a sandwich and go into the gardens and spend an hour on her own in the sunshine if it was only to get away from the stink of cosmetics, perfumes and all the rest of it. She'd had Glamour!

She turned down the lane and pulled up short as Kim sauntered out of the entrance to the car park just ahead of her. He gave her his familiar grin.

"Hullo, Peg. Thought I might catch you."

"What are you doing round here at this time of the day?"

"I've got a note for you from Aunt Annie."

"Oh." Guinea took it from him and slit it open anxiously. "Nothing wrong with Monnie, is there?"

"No. But if I know Aunt Annie's style of letter-writing all she's told you is that Monnie's getting on as well as can be expected, and that's all for now."

Guinea put the note in her bag. "That's just about it. But how is she really, Kim?"

"Not too bad, considering. She's practically slept the clock round since she came, and whenever she opens her eyes Aunt whips up an egg flip and pours it into her."

"Aunt Annie's been marvellous. I hope it's not too much for her?"

"It's right up her alley, actually. Don't you worry too much about the kid, Guin. I'll bet my bottom dollar she'll be as right as a bank before long."

Guinea nodded thoughtfully. She hoped he was right. One thing was certain, if anyone could do anything for Monnie it was Aunt Annie.

"Paypee! paypo!" A newsboy shouting on the corner roused her.

"I must get a paper, Kim, there's something I want to have a peek at."

Kim whistled to the boy, dropped two pennies into his palm and opened the paper. "What was it you wanted..." he began and stopped short. "Hey, Peg. Take a dekko at this. 'KEEPER OF DISORDERLY HOUSE GETS SIX MONTHS'."

"Where?" Guinea peered over his arm at the short mid-day news item.

> *Grace Louisa Smedley, 42, was given a maximum sentence of six months hard labour at the Women's Penitentiary, Long Bay, at Central Police Court today for keeping a disorderly house.*
>
> *The prosecuting sergeant pointed out that it was Smedley's first offence. The magistrate said there were*

701

certain features of the case which impelled him to give the maximum sentence.

Guinea looked up in disgust. "Wouldn't it!"

"Maximum sentence...six months..." Kim read the words aloud to make sure. "It can't be six months. Why, I knew a bloke who got that for pinching spare parts from a garage where I worked."

"Just shows you the rate they value girls at. Here, give me the paper." She almost snatched it from his hands.

"Hey, keep your hair on, Peg. I know it's rotten, but I'm not responsible."

Guinea didn't answer him, she was running her eyes down the columns of the centre pages.

"What else are you looking for? Wasn't that what you wanted to see?"

"No, it wasn't." She folded the paper in two and began a minute search of the back page. "If you must know, the sister of one of the girls in the Marie Antoinette died yesterday after an abortion and I want to see what the paper's got to say about it."

"Poor kid. Where's the bloke?"

"Somewhere up in the Islands."

"Hell, that'd rock you, wouldn't it?"

"I can tell you it rocked me."

"Did he walk out on her?"

"No. But he was married. Oh, here it is...it's just the same as the morning paper. That's a comfort, anyway."

"Why, are they frightened there might be a stink?"

"We're all frightened. Practically everybody in the salon helped her one way or another, and we're all scared out of our lives our names'll get in."

"Crikey, that wouldn't do your mother any good just at the moment, after what she's been through already."

"That's what I was frightened of. Poor old Bessie down in the powder room was decent enough to take the kid home after it was done and they've nabbed her for questioning."

"What rotten luck!" Kim slipped an arm through hers.

"Well, we can only hope for the best, and meantime it's no good worrying. What about a bit of lunch?"

Guinea nodded.

They stood at the corner for a moment, looking down Martin Place on the gaily striped marquees and waving flags of a charity fair. The sky was blue and cloudless after the rain and the sunshine poured down on the surging midday crowd. The air was full of the sound of shouting spruikers, the clatter of whirling chocolate wheels and lively band music.

"Come on," Kim urged her, "let's get going. I have a feeling that it's my lucky day, so we'll hop over and have a couple of tickets on the chocolate wheel."

They pushed their way through the crowd to a platform where a comedian was rattling off wisecracks and selling tickets as fast as he could hand them out.

"I'll have the last two," Kim called.

The wheel spun round and finally came to a standstill with a clacking of the leather tongue against the pegs.

"Twenty-seven!" shouted the spruiker. "Who has number twenty-seven?"

"What did I tell you?" Kim crowed, pushing the ticket in front of Guinea. "Here you are," he called. "Twenty-seven right here."

"Ah, my friend," said the comedian. "Just you wait — I have a nice surprise for you. I hope your wife's a good cook."

One of the attendants bent over a crate and took out a duck, quacking loudly and flapping its wings. He thrust it at Kim, who took it unwillingly amidst roars from the crowd.

"Duckling and apple sauce for dinner." The comedian took up the laughter and turned to Guinea. "Now's the time to show you know the way to your husband's heart."

"He's not my husband."

"What?" shouted the comedian, preparing to leap down from the platform. "Not your husband? Oh boy, let me out of this, I'm going to join the queue."

Kim tucked his arm through Guinea's. "Nothing doing," he called back. "I'm trying to screw up enough courage to ask her myself."

The crowd parted good-naturedly to let them through, the duck still quacking and Guinea laughing as she had not laughed for days. They went down past the War Loan platform and the band, and everywhere laughing faces turned to watch them.

When they halted at the Pitt Street crossing to let the stream of traffic go by, a woman in front of Kim screamed and turned on him a furious face.

"How dare you!" she glared at him, shaking peroxided curls. "Do you call yourself a gentleman?"

Kim went scarlet and looked at her in astonishment. The duck lifted up its head and turned a beady eye on them. Guinea choked back her laughter.

"What the devil's wrong with her?"

Guinea pointed to the duck and spluttered. "He...he bit her behind. She must have thought it was you."

"Huh!" Kim snorted. "If I ever come down to that I'll start on someone a bit younger."

There was a yelp behind him. He turned with a startled look. A middle-aged woman had a hand clapped to her lapel. "You ought to be reported to the police, carrying an animal like that round the town. The brute's ruined my orchid."

"Let's get out of this before I'm lynched." Kim took Guinea's arm and hurried her across the road. "Did I say something about my lucky day?" he groaned, pulling out a handkerchief and mopping his face. "And as for you," he said putting his hand round the duck's yellow bill. "You lay off. You ought to be ashamed of yourself, pinching blondes and orchids. I reckon I'll christen you Uncle Sam."

Guinea leaned against one of the GPO pillars and laughed till she was weak.

"Here," Kim thrust the duck at a passer-by, "take it home for dinner, will you, pal?"

The man gave him a suspicious glance and hurried on.

He offered it to a woman. "Madam," he pleaded, "there's a meat strike on. This might save your husband's life."

The woman swept on with her head in the air.

He looked at Guinea helplessly. "What are we going to do? We can't take old Sammy in to lunch with us."

"Come on, we'll pick up some sandwiches at Wynyard," she suggested, "and then go up to the park."

"Nice kind of celebration," Kim grumbled, following her across Martin Place. "The next thing you'll be slinging in my teeth is that your Yank boyfriends never take you into parks — at least, not to eat sandwiches."

"Oh, come off it. No Yank has ever won a duck for me, so that's one thing you've got on them."

They went down George Street and crossed over to Wynyard, where the midday crowds were flowing down the station ramp.

"You wait here," Guinea said, "and I'll see what I can rustle up."

"And don't be too long about it." Kim mopped the leg of his trousers gingerly. "I don't like this bird's habits."

He stood at the edge of the footpath, his face set in a strained grin. The lunch crowd laughed as they went past him; the people waiting in the wine queue beside the hotel stared at him with blank, unmoved faces. Guinea came back carrying a paper bag, a bottle of milk and two straws.

Kim groaned at the sight of her. "Is that all you could get to drink?"

"And lucky to get it."

"Well, all I can say, after a week in Sydney, the best thing the Yanks can do with what they've left of the place is take it back to the States with 'em."

"I'll pass on the suggestion." Guinea gave him a wicked grin. "You know, you look like something out of Walt Disney."

"Yeah?" Kim squeezed a protesting Uncle Sam closer, "and what's more, I feel like it."

The little park in Wynyard Square was crowded with people who had come out to spend the lunch hour in the sun. Kim and Guinea sat down on the grass and Kim set the duck beside him, untying its feet and tethering it by one leg to a tap. He let the tap run and it gobbled up the water thirstily, quacking round them hopefully while they unwrapped the sandwiches. Passers-by stopped to watch and passengers leaned out of the waiting buses.

Kim broke a sandwich in half and gave Uncle Sam a piece. "Luck!" he mourned. "I hang round the back of the SP half the morning to make sure of getting hold of you at lunchtime before one of your brass hats snaps you up and then when I try to get you off somewhere private for lunch, what happens? I get a bloody duck tied round my neck like an albatross and half the population of Sydney lines up thinking we're on exhibition."

Guinea flipped the cap off the milk bottle and dropped in a straw.

"Listen, Peg, I brought you out to lunch specially to ask you something, and I don't care if they start selling tickets to watch us and put a microphone up to broadcast what I'm saying, I'm still going to say it. I'm here to propose to you."

Guinea looked up at him and went on sucking at her straw. "Yeah! I seem to have heard your propositions before."

Kim leaned over and took the bottle from her. "Put that down and listen to me. You haven't heard this one, this is a newy." He stretched himself out flat on the grass, threw his cap down beside him and put his hands under his head. "Stretch out here beside me, and stick your lug over near me so you won't miss a word of what I'm saying. And if you look up you'll only see trees and the tops of buildings and the sky and you can forget that half the population of Australia is queuing up for the greatest love scene in history."

Uncle Sam wandered up and began to sample the gold wings on Kim's cap. He snatched it away. "Hey, lay off, that's sabotage. Hell, I'll never get started."

Guinea stretched out on the grass, her head touching his shoulder, her eyes on the blue sky that seemed to rest on the tall buildings framing the Square. A stunting bomber dived above the high arch of the Harbour Bridge and came in low over the park, swooping down with a roar. It zoomed up

706

again in a silver flash. Three fighter planes plummeted out of the upper air to engage it in mock combat.

Kim blew a raspberry after the planes. "Aw, go do your War Loan stunts somewhere else," he admonished them. "I'm off duty." He turned to Guinea and his voice was urgent. "Now, before those noisy cows come back again, will you..." the rest of his sentence was lost as another dive-bomber zoomed above York Street.

"What did you say?" Guinea shouted.

Kim moved closer and whispered against her ear. "I said, will you marry me?"

She lay absolutely still. The grass was cool under her head, she could feel it short and springy against her bare legs. High up, the trails of the fighter planes were scrawled across the sky.

"I mean it," Kim whispered. He swore as he heard the rising roar of the returning bomber. "Yes or no? Quick, Peg."

The zooming plane blotted out all other sounds.

"Did you say it?"

"No."

"You mean you didn't say it or you said 'No'?" Kim's voice was unsteady. "Crikey, if you knew how cheesed off I've been this whole week thinking what a mug I was not to have married you on that final leave..."

"Don't get romantic," Guinea warned him, "a lot of things have happened in the four years since then, and quite a lot of them you wouldn't like at all."

"Let's wipe all that," Kim brushed it aside. "I've done a lot of things you wouldn't like, either. If we started sorting out our hectic careers we'd probably break even. You don't ask me any questions — I don't ask you any."

"That's not the point."

"Well, if you must have it, I'm willing to admit here and now that I've been all kinds of a heel."

Guinea broke off a clover blossom and chewed it. "I don't think it'd work," she said at last.

"Why not?"

"We know each other too well."

"What do you mean?"

"There'd never be any of that mystery stuff about me; you know — all the romantic guff men seem to think so important."

"Mystery, phooey!" Kim retorted. "I've had all I want of this 'sweet mystery of love' bunk. I find that when I've been six months in the jungle, any girl I get hotted up about is full of mystery to me till I've slept with her. And while that mightn't be anything to boast about, at least it's taught me that in the end every girl's the same unless she's your own girl. And you're my girl, Peg, though I wasn't sure about it myself till the other day at the court. You're all the mystery I want."

Guinea lay looking up at the sky. A screaming Beaufighter swooped down on the bomber and went up again in a silver arc.

"I've only got another week," Kim went on urgently, "we could rush it through. Maybe Monday. Somehow I just can't face the thought of going away this time without being married to you."

The sun was beating through Guinea's thin frock and she watched the leaves of a golden poplar making patterns against the sky. She could hear the drone of the bomber a long way off and, nearer, the staccato beat of the fighter engines. Buses lumbered heavily along the street; the ground was shaking with the vibration of an underground train. Uncle Sam was quacking deliriously at something he'd found, and the crowd went by laughing.

The poplar leaves turned over lazily in the breeze and she was filled with a deep sense of peace. Maybe it made her feel good to have Kim come crawling back to her at last. Maybe it was something else...

"Let's toss for it," she said suddenly.

Kim sat up and looked down into her face; he was frowning and his mouth was set tight.

Why, she thought, I've never seen him look like that. He

708

really means it. If he never meant anything before, he means this.

"I'm not very good at speeches, Peg. They're not in my line. But if you want any guarantee — you know, about being able to trust me and all that — well, for what it's worth, I've just quite suddenly wakened up to the fact that I could be the faithful kind."

Her eyes met his and she looked at him for a long time. "Give me someone worth being faithful to, and so could I."

"I don't know if you feel that I come up to those specifications, but if you give me a chance I'll try to prove it."

She stared up at him and then past him. The mock battle was still going on. Her mind followed the planes. If I marry you, she said to herself, then I'll never have any more peace. It'll start all over again. All the time you're away fighting, part of me will be there, too. I wonder if it's worth it.

Uncle Sam waddled over and pecked at the red chevrons on Kim's sleeve. He ran a hand down the duck's gleaming neck feathers.

"If it's love you're wanting me to talk about, Peg, I can turn that on, too."

"I've heard you."

"Then we'll skip it. Right now, what I'm asking you to do is to marry me — for keeps. Compared to what some of your other boyfriends can offer you, it mightn't seem much of a bargain to share my deferred pay when I come back and help to build up a rundown garage. But the way I see things, that's not all there is to it. It mightn't be easy, but it'll be fun and we'll be together and somehow, I can't think of anything better than spending the rest of my life with you."

Guinea turned her face away. She wasn't sure she wanted any more of love. Not the kind of love she and Kim had had anyway. It hurt too much.

His voice was unsteady. "You know, Peg, it suddenly struck me I'd rather like to have a kid like you. Maybe that's what all this love business really boils down to."

Guinea's heart thumped. For keeps? And a kid of

Kim's. She lay silent staring at the planes.

"Well," he said at last, "what's the answer?"

"Let's toss for it." Her voice was clear and lazy.

He stared at her. She smiled back at him. There was a long pause.

"Do you mean that?"

"Huh-huh."

"OK. If that's how you feel about it. But somehow, the way I look at it, it's a damned big thing to rest on the toss of a coin. But if that's the way you want it, I'd better find a brown." He took a penny out of his pocket and tossed it experimentally. "It's a new one if that's any help."

"I hope it's not a double-header."

"What a woman! You wouldn't trust anybody, would you?"

She looked at him without smiling. "I might, you never know."

"Well, here it goes."

He spun the penny high in the sunshine and called "Heads". The lunchers near them turned to watch. It came down on the grass.

"Tails! Well, I can take it."

Guinea looked at him, half smiling. "You'd better have three tosses for luck."

He flashed a quick glance at her. "Whose? Mine or yours?"

"That depends."

He tossed again. The conductor on a passing bus leaned out and bawled, "Let the angels see 'em!"

"Heads!" Kim called again and it came down heads.

He rubbed the penny between his palms and spat on it. "Now here goes for the lucky last." It soared again, the new bronze sparkling in the sun. "Heads!"

It landed between them — tails.

Guinea picked the penny up and looked at it, turning it over and over. Then she rubbed it between her palms, breathed on it and handed it back to him, putting her hands under her head and yawning with a pretence of unconcern.

"Maybe you'd better keep tossing until it comes right."

Kim gave a whoop and all the heads turned round to look at them again. Uncle Sam quacked from the garden bed. Kim flicked the penny high in the air. "There it goes," he said, turning on his elbow and looking into her face. His hand closed over hers.

The new penny went up, spinning over and over against the blue sky. It came down on the edge of the garden, but neither of them bothered to look.